**"STOP THIS, MY LORD.
YOU CANNOT TELL ME OUR MARRIAGE
IS OVER AND EXPECT YOUR RIGHTS
AT THE SAME TIME,"
SUMMER SAID WITH CONTEMPT.**

"Can't I?" Ruark asked silkily. "I can do anything I please. I am still master of my own hall."

"I'll fight you," she vowed.

He laughed deep in his throat. Such a promise only spurred him. He reached out strong hands to take her by the shoulders, but she shrugged from her bed gown and ran.

His arm swooped down to catch her ankle, and as she tumbled to the carpet he was on top of her in a flash. As he bent to take her mouth, she managed to free one hand and rake his flesh. "Damn, you little wildcat, do I have to tie your hands?"

"Leave me alone . . . damn you to hell," she spat out.

"That's it!" he exploded. "Don't say I didn't warn you. . . ."

THE
Pirate
AND THE
Pagan

VIRGINIA HENLEY

ISLAND
BOOKS

Dedicated to Adele Ellis, my very first fan,
and to all my readers who are so loyal.
I deeply appreciate it.

Published by
Dell Publishing
a division of
Bantam Doubleday Dell Publishing Group, Inc.
1540 Broadway
New York, New York 10036

ISBN: 0-440-20623-5

Printed in the United States of America

Published simultaneously in Canada

December 1990

10 9 8 7 6

RAD

Five and twenty ponies trotting through the dark—
Brandy for the Parson, 'baccy for the Clerk;
Laces for a lady, letters for a spy,
Watch the wall, my darling, while the Gentlemen go by!

Them that asks no questions isn't told a lie.
Watch the wall, my darling, while the Gentlemen go by!

Rudyard Kipling, "A Smuggler's Song"

1

"**W**hat a beautiful cock!" she murmured under her breath. The young woman was wildly beautiful in a dark, unconventional way, and her personality and way of life matched. She gazed at it for long, silent minutes in wonder. It was without doubt the biggest cock she had ever seen. Her eyes actually dilated with pleasure as she closed them and reopened them slowly to make sure she hadn't imagined its great size. Pleased beyond belief that she would soon possess it, she licked her lips in anticipation.

Truly it was a magnificent specimen. She held her body perfectly still and coaxed him with a soft, seductive voice. "Come, my big boy, another few inches and you are mine. Don't be shy, don't retreat, after all 'tis only a little sin I'm committing," she whispered coaxingly. "Our chance encounter will soon be consummated," she soothed with confidence.

"You're a very big cock—I hope you fit—never mind, I'll cram you in somehow," she said under her breath. She begged prettily, "If I reach out my hand, will you let me touch you, stroke you?" Better not, she thought as he looked ready to bolt.

Now she was face-to-face with the act, she wondered wildly if she could go through with it. She'd never done it before, although she had contemplated it for weeks, but she knew after this time she would probably do it again and again. For a moment its size frightened her. What if it hurt her? It could probably do her irreparable damage given half a chance. She pushed her fear to the back of her mind, took a deep breath, and plunged upon it.

The fat rooster squawked so loudly and flapped his black wings so frantically that she almost lost it, but the fierce hunger in her belly made her hang on determinedly. Then she closed her eyes tightly and wrung its neck until it was very, very dead.

Lady Summer St. Catherine had an abundance of jet black, shining hair which fell heavily below her shoulders and curled on the ends into great natural ringlets. Her black-fringed eyes were a changeable shade of hazel, sometimes soft brown, more often leaf green and they were tip-tilted at the corners giving credence to her nickname, Cat, which she preferred because she felt her full name to be laughably pretentious. Her mouth was wide and capable of a sulky pout, a firm-lipped determination, or a dazzling laugh, but it was as red as crushed strawberries. Her skin was the color of rich Devon cream, a vivid contrast to her billowing cloud of jet black tresses.

Cat was slender and long-legged as a colt with small, high upthrusting breasts which strained the laces on the too-tight boy's shirt she wore. She also had on a pair of ragged knee breeches and scuffed boots which her young brother Viscount Spencer had outgrown.

Viscount Spencer St. Catherine also hated his name and answered only to Spider. The Cornwall estate where they lived was called Roseland, and though it stood on five acres with a once-splendid manor house, it could not boast of one servant or gardener and had an overgrown, unkempt air of neglect. Cat's mother was dead, her father alive, and she fervently wished it was the other way about since she had nothing but hatred for her father. He was and always had been a selfish, ruthless drunken swine who indulged every vice known to man.

Her mother had died giving birth to Spencer when Cat was only three. Years later, she'd learned through servants' gossip that her mother had almost died when she was born and the doctor had told Randal St. Catherine in no uncertain terms that another child would kill her.

"The useless brat's a girl!" he had raved. "I'll not stop trying till she gives me a son."

" 'Twould be deliberate murder, Randal, if she conceives again," the doctor had warned.

St. Catherine shrugged. "Then I'll be free to take a new wife—a younger, healthier woman to satisfy me in bed." But by the time his wife had given him his son and conveniently departed for heaven, the arrogant St. Catherine's world had been turned upside down by civil war. Parliament had decided to run the country with Oliver Cromwell's heavy hand at the helm. St. Catherine found it expedient to turn his coat, for being loyal to the old King could get your lands and money confiscated and it became a crime to be a member of the aristocracy.

So he had paid lip service to the austere "new order" which banned drinking, whoring, and gambling along with every other vice designed to make a gentleman's life tolerable. It didn't take many years for this new order to become tarnished, for Englishmen soon realized they had gone from bad to worse. With sinking trade and bad harvests, men everywhere were poorer with long unhappy faces atop their dull, worsted garments. The larger cities and towns were filled with Cromwell's spies and a breath of protest could carry you off to prison. Cornishmen were not quite as docile as the rest of the English, and while the ones with honor and integrity such as the Grenviles and Helfords risked their wealth and their lives to help restore the Stuarts to the throne, others such as St. Catherine took advantage of their isolated estates to further their own ends.

Roseland became no better than a gaming hell where forbidden cards, dice, and liquor became the order of the day. St. Catherine did not play on the square and soon cheating at cards became second nature even to his children.

In 1660 when Charles II was joyously embraced by one and all, St. Catherine was no exception. He took himself off to London and for the past few years had been slowly devoured by the dissolute life of the wicked city. The only reason he ever returned to Roseland was to denude its walls of its valuable paintings or sell off the last of the horses.

The last time he'd been home four months since, Cat had removed her beloved black Ebony from the stables and stayed out all night with him. Finally, Rancid, as she called her father, had driven off in a rage, cursing the young hellcat to perdition, and taking all of his servants with him.

Cat made her way through the tangled overgrown estate which

bordered the well-kept lands of the Helfords. She had only actually trespassed once on the magnificent Helford estate. The night she had protected Ebony she had ridden him onto the broad acres attached to Helford Hall and hidden in one of the many yew glades which were part of the formal gardens. The clipped yews formed high dark walls which kept out even sunlight and would be cool on the hottest days. Deep within the mile of yew walks it was remote, silent, and more than a little eerie, almost threatening.

The Helford estate boasted over five hundred acres, but these ran back from the seacoast along the Helford River right up to the town of Helston. The house itself stood atop the cliff's edge like Roseland, but they were over a mile apart and only Helford Hall's clustered chimneys, turrets, obelisks, and widow's walk were visible from the St. Catherine property. Of course they were only visible when the coast was free from heavy fog or sea mists.

Cat hummed a tune to herself as she strode along, swinging the large rooster by its feet. As she neared the house she waved gaily to her brother and called, "Spider, did you manage to get the eggs?"

At sight of her he stopped dead in his tracks, a black scowl descending like thunder upon his brow. "Hell and damnation, Cat, you send me to steal eggs, a job any five-year-old could manage, while you sneak off to throttle a cock!"

She sighed, knowing his male vanity had been injured. "Spider, I swear to God he walked right through a hole in the fence, straight into my path. I damned near tripped over him. What did you expect me to do? Ask him to hang about while I ran off to look for you?"

"All the same," he said grudgingly, "butchering is no job for a lady."

She nodded solemnly, "Fowl play."

He broke into a grin. "Christ, it's a big bugger. I bet it put up a hell of a squawk."

She laughed now, remembering. "I thought the bloody gamekeeper would come running. Still, I was ready to defy him if he had. Possession is nine-tenths of the law and the cock was on our land."

Spider said, "That bastard is the reason there are no rabbits left for me to snare. Can't have rabbits nibbling precious Helford shrubbery."

They made straight for the kitchen door. Roseland was a picture at this time of the year. Its soft red-brick walls were covered with flowering vines. Honeysuckle had overgrown each arched doorway and early pink roses and spring violets vied with a sea of daffodils which spread out under the fruit trees now covered in blossom. The lawns in close to the house were a lush green and looked well tended, but that was only because she tethered her horse Ebony and Spider's pony there so they could crop it. They had no oats or fodder for their animals and so the thick green lawns must suffice.

At the back of the house Cat always planted a kitchen garden, for they relied upon the vegetables she grew to keep them alive. They had used up all last autumn's harvest as well as the last of the apples. This time of year the gardens were very pretty but pretty didn't fill your belly. The only things that were big enough to eat were young green onions and a few new potatoes no bigger than marbles. Cat sighed as she put water on the fire to boil. First she'd have to pluck the cockerel, then clean it, long before the savory smell of the cooking bird would permeate the corners of the kitchen.

"The old man's been gone a hell of a long spell this time," said Spider.

"Four months," confirmed Cat.

"I wonder when the hell he'll be back?" said Spider, not quite allowing concern to creep into his voice. "Not that I care if I ever see him again, but at least old Rancid always brings lots of food and drink and servants to do the work."

"Lightning blast the man!" Cat muttered. "We'll have to mend the boat. We can live on fish if we have to. After we've gorged ourselves on purloined poulet we'll go down to the cellars to see if the tide's washed up anything we can use, and you can assess the damage to the family yacht."

The manor house was built on a rocky cliff. Its cellars had been built around natural caverns of the ocean and a secret tunnel led into a cave which flooded at high tide. At low tide the cave often contained a barrel of brandy or some other contraband lost from a smuggler's ship. They had moored their little wooden rowboat at the mouth of the cave after it had been battered in the last storm.

Spider fell asleep at the kitchen table waiting for the food to cook. Cat's heart was wrung as she looked down at the boy. He was only fourteen, although he always insisted he was as close to fifteen as dammit is to swearing. He was so thin and this last year he had grown like a weed, so that his wrists and ankles stuck out a mile from his shrinking, shabby clothes.

Lady Summer St. Catherine did not mingle with the towns-people but kept aloof for fear of being laughed at. A lady without money, clothes, or servants was a figure of fun and she had put up forbidding signs on the gates that warned "Keep Out! Trespassers will be shot!" She had Roseland and that was all she needed.

Spider on the other hand mingled freely with the youth of the district and was accepted as one of them. His friends were sons of farmers, fishermen, and tavern keepers, but they had no idea he was a viscount, and assumed he was a stableboy from one of the large estates.

As she prepared dinner Cat daydreamed over how her day had begun. Dawn was a special, private time for Cat. She had done the same thing this morning that she had done each day of her life until it had become a ritual. Whatever the weather, she rode Ebony for miles along the empty sands and saluted the sunrise.

This southern shore of Cornwall was semitropical with warm coves and inlets. Its low cliffs were covered with exotic wildflowers, its air soft, come rain or shine. Often the dawns were misty before the sun burned off the wisps of fog. The strong breezes which whipped her black hair about her wildly as she rode were often as not warm and seductive. This soft southern shore was in stark contrast to the north Cornish coast such a short distance away. There the weather was cruel, the craggy cliffs bare of vegetation as they towered over the storm-tossed Atlantic. This contrast of the elements seemed to account for the devils which surged in the blood of certain Cornishmen and women. At least Cat lay the blame there for the devils which surged in her own blood. How else could she explain the intoxication so close to madness which brought her each dawn to the edge of the sea?

Her mind came back to the task at hand. If she didn't stop daydreaming, they would never eat. She sighed over life's cruelties. Poor chickens gave eggs all their lives and ended up between some-one's knees, being plucked. Still, this was a rooster and she'd be damned if she'd waste pity on the male of the species!

2

Their plates, licked clean, had been pushed back on the table to make room for their feet as brother and sister lazed before the warm fire, replete for once. Spider's eyelids kept drooping over his eyes, but he was grinning from ear to ear.

"I wonder what Lord Helford would say if he knew we'd dined on his generosity tonight?"

"Bah! He's so rich he keeps fifty servants kicking their lazy heels, supposedly looking after an estate he never even visits. Lord Bloody Helford can rot as far as I'm concerned. I hope he has a miserable night, wherever he is," she said, licking her fingers one last time.

Lord Helford, as it turned out, was having anything but a miserable night. He had just dined sumptuously at Arlington House with the most important men of the realm. Baron Arlington, the secretary of state, employed the most superlative French chefs and was renowned as London's host supreme. Tonight had been neither ball nor banquet, but simply a meeting where business was discussed, and yet the food had been as lavish as the entertainment had been daring.

Madame Bennet's Naked Dancing Girls were served up as appetizer along with the smoked trout and the latest sensation from France called champagne. The men at table who had so wished had made their selections for postmidnight assignations, and then they dutifully attacked their food and the pressing business at hand.

King Charles II's face had settled into moody lines of cynicism as he listened to the advice offered him.

The Duke of Buckingham weighed up the men in the room, trying to pinpoint each one's vulnerability so he could use it to best advantage at some later date.

Sir Thomas Clifford, Lord Ashley, and the outspoken Scot, Lauderdale, seemed to be arguing, while Jack Grenvile, newly created Earl of Bath, and Lord Helford both looked on with tolerant amusement.

"Gentlemen, the Dutch fleet is trying to run England off the map and I'd like to know what we're going to do about it," said Charles bluntly. He smarted from the humiliation of the ships Holland had captured. The British navy was his pride and joy. He knew that the only way to make his nation a great one was by her sea trade. England must rule supreme over the seas of the world or she would be poor forever.

"At the risk of becoming a repetitive bore," drawled Buckingham, "the only answer is war."

Charles said, "Wars cost money, George. We're not all as flush in the pocket as you." George Villiers, Duke of Buckingham, had one of the largest private fortunes in England.

Buckingham said blandly, "What about the dowry?"

Charles rolled his dark eyes. "The three hundred thousand pounds is not yet in my coffers and my spies tell me Portugal is now offering over half of it in sugar and spices instead of gold."

"Sugar and spice and everything nice," said Buckingham maliciously, "that's what you get for trusting all to Clarendon." Edward Hyde, Earl of Clarendon and Chancellor of England, was conspicuous by his absence. He was hated by all but the King.

"Portugal didn't marry me," said Charles, "it married English sea power. That's why they gave us their prized colonies of Bombay and Tangier. The Dutch are now making a mockery of that sea power."

Every man in the room had made a great deal of money over the last three years, recouping all their losses of the lean years they had spent in exile. But only a fool would have been unable to make a fortune in London with its relaxed policy of free enterprise. So now it was their responsibility to see that England prospered as she should.

"Everything always boils down to money whether you're discussing a whore or a nation," said Lauderdale bluntly.

Charles sighed. "I need more money for ships, more money for spies, more money for bribes."

"We must continue to harry the Dutch fleet without actually declaring war on them," said Arlington.

"Two years we've been coursing that hare and haven't caught it yet," said Charles cynically.

"Grant me letters-of-marque against the Dutch," suggested Ruark Helford. He had been one of Prince Rupert's Privateers preying on Parliament's shipping while Cromwell ruled.

Jack Grenvile grinned. "Breathes there a Cornishman who isn't a pirate at heart?"

Ruark quipped, "You should certainly know."

Charles looked at Ruark. "You could be effective in Cornwall, Ruark. Smuggling is rampant. No wonder my tax coffers are bare. Every man and his mistress finds a way to get 'round paying excise tax. Everything imported here is supposed to be taxed whether it's tobacco from America, wine from France, or Venetian glass. So what happens? Instead of sailing into London and paying the taxes, they slip it in the back door along the Cornish coast. I've decided to make you the magistrate and high commissioner of the whole region. Catch and punish the smugglers and we'll see the tax money roll in."

Helford raised his eyebrows slightly at Charles, who nodded imperceptibly in answer. Yes, there would be a great deal more involved than catching petty smugglers. A base in Cornwall was an excellent cover for international spying.

" 'Od's Fish, I don't know why you bother us for advice when you seem to have all the answers," drawled Buckingham.

Clifford quipped, "Well, so long as one of us uses his brains, that leaves the rest of us free to indulge our other organs."

The meeting broke up at midnight and Lord Helford walked back to the palace with the King. They cut through the old Mulberry Gardens west of the palace.

"Never thought I'd live to see the night you went dutifully home to a wife," said Ruark, laughing.

Charles gave him an amused look. "I'm not the only one present who needs an heir . . . you're not that much younger than I."

Helford sobered. "I could tolerate a wife if I didn't have to see her outside the bedroom."

"Tolerance with women isn't your long suit, Ruark."

The two men could have been brothers. Both had the animal strength of a six-foot physique, black hair, dark skin, and impeccable manners.

"This business of smuggling," Charles said quietly. "The goods coming in aren't nearly so damaging as the information that's being smuggled out. Put a stop to leaking my navy's secrets to the Dutch for me, Ru."

"I'll finish up my business in London and as soon as you sign my letters-of-marque I'll be ready to leave."

"Perhaps I should ask you to seek out your brother Rory and give *him* the letters-of-marque," said Charles.

Ruark Helford stiffened. "Rory's dead," he said quietly.

"A convenient rumor the scoundrel circulates for some dark reason of his own, I have no doubt," said Charles, unable to keep the amusement from his voice.

"Is that an order, Your Majesty?" he asked coldly.

Charles nodded his head. "I think his services will be invaluable to me."

"Give my regards to the Queen, Your Majesty," said Ruark Helford, bowing formally.

Charles hid a grin. He knew he had hit a sore spot mentioning the pirate Rory. "My regards to you mistress. I don't envy you explaining why you must desert her for Cornwall."

Ruark Helford's brows drew together slightly. "I don't explain myself to women, Sire."

Charles laughed. "One day you'll meet your match, Helford. 'Tis the fate of all libertines, my friend."

Cat stretched her arms above her head and stood up from the kitchen table to light the lantern.

"Where are you going?" asked Spider between great yawns.

"I forgot to go down to see if the boat can be repaired."

"We can go in the morning," protested the boy.

"It's low tide now. I can go alone, you go on to bed."

" 'Course you can't go alone," he said firmly, all sleepiness gone from his voice. "If I don't look out for you, who will?" He asked the question with the inborn arrogance of a grown man and suddenly she felt such a pang that the boy she had looked after for years would soon grow into a man. For one brief moment she wished he would never turn into a man, for she hated them, but then she chided herself for having such wicked, selfish thoughts about her young brother.

Cat held the lantern high as they walked through the cellars, and on into the caverns hollowed from the cliff's rock. The salt tang of tidewrack assailed their nostrils as they bent their heads to go through the narrow passage into the cave. As she emerged from the passage and lifted the lantern, Cat was startled by a bright, flickering light from the sea. It was close in, almost in the shallows, and both of them knew in the same instant that it was a ship's lantern which thought their own light was a signal. Quickly Cat snuffed out her lantern, and as she did so, Spider pointed out a ship. It looked like a small French frigate. Its sails had been furled, but it was now in the business of hoisting sail as fast as it could. Voices carried clearly across the water. *"Vite! Patrouille marine!"*

Both of them had a smattering of French, and knew the ship had spotted a navy patrol boat. They peered out across the dark, choppy waters and saw it quite a way off, but resolutely closing the distance.

"Dans la mer!" came an order, followed by four muffled splashes.

"They're dumping cargo into the sea," Cat translated. "If they are caught and searched, there'll be no evidence unless the patrol takes time to fish it out of the drink."

A sailor called a question, *"Planche à bouteilles?"*

The answer came quickly, *"Oui, oui—embariller—sel, sel."*

"What did he say?" asked Cat low.

"Sel is salt. *Embariller* means packed in casks. Must be fish," said Spider in disgust.

"No, no—he asked the captain if he should dump the *planche à bouteilles* as well. That's a wooden crate of bottles. I know what they've done!" said Cat excitedly. "They've packed the stuff in rock salt so it'll sink. It'll take a few hours for the salt to melt, then around about daybreak the stuff will float up."

Spider said in wonder, "Isn't it amazing how somebody's misfortune is somebody else's gain? The world has a kind of balance to it, y'know?"

"But we've got to be quick and cunning." Cat laughed. "We'll go up to the kitchen and get a couple of hours' sleep by the fire. Tide will be rising by then."

* * *

Sunrise was still a good hour away and they had accomplished everything they'd hoped for. The sea had thrown up four large casks of brandy and five cases marked *vin de champagne,* holding fifty bottles in all. Cat had never heard of champagne, but *vin* was wine and the tide had done almost all the work for them. For the small price of a thorough wetting they had secured the contraband, lined it up in the cave in front of the entrance to the passage, and they now stood in the cavernous cellar waiting for high tide and the indraft to float it all "home."

Later that morning, as always, Cat, mounted on Ebony, greeted the golden dawn. Today, however, she expected to have company on the lonely stretch of sand. She sat alert, watching the distance, then as two tiny figures became visible around the far headland she urged the black horse faster and faster until the blood of both surged recklessly. The tide was still high enough to cover the horse up to its hocks and she deliberately splashed the two men who were obviously looking for something.

"G'day, m'lady," they muttered, abashed to be caught there so blatantly.

She nodded aloofly and waited. One of the men finally spoke. "Did ye see aught up the beach, m'lady?"

Her eyes narrowed. "You're not wreckers, are you?" she asked boldly, allowing a hint of loathing to sound in her voice.

Quickly they denied it vehemently. "Nay, nay, lady. Engaged in a spot of honest smuggling, that's all, I swear it."

"If I thought you were connected to wreckers, I'd turn you over to the militia instantly!" she warned again.

"Nay, nay," said the younger man, "my dad here's the tavern keeper at Mawnan. We were expectin' a delivery o' brandy."

"I've ridden for miles this morning; the beach is empty, I'm afraid." She smiled. "Well, you can't trust the French, y'know."

"No, m'lady," they muttered, and knew she lied.

She touched her heel to her horse's side, then as if she had second thoughts stopped and said, "If you've the money, I could let you have four kegs of brandy and say, fifty bottles of French wine from my father's cellars."

They looked at each other shrewdly, wondering how St. Catherine's wench had managed to locate and secure the stuff before they had. They shrugged. There was nothing they could do, for she'd have the militia on them as soon as look at them.

"Bring a wagon to Roseland this afternoon and I'll have one of the servants fetch it up from the cellars," she said airily as she turned the black Barbary and took off like the wind.

3

Lord Randal St. Catherine could smell his own sweat for the first time in his life and it smelled of fear! His luck had been all bad lately until he was reduced to one elegant satin suit and his well-sprung coach. He knew that tomorrow he would have to leave for Roseland. Then his luck seemed to change and it turned out to be a fateful night for him. It went by many names, but luck, fate, or destiny chose to stand at his shoulder this night as he sat at a gaming table at the Groom Porter's Lodge.

Early in the evening he had begun by dealing from the bottom whenever it was his turn, but as the night wore on he found he need not slur and knap to win, for the right cards seemed to be falling into his hands by divine power. It was as if he had made a pact with the devil. Whatever cards he needed to win, he turned up.

When his winnings reached four thousand pounds, he had enough sense to quit the table. He ordered a double brandy, giving silent thanks that he'd not had enough money in his pocket to buy it before he'd begun to play as he usually did.

As he stepped out onto the cobblestone street he found it unusu-
ly deserted. Stripped bare of humanity, the buildings looked ugly
decayed. Centuries of rottenness, overcrowding, and greed

made London a stinking cesspool of corruption and he knew he was as much a part of it as the open sewage kennels which ran along the sides of the streets.

The upper stories of the houses and buildings overhung one another, shutting out the light and the air and cloaking the night with a sinister pall.

"A pox on all coachmen!" he muttered as his eyes darted up and down the street, trying to decide in which pub he would find his man. He walked to the corner and glanced through the diamond-paned windows of the Rose and Crown, then turned the corner and spat an obscenity as a dark cat slunk across his path.

He saw his coach down a dirty side alley across from the Cock and Bull and knew he'd found his quarry. He glanced to left and right furtively before going into the alley, for London streets were unsafe for beggars, not to mention those with a fortune in their pockets. He heard a muffled step, glanced behind him, and saw only a well-dressed figure, a wide-brimmed cavalier's hat pulled low across the face.

He quickened his steps toward his coach. Inside was an iron bar used to lever the wheels from mud. His hand reached out to open the door as he heard the unmistakable sound of a sword stick being drawn from its sheath. It was then he smelled the fear on himself. He turned to look into the face of death and took the steel. It slipped between his ribs as if he'd been a rack of lamb skewered by a French chef.

As the strange metallic taste came into his mouth he knew at his heart root this was no random robbery, but a deliberate and calculated assault by a gentleman he had had the bad judgment to cheat. Someone as ruthlessly cold-blooded as himself. By the time his coachman found him he was lying in the gutter where he belonged, yet he still clung to life by a thread.

"Lil," he whispered, "Lady Richwood . . ."

His driver, afraid to make a run for it, lifted him into the coach and just barely made out the grating words, "Cockspur . . . Street . . . Number 5 . . ." He climbed on top and whipped up the horses. He could make no time on the twisting streets until he reached the Strand, then he let the horses have their heads until they were past the bend in the River Thames, and it took all his strength to steer them round the corner into the short Cockspur Street.

He lifted St. Catherine from the coach and struggled up the steps at the fashionable little house which was number five. A liveried footman answered the door, but the burly coachman brushed him aside and pushed into the reception hall on the first floor. The coachman tried to set St. Catherine on his feet, but knew if he let go of him altogether, he would collapse.

A very attractive woman perhaps in her late thirties appeared after a few minutes and stood staring in disbelief. Finally, St. Catherine gasped, "Lil . . . I'm dying!"

"So I see," she drawled in a beautiful, provocative voice. She was never at a loss for words and tonight was no exception. "Randal, darling, I wonder why it is when life deals a man a low blow and the world decides to turn its callous back upon him, the first person he turns to is his closest female relative?" She paused dramatically, yet did not seem to take a breath as she continued, "No matter how shabbily or dishonorably he has treated that female in the past?" She paused again, smoothing the folds of her elegant silk gown. "Shall I tell you the answer, darling? It is because a woman, no matter how harshly she has been treated, will not shut the door in the face of a brother, even though that brother be an enemy."

"Lil . . ." he gasped, his face whiter than death, "send . . . for . . . my . . . daughter."

"Oh, I shall, Randal, never fear." She motioned her hand for the coachman to take him upstairs. "You always were the most inconsiderate brute alive. Even in extremis you had to bleed all over my new carpet," she drawled. Over her shoulder she casually bade the footman, "Secure the coach and horses in the carriage house, James—I'm sure he won't have a crown to his name."

Lil dismissed an upstairs maid and led the way into a small, luxurious bedroom. "Disrobe him," she ordered his man as he laid him on the bed. She glanced at the wound dispassionately. It frothed and bubbled bright red blood with each shallow breath he drew. Without a word she whipped a sheet from the bed, tore off a long strip, and bound it tightly about his ribs.

"Doctor . . ." It came out in a rattle.

"Doctor?" Lil gave a droll little laugh. "Surely, darling, you mean undertaker."

"You're . . . hard . . . Lil!" he rasped bitterly.

"Yes, Randal, hard. Shall I tell you why?" she drawled. "You ⸻ved me out of Roseland on my arse when I was fifteen, and ⸻se I was particularly partial to eating every day, I soon ⸻ to live by my wits. To save myself I had to marry an old man. Didn't expect that, did you, Randal? Didn't expect I'd become Lady Richwood? Then when you thought he might be of some use to you, you latched onto my husband until you bled him dry. Well, he may have died penniless but Lord Richwood was my means of being presented at Court and that, Randal darling, is the only way I've survived. Now I'm particularly partial to servants, silk gowns, and security."

"Whoremonger!" he said, sneering.

She made a small moue with her lips. "Introductions, Randal. Discreet liaisons between young women of breeding and gentlemen of His Majesty's Court. Someone as coarse as you would naturally call it flesh peddling and that, darling, is what has made me hard."

She swept from the room, taking the coachman with her. "Come, I'll pay you what wages he owes you," she said, speaking briskly for the first time.

"Shall I come round tomorrow?" he asked uncertainly.

"If I were you, I'd cut my losses. Let's face it, if he were rich as Buckingham, he still couldn't bribe the Grim Reaper to overlook him for more than another day or two."

The driver touched his forelock and departed thinking she was a crafty bitch to secure the coach and horses. Still, it was a bleeding miracle she'd given him his wages!

Lil dispatched a footman for a doctor and sat down at her desk to pen a hurried note. She stroked her chin reflectively for a moment with the goose-feather quill, then in an elegant scrawl wrote:

Lady Summer St. Catherine:
Your father has suffered a critical accident. Come immediately.
                    "Auntie Lil"
                    Lady Richwood

She addressed it to Lady Summer St. Catherine of Roseland and gave orders that it was to be put on the mail coach for Plymouth immediately. Then she stared out the long window into the night-darkened streets. "Well, Lady Summer, you've had all the advantages of the fine upbringing I was denied. Let's see how you cope with this fine mess. The pain and the expense can be yours; I want none of it!"

She walked slowly through the house, picked up a decanter brandy, and thought, Funny, but I'm not really hard at all. S brushed away a tear and carried the brandy up to her brother. She knew she was in for a long vigil.

"Death and damnation!" swore Cat as she read the note from her aunt. "Wouldn't you just know it? The first money we've ever had and now I have to waste it traveling up to London. It's just so damned typical of him!"

"Did something happen to Rancid?" asked Spider.

"This letter is from Auntie Lil—his sister. Apparently he's had an accident and wants me immediately."

"He's most likely been wounded in a duel by an outraged husband he's been clapping horns on."

"What woman would look at him? He's never sober these days. More likely he's been caught cheating at cards. Now that he needs a bloody nurse, I'm the candidate."

"It's over two hundred miles to London. How long will it take to ride that far?" he asked doubtfully.

"I hate the thought of ruining Ebony on such a journey. Hell and fury, Rancid isn't worth it. Why don't we go down into Falmouth and see if someone's sailing to Portsmouth today? I can take the London coach from there."

Cat was worried to death to leave Spider on his own, but did not dare to mention it. Her brother wondered wildly how he could let Cat go to such a far-off, wicked city but knew better than to suggest she needed an escort.

Knowing how bitter cold it could be aboard ship, she donned a wool pea jacket and pulled a knitted cap over her tightly braided hair, and they set off at a brisk pace for Falmouth. A casual observer would have taken them for brothers.

It was only a mile and a half to Falmouth's waterfront taverns, and Cat strolled in as nonchalantly as Spider did and struck up a conversation with the seamen drinking there. She paid for two half-pints of ale and began to make casual inquiries. There were quite a few vessels anchored just beyond the seawall, and by asking the right questions and being observant, they soon learned one was obtained by an American. Cat joined him at his table and leaned until her chair was balanced on its two back legs.

"Carolinas?" she asked lazily.

"Virginia," answered the blond giant.

"Expect you've blown off course."

"Could be," he answered noncommittally.

"I expect you're headed for Portsmouth or London."

"Could be," he repeated.

"What cargo?" she asked casually.

"Fish!" he said very deliberately.

Her heart lifted, but she dared not let a grin escape. She finished her ale, wiped her sleeve across her mouth, and eased the chair back onto its four legs.

Her eyes slid over to Spider and as if on cue he said, "I suppose you want to unload your cargo before you run up the Channel?"

The American nodded. "Ship'll run up the Channel a helluva lot faster with an empty hold."

"Suppose," said Cat, "just suppose I supplied storage space for these barrels of fish. That way you could get your ship through London customs and then find a high-paying customer for your cargo. 'Course you'd have to ship it overland, but you could pass that cost on to your buyer."

While the American skipper was making up his mind about trusting them, Spider said innocently, "I hope your fish won't spoil. I hope it's well salted."

"What do you get out of this?" the American asked bluntly.

"As soon as we stow the cargo, you take me on an overnight run up the Channel to Portsmouth." The bargain was struck and the American went to gather his crew.

Cat said to Spider, "While I'm gone I want you to take the tobacco out of those barrels and conceal it. Take a bit of that money we've got and buy some cheap fish to replace it.

"Say no more." Spider winked.

"When they come for their 'fish,' there won't be a bloody thing they can do about it," she said, her eyes sparkling with the mere idea of the sting.

When they got into the longboat with the crew to row out to the ship, Cat ran alarmed eyes over the sailors. They were a mighty rough-looking crew, no better than criminals. A shiver of fear ran up her back and she pulled her woolen hat down low and turned up her collar. When she got the opportunity to speak to Spider, she whispered, "When we get to the caverns, go upstairs and get a pair of Rancid's pistols; one for each of us."

He nodded quickly in full agreement. The unloading, however, went off without incident. There were only forty barrels to unload and Cat surmised they must have already smuggled most of their cargo into France. The wind changed to a strong westerly and Cat gave Spider a brief wave. She could not afford a tender farewell in front of the American, but she did not need to put into words that she would be back as quickly as she could.

Aboard the *Seagull* on the upper deck she made herself comfortable on a coil of rope with her back against the taffrail. Cat loved the sea. It filled her with excitement. There was nothing quite so wild—untamed—unpredictable. The sea would never allow anything or anyone to control it. It was never safe, always dangerous, and her blood sang with a feeling of "oneness" and total freedom.

In the early hours, somewhere between midnight and dawn, Randal St. Catherine roused his sister where she sat napping in the chair beside his bed.

"The doctor . . . said I was finished . . . didn't he?" he gasped.

Lil bent close to catch his words. The candles clearly showed his dreadful gray pallor and eyes already beginning to film over. Lil reached for the glass and decanter. "Have some brandy, Randal, you were always particularly partial to good brandy."

He grasped the decanter in a feeble hand and shook his head. "Book . . . papers . . . hidden . . . under seat." He coughed and choked, then managed to say, "Summer . . . she'll know . . . black ma . . ."

"Black man?" Lil puzzled. "You mean you have a book hidden under the seat in your carriage and you want me to see that your daughter Summer gets it? I'd better go and see if it's still there." She took one of the candles and hurried from the room. She knew the book must contain some valuable information or he wouldn't have it concealed. At first she couldn't find it, then to her relief her hand closed on a sealed paper and a small, leather-bound volume tucked at the back, and she pulled them out and opened up the book. She held the candle close to see what was written on the pages, but it told her nothing. She recognized the names of places in Cornwall; there were dates and names and what might be ship's names but that was all. She hurried back upstairs with a dozen questions on her lips, but she saw immediately she would never know the answers. Randal had deliberately drained the decanter and the brandy had killed him.

Cat arrived in Portsmouth just as dawn was breaking. The gulls screamed and circled, hoping the ship was bringing in fish, and she smiled to herself as she thought of the cargo of tobacco safely concealed beneath Roseland.

From Portsmouth she had lots of time to take the early-morning mail coach for London. The fare they asked seemed outrageous to Cat, so she haggled and finally agreed to ride outside the coach next to the driver for a cheaper rate. Each time they came to a steep incline the carriage stopped and all passengers disembarked to trudge up the hill on foot, so it wasn't until five weary hours later that the coach pulled into Lud Lane off Gresham Street.

Cat had paid little attention to the open meadows of sheep and cows, nor had she noticed much difference in the villages which clustered on the outskirts of the city, but once she spotted the spires of hundreds of churches dominating the skyline she felt her excitement begin to well up inside her.

Soon her senses were reeling. Her ears were assaulted by the mixed cacophony of church bells, river traffic, porters, vendors, draymen, and the babble of a thousand voices. Her nose was assaulted by the unpleasant stench of open sewers, rotting vegetation, sweating horses, and unwashed humanity.

Her eyes darted about; she wanted to experience every detail of the greatest city in the world. London was walled, and after they passed over the great bridge which actually had houses and shops built on it, they passed through one of the entrance gates into the city.

To Cat it seemed overcrowded wherever she looked and she wondered what had happened to draw all the people. Gradually she realized it must always be like this. Her eyes were huge in her face as she saw magnificently dressed men and women in satins and velvet walk past filthy cripples and beggars. Some of the ladies wore black masks over their faces; others, obviously housewives and servants, were doing their shopping.

All the places of business had signs hanging outside their premises and apprentices stood in the doorways hawking their goods. Porters staggered under huge boxes of goods, others pushed handcarts over the cobbles, their loads piled so high they were in danger of toppling over.

She saw children singing for pennies, pickpockets and wig snatchers plaguing the crowds, cavaliers on horseback, and drunken fops outside taverns. The traffic slowed the coach to a crawl as they waited for hackney carriages, merchants' wagons, and sedan chairs. Cat learned a few choice curses she'd never heard

before from the driver as he waved his whip and threatened ana-
tomical indignities with it if they didn't "make way."

Cat was caught up in the violent energy of the place and she
instantly recognized that she would have to be constantly on her
toes here if she expected to be one step ahead of anyone else.

Next to the coach station in Lud Lane was an inn called the
Swan with Two Necks and she asked a young barmaid scrubbing
the steps how to get to Cockspur Street.

"Oooo, 'oity-toity," replied the wench upon hearing the fashionable address.

"Silly bitch, speak English," said Cat, annoyed.

"Well, I never!" said the maid, picking up her bucket and throwing the dirty water over Cat's dusty boots.

Cat grabbed a handful of her hair and said, "Tell me how to get
to Cockspur Street or I'll mop the bloody road with you."

"Lawks! Leggo! Murder!"

"It will be murder if you don't tell me," Cat threatened.

"Down Fleet to the Strand . . . straight down the Strand
nearly to the palace."

Cat murmured under her breath, "Look out, London, here I
come, ready or not!" At that moment her stomach rolled so loudly,
a mangy mongrel jumped aside and she let out a peel of laughter.
She bought a veal pasty from a pieman to stave off her hunger and
strode off toward Fleet Street.

Every detail fascinated her. She glanced in every shop, here an
apothecary offering cures for impotence, there a secondhand clothing shop offering dead men's boots, and on each and every corner
stood a tavern named after Charles II, either the King's Head, the
King's Arms, or the Royal Oak. She saw boy chimney sweeps, soot
black from head to foot, and a rat catcher with dead rats and mice
hanging from his hat.

By the time she had followed the Strand around the bend in the
river and located Cockspur Street she was dusty, dirty, and foot-
sore. She noticed that in this part of town the streets were clean
and the houses immaculate. She ran up the steps of number five
and knocked loudly. A footman opened the door, looked down his
long nose at her, and said, "Get away from this house, you varlet."

In a flash her boot prevented him shutting the door in her face.
She reached inside the jacket and pulled out a pistol. His eyes
rolled up into his head and he cried, "Help! Robbers!"

A woman's voice drawled, "James, whatever is the racket, don't you know the house is in mourning?"

Cat looked over the sophisticated woman from head to toe, taking in the platinum curls, the painted face, the silk gown, the ivory fan, and the white Persian cat on a silver leash, and said uncertainly, "Auntie Lil?"

The small woman looked at her blankly.

"I'm Summer, but I prefer to be called Cat." She tucked the pistol away and pulled out the letter. Lady Richwood's mouth fell open. Recovering only slightly, her hand at her throat, she said, "How extraordinary! How did you get here?"

"I walked."

"How extraordinary! Come in before anyone sees you." As Lil stood staring at the young girl who was her niece, her heart melted like snow in summer. "Oh, child, whatever has he done to you?" she cried. She had been prepared to thoroughly dislike Lady Summer St. Catherine, thinking her the spoiled and pampered heiress of Roseland, but the girl she saw before her had obviously had no advantages whatsoever. In fact, by the looks of her, she had been neglected shamefully. "Come and sit down, darling, I'm afraid I have some upsetting news for you." She took a deep breath. "Your father died last night."

Cat pulled off her woolen cap and her hair fell about her shoulders untidily. She felt nothing. No sorrow. No joy. "I feel numb," she said, sitting down hard on the elegant brocade settee.

"Summer, my poor darling, you don't need to explain things to me. He was my brother. I know what a swine he was. He isn't in the house—the undertaker took him for burial to St. John's-in-the-Wood. . . . I didn't know if you would come."

"There's no money to pay for it, what will I do?" asked Cat helplessly.

"Well, I think we've both had experience in coping when th[ere's] no money." She removed the silver leash from the white P[ersian] cat and it jumped up on the brocade settee. "First things fir[st,] look like you haven't eaten in a week."

"I've eaten twice."

"Today?"

"No . . . this week."

"Oh, darling, you are droll. We need something to [warm y]ou up. For dessert we'll have strawberries. I'm particular[ly partial to] strawberries," she drawled. "I'll feed you and bathe you, and then we'll do what women do best. We'll talk, darling."

Lil found her a snow-white nightgown beribboned and decorated with lace. It was easily the prettiest garment she had ever worn. Her freshly washed hair curled damply about her face as she sat beside the bedchamber fire to dry it.

"Now then, darling," said Lil in her beautiful, husky drawl, "your father asked me to give you this book and these papers. Said something about a black man which made no sense."

Cat unsealed the large parchment and slowly began to decipher the legal words. Suddenly she jumped up and sent her stool flying. "The man should burn in hell!" she cried. "He's mortgaged Roseland to the hilt and the note is due! My God, if he wasn't dead, I'd kill him!" She paced the room and tore open a second paper. "Oh, no! It's a bill of sale for my horse, Ebony. Rancid old bastard! I've got to get home . . . I've got to get some money . . . but how?"

"It has always been my experience, Summer darling, that since men control all the wealth, it is only logical that a woman who needs money must get it from some man."

"You mean marry for money?" asked Cat with loathing. "I don't think I could ever marry, not even for money. All men are vile and selfish. If I married someone wealthy, my money problems might be solved, but my other problems would just be starting and I'd be saddled with him for the rest of my life. The last thing I want is marriage!"

"Oh, darling, it isn't as simple as that. In London marriage, I'm afraid, is completely out of fashion. Liaisons are all the rage now, you see, but in your case even that would be almost impossible."

"Why?" asked Cat bluntly.

Lady Richwood hesitated then decided to speak plainly. "You are out of fashion. They are mad for blondes at the moment. Black hair on a woman is considered ugly, foreign, Portuguese like the poor unfortunate Queen. Darling, let me be blunt with you. You stride about in boots like a man, swearing and saying exactly what you think. Men don't want that. They want a painted doll who smiles sweetly, eats like a bird, dresses like an angel, has the manners of a lady, someone who is dainty, amusing, and acquiescent."

"Acquiescent?" repeated Cat suspiciously.

"Someone willing to do whatever they ask in bed," supplied Lil.

"So that's what liaison means," said Cat, shuddering. "Men are ugly evil. In this world men do all the taking and women do all the giving. It's not fair! You are suggesting I sell my body for money to some lecherous old man. I'd much rather steal the money. It wouldn't bother my conscience to steal from a man."

"Darling," Lil said patiently, rolling the word about her mouth until it came out like a caress, "in London men keep their wealth safely deposited with a goldsmith or banker, it's not left lying about for thieves. I think you have the spirit to be a great adventuress. Why not turn the tables for once? Use men the way they usually use women. You have great 'potential' beauty, darling, and if you are the clever girl I think, you could save Roseland and live the rest of your life in luxury. By the use of flattery and promises I'd be willing to bet you could get your hands on some dear man's fortune, and when it came time to pay the piper you could get away with actually delivering very little. That way he'd be 'giving' and you'd be 'taking.' "

Cat's sense of humor came to her rescue. "Well, I must admit the thought of turning the tables on some wealthy swine is tempting. My brother could help me to fleece him. Poor Spider is a lord whose life has been more meager than a stableboy's." The smile evaporated. "I couldn't do it," she decided firmly.

"No, darling, you're quite right, you couldn't do it," said Lil. "Why, you've never even held a fan in your hand. The fan has a whole language of its own dedicated to flirtation. You don't know how to dress or how to dance. You probably don't even know how to walk in high-heeled slippers, and I bet you couldn't giggle if I paid you," said Lil, using reverse psychology. "No, I doubt you could become a man's mistress, let alone receive a respectable offer of marriage."

Cat was stung by her words. If she set her mind to it, she could wrap a man about her little finger, aye, and get him to propose. Then she laughed out loud as she realized Lil was teasing her. Ruefully she said, "It's the only way to save Roseland, isn't it? Much as I hate the idea, I fear you're right. I'll have to learn all the tricks. I'll have to learn how to become a lady. I'm a wonderful mimic. . . . Let me show you." She grabbed Lil's ivory fan and spread it flirtatiously. Then she drawled huskily, "I could be particularly partial to a rich gentleman."

Lil laughed. "Oh, darling, you have me exactly!"

"That's because you fascinate me! Everything you say sounds deliciously suggestive, even when you're talking about strawberries."

Lil laughed delightedly, then she said practically, "We'll sell his horses and carriage to pay for the burial and we'll get you some pretty clothes with whatever is left over. In the meantime I'll lend you whatever you need."

"Oh, I shouldn't waste money on clothes," said Cat doubtfully.

"It isn't a waste, Summer. If you are to catch a gull, you must first bait the trap. Get some sleep now. Tomorrow afternoon I'll take you to see a play. 'Tis about a maid who masquerades as a titled lady and manages to catch an earl. That lesson shouldn't be lost on you, and then," she drawled without taking a breath, "in the evening I'll take you to a party Lady Shrewsbury is giving. If you keep your mouth closed and your eyes and ears open, you will see how to conduct yourself in society. The rest will be up to you. I know you are anxious to return home and I think your prospects for marriage would be much greater in Cornwall than in London, darling. The men at Court are rather jaded where women are concerned. They are onto almost every female trick in our vast repertoire."

"Good night, Lil. I appreciate all the help and advice you can give me. I'm woefully ignorant."

"Well, darling, starting tomorrow you are to drop the ridiculous name of Cat. Summer is a beautiful name; a name to make a man remember you."

Summer climbed into bed and picked up the small book her father had left for her. She glanced through the pages with a slight frown, not knowing exactly what all the prominent names meant and then suddenly it struck her. As soon as she read the words "Lizard Point" and the date, a sickening feeling of revulsion swept over her. It was one of the nightmares she had tried to blot out of existence, but here it was all neatly listed, page by sickening page.

A few years back she had followed her father one night as he'd ridden from Roseland. She had been insatiably curious about what lured him out on a night when a gale was blowing up. They had ridden to Lizard Point, where the lighthouse warned mariners of the treacherous rocks. A southwest gale always drove ships inshore and she watched in horror as her father joined a group of wreckers. They had put out the light of the beacon atop the cliffs and built signal fires below on the treacherous shore to lure a ship onto the rocks.

She threw the book aside and closed her eyes. She could still hear the screams of the victims when the great ship broke and splintered as it was driven aground. At dawn when the gale had subsided, she looked down a hundred and eighty feet from the cliffs above and saw all the poor drowned bodies. Her father hadn't said "black man," he'd said "blackmail." She could use this book to blackmail prominent families. As if she'd make money from wrecking! Now she remembered why she hated her father so much. All men were created evil.

Suddenly she was filled with a burning need to even the score. She would accept Lil's challenge to get the money she needed from some wealthy man. She was sick and tired of being a victim. She would enjoy turning a man into one for a change.

4

"There isn't a woman alive who can be trusted," said Ruark Helford, picking up his cards negligently.

"I've known since I was in my cradle that only a fool would trust a woman," answered Charles Stuart in his lazy, cynical way.

Buckingham had just let Ruark know that his mistress had been seen flirting with the Duke of York. They were all playing cards in Her Majesty's drawing room, the gaming tables piled with gold crowns. Catherine's rooms had become the fashionable gathering place for the courtiers and ladies only because Charles chose to spend his evenings there lately. He was doing his very best to be a dutiful husband and had succeeded admirably except for the one bone of contention which stood between him and his queen, namely his long-standing mistress, Barbara Palmer.

Charles looked across the room at Barbara now and she raised her eyebrows to him in a mute question. He did not commit himself and merely lowered one lazy eyelid in a wink. He sighed. She had such a voluptuous beauty, how could he resist her mahogany-colored hair spread across the pillows or her generous breasts, which filled his hands to overflowing? If only she were a little less tempestuous, a little more malleable . . . a little less domineering, a little more submissive . . . a little less extravagant, a little more prudent . . . a little less demanding, and a little more faithful.

Lord Helford's face was impassive but beneath the facade he was irritated by Buckingham. He had never liked the man, but knew he made a better friend than enemy. As for Ruark's current mistress, Ann Ashley, he didn't disbelieve that the jade had been flirting with the King's brother James. He had told her he was leaving for Cornwall soon, but dammit, he thought irritably, she could let the sheets cool off before replacing him in her bed. Ann had asked him to take her with him, hinting at marriage. The fact that he'd politely but firmly declined was doubtless the reason for her blatant behavior with James. He had more good sense than to marry his mistress. Women were all alike, he thought cynically—every last one of them looking to sell themselves to the highest bidder.

His mind went back to the first young woman he'd ever kept. It seemed impossible, looking back, that he'd ever been that naive, but he'd been taken like a trout on a hook. He'd paid over a year for the child she had borne until one night when too much liquor had been imbibed, his friend Sandwich admitted he'd gotten the girl with child before he introduced her to Ruark. Well, that had been the first and last time he'd ever let a woman make a fool of him.

It didn't take Buckingham long to see that the King and Helford were preoccupied with their own thoughts, and he took instant advantage until the pile of gold crowns on the table became his. The money he won meant little to him, but the sense of power he experienced as he stretched out his hand for his gains, observing his opponents' faces, gave him deep satisfaction.

Disgusted, Charles rose from the game and went to stand behind Her Majesty. Catherine had acquired a taste for gambling and knew herself to be very wicked because of the habits she had picked up at her husband's court. He bent low to whisper into her ear and she took his advice and immediately won.

It was close to midnight and Charles bent again to her ear with a more amorous suggestion. The company could not leave before the Queen, so when she reluctantly arose and summoned one of her ladies, not a few of the assembled guests were relieved. It was fortunate there had been no dancing planned or it might have gone on until five or six in the morning.

More than an hour had elapsed before the King's last gentleman of the bedchamber departed. In brocade dressing gown Charles

made his way to Her Majesty's privy apartment, his beloved spaniels at his heel. To his consternation Catherine knelt at the small
altar she had had set up in her dressing room, and two of her ladies
she had brought from Portugal were still in attendance.

He coughed discreetly, hoping they would take the hint and
depart, but they did not. Charles, usually good-natured and well
mannered, patiently waited another twenty minutes while his de-
vout little wife finished her prayers. Finally he opened wide the
door between the bedchamber and dressing room, affording the
dogs entrance to the other chamber. He knew full well her attendants did not have the inborn love of dogs that most English did
and he hoped to chase them away by this gesture. Obviously it was
not working, and feeling irritated, he went through the adjoining
door to expedite matters.

Catherine knelt in her voluminous nightgown, her face uplifted
to the cross upon the wall.

"My dear, come to bed, you will catch your death there upon
your knees."

"I won't be a moment, Charles," came the soft little voice, but
he received a quelling look from the Countess of Penalva.

Charles's lips tightened. "You ladies may withdraw," he said
firmly.

Penalva and Countess Ponteval, her constant chaperons, exchanged glances and raised their brows at Catherine.

Charles's temper frayed a little, yet he spoke to them with humor. "'Sblood ladies, I don't think Catherine needs protection
from me. She is my wife and I get to use her seldom enough with
you constantly standing guard over her."

They disapproved of everything about Charles Stuart and made
no effort to hide their feelings. With great reluctance they departed
with an air of abandoning an innocent lamb to a wolf.

When they were alone, Charles strolled up behind Catherine and
said softly, "My love, when you are without sin, why do you find it
necessary to spend so much time on your pretty knees asking
God's forgiveness?"

She turned from the altar with a determined look of defiance on
her face. "I'm not praying for myself, Charles; I'm praying for
you."

"Ah, my love, if you stayed upon your knees throughout eternity, I doubt me you could get all my sins forgiven." He smiled at
her and his swarthy good looks almost melted her heart. He took

her hands into his and firmly lifted her from her knees. Then he whispered, "Come to bed, Catherine." His head dipped low to kiss her, but she turned her face from him and by doing so confirmed what he had suspected. The delayed bedding was a deliberate tactic, a prelude to an unpleasant matter she wished to discuss.

Charles sighed. All he wanted was a pleasant hour's lovemaking, during which, if he was lucky enough, his seed would fill his little queen with an heir to the throne. God knows, he knew better than to expect passion from her. She could never satisfy his deep sensuality and he accepted that with a good grace and treated her with gentle kindness, but her reserve and reticence in all things sexual were beginning to weary him.

She allowed him to lead her into the bedchamber, but not to bed. "Charles," she began bravely, "there is a course you are determined upon which will destroy my happiness completely."

"Surely even I could not be such a brute, Catherine," he demurred.

She flushed because Charles had been kindness itself to her. Others may have laughed at her foreign clothes, speech, and manners, but never Charles. A tiny sob escaped her lips. "It is *that woman* again," she said, lifting reproachful eyes to him.

Charles kept a wise silence.

"It has come to my ears that she has demanded you make her a countess." She stamped her slippered foot in determination. "I do not wish it!"

"My dear, if I choose to honor Mrs. Palmer, try to understand that it in no way dishonors you."

" 'Tis like a slap in the face to flaunt her before me." Catherine's sallow face flushed a dark red.

Charles glanced wistfully at the bed where the two spaniels had stretched out to make themselves comfortable, then he sat down on its edge. "Catherine, there is no dishonor to have been mistress to the King. You wish me to end the liaison, but it would be most unkind of me to simply cast her off. The whole court would ostracize her. Like a wolf pack they would rend her to shreds. By bestowing the honor of a title upon her, I fulfill my obligation to the lady. Surely you will be generous in this, Catherine."

"What obligation?" she flared.

Charles had a dominant mother who had tried to bully him all his life. Simply because he was good-natured, most women thought they could control him. They could not. "She has just borne me a son. It is no secret."

Catherine burst into tears. "I've heard the whispers . . . you think I'm barren!"

He gathered her close and tipped her face up to his. "I think no such thing, sweetheart. I'll put an end to the whispers tonight," he said, drawing off her nightgown and removing his brocade robe. In the wide bed, he nudged the dogs over with his long thigh and took Catherine into his arms. She hid her face against his broad chest and bathed him with her tears. With infinite patience he cradled her until she had cried herself out. She was extremely slim and her breasts were as underdeveloped as a girl of eleven, but he stroked her gently and thumbed her tiny nipples. He kissed her a half-dozen times then murmured firmly, "The matter of Lady Castlemaine is closed." He purposely used the title he was about to bestow upon Barbara.

In a small voice Catherine said, "I'm afraid it isn't." She hesitated a moment then blurted, "I asked Chancellor Hyde not to allow Parliament to sanction her title."

Charles was furious. Though the Queen seemed sweet and biddable in most things, in this she was determined to thwart him. He threw back the covers and set his long legs to the carpet. "Good night, madame," he said coldly.

"Charles, where are you going?" she gasped piteously.

The King did not bother to reply. He thought his destination was patently obvious. He went out through the privy garden and took a shortcut to King's Street which ran through the palace grounds. Barbara Palmer's fashionable house was situated most conveniently. It was almost 2:30 in the morning, but he felt confident that she would welcome him with open arms.

Her household servants did not bat an eye as the King of England made his stealthy way up the stairs to milady's chamber. Barbara was in bed, fortunately alone, but when she heard the familiar step she was awake instantly.

"Don't get up, darling, I'll join you in a moment," Charles said, removing his coat.

Barbara threw aside the covers, lighted a dozen candles, and stood before him, her ample charms displayed in a pale lavender nightgown. His eyes darkened with desire, but she held up a forbidding hand. "Sire, we must talk."

He sighed. She wouldn't use a formal title unless she wished to discuss something serious. "We'll talk later, Babs, just looking at you has made me hard as marble." He was on her in two long strides. His practiced, skillful hands pulled the straps of her nightgown from her shoulders, baring her heavy breasts to his heated gaze. He lifted one in his strong, brown hand and bent his mouth to the succulent, dark aureola. He knew he could rouse her to scalding passion in moments with his hands and mouth. She tossed her magnificent head of mahogany-colored hair and cupped his hardness with one knowing hand. As he groaned his need she placed her other hand on her own breast and deliberately pulled the nipple from his mouth. "We will talk now. Your marble rolling pin can wait till later. Charles, I heard something today that made me want to die!" she said dramatically. "There is a conspiracy afoot to make sure I never receive the title you have faithfully promised me!" She clutched the lavender gown to partially conceal her breasts.

"Barbara, you know I will do everything in my power to see you created Countess of Castlemaine," he soothed. "Come to bed, your king needs your services."

"Everything in your power!" she scorned. "Anyone would think that old man Hyde has more power than you. Get rid of him, Charles!"

"In a way Edward Hyde does have more power than I. He is my chancellor, Barbara, and the head of Parliament."

"Well, if you intend to let everyone dictate to you, including your wife, I can clearly see your promises are just empty words."

"Her Majesty does not dictate to me," he said ironically, "but you, my love, fight me tooth and nail every chance you get. I swear 'tis so you can display how lovely you are when you are angered," he said in a coaxing voice as he moved close and slid one strong hand up her arm to rest on her bare shoulder.

She flung his hand off. "I always allow you to take advantage of me. You think everything can be settled in bed," she stormed.

"So most things can, love. Come, Barbara, you know your need is as great as mine." His hand moved to cup her magnificent breast again and she moaned low in her throat. "No, no, noooo, Charles, not this time. When I think of the sacrifices I've made for you, my blood runs cold and now you won't even take my part against them!"

"Sacrifices, Barbara?" he asked, thinking of the money, houses, and jewels he'd lavished on her.

"I'm the scandal of Whitehall—the whole court knows you're at me in daylight hours as well as at night. I've sacrificed my reputation, I've sacrificed the goodwill of my husband." She threw open the bedchamber door and cried dramatically, "Come with me to the nursery and I'll show the other sacrifices I've suffered for you."

"Barbara, be still! It would be cruel and thoughtless to waken the children at this hour." He sighed deeply. "I wish you could find it in your heart to be generous toward me, Babs. I've just spent a miserable two hours with Her Majesty over you."

"Have you?" She looked inordinately pleased, and went to pour herself a glass of white Rhenish wine. As she walked before the fire her luscious curves were silhouetted through the sheer nightgown and Charles bit down hard on his lip to prevent himself from seizing her and forcing compliance.

He said shrewdly, "You aren't going to let me into your bed, are you?"

"Not until this matter is settled, Charles."

He lifted her velvet bedgown in his long fingers. "Then for God's sake put this on . . . you're driving me mad!"

"Did you know that Her Majesty expressly forbade Hyde signing my title?" she demanded.

"Clarendon isn't the sort of man who would let either Catherine or myself sway him from his duty," explained Charles.

Barbara screamed, picked up a flacon of expensive perfume, and threw it against the wall. "Clarendon? Clarendon?" she screamed like a demented parrot. "So it's true . . . you've given him an earldom while denying me my title!"

"I've denied you nothing, Barbara."

She cried hysterically, drowning out his words. "I've been like a faithful wife to you and this is the thanks I get . . . cast aside like an old shoe!"

The King smiled cynically. "Wives are notoriously faithless and you're no exception, and as for that last accusation about casting you aside, one glance will show you I'm ready, willing, and eager to make love to you the rest of the night. Trouble is, Barbara, I believe you derive more pleasure creating a scene and watching me beg than in lying with me."

His words infuriated her. "You know that's not true. I'm the most passionate woman you've ever made love to! I'm the only woman who can match your sensuality. I'm always eager to satisfy any new tastes for which you develop an appetite."

"Yes, that is true," he said wistfully, "but for eleven years I went hat in hand across Europe. My begging days are over, Barbara." He donned his purple velvet coat and clapped his hat upon his head. "See an apothecary about these vapors, madame, I find them increasingly tiresome," he warned. "I bid you good night, or rather good morning!"

5

Ruark Helford was faring no better than his monarch. After he left Her Majesty's drawing room he made his way to the fashionable house he had rented in Tothill Street for Mistress Ann Ashley. He let himself in quietly then realized there was little need for quiet since she was not yet at home.

He made himself comfortable by removing his hat and coat and helped himself to a bottle of burgundy. He could not question her maid as she was nowhere to be found and so he sat back to wait with his feet propped up casually on a polished table.

After an hour and the burgundy had both disappeared he was spoiling for a fight. He opened a small drawer in the table and began to leaf through Ann's bills. The muscle in his jaw clenched like iron as he found she had run up five hundred pounds in clothes and jewels this week alone.

She came in with her maid, saw the look on his face, and said quickly, "Leave us, Millie."

Ruark Helford greeted her with neither word nor kiss, and she saw by his stance that he was in a very dangerous mood. She threw her fan, muff, mask, and cloak into a chair and began to undo her gown. She knew she must get him into bed as quickly as possible. She said breathlessly, "Ruark, darling, I thought you were with the

King tonight. If I'd been expecting you, I wouldn't have dreamed of going to Elizabeth Hamilton's supper party."

Still holding the bills, he regarded her figure from head to foot and she babbled, "I needed a new gown, Ruark."

He slanted an eyebrow. "One?"

"Well, three then . . . and I thought perhaps you'd like to make me a gift of the pearls as a sort of goodbye present." She pouted prettily. "I wish you weren't leaving for Cornwall, darling, I'll simply die of loneliness."

She had removed her gown and stood before him in her busk, a small corset which uplifted her breasts, and a pair of lace stockings with pink garters. She prayed the dishabille would divert him. It did not.

"Are there any more of these or is this the lot?" He casually waved the fistful of bills.

She approached him carefully. "You've spoiled me so much, my love, let me thank you in the way you love best." She removed the busk and he glanced down at her small, pretty breasts and tiny waist. She stood on tiptoe and slid her arms up about his neck, bringing her bared breasts in contact with his wide chest.

He removed her arms from his neck and stepped away from her.

"What's wrong?" she demanded, eyes blazing. "You act as if you don't want me to touch you!"

"I don't," he said simply, "not until I've learned where you've been."

"I told you I was at a supper party—"

"Ann, don't insult my intelligence," he warned. His eyes were so cold, she reached for a silk robe to cover her nakedness.

"You've been listening to gossip. There's always someone at Court ready to run to you with lies."

"The rumors link you with the King's brother, James." He said it flatly and awaited her denial. It came in a great rush of protest. She ran the gamut from anger to swearing before God, to the prettiest tears to which a man had ever been subjected. Finally she threw herself facedown upon the bed and waited for the mattress to dip, telling her she would be in his arms in another moment.

She waited in vain. Fear crept up her spine. She could never manipulate Ruark Helford the way she could other men. That's what made him so damned attractive. His face was always dark, hard, and impossible to read. His mouth had a hint of the ruthless savage about it. It was the kind of mouth that made a woman die for his kisses. She felt the danger in the room ready to explode, and it made her breasts tingle and the spot between her legs throbbed with the ache to have him fill her.

She cursed herself for a fool for flirting with James, Duke of York, before Ruark was out of the picture, but when he'd told her he was returning to Cornwall, her loss had been so great, so devastating, she had acted irrationally. Her loss wasn't just financial—one rich man could always be replaced by another rich man—her loss was emotional and physical. She had allowed herself to fall in love with him and allowed herself to dream of marriage.

She could never quite believe her own good fortune in attracting the most virile, desirable male at Court. He could never be replaced by any other courtier save a royal one, and that was the reason she'd encouraged the King's brother. She rolled over onto her back and temptingly stroked the sole of a lacy foot along her other leg. She asked breathlessly, "Are you going to punish me?" She needed his hands on her body, one way or another.

His hazel eyes darkened to deep brown and he half closed his eyelids to mask the pity in them. "You will be punished for your actions, my dearest Ann, but not by my hand." He hesitated, then said quietly, "James has syphilis."

Her eyes widened in fear and the blood drained from her face. Ruark silently picked up his coat and his wide-brimmed hat. "I'll take care of the bills," he said quietly, and took his leave.

Two tall, dark men walking from opposite directions came face-to-face in Birdcage Walk. Ruark Helford swept off his hat in deference to his king. Charles's cynical voice drawled, "Nothing like a stroll in St. James Park at four o'clock in the morning."

"No, Sire. 'Tis the only way to avoid the riffraff," replied Helford sardonically.

"I'm rather fond of riffraff," mused Charles.

Helford raised an eyebrow to mock himself, "I think we're in the same boat, Sire."

"Women!" snorted Charles. "Where the hell can a king get laid?" He lifted his head to see that the first faint rays of dawn lightened the sky. "A fast game of tennis until daylight? It's the only sport we'll get this night."

Ruark bowed his acceptance. "If you don't think we'll get carted off to Bedlam with the rest of the lunatics." His body screamed for action. He would have preferred being behind his ship's wheel in a storm, or riding a blooded stallion across the moors, but in a pinch a brutal game of tennis might rid him of his spleen.

They walked briskly through the park to the tennis courts, and as they passed the grassless alley where they played pall mall with wooden mallets, sending the ball through hoops fifteen feet from the ground, Charles said, "I'd prefer a game of pall mall but I don't suppose we could round up eight other fools at this hour."

Their play was so fast and furious they were soon shirtless. The two athletic, powerful men were so well matched it took two full hours of play to determine an even number of games won by each would have to be called a draw.

As the two companions donned their shirts and coats, Charles said, "Ruark is an Irish name isn't it?"

Helford nodded. "My mother was Irish."

"That gives me an idea, by God! I'll put Barbara's title through the Irish peerage since Clarendon refuses to sign it!"

"Brilliantly devious, sir," said Ruark, flashing white teeth.

Charles said seriously, "One learns to be devious when dealing with women." The two men were walking across St. James Park toward Whitehall when the King got another brilliant idea.

"Auntie Lil!" he said, stopping in his tracks.

"I beg your pardon?" said Ruark.

"We'll call on Auntie Lil . . . she's right here in Cockspur Street. I've a mind to be introduced to some pretty young thing, and what better place than Auntie Lil's?"

Ruark demurred. "I was introduced to a young woman at Auntie Lil's once . . . before I was done, she cost me a fortune and wasn't even virgin."

Charles laughed. "Virginity isn't all its cracked up to be—just thinking of all the necessary breaking in fatigues me."

Ruark knew he was thinking of Queen Catherine.

"You know, Ru, in my experience, which is rumored to be extensive, women are all the same."

Ruark silently disagreed with him. If he could meet an attractive lady who hadn't slept with the King and half his court, he'd probably consider marrying her.

The King continued, "On the surface Catherine and Barbara seem worlds apart, yet underneath both use sexual favors to get their own way. Then if they don't get their own way, they withhold those favors."

"Well," said Ruark, "there's not much point in my going to Lil's

with you, Sire. I'm for Cornwall in a week's time and the last thing
I need is a female entanglement. I've only just managed to extract
myself from one."

"Helford, you swore an oath to support your monarch in any
undertaking. As your superior, I command you attend me."

Ruark lifted one brow, dark as a raven's wing. "I have no superior, Sire."

Charles looked at him with admiration. " 'Sdeath, I do believe
you speak the truth." Charles's face was transformed by a lazy,
charming smile. "As my friend, come and give me moral support."

The white Persian cat had chosen to sleep in Summer's chamber,
but by the door scratching it was now doing, it obviously needed to
go outside. She threw back the covers, hesitated a moment over
going downstairs in the snowy nightgown so exquisitely trimmed
in ribbon and lace, then she scooped up the small ball of white fluff
and ran downstairs. She reasoned that before six in the morning
none would be about.

She was startled by a knock on the front door just as she was
about to open it and fell back in wonder as two tall, dark gentlemen stepped confidently into the foyer. The cat, alarmed,
scratched her and jumped from her arms. "Oh, you little hellcat,"
she murmured as her eyes went wide over the magnificently garbed
pair of gentlemen callers. One was dressed in purple velvet with
gold braid, the other in black velvet with a powder blue ostrich
feather sweeping from his wide-brimmed hat. Powder blue, begod!
She'd never seen anything like it in her life.

Her eyes began at their thigh-high cavalier boots and traveled
upward to their black, shoulder-length hair and frankly assessing
eyes. One of the men held her gaze for what seemed a lifetime as
panic rose within her at her state of undress. Relief swept through
her as one of her aunt's footmen stepped into the foyer and she fled
upstairs, her black cloud of hair in wild disarray and her cheeks
stained crimson.

Ruark Helford stared up the stairs long after she had gone. The
girl's looks had almost bowled him over. Her darkly dramatic features were exotic, unusual, almost mysterious, and she was physically exciting in the extreme.

The pristine nightgown she wore with the little bows all up the
front sent his imagination soaring. Today's fashions were so voluminous a man couldn't gauge a female's figure accurately until he

actually stripped her of her whalebone and padding, but the prim white garment had fallen about her in soft folds which hinted at the delicious swell of high-pointed breasts and round bottom. When she ran up the stairs, he'd actually glimpsed bare feet and slender ankles and he prayed that the limbs above the ankles were lithe and slim.

He had already made up his mind about one thing. The first time she came to his bed he wanted her in that white thing with its row of ribbon fastenings. The thought of opening them one by one made his throat go dry. There was that about her which suggested a man might find unmatched, pleasurable fulfillment if she would ever deign to bestow her favors.

Though he knew he had never laid eyes on her before, she reminded him of something or someone. He imagined himself deep inside her and he was instantly swollen with lust.

Ruark Helford said to the King, "I feel it only sporting to let you know I'm in the running after all."

"Not a chance, Helford! Gad, I believe that's the first unpainted face I've seen in two years."

"Fifty pounds say I taste her first," wagered Ruark.

"You are ordered to Cornwall, Helford, and I see no possible reason for delay."

Summer's auntie Lil was about to descend the staircase as the breathless girl flew past her. Lil's eyes narrowed with speculation as she saw Charles Stuart larger than life in her foyer. At the foot of the staircase she swept into a deep curtsy and drawled in her plummy, provocative voice, "Your Majesty, you honor me by your visit but must it be before six in the morning, Sire?"

"Lady Richwood, your humble servant, madame," Charles said, smoothly raising her jeweled fingers to his lips. "We are such intimate friends I believed I should be welcomed at any hour."

She slid her eyes over the King's companion. "Lord Helford, I believe you near frightened my niece to death with your dangerous good looks," she drawled suggestively.

"Your, er . . . niece," said the King delicately, "has caught my eye and I beg an introduction."

Lady Richwood stiffened instantly, and to show the King of England he had committed an almost unforgivable faux pas she dropped the drawl and spoke crisply. "Gentlemen, that really is my niece, Lady Summer St. Catherine. I summoned her to London because of her father's health. Sadly he passed away yesterday. We are in mourning."

It was an age of loosest morals, but strictest manners.

"Lady Richwood, forgive us for clumsy fools. My deepest condolences, madame, on the loss of your brother. Helford, your suggestion to come here today was most ill timed."

Lil Richwood's voice softened immediately as she drawled, "You are quite forgiven. . . . I'm particularly partial to tall, dark cavaliers."

Both men bowed formally and very deeply before they departed.

6

untie Lil swept up the staircase, her eyes narrowed in speculation. She reassessed her niece with shrewd eyes before she answered the question that had burst from her lips. "It was His Majesty the King, darling, and he was definitely interested in you. But if I arrange a liaison, you will have to be a very clever girl to hold his interest more than briefly. Your competition would be formidable. However, it would be a way out of your financial difficulties."

A little maid brought a breakfast tray with fruit and croissants and chocolate to drink. Lil grimaced at Summer's healthy appetite. Slowly, between bites, Summer asked, "Do you mean share the King's bed . . . for money?"

Lil watched her face carefully as she explained, "An alcove, a bathing chamber, a carriage, or wherever else he decided to have you, not just in bed. When your tail's for sale, you might as well sell to the highest bidder."

Summer shuddered. Then slowly she licked the honey from her fingers and asked, "Who was the other man?" She knew she could never land such a big fish as the King, at least not yet. She was willing to start smaller.

"Ah, darling, I don't think you'd be Ruark Helford's type. His current mistress, Ann Ashley, is like a porcelain doll."

"Helford?" repeated Summer with great interest.

"Yes, Lord Helford owns that great estate next to yours in Cornwall, though he's not been near the place in years, I'll warrant you."

"Hell and furies, so that's Lord Helford?" mused Summer in disbelief. "I pictured him a fat, old swine." She laughed. " 'Tis not a week since I wished him a miserable night." Her eyes narrowed. "When I think of the wealth of the bloody Helfords, it makes my blood run cold. Spider and I have gone hungry for years while the lowest of his servants has lived off the fat of the land." Silently she told herself he wasn't actually repulsive, not for a rich man.

"Darling, wouldn't it be divine justice if you could get your hands on Helford's money? If you successfully pursued him, it would even the score!"

Summer wasn't convinced. She said doubtfully, "He looked at me very strangely."

"How?" asked Lil.

"Like he wanted to devour me," she said.

"That's exactly what he might do, darling; he's dangerous." Lil could see her grudging reluctance and knew she could only convince her if she presented him as a challenge. "You need a man you can lead by the nose, and though you got only one glance at him, I think you know Ruark Helford couldn't be led by a woman. Perhaps an older man would be easier to control, someone who wasn't blessed with Helford's devastating looks."

"I wouldn't call him handsome," said Summer, tossing back her hair, "though I wouldn't call him unattractive either."

"It would take a great deal of cunning to outwit Helford. If you don't think you could rise to such a challenge, let's consider another."

"No-o," said Summer, narrowing her eyes in anticipation and acceptance, "I think Ruark Helford will fit my plans very nicely."

"All right, darling, but don't say I didn't warn you! I'll find out what's going on in his life at the moment."

"How will you do that?" asked Summer with keen interest.

"My servants will find out from his servants, of course. The household grapevine—a veritable cornucopia of invaluable trivia."

"This morning I intend to see the man who holds the mortgage on Roseland. I must try to stop him from foreclosing. I will bargain with him for time, but, Lil, I know I would fare much better if I had something decent to wear."

The maid returned for the tray. "My niece and I will be upstairs in the wardrobe and cannot be disturbed for any reason." She took Summer's hand. "Come, darling, I think it's time you met Dora."

To Summer's amazement she discovered the top floor of the fashionable house in Cockspur Street was set aside for clothes. The two wardrobe rooms were presided over by Dora, who had been a wardrobe mistress at the Theatre Royal. She was a small round woman with cheeks like red apples.

Large windows ran across one wall and mirrors across another. No wonder Auntie Lil was always turned out immaculately. By way of explanation Lil drawled, "This inventory is my stock-in-trade, Summer. You'd be amazed that my well-bred young women who know exactly how to act and what to say in society haven't the slightest idea how to dress. Dora is a treasure; a miracle worker. To keep expenses down she reuses the expensive furs over and over on different cloaks and capes and hoods. The same with the exquisite beadwork and lace panels. Ribbons are the latest fashion imported from France, so by using a few hundred yard of ribbon she's transformed dozens of gowns." Without seeming to take a breath, Lil said, "Now, Dora, what do you suggest?"

"Her coloring is so vivid she will look good in almost anything. But of course if it is a spectacular effect you wish, we must pay attention to every detail. If she were being presented at Court, she would be an overnight sensation in flame-colored silk with poppies in her hair."

"Can't be done, Dora my dove, technically she's in mourning."

"Ah, then we have to be more subtle. Her colors will have to be black and white, any shade of mauve, lavender, or purple . . . gray is good also. She may wear any color on the street if she is disguised with a black velvet vizard mask . . . we have many styles."

Although Summer had never been exposed to fine clothes in her life, with unerring feminine instinct her hand fell on a pale gray velvet cloak edged in soft gray fox. Its lining was amethyst satin. "She has the eye for elegance," approved Dora. "A gray fox muff goes with that cloak and we shall pin a spray of amethysts to it . . . just so."

Summer gasped as the woman opened a many-tiered jewel box and extracted the amethyst pin.

"Glass beads, darling. The trick is to wear them with the confidence of an empress," explained Lil. "We will keep the furs for later, Dora. This morning we must go to visit the man who holds a mortgage on her estate. She must appear to be a well-bred lady in deepest mourning who has prospects. We must convey the illusion that she will redeem the mortgage if given a little time."

Dora pursed her lips and nodded her head a dozen times as if she were acknowledging some invisible advice, then she pulled out a cream velvet walking suit with braided black frogs. She chose a high-crowned, cream-colored hat adorned with a black ostrich feather curling down the cheek and under the chin to match the suit exactly, and to finish off the outfit was a pair of black kid gloves, a black fur muff, a black enamel fan, and a black silk handkerchief for the tears.

"How in the name of God will I manage a mask, a muff, a fan, and a handkerchief?"

Lil ignored her. "Dora my dove, she'll look like the King's latest mistress. Ah well, I suppose that has its advantages. Summer, you'll make me look a positive drab. I'm afraid it will have to be the black sable for me." She caressed the luxurious fur lovingly. "I'm particularly partial to sable," she cooed.

Dressing became a totally new and exciting experience for Summer. She had never even worn a lady's hat in her life, so the silken stockings, ribboned garters, and high-heeled shoes astonished her almost as much as the busk, an invention which contorted the female form by reducing the waist and lifting the breasts. The effect might be unnatural, but it was also provocative and alluring and made her breasts swell above the neckline of any gown chosen.

Since she could not manage the muff and fan as well as the long handle of a face visor, she chose instead a simple black eye mask held in place with ribbons tied beneath the saucy hat.

When she was ready, Dora beamed and Lil clapped her hands. "Darling, you amaze me. You look more like you just arrived from Paris than Cornwall! I swear by the time you've painted your face for the evening and chosen your patches, you'll be so addicted to life in London, you'll never wish to leave."

A great rush of guilt rose up to almost choke Summer as she pictured poor Spider coping on his own with the barrels of contraband tobacco and almost nothing with which to fill his young belly. Auntie Lil allowed her no time to dwell on her thoughts as she'd ordered her small carriage be readied to take them into the city.

As Summer emerged from her aunt's house and descended the

steps to the street and the waiting carriage, she did not notice the mounted figure of Lord Helford.

Ruark was on his way to the Pool of London, where his ship was being readied for the voyage to Cornwall. He had taken a short detour from the Strand up Cockspur Street for some compelling reason he couldn't explain to himself. When he spied her followed by Auntie Lil and a footman, the reason became crystal clear to him. "Summer," he breathed, "Lady Summer." She was absolutely exquisite!

Solomon Storm, the moneylender, lived in Cheapside in the City of London proper. Ruark Helford followed Lady Richwood's small carriage down the Strand to Fleet, down Ludgate Hill, and over to Cheapside. He watched Summer emerge from the carriage and head toward where the goldsmiths and moneylenders did a brisk business paying out at a comfortable interest rate of six percent. Since there had been a death in the family, he assumed that Auntie Lil had wasted no time in taking her to collect some of her inheritance.

Reluctantly, he left them to their business and carried on toward Lower Thames Street and the Pool of London.

Solomon Storm ushered the two women into his office, noting with a shrewd eye their elegant clothes. Lil cocked her head on one side to watch Summer. She was ready to jump in the moment the waters threatened to become too deep for the young girl.

"Good morning, I'm Lady Summer St. Catherine," she drawled in her attractive voice. She handed him a paper and lied without batting an eye. "I've come to make arrangements to pay this mortgage and reclaim the property my father squandered."

"My dear Lady St. Catherine, I am by no means certain I will allow you to redeem this note. As you can clearly see by the date, it is overdue by a few days. With interest it amounts to eighteen thousand pounds, and I could easily sell the note for nineteen to a land speculator who buys and sells country estates."

She gave a little laugh of disbelief. "Nineteen thousand pounds?" she asked incredulously. "My dear Mr. Storm, the art collection alone is worth more than that. The property adjoins Lord Helford's, you know, and after the wedding . . ." Her hand flew to her mouth. "My dear Mr. Storm, I beg you to forget what you just heard. I'm in such an awkward position, you understand, being in mourning, we have to keep the engagement a secret. I can rely on your discretion, Solomon?" she asked intimately. "Let me see if I can explain my position without using names. The Cornwall gentleman will generously buy back my estate for me, but in the meantime I find myself short of funds. Why don't you add a couple of thousand more to this mortgage, at, say, eight percent for thirty days and I will be able to get on with the sad duty of burying my poor father." The black silk handkerchief was lifted to tear-drenched eyes while Solomon Storm pursed his lips.

The tears did not move him one iota, he had seen women cry before, but there was something about this particular lady, something indefinable. She would never be defeated, no matter the odds. "Nine percent?" he suggested.

"You drive a hard bargain, Solomon Storm. Nine percent it is!" she drawled flirtatiously.

In the carriage Lil Richwood looked at her with new eyes. "You don't need to see a play, darling, you're a better actress than the ones on the stage."

Summer grinned. "I want to buy my brother some new clothes, do you know of such a shop?"

Lady Richwood directed the coachman to drive to the Exchange. "Summer, you bought a little time and money, but when it's gone, you'll be in a fine mess."

"With enough time and enough money I could change the whole world. With a little time and a little money I should be able to change some things . . . who knows?" And she gave Lil a secret smile filled with mystery.

They arrived at the playhouse in upper St. John Street after five straight hours of shopping. Summer had walked away with four hundred pounds' worth of finery by parting with a hundred in cash. The remainder of the bill was to be settled anon.

Inside the theater she was filled with a restless excitement as she closed her nostrils to the overheated smell of the unwashed crowd. She enjoyed the stir she caused by arriving late, not minding at all the men's frankly assessing stares or the drop-dead looks from the women. There was so much to see all at once that she had to absorb it a little at a time.

Velvet curtains had been drawn aside to display a small stage with painted scenery screens and tall lighted wax candles which illuminated the stage like a picture in the darkness. It did not take long for her to realize the audience was more important than the play. A buzz of conversation, flirting, and laughter made it necessary for the actors to shout above the noise, and they even occasionally entered into heckling matches or ribald remarks with the audience.

The pit was filled with crowded benches of young men and bizarrely painted harlots. Above was a balcony of small luxurious boxes where ladies and gentlemen of quality had come to be seen. High above was a gallery of cheap seats known as "being up in the God's" where apprentices thought it their duty to be rowdy and boo, whistle and catcall the entire performance.

During the intermission, pretty girls sold oranges and lemons, drinks and sweetmeats, and Summer was both fascinated and repelled by the scandalous way the men touched and fondled the orange girls. It seemed that the lowest neckline, the highest skirt, the sauciest behavior reaped the most sales.

Summer absorbed it all like a sponge. Though she listened to the play, her eyes again and again strayed to the fine ladies in the audience. She noted their clothes and jewels and hairdos, but mostly she watched their gestures, how they whispered archly and plied their fans and flirted and displayed themselves like peacocks. She could do all that!

By the time she arrived at the Countess of Shrewsbury's party she had acquired an air of confidence which clearly said, "Here I am, if you're not looking at me, you're wasting your time!"

And look they did. Her cloak was the deepest shade of royal purple velvet. She removed it to display a gown the palest tint of mauve, fashionably low cut to display Auntie Lil's imitation amethysts. Though it was not a costume ball, she had chosen to wear a tiny black lace mask and carried a black lace fan. Because of her mourning, she excused herself from the dancing, but in reality she did not know how to dance one step. Before the end of the evening, however, by paying undivided attention, she knew how to dance a courante, a pavane, a minuet, a saraband, and a pendant gavotte.

Sitting quietly with her features half-concealed made her the center of attention. The men clustered about her and the women whispered. Buckingham was without a mistress at the moment, and he arrived late and spent his time at the gaming tables. Though she did not dance, Summer indulged in cards and she found herself sharing a private joke with Buckingham when at the same moment each realized the other was cheating. Gallantly, he let her win but she withdrew from the gaming and knew instinctively he was a most unsavory man.

Supper also was an education for Summer. The buffet table fairly groaned beneath its load of mutton, capon, beef, jellies, trifles, and syllabubs. The women who partook of the food and drink heartily were by and large boring lumps whose figures had gone to hell long ago. The women whom men paid attention to ate like birds, almost to the point of affectation. A tiny nibble or a sip, then a whole plateful of food was set aside. It was obviously fashionable to pretend no appetite in front of a man. Neither did men indulge in deep or intelligent conversation with the fair sex. Fashionable females tended to fall into two categories. Either they were shallow, sweet, and silly like Frances Stewart or they were practiced voluptuaries such as Barbara Castlemaine and Anna Maria Shrewsbury. The men adored both types but obviously respected neither.

On the carriage ride back to Cockspur Street, Summer rested her elegant new coiffure against the velvet squabs and fingered the tiny black patches stuck to her painted face. In twenty-four hours the world had been opened up and revealed to her. She had become an entirely different person and she had met her *victim*. Here was her one great chance to save Roseland and even the score with the rich for her life of poverty. She smiled into the darkness. If she went about things in the right way, she might even have some fun to boot—at Ruark Helford's expense, of course.

Lil Richwood watched her beneath lowered lashes. She had been a total success tonight. Six men had made outright offers for her and four others had made overtures, but Lil wouldn't have told her for a thousand pounds. There was no way she was going to introduce the beautiful, vibrant girl into the life. It was too tempting, too seductive, and before you came to your senses, it was too late. The name on everyone's lips would be Lady Summer St. Catherine. She must get her back to Cornwall before she took those first tentative steps down the road to perdition.

7

Summer sat in the small breakfast room pensively sipping her chocolate. Guilt nagged at her for leaving Spider alone for so many days, but she reasoned that he was beginning to chafe at her mothering him and was probably delighted to be fending for himself, as a man.

Lil came in with sparkling eyes and Summer could tell she had news. "Darling, the most extraordinary thing! The King is sending Helford back to Cornwall."

Summer's quicksilver thoughts raced about to put this exciting information to advantage when Lil's drawl dropped a bombshell.

"He's been appointed magistrate of the whole of Cornwall to put a stop to smuggling."

"Oh, no!" cried Summer, all her lovely prospects lying shattered at her feet and a small curl of fear threatening to knot inside her stomach. Again she saw clearly the dark, piercing eyes, the hard, dangerous mouth, and the risk and challenge he represented sent a shiver of excitement through her. She loved to sail too near the wind and knew in that moment she would hazard everything. Fortune favored the bold!

She saw her situation clearly, knew she was in danger of getting her fingers badly burned as she would constantly be between two fires, but the simple truth hit her.

She had chosen him.

She was going to get him.

It was fate.

She pushed the chocolate cup away, stood up decisively, and said, "Where can I go to meet him again?"

Lil made a moue with her lips. "It will be difficult if not impossible. The reason he wasn't at Anna Maria Shrewsbury's last evening was because he's readying his ship. He's leaving at the end of the week, so I don't suppose he'll be socializing at all."

"Where is his ship?" asked Summer.

"In the Pool of London, of course. Oh no, darling, you can't possibly go wandering about the docks," insisted Auntie Lil. "There are limits to what a lady may do and still remain a lady. Perhaps we could get away with a discreet note asking him to call."

Summer shook her head. "For God's sake, Lil, I was on the docks in Plymouth and sailed to the docks of Portsmouth. How the devil do you think I got here? I'll not wait about for discreet notes. I'll go this morning."

Lil took hold of both her hands and made her sit on the small satin-covered settee while she imparted some much-needed advice. "Listen to me, darling. You must make him think you are a lady. If he thinks you're anything less, he will love you and leave you as casually as he would buy a jewel or a horse. You must accept nothing less than carte blanche."

"I know that's French, but I don't know what it means exactly."

"It means full powers of a mistress," Lil explained.

Summer squeezed her hand. "Don't be so serious. I promise I will accept nothing less."

Lil sighed and relaxed her hold. "I'll send the little maid with you, who brought your chocolate this morning."

"Oh, no," said Summer. "I want that older woman with a face like the back of a fishcart."

"She isn't a waiting woman, darling, she's the terror of my kitchens," explained Lil.

"He won't know that," pointed out Summer. "I'll take that haughty old footman, too. The one who looks like he just smelled something disgusting."

"Very good, Summer," drawled Lil with admiration. "You play the game rather well."

The corners of Summer's mouth turned up in a secret little

smile. "I think I'll borrow that delicate pale gray outfit today. I might as well leave the lovely clothes I bought packed. After all, I'll be sailing home at week's end."

Lil Richwood would have bet money on it.

The unusual trio left their coach at the first dock and the two servants followed behind Summer as she carefully scanned each ship and passed on to the next. Suddenly she saw him, but immediately pretended otherwise. She gave all her attention to the names painted on the ship's sides until he was almost upon her.

Lord Helford swept off his hat. "Lady Summer," he said warmly.

She looked up at him, then sank to her knees before him. "Your Majesty," she breathed.

He immediately took hold of her hands to raise her and a slight frown marred his brow. "I'm not the King," he said, puzzled.

Her eyes flew open in surprise. "Oh, surely my aunt wouldn't play such a cruel trick on me?" He stood holding her hands, looking down into her lovely face framed by the pale gray fox fur of her hood. She said hesitantly, "After you left, I asked my aunt who the tall, dark gentleman was and she told me it was the King." Her lashes swept to her cheeks and she blushed prettily.

Ruark threw back his head and laughed. The corded muscles in his bronzed neck stood out strongly. She cast him a reproachful look at his amusement. "The other man was the King. Forgive my terrible manners for laughing at you, Lady Summer, but in truth I don't know whether to be flattered or insulted."

She looked at him innocently, but she knew damned well he had been flattered to have been mistaken for the King or she wouldn't have made the deliberate mistake.

"Ruark Helford, at your service, Lady Summer. Whatever are you doing here on the docks?" he asked.

"I'm looking for passage home to Cornwall. I arrived on the *Seagull,* an American ship, but I don't seem to be able to locate it here," she said breathlessly.

"Cornwall?" he asked with disbelief.

She extracted her hands from his and slipped them into her pretty fur muff, out of his reach. "I'm going home to Roseland. It's mine now," she said delicately without mentioning her father's death.

"But Roseland is the next estate to mine," he said with delight.

"What an amazing coincidence," she said with wide-eyed wonder. "You must be *Lord* Helford."

"There are no coincidences. It's fate, Lady Summer. All things happen for a purpose. I shall take you home on my ship."

"You are too kind sir, but I couldn't possibly put you to such inconvenience," she demurred.

"As a matter of fact 'tis the most convenient thing in the world. I leave for Cornwall day after tomorrow by order of the King." His face was hard and serious. "I won't take no for an answer. I couldn't possibly entrust you to an American captain."

She took a deep breath. He liked to take control. He was clearly a man used to having his own way. "Come aboard now and I'll show you my *Pagan Goddess.*"

Summer glanced behind her at the forbidding faces of her attendants. "Ah sir, I don't think they would permit me to do such a thing."

"Dragons," he muttered. "My dear Lady Summer, you do not need permission from servants to do anything." He raised his voice and said with authority, "I am taking your mistress aboard my ship. Be good enough to wait."

His firm hand was under her elbow guiding her up the gangplank and he couldn't believe this stroke of good fortune. Lady Summer had been the name on everyone's lips at Court, and he assumed she would take the opportunity offered her to become its latest courtesan, to be feted and fawned upon and, yes, fucked, if he was going to be honest. First by the King and then by the King's cavaliers when he grew negligent. That she was innocently unaware of the stir she had caused and was returning home to Cornwall was almost unbelievable.

Sailors swarmed both above- and below-decks as he ushered her down to his cabin. "Let me take your cloak," he said, his strong hands already undoing the tie at her throat.

She clung to the velvet and fur creation, her voice catching in her throat as she said breathlessly, "Ah no, Lord Helford. I don't know the mores and manners of London very well, but I'm sure we shouldn't be alone like this."

Her soft words were so suggestive and provocative that his semiarousal hardened like iron and it was an effort for him to remove his hands from her. She dropped her lids over her curious eyes and stole a look at a movement she'd seen in his tight white breeches. What she saw alarmed her. He didn't seem to be shaped like other men. How odd that she hadn't noticed it before because it was really quite pronounced.

His fingers itched to undress her. How could he possibly have her this close and not begin to make love to her? Her perfumed breath came to him and his own mouth went dry with the need to taste her. His shaft moved forward of its own volition with its great need to be plunged deep inside her. My God, what was the matter with him? He was reacting to her as if he was an untried boy about to taste intoxicating female flesh for the first time.

His jaw muscle hardened and he said, "You are right of course. Forgive me for taking advantage of such a lovely lady. Tomorrow I'll send someone to Cockspur Street for your boxes and I'll speak to your aunt personally to allay any fears she may have about your complete safety."

Summer's female instincts guided her infallibly at this crucial moment. She sensed he was waging a battle both physically and mentally, and womanlike, she knew she must tip the scales so that he lost the battle. She took his hand and held it tightly as she looked way up into his face. "Thank you, Lord Helford. I shall put myself into your hands completely."

He swallowed hard.

"I know I can trust you," she breathed. And then she was in his arms, his fierce mouth taking that which he could deny himself no longer. She was so small and her curves fit so nicely into a man's arms, emphasizing his masculinity. Never had he felt so strong and dominant, yet at the same time so protective.

Her mouth tasted like sweet wild strawberries and he was amazed at the inexperience he discovered. If he was any judge of females, this one was untried, and the thrill of his discovery raced along his nerve endings to fill his senses with the taste, the feel, the scent, and the innocent promise of virginal, female flesh.

Summer felt herself engulfed. His strength and masculinity totally overpowered her as her soft body was molded to his, her lips crushed beneath a mouth so demanding it made her pliant and without a will of her own. Her eyes wanted to close; her lips wanted to open; her arms wanted to slide up about his neck. She recovered herself just in time. This wasn't a game, it was a calculated role she was playing. If she lost control of the situation from the beginning, she didn't stand a chance. Lil had emphasized that she must make him think she was a lady or he would treat her as a casual love, which was exactly what he was doing!

She was angry with herself over the potent reaction he'd had on her and she vented that anger on him. "I should never have come aboard your ship, sir," she gasped, her color high. "I have been warned about men like you. Now I realize why my aunt insisted I be well attended. I never would have dreamed a gentleman would insult and manhandle a lady in such a fashion," she cried, outraged. "An American captain would be infinitely preferable." She flashed him such an accusing look because he had betrayed her trust that he felt a stab of shame. Without another word she turned and left, quitting the ship without a backward glance.

He came abovedecks in time to see her stiff little back disappear down the dock escorted by her dragons. "Damn," he cursed, then used a filthier word to express the disgust he felt with himself. Now she'd never take the voyage home to Cornwall with him. His eyes darkened, his fists clenched, and his jaw knotted. By heaven and hell she'd sail with him if he had to carry her off in the night like booty.

Next morning his note of apology arrived accompanied by masses of cream-colored roses. Auntie Lil drawled dryly, "I take it you will put the dashing cavalier out of his misery and forgive him at the last moment?"

Summer laughed delightedly. "You know, Lil, if I didn't know my American was way off in Portsmouth, I'd be tempted to thumb my nose at Lord Helford and sail home on the *Seagull.*"

"Darling, you'd have a duel on your hands and you know Charles has forbidden them."

Summer sighed. "I'm particularly partial to the forbidden."

"Then Helford should suit you to a tee, you little hellcat. Seriously, I'm going to miss you dreadfully. Do let me know how you go along. It may not be as easy as you're assuming despite the cream roses, Summer. I don't believe Helford is a man you can lead about by the nose, or any other prominent appendage for that matter."

Somehow Summer knew she was alluding to his male parts and immediately she said, "Lil, I'm so shamefully ignorant, I'm going to ask you some questions which will probably embarrass you."

"How novel; I haven't been embarrassed since I was twelve, darling."

"What . . . is a man like . . . down there? Oh, I've seen my brother when he was a little boy of course, but Lord Helford . . . I mean . . . he seemed . . . there was such a big bulge. . . ."

Lil's trill of amusement stopped and she became suddenly serious. "I wouldn't dream of sending one of my girls off for a tête-à-tête with a gentleman without thoroughly briefing her step-by-step on everything appertaining to the male, from what he looks like to what he will expect her to let him do to her, but in your case I don't want to do that. No, no, don't be offended, darling, let me see if I can explain this to you. Innocence cannot be simulated. It is a rare and precious gift which a woman can give to a man only once in her lifetime. If a man is a connoisseur of women . . . if he's sensitive and appreciative, he will savor that gift for a lifetime. It is so much more meaningful for a woman to have the mysteries of sensuality explained to her by a loving man; I wouldn't deprive you of the experience. And the deep pleasure it will give the man to tell you and show you and instruct you will be like an aphrodisiac. He will remember it always. It will come flooding back to him to almost unman him and it will give you a power over him that is almost mystical."

Summer licked lips gone dry. Oh, how she would enjoy having a mystical power over Lord Ruark Helford.

Lil continued, "Fortunes are paid for innocence, so it is like having an ace up your sleeve. A man is drawn to it irresistibly, lured by his instinct to hunt, to snare, to dominate, to possess that which no other man has captured. It is even possible to play the card skillfully enough to exchange the innocence for a wedding ring."

Summer's eyes sparkled with excitement.

"Oh, darling, I shouldn't have said that. Helford is definitely experienced enough to pluck a woman's innocence without paying the *ultimate* price, but what I'm trying to impress on you is not to let him have it without paying a fortune."

8

$\sim$

King Charles had been in his laboratory most of the afternoon. He had a passion for chemistry and the room was lined with shelves holding jars of powders and pastes and bottles of colored liquids. Alchemy fascinated him to the point where he was an easy mark for any quack's nostrums. He had a vast collection of books on the subject, all beautifully bound in leather, and some of these volumes touched upon witchcraft and wizardry.

No one ever dared to disturb him when he was working in his chemical laboratory as it was an unwritten law that he wished to be private. No one dared, except of course Barbara. She entered the long room with its open casements which let out the peculiar odors and vapors of Charles's concoctions.

When Charles heard someone enter the room, he frowned and set down the beaker of oil of prima materia he had just carefully measured out. When he saw that it was Barbara, however, he gave her a lazy smile of welcome.

"Charles, I thought I'd better warn you that the monsieur returned unexpectedly from the country this morning, so plans for tonight will have to be canceled."

"Not canceled surely, sweetheart? Can't we move them ahead to this afternoon?" he suggested with a healthy leer.

"What, here?" she asked doubtfully, glancing with unconcealed distaste at all the odd paraphernalia.

His eyes never left her luscious breasts as he reached for a glass container holding a golden liquid. He poured some into a glass and offered it to her.

"Charles, are you trying to poison me?"

"It's wine, sweetheart." He sampled some himself to show her it was no mysterious concoction. "We'll share a loving cup and a pleasant hour." He gathered her to him in one strong arm and held the golden wine to her exciting lips. Charles's heavy eyelids drooped at the sensual feel of her body pressed against the hardening length of him.

"Do you have any of that stuff you were telling me about?" she asked in a husky voice.

"Stuff?" he puzzled.

"Amyl something-or-other that one inhales to make the climax harder."

Charles chuckled. "Yes, I have a vial or two about somewhere. It's an amber liquid that tastes and smells of pears. You inhale it deeply just before you are ready to come. Would you like to try it, you wanton little wench?"

"Why not?" She slanted him a glance.

"Why not, indeed?" he echoed. "Let's see, it's over here on this shelf with the other items which induce lust."

Barbara's curiosity was piqued. "Really?" she asked, moving toward the fascinating containers. She lifted a small jar, removed the lid, and sniffed. "Mmm, what are these? They smell like violets."

Charles looked at the small purple gelatin capsules and grinned at her. "Intimate as we are, love, I blush to tell you what the apothecary said these were invented for."

"Oh, Charles, tell me," she urged.

"Well . . . you insert one up past your sphincter before you make love, then if you pass wind in bed, it smells like violets."

Barbara fell against him with laughter. "Darling, I must have some. It's quite an art to be able to do disgusting things delicately."

He gathered her close and looked deeply into her eyes while he pressed his swollen member against her soft belly. "I rather like you to do disgusting things . . . disgustingly."

"I know you do," she whispered, undoing the laces on his cod-piece.

"I enjoy taking you in broad daylight so I can watch you warm and flushed with passion." His hand slid down inside her bodice and the slow, languid strokes of his fingers upon her throbbing peaks soon sent excitement hurtling through her body. He loved the way Barbara responded instantly to arousal, rather like himself.

"How about some of these creams you can rub on to provoke lust?" she suggested.

"God's flesh, you above all others should know I need no nostrum for that."

"There's always room for improvement," she teased. "Here . . . let's try this . . . it says it's made from white mustard seed . . . it says it bringeth heat to the parts," she said, giggling, as she took a firm hold on his erection and dipped her finger into the pot of cream.

"Careful, Barbara, just a little dab, you don't want to burn the damned knob off!"

Barbara couldn't stop laughing as Charles pulled up her voluminous skirts to fondle her bared thighs. "God's flesh, you never wear undergarments and I swear whenever you come into the same room, my mind fixates on your nakedness."

Their tongues began to parry and thrust and Barbara put an extra large dab of the cream on the head of Charles's shaft. His large hands slipped over her bottom cheeks and held her imprisoned while he impaled her with his great weapon. "Serves you right, it will rub off inside you and then we'll see whose parts are heated," he teased hoarsely.

She gasped with pleasure at the fullness of him, then her insides felt as if they were afire with the heat of their joined bodies. The friction of his movements turned them both hot and swollen until they thought they would go mad from their heightened sensitivity.

Charles braced his legs wide apart to hold Barbara pressed against the cabinet. They were both oblivious to the tinkling of the glass bottles as their vibrations made the colored liquids foam and splosh wildly upon the shelves. Barbara was ready to scream with her excitement. Charles, always slow to reach full peak, still had a measure of control. He reached for the vial of amyl nitrite and held it so they could inhale the pear fumes deeply. They exploded together. Barbara let out the scream which had been building in her throat as she felt her blood pounding from the top of her scalp to the soles of her feet, then she fainted and collapsed upon him.

Charles had never experienced anything quite so volatile either. He carried her over to the open window and sat her upon the sill. She opened her eyes, still dazed from the finesse of his lovemaking. "Barbara, are you all right?" he asked anxiously.

"Oooh, I'm more than all right," she purred.

The Queen glanced up from the courtyard on her way back from evening prayers. She saw Barbara and Charles at the window of his laboratory and thought wistfully that Lady Castlemaine must be helping the King with his experiments.

Later in the day when a seaman came to collect Summer's boxes, she sent him back to the *Pagan Goddess* empty-handed.

Ruark Helford was forced to come for her himself, pledging his responsibility for her safety to Lady Richwood. His impeccable manners were in full display, much to the private amusement of the two women, and Summer finally allowed her aunt to persuade her to change her mind and sail with Lord Helford.

His pulse began to pound when he handed her into his carriage entirely alone. She was sailing without a tiring woman, a ladies' maid, or a chaperon of any description. Inside the dark carriage the silence stretched between them. The tension was thick in the air and it was charged with sensuality. There was no way to hide the fact that the male had scented the female and would pursue her.

His voice came rich and low through the darkness. "You must think it odd that I came at such a late hour for you, but we'll have floodtide around three in the morning to carry us out to sea."

"You forget, Lord Helford, I am a child of the sea," she said softly.

"Of course. 'Tis said we Cornish have salt water in our veins and fire in our hearts," he added warmly.

"And more guts than brains," she added pointedly.

He raised an eyebrow at the lady's language, but took the rebuke seriously. "Well, London has its diversions but for a man who thrives on an active life 'tis too confining. I for one am happy to be going home to Cornwall . . . it's been a long time."

It was on the tip of her tongue to ask him about his appointment as magistrate but she knew she must be wary with this man. In a way he was her enemy. Any way you looked at it, he represented the law, the authority, the power of the Crown, while she was up to her pretty little neck in smuggling. A thrill ran up her spine. Being neighbors was going to be the challenge of a lifetime.

"How about you, Lady Summer? Will you miss London?" he asked casually, yet he felt a deep need to know.

"I cannot miss what I have never known, my lord. I have always lived quietly," she said softly. "I love my freedom, but above all I think I value my privacy."

'Ods blood, he thought wryly, that's the second time in as many minutes she's tried to teach me my manners. Such a prim and proper lady. I'll have to see if I can change all that!

The carriage slowed, and when Ruark Helford opened the door, the smells and sounds of the sea rushed inside. As he arose, his hard thigh brushed against her leg, hip, and then her arm and she knew without a doubt it had been deliberate. He jumped lithely from the carriage and held up his arms to assist her descent. She held her beautiful head high at a defiant tilt; every line bespoke outraged innocence. She hesitated a full minute before she deigned to place her hands in his.

The moment their fingers engaged she swept her lashes to her cheeks and he imagined she blushed at the intimacy. 'Ods blood, if she blushed when their fingers touched, what would happen when his mouth explored all her most secret places? The anticipation was almost unbearable. The ache she had set up in his loins was pleasurable yet painful. He fought the urge to sweep her up into his arms and carry her to his berth, but promised himself he would do exactly that in the not-too-distant future. He ushered her aboard with a strong, steady hand at her elbow to make sure she did not misstep in the darkness.

All hands were on deck and stood smartly to attention as the master of the ship came aboard. In the faces closest to her she saw respect—or was it fear?—reflected by the ship's lanterns.

"Mr. Cully," his harsh voice rang out.

"Aye, aye, sir," came the immediate reply as a wiry-looking sailor of indeterminate age stepped up smartly and saluted.

"My lady's boxes," said Ruark Helford crisply.

Summer shuddered. He who must be obeyed, she thought with a slight tinge of apprehension. Much to her surprise he did not show her down to his cabin but took her to a small, well-appointed cabin located forward in the bow.

"You will see I am observing all the proprieties," he said huskily. "I knew if I offered you a cabin adjoining mine, you would refuse."

Summer let out a tiny sigh of relief. At last he had gotten the message that she was a lady. She could afford to unbend a little. She looked up at him and reached out a hand which aimed for his arm, but managed to fall upon his broad chest. "You have been so very kind to me, Lord Helford," she murmured, and she felt the strong beat of his heart beneath her hand. In one more second she knew she would be swept up in his arms, but at that very moment Mr. Cully pushed open the cabin door with his knee and swung two heavy boxes from his shoulders.

Ruark looked down at her ruefully. "When you have everything you need, lock this cabin door until morning. That is an order. Good night, Lady Summer."

When he had gone, she leaned her back against the door and threw her muff into the air with a little whoop of joy. Before she was done with him she'd have him eating out of her hand like her stallion Ebony. Mr. Cully returned with the last of her luggage, showed her the little cabinet which contained water, soap, and towels, then drew the leather curtains across the latticed window from which could be observed the deck and above that the quarterdeck if you crouched at the right angle upon the cushioned window seat.

"May I have a little wine, Mr. Cully?"

He indicated a rosewood panel in the wall and showed her how to open it. Inside silver goblets and a decanter of wine were fastened in brackets and a solid silver box held dry biscuits. He said in broad cockney, " 'Is nibs runs a tight ship, m'lydy." He touched his forelock and spirited himself through the door like a wraith.

She pushed home the bolt. "Well, Ruark Helford, I'll obey the first order you've given me . . . after that we'll see!"

After Summer examined her surroundings, reading the barometer which indicated a storm, twirling the globe of the world in its wooden frame, and feeling the soft wool blankets which made up the berth, she sipped two glasses of the full-bodied red wine, turned the oil lamp low, and undressed.

She didn't want to disturb the beautiful new clothes she had packed with such care and slipped into the bunk naked. The ship still at anchor rose and fell gently, lulling her to sleep. Vaguely she became half-aware that the ship was moving and the wind had picked up considerably. She turned over and went back to sleep.

She was rudely awakened by a thudding roar as a great wave hit the deck and the cabin stood on its end. She realized they must be out in the North Sea, being buffeted about by a gale before they could turn into the Strait of Dover. She threw back the blankets and staggered across the cabin to a porthole. The storm outside was raging. Rain swept horizontally across the heaving seas. As she struggled to shut the port she heard a man's voice roar over the thunderous storm, "Hands to braces in the maintops," and the ship gave a sharp plunge before she was brought around to the wind again.

Summer's pulses raced. It was an exhilarating experience to be in a storm at sea. It was frightening and exciting at one and the same time and her blood sang recklessly. She would have given anything to be on deck at this moment, but she had more good sense than to distract the sailors when the ship was in peril.

She hugged herself. Ruark must have known about the storm, yet it hadn't entered his head not to brave it. She clung to the braced window seat as the ship pitched and plunged. It seemed to climb upward over a mile-high mountainous wave, then wallow down into the trough.

Gradually the heavy weather lessened until the ship merely rolled about from side to side. The danger was past, but Summer knew a need to release her pent-up energy. She began to sway with the ship, keeping up with its undulating rhythm. Her dancing grew wilder, spinning and turning in an abandoned frenzy. Her black cloud of hair flew about her naked limbs until it was a great disheveled mass. She flung her head back in ecstasy as if she would sacrifice herself to some ancient sea god.

Ruark Helford had had no time to spare for his passenger until he had safely weathered the storm, but now that the sea was less heavy he thought of her immediately and imagined the great fear she must be experiencing, alone in the little cabin. His eyes were drawn down from the quarterdeck toward the cabin's latticed windows, and as his eyes focused on a chink of light through the leather curtains he was rooted to the spot as he saw the wildly erotic dance of the completely naked girl. He was stunned. Could this untamed creature be the same innocent young lady he'd brought aboard earlier? He was mesmerized by her beautiful young body, spinning and twirling, her cloud of black hair alternately concealing then revealing her full, rounded breasts. He'd never seen a female act so abandoned before, not even dancers in Turkish brothels. And yet her natural grace and total lack of artifice lent a piquant innocence to her uninhibited display. Something inside him was irresistibly drawn to her free spirit.

He knew the storm had affected her to the same degree it had him. Its danger had excited her to such a pitch she had to expend her energy in a lavish, excessive physical outburst. If he made love to her, he knew she would be capable of the same wild excess, the same delirious abandon. His blood was high, his pulses pounded from battling the raging seas, and he, too, needed release. His tongue licked the salt from his lips and his eyes devoured the long slim legs crowned with a triangle of black, silky ringlets. Her arms flung out as if to summon a lover. My God, she was like a pagan. And then he knew exactly where he'd seen her before. It was as if she had posed for the figurehead on his ship, the *Pagan Goddess*. All his senses cried out for her. She was utterly different from any other woman he had known. His blood, already intoxicated by the storm, was now enflamed with lust.

He turned the wheel over to his second-in-command and stalked a direct path to her cabin. "Summer," he called against the door, "let me in."

There was dead silence.

"I must see for myself that you are safe. Open the door," he commanded.

Again there was dead silence. Summer pressed against the inside of the door listening to the desire in his deep voice. She smiled and disobeyed his command.

The command changed to a subtle threat. "I won't leave this door until you open it and let me see that you are unharmed." He knew that if she opened the door to him, she would be symbolically opening her body to him and inviting him inside where he hotly lusted to be. The threat changed to a plea. "My lady, please open the door. The moment I see you are unafraid I will leave you to rest."

"I'm perfectly all right, Lord Helford," she replied. Then in a husky, teasing voice she whispered, "In fact . . . I've never felt better."

His arousal was so strong, he knew he must have her. "Let me see for myself," he commanded.

"We both know I cannot risk opening this door." The warm sensual tone of her voice belied her words.

"Risk?" he challenged.

"It would deny propriety, my lord, to admit you to my cabin in the middle of the night."

His hands were on the door to force it when he realized he was in a reckless mood, savage enough to force her once the door had yielded. He didn't want to rape her, he wanted to exert such a strong power over her that she would yield herself to him in extravagant abandon.

"Good night, Lord Helford," she teased.

He put his ear against the door and heard her deep breaths whispering against the polished wood. "Summer?" he begged low, desire refusing to be denied.

Her eyes slitted like a cat's when it was being stroked and the corners of her mouth lifted in a smile of triumph as she tiptoed across the cabin and slipped into bed.

9

 By morning it was as if there
had never been a storm. The English Channel seemed calm as a
duck pond and she surmised they must be somewhere off the Isle
of Wight. She hummed a little tune as she bathed and dressed in
the pale lavender silk with its prim high neckline. She heard a tap
on the door and called, "What is it?"

"Breakfast, m'lydy," came the voice of Mr. Cully. She unbolted
the cabin door for him and said, "I could have gone to the galley.
Thank you very much. When I've finished, I'm going up on deck
for some fresh air."

Mr. Cully shook his head. "Wouldn't do that, m'lydy . . . trouble brewin'."

"What sort of trouble?" she asked.

He shook his head again. "Best stay syfe in yer little mouse'ole."

"What's up?" she demanded.

He hesitated then blurted out, "A floggin' . . . Cap'n found a
man drunk on watch." He bobbed his head and ducked out.

Surely Helford wouldn't order a man flogged for taking a drink?
Especially after the horrors of sailing through that storm. She
pushed the food aside and reached for her cloak.

When she arrived on deck, she realized with horror that she was
too late. Not only had Helford ordered the flogging, he was carry-

ing out the punishment himself. The sailor had been stripped to the waist and lashed to the mast. His back was already bloody. Helford stood wielding a bullwhip, immaculately garbed in navy breeches and snowy shirt and stock. His long black hair was clubbed back into a cue as neatly as if he wore a wig.

Outraged, she ran across the deck and cried, "Stop!"

He looked at her with disbelief. "Go below!" he commanded.

"No!"

His eyes narrowed dangerously. "No? On my own quarterdeck you dare to say no?"

She swayed forward and he saw that she was close to fainting. A foul oath fell from his lips as he threw down the whip and strode to her side. "Cut him down," he called over his shoulder, then he took hold of her wrist in what felt like an iron vise and half dragged her belowdecks to his cabin. The cabin door crashed back against its frame.

"What in the name of God was that all about?" he demanded. His eyes were cold and hard and glittering with anger.

She stepped back from him, half afraid. She had stopped the whipping, so there was no point in exacerbating his temper. Breathlessly she said, "A flogging is so brutal."

"He got off easy . . . I should have hanged the bastard; and will next time."

"For drinking?" she asked hesitantly.

"He may get blind drunk anytime he likes, except under my command, when he is on watch. Our lives and my ship are in the hands of my sailors when they are on watch. I was the most detested officer in His Majesty's navy because I insisted on discipline. Soon I'll be the most detested man in Cornwall. I've been appointed high commissioner and magistrate to put an end to the blatant smuggling. The trees will soon bear the fruit of my hangings." He stopped and bit his lip.

"I shouldn't have interfered," she murmured. It was the closest she'd ever come to an apology.

Suddenly he saw himself through her eyes and he winced inwardly. A well-bred lady who had lived a sheltered life in the country must have been shocked to the core by what she had seen up on deck.

Summer was glad she had held her tongue. She had almost flung at him the terrible accusation that because she had bolted her door against him he had vented his spleen on the first hapless sailor he had encountered. Now she realized she had had nothing to do with it.

"Lady Summer, I should never have exposed you to such brutality. Do you forgive me?"

She nodded slightly.

"Show me you forgive me by taking supper with me this evening. I have to make port in Plymouth this afternoon, but I will have you home by ten o'clock tonight."

"I am happy not to have to spend another night aboard," she said softly.

"And supper?" he pressed.

"If you insist, Lord Helford," she conceded graciously.

When she returned to her cabin, she removed the gray velvet cloak and sat down upon the cushioned window seat to think. She had a few very tricky problems which she must work out if she was not to drop her candy in the sand. No doubt remained that Lord Helford was in pursuit of her . . . that was good. She had only slightly less than a month before the mortgage came due again . . . that was bad. He was already deeply attracted to her and couldn't hide the fact that he longed to woo her . . . that was good. She was a smuggler and he was the law . . . that was bad.

Her objective was to become wife or mistress within the month, and this would require a delicate balancing act. She must seem to hold him off with one hand while luring him on with the other. One thing was certain. He must not get a look at Roseland until she had bagged him. To let him see its run-down condition, dearth of servants, and the near-poverty conditions she and Spider had survived would ring a death knell to her liaison with the wealthy Lord Helford.

For the King to have given him this appointment, he would have to have a keen eye and the mind of an interrogator. She must never underestimate him. Summer sighed. She wished she could be herself with him. She wanted to ride with him across the wild moors and wear her breeches. She wanted to curse and swear at him and make him laugh. She wanted to cheat him at cards and beat the pants off him . . . pants off him, her mind repeated, and she blushed. She put her hands to her burning cheeks. She must keep her mind on the task at hand. She must never allow her emotions to gain control of her. She would have to be devastatingly devious to bring her plans to fruition. She needed access to his fortune to save Roseland. The wild rides, the curses, and the card cheating must never happen. She was supposed to be a well-bred, gently reared heiress. Still, she didn't exactly hate play-acting the role of a lady. It was all very diverting to ply a fan and balance on pretty high-heeled slippers and lower her lashes over her bold eyes.

Her mind flashed back to the orange girls at the theater. Their sauciness certainly attracted the men. Then she remembered how her demure behavior had almost had Helford panting. She'd try both; that should keep him off balance!

She contemplated changing her gown for dinner then decided against it. Earlier she'd worn her cloak, so he hadn't really seen the dress, and it had a high frilled neckline which could only be described as modest. If she changed her gown for something fancier, his male vanity would be flattered that she was making a display just for him.

She did decide, however, to put up her hair in a more sophisticated style. With her brush she piled it all high and fastened it with combs decorated by silk violets, allowing just one fat curl to fall down over her shoulder. Then she picked up a matching fan and practiced in the mirror. She also discovered if she took a few slow steps then turned quickly, her silken petticoats swished and whispered seductively.

When his low knock sounded on her cabin door at suppertime, Summer was ready. She was ready for anything! Her eyes widened at the elegance of the small table which had been set up in his cabin. Heavy damask linen, sterling silver, crystal goblets, and wineglasses had been laid out and its center was a mass of cream-colored roses and tall scented wax tapers.

"Wherever did you get the roses?" she asked.

"My men scoured Plymouth this afternoon," he said, smiling down at her.

A bubble of laughter escaped her lips at the incongruous picture the hard-bitten sailors must have made. He held her chair and his hands managed to brush her shoulders as she sat down, but it was only for the merest second. "You will have a little Chablis." He made it sound like an imperative as he picked up the bottle to pour.

"I am unused to wine, Lord Helford."

"You have many pleasures yet to taste," he said boldly.

Summer looked deeply into his hazel eyes to show him that she understood the sexual connotation and said slowly, "You mean the food; yes, it does smell delicious."

He lifted the silver cover from a soup tureen and served them a creamy lobster bisque. She gave up a silent prayer of thanks to Auntie Lil for teaching her the intricacies of the array of cutlery.

Should she toy with her food as she had seen the coquettes do at Anna Maria Shrewsbury's? She found it impossible to do so. She had missed too many dinners in her lifetime. Summer felt it a sacrilege to waste food.

He looked on with approval as she heartily dipped the large prawns into the melted lemon butter. He thought her face in the candleglow the most arresting he had ever seen. Her cheekbones were high, her eyes slanted upward at the corners, her skin was smooth as heavy cream, and her lips were full and red as crushed strawberries. Her face was as exotically delicate as a vanilla orchid.

She knew she must begin to lay the groundwork for her campaign. As he served the next course and refilled her wineglass she sighed. "I have so much to do when I get home, I don't know where to start, Lord Helford."

"Do you think you could find it in your heart to call me Ruark?"

"I should not," she said quickly.

"But?" he pressed.

She hesitated. "Perhaps." She continued, "My father was a most eccentric man," she said softly. "He could not abide servants about him. It was just as well really, because he was difficult . . . impossible . . . to work for, and one by one they all left."

"You cannot run Roseland without servants," he asserted.

"I have somehow managed to do so. However, all that will change now," she said.

He had taken it for granted that Lady Summer St. Catherine had been spoiled and pampered. Perhaps it was not so.

"It is also just as well that I will not be receiving visitors. The estate has been sadly neglected and I must begin restoration and repair immediately."

"Surely you will make an exception for this visitor, Lady Summer?"

"Lord Helford, you are doubly barred!"

"Ruark," he reminded. "Why so?"

"Because I am officially in mourning and because . . . I am alone at Roseland. You must promise you will not compromise me, my lord," she beseeched.

The food was forgotten. He came around the table to her. "I want to see you," he said firmly. "Do you not have a male relative to whom I may apply for permission?"

She caught her breath. Surely he wouldn't ask a male relative for permission to make her his mistress. She stood to face him. "There is no one, save my young brother and Lady Richwood of course."

He smiled down at her ruefully. "And I've already pledged your safety to her, haven't I?"

"I shall come to visit you," she offered.

"Promise me?" he asked solemnly.

As she looked up into his face his fingers reached up and took the violet combs from her hair. It tumbled down over his hands in a silken mass and his mouth took hers in a long, lingering kiss. A shock rippled through her body as the teasing dalliance of his tongue prepared her for bolder play. He was holding her much too close as his lips turned forceful and his tongue thrust demandingly into her soft mouth. She stiffened and pulled back but not before her insides had felt like molten silver sliding downward into her limbs from the onslaught of his probing tongue. She had had no idea that being in a man's arms could produce this liquid heat that made a woman long to be ravished, plundered, conquered. Just once in a lifetime every woman should be kissed by a dangerous man.

When she managed to pull away from him, she looked so vulnerable and trapped that he felt a moment of shame. "I shouldn't have given you that kiss. I was taking advantage of you," he admitted. His thoughts belied his words. He was glad he had kissed her. He wanted to kiss her so thoroughly there would be no breath left in her body. He was aware for the first time of a stunning weakness in his body at the contact with her. She threatened to make him lose control.

His words echoed over and over in her brain. "I shouldn't have given you that kiss." Surely he didn't regret it? She could have sworn he had been as shaken by the shock of their touching mouths as she had been. She would find out. "If you shouldn't have given it to me, I must give it back to you," she said simply. She went up on tiptoe, slipped her arms about his neck, and fitted her soft mouth to his.

He was totally unprepared for the effect it had on him. When she lifted her mouth and fitted it to his, she demonstrated an innocent sensuality, if such a contradictory thing were possible, which heightened his pleasure so that desire ran like wildfire from his mouth, through his heart, and straight to the tip of his shaft. The taste she allowed him set up a craving for more. She had the power to throw him off balance by luring him, then forbidding him, then luring him again. Her unusual, exotic beauty seemed to have a mystical power over him, and her sweet inexperience was like an aphrodisiac, attracting him a thousand times more than the artifices of his most experienced past lovers.

This child-woman had walked into his life and enchanted him. Conflicting emotions besieged him as he held her captive in his arms. He wanted to ravish her, to make love to her until she screamed with passion, yet he felt a fierce protectiveness toward her. He also knew a need to own her body and soul. This possessive desire was entirely new to him. He would make her his mistress despite the fact that she was a lady. He would simply have to school himself to go slowly so that he didn't frighten her, didn't destroy the magic which flowed so devastatingly between them.

She closed her eyes and melted against him. The pure physical thrill of his masculinity made her nipples ruche with pleasure and a strange hot prickling tingle began between her legs. When she lifted her trembling mouth from his, she said huskily, "I think it best if Mr. Cully takes me home when we make land tonight."

"You will come? You promised," he commanded.

"Good night, Ruark," she said softly.

"Summer's promise," he murmured after she had departed.

10

Spider's eyes widened in amazement as he circled round his sister, taking in the luxurious velvet cloak trimmed with fox fur. What he saw made him uncomfortable; he feared that after London, Cat would never be the same again.

"I have so much to tell, but first of all you'd better know that I was too late, Father had already died of his wound before I arrived." She noticed her young brother's eyes were glassy with tears. She didn't think it could be sorrow which caused them, as their father had always been particularly brutal to Spencer. Perhaps it was relief or more likely regret for what might have been, could have been . . . should have been.

"Auntie Lil was very kind to me; I liked her excessively. Father unfortunately left us a wonderful legacy . . . he mortgaged Roseland to the hilt and I've to come up with twenty thousand pounds in a month or it will likely be sold out from under us."

"Rancid old bastard," spat Spider, clenching his fists with impotence.

"He had a bill of sale on him for Ebony, too. They haven't been to collect him yet, have they?" she asked anxiously.

He shook his head quickly to reassure her, but his heart had sunk. He'd been dying to tell her of the smuggling deals he'd arranged to earn them some money, but in the face of a twenty-thousand-pound debt it amounted to no more than pissing in the sea. "What the hell are we going to do?" he asked her.

"I have another piece of news. Lord Helford has returned to Helford Hall. I sailed home on his ship. I think he's quite taken with me, so all I have to do is get him to propose before the mortgage is due and we'll save Roseland."

"Propose to you or proposition you?" he asked bluntly, his eyes blazing.

"It doesn't matter which," she said quickly.

"I won't let you sacrifice yourself to that fat, old swine," he said flatly.

"Spider, he isn't fat and he isn't old. . . ." Her voice trailed off; she wasn't as convinced about the swine part. In her experience all men were capable of being vile. "There's just a tiny fly in the ointment . . . the King has appointed him high commissioner and magistrate to eradicate smuggling."

Spider dropped onto a kitchen chair like a bag of sand. "Christ, girl, are you insane? I've fifty barrels of brandy coming in tomorrow night."

A look of panic crossed her face. "What about that tobacco?"

"I sold it yesterday, thank God. But what about the brandy?"

"What time is the tide?" she questioned.

"Early . . . just at moonrise . . . a few minutes after nine . . . it should be safely stowed by ten."

"I'll keep him busy," she promised.

"Will you keep all his nights busy?" He sneered.

"Spider, it's not like that; he thinks I'm a lady."

He looked at her as if she really was cracked, then he laughed so loud he fell off the chair onto the kitchen floor.

"I think it would be best if you and Ruark Helford did not meet," she said stiffly.

"Suits me, I can't take all this lord-and-lady stuff," he said, wiping tears of amusement from his eyes.

"Is the brandy coming off a Frenchie?" She deliberately changed the subject.

"Well, naturally it came off a French ship originally, but I'm buying it from a privateer who unburdened the Frenchie recently."

"You mean a pirate. What's his name?"

"Bulldog Brown," he said on a challenging note.

"Ugh." She shuddered. "That's the one who had part of his nose bitten off in a fight. For God's sake, be careful, Spider."

He waved his hand airily with the negligent arrogance of the titled class and she remembered the clothes she had bought for him. She opened one of the boxes and pulled out the black velvet suit and long, black, calf-skin boots. "I brought you some new clothes."

He gingerly felt the black velvet between thumb and forefinger and eyed his sister with distaste. "If I pranced around in this fancy stuff, I'd be the laughingstock of the town. Viscount bloody Spencer would soon have his teeth knocked out."

"You're a bloody lord now," she reminded him, "not a viscount. In London men wear pink satin and powder blue ostrich feathers," she said, remembering.

"Don't try to gull me, Cat, I'm not exactly a kid anymore, or hadn't you noticed?"

She sighed. "I noticed," she said with regret, closing the lid on the box of clothes.

"Come on, I'll carry these boxes upstairs for you. I know you'll want to unpack all your new clothes before you go to bed. These are the first pretty things you've ever had, aren't they, Cat?" He smiled sweetly at her. "It's good to have you back."

Ruark Helford had slept only fitfully the first night back in his home. Restlessly he had arisen before dawn to roam about the half-forgotten halls of the estate. It was so beautiful he didn't know how he had been able to stay away from it for so long. He went up on the high widow's walk to watch the sunrise—up among the gilded weathervanes which were fashioned after sailing ships—up among the twisted chimneys of Helford Hall. He looked out to sea as the golden dawn turned it into a rippling mass of molten gold, while behind him the dark green yew walks held pockets of mist which wouldn't burn off until the sun was full.

Summer had arisen before dawn to spend some time with her beloved Ebony. The sunrise was going to be spectacular; the air was soft with a hint of the warmth that the day would bring. The breeze off the sea was playful and she couldn't wait for a fast gallop down the deserted beach. Without bothering with a saddle, she slipped on a bridle, caressed the velvet nose, and was astride the tall animal in minutes.

She rode down the coast five or six miles at a leisurely canter, but when they turned to head home, she felt Ebony quicken between her legs and she let him have his head. He surged forward, thundering through the surf, sending up sea spray to make her shirt cling wetly to her breasts. Her hair flew about in wild disarray and she clung to the horse's mane for support, whispering encouragement into his pricked-back ears to gather ever greater speed.

Ruark Helford's eye was caught by a movement way off in the distance, down the beach, and he watched curiously as the speck became horse and rider and then to his astonishment the rider became Summer. There was no mistaking the wild, wanton pagan, her spirit as free as the wind and the sea.

This girl was nothing like the shy, proper, Lady Summer who always stood at arm's length with downswept lashes. Desire raged through him uncontrollably.

Desire to tame her.

Desire to mate her.

Desire to bury himself deep within her.

The damnedest thing was that even at her most prim, with two guardians at her back, she aroused him. Even from up here she looked naked to the waist. The vision of her magnificent, proud breasts thrusting through the wet shirt was too much for him. He must go down to the beach, to her.

He strode from the house and took the path that led down the cliff to the beach, but she was nowhere in sight when he arrived. He could hardly credit that she had disappeared so quickly and reasoned that she must have turned inland to ride up the Helford River. The tide had washed away her hoofprints and the beach was deserted in both directions as if she had been an apparition. A foul oath was snatched from his lips by the playful sea breeze. Frustration almost choked him, and yet he knew her elusiveness merely whetted his appetite and hardened his determination to have her.

Lord Helford had to contend with a mountain of paperwork and dispatches connected with his new post, yet a dozen times that day he threw down his pen with the intention of riding over to Roseland. He was torn between the need to see her and the desire to keep his promise.

Finally he gained control over his yearnings, reasoning that if he could not keep his word for at least twenty-four hours, she might develop contempt for him. He hoped against hope that she would visit him before the day was over.

By early evening he had given up hope and took an early dinner
in the vast, elegantly appointed dining room. He was totally unused to the feeling of loneliness which assailed him. Usually so self-
sufficient, he put his mood down to the fact that he had grown used
to stinking, brawling London with all its violent energy. The
change from the city to the country would take some adjusting. In
London all was noise. On the streets people shouted and pushed
and laughed and exchanged clever insults; here the silence was
deafening.

He threw down his napkin and pushed back from the table. His
longtime steward Mr. Burke approached him with an easy famil-
iarity. "Ruark, there is a young lady outside to see you, sir." He
had come from Ireland with Ruark's mother, Lady Rosalind, when
she had come to wed the first Lord Helford and had outlived them
both. Though it seemed natural for Burke to use his master's first
name, Ruark would never have dreamed of calling his man anything but Mr. Burke.

"Didn't you invite her in, Mr. Burke?" he asked as his eyes lit
with pleasure.

"I did, but the lady is unchaperoned and naturally awaits you
without," said Mr. Burke, his face as impassive as if he had announced that dinner was served.

Ruark's eyes widened at the sight of her. It was dusk, yet it was
as if she were surrounded by her own light. She is Summer, he
thought, dazed. She was mounted upon an expensive piece of
horseflesh which he knew was a black Barbary. She wore an elegantly cut riding dress in a ridiculously impractical shade of primrose yellow, and he had never seen a lovelier vision in his life.

"You are shocked because I'm not in mourning," she said.

He shook his head. "Nothing you could ever do would shock
me," he assured her.

It will . . . I promise you . . . it will, she thought wildly.
"Well, I cannot be a hypocrite; I do not mourn him," she said,
putting an end to the matter.

He tried to envision her as he had seen her at dawn, but he could
not. This young woman was as elegant as if she had been riding in
St. James Park. "I'm so glad you came," he said, moving to the
horse's side and holding up his arms to her.

"I came as a supplicant," she said solemnly.

As his strong arms lifted her down to him his heart slammed

inside his chest and it was not from exertion. "Anything," he murmured.

"I'm having the stables refurbished. I vow they are so dilapidated, a strong gust of wind would collapse them. Could I trouble you to stable Ebony until the work is finished?" When she coupled a lie with the truth, her conscience bothered her not at all.

"It is no trouble," he assured her, happy that he would see her more often now.

As they walked to the stables she embroidered her tale. "Don't be alarmed if there is a steady parade of wagons coming and going, they will just be workmen."

Inside the large, airy stables Ruark led Ebony into a loose box so he would have freedom without being tethered. He unsaddled the Barbary and took the bridle and bit from him as well. "He's a beautiful animal," he said with admiration, running his eyes down the glossy flanks.

"I'm particularly partial to him," she said in a throaty, provocative drawl.

The scent of hay and leather drifted in the air and Ruark's arousal was instant and pronounced. He wanted to pull her down into the hay and romp and roll until they were both naked and he had her pinned between his thighs. His eyes licked over her like a candle flame and he realized the impossibility of such wanton behavior. Her primrose habit was spotless, her coiffure the very latest style known as 'heartbreak.' He must remember she was a lady . . . and an innocent one at that.

Reluctantly he summoned a groom. "Lady St. Catherine will be stabling her mount here for a few weeks. See that he receives the very best of care."

As they walked from the stables, she said softly, "How can I ever repay you, Lord Helford? Each day I seem to be more and more in your debt."

"Come and have a drink with me. Let me show off the hall to you." It didn't sound like a request.

She shook her head regretfully. "You know I cannot," she said softly. "Show me the gardens."

"It is dark," he half protested.

"The moon is rising," she assured him.

"Smuggler's moon," he murmured, and she shuddered involuntarily.

The intoxicating fragrance of the night-scented blooms stole to

them as they crossed the velvety lawn separating the house from
the formal rose garden. They passed beneath an arch clustered
with heavy, dew-drenched blooms and Ruark's keen eyes searched
the darkness until he found what he sought. He left her side for a
moment and returned with an armful of cream blossoms. "I think I
shall always give you cream-colored roses," he promised. They
moved on to the eerie yew walks in deep, black shadow. "You
aren't afraid?" he asked.

She shook her head. "Not with you beside me," she answered
him.

As they walked side by side he reached for her hand. Her fingers
curled into his and he wished he could stay handclasped with her
until dawn. "These yew walks are reputed to be haunted," he said,
then stopped and looked down at her. "You haunt me," he said
huskily. The moonlight hardly penetrated the tall yew walk where
they stood. As she gazed up at him his face was all shadowed
planes and stark cheekbones. His eyes were half closed and she saw
the black smudge of thick lashes which concealed the desire she
knew smoldered there. The slant of his jaw emphasized the arrogance of his mouth which could give a fierce curse or an unbelievably heartrending kiss.

He cupped her face in gentle hands and dipped his head to
capture her mouth. The moment he tasted her, the kiss changed,
becoming hot and sensual. His hands left her face to crush her
against him. She could feel something hard as marble against her
belly and dimly realized it must be his shaft.

He could feel the tremors flowing through her body and his
strong brown hand came up to brush against her breast. She shuddered with pleasure. She could no longer deny the great attraction
she felt for Ruark Helford. His sensual masculine appeal made her
weak with yearning. Her defenses against him were crumbling and
she realized her feelings for this man could undermine all her
plans. She desperately wanted to believe that he was different from
other men. She longed to trust him, hoping he would always be
loving and generous toward her. She wished he would fall in love
with her and ask her to marry him so that she would be safe with
such a strong protector. She dared to hope that he was beginning
to care deeply about her, for she realized she could begin to care
for him. But she knew if she gave herself to him before he had
made a definite commitment to her, he would not value her.

She tried to push his hand away and with a ragged moan cried, "Ruark, please."

He lifted his head momentarily, but didn't think he could stop. "I will trust you implicitly. . . . I will let you set the pace, Ruark," she said softly, knowing they were the only words to stop him.

He groaned. He knew she was virgin. The sweet trust in her voice made him curse. "Dammit, Summer, you shouldn't trust me. You mustn't trust me! I want to be alone with you . . . I want to make love to you. Go . . . go now, run before I take your maidenhead!"

She laughed prettily. "I won't run from you, Ruark. I know you will protect me with your life," she said simply.

"I'm going to seduce you, Summer," he threatened, to give her fair warning.

"I don't care, Ruark. If that is what you want, then seduce me."

He groaned hoarsely and bit back a curse. He drew her to a bower and pulled her to the seat beside him. "Forgive me, love, for my rampant male behavior. I should be shot."

His mind searched desperately for safe ground and he turned to the subject of his work. "It's a good thing I'm going to be kept busy here. Tomorrow I have to visit the local militia and read them the riot act. They've been so slack, smuggling and even wrecking goes on under their noses. I intend to tear a strip off someone. I've got reinforcements coming down from the Bristol garrison. Then I'll inspect the Marine Patrol and their ships and point out their shortcomings. I'm going to be a very popular man," he said ruefully.

"Will you have to be away from home often?" she asked ingenuously.

"Yes, I'll have a circuit of courts at Falmouth, Penzance, Newquay, St. Austell, Bodmin, Saltash, and Plymouth."

"Plymouth is in Devon," she ventured.

"Yes, but I have jurisdiction. You see, it's too easy for Cornwall criminals to run across into Devon and think themselves safe from the long arm of the law."

"You won't really have to sentence people to death, will you?" she asked in a small voice.

He hesitated, then told her the truth. "I'm afraid so, Summer, but I will always be fair, impartial."

"*I* trust you," she said softly.

"That is unwise," he murmured.

"I throw myself upon your mercy," she said, laughing.

"I am known to be merciless," he admitted.

Her heart beat thickly with fear, for she knew he spoke the truth. Surely Spider would be finished with the business by now. She arose to walk slowly back toward the hall and he followed, keeping his dangerous hands stuffed into his pockets so they would not reach out to crush the delicate primrose.

As they approached the house, Mr. Burke came to the door with a lantern in his hand.

"Thank you, Mr. Burke, I shall see the lady home."

Panic rose in her throat. She gasped, "I'll not scandalize your servants."

"Mr. Burke would not tolerate such gossip among his staff," Ruark asserted.

"Then Mr. Burke is a most upright man." She smiled at the Irishman. "Would you do me the honor, sir, of lighting me home?"

Mr. Burke bowed formally and glanced at Ruark. "The lady knows what is correct even if the lord does not," he said dryly.

11

As soon as Summer looked down from her window and saw a man leading two horses, she knew it was the fellow who had bought Ebony. She sent a silent prayer to St. Jude that she had acted promptly in removing her stallion to the Helford estate and shouted down to the kitchen where she could hear her brother boiling the kettle for breakfast. "Spider," she called urgently, "go out the back way and get your pony out of the stables. Better clean up the horse droppings, too . . . spread it on the kitchen garden."

She grabbed an old gown which had gone to the rag bag a year ago and tousled her hair untidily with both hands. Automatically she thrust her knife into her belt, then she ran lithely down to the kitchen, chopped a spring onion, and held it to her eyes until they watered with irritation, then went outside to face their visitor.

She looked at him with red-rimmed eyes. "Did you bring us food, sir?" she asked hopefully.

"No," he answered, slightly annoyed. "I'm here on business. Is Lord St. Catherine here, girl?"

The tears spilled over onto her cheeks. "My father is dead, sir," she whispered.

The horse man frowned. He eyed the raggy gown apprehensively. "I have a receipt here for a black Barbary I purchased from St. Catherine a month back. I've come to collect him."

"Sir, what is a black Barbary?"

"A horse, girl, a horse!"

"It has been a long time since we could afford to keep horses, sir," she said with embarrassment.

"Who is in charge here? Show me to the stables," he demanded.

"No one is in charge," she said helplessly. He didn't dismount, so she walked meekly beside his horse to the stables. He tied his horses to the hitching post, dismounted and fastened the reins of his own horse securely. Then he strode inside, saying, "I'll take any livestock you've got if there's no horse."

He came to a full stop when he saw that the stables were empty. Just then Summer's tummy gave a loud roll and he looked at her in disbelief. He knew now what he had only suspected; namely that he had been cheated. What made him livid was the knowledge that he had been a fool to pay money out before he'd received the merchandise. Greed had prompted him to do such a thing, of course. The price asked for the Barbary had been a fraction of what it was really worth.

"No horses, no livestock . . . then I demand my money back," he said aggressively, and his voice echoed about the empty stables.

"Money?" she asked quietly as if she'd never seen such a commodity. "Sir, we don't even have food."

His eyes narrowed as he looked beyond the raggy gown. She might be a bit of trash, but she was magnificent trash! His eyes gleamed with speculation as he decided he would have something for his money. What better place than a deserted stable? He'd never coupled with a female this young and beautiful in his life. He was suddenly harder and randier than he had been in months. If his luck held, he'd keep her in the stables long enough to enjoy her tender flesh two or three times. If she resisted, he knew ways to force her to his bidding. Spirited fillies sometimes needed a taste of cruelty before they were ready for total obedience. If he hurt her, it was no more than she deserved for cheating him out of what was his. His eyes narrowed and his mouth twisted into a leer.

Before he took one step toward her, however, she had her knife in her hand.

"Cat," came a voice from the stable door. He whirled about to see a male version of the girl, also with glinting drawn knife.

"Spider," she answered, and the two began to slowly close in on him. The hair bristled on the nape of his neck as he realized the pair who used code names were primitive, uncivilized, savage. He took to his heels and ran. He mounted his horse with a filthy curse as he saw the lead rein had been cut and one of his horses was missing. He thought better, however, of inquiring after it.

Summer looked at her brother with admiration. "Where did you put your pony and the other horse?"

He winced. "Actually I put them in the back kitchen." He took off at full speed to assess what havoc they might have wreaked.

"Spider, I'll brain you! As if the place isn't in enough shambles," she cried, taking after him. They reached the back kitchen door together and collapsed upon each other mirthfully as they saw the big bay gelding and Spider's pony had devoured every scrap of their food. Gone were the freshly baked loaves, a basket of apples, a bag of oats for their porridge, and the pan of cream to go on it.

Spider said, "I could nip next door and steal some eggs."

"Don't you dare," cried Summer in great alarm, then she caught the teasing gleam in his eye.

"There's a ham in the larder. Let's hurry and eat before the wagons arrive for the brandy," he urged.

"You mean they're coming in broad daylight?"

"Don't tell me you're turning into an old woman," he scorned. "Oh, Spider, you'll give me a heart attack," he mimicked in falsetto.

She glared at him and bared her teeth. "I don't get heart attacks; I give them!"

Later in the day when they counted up their money and were about to lock it safely in their cash box, she said with pride, "We have almost three thousand pounds with what I brought back from London. Oh, Spider, I don't know how you've done it."

He grinned happily. "Only another seventeen thousand to go, don't despair." He filched a sovereign from the box before she locked it and tossed it into the air. "Don't wait up for me, Cat," he said, winking.

The candles had burned themselves out when suddenly Summer came wide-awake. She sensed something was not as it should be and fumbled to light a fresh candle. She reached for her crimson velvet bedgown, took up the candlestick, and went downstairs. In the front hall Spider leaned back against the door, his face ashen.

"What's wrong?" She ran to his side, her heart beating wildly in her throat.

"Militia," he whispered, "took a shot at me."

"My God, what were you doing?" she whispered furiously.

"Nothing . . . well, nothing much . . . stuff's still in the cave. Almost caught us red-handed . . . had to make a run for it," he said breathlessly.

They nearly jumped out of their skins as a loud hammering came upon the door. Summer jerked her thumb toward the stairs and he silently disappeared up them.

"Open in the name of the law," came an order in a voice which almost froze her blood in her veins. She waited silently until he hammered on the door again, then she flung it open and held her candle high. It showed her a burly young man with a florid face and small, piggy eyes. "Who are you?" she asked. "What is the meaning of this?"

"I am Sergeant Oswald, Falmouth Militia," he said with authority.

"And so?" she demanded.

"I have reason to believe that this household is involved in smuggling." He took a step forward with one boot touching the threshold. Summer did not move back, but thrust the candle closer to his face.

"This household, as you put it, consists of one lady. How dare you accuse me, Sergeant?" She sensed one or two men beyond him in the darkness and knew her only weapon was to humiliate him.

"We followed the felon here. No doubt he is one of your servants or grooms. Stand aside while we search the house."

"You pompous ass!" she flared. "Are you aware that it is the middle of the night, Sergeant? Are you aware that I am alone here, in a state of undress, Sergeant? Are you aware that this household is in mourning, Sergeant?"

His neck flushed until you couldn't tell where his bright uniform began. "If we find neither culprit nor contraband hidden within, we will leave you in peace, m'lady."

"You would find neither, Sergeant. You may take my word for it. Good night."

Oswald thought of Lord Helford's cold fury and contempt and the verbal flaying Helford had subjected him to that morning. "The new magistrate has ordered that we search any household under suspicion."

"Then the new magistrate is a bloody fool," she asserted.

"Fool he may be, but he is a black-tempered authoritarian and I dare not disobey his orders. We must search your house."

"You may search my house, Sergeant, when you have shown me your search warrant."

"I don't have one yet. I didn't think it would be necessary," he said with narrowed eyes.

"Let me assure you it is imperative! I suggest you go and get the warrant and come back."

"It is the middle of the night," he spat.

"Since you have ruined my sleep, I think it only fair that you ruin the magistrate's sleep, or you could return in the morning, Sergeant, at a more civilized hour," she suggested sweetly.

He pressed his lips together in rage and spun on his heel.

Summer threw home the bolt and climbed the stairs on very shaky legs.

Spider, still dressed, lay stretched out on his bed. "The whole story, if you please," she said quietly.

"It wasn't wrecking," he said quickly. "Somebody else must have done that. When we saw the vessel, it was floundering. Belgian or Dutch, so where's the harm?"

"We're not at war with Holland yet," she pointed out.

"Anyway, the wreckers had already looted her before we got to her. All the casks were gone except the broken ones. It was gin by the smell of it."

"What's in the cave?" she asked.

"I've no idea what it is. It could be worthless, for all I know. It's wrapped in oilskins."

"Well, whatever it is, we'd better go down now before the tide carries it out again."

"Perhaps that would be best. If they search the house in the morning . . ."

She stood like a pagan in her crimson robe. "We are part of the sea; we will give up nothing."

There were six heavy oilskin-wrapped bundles. It took them three trips each to carry the contraband into the cellars and another three trips to fetch it upstairs. Summer knelt before the bundles and carefully unwrapped one of the oilskins. Her breath caught in her throat as the candlelight revealed the beauty of the rich cache. "It must be Brussels lace," she said in awe, reaching out to touch the fine, costly material.

"Who the hell can we sell that to?" asked Spider with disappointment.

"We must find some way of getting it to Auntie Lil. It's worth its weight in gold. Of course we'll have to settle for less than its true value, but it will bring us a few thousand."

"Where will we hide it?" asked Spider.

"In my bed, I think. I'm reasonably certain I'm the only one with access to my own bed," she said decisively.

She arose at dawn as usual, but it was not to ride the beach. She chose with care the loveliest day gown she owned. It was a cream linen decorated with pale green ribbon loops. She fastened some cream-colored roses into her hair and went to awaken her brother.

He blinked at the vision before him. "You're going to a ball?" he asked, bewildered. Then he guessed again. "You're getting married!"

"No, silly. This is a day dress, and a simple one at that, I warrant."

"Well then, it's for *his* benefit," he grumbled.

"No, Spider, it's for yours. I have to get to Lord Helford before Sergeant Oswald does. Ruark will have to choose between us."

Spider grinned. "That bastard Oswald doesn't stand a chance, does he?"

"No, I'm afraid he doesn't," she said honestly. "Now come and hitch your pony to that little ponycart for me."

"You know how to do that; you've done it dozens of times," he said, yawning.

"Not in cream linen, I haven't, you lazy dolt."

As she came up the long driveway to Helford Hall she saw that Ruark was just ready to depart. A groom held his saddle horse while Mr. Burke stood by holding a stirrup cup. The moment Ruark saw her he came toward the cart, but she jumped down in a flurry of petticoats and ran to him. He took her hands in his, wondering how she could possibly look so delectable at six o'clock in the morning.

She looked up at him with distress clearly etched on her lovely brow.

"You're trembling, love, what is it?" he demanded.

She opened her mouth to speak and closed it again hesitantly.

"Come inside and sit down," he urged.

"Well . . . I . . . well . . . I." She hesitated breathlessly. "Well . . . I . . . will," she said, allowing him to persuade her.

With a protective hand at the small of her back he led her through the entrance hall to a small salon with comfortable chairs and a cheery fire. "Some coffee, Mr. Burke." He sat down across a small inlaid table from her and said anxiously, "Tell me what's amiss. Something has frightened you."

"It was a man," she said, low. "He came in the middle of the night demanding entrance. I was alone . . . undressed . . ."

His eyes blazed with fury; the muscle in his jaw clenched into an iron knot.

Mr. Burke's voice carried to them as he answered the door and bade Sergeant Oswald wait in the entrance hall. Summer looked through the doorway of the salon.

"Ah, no . . ." she cried, her hand going to her throat in alarm.

"Was that the man?" Ruark demanded.

Summer closed her eyes and nodded imperceptibly.

Ruark strode into the entrance hall and Sergeant Oswald saluted him smartly and said, "I'm sorry to disturb you, Lord Helford, but I need your authorization for a search warrant for your neighbor's property."

Helford took a threatening step toward the militiaman, who stepped back in alarm. Ruark ground out, "Yesterday, Oswald, I questioned your gross incompetence. Today I think I have my answer. Do you drink, Sergeant?"

"Yes sir, no sir, not on duty, sir."

Ruark was enraged that this ruddy-faced lout had seen Summer in her nightclothes. "What other explanation could you possibly have for harassing Lady St. Catherine in the middle of the night?" he thundered.

"Sir, we chased a suspected smuggler onto the St. Catherine property. She refused to cooperate and let us search for him."

"And if you had chased him onto my property, that implicates me in smuggling, does it?" he demanded dangerously.

"No sir, not at all, sir," Oswald answered, standing at rigid attention.

"By God, Oswald, I should have your commission for this," said Helford, trying to control his anger. His voice quietened, but it was much more deadly as a result. "If you or your men ever set foot on Lady St. Catherine's property again, I will take disciplinary action. Do I make myself clear, Sergeant?" he asked silkily.

"Yes sir." Oswald's eye caught a movement across the hall.
Summer stood in the doorway with a complacent little smile on her
lips, then she moved back into the salon. Oswald swore she would
one day rue the victory she now savored over him.

12

For the next three days Summer saw nothing of Ruark Helford. He was gone on official business and she chafed at the wasted days that were melting away. She had only three weeks left until the mortgage was due.

On the fourth day at dawn she collected Ebony from the Helford stables and rode out along the deserted beach. The sea air was brisk and cold and she wasted little time in covering the usual five miles then turned and rode back.

Halfway home she saw Ruark riding to meet her. For a moment she felt panic that he would see her in breeches and shirt with disheveled hair, but since there was nothing she could do about it, she waved gaily, genuinely glad to have him back.

He called to her, and though the wind tried to snatch his voice away, it was so strong it carried clearly to her. "You'll freeze to death in that thin shirt. Let's go up to the house. I want to talk to you."

She shook her head, letting the breeze blow her hair into a dark cloud. She noticed he, too, was in shirt sleeves.

"Then let me build a fire with some driftwood," he suggested hopefully.

She nodded her pleasure and pointed to a small cove in the rocks. They dismounted to gather an armful of wood and Ruark stacked it and set it ablaze. Summer pointed to a large mass on the sands which looked like resin. "There's a lump of ambergris washed up on shore."

"Ambergris?" he echoed. "My God, it would be worth its weight in gold in London."

"For what, pray?" she asked, laughing.

Ruark thought perhaps that even if he told her it was a rare aphrodisiac, she probably wouldn't know what he meant. "A sort of tonic," he said, and sat down with his back against the rocky cliff and held up his hands for her to join him.

She hesitated.

"You're angry with me for spoiling your solitude. You've told me plain enough you like your privacy."

"Of course I'm not angry with you. I just don't like you to see me dressed in masculine attire."

"Masculine?" he echoed, thinking how womanly she looked with the wet shirt clinging to her breasts.

"I missed you dreadfully."

"Did you? Did you really, Lady Summer St. Catherine?" he asked, his eyes hungrily devouring hers. "Then why won't you come and hold hands with me?"

She hesitated again. "I like holding hands with you," she confessed. "If only you won't do that thing that frightens me," she said in a rush.

He searched her face. "You mean kiss you?"

She shook her head. "I'm even shameless enough to like being kissed. I mean the other thing you do," she said, her face growing warm even in the cool breeze.

"Sweet, I'm at a loss; what is it I do to frighten you?"

"You make yourself . . . grow . . . enormous."

"Oh God," he swore. Very gently he took her hands and eased her down beside him. He kept his voice low and intimate. "I don't make myself grow . . . you do."

She gazed up at him, realizing this was one of those moments when he would reveal another piece of the puzzle to her. The mysterious male-female secrets which attracted and repelled her at the same time. She wanted to pull away; she wanted to melt into him.

"When you are near me, I have no control over it at all." He started to harden and dropped his eyes to her mouth. He realized his mistake immediately as his shaft jumped and lengthened. "I just see you, or hear you laugh or smell your perfume and I become aroused. Hell, you don't even have to be there at all, just thinking about you, thinking of touching you, and the damnable thing has a will of its own."

She loved the idea of not even having to be there to affect him. Her fear was slowly dissolving and in its place a great curiosity was growing. She ran the pink tip of her tongue over her top lip, unconsciously teasing him.

He knew he must taste her. "I've hungered for you," he said hoarsely as his mouth took hers in a demanding kiss.

She shivered at his touch. "You're wet," he said, concerned, as his brown hand brushed her breast through her clinging shirt. He was on his feet immediately to make the fire twice as hot for her. He loped down the beach to gather a great armful of driftwood and came racing back to their haven. He took off his wet shirt then slipped down again beside her with his back against the rocks.

She raised her long lashes to appraise his naked chest. "I know it's wicked of me, but I'm wildly curious."

"Curious about my body?" he asked huskily.

She nodded. "I cannot help myself . . . I have a burning need to look at you . . . to touch you . . . to know what you feel like when my hands and fingers explore you . . . and if it's wicked, I no longer care."

"Sweet love, it isn't wicked, it's natural and beautiful. Don't you know I have exactly the same needs? I can't keep myself from touching you when you're this close. Be bold, my darling, touch me. Give me one glimpse of that wild little pagan I'm falling in love with."

She moved to kneel in front of him and reached out her fingers to touch the furry pelt and the heavy muscles. He held his breath, keeping an iron control on himself. The last thing he wanted to do was frighten her off when she was this close.

With her eyes on his she slowly began to unbutton her wet shirt. Then very deliberately her eyes lowered to the place between his legs. He held his breath as hot desire pulsed through him, not quite believing what she was actually about to do. His balls tightened and he knelt up in front of her to let her see the full physical change she made in him. The blood surged and pulsed into his shaft, swelling, filling, lengthening, hardening it until the bulge threatened to burst from the confining breeches.

Her eyes widened with pleasure at the power she had over him.

Very slowly she removed the shirt and held it out to the fire. She was an irresistible combination of pagan and innocent.

His mind centered upon her naked beauty.

I've done this before, she thought, yet that was absurd, for of course it was the first time. The silence which stretched between them was a conversation without words. Then with reverence he reached out to cup the beautiful globes and bent to bestow a kiss upon each. "These are more aphrodisiac than any ambergris," he breathed, and then she felt the velvety caress of his tongue as he licked her nipples until they sharpened into dusky pink darts.

She was without shame, without reserve, and she thought with pity of all the women who were shy or reluctant when they loved. Ruark was both fierce and gentle with her at the same time and she knew as he took possession of her mouth that she loved the things he did to her, loved the way he made her feel and in spite of the fact that she was not yet ready to trust any man, she knew she could love him if he delivered her from her difficulties and fate was kind to her.

With his hot mouth on hers she felt half mad with passion. It raged in every part of her, her head, her heart, her belly, her naked breasts. Her frenzied hands longed to cup him, fondle him, crush him, yet they fluttered wildly over the forbidden male weapon while she gathered her last drop of courage to seize what she wanted.

"Cat!" The shout came from the clifftop above them.

She gasped and snatched up her shirt. "It's my brother Ruark. I must go."

Reluctantly he brought her horse and helped her mount its bare back. He looked into her eyes which were alive with silent promises, like windows into paradise. His heart soared wildly that she felt as he did, the same flame, the same longing. He picked up the ambergris and handed it to her. "It must have magic powers."

"What the hell were you doing down there?" Spider demanded, his lip curling.

"Minding my own business; something you seem incapable of," she said haughtily.

"You let him kiss you—on the mouth," he accused.

"I did," she added, silently relieved he hadn't realized she had been half naked.

"Did you worm out of him what he's been up to the last three

days or were you preoccupied with other things? Did he tell you he
took possession of that Dutchman we looted? Did he tell you he
captured a Frenchie plundering the estates along the coast by
Penryn? They slip across from Brittany all the time, but they've
never been caught before. He must have eyes in his arse. We'll have
to be more cautious. He means to enforce the law."

She pushed away a quiver of apprehension, knowing full well
that if you played with fire, you eventually got burned. Her eyes
fell upon the tall weeds growing everywhere. "Well, if we are to
have any vegetables at all this year, I'll have to tend the garden
today. Is that an innocuous enough occupation to suit you?"

He grinned at her, all animosity forgotten. "I'll help you," he
offered.

Summer was mortified to her bones as she looked up from kneeling in the dirt to see Mr. Burke approaching her. She jumped up to
brush the soil from her hands and her faded, drab gown. She wore
a rag over her hair and she touched it self-consciously as Mr.
Burke said, "Good afternoon, my lady."

She glanced at Spider, kneeling in his usual raggy attire, and her
heart sank. The game was up! When Helford's servant reported to
him about the overgrown tangle and air of shabby decay at Roseland, Ruark would cease to be interested in her.

"Lord Helford requests your company at dinner tonight, Lady
Summer. The invitation naturally includes your brother, Lord
Spencer."

She was flushed and stammered a futile excuse, yet not by a look
or a word did Mr. Burke indicate anything was amiss.

"We accept," said Spider coldly.

Summer gasped.

"Very good, sir. Lord Helford will expect you at six." Mr. Burke
bowed politely and took his leave.

"Are you mad?" Summer cried, then she sank down on her
knees among the cabbages and cried.

Later, as she dressed for dinner at Helford Hall she wondered
just how she would face him. She had toyed with the idea of refusing to go, but if she didn't show up, he would probably come and
get her and his actually seeing Roseland would be worse than hearing of it from Mr. Burke.

"Cat, where's my suit?" called Spider.

"What suit?" she asked absently.

"That black velvet thing you brought from London."

She took the beautifully tailored suit and soft, black thigh boots into his room and selected a white shirt which wasn't too frayed from his wardrobe. "You'll have to remember to call me Summer tonight, not Cat, and even worse than that, I'm going to call you Spencer," she warned.

He glowered at her with dark brows as she watched the clothes transform him from an urchin into a fashionable young gallant. Arrogance was written all over him and she was suddenly afraid he would demand to know what Helford's intentions were regarding her. She sighed. It wouldn't really matter if Mr. Burke had had a chance to disclose their poverty.

What a little fool she'd been this morning to lie in his arms naked to the waist. Tonight she'd face exposure of another kind and she needed the courage of a magnificent gown. It would have to be the crimson velvet whose skirt was shaped like an inverted tulip and the low-cut décolletage was shaped like delicate petals cupping her breasts.

She surveyed herself in the old mirror which needed resilvering and longed for rubies to clasp about her neck.

Spencer rode the big bay gelding, taking his sister up before him. Before she entered the hall she took a deep breath, squared her shoulders, and entered with all the pride of a cat.

As Mr. Burke took her wrapper he let one eyelid slowly close. She looked at him in disbelief and her spirits dared to rise. By St. Jude the Martyr, he didn't intend to tell Ruark Helford her secret. They were conspirators and it felt wonderful. She glanced back at her brother and her spirits plummeted again. She could see he was spoiling for a fight. As he surveyed Lord Helford with narrowed eyes and curled lip, he looked like a lean hound with raised hackles.

Ruark came forward to greet her and she prayed that he would not kiss her . . . kiss her on the mouth as Spider had so quaintly put it. Ruark's eyes warmed her and told her without words how beautiful she looked. Then he took her hand, turned up the palm, and placed a kiss within.

"Lord Ruark Helford, meet my brother, Lord Spencer St. Catherine."

The greetings were low murmurs exchanged stiffly as they measured each other warily. Drinks before they went in to dinner were offered and accepted with impeccable politeness, and Summer thought she would scream if this frosty formality went on much longer.

When at last they went in to dine, her heart was warmed by the lovely cream-colored roses Ruark had set by her plate and they exchanged swift, meaningful glances. He tried not to stare at her, but it was difficult. She was exquisite as a cameo. And she had an elusive quality about her that was so hard to define. What was it? Fascination, he decided.

The tension in the air between the two men was so thick you could have cut it with a knife. Whatever subject their host broached, Spencer managed to work into his reply that his sister, Lady Summer, had led a most sheltered life and was unused to men and men's wicked ways. He was more pointedly protective than any parent would have been and Summer was mortified that her brother was making it insultingly plain he was preserving her overripe virginity.

Finally she could bear it no longer and took over the direction of the conversation herself. "Lord Helford, is it true you took possession of two foreign ships this week?"

"So," he said, his eyes sweeping over brother and sister, "my business is common knowledge in these parts, I see."

She lifted the corners of her mouth. "The very walls whisper of the exploits of High Commissioner Helford. What will you do with the ships?"

He seemed to weigh his words carefully before he answered. "The Dutchman had been picked clean." He grimaced. "The work of wreckers. It carried only a skeleton crew, so one or two bodies might soon wash up. I'm sending the ship to Plymouth. His Majesty is building up the navy at last."

She dared not look at Spider, for they held contraband which would connect them with the brutal, bloody business of wrecking. Quickly she asked, "And the other ship?"

"We caught the raiders red-handed, so her cargo was intact. I'm sending it to London tomorrow."

"I suppose you'll make her crew swim back to Brittany?" she jested.

His face became grim and hard. "Piracy carries the death penalty."

The delicious minted lamb turned to ashes in her mouth. Then almost immediately her brother saw a spark of defiance come to her aid. Her great cat's eyes hid their fear for an instant under white lids, then flashed out with renewed fire, her sensitive nostrils flaring. "Lord Helford, I wonder if I could impose upon you to carry something to London on that ship?"

Spider almost choked on his wine.

"It is no imposition, Lady Summer, to perform a service for you," he said formally, but his eyes were alive with the sight of her and belied the formality.

"My father left his sister, Lady Richwood, some valuable paintings. If Spencer crates them and delivers the crates to the ship in the morning, would you instruct one of your trustworthy seamen to deliver them to Cockspur Street?"

"Consider it done," he said, smiling.

Spider marveled at her coolness, but by the set of her chin she wasn't finished with Helford yet.

"Lord Helford, you were once a pirate yourself, were you not?"

His eyes narrowed. "I served the King as a privateer under command of Prince Rupert."

Spider's mouth fell open, all reserve gone completely, as he asked with boyish enthusiasm, "You served under Rupert, sir?"

Summer may as well not have been present after that as the two men warmed to their subject. Rupert the Devil, Rupert the Military Genius, Rupert the King's Cousin, Rupert the Soldier-and-Sailor Prince, Rupert the Universal Admiral, dominated their conversation.

Summer almost fell asleep as the tales of Rupert began with his birth. "Did you know the first words he ever spoke were 'goddamn'! He was fully trained in arms by the age of eight and in the army before he was thirteen."

It was over an hour later that Summer heard Ruark say, "Next time he comes to Cornwall you must meet him. He loves us Cornishmen, says the sea puts a tantalizing tang in our nostrils."

As her eyes went back and forth between the two she sat stunned as they lifted their glasses high and burst into a sea chanty, "Damn 'em, and ram 'em, and sink 'em to hell."

Summer got to her feet. "Spencer, it's very late."

"Oh, is it?" he asked, surprised, then he saw Summer's compressed lips and Ruark's secret amusement and said reluctantly, "I'll get my horse."

The moment he left the room, Ruark slipped his arms about her and drew her to him. She put back her head and gazed up at his laughing eyes. "I had a wretched evening," she whispered. "Half the night I was miserable thinking he was going to demand if your intentions were honorable and the other half, you devious devil, you had him eating out of your hand."

"You are so beautiful tonight, I don't know how I kept my hands from you." As he gazed down at her he had an unimpeded view of her neck, shoulders, and breasts. "This gown cries out for jewels. What do you like?" he murmured.

She drawled, "I'm particularly partial to rubies."

His lips brushed hers softly. "Rubies would be perfect. Good night, love. Come back to me soon."

To add insult to injury, Spider, on the ride home, said, "You know, Cat, if you intend to wed Lord Helford, I think you'd better reform."

"Before or after we smuggle the Brussels lace aboard his vessel?" she asked dryly.

Next morning the fog lay thick upon the sea, blanketing everything farther than a foot from her nose. The weather never deterred Summer from her dawn ritual, however, so she donned her breeches and walked the mile to the stables at the Helford estate. The grooms and stableboys were familiar with her long-legged figure by now, but this morning they only nodded politely instead of the usual friendly greeting.

Ebony whinnied his welcome, however, as she moved forward into the loose box and picked up his bridle. She turned quickly at a sound behind her and saw the tall, broad-shouldered figure of Ruark enter the box with her.

"I don't like it," he said gravely, looming over her in the dawn's half-light.

"My masculine attire?" she asked, laughing.

"Masculine?" he puzzled, remembering she'd said that before. The figure-revealing breeches and lawn shirt showed off much too much woman in his opinion.

"No, love, I don't like you riding in this fog. It's dangerous."

"That's the reason I love to do it," she teased. "What music, drink, or love does for most, danger does for me."

He groaned and pulled her into his arms. Her words had hardened him instantly. He pressed her against his arousal and dipped his head to taste her luscious mouth. He was dressed in formal navy blue as befitted his office and regretted that if he laid her in the hay, he would be covered with the telltale straws. "When are we going to have more than a few stolen minutes together?" he murmured thickly against her mouth.

She gave him a tiny kiss. "This week?" She gave him another tiny kiss. "Next week?" She kissed him again. "Sometime?" And again. "Never?"

"I swear I'll run mad if you keep teasing me. Next week will be even busier than this one. Charles's mother and sister are coming from France for a visit. They'll be sailing into Portsmouth in a fortnight, so next week Charles and a lot of the court are coming first to Plymouth while he inspects his navy firsthand."

"Will he go to war against Holland?" she asked.

He kissed her nose. "You ask too many questions. I'll be away tonight. Will you come tomorrow night?"

She clung to him in the dimly lit privacy of the loose box, trying to control the restless devils inside her who fought and struggled for release. She wondered if all women in love were torn between two impulses. She longed to throw modesty to the winds and urge him to make love to her, and yet the thought kept intruding to be cool, aloof, utterly detached. Perhaps she should die rather than be the first to admit a thing so personal and intimate as love. "I don't know if I will come or not," she said with brutal honesty. "I know I should not, but if I cannot keep away from you, than I shall come."

"Summer, by letting me set the pace, you are forcing me to act honorably toward you." He ran a possessive hand down her back. "God's flesh, 'tis the hardest thing I've ever had to do."

"Act honorably?" she murmured, full of devilry.

He laughed. "Oh God, I want to be so dishonorable with you."

"Mmmm," she said, licking her lips over the thought. Her restless horse, tired of waiting, walked out of the stall without her and she pulled out of Ruark's arms to follow him.

He whispered huskily, "I'll come home early tomorrow night, and I'll try my best not to act dishonorably."

She wrinkled her nose. "Then perhaps I won't come after all," she teased unmercifully.

13

After her morning ride Summer kept Ebony to crop the lawns and was thankful she wouldn't need to water the vegetables today because the heavy morning fog had taken care of that chore.

Spider fashioned three wooden crates which looked as if they might hold paintings while Summer wrote a letter about the Brussels lace to Auntie Lil. She packed the lace lovingly, making good use of the oilskins, and Spider nailed the crates closed.

By eight o'clock he was on his way to Falmouth in the ponycart and Summer reckoned the lace should add another couple of thousand pounds to their savings. She carried water from the well and set it to boil for the washing, then as she scrubbed the linen her mind never left Ruark Helford.

All her time was running out and she knew he must make her his mistress soon if she was to obligate him with her debts. Once they had become intimate, she hoped he would be loving and generous enough to forgive her deceptions. She would have to choose very carefully the perfect moment when she would confess all.

He was going away again next week and heaven only knew when he would return once he was reunited with the King and court. So she decided she must make it happen. Tomorrow night he must make love to her!

When Spider returned, he had brought food from Falmouth. He unhitched the cart and set his pony to crop the lawns with Ebony. Over lunch he told her how smoothly it had gone when he carried the crates aboard himself and stowed them in the cargo hold. Lord Helford instructed Mr. Cully to deliver them to Lady Richwood when the ship docked in London and then, Spider said, the magistrate had ridden off to Plymouth, no doubt to condemn the poor bastards from Brittany who were imprisoned there, awaiting their sentence.

Later in the afternoon when Spider saddled the bay, she asked him where he was going. "When I checked the lobster traps this morning, they were empty, so I thought I'd ride up the Helford River and do a spot of fishing."

She sighed with relief, for he was getting to an age where he wasn't going to listen to a woman's admonitions to be careful, not even his sister's. When he hadn't returned by dusk, she felt uneasy, then when it turned full dark, she could not dispel a nagging worry. When a knock came upon the front door, her heart plummeted. A shabby urchin handed her a scrap of paper. "Spider's been taken," he said breathlessly.

"You mean arrested?" she cried.

He nodded. "Excise men."

She felt the blood drain from her face. She closed her eyes and grasped hold of the lintel. "Where have they taken him?"

The boy shook his head, so she looked at the paper on which were scrawled two words, "Falmouth jail." "Aren't you the Penrose boy from the tavern in Helston?"

He nodded. "They got my da' an' my brother, too," he gasped.

She thanked him and gave him some coppers. "Run home to your mother, she'll need a strong lad like you."

She wondered if she might be able to bribe Spider's way out and ran upstairs to get money from the cash box. Should she get dressed up, sweep in telling them she was Lady Summer St. Catherine, and demand his release? No, if she knew Spider, they hadn't the faintest idea who he was, so it would be best to dress shabbily this first time and hope she could learn something.

She put on her gardening skirt and wrapped a shawl about her, then she rode the pony to Falmouth. She put the shawl over her head and had no trouble gaining access to the prison. She wasn't the only woman hastening to the jail this night. All those who had been arrested for unlawful importation were housed in a common cell and not a few of them stood at the bars talking to their anxious womenfolk. Her brother motioned her over quickly. "Don't worry about me, Cat, I'm fine. The short, thickset man over there is Bulldog Brown . . . they've got me down as Spider Brown. We don't come up before Helford for three weeks, so for Christ's sake promise me you won't let this spoil things for you. Don't dare tell him or he'll never wed you!"

"You can't stay here for three weeks," she protested.

" 'Course I can. We'll just sit here and eat our heads off."

Penrose grinned at her. "I'm going to offer our jailers some cider from the pub to keep us in good stead."

"You see?" demanded Spider. "A deep draft of local cider will have us lying in the gutter every night with our toes in the air, so stop worrying about me and get on with more important business."

She nodded. She wouldn't tell him she'd brought money as a bribe. She didn't want to give him false hopes if it didn't work. She turned to seek out an officer, but before she could leave, Spider had her firmly by the wrist. "Promise me you'll pretend all is well when you see him."

She bit her lip and whispered, "I promise."

"Good girl. Now I have a really lousy job for you, Cat, but you've got to do it." He looked at her anxiously. "That bastard Oswald who caught us shot the bay out from under me. I don't think the swine killed him—he just left him there on the beach. You'll have to go and finish him off, Cat."

Her heart flooded with anguish. What sort of swine would leave a horse to die a slow agonizing death as its lifeblood seeped away? She felt for her money and hurried to the ward room. Fate was laughing at her this night. Sergeant Oswald sneered, saying, "Well, well, if it isn't Helford's whore. There's no denying it this time. I caught them with the barrels. Which one are you connected with?"

"I came on behalf of Mrs. Penrose at the tavern. You have both her husband and her son," she said quietly.

He leered down at her, his red face sweating. "I don't think spreading your legs will do you any good this time."

She couldn't get away from him fast enough. She urged the pony into a fast trot, wishing Spider had ridden this surefooted little beast who knew the cliff paths so well and probably wouldn't have been spotted in the dark.

Back home at Roseland she carefully loaded one of the pistols, put some fresh water into a bucket, and climbed down the cliff path to the beach. Halfway down she spotted the bay lying on the shingle, his maimed body making a grotesque mound in the moonlight.

Summer prayed he was dead, but before she even got close she could hear him heaving. She knew he would be unable to eat—that's why she hadn't brought an apple or oats—but she knew with his lifeblood trickling from him, he would have an unbearable thirst.

She dug the bucket of water down into the sand beside his muzzle and with soft soothing words lifted his head to help him drink. He drained the bucket, his great sides heaving and quivering with the effort. "Good boy," she whispered as she put the pistol behind his velvet ear and pulled the trigger.

It flashed and kicked in her hand, and if she hadn't been kneeling, it would probably have knocked her off her feet. She sat quietly a long time to make sure he was dead, then when the eternal tide crept up to wash about his hooves, she arose and let the sea have him.

That night she didn't sleep, of course. Her feelings were so intense she felt like screaming. If she could scream loudly enough, she felt that some of her tension might dissolve. She agonized over her brother, but at least she knew the Falmouth prison was no hellhole like the larger one in Plymouth. Finally she realized that Spider was right. The best way she could help him was to carry through her plans to secure her position with Ruark Helford and she had no more days or nights to waste.

Now that the moment had arrived, she was suddenly reluctant. She realized with dismay she was battling her conscience. Until now she hadn't realized she had a conscience. What sort of person could deliberately and dishonestly use someone they cared about for financial gain? She lay quietly, weighing the alternatives. If she were the only one involved, she would have abandoned her dishonest plans. If she lost Roseland as a result, then so be it; but now that Spider was in such serious trouble, she knew she would have to carry on with the deception. She would use Ruark to help her brother, but she promised herself fervently that she would never cheat him. She would be faithful and generous and give back in full measure whatever he did for her.

The warm fog the day before had been a prelude to the subtropical weather the gulf stream had brought this heavenly summer

day. In the afternoon Summer took a long bath and washed her
hair, letting the sun dry it until it was a dark mass of silken curls.
Then she opened her wardrobe and went over its contents.

She had only one gown left which Ruark hadn't yet seen. It was
a white, silk organdy with puffed sleeves, a low, heart-shaped neckline, and a skirt billowing with yards and yards of delicious organdy from the tiniest waist.

She put on lacy stockings and shift, blushing as she did so, for
she knew before the night was over his eyes would see everything
beneath the gown. Its waist was so nipped in, she found it difficult
to breathe, or was it the thought of what was yet to come which
made her so breathless?

By early evening none of the heat had left the day, so she didn't
bother with a cloak. She made sure the house was safely locked up,
and since she hadn't returned Ebony to the Helford stables the day
before, she rode him back now, very slowly, so that she wouldn't
be disheveled when she arrived.

At the stables there were a half-dozen grooms and stableboys
ready to help her dismount and care for Ebony. She smiled her
thanks and walked slowly up to the hall. Mr. Burke met her at the
front door and led her to the south wing, through tall French
doors, out onto a terrace where a profusion of bougainvillea and
other tropical blooms had turned it into a sheltered paradise.

Ruark had been sitting on the edge of a fountain until he saw
her, then he arose and came forward eagerly. "Sweetheart, I was
afraid you wouldn't come."

"I don't believe you've ever been afraid in your life," she said
prettily, laughing up into his eyes.

He took both her hands, holding her at arm's length to drink in
her beauty, then he enfolded her in his arms for a moment of
delicious possession. 'Ods blood, she *would* wear white tonight. It
was like a symbol of her purity. He pushed away the thought with
determination, for his mind was made up. He would wait no
longer.

He stooped to pick an exotic, flame-colored hibiscus and offered
it to her. She gazed up at him with unfathomable eyes. She knew
tonight would be different. Before, he had always given her cream-
colored roses. She reached out for the flaming hibiscus and Ruark
knew that tonight she would come to him fully.

He was instantly conscious of the blood flowing hot and thick in
his veins and of the heavy, unbearable ache which suddenly

flooded his loins. Keeping hold of her hand, he drew her to the fountain. Its centerpiece was a small dolphin carved from jade with the water spouting high from its mouth, then falling into a three-tiered waterfall. The pool was lined with jade green tile where the orange and black carp made a startling contrast.

"It's like paradise," she murmured, her eyes sweeping the flowering trees which enclosed the terrace. Yellow laburnum dangled its blossoms next to the mauve blooms of a glorious magnolia. Small flowering almond were backed by large masses of fuchsia-colored rhododendrons.

"I had it copied from an Ottoman palace in Algiers on the Mediterranean."

Summer's eyes widened. "There are so many things I don't know about you."

"And I you," he said huskily, "but we can remedy that." He brought her hand up and pressed a kiss to the pulse in her wrist and smiled as it fluttered erratically. Holding her eyes with his, he said, "Some people can know each other in a few hours, but with others it takes a lifetime. Which do you suppose it will be with us?"

She shook her head and said softly, "I hope our time together is not too fleeting . . . like these beautiful blooms . . . they'll all be gone in a week . . . it seems such a waste."

"Beauty enjoyed at its peak is never a waste," he said suggestively. "That is why I thought we should dine out here this evening."

A footman was putting the finishing touches to a small table he had set up just outside the tall French doors and Ruark, still hand-clasped, led her over to it. Summer didn't think she'd be able to eat a thing. A million butterflies' wings were fluttering inside her stomach and the hot evening was not conducive to a large meal.

Ruark held her chair and obediently she sat and unfolded her napkin. He took his place across from her so that he could make love to her with his eyes. He poured her a goblet of pale Chablis and their fingers touched intimately as he handed it to her.

Her eyebrows rose slightly, questioning him on its potency. He was pleased they could communicate without words. He shook his head to assure her it was harmless enough and she sipped it delicately, letting the cool liquid stay on her tongue each time before she swallowed it.

The meal had been chosen with a sure hand to appeal to both the eye and the palate on such a hot night. The footman served smoked salmon and cucumber aspic as a first course, and Summer sighed with delight at the marked contrast it made from the usual rough fare she normally ate. Then came cold capon with cherry sauce and chilled asparagus spears.

She blushed as she tasted the capon, thinking irreverently that this wasn't the first time she'd dined on one of his fine cockerels. He noticed her cheeks of course, for his eyes never seemed to leave her face.

His hand closed over hers and he urged, "Tell me what prompts your lovely blush."

She let her lashes sweep to her cheeks. "It's secret, Lord Helford."

"I insist upon Ruark. Surely you are not too shy to use my Christian name?"

She lifted her lashes and gave him a dazzling smile. "I am not shy, Ruark; everything I say and do is imprudent, I fear." The sexual tension stretched taut between them. The very air seemed to hold its breath.

At her words his flesh reacted instantly, swelling, filling, aching for her. Her eyes were on his mouth and immediately she imagined it kissing her own, then going lower to taste the hard little fruits of her nipples as he had that morning on the sand.

Ruark's eyes were dark and intense with passion. Always when he thought of her, he wished himself deep within her. His eyes lingered on her lips and he longed to watch them open and cry out with passion as he sheathed himself to the hilt inside her.

The footman hovered with dessert, but they were oblivious to anything but each other. It was as if they were alone in the universe. He arose and came around the table to lift her against his heart. "My darling, your beauty has no equal." He set her feet down upon the terrace flagstones, but hugged her to his side with one possessive arm. They wandered down the garden toward a huge outdoor chess set with life-size carved knights and rooks.

"Were these also at the palace in Algiers?" she asked in wonder.

"Actually we played with real people, slaves whose only purpose was to stand patiently while we made our moves."

"How decadent," she condemned.

"Yes, everything is decadent in Algeria, but they certainly know how to go about some things better than we do."

"Such as?" she challenged with raised chin. The carved king sat upon a throne and he lifted her until she was sitting in its lap and on an eye level with him.

"They train their women in ways to please men. A beautiful woman's main purpose in life is making love, and she is kept locked away in a harem where other men can never see her." His lips brushed hers.

She said breathlessly, "Surely that isn't what you want for me?"

"Of course it's what I want, if I'm being truthful."

She could feel the heat from his strong hands as they encircled her waist. His thumbs caressed the organdy beneath her breasts. She giggled. "I prefer the way it is in England, where I may sit upon the King's knee if I so desire."

"You little witch. If Charles ever looks at you, I'll kill him." He lifted her down from her wooden perch. The evening shadows had begun to lengthen and he drew her inside the maze, where they were completely private. "I'm going to taste you now," he said raggedly. His hands brought her closer until his hips just touched her. His nostrils flared with the scent of her and his hand slipped up beneath her hair to hold her head captive for his ravishment.

"Open your mouth to me, darling, I want you to know what it feels like when a part of me is inside you."

She felt the thrill of the kiss all the way down to her knees. She clung to him so that she would not fall. His hands burned her through the delicate material, his mouth also was burning hot and ruthlessly demanding. A curl of fire began in the pit of her stomach and stretched its fiery fingers upward to her breasts and downward to between her legs. She cried out, "Ruark, Ruark," as her need awoke and grew apace with his.

"I can't let you go tonight," he told her fiercely.

"I know that," she said softly, feeling his hard erection pressed against her until she learned how it throbbed and pulsed.

He tried to still his blood so that he wouldn't take her under the hedge like a servant girl. He knew this was her first experience with a man, and if he wasn't careful he would rush her through her deflowering with alarming speed. Though he was almost consumed by a towering lust, he managed not to undress her while they were still outdoors.

Instead he gathered her beneath a powerful arm and led her back to the hall. As they passed the table outside the French doors she picked up the flame hibiscus and tucked it between her breasts. He took the wine which had been left to cool, and oblivious to the world, they entered a small sitting room with a comfortable couch and sank down upon it in the darkness. The room was so shadowed that only the whiteness of her gown and his fine shirt could be discerned in the velvety dark. He pressed her back against the cushions, intending to enjoy her to the full.

Because she was a maiden, she had been bound by a strange reserve until now when she knew their moment had come. "Oh, Ruark, I love you so much," she cried.

His hand had just begun its ascent under her gown and up her leg. Her words made him realize he was about to ravish her with lust when she deserved to be initiated with love.

Summer knew she would not draw back now. She wanted what he wanted. Whatever happened to him would happen to her, any feeling or movement or sensation would be shared by both. Love happened when two people had no barriers between them, no shame, no reserve, no pride even.

His hands slipped beneath her back to undo the tiny buttons of her bodice, but her hands were there before his to aid his possession of her. However, as his fingers encountered hers, he thought she was trying to prevent him from removing her gown and he sat up and uttered a mild oath.

He lit a candle and gazed at her exquisite loveliness in the candleglow. "My Lady Summer St. Catherine, will you marry me?"

One heartbeat passed.

"My Lord Ruark Helford, I will."

He groaned and took her into his arms. She hoped that in the morning he would remember his proposal, but she was so much in love with him it didn't really matter.

14

Ruark arose from the couch
and straightened his clothes. Then he lit all the candles in the
room. Under the blazing light Summer felt the need to rearrange
her gown and smooth her wildly cascading curls.

Ruark went to the door and summoned Mr. Burke. Summer's
cheeks were flushed, and her breath caught in her throat as she
heard Ruark say, "I'm sorry to put you to the trouble, Mr. Burke,
but would you be good enough to go down to Helston and fetch
the parson?" As he turned back to her, he saw that her eyes were
like stars and he knew he had made her happy. He plucked the
hibiscus from her breasts and bore it away with him. "Wait just
where you are, darling, I have something that will go much better
with your lovely wedding gown."

She sat entranced, thinking surely her heart would burst with
happiness. Lord Helford had actually asked her to marry him. She
wasn't dreaming. He'd sent for the parson!

Ruark came back downstairs with a set of velvet jewel cases. He
held out his hand and drew her to the tall mirror set above the
mantel of the fireplace. The large case held a high necklace with six
strands of rubies. Summer gasped as he clasped them about her
neck and bent to place a kiss upon her exposed nape.

"These aren't for me?" she asked in disbelief.

He took out matching bracelets and slipped them over her wrists. "I heard a rumor that Lady Helford was particularly partial to rubies." He picked up the matching ring and slipped it into his pocket.

"Lady Helford," she breathed, wondering if she would faint dead away before the parson could be brought.

Ruark bade a servant fetch two cases of wine from the cellars and another to carry in a couple of hogsheads from the alehouse, while Summer, womanlike, admired her reflection in the mirror and held up her arms to catch the reflection of the bloodred rubies.

It was a half hour before Mr. Burke returned with the agitated parson. He was a large man with a shaggy, gray head and an air of authority.

"Welcome to Helford Hall; I have asked you here to perform a wedding ceremony, Mr. Rashleigh," said Ruark, offering his hand.

The clergyman ignored the hand and drew heavy gray brows together. "I've already explained to your man that will be impossible; however, the fool insisted I explain matters to you myself."

Ruark's eyebrows rose slightly at his tone. Summer glanced apprehensively at the men, clearly recognizing that both liked to be in control of all situations, and a small battle of wills was inevitable.

"In order for a marriage to take place, banns must be posted," he explained with exaggerated patience. "When your proclamation of marriage has been read out three times from my church, I shall be happy to consecrate your union, Lord Helford."

Ruark smiled blandly. "I am the head magistrate in Cornwall. I have the power to waive the banns, and I do so, Mr. Rashleigh."

The parson opened his mouth to speak and closed it again firmly as he thought better of it.

Summer and Mr. Burke exchanged a significant look—one that said, had there ever been any doubt whose will would prevail?

Ruark told Mr. Burke to assemble all the servants in the hall. He held the door for the clergyman and said quietly, "Fifteen minutes, Mr. Rashleigh."

When they were alone, Ruark closed the distance between them and gathered her close.

"Do you always get your own way so easily, milord?"

"Always," he said, his eyes playing with hers.

"With women, too, milord?" she pressed.

"Especially with women," he teased.

"Perhaps I shall prove the exception," she said boldly, and withdrew from the circle of his arms. He slanted an eyebrow at her, but she turned to the mirror to adjust her curls. Let him wait and wonder. She was not going to let this wealthy, arrogant young lord think she was easy. She had been the first to declare her love, and yet, she told herself, it had definitely been that passionate declaration which had made him propose.

She watched his image behind her deep in the mirror and hated with a passion all the women he'd known. She couldn't bear the thought of his mouth tasting another. He was hers and she'd never, ever share him! The thought of kissing brought her eyes to Ruark's mouth and she began to tremble.

He was beside her in an instant. "Love, what is it? Are you unsure about doing this?"

She turned from the mirror and looked into his eyes. "I want to do it with all my heart," she told him truthfully.

"That is indeed fortunate, for I cannot give you up. I want you and I want you tonight." She thought his eyes were like emerald fire as he took her hand and led her to the great hall.

Panic took hold of her for a moment when she saw the vast assembly of servants. She was living a lie, one which would be revealed any moment. She had lived like an urchin, running wild, catching meals whenever the opportunity presented itself. How could she masquerade as a great lady and run a household of fifty servants? Then she saw Mr. Burke eyeing her with approval and suddenly it was all right. Somehow she would pull it off.

She was the center of attention and somehow it had been inevitable that she wear the white gown tonight. With Ruark's strong arm at her back she stood proudly beside him, allowing the servants to satisfy their curiosity about her.

He held up his hand and the hum of low voices was stilled. "This is Lady Summer St. Catherine, who is to become my bride tonight. She is the first bride to come to Helford Hall since my mother came over thirty years ago." The servants applauded in unison. "I want you to be part of our wedding. I want you to open your hearts to her and take her inside, as I have. It is some sort of miracle that I found she has lived just next door her whole life. I like to think she has been waiting for me her whole life."

I have, thought Summer. It was like a revelation. What strange thoughts flitted through her head as large, craggy-faced Mr. Rashleigh helped them exchange vows. First she noticed that the parson had tobacco stains on his fingers and knew with a certainty he was not averse to a bit of honest smuggling. Then she noticed that most of the servants were fat with the exception of those who worked in the stables. They had gorged themselves on the bounty of Helford Hall while she and Spider had almost starved. Then she heard the clergyman admonish Ruark, "Husband, love thy wife as you would your own body. A man shall be joined unto his wife and they shall become one flesh. This is a great mystery."

Very soon Ruark would indeed join his body to hers, and she cast him a swift apprehensive glance. She thought with alarm, He is so solemn, so controlled. His dark hair was clubbed back severely, his brooding thoughts unreadable. Suddenly she had the urge to see him disheveled and wildly out of control. She knew the need to shatter his composure into a million pieces and a small wicked voice inside her taunted, Will you be the one to do it?

"I will, I will!" she vowed, and the assembled servants murmured their approval that the lady had put her whole heart into her response. Now the bloodred ruby ring was pushed on her finger and he was bending to give her the matrimonial kiss, and instead of closing her eyes, she looked into his to see them darken with desire. She was aware of how her loveliness affected him by the way his avid eyed devoured her.

"You look happy," she murmured.

"I have very simple tastes; I am always satisfied with the best." He hugged her to him quickly before he turned her to face the staff. Mr. Burke stepped forward to present her with a great ring of chatelaine keys and one by one the scullery maids, the kitchen maids, the cooks, the upstairs maids, the parlor maids, and the housekeeper came forward to give their curtsy to the new mistress. There was a strict pecking order and Summer learned it for the first time.

Next came the males of the household. First were the spitboys and the bootboys, followed by the stableboys. Next came the gardeners, the grooms, the footmen, the fat gamekeeper, and lastly Mr. Burke, who completed the circle and took back the symbolic keys. Summer gave him a grateful smile and in response his left eyelid closed in a solemn wink.

The footmen were busy serving everyone drinks so they could toast the new bride and groom. The women took wine, while the men were served ale. Ruark took the glass from Summer's hand and put it back on the silver tray. "You'll need no wine to fire your blood, my darling," he murmured low. He was in a fever of impatience to get his new bride alone. He had included the servants because he wanted to do things properly. She was Lady Helford and he wanted them to love and respect her, wanted every last one of them to know that she was his virgin bride. But his frustration mounted relentlessly as he waited for everyone to leave. It took a will of iron to suppress his raging hunger.

Finally the servants filed from the hall and began buzzing like hornets. By the time they were alone, she could feel his nearness reaching out to her. She looked at his mouth, imagining it covering her own, and grew faint with desire. He took her small hand in his strong one, but instead of leading her upstairs as she expected, he took her through the front door.

She looked at him with a question, then he swept her up into his arms and carried her over the threshold. She slipped her arms about his neck and whispered provocatively, "Carry me all the way to bed."

Lord God, how lucky could he get? His virgin bride was in a playful and seductive mood. With his arm beneath her knees he started up the stairs. "You've never even seen the house, love, but I beg you won't ask for a tour tonight," he teased. At the top of the magnificent staircase he turned into the south wing and entered his suite.

"There's something else I've never seen that's much more important."

He set her feet to the thick carpet but held her touching him all the way down. "What, darling?" he asked huskily.

"I've never seen a naked man . . . and I want to." She removed the black ribbon from his clubbed cue and ran her fingers through his hair, tousling it until it fell wildly about his shoulders. "You undress first," she suggested wickedly, thoroughly bemused he was more than happy to do anything she asked.

"Wed half an hour and already you're being cruel to your husband," he said, removing his shirt. "Do you know how long I've waited to see your legs? I've never glimpsed more than your ankles."

She laughed and lifted her skirts to display her lacy stockings. Ruark's mouth went dry. Her legs were so long and slim he couldn't believe it. She dropped her skirts and watched as his hands undid his belt, growing more and more excited as his strong body was slowly bared. She didn't lower her lashes and blush, but looked at him intently, her eyes taking in every detail of his splendor.

His hands stopped just short of removing his breeches. He had opened them and lowered them to his hips, but he was so afraid of alarming her and destroying the playful mood that he suddenly sat on the edge of the bed to remove his boots. He held out his hand to her in invitation. "Come close, let me touch you," he begged.

She came to him slowly, shaking her head in denial. "No, I want to touch you first." She sat down beside him on the bed and reached out a finger to trace the strong line of his jaw. His shoulders were impossibly wide and well muscled and her hand caressed him, her fingers delighting in the heavy mat of crisp hair which narrowed into a dark line running down his belly and spreading out again just at the place his pants still covered his groin.

She reached out her hand to touch him, but hesitated as if the feel of him would be too much to bear in her great excitement. Gently, he covered her hand and slowly forced it forward to brush over his swollen phallus. The moment she touched him his manroot jumped wildly as it filled with more blood.

"Oh!" she said in surprise, and quickly withdrew her hand.

"Ah love, don't stop touching me," he begged.

She reached out to him again because she couldn't help herself, but carefully avoided the still-unknown, mysterious male organ. "Ruark Helford, you are tempting as sin," she breathed as her palm caressed the slabs of muscle in his chest.

His arms crushed her to him and with his mouth against hers he said, "You know nothing of sin . . . yet!"

"I'm not finished looking, I've only just begun."

He laughed with pleasure deep in his throat. He rolled her beneath him and spread her arms wide. He hung above her, falling deeper in love with every heartbeat. "Is your curiosity not satisfied?" He laughed.

"No, it will never be satisfied," she breathed.

He kissed the sweet corners of her mouth. "Am I as you expected so far?"

"No, no. You are much more exciting than I ever dreamed and . . . and you feel so big . . . here." Her hand escaped his and went to the place between their bodies where his hardness pressed into her soft belly. Her hand found the opening in his pants and the tips of her fingers grazed the head of his shaft. It felt like she had burned him. "I didn't expect you'd be covered by black hair down there, but I love it!"

"Don't you have black curls between your pretty legs?" he teased.

"Yes, how did you know?" she asked ingenuously, and he was reminded with a jolt of just how inexperienced she was.

Ruark's hands slipped beneath her back to deftly undo the tiny buttons at the back of her lovely white gown. It reminded him of the white nightgown she'd worn when he first glimpsed her, and his throat went dry with desire. When she felt him undressing her, she slipped her arms from her sleeves and allowed him to remove it entirely.

She lay beneath him in her lacy shift and stockings, and he devoured her with eyes which were stained almost black with suppressed passion.

"I'm going to stand up now to take off the rest of my clothes," he warned her gently.

She sat up, her eyes like saucers as his hands moved to his hips to slide off his breeches. From the crisp dark hair his shaft rose up proud and blood-crimsoned.

"Ru!" she cried, half-afraid, half-mesmerized. His legs were like columns of marble, his thighs bulged with hard saddle muscles. He reached down to pull her up into his arms and he was relieved when her hesitation was only a slight one. His hands immediately went to the straps of her shift to remove the barrier of lace which stood between their naked bodies. "I wondered what my breasts would feel like against your fur pelt." He groaned as her shift fell to her hips and she stood on tiptoe to fit her breasts closely against his chest.

"Now *I'm* not finished looking," he said as he held her away from him at arm's length.

Her skin gleamed like a tropical pearl, as if it were dusted with translucent powder. She aroused him to near madness. Though she'd never been with a man before, she was totally unself-conscious. His hands caressed the silken mass of her hair, wondering at its fine texture and shining blackness. The feel of it between his fingers excited him and he took up a curling tress to taste it. Summer reached out to feel the coarser texture of his hair as it fell upon his shoulders, and as he had done, she brought it to her mouth to taste. He shuddered.

Her eyes were slanted with desire, making her the most beautiful woman in the world. "Lord God, you are exotic as a tropical storm," he said, and buried his lips against her throat.

His hands eased the lacy shift over her hips and it fell to the carpet with a whisper, then he picked her up and sat her on the edge of the bed. For the first time she became aware of her surroundings. Her eyes widened at the size of the massive four-poster with its brilliant teal-colored curtains. On one of the pillows lay her flame hibiscus as a symbol of her deflowering and she realized that like herself Ruark was a true pagan at heart.

As he knelt before her to remove her lace stockings, she watched every minute detail of his expression. She watched his eyes grow heavy-lidded with smoldering desire. Her gaze lingered long upon his mouth, longing for its tenderness and its fierceness. He opened her legs to gaze between and she gave him back his own question. "Am I as *you* expected?"

"Exactly! I've pictured you for weeks." He lifted her foot to his lips and placed a kiss upon its sole. "I lie, you are a thousand times more lush than I dared dream." Then, because he hoped he could say anything to her, no matter how intimate, without shocking her, he said, "Whenever I pictured you, I saw myself lying between your legs."

She slid from the bed until she knelt touching him. His shaft rose up between their bellies like a steel rod with a head of velvet. "Initiate me in the mysteries of sex," she invited, and he knew in that moment that he loved this woman beyond discretion, beyond reason.

He slid his long, rampant maleness between her legs and his neck arched back as a groan of sensual pleasure escaped his lips. He slid back and forth across her lips and she gasped with hot pleasure. The slow strokes brought exquisite sensations as if she, too, were swelling; each caress made her more sensitive until she wanted to scream with excitement.

"Oh, Lord Jesus, I've dreamed for weeks of being deep inside you. Let me lift you onto the bed before I slide inside you," he gasped.

She laughed. "That would be impossible, Ru, don't tease me."

He was swept with a wave of misgiving. She was so loving and trusting because she thought this was all he would do to her.

"Oh, I love it so much, Ru, do it again," she begged, and arched against his hardness. She was so unbelievably eager, he knew he wanted her this way for the rest of their lives. This first time he wanted her pleasure to be so great she would remember it always. He knew he must not do anything which would bring her the slightest twinge of pain. She must not connect this intimate play with pain or even discomfort. He realized he had set himself an almost impossible task.

He lifted her to the bed, opened her legs wide, and knelt between them. His hands slid beneath her thighs and he lifted her closer until her bottom rested on his folded legs. Then with his fingertip he traced the tiny folds she offered so trustingly.

A cry of pleasure burst from her lips and she opened her knees wider to aid his ministrations. He took the head of his shaft in his hand, inserted the tip, and rotated it in a circular motion around the tiny pink bud of her womanhood. She moaned and writhed in abandon.

"Dear God . . . don't move," he ordered, and she stopped for the space of two heartbeats. It was enough for him to clamp an iron control on himself and continue the slow, delicious, circular rhythm.

He watched her face, watched her eyelids become heavy with the enormity of her pleasure, and her head moved from side to side as she begged, "Ruark, please, please." She knew not for what she begged, but mercifully he did. Deliberately he stopped moving around her bud in a clockwise direction and started circling it the opposite way. Immediately she quivered as if something had exploded between her legs and the opening of her sheath closed over his tip in convulsive possession.

His mouth tasted hers as she cried his name. "Did you like that, little love?"

"Oh, Ru, I loved it . . . and you really did slide inside me," she said with wonder.

He swallowed hard and drew a couple of ragged breaths. "We'll go a little deeper next time," he ventured, to carefully gauge her reaction.

"I have so many questions," she said breathlessly.

He breathed deeply to quiet his raging lust. "Ask me anything, love."

"Can . . . can we do it tomorrow in daylight or do we have to wait until bed?"

"God's flesh, we don't have to wait five minutes." He lowered his mouth to kiss the softness on the inside of her knees, then opened her legs again to fit himself between. This time he placed his thumbs on either side of the pretty pink lips between her legs and gently pressed until she opened a little. He pushed the smooth, marblelike head of his long shaft inside her opening until he felt her stretch and then withdrew it. He did this over and over with a slow rhythm that set up a singing in her blood.

Her sheath felt like velvet and she was so fevered she scalded him each time he entered. He did it over and over and each time imperceptibly his thumbs forced the opening wider so he could penetrate a little bit deeper. Finally he could see she could take half his length without pain, but any more than four inches of shaft would have torn her hymen.

She grew so aroused and frenzied he almost lost control and drove himself to the hilt, but he was discovering that he loved her with his heart and soul as well as his body and knew he must sacrifice some of his pleasure to bring her to exquisite bliss. She was half-mad with passion, crying and biting his shoulders with sharp little teeth, then he felt her muscles spasm all the way down her legs and she arched up off the bed to impale herself on him, but he had grasped his shaft instantly to withdraw it.

His shudder was ten times more violent than hers. She looked down to where they had been joined and saw with amazement the hot, thick lovemilk spurt inside her. He collapsed onto her and she welcomed his weight, but when he rolled beside her, she mourned the loss and rolled against him.

The tips of her breasts burned holes in his chest and his shaft was scalded by the heat between her legs. He whispered smoldering love words which told her in explicit, decadent detail what he was going to do to her. He told her how it would make her feel, how it would make him want more. He told her how long he was going to make love to her and how many times he was going to make love to her and how many different ways he was going to make love to her. His hands explored every soft curve until she moaned and writhed and arched and finally screamed her need.

Her scream told him that her mouth needed his attention and he took it in a demanding kiss, parting her lips to thrust his tongue in deliciously deep. Then her tongue fought his until finally he relented a little and allowed her entry into his mouth.

As they lay breathlessly entwined, Ruark said wickedly, "I've just had a diabolical thought. Perhaps I should keep you virgin for the whole honeymoon. I should keep you at the peak of your arousal so that you would respond to my lightest touch. When I take you to Stowe, it would drive the other men mad to watch you touch me, cling to me, hunger for me."

She sat up in the bed and gazed down at him in disbelief. "I'm still virgin?"

"Technically, yes . . . I haven't yet taken your maidenhead."

"And you want to keep on doing this every night of our honeymoon?"

"No, darling love, I'm just teasing you."

"I don't mind, Ru darling, but I think it only fair to keep you at the peak of your arousal, too," she teased. She slid down his body until her face was on a level with his flat belly, then she probed his navel with her pink tongue and he was lost, lost.

"If you want the truth, I could not summon that kind of control again if my very life depended on it. In truth, I can wait no longer," he said, pushing her back upon the pillows, towering over her with the blood beating in his throat, his loins, even the soles of his feet.

"Will there be pain?" she asked softly, not really afraid.

"There will be pain, love . . . at first, until I stretch your small sheath to fit me and tear the hymen, but after I've loved you two or three times more there should be only pleasure."

"I will ignore the pain and concentrate on the pleasure," she whispered.

He separated the tiny folds between her legs, experimented for a moment with one finger until he touched the sensitive little bud of her womanhood and felt her arching response, then he positioned the velvet head of his shaft and slowly thrust inside her.

Summer was surprised that there was no pain for the first part of his penetration and she relaxed her muscles and her guard. Then his fingers opened her to accommodate his great size and he thrust home sharply and deeply.

The pain for one second was unendurable as his weapon split her hymen and rammed all the way inside her. She screamed in spite of her determination not to.

"Stay with me, darling," he urged raggedly.

She took a deep breath and he held himself absolutely still so she could endure the impaling. The new and strange sensation of being filled with his long, thick manroot was not altogether unpleasant.

The feeling that it was too much, too big, too soon, subsided slightly and as she held her breath she could feel it pulsing, burning, expanding, and she lay in wonder as she realized she could feel his heartbeat inside her own body.

Then Ruark began to kiss her and move rhythmically in and out and in a very few moments she caught the magic and let him take her with him to the edge of the universe. They clung there for heart-stopping moments then flung themselves over the edge in an ecstasy of abandon.

Ruark cried out as he felt his seed start and she joined his cry as he erupted into her, making all her muscles contract down her long legs to her very toes. She had never known anything on earth to compare with this melding, becoming one flesh.

They clung together in the warm nest they had thrashed out in the massive bed, savoring these precious moments when they could lie naked together. Each knew nothing would ever be the same again. Summer sighed to her very soul as she luxuriated in her husband's fierce embrace. All her troubles would be over now. She had never felt more safe or secure in her whole life.

She smiled across the pillow into Ruark's eyes, suddenly sure in the knowledge that not all men were evil as she had imagined. She was lucky to find one of the rare exceptions.

"Do you still love me?" he whispered fiercely.

The corners of her mouth went up languidly. "With my heart, I thee love; with my body, I thee honor."

He knew he possessed someone very rare. Here was a woman to cherish and savor.

Drowsily she asked, "Did you say something about Stowe?"

"I'm invited to Stowe for the next three or four days, so that's where we'll have our honeymoon," he murmured, tucking her head beneath his chin.

"But isn't Stowe a great mansion? The most important family in Cornwall, the Grenviles, live at Stowe," she protested.

"Mmm, it is big and fancy, two footmen behind each chair in the dining hall and a ladies' maid for every female guest. Only place that can decently accommodate the King and court, aside from Plymouth Castle, which is nothing more than a barren pile of rock." He kissed her temple. "But I assure you, Jack and Bunny Grenvile are the easiest, most casual men in the world. No airs whatsoever."

"Heaven be praised." She sighed with relief, then as all his words filtered through her drowsy mind she sat bolt upright. "The King and court?"

He sat up instantly, drawing her down in strong arms. "In the morning you can collect your maid and your clothes and bring them over here. We won't leave early. Whatever you need I'll buy for you in Plymouth."

"I . . . I let my maid go, she didn't suit," she murmured.

"You don't much like servants do you, darling?" he asked, amused at such an oddity.

"I like Mr. Burke," she said truthfully.

"And Mr. Burke likes you, my love. As a matter of fact I think you've taken the place of my mother in his affections. They came from Ireland together, you know. He was fiercely protective of her."

"Ru? Must we go to Stowe?" she whispered.

"I'm summoned by the King, darling, and I'm certainly not going without you. You've met Charles, you've already made a conquest of him, so I don't know why all the reluctance."

That's just the trouble, she thought worriedly, *you don't know.* You don't know that I've never dined elegantly or danced. I've never mingled with lords and ladies, earls and countesses, Kings and Queens. I don't know which fork to use, or which dress to wear, or how to address a duke. And Lord God, I don't know how I'm going to go running off to Stowe with Spider rotting in prison.

His low, rich voice brought her thoughts back to him. "Sweet, let me see you again." He turned down the covers so his eyes could roam where his hands wished to follow. Her red drops of blood were scattered across the sheet like rubies. The effect upon him was instant and marked.

She watched his erection rise up hard as marble and knew she possessed a new and thrilling power over this magnificently powerful man. His hands roamed over her, teasing, caressing, exploring for a long time until she sprawled wantonly, letting the pleasure build and recede, then his lips and his mouth and his tongue played with her until she tossed and arched wildly in a fever of need.

He spread her thighs apart and entered her with one deep plunge. She responded to his thrusts immediately and wrapped her legs high about his back. She fulfilled all his erotic fantasies of being deep inside her, but he had never dreamed she would be this tight or this hot.

They wore each other out with passion, then with limbs still entwined they fell asleep, totally sated for the moment. Rarely had two lovers been so well matched or so deeply in love after only one night.

15

When Summer opened her eyes, it was still pitch dark outside and she had no idea what the hour was. She became fully awake instantly when she realized Ruark was not in the bed with her. She had never felt so alive before in her life.

She was filled with such vitality and energy that she felt a compulsion to greet the dawn with her pagan ritual as a form of celebration, a thank-you to the gods for their splendid gift of Ruark Helford.

The air was soft and warm, the subtropical weather still blessing this sheltered, magical corner of Cornwall. She picked up Ruark's fine white shirt from the chair and slipped her arms into the long sleeves. It covered her thighs and for Summer this was enough. The faint, delicious scent of her husband lingered upon the garment and filled her senses. Her delicate nostrils flared at the maleness of the fragrance.

On bare feet she crept from the house and made her way to the stables. All was in total darkness as she led Ebony from his stall, not bothering with either saddle or bridle.

Astride the horse, she used only her knees as he delicately picked his way down the face of the cliff, then once she was down on the sands, she threaded her fingers through the black stallion's

flowing mane and dug in her heels. With a great surge of power he
leaped forward in the ride which brought him as much pleasure as
it did his mistress.

A faint light was just beginning to show upon the horizon beyond the sea at the edge of the world. Summer felt her blood racing
through her veins. She was transformed. She was invincible. She
was in love!

Suddenly out of the darkness loomed a rider bearing down upon
her in a relentless gallop. She had only time to take a deep breath;
no time whatsoever to swerve from his path. But the other rider
was so expert he came alongside her with only inches to spare,
reached out strong arms, and, lifted her from Ebony onto his own
mount.

"Ruark!" she cried exultantly.

"I knew you would come, it was inevitable," he said triumphantly.

He was naked, she realized as her arms went about his body for
support. With a joyful cry she flung off his shirt and pressed herself
against his bare, muscular body, then like riding on the wind, they
thundered down the deserted beach to greet the dawn.

On the way back it became a daring race with the tide as it swept
in to hurl itself against the rocks of the cliff. Ebony had followed
the other horse up the shore and back and stayed close as they
tackled the steep bridle path back up the face of the cliff. Ruark
unrolled his cloak where it lay on the saddle and wrapped it about
himself and Summer just in case some of the servants were about
early.

They slipped through the French doors in the south wing and
gained the sanctity of their bedchamber before dawn had spread its
pink fingers up the sky. They were laughing and carefree as children, totally happy in the moments they had stolen from the rest of
civilization.

"I watched you ride like a pagan the first morning I was here. I
went up on the roof to the widow's walk and became enchanted by
your spell."

She turned to gaze at his splendid male body. "Today we were
pagans together. I'll remember it always."

He closed the distance between them in three strides. "Darling,
you must promise me you'll never ride before daylight, and it goes
without saying, I hope, that you must never ride naked. This coast
is a haven for pirates and smugglers and is extremely dangerous."

"Danger excites me," she said, standing on tiptoe to kiss him.

He kissed her back fiercely. "You remind me exactly of my beautiful figurehead on the *Pagan Goddess*." He carried her to their bed, but when he let go of her, she stood up on the bed, put her back against one of the carved posts, then put her arms behind her to suspend herself in the same pose as the figurehead.

It thrilled him deeply that she was so natural and artless with him. No trace of self-consciousness marred their love play. He took hold of her lovely legs and pulled her down onto the pillows. He straddled her and bent to give her a dozen kisses, then he rolled with her until she lay on top of him. "Let's make love while the reckless pagan mood is still upon us," he invited.

She needed little urging. She ran her fingers over the crisp dark hair of his chest, then fastening them in the black curls on his head, she drew up his face to hers until their mouths fused. Then her legs stretched and her body opened to receive him. Instantly her body contracted as if to seal that part of him inside her forever. They were aroused to such a pitch she felt she could never absorb enough of him.

When they reached the peak of their endurance, they erupted and spilled together, and she fell trembling upon him and sobbed from the great release she had received.

Ruark cradled her and soothed her. "My baby, my honey love, don't cry, life is too short."

She dashed the tears from her cheeks and gave him a dazzling smile. "Lady Helford has a thousand things to do this morning, if you will release me from this bed."

"I will release you on condition you let me watch you take your bath."

"Watch me? Surely you will join me?" she tempted wickedly.

He needed no urging and went himself to carry in the large slipper bath.

"Ru, I was teasing," she gasped.

"I was serious"—he grinned—"but I'll tease you if you wish." For the first time she blushed.

He summoned maids for hot water and built a fire so she wouldn't be cold. Though it was still very early, light had begun to stream through the tall windows, and when she realized their nakedness would not be half-shadowed or bathed in candleglow, a thrill ran up her spine. He enjoyed looking at her so much, he made her feel very beautiful. She eyed his great length doubtfully. "Will it hold us both?"

"Only if you sit in my lap." He leered at her wickedly as he lifted her to stand in the water and climbed in behind her. He sat down first and made a chair for her with his knees, but before she could sit, he pressed a kiss upon her bottom. "Has anyone ever told you what a pretty bum you have?"

"And who, pray, would tell me such a thing?" she asked primly, suffused with blushes.

His heart melted. He pulled her to his lap and enfolded her in his arms. "Sweet, I'm sorry to use you so familiarly. Most ladies would be in shock by now at the things I've done to you. I'm so lucky that you're generous with me." He closed his eyes and buried his face in her hair. It smelled of the sea. He was enthralled to discover he loved absolutely everything about her.

Shyly she handed him the sponge so he could wash her back, but he tossed it across the room and whispered against her neck, "I'm going to use my hands." No sooner were the words out of his mouth than his hands cupped her breasts, lathering them with scented soap, then playing with them by drawing circles and elaborate patterns across the peaks and valleys. Then on the pretext of searching for the soap, he dipped his hands into the water between her legs until she was squealing from his teasing fingers.

Gasping, she twisted against him and he took possession of her tempting mouth, unmindful of the great splosh of water their playful bodies displaced.

Summer insisted it was only fair she be allowed to lather him, and when he lifted his arms, she tickled him unmercifully. When she kissed his armpit, the gesture was so intimate, their laughter ceased. They gazed into each other's eyes, then very tenderly he touched his lips to every part of her body.

When at last she was able to return to Roseland, sweetly refusing Mr. Burke's offer to accompany her and help bring her things to Helford Hall, she changed into an old skirt and shawl and rode the pony down to Falmouth. She was extremely relieved to find no trace of Sergeant Oswald about the prison as she made her way as unobtrusively as possible to the common cell.

Spider looked no worse for wear and was in a most cheerful and cheeky mood. "What the hell are you doing back here, Cat? I forbid you to come again."

"I had to see if you were all right."

He winked. "I see more meals here than I ever saw at home."

"Spider, Lord Helford and I were married last night," she said, low. "I haven't told him about you yet, or about the damned mortgage on Roseland."

Spider seemed to take it for granted that she would have become Lady Helford as she had schemed to do. "For God's sake, Cat, don't tell him yet. Wait until you have him eating out of your hand before you breathe a dicky-bird about your 'difficulties.' "

She nodded quickly. "He's taking me to Stowe for a few days, but I'll tell him before your case comes up before him, I promise. Everything will be fine, Spider. He's wonderful. I know he'll do anything I ask."

Spider grinned. "Stop worrying; go and enjoy yourself."

Two hours later she drove the ponycart up to Helford Hall. She had carefully packed all her pretty clothes from London into two small trunks and instructed a footman to put them directly onto the traveling coach which stood on the driveway waiting for the team of four carriage horses to be brought from the stables. She wore the primrose yellow riding dress, and when Ruark saw her, his eyes swept over her possessively. "You look delicious, darling. How in the world did you manage to transport all your belongings so quickly?"

"Oh," she replied, dissembling, "I only brought a few things to take to Stowe. I couldn't find anything fine enough to wear before the King and court. I'm afraid I'll shame you with my rags."

He swept her from head to foot with amused eyes. "If this elegant, impractical primrose outfit is any indication of your wardrobe, you'll make the other women look like damned crows. However, I'll take you to Plymouth tomorrow so you can do some shopping if you like," he offered indulgently.

"Oh, thank you, darling. I'll just run upstairs and get my rubies."

When she entered their bedchamber, she was surprised to find a half-dozen maids and the housekeeper gathered about the bed. They stopped talking as she came into the room and the two youngest ones lowered their eyes and blushed. Then she realized with amazement they had gathered to see if there had been blood on the sheets as befitted a virgin bride.

Suddenly Mr. Burke appeared in the doorway with an armful of fresh linen. He immediately realized what the nosy women were up to. In a cold, stern voice he announced, "I shall take care of Lady Helford's chamber this morning. Be about your business, ladies."

They left immediately, thoroughly abashed. Summer picked up the velvet cases which held her precious rubies and said softly, "Thank you, Mr. Burke. I haven't even had time to see all of the house yet."

"When you get back, I'll give you the grand tour."

"I'm so glad that you will be here waiting for me when I return." The two were already firm friends and allies.

The roads of Cornwall were steep and craggy. They were also narrow, precipitous, and dangerous, particularly for a coach-and-four. A safe journey depended in part on the stamina of the horses and the skill of an experienced coachman.

A face-to-face meeting with another carriage or cart required that the one heading uphill back down to a wider place called a lay-by. Sometimes the road followed the windy edge of the endless cliffs and sometimes it wound slightly inland, hugged by hedges and a profusion of wild flowers.

From the wind-whipped headlands one could view the coastline riddled with little bays and hidden caves and crevices, and beyond, the sea's mad exhilaration filled the observer with wild enthusiasms. Together they admired this Cornwall of theirs.

"The whole three hundred miles of coastline is indented by coves and inlets." He shook his head. "It is a perfect place for smugglers . . . no authority on earth can stop such determined men."

She shuddered. "Let's not talk of such things. Most people tell tales of smuggling filled with adventure, derring-do, and romance, but I know the reality is filled with gore and drear and pain down every pathway. You don't employ informers, do you? For some, betrayal and informing are a way of life."

"I thought you didn't wish to talk of such things," he said, evading her question.

She smiled at him. "I swear Cornwall blood sets us apart from others. There are times when you cannot dispel brooding, dark moods and then there are the times when restless devils inside us struggle to be set free. My worst fault, I suppose, is feeling passionate over absolutely everything."

His mouth looked hard, almost cruel, as he said, "I thought I was totally responsible for kindling your passion." Then she saw the teasing light in his eyes and laughed.

"What is your worst fault, Ru?"

The teasing light faded from his eyes as he became serious. "I have an explosive temper, which I try to keep under control. Unfortunately every once in a while"—he looked off in the distance as if remembering, regretting, then he looked at Summer, gave her a quick smile and finished his sentence—"it escapes and runs riot over everyone and everything."

She wondered if he was warning her. "Ruark, were you born at Helford?" she asked.

"No, I was born up the north coast at a place named High Tor. A wild and barren place where the whip of the wind never ceases. A place too stark and craggy for anything but stunted trees and screaming gulls and flying spume."

"That accounts for your dark side, your moods," she said lightly. "I, on the other hand, was born at my mother's home on the Roseland Peninsula. A place filled with bloom and beauty which runs up the sheltered valley cleft from the sea."

He smiled at her indulgently. "That's why your home was named Roseland and you were named Summer."

"Of course," she said lightly. She couldn't bear to tell Ruark the truth about her unhappy origins—she almost wanted to believe her lies herself. She, too, had been born on the bleak north coast, where her mother had been temporarily abandoned by her brutal father. Rumor had it that winter had been the longest in memory, and when her child was finally born, she had called her Summer in defiance.

"Well, Lady Summer Helford, you are extremely beautiful today. I would hazard a guess that marriage agrees with you." He began to make love to her with his eyes.

"You know, Ruark, I never ever thought that it would. I quite hated and detested men until I met you."

"I, too, dreaded marriage, but the truth is, sweetheart, there's nowhere on earth I'd rather be than in this damned uncomfortable coach with you in my lap." He lifted her from the opposite seat onto his knee. He could not keep his hands from her shining black tresses, and as he lifted a silken curl from her shoulder it twined possessively about his fingers.

She was so close he could see the delicate blue veins in her eyelids and see the golden tips on the ends of her feathery black lashes. She reached up a finger to trace the faint blue-black shadow which remained even when he had shaved closely, and when she touched him, he jumped as if he had been burned.

He kissed her temples, her eyelids, and finally took possession of her mouth, needing the taste of her as if he were starving. She felt his arousal begin against her buttocks and the memories of their first night together came flooding over her. His avid fingers undid the buttons on the jacket of her riding dress and he reached inside to cup and fondle a soft round breast through the thin material of her lacy shift.

It was obvious to him from her little cries of pleasure that no man had ever played with her before. His manhood, prompted by a virile hunger, strained to be free from the constraints of his garments and he shifted her a little so his swollen organ nestled in the cleavage between her bottom cheeks. Each time his thumb brushed across her nipple, she squirmed and sighed. Each time she squirmed she squeezed the tip of his upstanding shaft with her buttocks until he was almost mindless.

Finally he knew he must divert attention from the hot center of his pleasure or he would disgrace himself. He laid her back against the seat cushion and reached a strong, brown hand beneath her skirts. He caressed her leg, going ever higher to that delicious bare space on her thigh above her stocking. Very slowly he slipped off a garter, then peeled down the stocking and removed it. Then his bold hand began its journey up the other leg.

"Ruark," she protested, "you can't undress me here."

"Can I not, my little innocent?" he challenged.

She gasped as he drew off the second garter and stocking and waved them in triumph. His questing hand again found its way beneath her skirts and her heart quickened its pace. His caresses continued following the soft inside of her thigh, then his fingers became bolder, intruding into the private center of her woman's flesh. He half lifted her against him and her low moan was taken from her by his deep kiss. The slow, strong, strokes of his fingers set her whole body ashiver and it was pointless for her to try to deny that she wanted it, loved it!

Suddenly a small wave of panic swept over her as she felt the carriage slow and turn into a private drive. She struggled against Ruark's insistent fingers, but he persisted, murmuring, "Almost there." His words, purposely, had two meanings, she realized as a shivering shudder went through her and she curled against his hand.

It was indeed fortunate the sycamore-lined driveway was a long one, for they had already passed the gatehouse and she barely had time to button her bodice, pull down her skirts, and find her shoes. She had no time whatsoever to compose herself. The coach came to a halt before a massive house and the coachman was opening the carriage door before Ruark tucked her stockings and garters into his pocket with a wicked grin.

16

Sir John Grenvile, newly created Earl of Bath by His Majesty, strode from the iron-studded front door to greet his old friend. His eyes widened as he saw the beautiful vision in primrose and a familiar voice said, "Jack, I decided to take you up on your invitation. Stowe will be a perfect setting for our honeymoon."

Summer was almost panting, as if she had run down the driveway, and Jack Grenvile took possession of both her hands and took the liberty of a kiss upon her cheek. My God, Helford married was more than a mild shock. However, he had no need to look to the lady's waistline to see if it was a marriage of necessity, for it was clear the beauty had only just been introduced to amour and the insatiable demands of a bridegroom by her blushes and gasps.

Ruark winked at his friend over his bride's shoulder. "We were wed only last night. Jack, this is my wife, Summer."

She tried to curtsy, for she knew he was an earl, but for the life of her she couldn't remember how to correctly address an earl. It was definitely not "Your Earlship." Jack held her hands firmly and would not let her curtsy. "You dog, wait till Bunny sees her. Come in, nearly everyone's here but the King."

They followed their host into the great hall and Summer pinched Ruark to get his attention and whispered, "Is Bunny his wife?"

Ruark's eyes sparkled with amusement. "No, love, Bunny is his brother, Bernard Grenvile."

She was mortified to see the great gathering of cavaliers and fashionable ladies in the great hall, especially with her stockings and garters in Ruark's pocket. She cast him a look of outrage, but his grin only widened.

Then suddenly she became the center of attention as the introductions were made and the news spread that she was a brand-new bride. The magnificently dressed cavaliers swept off their wide-brimmed hats, sweeping the carpet with their plumes as if she were a queen. Each declared, "Your servant, madame" or "My services, madame" with gallantry and appraising eyes.

The respectable wives present received her warmly because she was wife rather than mistress and the fashionable women of the court who had slept with most of the men who had endured exile in France with Charles came to speak with her because she was beautiful and obviously competition.

It was impossible for her to remember names or titles, so she gave up trying to take it all in at once. She did absorb some of it. Lord Buckhurst was the youngest male present. The Grenvile brothers had auburn hair, and the good-looking man of about fifty was George Digby, the Earl of Bristol.

She was introduced to Sir Charles Berkeley, Harry Killigrew, and Henry Jermyn, but she couldn't tell one from the other. Summer had a much easier time with the Cornwall families, probably because of their accents and because their clothes weren't as flamboyant as the Londoners'.

She met the Arundells, who owned Pendennis Castle, Richard and John Carew from Antony, and Sir Richard Robartes, an extremely wealthy merchant and banker who made his money in the tin trade. These were the old, noble families of Cornwall, whom she had never in a million years dreamed she would ever meet.

She was fascinated by Sir John St. Aubyn, who had bought St. Michael's Mount, a place in her mind akin to Mount Olympus. He told her how at high tide it became an island and had originally been a monastery which had stood there for over five hundred years.

She met Lady Anne Carnegie and Elizabeth Hamilton and learned from them that Barbara Palmer, newly created Lady Castlemaine, had arrived with an entourage of attendants but had retired for the afternoon. The King was in Plymouth with the

Duke of Buckingham and the Scottish John Lauderdale and they wouldn't be arriving until tomorrow.

The men crowded round Summer, offering to show her the pond, the medieval dovecote, and the great gallery with its magnificent plasterworks decorating the long ceiling, vividly depicting stories from the Old Testament, which had made Stowe famous.

Finally, Ruark's scowls and black looks informed the eager men that if his wife needed escorting anywhere, he would do it and at the moment the only place to which he intended escorting her was to their private bedchamber.

The room assigned them on the third floor was elegantly appointed with gold brocade window curtains and bedhangings. The carpet was worked in blue and gold and the furnishings looked as if they had been brought over from France. "Oh, how lovely," cried Summer when she walked in. A gilt slipper bath stood in one corner behind an ornate screen and a tall wardrobe with mirrored doors stood next to it.

"If this is more to your taste than our bedchamber at Helford, feel free to redecorate, darling. I suppose my room is furnished in very masculine taste." He was being indulgent with her and she loved him for it.

"To tell you the truth the only thing I saw last night was you, Ruark," she said, blushing. They were not yet alone. A maid and a manservant had been provided for them by their host and they busied themselves unpacking and hanging the clothes in the wardrobe. Servants always knew everything about guests by way of gossip, for they were in a position to know intimate secrets. The man and girl knew this couple was honeymooning and worked rapidly so that they could be left alone for a couple of hours. The manservant brought a decanter of wine and glasses and the maid drew the curtains and turned down the bed, murmuring about an afternoon nap, then they discreetly withdrew.

Summer threw wide the curtains to let in the afternoon sunshine, saying with scorn, "Naps are for babes and old people."

Ruark's arms slipped about her from behind and fastened beneath her breasts. "I think 'nap' is just a euphemism, darling, for other things we will do in bed."

"Oh," she said, realizing her naïveté. "But won't we be expected downstairs? I know our host and hostess must have all sorts of things planned for our entertainment."

"Nothing as entertaining as what I have planned," he said, nuzzling her neck and biting her small ear.

"But Ru, if we don't go back down, they will guess what we are doing up here."

"Exactly! And every last one of them will be green with envy." His hands cupped her breasts and pulled her back against his body so that she could feel he was ready for love. "Leave the drapes open, my darling, the first time I take you in broad daylight I want to see your body flush with passion." He turned her from the window and took her in his arms.

The intensity of his kiss gave evidence of his starved senses. Her eager hands helped him as he undressed her then aided in his own disrobing. Each time she glimpsed their naked bodies in the tall mirrors, shards of excitement stabbed through her until the hunger of her loins became insatiable.

With a growl of passion he lifted her high then brought her slowly down his body. His crisp mat of hair rubbed first her thighs, then her mons and belly, and finally her soft round breasts as her body slid down his. He brought her down directly onto his upthrusting shaft, impaling her with pleasure, then with his hands cupped beneath her buttocks he walked directly up to the mirror so that she could watch what he did to her. He played out the penetration game to its limit, knowing it was one of the most pleasurable parts of love play for a woman, then he carried her to the bed so that his body could fulfill its purpose.

Ruark's mouth was unbearably tender as he kissed her face, lingering on her eyelids and along her lovely slanting cheekbones, then his mouth found hers and he began to kiss her less gently. Gradually his mouth became demanding, punishing with urgent hunger.

Summer knew he had been denied too long. She reached down toward his hardness.

"Don't!" he ordered. "I'll spill myself on you."

His words aroused her further, knowing, as she did, that her hands could drive him as wild as his did her, and make him lose control of himself. Then all thought vanished with the impact of his hungry lovemaking and she learned the devastation of his possession when it was urgent and fierce and frantic.

When he was finished with her, she was only a heartbeat away from semiconsciousness and she fell deeply asleep in his arms.

* * *

After a small knock the maid entered their bedchamber and Summer scrambled behind Ruark and peeped over his shoulder.

"I weel draw your bath, madame," the little maid said in her French accent. "If you weel tell me which gown you weel wear tonight, I can do your hair verry special to match, no?"

"No," said Summer.

"Yes," said Ruark.

The maid set the fresh sheets she was carrying on a small table beside the bed, and Summer blushed hotly at the fact that the maid had known the bed would need changing after their lovemaking.

Ruark said, "Madame will wear her white gown tonight as befits a bride."

"Oh, Ru, 'tis so plain, did you not see the gorgeous brocades and satins the ladies wore downstairs? And that was just for afternoon. Imagine what they will wear tonight!"

"Sweet love, wear the white for me tonight and tomorrow I'll buy you a dozen brocades and satins," he promised.

The manservant brought them a light meal on a tray, for the formal dinner at Stowe would not be served until eight. The maid took out a busk for Summer to wear beneath the lovely white organdy and it made quite a difference to her appearance. The short, tight little corset forced her breasts high and took two inches off her waist. Then the maid showed off her skills as a hairdresser. She arranged kiss curls about Summer's face and swept the rest up into a style known as "Heartbreaker." When her dress was carefully donned, more than half of her beautiful breasts were exposed and she called Ruark to put on her rubies so she could gauge his reaction.

He was wearing midnight blue satin breeches and his arousal at the sight of her was quite visible. "Is it necessary to expose your breasts in that fashion?" he asked, frowning.

"Mais oui," assured the maid, "thees way no one weel whisper that they are false."

Ruark took up the ruby necklace and smiled into Summer's eyes. "There's not much point in wearing these . . . no one will even notice them."

"Oh, darling, I'd feel naked without them."

"You would be naked without them," he teased.

She slipped the bracelets up her arms and admired her reflection in the looking glass.

His lips brushed her ear. "I'll have to buy you some more jewels."

"No, Ru, you've already been too generous," she protested.

"I'm very vain about my wife. I enjoy giving you jewels and trinkets. Let me spoil you. Come on, I want to show you off downstairs."

"Can we look at the gardens first?" she pleaded, slipping the ribbon of her fan over her arm.

He fastened a slim sword on his hip. "I might need this to keep the men away from you. They'll be jumping out from behind every bush."

The magnificent ivy-covered home of the Grenviles stood in a two-hundred-and-fifty-acre park. Its gardens were on many different levels as they descended the valley below the house, and contained ponds, rills, old yew hedges, terraced flower borders, and trees which bloomed in their turn every month of the year—from camellias, azaleas, and magnolias to the great copper beeches which shaded the walks.

All the ladies had decided to view the gardens at the same time and had persuaded the gentlemen to escort them, but none would venture beyond the stone walks for fear of soiling their fancy evening slippers. None, that is, except Summer, who took her husband's hand and led him to the more lush and secluded garden paths. They came upon a small spring with mossy walls which opened up into a brook with floating wildflowers. Summer was enchanted by it. "Oh, Ruark, could we have a water garden?"

He pulled her into his arms. "You may have anything you desire."

She sighed blissfully and leaned against him. She loved him very much and knew just how lucky she had been to find such a generous and loving man, who was going to take care of all the worries that had dogged her young years. She felt she had been kissed by the gods!

On the way back they stopped in at the cider house and shared a loving cup. It was so strong she pretended to stagger and he offered to carry her. She shook her head, laughing. "We'd cause a scandal. Wives aren't supposed to love their husbands, 'tis unfashionable. You had better pick a lady to receive your attentions at dinner. The lovely Lady Castlemaine perhaps?"

"She's no lady," he said low, giving her his undivided attention. "She's too overblown for my taste and another drawback with

Babs is her fecundity. All Charles has to do is throw his breeches on the bed and she's up the stick."

By this time they had reentered the house and there across the room was the woman they were discussing. Summer couldn't stop laughing. He bent his lips to her ear. "She's also . . ."

Summer gave him a sharp slap with her fan and hissed, "Ruark, stop!"

Barbara Castlemaine swept across the room to them. She wore a wine-colored gown in the identical shade of dark red as her hair. The gown was the latest fashion, split down the front to expose a gold-tissue petticoat, and the sleeves were decorated with yards of gold ribbon. She wore a necklace and matching ear bobs of golden topaz.

"Helford," she drawled, "I don't believe I've had the pleasure." She was looking Summer up and down critically, thinking the white gown ridiculously missish, but the rubies were not to be dismissed lightly.

Ruark's manners were faultless. He bowed low and said, "My Lady Castlemaine, may I present my wife, Lady Summer St. Catherine Helford?"

Her eyes narrowed. "Ruark Helford married? Since when?"

"Since last evening at this hour," he said.

Summer flushed and fanned herself furiously.

A little pigeon to be plucked, thought Barbara. She smiled archly at the bride. "I believe we already have something in common, besides our taste in men, of course. Obviously we both like jewels. I'll enjoy a game of trick track with you after dinner." Then Henry Jermyn approached and Barbara took his arm and swept off.

"She wanted me to think you'd slept with her," said Summer furiously.

"Yes," said Ruark.

"Yes?" repeated Summer hotly.

"Yes, she wanted you to think that. I wonder if poor Jermyn has been elected stud until Charles arrives?"

"Ru, stop!" She again slapped him with her fan, but her good humor had been restored.

"What would you like to see? There's a boring collection of arms and armor in the great hall or there's some fascinating plasterwork in the long gallery. In fact, I think there's a likeness of us depicted there," he said gravely.

"I think that highly unlikely—show me."

They strolled through the long room, which vividly depicted Bible stories from the Old Testament. "There you are!" His face was a perfect mask of gravity as he pointed to Eve in the Garden of Eden. "Just like you this afternoon . . . naked, holding a round thing in your hand."

She gasped, "That's an apple," and spun about quickly to see if anyone had overheard the outrageous remark. No one was within earshot, so she turned back to the fresco, pointed to a naked Adam, and said, "And there's you."

"No, it isn't. That fig leaf is far too small to cover my parts."

"Since such a beautiful woman consented to marry you, I've noticed an increase in the size of your head, too!" She laughed up at him.

He immediately kissed her.

"You mustn't kiss me in such a public place," she said, blushing.

"If you want me to kiss you in a more private place, you'll have to wait until we're in bed," he teased.

She sobered and said softly, "Will you take me to the private chapel?"

The chapel was small, but very beautiful. It even had a shrine dedicated to Sir John Grenvile, who had sailed to the Indies with Sir Francis Drake. Ruark watched his wife's delicate profile as she knelt to pray. Suddenly her shoulders drooped and he wondered what in the world was making her so sad.

Summer was praying in earnest. "O Holy St. Jude, Apostle and Martyr, great in Virtue and Rich in Miracles, near kinsman of Jesus Christ, Faithful intercessor of all who invoke your special patronage in time of need, to you I have recourse from the depths of my heart and humbly beg you to help my brother Spencer. Please make Ruark love me enough to take care of the mortgage on Roseland and free my brother from prison."

"Darling," Ruark murmured.

Summer opened her eyes and arose from her knees, searching his darkly handsome features.

"Let's exchange our wedding vows again here while we're private."

Her eyes widened. "What a lovely thought. You are so romantic."

They faced each other and held hands.

"I Ruark take thee Summer to my wedded wife, to have and to

hold from this day forward, for better or for worse, for richer for poorer, in sickness and in health, to love and to cherish till death us do part, according to God's holy ordinance; and thereto I plight thee my troth."

Her throat had a lump in it at the deep sincerity of his words. Then huskily she said the vow back to Ruark, adding of course, "to love, cherish, and to obey." Then Ruark fingered the bloodred ruby he had placed on her finger last night and repeated, "With this ring I thee wed, with my body I thee honor, and with all my worldly goods, I thee endow." She offered silent thanks to St. Jude, for already he seemed to be answering her prayer.

17

R̲uark slipped a possessive arm about her and they emerged from the chapel to join the vast company for dinner. The great dining hall was ablaze with candlelight. It reflected from the crystal goblets of water and wine and from the heavy silver service which would serve one hundred in the same identical pattern. Each place setting boasted a display of ten knives, forks, and spoons in the heavily ornamented Sterling which was crested with an ornate *G* for Grenvile.

Panic arose in Summer as she viewed the formal tables, wondering how on earth she would get through the meal without exposing her ignorance. She realized with dismay that Ruark had been literally telling the truth when he said there were two footmen to stand behind each guest's chair to serve, any one of whom knew more about dining etiquette than she would ever know.

Ruark chose to sit next to the Arundells from Pendennis Castle and Summer listened attentively to their conversation. What she heard banished the worry over which fork to use, for here was Ruark making plans with John Arundell to entertain the King and whoever else wished to accompany him.

"I know Charles will want to pay a nostalgic visit to Pendennis Castle, so I propose to open Helford Hall for the court's entertainment. It wouldn't be for more than a couple of days because they must be in Portsmouth next week for the arrival of Queen Henrietta Maria and Minette," Ruark said to John.

Arundell's wife gave Ruark a most grateful smile. "How very generous of you, Helford. I must admit I'm at a loss when it comes to entertaining these fashionable town people." She bent confidentially toward Summer and said, "Their sleeping arrangements resemble nothing short of musical beds, so gossip will have it."

Ruark saw the look of dismay etched on his wife's lovely features and took her hand beneath the cover of the damask cloth. "Stop worrying, my sweet. We shall supply the wine and card tables and they will entertain themselves, and I doubt if all of them will come."

Somehow she wasn't in the least reassured.

Ruark said, "John's father, Colonel Arundell, held Pendennis Castle for five months in a siege by the Parliamentarians. In the end it was hunger not force that beat Pendennis and the emaciated garrison marched out with the full honors of war."

John Arundell gave them a deprecating smile. "I think every last one of us had heroic fathers . . . all the King's brave men," he said, shaking his head.

The dinner served was sumptuous. Some dishes were totally foreign to Summer and she took only a tiny amount in case they proved unpalatable; however, there were so many courses served, she was soon shaking her head when the footman pressed her to take more.

Muscians strolled about with violas and lutes, much as they must have done in medieval times, although now of course there was no throwing the bones to the dogs; the long-nosed footmen saw that everything was kept immaculate.

The formal dinner had lasted two hours, so it wasn't until after ten o'clock that the assembly moved en masse to the gaming tables to indulge their passion for cards. Soon the tables were piled high with gold coins.

Ruark gave his wife a small bag of gold, squeezed her hand, and encouraged her to sit with the ladies while he joined Jack and Bunny Grenvile at dice. The room was soon filled with laughter, the whisper of cards being shuffled, and the *click-click* of dice tumbling from their wooden casting boxes. The players moved from table to table, changing from bassette or whist to ombre or trick track.

Whenever Summer found herself playing beside a gentleman, he offered to let her play from his privy purse and she marveled at the easy and negligent way they gambled away their wealth.

Finally Summer found herself sitting at a table with Barbara Castlemaine, Anna Maria, Countess of Shrewsbury, and Lady Anne Carnegie, who, up close, was ridiculously overpainted. Barbara had a reputation for betting heavily and losing more than she won. "Gads, I swear I'm bored to death with this godforsaken country. I'll be glad to get back to England, I'll warrant you," Barbara said, yawning.

Summer was stung and rose to the bait. "Cornwall is England, Lady Castlemaine. It was the only county to remain loyal to His Majesty."

"Gads, that was all so long ago, but I swear 'tis all you hear about here at the back of beyond. Lady Anne, those are fine sapphires you are wearing tonight. Why don't we play for our jewels instead of money, just to make the play the tiniest bit interesting?"

The Countess of Shrewsbury knew her friend Barbara was hardly interested in sapphires. No, it was Helford's bride's rubies she had her eye on. Barbara had a small collection of rubies and her fingers fairly itched to add to that collection.

After a very short time of play Barbara began to win every hand. There was absolutely no way Summer was going to lose the Helford rubies to Barbara, so she began to cheat blatantly. Barbara didn't dare accuse her of dealing from the bottom because that's exactly what she had been doing herself, though less skillfully.

After an hour's concentrated play Summer became the new owner of Barbara's topaz necklace, Anne's sapphires, and Anna Maria's pearls. Only Lady Anne looked worried. "What in blazes am I going to tell Lord Carnegie when he asks where my jewels are?"

"You know I rather like men, but husbands are a breed apart," drawled Barbara. "Tell him what we all say when our jewels go missing . . . tell him they were stolen by a highwayman."

"The practice is common enough he just might believe it," agreed Anne Carnegie, looking relieved.

"Did you go to see Gentleman Jackson, the famous highwayman, hold court at Newgate last month?" asked Barbara. "I swear he had a greater audience than Charles that day. Gads, it was the drollest thing I've seen in an age and more than one titled lady gave him 'come hither to bed' invitations."

Anna Maria's coarse laugh rang out. "Perhaps I should give him a try. We're all looking for that one man in a million who can produce the triple orgasm. How was that contortionist from the circus, darling?" she asked Barbara spitefully.

"Shut your mouth, Anna . . . anyway he was a trapeze artiste." She changed the subject back to highwaymen. "Did you hear that the Duke and Duchess of Mazarin were stopped and the damned fellow took the duchess in the bushes. When he was finished with her, he relieved the duke of fifty pounds for doing his drudgery for him!"

Anna Maria's great whoop of laughter rang out and she begged, "Stop it, Barbara, before I pee myself."

Ruark and Jack Grenvile strolled toward the ladies. Jack said, "You're a lucky devil, Ruark, she makes all the other women look well used and shopworn."

Ruark stopped behind his wife's chair and cupped her shoulders in his hands. "It's after midnight, darling."

"Gads, in London we'd just be starting to wake up. After we tired of gaming, we'd dance till morning," complained Barbara.

"You forget, Lady Castlemaine, they are on their honeymoon." Jack Grenvile laughed. Though he was her host, Barbara was none too pleased that he had been created Earl of Bath. "If Lady Helford is as good in bed as she is at bassette, then you both have the devil's own luck," Jack went on.

Ruark's manners were impeccable. Not for the world would he make a surly remark to mar the hospitality of his host and friend. He drew Summer from her chair, bowed low to the ladies, and bid his friend good night.

Just as they were about to ascend the stairs Summer spied Lady Anne Carnegie looking rather woebegone. On impulse she took the sapphires from her bag and handed them back to the overpainted young woman. "I would not like to cause trouble between a husband and wife," she whispered.

Lady Anne, her mouth open, was bereft of words, but her eyes bespoke her gratitude. Summer felt much better about the whole thing. Her own relationship with her new husband was almost perfect and she could not bear the thought of causing angry words between another husband and wife.

The maid and manservant sat awaiting them in the blue and gold chamber. Summer wanted to dismiss them immediately, but Ruark was busy giving his valet instructions about which clothes to lay out for morning, so she did the same and told her maid she would be wearing her cream velvet walking suit, trimmed with black braid. She would also need the matching hat with its sweeping black ostrich plume and the fur muff. She would not bother with a face visor which she rather thought was an affectation of London. She heard Ruark tell his man that he would need his magistrate's wig and robes packed, then he poured them each a glass of white Rhenish and waited rather impatiently for the man to finish his duties. When the maid began to take the pins from Summer's hair, Ruark dismissed her with three words. "I'll do that." The valet set the traveling case beside the door, and Ruark slipped a couple of gold coins into his hand then turned to smile at his wife.

Summer's conscience had begun to nag at her. "Ru, there's no need to go all the way to Plymouth tomorrow if you'd rather be here with your friends. I suddenly find extravagance fills me with guilt."

"I've had word that I must go to Launceston Castle for the assizes tomorrow. The town prison is inside the castle and at the moment it's holding some very important prisoners. You can watch me hold court tomorrow if you like. After we're done it's just a short sail down the Tamar River to Plymouth." He drained his wine and came to stand before her. "You are so unearthly fair." He bent to brush his lips across hers and her mouth opened slightly to receive his kiss. "You are generous enough to give me everything I desire," he said huskily, removing the pins from her hair so that the silken mass fell over his hands, "so why shouldn't you have everything you desire?"

She sighed. "I think perhaps I already have that." Her head fell back in sweet invitation. Never had he felt a desire like the one that overpowered him now. He wasted no time removing his clothes then he lifted her dress over her head and buried his face in the exaggerated upthrust of her breasts before he removed the tiny busk. He lifted her onto the bed, still adorned in her rubies and her lace stockings and garters, and murmured thickly, "You may keep your stockings on now to make up for this morning when I robbed you of them."

He towered above her, gazing down at the desirable picture she made against the silken sheets. "You look absolutely decadent making love in your jewels and lace like some goddess queen." His lips traveled to all his favorite places until her skin became so sensitive his mouth felt as if it was burning her, setting her whole body ashiver. He lifted her breasts with his palms and his tongue teased her ruching nipples, then licked the silken skin beneath each delicious globe. His lips traced her rib cage, and his hot mouth trailed down across her belly to tongue her navel. Then he kissed her lacy knees and traveled up to the bare expanse of thigh where her stockings left off. Finally he rained kisses on her swollen mons, his lips teasing the dark curls between her legs.

"Ru!" she cried in protest. His head lifted and he raised himself above her so his mouth could plunder her lips again and taste his name, which she cried out with such yearning.

Their needs became a greedy search for more and her heart cartwheeled over as his plunging hotness penetrated her like a flaming blade. With avid arms she pressed him close, then her hands slipped down over his hard flexing buttocks and her mouth sought out his small, flat nipples and sucked until they became diamond hard.

His body was fiercely demanding and his blood sang with delirious excitement. She cried out as she reached her climax, but Ruark ignored her plea for him to stop. He scythed deeply in and out until she thought she could not bear it, then miraculously she began to build again. Her cries of "stop" changed to cries of "please don't stop." He urged her on with heated love words, blushingly intimate and explicit. Now his hands reached beneath her to perfectly cup her bare bottom and help lift her to meet his savage downward thrusts and she cried out into the velvet darkness as she peaked again. He was teaching her boldness.

He rocked against her pulsing erect bud just below her mons and she began a countermovement against him, twisting and writhing to escape his demanding shaft, but then deep within her something blossomed like a flower, unfurling its petals and then its center core. He withdrew his erection all the way, arched himself high above her, then plunged, sheathing himself to the hilt and crying her name with a hot rasping sob as his burning seed spurted high inside her.

To be part of him like this was all she would ever ask of heaven. It was a long, languorous, delicious spiral back down to earth. She smiled with deep satisfaction as she now realized what Shrewsbury had meant when she had spoken of triple orgasm.

Ruark handed Summer down from the carriage in the square bailey of Launceston Castle. The shell keep had stood since the twelfth century. Royal troops had been garrisoned there during the Civil War and it had changed hands no less than four times.

"This place used to be dubbed Castle Terrible because of the filthiness and squalid conditions of its jail." His face was grim as if the castle held bad memories for him, and yet, Summer reasoned, he would only have been about fifteen when Cromwell's army had forced the Stuarts from Cornwall.

She saw that the town of Launceston was shaped like a camel with two humps. The two hills were called St. Thomas and St. Stephen, and she now understood why this town was called the gateway into the rest of England.

She looked up at the castle and indeed its bluestone and shale tiers gave it a menacing quality. Summer was surprised that the townspeople were gathering and realized they had come to sit in the court over which Lord Helford would preside. Before he left her in the crowded great hall, he put his fingers beneath her chin and looked into her eyes. "That rakish ostrich feather is so damned fetching I want to kiss you right here before the whole court." She stepped away from him quickly because she had learned he was fully capable of taking liberties while people gaped.

A short time later when he took the dais, she hardly recognized him in his magistrate's wig and robes. The prisoners were led out. There were twenty-five men, all in shackles, but one stood out from all the rest. The first man was corpulent with a jowly, red face. His clothes, though filthy from his imprisonment, were expensive and fashionable. The other two dozen all looked alike to Summer. They were thin to a man, with a mean, sly look about them like a cur that you would not dare turn your back upon. She could not stifle the urge to shudder, so loathsome did they appear, and when the Crown read out the charges, she understood the reason for her revulsion. They were wreckers!

The corpulent man was William Godolphin, who owned tin mines in the area. There were many witnesses to give testimony against the wreckers who hid in the mines while ships were lured onto the rocks, then emerged to murder and plunder as the helpless ships were smashed to smithereens on the jagged coastline. None of the witnesses was brave enough to give evidence against William Godolphin, but he had damaged himself by being found in possession of over ten thousand pounds' worth of cargo from wrecked ships.

Ruark's face was hard and set in grim lines as he listened to the evidence given in court. Then an eyewitness to a wrecking began to give lurid details of how the ship had come aground in the shallows and its passengers, though terrified, were halfway to saving themselves and their children by wading in carrying their little ones on their shoulders. The wreckers had stoned their victims, breaking their arms and legs with cruel, jagged rocks so that they drowned in four feet of water rather than let there be witnesses to their filthy trade.

Ruark's countenance was black with suppressed fury. He banged his gavel heavily. "Bailiff, clear this court of women and children before any more evidence is given," he ordered.

Summer was trembling. It had brought the horror of Lizard Point back to her vividly. Her heart went out to Ruark. His appointment by the King was not a pleasant one. She went up upon the ramparts where she could see for miles each way along the freshwater shore of the Tamar, which almost severed the rough triangle that was Cornwall from the rest of the country. She could see the Tors of Dartmoor, those massive sentinels of stone which had stood there since the hand of God had created them. They had such strange shapes, those long stones which stood on end as if they were leaning against the wind.

The moors were untamed and dangerous, fit only for wild ponies and sheep, ravens and buzzards, and yet their solitary beauty tore at her heart. She closed her eyes to let her soul fly free and was immediately comforted.

Ominous dark clouds swept in and she felt the first sharp needles of rain. She ran down to the coach, and when she saw their driver huddled in his greatcoat, she took matters into her own hands. "Is there not an inn where we may be comfortable until Lord Helford is done with his business?"

His face brightened then fell at what his lordship might think of allowing his new bride into a common inn, but Summer insisted and he had no choice but to obey her orders. They went over to the square, to a coaching inn named the White Hart with its magnificently arched Norman doorway. Summer ordered plain fare for 'twas what she liked best. Hot, mulled cider and Cornish pasties arrived and soon the coachman's diffidence at dining with his mistress melted away as their bones warmed in front of the inn's peat-turf fire.

It was midafternoon before Ruark was finished with the business of Launceston. His face had a closed, forbidding look about it when he joined her and she chose not to question him. After a large mug of cider, however, he gave her a small regretful smile. "I'm sorry your promised day in Plymouth didn't materialize, darling."

"It doesn't matter, Ru," she assured him.

"It matters very much. Drink up and fetch your muff—there's still time to take a barge down the Tamar to Plymouth Sound. We'll stay over tonight and go back to Stowe tomorrow." He bade his coachman stable the horses and take a room for himself at the White Hart.

"I brought nothing with me, Ruark, for an overnight stay," she half protested.

The darkness in his face lifted at last. "You have lace stockings? And rubies? What more do you need?" he teased.

She laughed with him, happy that thoughts of her were strong enough to lift his black mood.

18

They stood together at the barge's railing, his arm cuddling her to his warmth. She took off her pretty wide-brimmed hat, lest the wind steal it from her, and let it raise havoc with her black tresses. She almost reached up to snatch the black ribbon which clubbed back Ruark's hair so severely, but then decided a lord should not abandon decorum as she was wont to do.

When she saw the large harbor that was Plymouth Sound, it took her breath away. There were more ships anchored here than had been in the Pool of London. Ruark's knowing eyes scanned the vessels, taking a quick inventory. "Hello, what's this?" he said almost to himself.

"What?" asked Summer.

"Yonder is one of my ships on loan to the East India Company. Looks like she's limped into port." A frown creased his brow as he scanned the double-masted cargo vessel which was bristling with guns.

The *Golden Goddess* rode at anchor between two royal vessels belonging to the King. Ruark gave orders for the bargeman to pull alongside his ship and he cupped his hands and shouted, "Ahoy there!"

The next thing she knew Summer was climbing up a rope ladder and being pulled aboard ship with eager hands. The ship's master, Captain Hardcastle, had a bushy brown beard and prickly eyebrows above pale blue, twinkling eyes. He was a barrel-chested man, his shoulders humped with muscle like an ox.

"What happened?" asked Ruark with concern.

"The bloody Dutch is what happened, beggin' yer pardon, ma'am," said Hardcastle. "Three of us convoyed for safety; would have made it through the Channel and up to London if it hadn't been for the bloody Dutch, beggin' yer pardon, ma'am. They chased us all the way from Java."

Ruark grinned. "Didn't catch you, though!"

"Too bloody slow to catch a cold, beggin' yer pardon, ma'am, then the cheeky bastards sailed right into the Scilly's after us . . . imagine . . . right into our own waters. They're proclaiming themselves 'Lord of the Southern Seas.' " Captain Hardcastle spat deliberately.

"Well, they may have put a hole in your side, but they didn't get the cargo," said Ruark happily.

"Bastards sank one of the East India ships, though. We saved most of the crew and t'other ship's on its way to London."

"Bloody Dutch!" echoed Ruark. "I don't know why the hell we don't declare war on them . . . it'll come to that in the end anyway."

"Well, war or no war, the bloody Dutchman who was greedy enough to tail me into the Scilly's found a watery grave."

"You sank her?" asked Ruark.

He nodded. "With all hands."

"Good man. The King's here in Plymouth. I'll tell him what you did. Let's see what you've got," said Ruark, taking Summer's hand to guide her belowdecks.

The air was redolent with the heady tang of spices. "I've never smelled anything like this before. What is it?" she asked curiously.

"I've no sense of smell, ma'am, but they do say cloves and nutmegs are the strongest."

Ruark sniffed the air. "You've got cinnamon and green ginger and frankincense and what's that drug called . . . camphire, that's it."

"I've got everything—pepper, mace, aloes, tea." The captain nodded.

"Oh, how wonderful; may I have some?" asked Summer.

"Get one of the men to pack my wife some of each," instructed Ruark.

"Oh, I only meant tea—not everything," she protested.

Ruark grinned, delighted that he could give her the riches of China and the Indies. "This is nothing, darling. Wait until you see the bales of silks and damasks. Have you any fashions the London ladies are demanding?" asked Ruark.

Captain Hardcastle winked with relish and took them to a storage cabin. Summer couldn't believe her eyes. There were trunks filled with mantuoes—gowns worn open down the front to show a flash of elaborate petticoat. Other trunks held Indian gowns called negligees of the finest cobwebbed cotton embroidered all over with pearls and crystals. Ruark told her to choose and after great deliberation she picked a turquoise mantuoe and a pale green petticoat embroidered with silvery thread.

Ruark picked up another mantuoe which he said was melon color. She had never seen a melon, but the color looked like a sunburst. He piled her arms high with Indian gown negligees before they moved to another cargo hold which contained hundreds of bolts of cloth. A sigh of wonder escaped her lips as she drank in the exotic colors and textures laid out before her. They were so fine she hesitated to even reach out a hand to touch them until Ruark took some of the great bolts and unrolled them across the floor.

She chose a bolt of tissue-thin silk damask in pink as pale as the blush of dawn and another bolt of stiff, rustling taffeta which had the color and crackle of flames.

"And this," said Ruark, choosing the altobassos cloth of gold.

Some of the calicos and chintzes had fantastic painted patterns covered with sprigs of flowers, seed pods, vines, and trailing grasses. Others had native birds flitting about trees of bamboo and Summer thought what beautiful drapes and bedhangings they would make. She pictured how splendidly she could refurbish Roseland and tucked the thought away for another day in the near future.

Captain Hardcastle said, "I've cane chairs and lacquered cabinets and other furnishings."

Ruark shook his head. "The attics at Helford Hall are filled with the stuff."

"Oh, Ru, may I see them?"

"They are your attics, darling."

The light was fading before they were rowed to the quay. It took three sailors to carry the treasures Summer had plundered from the hold of the *Golden Goddess* and they staggered with laden arms behind Lord and Lady Helford as they made their way to the Shipp Inn.

No sooner had a hearty meal been brought up to their suite than a message was brought for Lord Helford. He opened the note and scanned its contents. "It's from the King. He asks I attend him." Ruark bit his lip, not really wanting to leave Summer alone.

"Where is he?" asked Summer, alarmed that His Majesty could be in the next room and walk in at any moment.

"He, Buckingham, and Lauderdale are aboard the *Royal Oak*." He looked hesitant.

Summer urged, "You must go. Please don't think me such a clinging, useless creature you cannot leave me alone."

"I'm sorry, darling. Married to me, you will find yourself alone only too often, I'm afraid. I'll order a chambermaid for you." He looked regretful. "Don't wait up for me, sweetheart."

As she undressed for bed she missed him terribly in spite of her assurances. She wanted to be undressed by him, she wanted to see his eyes as each part of her body was revealed, she wanted the feel of his hot mouth upon her skin as he tasted her. She knew she was being ridiculous.

She looked about the room piled high with his love tokens and felt comforted, yet the bed would be cold and lonely without him. She undressed and slipped naked between the sheets. Her breasts ached for him unbearably.

She was appalled at the prospect of entertaining the King and courtiers. As she lay alone her thoughts multiplied and her misgivings turned to fears. How could she possibly face such an ordeal? Ruark shrugged and laughed, thinking it a simple affair to entertain a king. All this to face when she returned to Helford Hall on top of Spider's imprisonment. It was not to be borne!

Finally she rolled into a ball on her side and cupped her breasts to still their pain. She never knew at what hour he returned, she only knew that when she awoke, she was cradled in his arms. Happiness flooded over her as the new day began and she stretched luxuriously in the warm featherbed, feeling delicious all the way down to her toes. She peeped at Ruark, hoping to catch a glimpse of him while he still slept, but his eyes were already loving her. All her fears and fancies of the previous night melted like snow in Summer. He laid her back upon her pillows and spread her hair in

a great fan against the white flax sheets. The backs of his fingers
brushed her cheeks, her throat, her shoulders as lightly as thistle-
down. His gesture was so infinitely tender, it brought tears to her
eyes.

His lips brushed her eyelashes, removing the tears, then moved
to her lips in the gentlest kiss he'd ever given her. She sighed and
moaned helplessly. Each curve of her body anticipated the caress
of his hands and his mouth. She watched his handsome, dark face
through slitted eyes, luxuriating in this private dawn where they
could lie naked together like this. She ran her fingertips over his
lips and he kissed them with reverence. Her breath caught in her
throat and she wondered if it were possible to die of love.

Ruark lifted her face to his with reverent hands as if he were
receiving a sacrament. When his hands caressed her breasts, he did
so with a delicate touch as if he were handling precious porcelain.
"I love you so much," he whispered. "Sweet, darling love, yield to
me."

Like a bloom of silken petals she opened her soft thighs. He
sheathed himself in her gently, sweetly. She had never imagined his
lovemaking could be so utterly poignant and beautiful. His mouth
never left hers. Their warm lips fused over and over until her
mouth tingled and felt bee-stung from too many kisses. His lovemaking was gentle and unhurried, and with closed eyes she drifted
away on pink clouds, smiling dreamily as he filled her with his
love. Her pleasure grew so intense she feared she might faint, then
suddenly at just the perfect moment they melted into each other,
her soft cry bringing him more sweet pleasure than he had ever
known. He kissed the soft tips of her breasts as she lay in his arms,
adoring him with her eyes. "How did I ever find you?" he murmured.

Suddenly he was afire to buy her something which would show
her the extent of his love. While she was at the dress shop, he
would go to the jewelers. "Take the bolts of cloth to the dressmaker and you can tell her what you'd like made up. When they're
ready, they can be shipped to Helford."

"I think I'll also take the mantuoes you gave me, then they can
be taken in if they don't fit me properly. The ladies will be pea
green with envy back at Stowe." He stepped from the bed, and as
her eyes swept down his well-muscled torso she knew the women
were already pea green with envy.

"You know it's really ironic that these fashions from the East that are all the rage are a direct result of little Catherine becoming Charles's queen. England got Bombay from the Portuguese as part of her dowry."

"Where is the irony, Ru?" she asked, puzzled.

"Oh, I forget you've not been to Court, love. Women can be such cruel bitches. They all hooted with laughter because Catherine wore the old-fashioned farthingales when she arrived," he explained.

"Fashion itself is a cruel bitch; the scarcer and more costly the commodity, the more it becomes the mode," she replied.

He threw her an amused look before he went into the adjoining room to shave. "That sounds brittle and jaded . . . so unlike you, sweetheart."

She bit her lip. She must remember not to swear in front of him, nor must she appear to be cynical and worldly-wise. Lord Helford thought he had married a sheltered, well-bred lady. He adored her innocence, and if he wanted her corrupted in any way, he would do the corrupting!

The most fashionable modiste in Plymouth had her establishment in the town square, so Summer did not have far to go. Lord Helford had a discreet word with the enterprising Frenchwoman who had fled to England to take advantage of the insatiable English appetite for anything French. He told Madame Martine he would pay double for any garment she could make ready today, so naturally the woman decided to make a month's sales in one day the moment he took himself off.

Summer's pile of purchases grew ever higher. She bought gowns, laced waistcoats, petticoats, crinolines, a dress with a fashionable train, and naturally each outfit needed matching shoes, stockings, undergarments, hats, muffs, fans, and vizards.

Madame Martine provided a light lunch whenever her clientele warranted it, and Summer ate her crab and cucumber sandwiches in the small fitting room while madame's seamstresses plied their needles.

Two women came into the shop to browse after lunch and Madame Martine excused herself to wait on them. By eavesdropping, Summer learned that they were none other than the Duchess of Buckingham and the Countess of Lauderdale. Quite clearly she heard Madame Martine say, "Ah, your ladyship, I am very sorry but that cloth of gold ees not for sale, eet belongs to Lady Helford."

"My good woman, I am the Duchess of Buckingham. Price is no object. Lady what's-her-name can await your next shipment."

Bess Maitland, the Countess of Lauderdale, chimed in, "Och, the lassie will never know. Palm her off with any old tale."

Summer stepped from the fitting room wearing only her shift and busk. "Lady what's-her-name begs to differ," she said angrily.

Buckingham's wife held the bolt of gold cloth possessively as if no force on earth could part her from it. The duchess's eyes narrowed, making her even uglier than usual. "Just who do you think you are?" she said, sneering.

Summer took a step closer. "I, madame, am the owner of that bolt of cloth you are clutching to your scrawny bosom."

Bess Maitland, who had enormous breasts, as a lot of the gentlemen of the court could testify, let out a bark of coarse laughter.

The Duchess of Buckingham was now an alarming shade of purple. "Do you realize who I am?" she shouted.

Summer's auntie Lil had told her all the gossip about Buckingham and how he'd held on to his vast fortune by marrying the daughter of the parliamentary general who had got the Buckingham lands. Summer's tongue ran away with her now. "Are you Old Noll come back from the devil to get me?"

Bess Maitland hooted and slapped her thigh in glee. Lady Buckingham raised the bolt of cloth as if she would use it as a weapon and Summer grabbed hold of its end. The two women pulled on the coveted cloth like two mongrels with a bone.

Suddenly the shop door was flung open to admit four elegantly clad gentlemen. Lady Buckingham gasped, "Your Majesty!" She let go of the bolt of cloth and Summer sprawled on her bottom, clutching the gilt fabric.

The King had eyes only for Summer and her delicious state of undress. He strode forward gallantly, beating the other men to it. "My dearest Lady Helford, allow me to offer you my hand, and my heart, too, if you'll have it."

"Thank you, Sire," she whispered, realizing the great homage being offered her.

Buckingham drawled, "I see you ladies have met." His bland face belied the amusement implicit in his dry tone.

Bess Maitland rolled her eyes at her husband, who was thoroughly sorry he had missed the fight, and Madame Martine looked as if she were going to pass out.

Summer backed into the fitting room, holding the gold cloth over her deshabille and not daring to meet Ruark's eyes. He called out, "We are invited to accompany His Majesty to Stowe, my lady." Then with faultless manners he bowed to the two women. "My ship has just arrived from the Indies. Why don't you ladies come and take your pick of cloth while we await Lady Helford?"

The King sat himself down on a carved settee and waved them all off. "Excellent suggestion, Helford. I'll rest my feet here and await the bride."

Madame Martine helped Summer into her own black and cream outfit with trembling hands. Finally she hissed, "Ees that really Hees Majesty?"

The lazy voice came from the other room. "No, no, of course I'm not the King. The wretched fellows were just pulling your leg, madame."

Summer stifled the urge to giggle. She couldn't hide from the fact that King Charles awaited her presence in the other room. She picked up her hat and muff and carried them out with her.

He smiled his sloe-eyed smile at her. His long legs were stretched out before him. "I've never seen you dressed before," he said outrageously, and her mind flew back to the day he had seen her in the beribboned nightgown.

She blushed. "Sire . . . I . . ." She curtsied, not quite knowing what to say to this King who was looking at her the way any ordinary male would.

He said intimately, "You must promise that when we are private, you will call me Charles." It was a command. "Tell me the truth, Lady Summer. Did you really live on the next estate to Helford or did the scurvy fellow make it up?"

"Yes, we were neighbors who never met until that day in London."

His warm brown eyes assessed her, frankly liking what he saw. "I never knew anyone called Summer," he mused.

She put her head on one side and replied, "I never knew anyone called Rex."

"Ha! The lady has wit. Though you have never been presented at Court, you are most welcome to come to St. James anytime." He took her hand and kissed it, then invited her to sit down with him.

Breathlessly she did so, not quite believing that this was really happening.

"Did you set Stowe on its ear? I'll bet the men have been lined up to dance with the new bride." He was openly flirting with her and she found she liked it.

"There was no dancing last night, Sire. The masques and balls are planned for after your arrival."

"I think perhaps I should warn you about my courtiers. Dancing's just an excuse to get their hands on a beautiful woman and ask for an assignation right under her husband's nose. Most of the damned scoundrels are cavaliers who've lived at the licentious European courts, remember."

"Oh, Sire, I don't think I need to worry. All the gentlemen at Stowe are Ruark's friends."

The King was highly amused. "Little innocent bride! The wives of your friends are the first ones you make love to; 'tis so convenient!"

She laughed. "Now you are teasing me, Sire."

"No, sweetheart, 'tis you who are teasing me." He sighed and patted her hand. "We'll give the marriage a few weeks before we try to corrupt you." His mouth curved into a smile below the slender mustache, and Summer realized he would always be more man than monarch.

19

On the barge ride back up the Tamar, the King and Ruark had their heads together the whole time. Bess and John Maitland, the Countess and Earl of Lauderdale, were almost comical in their suitability for one another. They were both redheaded, coarse in the extreme, with a bawdy wit which amused the King, but when they were together, they spoke with such a thick Scottish burr, none could understand them.

Buckingham's wife Mary suffered from mal de mer, which left him in Summer's company. She felt rather awkward over what had happened at the dressmaker's. "I'm afraid your wife won't care much for my company, your grace."

George Villiers's blond looks were godlike, but his tongue had a cutting edge which no one escaped, least of all his dull wife. "Well, you can't truthfully say you would care much for hers. I don't. Though we coexist, we do not coalesce, cohere, nor cohabit."

Summer heaved a sigh of relief. She knew Buckingham made a dangerous enemy and she would fare better in all circles if she had his approbation. He raised his quizzing glass to study her. "You are an unusual-looking female . . . rather exotic. I predict you shall become all the rage. Watch out for my cousin Barbara; she will hate you on sight."

Summer laughed. "The King has warned me about the men, now you are warning me about the women."

He raised an insolent brow. "And both of us rather redundant, for I fancy you could hold your own against either sex."

"That which doesn't kill me, makes me stronger," she quoted.

"Precisely. Yet it isn't your quality of survival which intrigues me. You have an air of mystery about you. You are an unknown quantity. I believe we see only the tip of the iceberg. Fascinating!"

Her heartbeat accelerated. She did not want this man examining her too closely. If he learned anything to her discredit, he would expose her for the sheer pleasure of it. Should she act silly or shallow to throw him off the track? No, he was shrewd enough to see through any sham. All she could do was turn the conversation to a subject which would hold his attention—himself. "You are the one who is fascinating, your grace. Rumor has it you are the cleverest as well as the richest man in England. In fact"—she paused dramatically—"I've heard it said 'tis you not Barbara who is the power behind the throne."

When they reached Launceston, Summer was relieved that she and Ruark were to have the privilege of carrying the King to Stowe in their carriage, while the Maitlands and Villierses had to hire three carriages, two of which were for baggage alone. She found Charles's company far more relaxing than Buckingham's.

They did not arrive until after dark, but Lady Grenvile had held off dinner until such time as the King arrived and it was almost eleven o'clock by the time the six-course meal was over.

Card tables had been set up in the long gallery and soon twenty of the great courtiers were playing bassette round a large table with a bank of over four thousand in gold before them. In the end it was Jack Grenvile who scooped up the winnings; and Lady Castlemaine, her face like a thunderstorm, quit the table and dragged Buckingham into a game of trick track which Summer had been enjoying with Elizabeth Hamilton and Anne Carnegie.

Barbara said petulantly, "I don't know why Charles had to create Grenvile Earl of Bath at the same time as I received my title."

"Then I shall enlighten you, dear coz," said Buckingham. "Jack's father Bevil died at Lansdowne leading his men into battle. Jack, who was only fifteen years old at the time, mounted his father's horse and charged the enemy. Charles will never forget those who have served him well." His mouth twitched as a droll thought struck him. "And that goes to show you where titles are concerned, our monarch considers fighting just as worthy as fucking."

"George, 'sdeath I swear you must be suffering from the pox again, you're in such an ill humor. When we get back to London, I suggest you see Dr. Fraser for some turpentine pills."

If Barbara thought to discomfit Buckingham in front of the other ladies, she was sadly disappointed, for he had an immediate rejoinder. "I'll never know why you recommend Dr. Fraser when he botched your last abortion so badly."

Barbara had the grace to flush. "Oh, George, you will have your little joke. Are you ready to play cards? I'll even play bassette if it will please you."

"My dear, the point of the insidious game is to outguess the others as to the order in which the cards turn up. Let's play something which requires a little skill."

"Oh good, we'll play ombre. We'll need a third. Lady Helford, would you oblige?"

Buckingham nodded imperceptibly to Summer and winked.

Barbara lost consistently until she became reckless. In a desperate attempt to recoup her losses she bet a thousand pounds. Summer was about to say the play was far too deep for her, but obeyed a signal from Buckingham to play. Through his clever manipulation Summer won the hand and Barbara was hooked into a reckless pattern of one thousand on the turn of every card. Thereafter Buckingham or Summer consistently won her money from her. She dropped ten thousand pounds in less than a half hour, three thousand of which was now in the hands of a happy Lady Helford.

The King strolled over to the table and his mere presence effectively put a stop to Barbara's extravagance. "I think I shall take pity on everyone and retire early tonight," he mused aloud. Etiquette dictated no one retire before the King. "I hear there is to be a great masque and ball tomorrow night. You ladies must take your rest, for I swear I'll dance you off your feet tomorrow." He looked at Summer as he spoke. Ruark, approaching the table, overheard Charles and saw the covetous looks he cast his wife. Charles glanced at Ruark and back to Summer. "You don't suppose Helford will be tiresome and monopolize you all evening, do you?"

Summer smiled her secret smile. "I'm sure he'll let me share my favors, Sire."

"Over my dead body," said Ruark, letting everyone within earshot know just exactly how tiresome he could be, if pressed.

As they left the gallery Summer could suppress her yawns no longer. Ruark said, "You're exhausted."

She nodded. "If we were at home, you would have to carry me to bed."

He immediately swept her into his arms and carried her up the staircase, completely ignoring the shocked and amused comments which floated up to them. She slipped her arms about his neck and murmured, "If I'm heavy, it's because of all the gold I've won."

Ruark dismissed the servants who were waiting up for them and said, "We won't need you in the morning." He undressed Summer quickly and laid her between the silken sheets, ignoring the nightgown which had been laid out on her pillow. Reluctantly, he gave up the idea of making love to her, which he'd been anticipating for hours. By the time he undressed and got into bed to pull her into his arms, her eyes were closing. "Tomorrow, we will sleep very late."

"Wouldn't that seem rude?" she murmured.

"The King will keep Barbara abed till noon, and when His Majesty sets the fashion, the rest of us must follow his lead. In the morning I will make love to you twice to make up for tonight." He brushed her dark curls back and kissed her temple. How was he going to endure being separated from her? he wondered, thinking of the mission the King had suggested for over the next few weeks.

"Ru," she said sleepily, "can we go home soon?"

"Yes, my darling. I don't enjoy sharing you with others. Perhaps we can savor a few days of solitude before the rabble descends upon us next week."

Early the next morning Summer awoke first and eased from the bed very carefully so she wouldn't disturb her new husband. She unpacked the many things he'd given her from the *Golden Goddess* and all of the lovely clothes from Madame Martine's, then she stood in front of the mirror and held up each gown, trying to select one for the King's ball.

She sighed with happiness as her eyes fell upon the lovely nightgowns and she slipped into the sheer black which opened down the front and fastened with ribbons just beneath her breasts. She heard the silk sheets rustle and thought Ruark had awakened, but when she returned to the bed, his eyes were still closed, though in his sleep he had thrown off the covers.

She was wildly curious about his body, so very quietly she knelt upon the bed beside him so that her eyes could explore him in detail. He looked younger in sleep, probably because his mouth had lost the hard, almost cruel look it had when he was awake. His shoulders took up most of the bed, so wide were they, and his neck was corded with long columns of muscle.

Her fingertips brushed the mat of hair on his heavy chest with a feather-light touch and she shuddered as the crisp hair felt springy and slightly scratchy. She remembered the feel of her breasts against his chest and her nipples stood out beneath the transparent black silk. His legs were so straight and strong, like the trunks of young trees, and between his legs was the greatest mystery of all. He was semiaroused even in sleep and she measured him with her eyes, guessing his shaft was about eight inches in length and as thick as the handle of a sword . . . a formidable weapon indeed. It lay along his thigh. She bent her head low to look at its underside and decided its head was heart-shaped. Below his shaft, very tight to his body, were two very distinct egg-shaped spheres nestled in black curls. Suddenly his shaft moved and stood straight up, reaching almost to his navel. Her eyes flew to his and she saw that he was awake.

"Damn," he swore. "I wanted you to think I was still asleep. I enjoyed your looking at me, but you have this effect on me I can't control." His eyes swept over her black-silk-clad body and he murmured, "You are delicious as sin." He reached out to undo the ribbons beneath her breasts and opened the negligee, then he pulled her down on top of him and the black silk floated down to cover their nakedness.

The saddle muscle in his thigh felt like marble and she straddled it to rub herself against its hardness. His body smelled of leather and the sea and sandalwood and something else she couldn't define, but it was definitely male. As she rode his thigh she reached out a tentative finger to stroke his pulsing erection. A drop of clear liquid fell upon her finger and she put it to her mouth and licked it. His eyes smoldered like emerald fire.

"I wanted to see what you tasted like," she whispered.

"And what do I taste like?" he demanded huskily.

"Salt," she softly.

He reached up to draw her face down to his and took her mouth savagely, using his tongue to arouse her to fever pitch. She needed more than his thigh and moved over him so that his thick manroot could penetrate her soft womanliness and fill her with his burning brand. Lovemaking was still new enough to cause her to gasp upon his initial entrance. She could have sworn he became larger every time he made love to her. As her tight sheath stretched to accommodate his great size and the pleasure became intense, Ruark gripped her with his thighs and rolled with her until he gained the dominant position, then proceeded to love her into submission.

Much later when Summer stretched luxuriantly and slipped from the bed, Ruark suggested, "Don't dress, darling, keep that black thing on. It was designed to give a man pleasure."

She fastened the ribbons beneath her breasts and brushed her hair. "Why didn't Charles bring the Queen?"

He lay propped on one elbow, watching her. "She's preparing for her mother-in-law's visit. She's traveling down to Portsmouth at the end of next week, I believe. Aren't you glad you don't have a mother-in-law? I am," he said wickedly.

She ignored his banter. "Ruark, why is Charles unfaithful to Catherine?"

He sighed. "Until she came to England, Catherine lived in seclusion in the royal palace of Lisbon. She probably only left it half a dozen times in her life. She never saw a man who wasn't a relative. She was surrounded by disciplinary, protective duennas and no doubt suffered from a surfeit of religion. She was more suited to becoming a little nun than to mating with our lusty monarch."

"Then you don't think she loves him the way I love you?" she asked.

"No man was ever loved the way you love me," he teased. "Come back to bed and love me again."

"Be serious, Ru!"

"I think she loves him very much, but our cultures are so different it will take her years to adjust. She was always dressed in those hideous rigid hoop skirts and it was a sin to show her feet in public, let alone her breasts. She likes the idea of love, but hates lovemaking. Charles, like every full-blooded man, longs for a woman whose senses he can arouse and who can arouse him."

"Like Barbara Castlemaine," she concluded.

He shrugged, not much interested in the King's affairs. "If she brings him happiness, I'm sure he shouldn't be condemned for a little illicit pleasure."

Summer put her head on one side. "Barbara won't bring him happiness. She'll punish him every day of his life for not marrying her."

"You're a shrewd little baggage." He darted from the bed, picked her up squealing and kicking, and took her back to the bed. He whispered, "To hell with Charles and Barbara, I want to see you on your pretty hands and knees for me."

20

A hunt was organized for the afternoon to replenish the Grenvile larder, but since hunting was anathema to Summer, Ruark joined the King and most of the other gentlemen, who were glad for a chance to be outdoors, well mounted on Grenvile Thoroughbreds.

When the maid came to do Summer's hair for the gala evening, she decided to wear it *à la négligence,* that is to say curled loosely about her shoulders. Summer's dark silken mass of hair had only one rival in that whole assembly and that of course was the mahogany tresses of Barbara Castlemaine. Summer decided to wear the vivid peacock-colored gown which opened down the front to display the pale green petticoat embroidered with silvery threads. She had an eye mask in the shape of a butterfly which was made from jade and turquoise-colored feathers and she carried a silver lace fan. She knew she was more beautiful than any other woman present. She knew that because of it, she would make enemies, but she didn't give a damn.

The weather was not kind to the elaborate plans Lady Grenvile had made for the masque, and so it was moved indoors to the long gallery. Alas, it lost something in the transition from leafy glade to the overcrowded gallery.

The titled ladies of Cornwall and their daughters put on an

amateur theatrical performance with a plethora of shepherdesses, milkmaids, and nymphs, gracefully coming forward to say their rhymes in an allegory whose underlying meaning was woefully blurred, and lost on everyone save the ladies who had labored over it.

The manners of the gentlemen were impeccable as always and they applauded and swore they loved it. The ladies from London were not so kind. Although they were highly entertained by its rusticity, their fans did not conceal their eyes rolling to the ceiling nor their voices from floating about the gallery.

"Lud, I was better entertained last month when we went disguised to Ram Alley in Whitefriars where we watched two naked women wrestle," Barbara whispered to Buckingham.

Lady Lauderdale leaned across her husband and hoarsely whispered back, "They should take their playlet to Bartholemew Fair, where the crowd could shie coconuts at them."

When the last lady had come forward to pay homage to the King, he gallantly murmured, "Most fetching."

Barbara's fan went up again. "Did he say retching?" she whispered to the company at large.

Buckingham nudged her, and under cover of the applause which ran around the room, he said, "Keep your voice down."

There were a few polite cries for "more" and Barbara, enjoying herself thoroughly, asked, "Did he shout *bore*?"

Summer turned around, looked Barbara straight in the eye, and said, "Perhaps you heard someone shout 'whore'!" It was wittily done, but though Ruark bit his lip to keep from laughing, he took Summer's hand in a hard grip and squeezed. She gasped and decided she did not like him teaching her manners in that way. She turned her face from him angrily and fanned herself. Her eyes narrowed behind the butterfly mask and she knew she would pay him back.

Tonight the great dining hall had been transformed. Instead of a formally set six-course dinner, there was a sumptuously laden buffet, a thing King Charles infinitely preferred at these gatherings. Small tables lined the walls where the guests could sit and chat before they went back to refill their plates. This mingling allowed the ladies to show off their clothes and jewels and indulge in their second greatest passion, which was gossip.

Without the distraction of dancing or cards the King and his advisers were able to discuss the problem of the Dutch, and the spying and smuggling which had become rampant in Cornwall.

Hundreds of dishes were set out along the buffet. There were smoked oysters, smoked salmon, and smoked trout. Molds of jellied eels and lampreys sat next to steaming dishes of prawns and muscles. Haunches of venison, kid, and lamb stood at the center surrounded by vegetable dishes which had been prepared with the new and extremely expensive spices from the South Seas. Some were hot like curry and cayenne pepper, others had pungent odors like cloves and cinnamon. Game pies, rabbit pies, and huge Cornish pasties cut into great slabs tempted those with heartier appetites, while others preferred the sweet desserts such as custard laced with nutmeg or traditional English trifle smothered with yellow, clotted Devon cream.

Since Queen Catherine had come over from Portugal, port wine was fast replacing claret as the wine of choice, and of course the ale and cider flowed freely.

The King spent time with his gracious hostess, the new Countess of Bath, and the Countess of Castlemaine's eyes narrowed in jealousy. Barbara was gowned in royal purple, her décolletage displaying a magnificent set of amethysts, and she thought their hostess looked insipid in her white gown and pearl necklace. However, she knew the pearls were priceless and had been handed down for generations.

Later, when Barbara saw her cousin Buckingham standing beside their hostess, she jostled his arm so that he splashed the Countess of Bath with port.

" 'Sdeath, George, they said you weren't fit to dine with pigs, but I defended you; I said, oh yes he is!" Those about edged closer, hoping to see the promised display of fireworks early. The Villiers cousins in a perverse way enjoyed besting each other in witty banter, but Buckingham usually came out ahead because there was no level to which he would not stoop. He apologized smoothly to Lady Grenvile. "Forgive me, dear lady, for my clumsiness, but upon your lovely white gown the wine looks like your heraldic crest—a scarlet banner with three gold rests." He loved to display his knowledge of England's aristocracy. "You exemplify your noble family motto."

Barbara was put out because she had no family motto or sentence adopted as a rule of conduct. She smiled smugly and drawled, "The King and I were discussing which crest I should adopt. I rather fancy a swan holding a golden horseshoe."

Here was Buckingham's chance to put Barbara in her place with his cruel wit and he didn't disappoint his audience. "I have the perfect motto for you Barbara. *'If it swells, ride it.'*"

Bess Maitland's coarse laughter rang out and she smacked Barbara on the back in appreciation. "'Sblood, top that one, if ye can." The smack unfortunately caused Barbara to swallow a fish bone, which rendered her speechless for fifteen minutes. A rare respite for her friends and enemies alike, one wag commented later.

The King was trying to enjoy Lady Helford's company but Summer was amazed at the number of courtiers who approached the King asking favors. When they were alone, she looked up at him and said, "Everyone wants something. I'm beginning to realize being a king isn't always enviable."

He smiled at her slowly, lazily, "I learned that from my father."

She looked into his eyes, which for all their cynicism were strangely tender, and she said softly, "I'm sorry, you've sacrificed so much for everyone, yet still they ask more of you."

"My sweetheart, you are wrong," he said sadly. "Every man in this room lost his father to the Stuart cause, and most of them sacrificed their lands and wealth to fight the enemy. Then, when we failed, a good number accompanied me into exile." He shook his head. "So gallant . . . so loyal . . . all my children . . . now I can deny them nothing."

Her eyes sought out her husband's powerful figure. He was one of these gallant men the King revered. She realized as their eyes met that Ruark had been watching her with the King. Suddenly she didn't want to pay him back for squeezing her hand to teach her manners, and she certainly didn't want to make him jealous of the King. He looked across the room at her hungrily and she put her fingertips to her lips and blew him a kiss and a promise.

The musicians with their lutes, citherns, and harpsichords were now assembled in the ballroom and group by group the guests wandered in, drawn by the magic of the music.

The King opened the ball, dancing with his hostess, the Countess of Bath. Her husband, Jack, partnered the Countess of Castlemaine, and the rest of the guests chose their partners. The Cornwall people chose to dance with their husbands and wives, while the London people chose anyone but.

It was a minuet, slow and stately, and when the stilted figures were complete, the ladies were passed on to another partner. Ruark reluctantly passed Summer over to Charles and partnered Jack Grenvile's wife. The King looked at Summer with deep appreciation. "Keep count of how many propositions you receive. I shall be most interested." She wagged her finger at him for teasing her and he laughed delightedly.

After the minuet came a slow pavane. It was a good dance for carrying on a conversation, not like the courante with its quick running and gliding steps, and Summer was asked to partner Bunny Grenvile. She smiled up at her husband's friend and said, "Do all the Grenviles have that attractive auburn hair, my lord?"

He whispered, "Yes, darling, upon our heads and in other interesting places. If you'd care to go for a little stroll with me, I'd be more than pleased to show you."

Summer gave a shocked little "oh!" The King, still within earshot, turned and raised his eyebrows in a question. She nodded in answer and the King threw back his head and laughed.

Lord Buckhurst begged her for a dance. He had a decided stutter, but it didn't inhibit his libido in any way. Before the dance ended he remarked, "Your b-bridegroom is much older than you, d-dearest Lady Helford. Should you ever wish for d-diversion with a man your own age, I pray you will give me every c-consideration."

"My dearest Lord Buckhurst, my husband has the most violent temper in England. Do you suppose it's his age?" she asked innocently.

The King called for one of his favorite country dances, Cuckolds All Awry, and Summer found herself being swung high by the very loud and very Scottish Earl of Lauderdale. His hair flamed like a torch and Summer blushed as she pictured what he must look like undressed. As he lifted her a second time his hands slipped up to cup her breasts and he leered at her and said something totally incomprehensible to her. She knew he had suggested something, and she knew that suggestion was both lewd and lusty, but she hadn't the faintest idea what it was. The King caught her eye and raised his eyebrows in question. Summer held up three fingers in reply and the King shouted, "Bravo!"

The men were all asking for a dance called the brawl, in which kissing was part of the routine. Summer found herself being swung up into strong arms and knew that Ruark had come to claim what

was his. As their mouths fused, the world faded away and there
were only two people who mattered in the whole world.

The dawn was gray as the footmen carried Lady Helford's baggage downstairs to the awaiting traveling coach. Without doubt
she had more pieces of luggage than any other guest, and the baggage rack plus the top of the coach were inadequate to carry everything. Some of the boxes would have to go inside and the lady
would be forced to share the seat with Lord Helford.

She had thanked her gracious hostess the previous evening,
knowing Lady Grenvile would not likely be abroad at the ungodly
hour Ruark would get on the road. As she descended the stairs she
saw Jack Grenvile in the hall below and called down to him; however, when she reached the bottom stair, she saw that it was not
Jack. It was obvious to her, however, that this man was a Grenvile.
He was somewhat older than Jack, with twice the arrogance in his
aristocratic face, and Summer was most curious about him. "I'm
sorry, milord, it seems I have mixed up one Grenvile with another."

She held out her hand, but the man said coldly, "Madame, you
are mistaken," and brushed past her.

"What an uncouth wretch," she muttered, "and what a miserable day for traveling."

The previous night's festivities had lasted until four in the morning, then Ruark's private entertainment had lasted another two
hours and she had had no rest at all. As Ruark handed her into the
carriage he noticed the dark smudges beneath her lovely eyes and
experienced a pang of guilt at his selfishness. He gave his coachman some last-minute instructions and climbed in beside his wife.
She put up her hand to stifle a yawn and he said, "Darling, I've
exhausted you. You must learn to say no to me when I'm too
demanding. Come, let me hold you while you try to sleep."

She gave him a grateful look and snuggled down into his arms.
She was asleep in five minutes.

As he looked down at her he was filled with tenderness. He was
so much in love with her that he knew he'd never have enough of
her. She was like the other half of himself, the half that made him
complete. Only a month ago he would have laughed cynically at
love. Marriage was a dull duty a man assumed for the purpose of
begetting an heir. Now all his previous thinking had been turned
upside down.

Her dark lashes made half-moons upon her cheeks and he thought he'd never beheld a lovelier face in his life. He couldn't believe they'd only been married for five days; it was as if they'd been together throughout eternity. He smiled to himself as he thought of the diamond necklace he'd bought her. It was like a waterfall of diamonds and he wanted to see her eyes sparkle when he gave it to her. It was to be an anniversary present . . . an anniversary of one week. He was vain about her and wanted her jewels to be finer than those given to any mistress, even the King's. She was his precious wife; she deserved only the best. He stretched out his legs and closed his eyes to doze, deeply content that she lay asleep against his heart.

They didn't arrive home until late afternoon and Summer knew that the most important person in her life for the next week would be Mr. Burke. Without his advice and guidance she would never be able to face entertaining the King and court. She was totally ignorant about food, wine, entertainment, and the pecking order. To top everything off she simply couldn't endure the thought of Spider being in prison any longer if she had the means to free him.

The mortgage money to Solomon Storm would become due about the same time as their guests would be leaving and she realized that distasteful as it was to confess all to Ruark, she would soon have no choice. It must be faced, and she knew she would only be able to breathe freely once she'd gotten the whole thing off her chest and unburdened herself to Ruark.

Summer found Mr. Burke the easiest man in the world to talk with. He had already set two maids to unpacking all the lovely things she'd brought back from Plymouth and she found herself telling him all about the exotic things the *Golden Goddess* had brought from the Indies.

He told her that they would select the menus together for the King's visit and then leave everything up to the cook, who had a small army of assistants to carry out her bidding. He informed her that Ruark would select the wines for his guests and set her mind more at ease by assuring her that Lord Helford was a superb, attentive host and all she would have to do was look beautiful.

"Mr. Burke, the sophisticated ladies from the Court of St. James laughed at the rustic masque performed at Stowe. We must put our heads together and come up with something that will catch their imagination. They are so easily bored."

"If I may be so bold, my lady, it is because they are shallow, hedonistic, and immoral. Someone as clever as you are will have no trouble setting a new pace with some unique frivolity, I'm certain."

Summer wished she had as much confidence in herself. She changed into boots and breeches and went to the stables to visit Ebony. Ruark had gotten there before her.

"I thought I'd give Titan some much-needed exercise. I see we both had the same idea. Will you ride with me, love?"

She hesitated only a moment. She would not be able to ride into Falmouth to the prison now. However, if she gathered enough courage to tell him of her brother's plight, she knew she would never have to visit the prison again.

"Ru?" she said tentatively.

"Yes?" he asked, looking fiercely into her eyes.

"I . . . I'll race you," she said, her courage fleeing before the sheer authority and power of this husband of hers.

They headed inland, following the Helford River. He allowed her to take the lead for a while, but in the end, like any red-blooded male, he could not let a woman best him. "I win!" he shouted triumphantly as he dismounted and waited for her to catch up.

"Unfair!" she cried. "I couldn't bring myself to ride through those pink samphires and crush their beauty." She dismounted to gather an armful of the pink flowers.

Ruark watched her with such intensity that she was drawn to him almost against her will. He stared at her as if he wished to imprint every last detail of her image upon his memory. The look upon his face took her breath away and made her heart beat with thick, slow strokes. Her arms filled with the pink flowers, she came to him and stood close in the warm, scented twilight. "Don't touch me," he warned, "I'm too full of wanting you."

She felt triumphant to know that she could make him lose control of himself and his words aroused her. "If you want me, take me. Here in the wildflowers,"

He undressed her slowly, kissing each lovely curve as he uncovered it, then his hand slipped down inside her breeches to play with her before he removed them. She stood poised for one brief moment, totally nude, then before he could disrobe she ran from him through the pink samphires just for the pleasure of having him pursue her and catch her and take the spoils of his victory.

He pulled her to the ground in a mass of yellow poppies and the golden pollen painted her breasts and thighs. They caught their breath on a ragged sigh and a sob for the sheer beauty of the moment. It was a perfect mating; when they coupled, they became the perfect male and female . . . a fusion of silken flesh . . . obelisk and sphere.

They were so aroused by their wild ride and the erotic setting of their sylvan glade that before he had penetrated her fully, she began to climax. As he felt her fluttering convulsions along his entire length he spilled into her with a low groan. "Let's go home to bed," he whispered urgently, and helped her to dress.

He took her up before him on Titan. She sat pressed in tightly between his legs, the inside of his muscled thighs gripping her legs and his hands caressing her sensitive breasts until she flung her head back and screamed from sheer excitement.

21

Early the next morning when Summer awoke, the bed curtains still cloaked them in intimate darkness. She sat up to push them back and let in the early-morning sun. Ruark reached up to pull her back to their warm cocoon and she lay in the curve of his arm, knowing he could never love her more than he did at this moment.

The waterfall diamond necklace was in a cabinet beside the bed and he wanted to give it to her now. He dipped his head to steal a kiss, but she stopped him.

"First, I have something to tell you, darling." She hesitated, her heart beating rapidly now that the moment was here. "I have some secrets that I have to confess to you," she said softly.

His look bathed her with love and tolerant amusement for her great confession.

She knelt before him with bent head and lowered lashes. "My brother Spencer was arrested on suspicion of smuggling with some other men—"

His voice like a whiplash cut off her words. "When?" he demanded.

"He . . . I . . . the night before we were married," she answered truthfully. "He's in Falmouth prison and I told him . . . I hoped . . . you would be able to release him." Ruark flung from the bed and reached for his breeches. The silence in the room was terrible. No one could have guessed at the panic that was rising within her. The only thing she wanted to do was confess all and receive her punishment. "Ruark, we had to dabble in smuggling, we were starving! My father gambled away everything we had. He sold the horses, the paintings, the furnishings. Roseland hasn't had servants in years. The stables are falling down, the grounds are overgrown, and the house in in total disrepair. When I met you in London, I'd just learned that it was mortgaged for eighteen thousand pounds. That debt has now grown to twenty thousand, and it's due next week or the London moneylender, Solomon Storm, will sell it." She took a great trembling breath.

"You little bitch!" he ground out. "You mercenary little bitch. You only married me for my money!"

Her lashes flew up. "No . . . Ru . . ."

His face was livid with anger. His mouth was set in a grim cruel line and his eyes glittered with cold fury. "Not only did you marry me for my money, but for my position of power as magistrate. By Christ, you had it all worked out in a neat little plan. Well, let me tell you that you and your damned brother knew smuggling was dangerous. You know by definition it is dishonest, and you know it is forbidden strictly by the law of the land. I neither can nor will, madame, gain his release from prison. He can rot!"

Summer was aghast. She couldn't believe the things he was saying to her.

"Women are all bitches . . . every last one. I've never dealt with a woman in my life who didn't betray me! I thought you were different. Have you any idea how much I loved you?" he raged.

She was trying to conceal her fear, but perhaps fear was what he wanted from her. She couldn't move. She felt trapped . . . kneeling naked in the bed . . . where only last night he'd worshiped her from head to foot.

"Love obviously never entered into our relationship once!" he lashed out.

The tears streamed down her face. She loved him with all her heart, yet she knew she was guilty of much deceit. Desperately she cried, "Ruark, how can you accuse me of not loving you . . . you must know I love you more than life." She could not bear to hear him accuse her, even though she was guilty.

"Like every vixen born before you, you are nothing but a deceitful liar. Christ!" His cry was like that of a wounded wolf. He remembered the diamonds he'd bought her and threw back his head in laughter, but there was no mirth in it. "What a bloody fool you made out of me. You're nothing but a little whore asking money and special privileges for sexual favors!"

"No, Ruark . . . please let me explain. We were desperate . . . we had no money, no food . . . and then the very roof over our head was going to be taken from us."

His anguish at her betrayal deafened him to her pleas. He'd never believe another word she uttered . . . and he'd never forgive her . . . never, ever.

She remembered how she'd lured him, hoping he'd marry her, but being willing to settle for mistress. But damn it all, that had absolutely nothing to do with how she'd fallen in love with him since they'd exchanged vows. She'd loved him since she'd laid eyes on him, if she admitted the truth. It suddenly infuriated her that he accused her of giving him sex for money. She put up her chin, her eyes blazing. "How dare you speak to me like that, you arrogant swine!"

"Lady Summer St. Catherine," he mocked, "my own pure little virgin."

She was speechless with anger, for none knew better than he that she had been virgin.

"So diabolically clever. You underestimate yourself. You don't need me—you don't need anybody!" he thundered. He smiled his wolf's smile. "Since you're so bloody clever, you can get your own mortgage money. Not one copper penny of Helford money will you get your grasping hands on."

"Sod off!" she screamed.

"No, madame, that's what you will do. I'm going to get an annulment!"

She was stunned. "You can't . . . the marriage has been consummated."

He said coldly, "You forget I am the magistrate—I am the law. It will be the simplest thing in the world for me to arrange."

She reached for her clothes and said icily, "I'll leave now, Lord Helford. I'm going home to Roseland."

That's when he approached the bed and struck her across the face. "You, madame, will do precisely as you are told. While you are still my wife, you will reside under this roof. You forget our guests are due to arrive in a few days."

She lay in a crumpled heap. It was true. She had forgotten. How could he possibly expect her to entertain the King and his courtiers under these circumstances? She was no match for him physically, but she used her tongue as a weapon. "I'll cuckold you with the first cavalier who asks me!"

His eyes narrowed dangerously. "If you are unfaithful to me while you are still my wife, I shall kill you. Once the marriage is annulled, you may do as you damned well please. You may keep these rooms for the present. I'll move to the north wing." The door slammed after him.

Summer was left feeling stunned, incredulous. The lovely dream couldn't end this way. She was totally shattered. She lay down upon the bed, curled into a ball, her heart broken.

In about an hour there came a low knock upon her chamber door and Mr. Burke entered quietly with her breakfast. She shook her head because she did not trust herself to speak.

"You must eat something, my lady."

"I cannot eat, Mr. Burke, so please don't press me," she whispered. She gazed with unseeing eyes through the tall window which overlooked the fountain, her hand pressed against her breast. "My heart hurts so very much."

"Lady Summer, he has a terrible temper and a stiff pride. It has always been so. Afterward he regrets the terrible things he has said, but his damned pride prevents him from apologizing."

"This has happened before?" she asked listlessly.

Mr. Burke nodded. "His father was cursed with the same Helford blood. They quarreled viciously and his father went to the grave without them reconciling. He's never admitted it but I know he deeply regrets his part in it, just as he will regret this between you two."

"I must get out of here. I'm taking a ride if he asks, Mr. Burke."

The servant said quietly, "He won't ask, my lady, but if you don't return, he will come and get you, even if he has to drag you back."

"I'll return, Mr. Burke, but don't expect me for hours and hours."

Summer went home to Roseland. She sat dejectedly in the deserted kitchen, wondering what on earth she was going to do. It wasn't in her nature to mope, as she had always preferred action. Soon a small core of anger deep inside started to spread through her blood. "Damn you to hellfire, Ruark bloody Helford!" she shouted. "You think I need you? You were right, I don't need anybody! I'll get the money for the mortgage on my home if it kills me," she vowed, striking the table with her balled-up fist. First, though, was the problem of Spider. She went over the alternatives in her mind. She had a pistol. She had jewels . . . perhaps she could bribe someone.

She gasped in fear as the kitchen door swung open quietly. Gathering her courage, she challenged, "Who's there? Speak up or I'll shoot your blasted brains out!"

"It's me, Cat, don't shoot!" her brother cried out in alarm.

"Spider! Oh, thank the blessed St. Jude. Did Ruark get you released after all?" she asked, a tiny spark of hope kindling in her heart.

"Ruark my arse!" he swore, shutting the door carefully and coming into the room. "They took me to an interrogation room and the bloody window was open. Can you believe such incompetence?" he crowed.

"You've escaped? Ohmigod, they'll come looking for you!"

"You forget, they don't know who I am, Cat." He grinned.

Her heart sank. "I told Lord Helford this morning."

"But surely I don't have to worry about that, you said you were his wife. Cat, were you lying to me?" he demanded.

"No," she said angrily, "but he threatened to annul the marriage when I told him about you and the mortgage."

"He can't get an annulment unless there's something wrong with him and he can't perform sexually," stated Spider.

"He's the law, he can do what he damned well wants."

"Did he fuck you or not?" Spider asked bluntly.

Summer closed her eyes, pressed her lips together tightly, and nodded.

"The rotten swine!" swore Spider. "Well, you've had a rude awakening."

"Aye." She laughed shortly. "One preceded by sweet slumber and seductive dreams, but I'm awake now thank God and have learned the most valuable lesson in life—to rely on myself in this world." Her mind was like quicksilver, examining each option and swiftly rejecting it. "Since we're smugglers, the first thing we have to do is smuggle you into Helford Hall. They won't look for you there. You can stay in the attic until we come up with a plan. I'll ride back now and await you at the French doors in the south wing. Let no one see you, least of all the servants."

Spider managed to avoid the Helford gamekeeper as he'd done all his life, but the gardeners were weeding and trimming out by the fountain and they looked like they would stay until the afternoon light was gone. He went by stealth from tree to flowering bush, making very certain he avoided all eyes.

Summer was at the French doors when she saw him slip up to the window. She reached out her hand to the door handle and a sudden step behind her made her whirl guiltily.

"Oh, Daisy, just put the flowers on that table please. Would you go and tell Mr. Burke that I have returned?" The maid curtsied and left the room. Summer quickly opened the doors so Spider could slip inside, but they both heard voices just outside the far door. She pushed him behind the heavy drapes and walked to the room's center. "Oh, Mr. Burke, I didn't ask Daisy to fetch you, I just thought I'd let you know I was back," she said lamely.

"While you were out, I took the opportunity to remove Lord Helford's things from your chamber, my lady."

"Oh," she said, knowing Ruark had ordered it so. She had to get rid of him quickly. "Mr. Burke, I think you were right. I think I should try to eat something."

He smiled gently. "I'll get cook to fix you a tray."

When the hall outside was clear, the brother and sister crept up the stairs to her room. Spider whistled low at the luxury of the chamber, but all Summer could see was the ghost of her husband lingering wherever she cast her eyes.

She lifted the lid on a beautifully carved sandalwood box and showed Spider her cache of gold. "I have almost six thousand pounds now. I've been thinking perhaps it's a good idea for you to disappear for a while. Take the money to Auntie Lil in London and she can get it to Solomon Storm and promise that the rest is coming shortly. She should have been able to sell that Brussels lace by now. Too, I have some very expensive jewels I won at cards and I hope to win more, but I'll have to find someone to sell them to."

There was a low knock upon the door and Spider dropped to the floor and rolled under the bed. Mr. Burke set the food down upon the bedside table. "I brought you some wine, too, my lady."

"You are always so thoughtful, Mr. Burke. Could you ask the servants to bring me water for my bath in about half an hour? Then I would appreciate it so very much if you'd tell them I want to be alone. Do you think you could keep them out of the south

wing, Mr. Burke? I'm not used to having servants about every time
I turn around. I feel I need some privacy the next few days."

"I shall see that you are not disturbed in any way, my lady," he
said with a crease of concern between his heavy brows.

The moment the door closed Spider crawled out from under the
bed. "I suppose that bloody bath you ordered is for me?" he ob-
jected.

"He may not have seen you, but by heaven 'tis a wonder to me
he didn't smell you. You stink of prison," she said, wrinkling her
nose. "When you've finished with the water, we'll wash those
clothes your wearing. In the meantime you can have a shirt and a
pair of your breeches back."

"You're not such a fine lady yet that you wouldn't rather be
running about in breeches, eh?"

She sighed. "I'll never be a lady, but when I think about it, they
must be very few and far between. The last thing the women of
Charles's court are is ladies!"

"The food smells good, let's eat before they bring that bloody
bathwater."

She lifted the covers and made him sit down in a comfortable
chair. "You have it, love, I'm not hungry."

He looked at her sharply. "You're so upset you can't eat, can
you?" he demanded.

"I'll be all right." Then she smiled to reassure him. "I'll have a
cup of wine." She sipped it reflectively while Spider wolfed down
the food. He's missed too many meals in his life, she thought, and
her resolve to get money hardened a little bit more. How ironic,
she mused, that I gave Ruark nothing until he wanted everything
. . . then I fell in love and gave him everything until he wanted
nothing.

Spider soon polished off the food and hid himself once more
beneath the bed, long before the servants brought the hot water. A
maid brought a pile of Turkish towels, pulled out the slipper bath
from its corner, and set the modesty screen about it, then a half-
dozen footmen carried in huge copper jugs of hot water. "Are you
sure you wouldn't like me to help with your bath, Lady Helford?"
asked the maid.

"Very sure, thank you. Good night," she said firmly, and closed
the door behind them.

Spider leered. "I wouldn't have minded her help."

Summer, hands on her hips, demanded, "Why are men always so . . . male?"

"I don't know, why is that?" he asked cockily.

She stood with unseeing eyes, staring out into the darkness to give him what privacy she could. Her mind was filled with images of another man. She could still feel the hardness of his mouth upon hers from this morning's love play. She closed her eyes and willed herself to put his image from her.

After the bath they each took a candle up to the attics. The furnishings stored up there took their breath away. There were silken Persian carpets, brilliantly colored cushions and ottomans, lacquered cabinets, cane chairs and daybeds. The small attic windows opened into the roof by the widow's walk and the tall chimneys of Helford Hall. Spider was pleased beyond measure. He threw a pile of brilliant cushions down to make himself a soft bed, and though he said nothing to his sister, the windows opening onto the roof would give him a way in and out without being detected.

Back in her chamber Summer was immensely relieved that at least her brother was safe and warm for one night. She would have whipped the young devil had she known that five minutes after she left, he was climbing down the thick vines which covered the stones of Helford Hall.

For Summer the night was endless. The things Ruark had said to her came back in minute detail. She could see the look in his eyes and the hard set of his mouth every time she closed her eyelids, but the unbearable part for her was being alone in the vast bed where so many intimate things had been done to her in such a few nights.

His scent lingered and her very skin remembered his touch. She felt she would starve if she never knew the security of his strong arms again. But the most painful thing she missed—and this brought a bright blush to her cheek even though she was alone—was the need to have him fill her. She ached unbearably for his long, thick manroot. She moaned softly as she remembered his shaft deep, deep within her. She was bereft.

She hugged her breasts tightly to still their ache, put her face into her pillow, and proceeded to drench it with heartrending tears.

22

The next morning when she quizzed Mr. Burke about her husband's whereabouts, he told her that Lord Helford was away and wouldn't return until the end of the week when his royal guest was expected.

In the afternoon Lady Arundell paid her a visit to coordinate plans for their visitors and she brought with her a list she had compiled of all the people they could expect. There were more coming than Lady Arundell had first assumed and she was in a flap about how to entertain them all. "I have no problem with space; Pendennis Castle has chambers enough to sleep them all, and of course His Majesty will definitely wish to again occupy the 'King's Chamber' in which he stayed over a dozen years ago before he escaped with his life to the Scilly Islands."

"Well, that is most fortunate, for of course we only have a few guest chambers at Helford Hall. I will check with Mr. Burke to learn the exact number."

"Oh, my dear, I'll put them all up if only you will entertain them through the day and long evening hours. You know I don't like to say things about anyone unless I can say something nice, but London people are not like us. I fear their appetites for ever new sensations and pleasures have jaded them for the simple, wholesome joys of country life."

"Lord Helford is looking forward to having them, and it will only be for about three days, I believe. I get butterflies in my stomach just thinking about it—I've led such a quiet life here in the country," Summer said politely.

Mr. Burke, her savior, served an elegant afternoon tea for Lady Helford and her guest, and instead of dispatching a footman to wait on them, he took it upon himself. After Lady Arundell had departed, Summer said to him, "I don't know whatever I would do without you."

He looked at the tea tray still laden with food. "I don't believe you've eaten a thing. I'll leave the tray and perhaps something will tempt you."

"Mr. Burke, have you any idea what Ruark, I mean Lord Helford, will do to entertain his guests? I can't seem to think straight."

"You won't need to consider the gentlemen at all. He'll organize a hunt and probably he'll take them salmon fishing in the Helford River. The King, I hear, particularly enjoys a spot of good fishing, but seldom gets the opportunity. I recall when Ruark was younger, old Lord Helford always organized horse races for his guests' entertainment. Our stables have the finest blood stock in Cornwall. The first Lady Helford brought her horses with her from Ireland. I understand Londoners are mad for anything which gives an excuse for large wagers. You'll only have to entertain the ladies for a couple of afternoons, for the evenings will be taken up with gambling. It's become an English addiction."

"I see," she said without much enthusiasm. "It's going to be very difficult to get through, Mr. Burke, now that Lord Helford and I are not even on speaking terms."

"Lord Helford's manners are impeccable, madame. Not by a word, a look, or a gesture will he betray that there is aught amiss in your personal lives. You may rely upon his finesse, my lady."

She thought unhappily—what was it Buckingham had said about his own marriage?—we coexist, we do not coalesce or cohabit! She gave him a brittle smile. "Well, we are the height of fashion . . . with our very modern marriage." Then she thought of Ruark's promise to get the marriage annulled and she clenched her fists into little balls of resentment. Damn him to hell. I'll show him! I'll give his fine London friends such unique entertainment they'll talk of it all season. I'll make Helford regret putting me aside if it's the last bloody thing I ever do!

The moment Mr. Burke's back disappeared through the door

she lifted the heavy tray of food and carried it upstairs. When Spider had relished every crumb, he wiped his mouth and said, "I've a bit of news."

Summer looked puzzled.

"His high-and-mighty magistrate certified there was no proof of unlawful importation or landing of foreign spirits and dismissed the case. The whole bloody lot of us got off scot-free!"

"Have you been out?" cried Summer in disbelief.

"I went right into assizes court and listened to the whole thing," he said cockily.

"Hell's gates, Spider, I've been worrying my guts to fiddle strings over you. The main reason I married Helford was to get you free. I've been hiding you under beds, giving you all my food . . . and the moment my back's turned you're off on a bloody lark!"

He drew himself up indignantly and demanded, "I wouldn't be much of a man if I didn't crave adventure, would I? Besides, if the shoe was on the other foot and I shut you up in the attic, you'd climb down that vine the minute the moon rose. Don't put the blame on me for marrying Helford. You're a willful little bitch who always had her own way no matter what, and nothing will ever change that, certainly not marriage—no, not to ten lords, let alone Helford. You know what? I feel sorry for the poor bastard. He doesn't stand a chance against you, Cat!"

"Go home, Spider," she hissed between clenched teeth. "Since you are no longer a wanted man, you can fend for yourself like I'm going to have to do."

He grinned at her and climbed from the window. Summer sank down onto the brilliant cushions. Why had Ruark dismissed the charges against the smugglers? Had he done it so her brother could go free? She hardened her heart. If he had, it was so that the fine name of Helford wouldn't be besmirched. She suddenly had an uncontrollable urge to sully him and his name. Hell's gates, before she was finished with him, she'd . . . She stopped the thought, knowing her deep hurt wouldn't be assuaged until she had inflicted pain on him. He had experienced her fire, now he would feel her ice. She would be so icily polite, she would freeze him to death. His impeccable manners, so revered by society, were nothing but a thin veneer over an uncivilized, brute male. She would like to break that veneer into a thousand pieces, aye, and would before she was done with him!

Helford stayed away until the last possible minute, but Summer kept herself busy making plans for their guests' meals and entertainment. The moment she knew he had returned she dispatched Mr. Burke with a summons for Ruark to attend her in the reception hall.

He braced himself for the inevitable confession and tears and with jaw clenched firmly with determination descended to the hall.

She saw that he was tanned and knew he had been at sea. His nearness set off a hammering in her heart, but she firmly ignored it, rustling the lists of names she held and plunging in with the efficiency of a general planning a campaign. "Lord Helford, here is a list of the guests we can expect tomorrow. The Arundells have made provisions to sleep them at Pendennis Castle each night, so you will have to provide room in the carriage house and stables for all the hired coaches and horses." Without glancing at him or even pausing for breath, she continued, "Mr. Burke assures me you will take the gentlemen hunting, hawking, or fishing and I would appreciate a copy of your planned itinerary so I may coordinate it with my plans."

"Your plans?" he questioned, sounding both annoyed and disappointed by the cool businesslike tone she used.

"Of course." She glanced at him coldly as if to rebuke him for being disorganized. "I've decided on a treasure hunt for tomorrow. Since everyone will be arriving at a different hour, they can join in any time they please. The secluded yew walks of Helford Hall will tempt both men and women to join in the game."

He frowned darkly. "It sounds risqué—no, in fact it sounds downright bawdy. You are openly encouraging them to play all sorts of games in the bowers, and you know damned well what treasures they'll be hunting," he accused.

"Of course," she said matter-of-factly. "They are all adults, I believe, and you've no idea how unutterably bored they were with the Countess of Bath's shepherdess fiasco."

He cocked an arrogant brow. "What do you intend to use for a prize when the winner is declared? What do you have of value?"

"The ambergris aphrodisiac, of course," she said as if he were a dullard not to have guessed. His frown deepened to a scowl, but before he could object, she hurried on. "The next afternoon while you occupy the gentlemen, I am transforming the tropical terrace and garden into a replica of that Ottoman palace in Algiers you told me of. All the silken Persian carpets and brilliant cushions and divan lounges are to be brought down from the attics. The ladies can wear veils and Mr. Burke has promised to oversee the cooks while they prepare exotic and spicy Eastern dishes."

"And how the hell am I to interest the men in salmon fishing when they glimpse your veiled ladies languishing about among the flowering almond?" he demanded.

"Really, Lord Helford. Use a little common sense, if you have any. Get them out of here early before we transform the gardens, then when they return, wet and weary from your bucolic expedition up the river, they'll stop their complaining and be delighted they came after all."

He noticed with annoyance that she was wearing a cream linen gown with cream-colored roses in her hair. She had deliberately put them there to provoke intimate memories, he told himself. Well, they were certainly doing that. The little bitch hadn't even thanked him for enabling her brother to escape from prison, he thought bitterly. "Have you any more plans, madame?" he asked in a sarcastic note.

"Of course I have more plans, I'm simply waiting to hear yours. They have insatiable appetites for anything unique. I thought perhaps if you were planning to race some of your Thoroughbreds, it would make an exciting change if afterward we had a seafood dinner down on the beach."

"On the beach?" he asked incredulously.

"How many of them have ever lit a beach fire and baked clams and lobsters and crabs?" she asked.

Though his expression remained unreadable, the idea appealed to him. "Probably none of them except the King. He and I have done that before."

"Good, he'll love the nostalgia it will provoke, trust me."

"Trust you?" he raged. "I have done that before also, madame. I might have known a clever, conniving female like you would come up with such exciting, illicit schemes for entertainment. You have planned everything down to the last detail, *as usual*," he threw at her with emphasis. "It's too bad I didn't know your true attributes when I married you!"

"My heart bleeds for you," she said with exquisite sarcasm. "The biddable little country girl turned out to have too much spirit for you to tame."

"By Christ, I'll tame you before I'm done with you . . . and that's a promise." He bowed and left her with her guest lists.

Summer was pleased with herself. She had treated him in a summarily offhand manner and it had angered him enough to make him threaten her. The rest of her day was so busy she hardly had a moment to think of him, but at bedtime, the night stretched before her empty and endless. She ordered a bath to pass the time and relax her so she would fall asleep the sooner, but the tantalizing water evoked such intimate memories that she soon stepped out and wrapped herself in a Turkish towel. She stepped before the mirror to brush her hair, but his image lingered in its depths. She saw him standing behind her, cupping her breasts; she saw him lift her up onto his shaft and slowly impale her; she saw him slide his pulsing erection up her back then turn her to face him so he could slide it over her breasts. She closed her eyes and smashed her clenched fist into the mocking mirror.

She sent for a flacon of wine and downed cup after cup. A line from a play by that fellow Shakespeare ran through her mind: "Give me a bowl of wine; in this I bury all unkindness."

But by the time the flacon was half-empty she wished desperately she hadn't had any at all, for her blood grew warm and she was all liver and lights. Toward morning she did manage to fall into a fitful sleep where she saw a tall, dark cavalier beckon to her. He was irresistible and all he had to do to make her follow him was to lift his finger. He held a bag of gold and selected a crown from it. Holding it out to her on his palm, he crooned, "You like gold, don't you, little wench?"

"Yes, Ruark," she answered.

"Will you sell me a piece of tail for a piece of gold?"

"Yes, Ruark," she readily agreed.

"I have a hundred crowns in this bag. Will you let me fuck you a hundred times?" He leered.

"Yes, please, Ruark," she begged.

When she awoke, she was covered with shame. The only thing that saved her from completely wallowing in self-loathing was the realization that this was the day the King and their other guests were arriving.

All morning and into the early afternoon the carriages and gilt coaches rolled up the long driveway to Helford Hall. The drivers, along with the grooms and stablemen of Helford, unharnessed the horses and took them into the dark, cool stables to be fed and watered. Though their guests would not be sleeping at the hall, nevertheless Summer had made the guest chambers available for the ladies so they could bathe, change their clothes, or rest in privacy. All the female servants, not just the chambermaids, were given special duties, even though some of the ladies high in the pecking order like the Countess of Castlemaine brought their own serving women.

Finally the King arrived accompanied by Buckingham, and Lord and Lady Helford came from separate directions to welcome their royal guest. Summer was wearing the very latest fashion from France. Her bodice was low cut and laced together to allow delicious glimpses of female breast to peep through the laces. Her full skirt was striped in pale and jade green and the flattering color made her eyes as green as emeralds. She curtsied deeply before Charles and he boldly took advantage of the opportunity presented and gazed down the front of her dress. He lifted her at last and took her hands to his lips. Her eyes met his and he murmured, "Little beauty." Then in a louder voice he drawled, " 'Sblood, some men have all the luck in their choice of wives, Helford."

"Welcome, Sire, it looks as if we are to be blessed by king's weather," said Ruark, ignoring the compliment about his wife.

Although the game of the treasure hunt had been explained to all the guests and they were eager to get started in their search for clues which would lead them to the treasure, most had been reluctant to set off before the King arrived. Now, however, as the King and Buckingham were given refreshments, men and women were choosing partners to help them win the game.

A great crowd was gathered about the table in the front hall, where the large lump of ambergris sat resplendent in a gilt casket which Summer had found up in the attics. It caused a great deal of ribald comment and set a bawdy tone for the afternoon's festivities.

The King was sampling some cider which Ruark said had been aged in applewood casks for five years. He grinned at Ruark. " 'Sblood, it's the first time I've seen Buckingham take an interest in something other than the cut of his coat in a twelvemonth."

The men were making private wagers on who would win the coveted prize and Summer was aghast at the great amounts of money being so casually gambled away.

"I wouldn't mind a lump of the stuff to analyze in my laboratory —purely for the sake of science, you understand," Charles said, winking at Ruark. "Lady Helford"—he beckoned—"I shall consent to play treasure hunt only if you will partner me, dearest lady." He turned to Ruark, who had a heavy frown between his brows. "There is method in my madness. The lady who made up the rhyming clues must know where the winning clue is buried."

"Ah, but Sire, I could take you along a false track, lead you down the primrose path so to speak, and you'd be none the wiser," Summer warned prettily.

"How can I lose if I spend an hour with you in a shaded yew walk, my beauty?"

She glanced at her husband in a cool detached manner and replied, "I do not wish to cause jealousy, Your Majesty."

"Oh, Ruark knows it is my duty to spend time with my hostess and Barbara can partner her cousin Buckingham if she wants to play the game."

Summer linked her arm with the King's and dipped into the glass bowl for the first rhymed clue:

"First seek out the leafy bower
Where you may measure every hour."

Summer handed it to Charles. "The first one is easy; they get progressively harder."

"Harder and harder," he whispered wickedly as they walked off in the direction of the sundial.

Charles tried to amuse himself with kissing games, but no matter how he pressed the lady she would not yield to anything adventurous. When Summer urged him to hurry or they would never get through all the clues which led to the treasure, he put his arm about her and whispered into her ear, "I need no aphrodisiacs, sweetheart. I'm accused of being in rut like a stag as it is."

"And with good cause, Sire," said Summer, eluding his arms and skipping away from him into the next deserted yew walk. For a moment she was dismayed to find it empty. Charles's long legs soon closed the distance between them and he finally managed to claim a kiss. He whispered into her ear again, "Sweetheart, a hostess really should do everything within her power to please a guest."

"Do I not please you, Your Majesty?" she asked, filled only with hurt and longing for her unyielding husband.

"Yes, you do, but could we not sit down and rest awhile in this cool grass in the lovely shade of these private yews?"

"They won't be private for long, Sire. Whatever would become of my reputation if we were caught lying in the grass together?"

"Little innocent . . . none of the court would dare come down the same secluded yew walk where I had taken a lady. They would avoid us at all costs rather than risk my displeasure."

"I see," she said softly, "but you would risk my displeasure."

"Sweetheart, not for all the world. If you are unwilling, we'll say no more about it."

Since the King had gone off with Summer Helford, Barbara put a good face on it and prepared to partner Buckingham. Barbara's friend the Countess of Shrewsbury said, "Dammit, Barbara, how is it you get two of the most virile men at Court?"

"George is my cousin, you know that!" protested Barbara.

"So? That never stopped anyone. Tell me the truth, have you never lain with him?"

Barbara whispered behind her fan, "George has peculiar tastes. He frequents a brothel in the Haymarket where they pander to perversion."

"Really?" drawled Anna Maria, sensing a challenge. She walked over to Buckingham and licked her lips. "I doubt very much if ambergris would work as well as other devices I could name."

Buckingham's eyes were on her mouth as her tongue outlined her lips again. She continued, "When the senses are slightly jaded, a man needs more voluptuous stimulation than powders to drink. Tell me, your grace, have you ever heard of the ingenious Oriental rings?"

"Anna Maria, I have heard of them and seen a demonstration of their efficacy, but, alas, I have never been able to procure any."

She smiled. "I happen to have a collection of Chinese curios Shrewsbury brought home from the East. He hasn't the vaguest notion they are sexual devices." She tapped his arm intimately with her fan.

"I think," said Buckingham, taking her elbow, "we would make formidable partners."

23

In the end it was Dick Talbot, a huge and handsome friend of the King's celebrating his thirty-third birthday, who was declared winner of the treasure hunt. Though he had so far escaped matrimony, he was rumored to have bastards sprinkled all over England. The prize was presented with great ceremony amid a veritable hailstorm of lewd, rude, and crude bon mots.

Summer stood on tiptoe to press a kiss to his ruddy cheek as he accepted the gilt casket from her hands and, taking the ribbing like a good sport, announced, "See, it's already working."

Dinner was served in the formal dining salon of Helford Hall. An immense oval refectory table accommodated the whole company of nearly one hundred. Summer, as hostess, sat between the King and her husband. Ruark's attentiveness almost undid her. How could he play the role of devoted bridegroom while despising her?

She gave the lion's share of her attention to Charles, but it was impossible to ignore her husband completely since he and Charles carried on a conversation with each other, and her presence between them inhibited their topics in no way.

Charles said, "I think Harry Killigrew deserves a prize for dallying in the gardens two hours longer than anyone else."

Ruark laughed. "Wild Harry, I heard, made love to not one, but two countesses this afternoon."

Summer's mouth gaped. "How can you laugh? I distinctly remember you saying that anyone caught with another man's wife should be shot!"

He winked at Charles. "The key word, my little innocent, was 'caught,' " he said with his wolf's grin.

"Oh!" she said, and deliberately turned her back upon him, but it did not free her mind of his strong image. She seethed as his insufferable laughter rang out over her head.

The King looked her over with appreciative eyes and said, "I see you have changed your gown, madame, I swear you must have more dresses than Lady Castlemaine." He pulled a rueful face. "This visit will cost me a pretty penny, I'll warrant."

She glanced at Ruark from beneath her lashes and said to the King, "I had to change my gown, Sire, the one I wore in the garden was covered with grass stains."

It was a blatant lie, for her gown had been the color of grass to begin with, but it had the desired effect on Helford. His eyes narrowed dangerously and she looked down at her plate quickly. Her eyes strayed to his powerful hands, and when she saw them clench in anger, she shuddered.

The King decided to rub salt in his wounds as any good friend should. "I told you, sweetheart, you should have let me spread my cloak for you."

At this moment Barbara had had enough of Summer Helford's monopolizing and she put her hand upon the inside of Charles's thigh beneath the table.

With the King's attention diverted from them for a few moments, Ruark took Summer's hand and squeezed it painfully. "I swear you must be the worst wife a man was ever cursed with," he said between clenched teeth.

"Oh no," she said with exquisite sarcasm, "that would be too great a coincidence!"

The kitchen staff of Helford Hall had outdone itself for this royal visit and the pièce de résistance to end the sumptuous meal was petits fours iced with the Christian names of every guest, a half-dozen of each, making a total of over five hundred cakes. It seemed everyone at table wanted to taste a Barbara, a Summer, or a Bess while the ladies fought over Charles and Ruark and the losers settled for a George or a Bunny. Some of the men who thought they were witty offered the ladies a Dick or a Roger and the meal ended in high good humor as everyone repaired to the gaming tables.

Ruark singled out Mr. Burke to compliment him on the successful menu and was annoyed when that worthy gentleman said, "All the credit must go to Lady Helford, sir." The real reason it annoyed him so much—if he were to be truthful—was that he wondered how on earth she managed so superbly. Until that fateful trip to London she hadn't known which fork to use or which form of address was correct. She'd run about in rags, yet here she was with better dress sense than any female he'd ever known. She plied her fan and fended off a king's compliments with the finesse of an experienced courtesan. She had such allure every man present was aware of it.

She had this exciting hidden quality about her which wasn't altogether explained by her deception, for even though he now knew the ugly truth about her, her hidden pagan qualities almost magnetized him. He might no longer feel love for her, but he still felt an overwhelming desire for her. He looked over at his wayward bride.

Summer's gown was ivory lace. She wore her mass of dark, silken curls swept up high off her neck to show off her rubies. As she moved from table to table, making sure her guests' glasses were refilled or making polite conversation, she was utterly dismayed at the amount of money she saw sitting so casually on the card tables. She was certain there would be enough money lost and won this night to pay off the dreaded mortgage which hung over her head so disastrously, threatening to steal her very sanity. Her quicksilver mind darted about every which way to devise a scheme whereby she could acquire some of the gold in that room. Damn, she thought, I should have auctioned that bloody ambergris off to the highest bidder and found a way of pocketing the receipts, she scolded herself. None of the schemes she dreamed up were practical and with a little sigh she sat down to try to win some money, but her attention was not wholly on her cards and she lost more than she won. There was no alternative but to cheat, she told herself righteously, but at the end of the evening all she had to show for her deceit was a miserable hundred pounds. At this rate she'd have a long white beard before she accumulated the thousands she needed. The festivities broke up at eleven because the guests had to travel by carriage to Pendennis Castle about four miles away.

Summer walked with the King and Buckingham to the royal coach, while Ruark attended the ladies. Charles said, "I'm looking forward to seeing Pendennis again. Zounds, I remember the last time I was there fifteen years past, I wouldn't leave, I wanted to stand my ground even when General Fairfax besieged the castle. I had more courage than common sense I'm afraid and had left it too long to escape. Your husband is the only reason I'm standing here today. Since we are the same height and coloring, he donned my clothes and made himself a visible target up on the walls of Pendennis for three days while I was taken by ship to the Scillies. The ship tried to return for him but had to stand three or four miles out to sea. It signaled the castle that I was safe, but the ship couldn't come in closer, and do you know what the damned fellow did? You guessed aright! He swam out to sea." Charles shook his head at the selflessness of such an act, but Summer knew it was recklessness that was in Helford's blood. She knew the demons which craved adventure, for she herself was cursed with them.

"Don't let on I told you, sweetheart," the King warned. "He'd not be best pleased if he knew I was trying to make him a heroic figure."

Buckingham drawled, "I'll wager she's already found him to be real flesh and blood."

Ruark and Barbara Castlemaine caught up with them. Summer gave him a measured look and said with a shrug, "He's a man . . . no more, no less."

She waved gaily to each carriage as it lumbered off into the warm night, then picked up her skirts to return to the house. When Ruark arrived back at the hall, he found she had assembled the entire household staff, which numbered almost threescore. She gave them her heartfelt thanks for a splendid job and told them she would need their special help tomorrow. She bid them good night, while a proud Mr. Burke stood smiling happily. "Oh, and by the way, Lord Helford asked me to tell you that he's raising everyone's wages." She swept her husband from head to foot with a cool glance and said sweetly, "Good night, everyone."

Ruark wanted to snatch her up, throw her across his knee, and deliver a damned good beating where it might do some good. He watched her bottom move from side to side as she ascended the great staircase and knew that wasn't the only thing he'd like to do to her. After the flogging he'd like to give her a good bedding. She'd put up one hell of a fight, he knew, but ached to force her to his will. He took one step after her, then stopped himself. That would be playing right into her hands. That would show her without a shadow of a doubt how he craved her, how he could not exist without her. Well, she could come to him and even then she'd have to come on her knees!

Summer threw the bolt on her bedchamber door. She'd never, ever allow him into her bed again. She vowed it to herself. She opened the doors that led out onto the small balcony overlooking the tropical garden and terrace and stepped out to look up at the stars. Tomorrow that garden would be transformed into a sultan's harem.

She heard a rustling sound and looked down in alarm. She sighed with relief as she saw Spider's familiar face approaching from the garden below to her balcony.

"I gather it was a roaring success? I perched in a tree at the end of the drive so I could look into the carriages, and finally got to see the King. Christ, the coachmen were so drunk it's a wonder they didn't tumble from their boxes. What the hell had they been drinking?"

"Cider, I imagine. Oh, Spider, you wouldn't believe how high the gold was piled on those gaming tables tonight."

"Perhaps I could join you tomorrow night and between the two of us we could relieve them of the burden of their wealth."

"No, Ruark knows you. He has a deadly temper, so please don't try any of your tricks," she warned.

He shrugged. "I've other things to do, Cat. There's a rumor about that the pirate, Black Jack Flash, was in these waters last week. Now there's somebody I'd like to do business with. He's the best at what he does. He's slick, fast, and his cargoes are unbelievable, so I've been told." He eyed her rubies. "Why don't you give me your jewels . . . perhaps I could sell them to him."

Summer was outraged at the suggestion. They were the only things of value she'd ever had in her whole life and she cherished them. The wonder of it was that Lord Helford hadn't demanded their return. He might yet, she thought bitterly. When the marriage was annulled, he could take back the jewels. She wouldn't give them up, of course. She would hoard them against the bad times. If ever the day came again when she was starving, then would be the time to sell the rubies. They were more precious to her than blood. "I have sapphires and a topaz necklace but I'm not giving them to you tonight. If you make contact with this Black Jack Flash, I'll do the negotiating myself. After watching the courtesans manipulate the men and Barbara blackmail Charles, I could handle Black Jack Flash with my hands tied behind my back. I'm dead on my feet, Spider, is there anything else you want?"

He grinned. "Half a crown would be good . . . a crown would be better."

She picked up a crown and handed it to him. "Be careful," she admonished.

He looked disgusted. "Stop making noises like an old woman." He waved his thanks and disappeared over the edge of the balcony.

Tonight she would not allow her thoughts to linger on Ruark. She had much on her mind and no room whatsoever for his intrusions. As she lay in the lonely bed drifting to the edge of sleep, all her thoughts began to jumble together. Thoughts of the day past mixed into those of the day to come. Black pirates stole piles of gold and she stood naked, save for masses of bloodred rubies. She fell into a sleep, them tumbled further into a vivid dream.

She was dressed all in black astride Ebony. The night also was pitch black and she was waiting, waiting for she knew not what. It seemed an eternity. Then suddenly she heard a low rumble. The moment she heard it, she knew exactly what it was and exactly what she would do. It was a carriage which careened through the blackness, its driver highly intoxicated. With deadly aim she leveled her pistol and called sharply, "Stand and deliver!"

A woman's pitiful voice cried out from the carriage, "Who are you?"

Ignoring the woman's cries, Summer yanked open the carriage door and gold coins fell in a waterfall to her feet. As the coach fled she cried into the night, "Tell them it was the Black Cat who robbed you!"

When she awoke at dawn, the details of the dream were still with her, and she felt as if she hadn't slept at all. She threw back the covers and put her long, slim legs to the carpet, knowing she hadn't a minute to lose. She had asked Mr. Burke to assemble all the male servants employed at Helford, under the age of fifty. This included the footmen, the grooms, stablemen, gardeners, and even the little stableboys and kitchen spit turners.

She put on a plain morning gown, brushed the tangles from her hair, and skipped breakfast completely. By the time she arrived in

the reception hall the men all stood waiting to learn why they had
been summoned and for a brief moment she felt too shy to ask
them what she wanted. Plunging in, she took her courage in both
hands and appealed to them for their help. "Before I go any further I want you all to know that this is absolutely voluntary. I
don't want any of you to do this because you think you are compelled. I will excuse any man and say nothing more on the matter."
She scanned their faces anxiously but all she saw written there was
curiosity. "Lord Helford is taking the gentlemen hunting or fishing
or whatever today and I am to entertain the ladies. The cooks will
be busy preparing spicy, exotic dishes from the East and the South
Seas, and I intend to transform the tropical garden and terrace
with the jade fountain into a sultan's harem. The attics are filled
with silken carpets and cushions and screens and all manner of
Oriental and Indian furnishings which I will need taken out to the
terrace before the ladies arrive. Now here's the part where I need
your help."

She took a deep breath and put her idea before them. "I want
you gentlemen to entertain my ladies. You need do nothing but
stand at attention and be guards of the harem. If a lady asks you to
get her food or drink, you will do so with a deep bow. I don't want
you to speak with the ladies; in fact it will be part of the game for
me to tell them you are forbidden to speak with them even if they
tease you and ask you questions. The footmen will do nothing
which they don't do in their everyday duties. For the grooms,
stablemen, and gardeners, however, it will be quite a departure."

She gave them all a nervous little smile and revealed, "It is
necessary that you wear a costume." She had taken the large bolt
of gold cloth and cut it into scarf-size pieces. She held up two
scarves and said, "You will each need two of these. One for a
turban . . . and the other for a loincloth. Mr. Burke will show
you how to tie them. Those who don't wish to participate may go
back to work." She expected half of them to leave. There was a
buzz of conversation among them and only one servant left. He
was a gardener who had an arm missing through an unfortunate
childhood accident. The rest of the men came forward with sheepish smiles on their faces to receive their gold cloths. The young
boys giggled and were removing their clothes before Summer even
had a chance to leave the room. The transformation was absolutely
amazing. She had known the footmen would look most impressive,
for they had all been hired for their attractive looks in the first

place, and of course each man was the six feet in height necessary
for any footman. The grooms, stablemen, and gardeners were a
pleasant surprise, however, for what they lacked in height they
made up for in sinew and hard muscle. No wonder they had
jumped at the chance to show off their physiques before the ladies.

When her guests arrived, Summer explained to the ladies the
theme of their afternoon and asked them to improvise a costume
and veil their faces. It turned into a contest with each trying to
outdo the others, as women in a large gathering always will. Their
ingenuity was astounding, with some wearing thin petticoats, some
in tiny busks, and some even came down in diaphanous night rails.
There was an abundance of bangles, beads, dangling ear bobs, and
bracelets upon ankles.

When they went out upon the transformed terrace, most of the
ladies couldn't resist picking exotic blooms to decorate their hair
or wrists. The hit of the afternoon, however, were the male Helford
servants in their gold loincloths. They stood immobile with arms
crossed over their bared chests and Summer explained to the ladies
with a twinkle in her eye that they could not speak because they
had had their tongues cut out, but that in no way diminished their
ability to perform any task the ladies might require of them.

The air was scented by the thousands of blooms in the tropical
garden and as well, Summer had incense burning at intervals along
the terrace. Rattan couches stood upon silken Persian and Indian
carpets and the multihued cushions were strewn all the way from
the French doors to the jade fountain. Red lacquered cabinets, like
no other red in the world for they were colored with cinnabar,
stood among the cushions holding trays of fruits and sweetmeats.
All the foreign treats had easily been bought in the port of Falmouth from the trading ships. There were oranges from Portugal,
grapes from France, olives from Spain, dates and figs from Mo-
rocco, and coconuts from heaven only knew where.

The ladies of Cornwall seemed just as delighted as the ladies
from London. They spent the afternoon alternating between warm
sunshine and shady flowering trees. They lounged upon the cushions, nibbling sweetmeats and exchanging delicious tidbits of gossip. A few of the energetic ladies played chess with the uniquely
carved, life-size chessmen and the rest contented themselves to
dabble their bare feet in the jade fountain and run a surreptitious
hand over the muscles displayed by the Helford palace guards.

Summer was delighted with the way the servants played their

roles, most discreet and aloof, yet she knew that one or two of the more sophisticated voluptuaries of the court made whispered assignations for after-dark frolics. She hid a smile as she watched Bess Maitland's fingers play about one man's loincloth and wondered what the countess would do if she realized the brawny fellow she itched after was the Helford pig herder.

24

As the afternoon hour grew late Summer urged the ladies to leave the terrace and dress for dinner before the gentlemen returned and caught them playing harem, but she noticed with a secret smile of satisfaction that they dawdled and lingered purposely, wanting the gentlemen to join them in this provocative setting.

When the men returned, they were both fascinated and delighted by what they found and insisted upon joining the females at their leisure. The setting lured them, the costumes fired their blood, and an impromptu game of forfeits began. The ladies had very little to forfeit besides their jewels and fans, and soon off came veils and the forfeits turned into kisses and other liberties.

The guests were most loath to give up this pleasure and Charles approached Ruark and asked him if they could dine in the sultan's garden rather than have a formal dinner in the dining room. Reluctantly, Ruark was forced to approach Summer to ask if it could be arranged. She couldn't tell if he was angry and disapproving or feeling tolerant of her arrangements. Of one thing she was certain —she saw no thanks or admiration for how delightfully she had managed to entertain his guests. To hell with him, she thought angrily as she appealed to Mr. Burke to serve a buffet supper al fresco on the terrace.

She decided to wipe the faintly condescending smile from Helford's mouth. She held up her hands for quiet so she could make a little announcement. "If you will all be patient, the servants will set up a buffet dinner out here. For the more daring gentlemen who have athletic physiques, I would offer fantastic gold turbans and loincloths. Who knows, perhaps we could hold a slave auction later if enough wine is imbibed to give us the courage!"

Ruark caught hold of her wrist as she was about to sweep past him. In a low, angry voice he demanded, "What the hell are you trying to do, turn Helford Hall into a brothel?"

"The Court of St. James is already a brothel, without any assistance from me, Lord Helford."

"In that case, madame, would you take a hundred pounds to lie with me tonight?"

Summer gave a short unpleasant laugh. "You dream, Helford! There isn't enough money in Cornwall to induce me to lie with you tonight, or any night for that matter. Pray address yourself to some other who is not quite so particular as I, sir."

He let go of her wrist and gripped her shoulders in his powerful hands. He deliberately squeezed hard until he knew he was hurting her. "Are you challenging me to take you by force?" he demanded, eyes blazing. "By God, I'd advise you to fear the consequences of playing with fire, madame!" He gave her another brutal squeeze before he let go of her and she swallowed her fear and laughed in his face, knowing she had wounded him. She made her way directly over to the King who hugged her and good-naturedly wrapped the turban around his head. He whispered, "I'd gladly put on the loincloth if you'd agree to a private showing."

"I'll have your tongue cut out for such wicked talk, Sire," she teased.

The entire company let their hair down, so to speak, and many of the guests declared it was the best time they'd had in memory. Unfortunately the one they declared it to was having a singularly miserable time of it, though not by word or deed did Ruark Helford let on.

By the time the ladies retired to the guest chambers to don the gowns in which they had originally arrived, most of them were slightly intoxicated. Summer couldn't have been happier, for she was ready to try gambling for jewels, since the coins from the previous evening had been so paltry.

Barbara Castlemaine was resplendent in black silk embroidered

with diamonds. She was wearing a diamond necklace to set off her
magnificent breasts and indeed they drew every eye. Summer wore
the tulip-shaped bloodred satin and her rubies, while Anna Maria,
Countess of Shrewsbury, had outdone them all. To attract Buckingham she wore a pale green gown embroidered with silvery
thread, and the necklace she had chosen to complement the dress
was an intricately designed dog collar of emeralds and jade.

Tonight the men seemed to prefer dice and most of them
sprawled on the floor on the cushions brought from the terrace.
Summer circulated politely among her guests, but she had her eye
on Castlemaine's diamonds and she realized she would not know a
moment's content until she had them in her possession. She spoke
a sweet greeting to the Earl of Shrewsbury but he was decidedly
surly to her. She thought he looked a bit green about the gills and
decided he'd had too much sack.

Barbara hailed her and asked her to join their table in a game of
pontoon. The object of pontoon was to score twenty-one or as close
to it as possible. If you went over, however, you went bust. She
played carelessly while the stakes were a few crowns, yawning a
few times to show her boredom.

"Am I keeping you awake, Lady Helford?" drawled Barbara in
her sultry voice. "Perhaps we could liven the evening with higher
stakes?"

Summer fingered her necklace. "Still have your eye on my rubies, do you, my lady Castlemaine?"

"Well, what do you say?" she urged.

"Oh, I couldn't," protested Summer.

"Come on; are you in, Anna Maria?"

"This is my lucky day, how can I lose?" asked Anna Maria
enigmatically.

"From what you told me, that was yesterday," quipped Barbara
with a leer, so Summer knew they referred to some liaison.

At last Summer permitted herself to be persuaded, but only for
the bracelets. She knew it was her only chance to acquire Barbara's
diamonds. She felt very confident as she sat with two kings in her
hand. She watched with delight as Anna Maria drew a card and
busted with twenty-two. Now it was all up to my lady Castlemaine,
who looked decidedly worried. Barbara's face clouded for a moment, then lightened again. With a swift exultant glance she
slapped down an ace and a queen and cried, "Pontoon!" Summer
went cold. She couldn't believe what had just happened to her. It

wasn't possible! It was absolutely inconceivable to her that the detested Castlemaine was the owner of *her* ruby bracelets. With stiff fingers she removed them from her arms and shoved them across the green baize toward Barbara. The blood pounded in her ears until she thought she was going to faint.

Anna Maria handed over her emeralds and immediately reached for her earrings with little concern for their value. "You'll have me naked before the night's over," remarked Anna Maria.

"Just trying to aid my dearest cousin," Barbara quipped.

Summer wagered her ruby necklace in a desperate attempt to win back her bracelets.

She bit her lip as she was dealt an ace and a nine, giving her a total of twenty again, which was difficult to beat, especially since she was in possession of one of the aces. Barbara Castlemaine wore exactly the same cloudy face as she had after the last hand and Summer's heart plunged to her slippers. However, this time Barbara's expression did not clear and Summer extended her hand triumphantly for her ruby bracelets.

"Just a moment, darling," cut in Anna Maria. "I told you this was my lucky day. . . . Pontoon!" She scooped up the bracelets but they were too tiny to fit over her fat arms, so she held out a pudgy hand for the necklace.

Summer was devastated. She actually felt the blood drain from her face at the unexpected turn of events. A feeling of unreality assailed her and she became disoriented. This must be a dream, she told herself, but gradually it came to her that the nightmare was very real indeed. With a fixed little smile on her face she excused herself from the gaming table. She knew she was going to be sick and slipped into the entrance hall and thus out the front door. Her stomach heaved and knotted, but she did not vomit much because her appetite had been almost nonexistent since the terrible fight with her husband. Nothing had gone right since that moment. As she knelt upon the grass, retching, she realized how low she had been brought.

She went very cold inside as if her heart turned to stone in her breast. She clenched her fists and stood up quickly. Never would she fall to her knees again . . . never! She walked briskly along the driveway until she came to the stables. Most of the grooms and stablemen were at supper, for they would be working late again tonight, harnessing the dozens of coach horses to the carriages for their short journey to Pendennis Castle.

She slipped a saddle onto Ebony and led him from the stable. A stableboy gave her a sidewise glance and she explained quickly, "I've had no time for poor Ebony today, and I'm sure all these strange horses bother him." The boy shrugged; there was no accounting for the odd ways of the gentry. She led the black horse deep through the garden and into one of the dark and deserted yew walks. There, very deliberately, she tethered him to a very strong yew branch.

When she returned to the house, she instructed a servant to take a couple of hogsheads of ale out to the coachmen waiting in the coach house, then she rejoined the guests, who were well into their cups and gambling heavily.

She made her way over to the King, sketched him a slight curtsy, and murmured, "Your Majesty, I am afraid I must beg your leave to retire. I am unwell. I'm afraid I indulged in too many spicy dishes this afternoon."

"Let me get Helford," he offered with concern.

"Ah please, Sire, the host cannot leave as well as the hostess. I beg your indulgence, Sire. I promise you I will be well if I can lie down for a while."

He kissed her hand, and as she withdrew the rumors began to circulate that perhaps the lady was already enceinte. On wooden legs she climbed the stairs to her chamber and, once there, threw home the bolt. There was something about the events of the evening which seemed predestined.

She washed her face and tried to stop her mind from remembering her dream from the previous night. However, as she mentally rejected the memory, she walked over to her wardrobe and opened the trunk she'd brought back from London. One by one she lifted out the articles of clothing she'd bought for Spencer. Her fingers ran along the plume of the wide-brimmed, black hat, then caressed the black velvet of the doublet and breeches. Finally she lifted out the high black calf-skin boots and closed the trunk.

She undressed slowly and with remarkably steady hands donned the black attire. Finally she admitted to herself that she was going to go through with it. She wasn't simply playing a game of dress-up to see what she would look like. There was absolutely no other way to get the mortgage money and recover her rubies; she'd been over every possibility until every other plan had been exhausted. According to gossip, highwaymen were thick as flies on a dog turd and the nobility actually bragged about their coaches being held up.

She put on the hat and stepped to the mirror. Her black hair fell to her shoulders exactly like a young cavalier's. She was tall and slim in the male attire. In the dark she knew she could easily pass for a young man, and yet she needed something which would definitely mark her as a man in the eyes of the people she was about to rob. She sat at her dressing table and, picking up the scissors, snipped a small amount from her hair. With steady fingers she fashioned a black mustache and fixed it in place with the glue she used to affix her face patches. She picked up a black velvet eyemask and tied it in place, then found her pistol. She carefully went over the details of her plan; she couldn't afford to make any mistakes. Now that she was ready, she hesitated, looking into the mirror. Her mouth went dry and her knees suddenly began to tremble. If she didn't go immediately, she knew she wouldn't be able to go through with it. She looked into the mirror and said to herself, "Toughen up!"

Her black riding gloves protected her hands as she climbed down the vine from her balcony in the south wing. She dropped to the ground, listened intently, then, when she encountered only silence, she melted into the darkness of the gardens. Ebony recognized her approach and whickered softly. She rubbed his velvet nose and murmured affectionately to him. "Carry me safely, my darling . . . I need your great strength," she whispered. She mounted and led him very, very slowly to the far end of the deserted yew walk, which was three or four acres from Helford Hall, and there she began what she knew would be a long vigil.

It would be a tricky business to single out the Shrewsburys' coach until it was quite close, but then she should recognize it easily, for they had brought one of their own with its coat of arms upon the door.

In the quiet of the yew glade she heard the rustle of small, nocturnal creatures as they prowled the night for food. Some were hunters, other poor devils the hunted; and she knew which one she would rather be. She tried to keep calm, for she knew she could easily transfer nervousness to her horse and spook him. A pair of bats swooped toward her then arced away at the last minute. Her mouth was dry, her palms inside her black riding gloves were wet. She remained absolutely stock still and silent, but her heartbeat thundered in her ears and she imagined her teeth to be chattering.

She clenched her jaw so tightly it began to ache dully as the minutes crawled past. She schooled herself to patience, for she most
likely had hours to wait yet. Of one thing she could be certain,
there was no likelihood she would doze off. Her body was pumping
blood and energy until she thought she would scream with the
forced inaction. Then suddenly she heard a low rumble. It was a
carriage which careened through the blackness. She felt panic rise
in her throat. Nobody should be leaving yet. She told herself that
all she need do was stand in the shadows until it passed, then ride
back to the house and go to bed. Then she heard herself whisper,
"Fortune favors the bold."

She peered intently into the blackness and recognized it was the
very coach for which she had been waiting. Don't question it, she
told herself sternly, just take advantage of it!

She rode out into the middle of the road, leveled her pistol at the
intoxicated driver, and roared, "Halt!"

The startled driver saw no one, but he pulled on the reins and
the horses slowed.

"Stand and deliver!" she bawled roughly.

"What the hell?" cried the coachman as he yanked the two carriage horses to a full stop.

She touched Ebony's side with her heel and he walked forward
three paces. She waved the pistol at the befuddled driver and ordered, "Tell them to stand down and deliver." He did nothing but
stare. The carriage door was thrown open and a red-faced man
stepped down in an apparent rage. He was not, however, even
aware of the highwayman. "I'm glad you stopped," he shouted in a
high rage. "I'm not going to Pen-bloody-dennis Castle tonight,
madame," he shouted at the woman inside the coach, "to be cuckolded again, thank you very much! Driver, back to London!"

The coachman, unable to make any sort of decision, did nothing.

The woman inside the coach said, "We cannot go back to London tonight, and besides we are expected in Portsmouth for the
royal visit."

"The court, madame, is a cesspool. We return to London tonight! If the Duke of Buckingham tries to sniff round you again, I
will call him out and shoot him for the vile coward that he is!"

The woman spoke again, very low.

"*I'll* cause a scandal?" he cried at the top of his lungs. "You have
already done that, according to the gossip that came to my ears
tonight. I won't allow you to drag my name through the mud,

madame. The title of Shrewsbury has always stood for something noble!"

Summer pointed her pistol into the air and pulled the trigger. Its discharge jolted all the way up to her shoulder, but she got Shrewsbury's attention at last.

"Who the devil are you?" he demanded.

Summer sketched him a slight bow. "The Black Cat, at your service, sir."

"What the devil do you want?" he snapped angrily.

"Your lady's jewel case and I'm on my way . . . my oath on it, sir!"

Shrewsbury turned back to the coach door, saw the case on the seat beside Anna Maria, and opened it. There lay a diamond necklace and a ruby necklace and bracelets which he had not given to his wife.

"What's these?" he roared. "Gifts from Buckingham?"

"The case, milord," Summer demanded in a deadly voice, "or I'll lighten your own pockets as well."

Shrewsbury grabbed the case from the coach.

"Leave it on the road and drive on," Summer ordered.

Shrewsbury, almost bursting a blood vessel by now, raged at his wife, "This is all your fault!"

Summer called to him, "I'll keep my mouth shut about your lady's indiscretion, my lord Shrewsbury, but if I were you, I'd give her a damned good beating!"

Shrewsbury looked in disgust at his coachman. "You . . . drive north!" He slammed into the coach and it lurched off, leaving Summer with an irresistible desire to bend double with laughter.

When the carriage was out of sight, she picked up the case and put it in her saddlebags. She had done it! She felt invincible. Her blood surged wildly with the thrill the danger had brought. Damn, it was easy . . . like taking candy from a baby. She felt slightly intoxicated . . . light-headed . . . light-spirited, and very merry.

She stabled Ebony at Roseland and took the jewel case up to her bedroom. She slipped her rubies into her doublet and put the jewels she had won at Stowe into the case with the diamond necklace and what looked like sapphires. Unfortunately Anna Maria had still been wearing her emerald and jade necklace, but Summer was ecstatic over the fortune in jewels she had acquired. Of course when she sold them, she'd never be able to get full value, but it would go a long way in paying off a great deal of the mortgaged

debt. She frowned . . . the time had all but run out. In fact tomorrow would be the day the debt fell due. Spider would have to
take what money they had to London to pay part of the debt. He
could ride into Plymouth and easily take passage on a ship going to
Portsmouth or even London, for the King and court would be
leaving for those ports after just one more day.

She made her way on foot back to Helford House. She had no
trouble climbing up to her bedchamber balcony undetected, for the
guests were just taking leave of their host on the opposite side of
the house. She locked away her precious rubies then carefully removed her black garments and put them into the trunk in the
wardrobe. She honestly believed at that moment her career as a
highwayman was over.

Suddenly she heard her bedchamber door being tried and caught
her breath in alarm. Thank heaven she had had the presence of
mind to secure it before she had gone out. She stood naked, torn
between searching her wardrobe for a bed gown and discovering
who was outside her chamber door. To reassure herself that the
door was still locked, she crept across the deep carpet without a
sound and placed her ear against the panel.

"Summer"—Ruark's voice brooked no refusal—"let me in."

A feeling of déjà vu swept over her as she recalled standing
naked behind his cabin door after the storm. She clenched her fists.
She hadn't let him in that night and she sure as hellfire wasn't
about to let him in tonight. She remained silent, willing him to
leave, when to her horror she saw the key being pushed out of the
lock, and a scraping metal sound came from the other side as she
realized he was picking the lock. Lightning blast the man! She
should have known it would take more than a lock to keep Helford
at bay.

She ran to her wardrobe and quickly pulled a velvet robe over
her nakedness and was standing in the center of the room with
hands on hips when he opened the door and let himself in. Ruark
wore only a robe and alarm bells went off in her head to keep him
at arm's length no matter what. "What do you want?" she demanded.

His eyes traveled the length of her slowly. Though they were
enemies at this moment, he had to admit her allure. He could not
love her, but he definitely wanted her . . . wanted to master her,
ravish her, seduce her to the point where she would beg him to

take her. His deep voice sent a shiver up her spine as he sounded concerned over her. "I heard you were unwell."

"I never felt better." She lifted her chin. "These people thrive on gossip."

"Yes," he said, slowly shortening the distance between them, "they are certainly gossiping about you."

"Really?" she drawled. "And what pray are they saying?"

"One rumor had you gambling away your rubies," he said evenly, watching her reaction to his words.

She flushed and her heart hammered in her chest as she realized the close call she had had. Triumphantly she unlocked her jewel case. Like a conjurer revealing a rabbit, she stood back to display her rubies. Her stubborn mouth and defiant eyes dared him to take them from her. Tonight, however, Helford was after another jewel.

"Another rumor which swept the hall when you retired said I had already gotten you with child." With the lithe, quick movement of a panther his hands parted her bed gown and his eyes swept down over the lovely curve of her belly.

"Stop this, my lord. You cannot tell me our marriage is over and expect your rights at the same time," she said with contempt, closing her bed gown over her nudity.

"Can't I?" he asked silkily as his thumb moved to undo the belt of his robe and it swung apart. "I can do anything I please. I am still master of my own hall."

She knew exactly how irresistible was his allure. For her own self-preservation she knew she must not allow him to break down her resistance. If he loved her and left her again, she would crave him for weeks. "I'll fight you," she vowed.

He laughed deep in his throat. Such a promise only spurred him to render her to complete submission. He reached out strong hands to take her by the shoulders, but she shrugged from her bed gown and, naked, ran to the other side of the curtained bed.

He threw the empty nightgown to the floor, deliberately took off his own robe, and began to stalk her. She knew he was dangerous, but danger always excited her and she knew she must keep her eyes from his magnificently muscled torso. She turned to flee, but his arm swooped down to catch her ankle, and as she tumbled to the carpet he was on top of her in a flash.

She raked her nails down his face, then down his chest.

"Stop it, Summer." He pinioned her wrists to the floor and hung over her until his wide shoulders blotted out the whole room. As he bent to take her mouth she managed to free one hand and again she raked his flesh. "Damn, you little wildcat, do I have to tie your hands?"

"Leave me alone . . . damn you to hell," she hissed as she took two handfuls of black hair and pulled savagely.

"That's it!" he exploded. "Don't say I didn't warn you."

He lifted her to the bed, kicking and struggling, and ripped the cord from one of the bed curtains. He secured her wrists above her head and fastened the cord to one of the bedposts, closing his ears to the profanities she screamed at him. When she was breathless from cursing, he hung over her again, the green flame of his eyes almost burning her with his towering lust.

Though she had put up a magnificent defense, it was in vain. She lay pinned between his powerful thigh muscles and his hands were free to caress her body in all the places he knew exactly she couldn't resist. Her breasts had ached so much for his love play that the moment his palms cupped and lifted them she moaned and remembered the feel of her nipples against the crisp, coarse hair of his chest. She prayed that he wouldn't take them into his mouth, but her pupils dilated with pleasure as he first kissed, then tongued, and finally sucked until her twin peaks became diamond hard.

His thighs pressed against hers, letting the velvet head of his marble shaft rub against her belly, just above her sensitive mons. After he roused her to near madness, he began to stroke and caress her, to gentle her like some wild creature until all her resistance was broken away. When the kiss came, it was unbelievably gentle, changing subtly to one of overwhelming sensuality. His lips traced her throat in old remembered patterns until she wanted to scream with need. All the while his lips brushed her ear and he whispered, "Yield to me, yield to me!"

The scent of him filled her head as he reached above her to untie her wrists. She thought she would never yield, she would die first, and yet . . . and yet . . . she knew she had a power over him. Her hands sought his hard body. Perhaps if she ravished him, he would never be able to bear their parting. Suddenly she was on fire for him and wantonly she let him know her body's needs. She was kissing him back sinfully, letting him know that his seduction had caused her body to beg him. Then she opened herself to the flame that was Ruark Helford.

Suddenly he took his mouth from her and sat up. "I needed to know that you are still trained to my hand . . . that I can still tame your wildness . . . that you will yield to me whenever and wherever I desire you, my little pagan bride."

She was panting with need and the painful ache of frustration as he picked up his robe and walked away. "You swine! I hate you!" she screamed, not caring if the servants or Mr. Burke or the whole damned world heard her.

25

The King's weather held and the next day was absolutely glorious. Ruark had organized races using his ten fastest horses. They drew lots among the men to see who the lucky riders would be and the serious business of placing their wagers began. Ruark had decided to combine the races with Summer's suggestion of cooking lobsters on the beach so the sands could be used for the races.

A large tent pavilion was set up down there and the house servants spent two hours carrying down tables and chairs, cushions and blankets to make the guests comfortable.

A lot of the ladies wore wide-brimmed hats to protect them from the sun, but Summer and a few of the more adventurous went bareheaded and let their hair fly loose in the sea breeze.

Since the King's great height and weight would be a disadvantage in a horse race, he contented himself with being a spectator. Buckingham was in charge of the betting and held all the money. Jack and Bunny Grenvile had both drawn lots to be jockeys, as had Lord Buckhurst, Sir Charles Berkeley, Henry Jermyn, and Wild Harry Killigrew. Three riders were men of Cornwall: John Arundell, Richard Carew, and Sir John St. Aubyn. The tenth man was George Digby, the Earl of Bristol. Ruark Helford chose not to ride nce he would have an unfair advantage in being able to choose his astest horse.

Only two horses at a time raced each other as the beach was not vide enough to safely race more at once, which made a total of ine races before a winner could be declared.

The men weighed up the horses very carefully before they made heir wagers, but the women bet strictly on the men. In each race hey either chose the better-looking man or a particular favorite. When the Earl of Bristol raced, every woman present bet heavily n him. Summer, too, placed a large wager on him, not because he vas the best-looking man at Court, but because he was astride Ruark's beloved Titan and she knew the horse's capabilities.

By being reckless enough to wager a thousand pounds, Summer ad doubled her money and was now in possession of two thousand. Only two horses remained which hadn't yet raced. One was idden by Wild Harry Killigrew, who was known to ride hell-for-eather as he did everything else in life. He was definitely the odds-n favorite with the crowd, but Summer put her whole two thousand on Jack Grenville. She knew he'd been in the cavalry and the tory of his mounting his father's horse after Bevil had been killed y the enemy gave her total confidence in him. The crowd creamed and cheered them on, championing Wild Harry, but Jack Grenville outrode him in every way. He showed such superb horse-manship, the crowd was swayed to his side and at the finish he was eing cheered on even by those who had bet against him.

By the time the final race was ready to be run, Summer knew without a shadow of a doubt who the overall winner would be. It came down to a race between Jack Grenville and George Digby—he Earl of Bath against the Earl of Bristol, but since the latter was mounted on Titan, she knew the race would be between the two orses, not the men.

Buckingham, of course, was hidden by the throng placing wagers. When it was finally her turn and she bet her whole four housand on the Earl of Bristol, Buckingham said, "You won't be lattered by the comparison, but you do things with abandon exactly like Barbara."

"All or nothing at all," said her husband's voice in reply to Buckingham.

"And I don't really give a damn which!" she threw at him. Her blood was up and she was in a mood to be reckless. She didn't need to watch the race; its outcome was a foregone conclusion. She'd show them abandon . . . she'd give them something to whisper about behind their damned aristocratic hands!

She climbed the cliff to Roseland, put on a pair of old breeches and boots, and rode Ebony down to the beach. By the time she got there, the races were ostensibly over and those who had bet on the Earl of Bristol were counting their winnings.

Ruark came over and took hold of her bridle; he knew she was up to mischief.

"Lord Helford, I challenge you to a race." Her voice rang out clearly and sparked a great deal of interest from the guests. Those who had whispered about her being pregnant were now not quite so sure of their facts. Those who had whispered about the Helford's great love match were also not quite sure of their facts.

"Think you that misbegotten bag of bones can beat Ebony?" she challenged.

Most thought Lord Helford would not take his young wife seriously, but the King murmured to Barbara, "Helford's got a hell of a pair of balls; I think he'll take her up on it."

"How much have I won, my lord Buckingham?"

"Eight thousand," he said, enjoying himself immensely. One of them would be beaten and brought low; it mattered not to him which.

Helford said, "You have the advantage, madame, Titan has already run three races."

She smiled her secret smile. "I know."

He bowed in acceptance and took Titan's reins from the Earl of Bristol.

"Double the course . . . there and back," Summer's voice rang out.

Once more he nodded, but his eyes narrowed at her behavior. She was aware of Ruark's temper, but heeded not the warning signs. They lined up at the starting post and as the flag was dropped Summer shot ahead of Ruark. She had her heart set on winning sixteen thousand pounds and wiping out the mortgage. She had confidence that they could win if they put their hearts into it, for they had made this run almost every day of their lives. Ebony was fresh and he carried only half the weight that Titan labored under.

She knew she was going to make the turn ahead of him. Elated, she glanced back and her eyes fell upon his hands. He held the reins strongly in check—he was actually holding Titan back! Her blood began to sing in her veins . . . he was going to let her win! In that moment she realized just how much she still loved him. Then he came up level beside her and shouted, "The loser comes to the winner's bed tonight."

She looked at him in disbelief. "Go to hell!" she shouted angrily, and dug her heels into Ebony's sides.

It was very simple really. All he did was give Titan his head and the powerful Irish Thoroughbred did the rest. He thundered past her just before she crossed the finish line. Summer's heart plummeted with her disappointment. Not only had she not won the sixteen thousand, but she had lost the eight thousand she had accumulated so easily that day. Ruark's maddening words echoed in her brain: "All or nothing at all."

Gallant Jack Grenvile lifted her down from the saddle and a small knot of the men who had been championing her gathered about her protectively. She gave them a gay smile and said, laughing, "In the end I couldn't shame my husband before such grand company."

They knew her horse had been defeated fairly, but there wasn't a man there who wouldn't have thrown the race to win her favor. She gave a rueful little shrug to Buckingham. "Since I called the tune, I'll have to pay the piper. See that Lord Helford gets whatever I owe him."

As he watched her walk away Buckingham thought she would most likely give Helford one hell of a lot more than she owed him before she was finished.

Barbara Castlemaine lounged in the tent pavilion, sipping champagne and eating oysters with Bess Maitland. As Summer came to get a drink Barbara called, "I'm surprised a rustic farm girl like you came such a cropper. Perhaps you bit off more than you could chew when you took on Helford for husband." She whispered something amusing to her coarse companion and they went off in peals of laughter.

"Unlike yours, my husband is somewhat old-fashioned. My husband would kill me if I cuckolded him. I hear your friend Anna Maria was dragged home in disgrace; her husband must be old-fashioned, too."

Barbara's eyes narrowed and Bess Maitland was all agog to find out the gossip on the Countess of Shrewsbury.

* * *

The King was a very strong swimmer who had to content himself with a dip in the Thames when he was in London, but today he took advantage of a calm ocean where the water was warmed by the gulf stream. Charles, Ruark, and a half-dozen of their friends swam out quite a distance and some of the more daring and adventurous ladies removed their shoes and stockings so they could wade.

Seabirds and kittywakes joined the party hoping for handouts, and daring seals and otters swam in close out of curiosity. Summer's heart ached. She wanted to swim out to sea and never return. She was a good swimmer but she'd raised enough eyebrows for one afternoon without disrobing and plunging into the briny.

The King came out of the sea and toweled himself vigorously. All the men except Ruark were coming out now and she shaded her eyes against the late-afternoon sun as she watched his head bob up and down behind the waves. Charles saw her pensive look and joined her. "He's very like you, you know; reckless to a fault." She smiled at the King, but it was a decidedly sad smile. "I can't remember when I've enjoyed a few days away from my responsibilities so much. If there's ever anything I can do for you, Summer, please come to me. Oh, I know you don't need me when you have Helford. He'll guard you with his life and you'll never want for anything, of course. Still, life sometimes has unexpected twists. Some of the missions I send him on are fraught with danger. . . ." The King's voice trailed off as if he had said too much. She looked up at the swarthy face with its black eyes and narrow mustache. He had a glowing charm which warmed her heart. Was he just reminding her that dealing with smugglers was hazardous for a magistrate or had he been trying to warn her that Helford was involved in a more dangerous game, like spying perhaps? Where had he been last week? she wondered. Where would he go next week? Before the trouble between them, he had hinted he would have to spend a great deal of time away from her. He hadn't confided in her, even when they had been so close and lovingly intimate. Why should she care? She had enough things to worry about, thanks to his high-and-mightiness. He could go to hell for all she cared!

She saw that the grooms had finished feeding the horses and were taking them back up to Helford Hall, so she took Ebony from the groom leading him and once again tethered him in one of the isolated yew walks. Her conscience told her that she should not play the role of the Black Cat again tonight, but she told herself fiercely that Helford had made it her only way out. Not a copper penny of his money would she ever have again, he'd told her, and this afternoon he'd proven his words. God rot his eyes!

The beach picnic was a huge success. They dined on lobster dipped in drawn butter, baked clams, and the salmon the men had caught yesterday, wrapped in herbs and leaves and baked on great stones in the bonfires. For those who did not care for fish, whole young boars were roasted in pits dug out of the sand.

As darkness descended they gathered round the fires and sang sea chanties, bawdy drinking songs, and the latest songs from the London theaters.

Only about half of the guests found a need for cards this evening. Gambling was a compulsion with them and of course the card tables were set up for their pleasure. But most of the company stayed late upon the beach, hating to leave the idyll and the informality of dining and singing out in the open.

Summer was very restless. Now that she had decided to play highwayman again she wished they would all start to say their goodbyes. There were a couple of things she could do, however, to make use of her time. She bade a footman take a hogshead of ale to the waiting coachmen and she looked about her to decide who her victims would be.

She decided she could stop only two coaches, more would be hazardous. Lauderdale and Buckingham were the King's traveling companions and stopping His Majesty's coach was naturally out of the question. She didn't want to stop a coach that had too many passengers; she couldn't watch them and control them all at once. Jack and Bunny Grenvile and their wives were traveling together and the ladies had brought their maids, so their coach was eliminated. What she needed was a woman traveling alone and preferably not Barbara Castlemaine.

She stepped into the salon to watch the gambling and her eyes immediately fell on the Duchess of Buckingham with her pudgy turned-up nose. What a damned hypocrite the woman is, thought Summer. She must have been brought up to be a pious Parliamentarian if her father was one of Cromwell's generals, and yet there she sat, addicted to cards and married to one of the most profligate men at Court. Summer watched her rake in about five hundred crowns with her greedy hands and marked her down for a rendezvous with the Black Cat. Of course with Buckingham and Lauderdale escorting the King, the duchess and countess would again be sharing a carriage.

"Sweetheart, come an' bring me luck." Harry Killigrew beckoned to Summer.

She strolled over to the table of men and gave him one of her prettiest smiles. Gad, how could he win so consistently when he was rolling drunk? No wonder they called him Wild Harry! She picked up a decanter of port from the wine table and refilled his glass. Suddenly she felt a hand caress her bottom. For a moment she couldn't credit it. While Harry was feeling her bottom with one hand, he was laying out a winning hand of cards with the other, and all the while so disguised, he sat at a forty-five-degree tilt.

Summer spoke to a friend of his, Henry Jermyn, who was a particular friend of the royal family and was rumored to have been on the point of marrying the King's sister Mary. "Will he be all right?" she murmured.

"Perfectly, Lady Helford. His back teeth are awash every night of his life. His man is used to pouring him into bed. Can't play cards worth a damn unless he's three sheets to the wind."

"His man?" echoed Summer.

"Little chap, valet, driver . . . mothers him completely."

"He needs smothering not mothering." Summer laughed. She could afford to laugh; she'd just found her other mark!

Suddenly an authoritative voice behind her said, "I think you are flown with wine, madame. Perhaps you should seek your room, Lady Helford." She turned, a sharp rejoinder on her lips, as she saw Charles and Ruark had come in together. She realized what she must look like standing laughing with the men, a wine decanter in her hand and Wild Harry's hand hovering about her bottom. Being sent to her room suited her plan so well that instead of indignation, she put her hand to her head and said, "I am only a little dizzy." She bowed with exaggerated dignity to the King and said owlishly, "With your permission, Sire."

He smiled down at her, thanked her for her wondrous hospitality, and bade her goodbye.

26

She carefully locked her chamber door, stripped off her female garments, and replaced them with her male attire. She made sure her pistol was charged and that she had extra balls and powder, then she glanced in the mirror. Good heavens, she'd forgotten to take off her makeup! She carefully washed her face, affixed the black mustache, then took her saddlebags out on the balcony and dropped them into the garden below. She went back into the room, pulled on her gloves and wide-brimmed hat, blew out all the candles, and prepared to follow her saddlebags.

Halfway down the ivy, she froze against the wall as she heard laughter and male voices. She was weak with relief when she realized some of the men had come into the garden to relieve themselves. Coarseness comes naturally to men, she told herself, they'll piss anywhere!

Deep in the secluded yew walk, she untethered Ebony and spoke to him softly as she strapped the bags on either side of her saddle. Each step was familiar tonight and she found that she was not trembling, nor were the palms of her hands wet. Her heartbeat was slightly accelerated, however, and she could hear it drumming in her ears. She decided to ride down the road toward Falmouth a couple of miles. If she stayed on Helford property, the carriages might come too close together for comfort.

She went slowly, quietly, and all the while her eyes were adjusting to the light. In the yew walks it had seemed pitch black, but now that she was becoming accustomed, she was amazed at how well she could see everything. She heard a coach approaching and walked Ebony into a stand of trees until she identified it. As she had assumed, the first coach held the King and his escorts. Four servants rode outside the coach with the driver and by their loud gibes at each other she could tell they were well oiled. She should not have too long to wait for the Duchess of Buckingham and the Countess of Lauderdale. In about ten minutes she saw a black coach approaching at a fast clip.

Summer rode out from the trees onto the road and then she realized with horror it was Castlemaine's carriage. Swiftly she galloped back into the trees, but not without startling the coachman so much he swerved the coach and pulled back on the reins. An angry tirade came from inside the carriage. "You stupid pricklouse, you almost tipped us over! What the hell is the matter with you, man?"

"Forgive me, my lady, I swear the horses were spooked by what looked like a headless horseman. I swear it must have been a ghost rider, my lady."

"What piss and piffle!" shouted Barbara. "If you can't stay sober when you drive me, I'll replace you. Do you have your pistol ready in case your ghost turns out to be a highway robber?"

"Yes, ma'am," said the driver, cocking his pistol.

"Then proceed and don't spare the horses! I knew I should have ridden with the King."

Ebony stood motionless in the shadows as Summer stroked his neck and whispered so that his ears pricked at the familiar voice. It would have been such a tactical mistake to hold up Barbara, for like Summer she had a reckless nature and might on the spur of the moment challenge a highwayman. Either that or proposition him, chuckled Summer, then where would she be? Also Barbara was so shrewd, Summer didn't feel confident enough to play the man in front of her. She was vastly relieved to see the back of Barbara Castlemaine this night.

In a very short time, perhaps only five minutes, another coach came ambling along. She knew it was the right coach this time, as she remembered the yellow carriage lamps. Boldly, without hesitation, she rode into the middle of the road, leveled her pistol, and commanded, "Stand and deliver!"

The reins fell from the nerveless fingers of the driver and the coach horses stopped of their own volition.

"Facedown on the ground!" she ordered the hapless man, and without a murmur of protest he obeyed the menacing black figure.

Bess Maitland stuck her head out of the window and shouted, "What are ye aboot, mon?" Then she saw the highwayman and quickly withdrew her bright red head inside the carriage.

"Outside!" ordered Summer. "Your maid too!" she called, beginning to enjoy herself.

"Maid?" screeched the duchess, climbing out after Bess Maitland. "Sir, I am the Duchess of Buckingham. I demand that you let us go unharmed. I'll have your head for this, sirrah!"

"Do you seriously think I'd believe the handsome duke would marry the pig-faced lady?" asked Summer in a deep voice. "You there!" She indicated Bess Maitland. "Is that pig-faced woman really the Duchess of Buckingham?"

"Aye, she is." Bess nodded, making the duchess purple with fury.

"Well, madame, I'm the Black Cat and I'm noted for my reputation with the ladies, but in your case I beg to be excused." Summer gave an elaborate bow and Bess Maitland burst out laughing.

"Ladies, you are free to go on your way when I have your gold."

Bess Maitland wasted no time turning over her money, but when she tried to separate Lady Buckingham from her heavy purse, she cried, "I'll see you hanged first!"

Summer aimed the pistol at her head. "Madame, deliver or die!"

Lady Buckingham swooned. Bess Maitland took her heavy purse, threw it into the road, then ignominiously stuffed the duchess into the carriage like she was a sack of potatoes. "Christ, how much do you weigh?" Bess puffed as she climbed in after her hapless companion.

The moths flitted about the yellow carriage lamps as Summer urged the prone coachman to arise and depart, then she jumped down to retrieve the heavy purses from the roadway and deposit them in her saddlebags.

Summer decided to cut back through the fields. In case the women decided to report the highwayman in Falmouth and set that damned swine Sergeant Oswald on her trail, she rode closer to Roseland and Helford Hall. She kept her eyes open for Harry

Killigrew's little valet-coachman, but though two hours had elapsed and every guest who'd visited had departed in their carriages, still there was no sign of Wild Harry. She wavered between sticking it out and giving it up. She wasn't really tired; the exhilaration of her daring escapade made her blood surge in her veins and, too, she was highly elated with the success of her attempts at being a hostess. She knew she'd done a superb job and that she would be talked of in London for weeks to come.

The King himself was smitten enough that if she was so inclined, she knew she could become his mistress. All in all it had been the most disastrous and the most successful few days of her life. She sighed deeply and was about to turn in the gates of Helford Hall when she heard the approaching carriage.

She turned Ebony about, galloped a couple of hundred yards off, and turned to face the coach. "Stand and deliver!" she barked.

The carriage came to a hurtling stop and Lord Killigrew, who had been in a drunken doze, yanked open the carriage door and promptly fell through it onto the road. His little coach driver had his pistol out, aimed at Summer's head, and discharged it without hesitation. Fortunately for her, Harry had lunged at his valet, shouting, " 'Sdeath, man, don't shoot! Can't ye shee it's my frien' Berkeley?"

"Berkeley's got sandy hair, sir. This is a holdup!" cried his driver.

"No, no, itsh a joke, Sam—just a sham. Can't ye shee he's wearing a periwig!" Killigrew waved at Summer. "Games up, Charlie, I'd know ye anywhere."

Summer shouted, "You're too foxy for me, Harry! Trouble is, old man, if I turn up without your strongbox, I'll be a bloody laughingstock."

"No trouble, Charlie, take the box."

When his valet vigorously protested, Wild Harry explained patiently, "It's just a sam, Sham! 'Sdeath, can't go about shootin' me frien's—don't have that many!"

Harry fumbled in the carriage for the strongbox while Summer leveled the pistol at the little coachman.

"Leave it on the road!" ordered Summer.

Wild Harry winked, tipped his hat, and climbed back inside. The coachman, angry but impotent, had no choice but to climb back up on the box and drive off.

Summer's knees were butter and her hands shook visibly as she tucked the pistol into her doublet. When she'd heard the pistol discharge and the ball go whizzing past her ear, she had almost fallen from Ebony. How she had ever kept her seat and carried on with the business, she'd never know. Did other highwaymen encounter a fiasco with every coach they stopped or was it just her? She dismounted on weak legs and discovered the strongbox too heavy to lift. She found the lid was securely locked and thought she would have to shoot it open. She was too close to the house to risk a shot, however, and first tried to break the lock with a jagged rock. The lock held firmly, but the hinges on the back of the lid caved in with her efforts and she transferred the money to her saddlebags. As well as the money, there appeared to be a small jewel case. She took that as well and when the strongbox was empty she found she could lift it.

She remounted Ebony and rode inland to the banks of the River Helford. There she hurled the strongbox far out into the raging water and made her way slowly back to Helford Hall. She tethered Ebony in the yew walk again, since it was fairly close to the south wing and her saddlebags were heavy. Wearily she glanced up at her balcony, thinking that after one last great effort of climbing the vine it would be all over and she would be home safe, when all at once she felt something like a sixth sense tell her that all was not right. She didn't know if she first noticed the fragrance of tobacco or the faint glow from her bedroom window, but she was alerted that Ruark was waiting for her. The first thing she did was put her pistol in her saddlebags and hide the bags behind the shrubbery. After a few minutes' deliberation she realized she had no option but to go up and face him. How she gained entry to her chamber mattered little at this stage of the game, so she hoisted herself up the thick ivy and swung her legs over the balcony. She removed her wide-brimmed hat and sailed it across her bedchamber into the darkness, thereby defiantly announcing her arrival.

She saw his dark shape stretched out full length upon their bed; the glow from his cheroot was bright red like a warning signal. "Good evening." His voice was filled with such quiet menace, she licked lips gone suddenly dry. My God, she was still wearing the mustache! Quickly she peeled it from her top lip and thrust it into a pocket. "It was," she said coldly, showing no surprise at his presence.

"Where the hell have you been?" he demanded.

"I've been out minding my own business," she said with great impudence.

He was off the bed in a flash, gripping her shoulders in harsh hands. "Never use that tone of voice to me again, madame." His voice was like a whiplash and a wisp of fear curled in her belly.

She put out her hands to ward him off and encountered his hard, naked chest. She drew in her breath sharply as if she had been burned. His hands left her shoulders and he lit the candles on the bedside table. His eyes swept down her body, taking note of the male attire. "Who were you with that you needed a disguise? It could only have been the King," he answered his own question.

His eyes burned into her like green flames in a mixture of hatred, anger, and lust. Oh, God, and lust, she realized suddenly. He had the black doublet off her before she realized his intent. She fled across the room in her tight little busk and the slim black breeches and boots. She glanced at the bedchamber door and saw that the key was missing. He grinned wickedly as she realized she was trapped in with him. Almost leisurely he lit another dozen candles in a wall sconce so that he could enjoy the scene to the full.

"Ruark, I've not been with the King or any man. I was out riding. I went home to Roseland . . . I thought it best to go dressed as a boy," she finished lamely.

"How odd that you should bother to protect my good name of Helford after your shameless behavior with the King these past two days."

"I have done nothing to deserve your jealousy," she swore. She prayed that it would not be a repeat performance of last night, that would be too cruel. "Why are you here?" she asked, stalling for time.

"I felt like a piece," he said crudely. "You've kept me waiting over two hours, it had better be worth the wait," he said, his eyes never leaving the swell of her breasts in the tight black busk.

"No," she said firmly, making it clear she wanted no part of this behavior.

"I'm simply claiming my winnings from our wager." His mouth looked particularly cruel.

"You bastard. How could you even insinuate that I'd wager my body!" she cried.

"Ah, I forgot how important money is to you. Your tail's only for sale, I bet." He fished in his breeches pocket and pulled out a crown. The insult was so blatant she reacted instantly, furiously.

With all her might she brought up her hand and slapped him full across the face. He grabbed her instantly, threw her to the bed, and pulled off her boots and breeches. Then he turned her over his knee and gave her bare bottom a tanning.

As his hand first made stinging contact with her soft flesh she cried out in pain. She realized instantly that he would turn a deaf ear to her cries and that she must do something more overt to protect herself. She bit his thigh, then she tried to move her mouth between his legs. "By God, you are outrageous enough to do anything!" He pushed her away from his vulnerable manhood. The second his hands let go of her she rolled off the bed clad only in the tiny corset. With the bed between them he gazed at her splendidly naked limbs as if mesmerized. He saw her through a bloodred haze of lust. My God, she was more sensual than any dream. Her breasts heaved, rising and falling back into the cupped busk until he thought he would go mad from the need to be deep inside her.

Very deliberately he stripped off the remainder of his clothes until he was completely nude. Then he simply lunged across the bed and grabbed her. She fought like a wild animal, with fists and teeth, grabbing handfuls of his hair, bringing her knee up between his legs. To his great credit, he never actually hit her, but by sheer force of strength he protected himself from her onslaught and at the same time allowed her to exhaust all her strength and energy. She was panting with exhaustion and realized her sharp tongue was the only weapon he'd left her.

"Your lust is disgusting," she cried.

"*My* lust? What about yours?" he demanded, then covered her mouth with his to stop her cruel retort. "I know only one way to stop you craving the King," he ground out. Suddenly she realized with clarity that he was about to reclaim his property and brand her as his woman. He towered above her, paused, ready to impale himself inside her in a brutal downward plunge.

"Ruark, don't ravish me!" she begged.

Her words arrested his descent as he hung above her. "Me? My God, you are the ravisher. Only a moment ago you had your mouth upon me, biting me," he groaned hoarsely. "Admit it, we both have needs only the other can satisfy."

She knew that he spoke the truth, but she was outraged that he thought it was all right to use each other without making up their quarrel and declaring their love. Perhaps beneath the surface man and woman would always be deadly enemies, she thought wearily, and closed her eyes. She bit her lips to prevent a cry from escaping as the weapon of her enemy-lover thrust deep enough to touch and break her heart.

Ruark's jealousy had eaten at him too much for him to enjoy her. Dear God, why couldn't they have gone on loving each other? Why had she deceived him? He had just taken her without love and knew he never wanted to do that again. He realized miserably that it was really all over between them.

She felt degraded . . . empty. It was the last time he would ever touch her, she vowed as she watched him leave in silence.

27

The next morning she awoke with chills and fever and a nasty sore throat, and though in the heat of her anger in the middle of the night she had vowed to leave this house forever at dawn, all she did was groan and turn over in the great empty bed.

A maid brought her breakfast early but she sent her away, and when she hadn't shown her face downstairs by ten o'clock, Mr. Burke came himself to investigate. He noted the broken lock, the odorous remains of the cheroot, and Ruark's breeches strewn on the floor. He removed all unobtrusively, and when he saw that Summer was unwell, he ordered her to remain in bed. "You have managed to exhaust yourself and now you are ill, all over that London rabble. With the exception of His Majesty, there isn't one of them worth a pinch of bat shit, begging your pardon, my lady."

"Oh, Mr. Burke, you make me laugh even when I'm feeling so wretched. I intended leaving Helford Hall forever this morning."

Mr. Burke pressed his lips together as if to prevent himself from saying something indiscreet. Instead he said, "This is your home, Lady Helford. You've seen the back of his lordship for a while. He's gone. God only knows where."

She suddenly remembered her saddlebags and wondered if she dare risk asking Mr. Burke to retrieve them. "My saddlebags are down in the garden behind the flowering rhododendrons. Could I trouble you to carry them up to me, Mr. Burke?"

"It is no trouble whatsoever, my lady." He went immediately.

"No trouble," she repeated his words to herself. "Every time I turn around I run into trouble."

Once her saddlebags were safely in her chamber she gratefully accepted a posset of camomile tea to soothe her fever and help her sleep. It was three days before she felt well enough to get out of bed.

Spider had climbed in her window a couple of times, but seeing how poorly she did, he did not press her about money and London. After three days in bed she felt amazingly well and rested, and after she had bathed and dressed she found enough courage to open her saddlebags and learn exactly how much money she had accumulated.

She took out the two purses she had snatched from the Duchess of Buckingham and the Countess of Lauderdale and was slightly disappointed that between the two of them they had only a thousand pounds. Wild Harry's strongbox added another three thousand, which wasn't too bad, but nowhere near the sixteen thousand she would have won if that bastard Helford hadn't snatched away her victory at the last moment. Mentally she added what she had taken dressed as the Black Cat to the money she had secreted away. It came to a glorious total of ten thousand pounds. That was half of the mortgage debt. She must get Spider on his way to London without delay and perhaps with any luck at all Solomon Storm hadn't sold Roseland.

When she opened Killigrew's jewel case, she was both surprised and delighted. There was a full set of sapphire shirt studs, another set of ruby studs, a man's diamond ring, an emerald ring, and an opal and onyx ring. There was a set of shoe buckles made from diamond chips and another pair of turquoise and pearl. Also there was a heavy silver knife with amethyst stones set in the haft. Summer decided to keep it. Whenever she rode to the beach at dawn, she carried a knife in her belt and this was a decided improvement over the plain little knife she used to gut fish. She also decided to keep the ruby studs. Castlemaine wouldn't be the only one with a collection of rubies. She quite enjoyed wearing a man's finespun shirt sometimes and the rubies would be a fine touch of defiant elegance.

She was the proud owner of a magnificent collection of jewels, though she hadn't the vaguest notion what any of them was worth. If she was lucky and if she could find a buyer, it just might take care of the other half of the mortgage.

She spent the next couple of days with her brother. They fashioned a money belt for him to wear beneath his clothes and his wily mind gave him the idea to fit a false bottom to the small trunk he would carry with him. She gave him their aunt's address in Cockspur Street and gave him a letter addressed to Lil Richwood, asking that she take the ten thousand to Solomon Storm and tell him the balance of the money owed was on the way.

She admonished him to keep a sharp eye out at all times, for the City of London was a wicked, vile place akin to hell and it was populated by people who lived by their wits.

"Oh, that reminds me," he said. "Black Jack Flash is in these parts again. His ship, the *Phantom,* was seen up the Helford River. If you encounter the ship, for God's sake get the hell away quickly, for he's in hiding and won't hesitate to slit your throat if you discover his hiding place."

She shuddered thinking of Bulldog Brown's ugly face.

"Cat, when I come back from London, I'll try to arrange a meeting with him to see if we can do some business together, but you must have a contact who'll vouch for you or he'll cut you up and use you for bait," he warned.

"Spider, I don't want you worrying about me; just look after this money, that's all you have to do. Here's a hundred pounds for your expenses—far more than you'll need."

"I'll guard it with my life, Cat, you know that."

She smiled and hugged him. She realized he'd grown taller than she in the last few weeks. "We'll ride to Falmouth at dawn. You can ride Ebony and I'll ride the pony, then I'll bring them back," she offered generously. She realized with a pang that at fifteen he'd become a man. It was only fitting that he ride the Barbary.

Summer cherished the freedom of her days, although she admitted with shame the nights were inconsolably lonely. She arose each morning while it was still dark and rode upon the beach as the day dawned.

Two weeks had gone by since she had seen her husband and she never gave him a thought. Never a thought until she was in her lonely bed at night and then he dominated the long, dark hours. Where was he? What was he doing? Did he think of her as often as she thought of him? Did his body cry out for her? What a ridiculous thought; the moment his body demanded pleasure, he would take it; she had no illusions about that. He wouldn't even pay lip service to being faithful.

She wondered if he had taken steps yet to annul their marriage. She hoped he had; she wanted desperately to be free of him, she told herself fiercely!

She had done nothing about the jewels, for she knew that in the small port of Falmouth there were no jewelers. There was possibly a small demand for such things in the lurid little seamen's taverns and brothels that were part of every port in the world, but she knew the jewels were of the best quality and wanted a good price for them.

The thought of Black Jack Flash lured her to ride along the Helston River each afternoon, but rumors of the pirate in these waters must have been just that, for she never even glimpsed a vessel. After two weeks of idleness she was frankly bored and sought to fill the hours of the day with anything which would take up time.

She washed her hair and tried on one of Ruark's fine lace shirts and inserted the ruby studs. She laughed into the mirror as she admired herself in her tight black breeches, for she looked like a lady pirate. She went up on the widow's walk to finish drying her hair, up among the twisted chimneys and sailboat weathervanes. She gazed east over the sparkling seas, shading her eyes to watch some passing whales far out to sea, then idly she walked around to look west along the Helford River. Was it a trick of the light or were her eyes deceiving her? she wondered. No, there was definitely something there tucked into a cove, beaneath the trees. Her heartbeat quickened. Could it be a ship? It was a possibility; one she would investigate. She put the lovely silver knife into her belt and ran down to saddle Ebony. As she rode she wondered if the ship had been there awhile and was only visible from the top of Helford Hall.

She dismounted a distance away and tethered her horse in a thick stand of trees where he wouldn't be easily seen, then by stealth made her way to where she thought the vessel lay hidden. It *was* a ship! She lay full length on her belly in the grass to look it over carefully. It was smaller and much lower to the waterline than the usual sailing ship. All sails were furled tightly and it was painted a shade of gray which blended into sea and sky in a successful attempt to make it invisible. It flew no flag, had no name or figurehead, yet she knew it was the *Phantom*.

She was so close she could hear voices and laughter. She could not make out what the men were saying for they seemed to be speaking in a foreign lingo. On her hands and knees she crept closer and saw two men who seemed to be splicing lines. They were very dark and foreign looking. They wore no shirts, only wide canvas pants and bright red scarves about their heads. She was most hesitant about making contact with the ship. She was dying to meet Black Jack Flash but at the same time a danger signal was ringing in her brain. What if he spoke no English? What if they slit her throat the moment she tried to board?

Suddenly the decision was taken out of her hands as a coarse sack was thrown over her and she was lifted bodily from her hiding place. She cursed and screamed and kicked to no avail. Whoever carried her was both massive and strong and took no more notice of her struggles than he would have a child's. Even though her head was covered, she knew she was being carried aboard. She heard men laugh and shout foreign words, then felt herself being taken belowdecks.

"You filthy swine! You son of a whore! Let me go!" she raged.

She was dumped unceremoniously upon the floor of a cabin, where she struggled inside the grimy sacking which encased her.

"It's a good thing Pedro doesn't speak English or you'd have him blushing with that salty language," a lazy, amused voice said.

"I know this ship belongs to that bastard, Black Jack Flash. I demand you take me to him," she said, finally emerging from the sacking. Her words died on her lips as she stared in surprise at the dark, bronze face. He had wildly curling black hair. At one temple there was a zigzag of white exactly like a flash of lightning. He was unshaven and wore a black patch over one eye. The other was bright green.

"Good God, you're a Helford!" she accused.

The resemblance to Ruark was marked, yet this man was completely different. He wore a permanent expression of amusement as if he refused to take life seriously. Where Ruark was intense, serious, and brooding, this man was young, with a teasing, laughing, outrageous personality.

She got to her feet and swaggered toward him with hands on her hips. "Don't bother to deny it. I know you are Ruark Helford's brother, for I'm married to him."

He laughed, his teeth showing white against bronzed skin. "Are you bragging or complaining?"

"Complaining, may lightning blast the man!"

He was more amused than ever and looked her over frankly, assessingly. "Since you've guessed my identity, I might as well admit I'm Rory, the black sheep of the Helford family."

"Oh no, I insist that distinction is mine. I'm Cat," she said in a challenging tone.

He laughed again. "Hellcat Helford . . . . it suits you."

He said something to Pedro, who grinned and nodded. She looked toward the cabin door and saw two dark, wiry men wearing red scarves and golden earrings. One was eating an orange and spitting the seeds on the floor and the other put a mouth organ to his lips and played a saucy tune. She compared these foreigners who looked like monkeys to the sailors aboard Lord Helford's vessel. God in heaven, Ruark would have had them flogged for disrespect. "Get out!" she ordered Pedro, waving her hand toward the cabin door. The massive man grinned and left and she slammed the door on their inquisitive faces.

She turned back to Rory Helford and said in an awed voice, "You really are a pirate!"

He saw her eyeing the streak of white hair at his temple and grinned widely as he ran his fingers through his hair. "Have you ever seen a raven with a white feather in his wing?"

She answered, "Yes, often."

"It's caused by an injury. Same thing with this—it's an old scar, the hair grew in white."

"Is that how you lost your eye?" she asked curiously, showing no pity.

He laughed again. "I have both eyes. This patch is only temporary. Powder flashed in the pan when I shot my pistol last night."

"Aren't you afraid of hanging?" she asked.

He said grinning, "Hanging's only half an hour's pastime."

"So you're not afraid to die?" she demanded.

"I won't die. Heaven doesn't want me and hell's afraid I'll take over!"

"Does everything amuse you?" she asked with a sneer.

"Most things . . . females in breeches with beautiful breasts in particular," he teased.

"Oh!" she said, pretending outrage, then suddenly she realized his laughter was infectious and a bubble of laughter escaped her lips. "You are clearly a selfish, conceited, mannerless swine who does exactly as he pleases, and yet I like you. Why is that, Rory Helford?"

"Because there is no pretense between us. You can be yourself and swear your head off and strut about in your boots and I don't rebuke you. We could amuse each other, I think. How the hell did you come to marry my brother? Please don't expect me to believe you fell in love with him."

"Love him? I hate him, plague take the man. I own Roseland, next door to Helford Hall. At least I did own it until my rancid father mortgaged every cobweb. When your precious brother found out I wasn't the wealthy heiress he thought me, that temper he's famous for took control of him. He swore I'd not get a copper penny of precious Helford money and told me to get it myself."

Rory almost fell from his chair with amusement. "You needn't have hysterics," she told him hotly, "I have every intention of getting it myself."

"The reason I'm laughing so hard is the touchy subject of mortgages. I imagine it exacerbated Ruark's temper because it's taken him four long years to pay off the mortgages on Helford Hall. Everything was mortgaged in the Stuart cause, you see. It's so bloody rich . . . I wish I could have seen his face. He just gets one paid off and you hand him another on a silver platter!"

"He's rolling in money . . . the swine won eight thousand pounds from me not two weeks ago."

He cocked an amused eyebrow at her. "You need money and you were foolish enough to lose eight thousand to him? You're not a very good businesswoman, are you?"

"Hell and furies, yes I am! I'd like to do business with you."

"Why in hell's name would I want to do business with a woman?" He laughed.

"For profit, of course. I can do anything a man can do," she insisted.

He tried to keep the amusement from his face but failed utterly at her preposterous assertion. "I don't do business unless it's to my advantage," he said. His eyes traveled down her body and back up again as if he were assessing her for his own private use. He thought how pleasant it would be to free those pert breasts from that lace shirt and toy with her nipples until they stood out like the ruby studs she wore. He'd like to lay her on the floor and teach her how to kiss a man, whatever sort of struggle she offered.

"I can offer you storage for any cargo you bring in," she stated boldly.

"Up at the hall?" He grinned.

"No, at Roseland. I've a cave opens into my cellars," she boasted.

"So, my little hellcat, you're up to your pretty neck in smuggling . . . tell me how in Christ's name you manage to keep all this from the magistrate?"

"Death and damnation, I should have kept it from him, but I was foolish enough to confess my sins." She grinned sheepishly.

"And expected absolution?" He grinned.

She changed the subject. "I have some jewelry I'd like to sell."

"Rubies?" he asked.

"No! I'm particularly partial to rubies," she drawled. "I have diamonds, pearls, sapphires, lots of stuff. Will you buy them from me?"

His eyebrows went up at mention of so many jewels but he shook his head. "I told you I don't like doing business with women, they have no stomach for danger."

"Try me," she challenged.

He stood up for the first time and she noticed his movements had the easy appearing grace of an animal, lithe and quick, yet at the same time appearing unhurried.

"Jake," he called from the cabin door. A blond youth about her own age appeared and had the audacity to wink at her. "Fetch two bottles of champagne and a barrel of oysters," Rory directed. He came back into the cabin and circled his prey. "Have you ever had champagne?" he asked.

She tossed her long black tresses and lifted the corners of her mouth with conceit. "Of course. I had a whole cargo of the stuff in my cellars two months back," she boasted.

He looked amused. He drew two comfortable chairs up to a low round table, sat down, and put his feet up on it. "Make yourself comfortable," he invited, taking two Venetian crystal glasses from a cabinet at his elbow.

Jake brought the bottles of champagne in one hand and the barrel of oysters in the other. He plunked both down on the table between Rory and Cat and left, but not before he'd winked at her again.

With a little shock she realized that the oysters were raw. She'd eaten oysters before, of course, but they'd always been decently baked or fried. Raw oysters were a mass of slippery gray slime and just the thought of swallowing one made her queasy.

Rory Helford filled their goblets with champagne, pried off the lid on the barrel, and said, "Dig in." He took a knife from his belt and picked up an ugly crustacean. He was testing her! The son of a bitch was laughing at her.

With all the assurance in the world, she took out her knife, slipped it into the shell of the barnacled creature, and exposed it to the light of day. She eyed it with distaste, then with a bravado she did not feel, she lifted it to her lips and tipped it down her throat. For one awful moment her throat closed and refused to accept the obscenity, then it slid down with a plop and she quaffed the champagne to wash it down into her stomach. By God, she'd done it! But now of course, she had the whole disgusting thing to do over, all the while looking as if she was enjoying herself immensely. She matched him oyster for oyster and glass for glass. He watched her with admiration as he ate and drank with gusto. She was a rare beauty, what man could resist her? Certainly not Rory Helford, he decided. He refilled her glass again and again and noticed she swallowed more champagne than oysters.

They were laughing over a tiny crab that jumped off one of the oyster shells and scrambled across the table, when all of a sudden a look of horror crossed her face and Summer and the oysters parted company. She moaned in terrible distress as she retched and spewed forth oysters afloat in champagne.

Rory was on his feet instantly. He picked her up with the greatest tenderness in the world and took her through an adjoining door into his bedroom. "Cat, forgive me, sweetheart, I've made you ill." He laid her down upon his bed and brought fresh towels and water. He removed the offending shirt and washed her face, throat, and breasts with gentle hands.

She felt so ill, she thought she would die. He slipped off his own black shirt and put it on her, tenderly brushing her hair back from her face. "I'll leave you to rest," he murmured. "Close your eyes for half an hour and I'll come back to check on you."

She turned her face into the cool, silken cover and wished she could die. Miraculously, little by little she began to feel better. Within a half hour the extreme nausea had passed enough that she began to take notice of her surroundings. She lay upon a scarlet silk cover; above her was a flame-colored silk canopy that billowed and drifted about in the sea breeze from an open porthole. Red silk

panels were tied back at the moment, but she could see that when
the ties were undone and let down, the occupants of the bed would
be enclosed in a flame-colored world which was exotic in the extreme, more so because the silk was transparent and would not
completely hide whatever took place there. Red-lacquered Chinese
cabinets stood against walls paneled in light wood which gave off a
fragrance. Summer realized it must be sandalwood. The carpet was
like thick, black, plush velvet. Good God, she thought, it's fortunate I didn't spew all over this. Then she thought wickedly, I'll bet
that would have wiped the damned amusement from his face.

She groaned. Hell and furies, how was she going to face him
after she'd embarrassed herself so completely? She sat up as she
heard him at the door and he came in carrying a steaming bowl.
The last thing she wanted was food. Her lashes swept to her cheeks
in chagrin and she muttered low, "You don't expect me to ever eat
again, do you?"

He laughed and said, "I made it for you myself. It's broth . . .
here, I'll even feed you," he offered. He lifted the spoon to her lips.
She blushed hotly, but opened obediently and after three or four
mouthfuls actually began to feel better.

"I'm sorry, I've never so disgraced myself in front of a man
before," she said shyly.

"That's all right. I've never had a woman in my bed who I didn't
make love to before."

Her blush deepened.

"But I'm giving you fair warning, little hellcat, I'm going to
seduce you."

She swung her feet to the floor quickly.

He laughed. "Not now," he teased, "you have a decided miasma
about you."

"Oh, you brute!" she gasped.

He laughed with delight. "I thought we'd agreed to be brutally
honest with each other? Why else would I warn you I was going to
have you?"

"That would be adultery," she said repressively.

"Something I've been known to indulge in from time to time,"
he said, amused.

"But I won't!" she swore emphatically.

"Won't you?" he challenged lightly

"What about the jewels?" she said, dismissing the subject.

He opened her hand and dropped the ruby studs into her palm.

"Not these, the ones I want to sell."

He cocked an eyebrow at her. "I'll have to see them first, won't I?"

"Will you be here tomorrow?" she demanded.

"My whereabouts are my business. Perhaps I'll come to you. We can contact each other through Mr. Burke."

"Mr. Burke?" she asked in surprise.

"He's had a soft spot for me since I was a boy. Does that surprise you?"

"It shouldn't," she admitted. "He's been a good friend to me also. He must have a weakness for black sheep," she said, smiling.

He went to one of the cabinets and took out an exotic-looking bottle. "Let me give you a present." He grinned wickedly. "It will make you smell even better."

She took out the stopper and sniffed appreciatively.

"Frangipani," he said.

She accepted it with a smile.

28

T hat night her dreams were un-
believable. She blamed it on what she had eaten because she
wouldn't admit, even to herself, that Rory Helford attracted her.
One dream led into another and he was with her in all of them,
mocking, teasing, laughing, touching, kissing, but when their bodies finally joined, it was Ruark who made love to her.

She didn't fall into a deep, peaceful sleep until morning and so it
was after ten o'clock when she opened her eyes and slipped from
the bed. The first thing she did, even before she dressed, was go up
to the roof to see if the *Phantom* was still there. When she saw he
was gone, a feeling of disappointment swept over her. She told
herself the disappointment stemmed from not being able to sell the
jewels today and tried to force her mind to other things, other
people. But when she returned to her chamber, her eyes fell on his
shirt which she'd worn home, and with a blush upon her cheek, she
picked it up to sniff the sandalwood and male scent of it. Death
and damnation, what was it about these Helford men that had this
stunning physical effect upon her?

She realized that before Ruark she had been unaware,
unawakened, and he had introduced her to the mysteries of sex in
such a pleasurable way that now she had needs and longings and
some nights she burned with desire. Yet up until now no other man

had aroused any sort of romantic feelings in her except Ruark . . .
up until now . . .

She washed and ironed his black shirt herself, fingering the embroidered *R* upon the collar and wondering jealously who had
done it. She tucked it away in a drawer then spent the rest of the
day in a quandary, trying to decide if she should take all the jewels,
and if not, then which ones should she select?

That night when the curtains were drawn and the candles lit, she
took out each piece, laid it on the bed, and tried to put a price on it.
She knew he would offer less than she asked and tried to establish a
firm price for each piece below which she would absolutely refuse
to go. She had a pretty good idea that the diamond necklace was
worth the most. She decided to take no less than five hundred for
it. Altogether she hoped to get at least three thousand pounds, but
if he refused that much, then she was prepared to go as low as two.

The next morning there was still no sign of the ship and again
she felt a pang of disappointment. In the late afternoon Mr. Burke
brought her an invitation card. She picked it up with indifference
from the silver salver he produced, wondering which neighbor had
sent it. Her eyes opened wide in surprise. It was an invitation to
dine aboard the *Phantom*. She decided not to question how Mr.
Burke got it, for he never ever questioned her.

She tried to suppress a feeling of elation, but found it impossible.
Since he had sent what amounted to a formal invitation, she decided to dress formally. She felt a great compulsion to look beautiful and knew the reason why. Here was a man who made it clear
he found her attractive and she knew there was no point in denying
she felt that same attraction. Rory Helford's mission in life seemed
to be to amuse himself, so why shouldn't she do the same?

She bathed, perfumed between her breasts with frangipani, then,
because he wore black, she donned a black lace gown slit up the
skirt to show off an embroidered petticoat, except she left off the
petticoat. She needed the freedom to ride, and besides, she decided,
the gown worn this way had a delicious shock value she couldn't
resist. Since Rory Helford urged her to be herself, he might as well
know from the start she was a pagan.

She wore black silk stockings, and to complete her outfit she
wore the diamond necklace that had once belonged to the King's
mistress. She swept her hair up atop her head and fastened the
diamond shoe buckles among her curls. She even selected a tiny

black patch shaped like a diamond for one cheekbone. If he was expecting the hellcat in breeches, he was in for a surprise.

She tethered Ebony beneath the trees in the early-evening shadows and carefully picked her way to the edge of the river and up the long gangplank. His motley crew stared openmouthed at the fine lady who came aboard. She wore no mask, nor carried a fan; Cat had no patience tonight for such affectations. She did, however, bring the jewel case. She went straightaway to his cabin, knocked politely, and entered. The door to the inner room stood open and she could see partway into his exotic bedroom. When he came through the door, he was not in black, but wore a loose white djellaba and bare feet. His skin looked so dark against the white robe that he almost did not look like a white man. He had shaved his beard but not the mustache. The black patch was gone from his eye and the zigzag of white hair at his temple made a startling contrast.

He did not laugh at her tonight, but the mocking amusement was still in his eyes as they swept over her from head to foot and came to rest on her breasts. Of course he wasn't looking at her breasts, she told herself, he was looking at the diamonds.

The way he looked at her made her blood thicken and she could not dispel an image of him in his white robe sprawled across his flame-colored bed. He waved his arm toward a cabinet holding a vast array of bottles. "I won't force champagne upon you tonight, you may chose your own poison."

"I suppose it is most unsophisticated of me, but I like sweet red wine," she challenged.

He smiled. "Then you will like Madeira." He added, "I hope you like French cuisine?"

She nodded hesitantly.

"Escargot—snails?" he asked.

A look of horror came across her face and he relented immediately, his wonderful laugh rolling about the cabin. "Cat, I'm teasing you." He handed her a goblet and clinked it with his own. "Let's drink to a mutually enjoyable relationship." Her lashes swept to her cheeks, but she touched her lips to the wine, acknowledging the toast.

He smiled at her as she looked over the elegant table laid with damask linen and silver. "You choose. Will we do business first or dine?"

"Why don't I just open this jewel case so you can peruse the contents while we eat?" she suggested.

He glanced once at the jewels, then fixed his eyes upon her where they remained throughout the meal. "Are they presents from admirers?" he asked casually.

Her mouth curved into a wicked smile as she touched her neck. "These diamonds were a gift from the King!"

He frowned for the first time and she laughed. "Now I'm teasing. They were a gift to Barbara Castlemaine. I won them from her fair and square at the card table. Well, perhaps not exactly fair and square."

He found it amusing that she cheated at cards and she thought to herself, My God, why can't Ruark be like this?

His eyes never strayed from her to the jewel case and she began to feel nervous. He is pretending disinterest so I'll lower my price, she thought in a panic. But she was entirely wrong. He was all virile male and the vision before him lured him to taste her rose-colored lips. The frequent glimpse of legs clad in black silk stockings tempted him to part her skirt and run his hands over her thighs and then slip upward to caress her buttocks. But most of all he wanted to slide her gown from her shoulders to reveal the magnificent breasts he'd seen yesterday, and since that is what he wanted most, he decided that is what he would do.

"Do you like peaches?" he inquired.

"I don't know," she answered.

He took a silver fruit knife, peeled and quartered a succulent peach, then came around to her side of the table. He knelt down and held a piece of the fruit to her lips. She took it from his fingers, gingerly at first, in case she didn't like the taste, then more boldly as she found out how delicious the fruit was. With the juice still upon her lips he bent forward and covered her mouth with his.

Her mouth resisted instantly, but as he increased the firm pressure her mouth softened and yielded to the warm thrilling sensation. He lifted his mouth from hers only a fraction so he could murmur, "I wanted you to wear the frangipani for me."

Breathlessly she said, "I did wear it."

"I wanted you to wear *only* the frangipani for me." His hands slid from her shoulders down her arms and carried the black lace gown down with them. Her breasts sprang from the confines of the neckline and he rolled his eyes heavenward in delighted appreciation of her charms. He chuckled in his throat, "Hellcat Helford, you have the most beautifully impudent breasts in the whole world; they cry out to be kissed." Still kneeling before her, he put his hands beneath her armpits and pulled her down to him, then he laid her upon the rug and kissed her everywhere from her temples to her navel.

"Please . . . no . . . Rory . . ." she gasped, having no will to struggle as she lay in his arms.

"You need loving." It was a statement of fact. He unclasped her necklace.

"My diamonds," she gasped.

His mouth covered her throat where they had lain. "They are unworthy of you."

My God, what was it about this man that made her feel as if she was the most desirable, the most beautiful woman who ever breathed? "Rory, I can't," she protested.

"I just want to look at you," he soothed. His fingers unfastened the back of her gown and he took it from her slowly, inch by inch revealing her creamy flesh to his laughing eyes. She half believed that he would only look at her and go no further.

He took off her black silk stockings, telling her she was far more beautiful nude than adorned in silk and diamonds. Indeed, all he allowed her to keep on was the frangipani. He even pulled off the tiny black patch from her cheek.

He did nothing but look. His eyes caressed and made love to every pore of her body and she thought it the most intimate thing a man could ever do to a woman. She had a lot to learn. He sat back upon his heels and gazed at her body anew, then he stood and looked down upon her from his great height, studying her as if he wished to remember forever the picture she made. Then he reached down and drew her up to stand before him. He opened his robe and drew her inside.

"Rory!" she gasped as if his flesh had burned her. Indeed her skin was so sensitive at this moment she wanted to scream each time his body came in contact with hers. "Please cover yourself," she begged, "I cannot resist you and hate myself for it!"

He laughed and fastened his robe. "Don't hate yourself, sweet Cat. Take your pleasure where you find it—a man would."

"Oh, I know, Rory," she said breathlessly. "I'm just not ready to be unfaithful to my husband yet."

He laughed softly and carried her to his inner bedroom. He laid her tenderly inside the flame-colored cocoon, spread her hair upon the pillows, and gazed down at her. When he reached down to touch her, her body jumped and he knew she was nearly mad with the need for him. His hands began to explore her body intimately and he said low, "You are trembling with need, darling."

She moved her head from side to side and moaned her denial. Rory's eyes were stained almost black with passion. Since she would not let him make love to her with his body, he must do so with his mouth. She inflamed him with desire to the point where he felt enslaved. She was like a narcotic in his blood as he explored her slender body. He knew her breasts ached for his touch, and as his lips and tongue touched each rosebud she moaned in her throat at the exquisite pleasure he brought her. His mouth traveled over and over from breast to breast, then slowly traced down across her pretty belly until his mouth was buried in the black silken curls at the top of her thighs. He murmured against her hot center, "Beautiful, beautiful."

His words were like a love potion to her senses and she quivered with anticipation until his tongue touched her with exquisite torture. As he penetrated her with his burning tongue a sob of pleasure escaped and convulsively she reached for him, not knowing if she wished for much more or much less.

Rory gave her no choice in the matter. His tongue explored thoroughly all the secret delights of her womanhood. His strong hands slipped beneath her bottom and he lifted her closer to his mouth so that his tongue could thrust deep inside her hidden softness. Every nerve in her body was centered where his mouth plunged with such sensual enjoyment. She panted and thrashed as wave after wave of incredible pleasure crashed over her until she screamed. Her very center jumped, exploded, then melted, leaving her unable to lift her heavy eyelids even to look at him.

His body screamed for gratification, but his iron control would not allow him to ravish her. Soon enough she would consent to all his needs. She was well worth waiting for. She drifted off to a warm, magic place as if surrounded and protected by flame-colored swirling smoke. She knew not if it was paradise, heaven, or hell and she cared less.

When she awoke much later, she was wrapped in his white robe. Her black gown and stockings were neatly laid beside her with a note which simply said, "I will bring you ten thousand pounds. R.H."

The blush would never leave her face again, she thought hotly as she remembered what he had done to her. True, she had not committed adultery, but what he had done seemed ten times more intimate than coitus.

She put on her clothes quickly, grateful that his laughing eyes were not there to see inside her very soul. The ship was dark and silent as if all slept. She crept off the *Phantom* and found Ebony beneath the dark shadows of the trees.

Her conscience and her dreams were filled with unrest, and when she awoke early the next morning, she was angrier with herself than she had ever been in her life. She had come away from the pirate without jewels or money or clear conscience and she was consumed by an impotent rage that he had taken such complete advantage of her. She took out her pistol and weighed it in her hand. She would go down immediately and demand the return of her jewels. If he did not comply, she would shoot him!

She ran up to the roof and eagerly scanned the river, but the *Phantom* was long gone. Her body demanded action. She rode Ebony with wild abandon, then she stopped at Roseland and on hands and knees weeded the whole vegetable and herb garden. By the time she was finished, she was hot and dirty, but she was not tired, nor had her anger at herself dissipated.

She began to worry about her brother, even though she told herself repeatedly he could not go to London and back in under ten days. When her mind strayed to thoughts of her husband and his safety, it made her angrier than ever. It was absolutely no skin off her bottom if the King had sent him into danger. What in the name of hellfire did she care? He was going to rid himself of her and she would no longer be Lady Helford. But if he made her a widow, she would be Lady Helford forever. A solitary tear rolled down her cheek at the thought of harm coming to him and she dashed it away angrily with muddy fingers, leaving her face streaked and woebegone looking.

She climbed down the cliff to the beach, stripped, and swam out about three hundred yards. How nice it would be to relax and just let herself drift away, then all her problems would be solved. Suddenly she was slapped in the face by a small wave. She swallowed a great gulp of salt water and gasped and spluttered for a few frantic minutes. A bit of a squall had come up suddenly and she had to stroke out strongly for shore. As she swam her determination hardened. She would survive her money troubles and her marital troubles. A woman's lot in this world was by nature much harder than a man's. She would use any means to beat them at their own game.

The Helfords had certainly taken what they wanted from her, so she would do the same with an untroubled conscience, and if by chance she couldn't get what she needed from the Helfords, why then there was always the King, a pushover for a pretty smile and a pretty pair of legs.

29

B efore Summer got into bed she slipped to her knees and prayed to St. Jude, the patron saint of hopeless causes. She was not in the habit of bothering God and His apostles over everyday problems but she felt desperate. She feared that Black Jack Flash and her jewels were forever out of her reach, and if she listened carefully, the sound of his laughter could be heard mocking her gullibility.

She sighed hopelessly and climbed into her lonely bed, hoping she would not have to again don the highwayman's costume and take to the road. No sooner was she asleep than she dreamed of Ruark. He came to her as a supplicant, begging her forgiveness. He told her how very proud he had been of her efforts to entertain the King and the court. He confessed how he really felt about her, how much he had longed for her and missed her. He told her how deeply he loved her and how he could not live without her.

She was in an agony of remorse. She was covered with guilt over his brother Rory and longed to confess all to her husband Ruark and be forgiven. But she knew exactly what would happen if she confided in him. His temper would flare out of control. He would do and say the most horrendous things to her and probably beat her to a jelly. She knew she loved Ruark and wanted him more than anything in the world, so she decided to keep her guilty secret. She suddenly felt him slip into bed with her and take her into his arms. She knew she had awakened from her dreams because this was better than any dream could ever be. His lips were against her ear, whispering, "Did you miss me?"

"Oh, yes, I was afraid something terrible might happen to you." Her arms twined about his neck and she lifted her mouth for his kisses. She clung to him possessively, her hands feeling the splendid muscles in his shoulders. "I was dreaming about you. I dreamed you came back to me and like magic you did."

His hands were sure on her breasts, her whole body, knowing all the secret places she longed to be touched, and she knew that no feeling on earth compared to his touch. He was so very tall that she could not kiss him and capture his shaft between her legs at the same time. She moved down his body until her cheek rested against the dark pelt of his chest and her tongue flicked out to taste his hard nipples. She arched her mons against him and immediately he nudged her thighs apart and thrust into her until she was filled with his hot, hard shaft.

Her hands caressed his broad back then slipped down to his buttocks. He rolled with her from their sides until his hard length was on top of her and she felt the muscles of his body grow taut as he gathered the power of his body to fulfill its purpose. "Ruark, I love you so much," she moaned against his chest.

"Cat, sweetheart, it's Rory," he said in a low, intense voice.

Her body contracted upon his so violently at his words that he cried out in a convulsive explosion and without any control over her own body she exploded the moment she felt his hot seed start. In the darkness her fingers trembled as they touched his face; she sought confirmation of his identity by running her fingers through his hair to search for the scar. The fine jagged line was barely perceptible, hidden beneath his long hair, but it confirmed her worst fears. "Rory, my God, what have you done?" she cried.

"Fallen in love," he murmured hoarsely, gathering her to him possessively. She hit out at him and struggled to light the candles.

She stared at him unbelievingly as he sat naked in the bed. "I thought I'd never see you again."

His laughing eyes caressed her face. "You knew the other night I hadn't finished what I'd begun. I'm not nearly finished with you." His gaze dropped to her breasts and he rolled his eyes heavenward as if giving thanks to the gods for such perfect wonders. He was the world's most outrageous man and she longed to laugh with him.

Amazingly she discovered she could not hate this man. He was a totally unscrupulous rogue, but every woman should be loved by a rogue at least once in her lifetime. All her anger was directed toward her husband, Ruark. Why hadn't he come to her? Why wasn't it he who had crept into her bed to make such passionate love to her? She threw on her bed gown and handed him his breeches. "You have just seduced me and you're not even sorry for what you have done!"

"Sorry? For making you purr, for making your body sing? I thought we agreed to be honest with each other . . . go on, tell me honestly that you are sorry."

"I'm sorry I ever met you . . . I'm sorry I ever met anyone named Helford!"

He drew on his pants with great amusement. "Are you? Shall I keep the ten thousand pounds I brought you?"

"Surely the jewels aren't worth that much?" she asked.

"Sweetheart, that's not the point. You need ten thousand. If you asked me for fifty thousand, I'd get it for you," he said simply.

"Oh, Rory." She bit her lip, wondering why she wanted to cry. "You can use the cellars at Roseland for cargo any time you have to," she offered.

"That's most generous of you, Cat." He sat down in a comfortable chair by the open window and stretched out his long legs. "Did you know the Dutch port of Stasia takes in a million pounds a year for warehouse space? The cargoes in these trading ports are beyond your wildest dreams," he told her.

"You sail into Dutch ports?" she asked doubtfully.

He grinned. "I don't fly the Union Jack, darling. My crew are all foreign, they come from every country in the world. The *Phantom* slips in and out virtually unnoticed, wherever she can make a profit."

"What kind of cargo do you carry?" she asked curiously.

He laughed. "Not always what you might expect. Sometimes my cargo is human."

She puzzled on his words for a moment, then realized he smuggled spies. The question was, did he smuggle people in and out of Holland or in and out of England? She dared not ask.

Suddenly he stood up and took her hands. "Come with me, Cat. Sail with me across to the continent. I'll show you exotic places you never dreamed possible . . . warehouses piled with treasures from the East Indies . . . sun-drenched coasts with miles of white, surgary sand where we could swim naked."

For one breathtaking moment she was tempted. "It's not possible, Rory." She hesitated a moment. "There's something I haven't told you . . . Ruark said he was going to have our marriage annulled."

He threw back his head and laughed. His neck columns stood out strong and brown and his white teeth flashed in his face. "If he is mad enough to release you, you're mine," he claimed with authority. Then his head dipped and his mouth claimed hers in a demanding, sensual kiss that showed her exactly how susceptible she was to him. His lips traced a fiery path to her ear. "You will sail with me; it's inevitable. You'll love me, too," he added with amusement. "In fact, I think you already do," he added outrageously.

"My windows and doors will be locked from now on," she warned him.

"It's your heart you had better lock." He winked and then he was gone, over her balcony.

What in the name of God was the matter with her? She had just committed one of the most unpardonable sins a woman could ever commit. The guilt washed over her in waves. The trouble was that while Rory was close, she was under his spell, then when he left, she came to her senses and the realization of their sinful intimacy overwhelmed her. She prayed for forgiveness and swore an oath that she would never be intimate with him again. If her husband had their marriage annulled, then it would be another matter and she might someday consider accepting Rory's love, but for the present she had to make him understand that nothing further must happen between them. She couldn't change the past, but she must take responsibility for the future.

At dawn she rode Ebony along the Helford River but there was no sign that any ship had ever been moored there. She spent long hours riding the beach each day and it was there she heard Spider call to her from the cliffs of Roseland. She had never been so glad to see anyone in her life. Her happiness was extremely short-lived, however, as her brother imparted his news. "I'm sorry, Cat, I was too late. When Auntie Lil took me to see Solomon Storm, he told me he had already sold the mortgage on Roseland. He wouldn't take the money, of course—he explained it would be up to the new owner whether he would redeem it for the twenty thousand owed or whether he would choose to keep Roseland. He warned me that the man would be a fool if he didn't keep the estate. He gave me this sealed letter for you. I didn't open it, though I was tempted."

She took the letter and swore a blue streak. "Damn, blast, and set fire to it all!"

"Cat, it's no good venting your spleen on me. We missed the due date on the loan. Solomon Storm showed me the papers Father signed and the ones you signed for the extra two thousand. He was within his legal rights to do so and I'm pretty sure we have no recourse."

"Damn, damn, damn," she cried. "I was absolutely counting on us owning Roseland, then I could tell his high-and-mightiness where he could stick Helford Hall! Oh, Spider, I have so much to tell you. I met Black Jack Flash . . . you're never going to believe this, he's Lord Helford's younger brother."

"The magistrate's brother is a pirate?" he asked in disbelief.

"Yes, it's true, honest to God. He's absolutely nothing whatsoever like Ruark. He's so easygoing, I swear he never stops laughing. He lives life exactly as he chooses and thumbs his nose at the entire world. You'll just love him," she promised.

Spider looked at her shrewdly. "Well, it sounds like you do, at any rate!"

Summer blushed uncontrollably. "Wait until you see him. His hair is streaked with a zigzag of silvery white at the temple. That's where the name Black Jack Flash came from. He's larger than life, he only wears dramatic black or white and his bed is hung with red silk panels . . ." Her voice trailed off as Spider's eyebrows went up.

"You've already shared his bed, haven't you, Cat?"

She ignored the question as they went in through the front door of Roseland. The scent of the climbing flowers above the entrance and the pearl gray doves perched cooing softly on the slanted roof brought a lump into her throat. She sat down on a faded sofa and broke the wax seals.

To Lady Summer St. Catherine:
On July 7 when your mortgage became overdue I sold it to Lord Ruark Helford of Cornwall. Please find enclosed a note from that worthy gentleman regarding instructions.
                                        Solomon Storm

As she read the name Helford her face drained of color. She tore open the note from her husband and read the following:

I took a notion to acquire Roseland for the twenty thousand pounds owing on the property. I plan to do some necessary renovations and will allow you to remain at Helford Hall until such time as the annulment is finalized. After that I will allow you and your brother to live at Roseland, even though this property is now legally mine.

RH

"That bastard!" she screamed.

"Who, Storm?" asked Spider.

"No! Lord bloody-rotten Helford. That's who bought the mortgage. My God, he couldn't get to London fast enough . . . he left here July sixth and paid off the mortgage on July seventh." She almost choked. "Read that! He will *allow* me to stay at Helford Hall until the annulment. *Allow* me! The whoreson will then *allow* us both to live at Roseland. Over my dead body will he *allow* me to do anything. I'll get Rory to help us."

There was a sharp rapping upon the front door that made her jump out of her skin. She opened the door angrily and looked straight into the face of the hated Sergeant Oswald. A militiaman stood respectfully behind him.

"What do you want?" she demanded.

"I'm here to question Spencer St. Catherine in regard to a robbery. The last time he was arrested he gave his name as Spider Brown but I've since learned the young felon is your brother."

"A robbery? That's preposterous, my brother has just returned from London. What's all this about, Sergeant?" she demanded in her most repressive voice.

"On the night of July sixth there was a complaint lodged by two very high-placed ladies, namely the Duchess of Buckingham and the Countess of Lauderdale, that they were robbed near here by a highwayman calling himself the Black Cat. I am certain the Black Cat is young St. Catherine," said Oswald with satisfaction.

"Sergeant Oswald, you are a very tiresome man. My husband, Lord Helford, warned you about harassing me, I believe."

"I know you're Helford's whore, but I doubt very much if you're Helford's wife." He sneered. "Your brother left a ship in Falmouth this morning and came straight here. I intend to search him for stolen money."

"As a matter of fact, Oswald, I happen to be both whore and wife, and when my husband learns of the way you just spoke to me, you will not only be court-martialed, but he'll probably order you flogged. As I told you once before, Sergeant, come back when you have a warrant."

Oswald smiled slyly. "As a matter of fact I have a warrant right here, signed by none other than Lord Helford, High Magistrate of Cornwall, to seize and search any person suspected of committing crimes of robbery or smuggling."

Summer snatched it from his hand and read in disbelief the undeniable signature of Lord Ruark Helford, Magistrate.

With obvious satisfaction Oswald stepped inside Roseland and ordered the militiaman to search young St. Catherine. Summer stood by in helpless humiliation as they manhandled her young brother and stripped him. Naturally they discovered the money belt containing the ten thousand pounds.

"That is *my* money, Sergeant Oswald. My brother, *Lord Spencer,* took it to London to pay off mortgages on our property," she explained reluctantly.

He sneered at her. "Then why didn't he do so? Your explanation is contrived horseshit, excuse my language, *Lord and Lady St. Catherine.*"

"I am Lady Helford!" she insisted.

"And I'm the Duke of Buckingham." Oswald laughed. "Come on, you young swine, I'm taking you in for questioning."

"You cannot arrest him; he's done nothing!" said Summer, blocking the doorway angrily.

Oswald smirked. "I'm not arresting him. I'm only taking him in for questioning. If he's done nothing, he'll be released, won't he?" He picked up the money belt.

"You can't take my money!" protested Summer desperately.

"Can't I? Who's going to stop me?"

"Sergeant Oswald, at the very least I want a receipt from you for the ten thousand pounds. You are a man of the law, and if we must abide by it, so must you, sir." Her eyes narrowed with hatred. "If I do not get a receipt from you, I shall tell Lord Helford that you tried to rape me."

"You forget I have a witness, you little bitch."

"And who do you think Lord Helford will believe, Sergeant?

You haven't the faintest idea just how much of a bitch I can be, if I set my mind to it."

Reluctantly he scribbled her a receipt for the money. Summer was prepared to go into Falmouth with her brother until Spider said to her, "It's all right, Cat, I'll let them take me in for questioning. If I'm not released by tomorrow, then you can come and pull the bloody prison down stone by stone."

Finally she agreed. She would go to Helford Hall immediately and see if Mr. Burke knew where Lord Helford was. Failing that, she would ask him to contact Rory for her.

30

Mr. Burke could not hide the fact that he was shocked over the way Sergeant Oswald had treated her. "Ruark is supposed to be home tomorrow, my lady, but whether it will be before nightfall I cannot say. If he does not come, I will consider it my duty to accompany you to Falmouth and vouch for the fact that you are indeed Lady Helford and we will demand your brother's release," he said. "Young Lord St. Catherine must be charged with a crime and stand trial before he can be imprisoned for any length of time. Once Ruark returns, he will put everything right. He may have a temper, but he is absolutely fair and impartial where the King's laws of England are concerned."

He scrutinized her closely, noting the purple shadows beneath her eyes. "Have you had anything to eat yet today? Then I suggest you go into the garden by the fountain and enjoy the sunset. Water has a very tranquil effect, so I'm told. I'll bring you a tray and some good strong cider."

Summer smiled her thanks. Mr. Burke was a rare treasure. He was like the father she had never had. No wonder he held a special place in the hearts of both Ruark and Rory. After she had eaten, she pulled out the letter from her husband and reread it. It was the most infuriating missive she had ever read. It was as if he had taken pleasure in selecting phrases which would flay her temper. One thing was certain, she must get the ten thousand back from Oswald, and together with the ten thousand Rory had given her she would offer it to Ruark in return for Roseland. She must make him understand that when she was no longer Lady Helford, she must have total independence. Surely a man who needed to be in control as much as Lord Helford would understand her needs. The words of an old Chinese proverb kept running through her mind: "Under another's eaves you have to bend your head." That would be intolerable to Summer.

She did not retire to her room until long after dark and even then did not undress and get into bed. Instead she sat by her open balcony window expecting the impudent face of Spider to appear over its edge any moment. She awoke with a start to realize she had been in the chair all night. She rode over to Roseland, hoping Spider was there, but in her bones she knew she would not see him. With a heavy heart she went back to the hall to seek out Mr. Burke.

"I'll order the carriage and the coachman will drive us to Falmouth. We'll take two liveried footmen and you must choose one of the maids to be your attendant. I think you should put on your most expensive gown and leave them in no doubt at all that Lady Helford is paying them a visit."

"You're right, of course, Mr. Burke. Tell Daisy I shall need hot water for a bath." Since the morning was on the cool side, she decided to wear the cream velvet walking suit with braided black frogs. She carefully took the high-crowned hat with its saucy black ostrich feather from its box, along with the black kid gloves, vizard mask, and enameled fan. As a last touch she clasped her ruby bracelets over the long black kid gloves and surveyed the result in her mirror. There! With a touch of lip rouge she'd be able to order even the pope about, not to mention some red-faced sergeant with a taste for vengeance in his pea-sized brain.

When she emerged from Helford Hall, the carriage, Mr. Burke, and the attendant servants were awaiting her ladyship's convenience. For one moment Mr. Burke felt sorry for the unfortunate Sergeant Oswald, for he was surely about to reap the whirlwind.

The large black carriage rolled up to the door of the Falmouth prison and the liveried footmen jumped down and opened the carriage door for Lady Helford. News of Summer's arrival reached Sergeant Oswald long before she strolled in to the guardroom with her servants in tow. She moved with the assurance of a prideful Siamese cat, and when he saw her, Sergeant Oswald knew a terrible moment of disquiet.

She raised her voice when she saw him and hailed him from across the room as if he were the meanest lackey. In a voice as richly plummy as Lil Richwood's she drawled, "Sergeant, I believe you've held Lord St. Catherine for questioning just a little too long. I'm here to see that any charges are dropped and I've come to escort him home. Oh, and Sergeant Oswald, you will be sharp about it, won't you?"

Actually Oswald's face lost some of its ruddy color. The woman would hardly walk in claiming to be Lady Helford when Lord Helford had arrived only moments before. When he hesitated, and seemed at a loss, Summer gave him an order. "Release my brother, Sergeant Oswald."

"I can't," he said lamely, "he's gone."

"You mean you have released him?" she questioned.

"No. Last night he was transferred to a more secure prison . . . because of his escaping last time . . . I thought . . . that is, it was decided to move him."

Her eyes narrowed. "To where, Sergeant Oswald?" Her voice had gone deadly quiet.

"Newgate," he mumbled.

For a moment Summer didn't quite understand. "Newgate? You don't mean Newgate in London?"

Oswald nodded, grim-lipped.

Summer began to scream. A red mist formed before her eyes and she was fast losing control of herself in hysterics. Mr. Burke tried to soothe her, but knowing the horror that was Newgate, he doubted he would be able to comfort her.

An authoritative voice demanded, "What the hell is going on down here?" Ruark Helford descended the stairs from an upper floor of the prison.

Summer looked up in disbelief. His face was tanned from being at sea somewhere, but the uniform cut of the navy blue coat and the severely clubbed-back dark hair emphasized his ironclad authority.

"You swine! If this is your doing, you bastard, I swear I'll get my pistol and shoot you!"

"Must I remind you, Summer, that you are supposed to be a lady?" he demanded in a voice cold as steel.

"No, Sergeant Oswald told me last night what I was . . . your whore I believe was his exact word. Would you mind telling him once and for all that I am also your wife?"

"This is indeed Lady Helford, Sergeant, though for how long is a moot point," he said between clenched teeth. "Would someone enlighten me about what is going on here?"

Summer took a deep shuddering breath. "Allow me to enlighten you. This pig arrested my brother and stole ten thousand pounds from me."

"Your brother's been arrested again? Christ Almighty, what are you two up to now?" he demanded furiously.

With narrowed eyes and bared teeth she said in a dangerously quiet voice, "My brother took the money to London to discharge the mortgage on Roseland, but discovered some scheming bastard had bought the place out behind our backs. This bastard has magnanimously offered to *allow* me to live at Helford Hall until my marriage is annulled and thereafter will *allow* me to reside at Roseland. To top off everything this bastard's lackey has shipped my young brother off to Newgate."

Mr. Burke stood staunchly beside Summer with a condemning look upon his face.

"Newgate?" asked Ruark with disbelief. "There's been some mistake. Though I have no jurisdiction in London, I'll look into it and rectify matters."

"You, sir, have done enough. I neither want your help nor need it! Charles is a personal friend of mine. What the hell do I need a lord for when I can get favors from a king?"

They glared into each other's eyes with unconcealed hatred. She knew she had wounded him with her last words. He knew a strong urge to flog her and fuck her, and if they'd been at home, he would have done both.

She raised her vizard to her eyes and said to Oswald, "My ten thousand pounds, Sergeant . . . please don't expect me to believe you sent that to Newgate."

Ruark glared at him furiously and he took an involuntary step backward. Then he unlocked a drawer and produced the money belt. Mr. Burke took it from Oswald and Summer turned upon her heel and swept out. In her ears, as she left, her husband's deadly voice ordered, "Sergeant Oswald; in my office!"

Summer threw herself into the vigorous activity of packing everything she and her brother owned both at Helford Hall and

Roseland. She realized she must seek Rory Helford's assistance
and asked Mr. Burke if once again he would contact Black Jack
Flash. When she had seen to every last detail, and not before, she
threw herself full length upon the bed and sobbed her heart out.
Her nerves were at breaking point. She was worried sick for Spider,
incarcerated in the bowels of Newgate, surrounded by horrors she
could only imagine.

She cried bitter tears for her lost love. She had been so much in
love with Ruark Helford she had allowed him to become her whole
world, her whole reason for being. That love had been shattered
into so many pieces she knew it could never be restored. Each
encounter with him now deteriorated from bad to worse. She
swore never to see him again. And she was being forced to leave
her beloved and familiar Roseland. Even Cornwall was to be left
behind as she moved forward to make a new life for herself in
London.

She was not naive enough to think a pirate would take her to
London without her having to pay a price, but she must look on
the bright side. Rory was a magnificent lover and he treated her
with tender concern. She was willing to pay the price if he insisted.
She was not quite so willing to pay King Charles's price. She hoped
she could offer something else of value to him in return for the
release of Spider, but in the end, if there was no other alternative,
she knew she would pay any price to save her beloved brother.

She became impatient with herself. Whatever was the matter
with her, shedding tears over a man who simply wasn't worth it?
She had twenty thousand pounds to spend as she pleased and she
would again enjoy the witty company of Auntie Lil. What more
could she ask? She knew if she was to survive, she must not let
herself keep reliving the past. She must wear it like a loose garment, take it off, and let it drop.

Every hour of the day found her climbing to the widow's walk to
see if she could glimpse the *Phantom*, but each time she was disappointed. Perhaps he wouldn't come to her rescue, perhaps now
that he had had his way with her he would discard her as his
brother had.

She came down from the widow's walk around midnight. She
hadn't expected to see the ship in the dark, but the smallest light in
its rigging would have been visible. She closed the French doors
which led out to the small balcony and with a troubled heart began
to undress for bed. A light tapping on the windowpane set her

heart thudding. She threw on her red velvet bed gown and prayed that somehow Spider had managed to again escape.

The tall, black-clad figure of Rory Helford stepped into her bed-chamber, the streak of white hair at his temple identifying him immediately even in the dim light.

"Oh, Rory, I've been watching for you all day. I had given up hope."

He grinned at her. "I do my very best work under cover of night."

"Rory, I have no one else to turn to. Will you take me to London?"

He laughed with delight, lifted her in his arms, and swung her about. "At our last meeting I told you it was inevitable that you would sail with me." His teeth nipped her ear and he whispered, "Can't I persuade you to sail to the Baltic Sea or the sunny Mediterranean?"

As she kicked, her bed gown fell open to reveal her lovely slim legs. "Put me down this instant, Rory. I have to get to London because my young brother has been sent to Newgate Prison."

He suddenly noticed all her baggage stacked and waiting.

"Oh, everything is in such a bloody, rotten mess," she wailed. "I sent my brother Spencer to London to pay off the mortgage, but it seems your brother was one step ahead of us. He acquired our property for himself. When my brother returned by ship to Falmouth, he was followed to Roseland. My husband commands a swine called Oswald. When he stripped and searched my brother, he naturally found the money on him. He swore he was just taking him in for questioning, but when he didn't return, I went to Falmouth and discovered they'd sent him to Newgate. Ruark was actually there in Falmouth. How could he have let it happen? I would have trusted him with my life once. How could I possibly be such a poor judge of character?"

Reluctantly Rory set her on her own two feet. "You have no trouble reading me like a book."

"What do you mean?" she asked.

He indicated the mountain of luggage. "You were very sure I would come for you, my beauty."

"No, to be truthful I thought you too had loved me and left me."

"Cat, my darling, if you think our brief encounters can be called loving, you have an awful lot to learn."

His outrageous words did wicked things to her body as she remembered the delicious forbidden wild feelings his mouth on her body had evoked. "Rory, I swore I wouldn't commit further sins with you," she cried.

His mouth curved into a hungry, sensual smile. "Then you'll have to unswear it, won't you? You'll have to come now under cover of darkness, but we won't sail until the morning tide. . . ." His voice trailed away; implicit in what he said was what would happen between.

"You intend to take me like a piece of pirate booty, don't you?" she demanded.

He was so tall she had to tip her head back to look up at him. In that moment he was the most wickedly desirable man she had ever seen. He reached out and took her shoulders between his powerful hands, but held her at arm's length so he could look deeply into her eyes. "Cat, don't be a hypocrite. Whenever we are within a hundred yards of each other, our bodies scream with desire. You know that if you put out your fingers to touch me, I am hard as marble . . . and I know if I put out my fingers to touch you I would find you wet and hot for me. We are two of a kind . . . made for each other. We fit together perfectly, magically, as a sheath fits the sword for which it was designed."

He lowered his head and took her mouth. It was an act of dominance and submission, each exulting in their chosen role. "Let there always be truth between us," he murmured against her lips.

"I'm finished with Ruark," she admitted.

"I love you, Cat," he vowed.

31

"I'll carry everything outside
and send two of my crew for your trunks. Are you ready?" he
asked her quizzically.

She threw her gray cloak over her bed gown, picked up the jewel
case which always held her rubies, and nodded.

"Most women wouldn't give up Helford Hall and a title so easily. It seems you're ready to leave without a backward glance."

"Things aren't important to me, Rory. It's people who matter.
I'll miss Ebony, but he and the pony will be well taken care of in
the Helford stables."

Much to her surprise, Mr. Burke appeared to help Rory carry
her trunks outside. She shook his hand warmly and thanked him
for everything he'd done for her, then she bade him goodbye.

"It's not goodbye, my lady, it's only *au revoir*. May the road rise
with you, and the wind be ever at your back, and may the Lord
hold you in the hollow of his hand."

The *Phantom* was not hidden up the Helford River but rode the
low tide off the beach below the hall. When they were safely
aboard, he looked down at her and said, "You know your way to
my cabin."

She hesitated for one or two heartbeats. Rory Helford wasn't asking. It was his ship and he was the master. If she went along to his cabin now, she was giving her consent to everything that would happen between them this night. She took a deep breath and with deliberation moved along the companionway to the cabin of Black Jack Flash. She stayed in the outer cabin, for at this moment she didn't think she could face the scarlet silk bed.

Rory Helford was so much more relaxed and informal than his brother Ruark. One or two of his belongings were left about negligently and this quality endeared him to her. Lord Helford was so damned rigid about everything, no wonder he couldn't allow her to bend the rules. She picked up a black leather vest and took it to the wardrobe. When she opened its door, she saw again that every article of clothing he owned was either black or white. Of course it was done on purpose, for dramatic effect. The streak of white hair against his shoulder-length black curls made an impact on her every time she saw him; the clothes would be an added contrast.

When she finally heard his light step outside the cabin door, she knew a moment of panic. He threw open the door. His tall body filled the frame. He looked at her tenderly and held out his strong hand. Slowly, trustfully, she placed her hand in his and to her great surprise he did not lead her to bed, but drew her close to his side and led her up on deck.

They walked to the rail in companionable silence. The stars were like diamonds scattered across black velvet. The breeze lifted and teased their hair and made the ship creak and groan softly as the water slapped against the hull. It was such an exquisitely beautiful night that it brought a lump to her throat. She turned to face Rory and said, "I'm so very afraid for Spider."

"I know," he said softly. He gathered her in his arms and she buried her face in his big shoulder. "I won't lie to you, love, Newgate isn't like Sunday school. Some parts are better than others, of course, so it all depends where he's lodged. One good thing about it, though, you'll be able to visit him and give him some money. Believe me, the place isn't run for charity and you have to pay a garnish for anything and everything. I only wish I could take care of it all for you, but I'm not supposed to be in London, I'm afraid, I'm supposed to be in Holland."

"I'll go to the King," she swore.

"Sweetheart, I'm certain Charles will help you, his weakness is pretty women, but remember he owes the Helfords much. Don't give him more than you want to, whatever that may be," he advised.

"Thank you for your good advice," she murmured wearily.

"Cat, I don't have to warn you about London, do I? You've been there before? I know you've more guts than a slaughterhouse, but the city and its inhabitants are both filthy and debauched and it's not just its whores who are peppered with disease; half the nobility at Court is rotten with it."

"You don't need to warn me of its wickedness," she assured him.

He grinned. "It's not wicked. You and I are wicked. It's evil. There's quite a difference."

"I'll be careful," she promised him.

"I'll come to see you at Lil Richwood's as soon as I return from Holland." He took her hand. "Come, let me take you to bed now, love. We can talk in bed."

Cynically she thought that was just one of the things men said to get you between the covers. "How long until we sail?"

"We'll go out on the flood. Three more hours."

She let him lead her down to his cabin. My God, the way Rory Helford made love, he could make three hours feel like three days . . . and nights!

The bedroom was as dramatic as Black Jack Flash himself. Her feet sank into the thick pile of the black carpet, which came up between her bare toes. Her red bedrobe made her look as if she belonged in this exotic stateroom. She watched Rory casually disrobe and prop the red silk pillows up for them to lounge against. His body was magnificent, with a splended breadth through his chest and shoulders. His whole torso was bronzed from exposure and his flesh had a smooth, hard surface. He patted the place beside him and she blushed as she undid the buttons of her bed gown.

The moment she let it slip to uncover her breasts his eyes rolled to the ceiling as if he had just entered a state of bliss. She giggled. "Rory, you do that just to make me laugh."

"And it works every time." He smiled.

She felt shy as she slipped into bed with him, but he gathered her up and sat her between his spread legs. He stroked her hair and his beautiful voice murmured in her ear. She couldn't believe it, he really did want to talk.

"Cat darling, the very heart of every binding relationship between a man and a woman is sexual, but I want us to have more than that. I'll give you all the love and laughter you can handle, but there are other things I can give you. You need my understanding, my friendship; you need my money, my strength; but most of all, right now you need my protectiveness. Tonight, more than anything else in the world, you need to be held."

She leaned back against his powerful strength and closed her eyes. She thought, Oh, God, Rory Helford, I could love you so easily.

He murmured against her hair, "I won't always be able to be there for you, though I would wish it otherwise, but tonight I *am* here for you. I'll listen if you want to talk, I'll be your rock if you just want to lean on me . . . and if you want me to blot out everything, I'll give you a loving that will render you mindless."

During the course of the next three hours he did all three. She fell asleep in Rory's strong arms and never felt him quit the bed to go up on deck. For the first time in weeks she slept peacefully without the disturbing nightmares.

When she opened her eyes at dawn, however, and tried to arise, she fell back with a groan. Nausea had swept over her the moment she had tried to sit up. She prayed that the seasickness would pass. She'd never live down the embarrassment of fouling his cabin again. She moaned softly as Rory entered the room carrying a breakfast tray for her. "Oh, Lord, you'll have to take that food away if you don't want to see me disgrace myself again."

He set the tray down outside the door and came back to the bed. He gently brushed back her tumbling curls and grinned. "A pirate's woman can't suffer mal de mer, 'tis unfitting."

"I'm usually a very good sailor," she said weakly.

He lifted her feet back into the bed and covered her tenderly. "Lie back until it passes. We are in no hurry. I have to arrive at the London Pool in the middle of the night then leave immediately. I never anchor there—'tis too much of a trap. I'll go and get you some dry biscuit and a little dry red wine."

Inconsequently she said, "Your eyes are as green as emeralds."

He shook his head. "They're really hazel like yours; it's the sea that turns them green. On land they are quite brown and nondescript."

"Rory Helford, there is absolutely nothing nondescript about you; you display like a peacock." The nausea returned and she closed her eyes in misery. As he shut the cabin door a fleeting thought came to her which she adamantly denied to herself. Of one thing she was absolutely certain, *she was not with child!*

Later in the afternoon when she felt better, she strolled up on deck to get the fresh, exhilarating sea breeze. She watched Rory covertly. He was such a handsome devil. He laughed with his crew, tossing gibes back and forth, and yet she knew that in a fight he would be a deadly, dangerous opponent. Beneath the devil-may-care attitude was the strength of coiled steel and she would bet her last crown he had a keen, cool, convoluted mind. One equally capable of dabbling in intrigue, setting traps, or plotting the downfall of an enemy. Spying would be child's play to Rory Helford.

She remembered the King had hinted that her husband went on spy missions. Could it be that the two brothers worked for opposite sides? She shuddered slightly. Her blood always raced with excitement at the mere hint of danger.

Rory caught sight of her and smiled lazily. He beckoned her to his side, where he stood braced at the ship's wheel. She couldn't help comparing his attitude to Ruark's. He would have ordered her below the moment she set foot on his deck. Rory, however, didn't give a damn if his sailors leered at her. Slowly she made her way to the bridge. Rory was naked to the waist, enjoying the feel of the sun and the sea spray on his bronzed skin. "Feeling better, sweetheart? Come, I'll let you sail my ship."

She could never really tell whether Rory was teasing or serious, but he stepped away from the wheel and let it spin wildly. As she dove to grasp it before the ship keeled over he laughed delightedly and came up close behind her as she stood with her hands upon the wheel. His strong brown hands covered hers and he whispered, "Here, sweet, let me show you. To keep a ship on a steady course is not difficult once you learn the secret. You must feel the wind on the back of your head. Never let it come past your left or right cheek."

Summer turned the wheel until she felt the wind on the back of her head, then she looked up at him over her shoulder. "Is that all?" she asked with disbelief.

He grinned and whispered in her ear, "As simple as making love, once someone has taught you its secrets."

Desire for him raced through her blood like wildfire. She knew she would never be able to resist the magnetism of his nakedness. The dark mat of hair on his chest drew her eyes and suddenly she didn't want her hands on the ship's wheel, she wanted them free to explore the thick slabs of muscle on his perfect male body, which was almost, but not quite, touching hers.

"Pedro, amigo, take over for me," he called down to the foredeck. The grinning giant with the golden earrings took the wheel from her hands, and as Rory led her below a rousing cheer came from the crew, making it quite plain they knew why their captain was taking the beautiful girl down to his cabin.

She was blushing profusely and protested breathlessly as he impatiently swept her up into his arms to speed their journey. He stripped off his breeches and was naked in seconds, but he drew out and prolonged the pleasure of undressing her. As he bared each delicious curve, he kissed and tasted it and she knew an overwhelming desire to lick the salt from his bare skin.

"I'm going to give you a rubdown with champagne. I promise you've never felt anything like it. It will make every nerve ending tingle until you'll want to scream from heightened sensitivity. Then I'll lick the champagne from your delicious body," he promised huskily.

The scarlet silk veils drifted about the bed, barely concealing the deeply sensual act of the lovers. Rory's hands had a magic touch, arousing her to a desire she had never felt before, then his mouth and tongue drove her to a frenzy. His finesse was such that she experienced everything from wild, carnal lust to a sweet, heartstopping gift of herself where they exchanged a whispered pledge of love. In the end he set out to make her laugh. He drank champagne from her navel, allowed her to shake the bottle until it sprayed all over them, and they playfully rolled about the silken bed like children.

He fell to the floor and she sprang after him like a lioness to bite and scratch him. The sight of her creamy body against the thick black pile of the rug made all laughter flee from his hungry face as he looked down at her. His eyes were stained almost black with desire as he poised above her, then he mounted her, and rode her to paradise.

Before they parted he held her to his heart. "Swear to me you'll sail with me any time I come for you."

"I swear it, Rory," she pledged.

"When, I can't bear to be parted from you, I'll come for you. Swear you'll drop everything to come to me?" he demanded fiercely.

"Yes, yes, yes," she vowed her commitment to him.

32

They glided up the Thames at four o'clock in the morning. London was a city which never slept, but at four in the morning it dozed a little, before it stretched itself at five to begin another day at the center of the world.

Rory hired her a carriage, loaded in all her baggage, and lingered long over his goodbye kisses. Summer arrived at Auntie Lil's along with the morning milkmaid at five o'clock. Lady Richwood was still abed, so Summer crept upstairs to the chamber she had used before and told the maid not to disturb her for the next five hours.

Promptly at ten o'clock Lil Richwood swept into the room like a gust of fresh air.

"Darling, I've missed you so much. Wake up and tell me everything!"

Summer opened her eyes and tried to sit up, but the moment she did so she was assailed with nausea. She moaned and lay still.

"Darling, you have morning sickness! Oh, what a clever girl you are to already be breeding the next Lord Helford," she drawled.

"No, Lil, I'm definitely not with child," choked Summer desperately.

"When was the last time you had your menses?" demanded Lil in a practical tone, her drawl disappearing.

"I . . . I can't remember . . . I haven't been unwell since before I was married, but—"

"Married! I was astounded when I heard you had actually pulled it off. Lord Ruark Helford bludgeoned into matrimony. It was all over London that he had taken you to Stowe for your honeymoon. So it wasn't necessary to become someone's mistress after all."

"Mistress?" she repeated, blushing hotly.

"How refreshing to see a lady who still blushes; a most rare occurrence in London." She stopped talking to take a breath, and as she did so she noticed the mountain of luggage Summer had brought with her. Her eyebrows went up instantly.

"I've left him," said Summer baldly.

"You must be mad," concluded Lil. "Women do take mad fits when they're breeding, you know. Tell me what all this silly fuss is about and we'll straighten it out, I promise you."

Summer sighed. "I might as well start at the beginning. I didn't have any difficulty getting him to believe I was a sheltered, wealthy, well-bred young lady. He made no secret of how he felt about me and I expected him to offer me carte blanche, but then he surprised me by asking me to marry him. My brother had just been arrested for smuggling and I was so afraid for him—the offer of marriage seemed to be the answer to my prayers about my brother and about the twenty thousand owed on Roseland. The whole trouble was I fell in love with him. Even before we were married, I knew I was falling in love, but afterward I didn't stand a chance. He held me in the palm of his hand. I was hopelessly infatuated . . . over the moon . . . I held nothing back, I gave him my heart and soul. He seemed to be in like case. Damn men, anyway, I should have known better. I waited until after the honeymoon to confess about Spencer's trouble and the mortgage. He went mad. Called me every name under the sun. Told me I was so clever at getting money, I could pay my own mortgage, for not one copper penny of Helford money would I get."

Summer hesitated over whether to tell her all of it, then shrugged and said, "He told me he would get the marriage annulled."

"Oh, darling, that's just Ruark's temper. When he finds out about the baby, of course he will forget all about a silly annulment."

"Lil, no! You mustn't tell him," cried Summer. "I'm not pregnant."

"No, no, darling, you must have the pleasure of doing that yourself," soothed Lil.

"Lord Helford was the one who bought the mortgage from Solomon Storm," Summer said bitterly.

"Ruark probably meant it as a gift for you," said Lil. "I know he must have been delighted with the way you entertained the King and court. Summer darling, I've heard nothing this past week but what unique diversions Lady Helford provided. Everyone is going to copy you. Lady Castlemaine is at this moment redoing a room in the Persian style. My sweet, when they learn you are in London, you'll be the toast of the town, and here you lie as if you had the woes of the world on your pretty shoulders." It was inexplicable to Lil Richwood why Summer suddenly burst into tears. "Oh, you mustn't spoil your face, darling. You have an entré to the court and I'm absolutely dying to see this Frances Stewart the King's sister has brought over from France."

"Lil, my brother's in prison again. This time he's been sent to Newgate."

"Why, he was just here a few days ago. Whatever has the young rogue done? I knew someone with his looks couldn't stay out of trouble long."

"He's done absolutely nothing. One of Lord Helford's sergeants has a vendetta against my brother and me. He searched him and found my ten thousand pounds on him and arrested him for robbery. It's all very complicated. I must beg the King's help. How can I get a private audience with him?"

"Well, Edward Progers keeps in discreet communication with me. I'll get him to arrange a private audience for you."

"Edward Progers?" asked Summer.

"His Majesty's page of the backstairs. He handles private money transactions, secret correspondence, and the like." She waved her hand airily, skipping over the bald fact that he was the King's pimp and procurer.

"I must get dressed. I'm going to Newgate to try to see my brother. I must try to get some money to him until I can gain his release."

"Speaking of money, darling, I owe you some you can have for Spencer. I sold the Brussels lace for a fortune. You don't know where you can get your hands on more?"

"Life is such an ironic bitch, Lil. The last time I was here lack of money made my life pure hell. Now I have money to burn and it doesn't solve one problem for me."

"That's not quite true, sweet. It will certainly help ease life for your brother. We'll have to be very careful how we dress for Newgate. The place is crawling with thieves and debtors."

"You mean you'll come with me?" asked Summer, quite surprised.

"Why, of course, darling. It's very fashionable to visit the place. It's called Lord Shaftsbury's pride and joy. The place runs the gamut from sumptuous to cesspool. When a nobleman is clapped up for some crime, he lives in luxury, paying to have everything brought in from meals to mistresses. Highwaymen who are unfortunate enough to get caught hold court in their rooms, where visitors pay to go in and visit them, like Gentleman Jackson. There was even a rumor going around that a certain king's mistress paid to sleep with him simply for the thrill of it. The place absolutely stank when they beheaded the thirteen regicides who condemned the King's father to death. Their heads were put on spikes to decorate London Bridge, but first they were sent to Newgate to be pickled and cured and then their bodies were thrown into a pit outside—oh, sorry, darling, I forgot your nausea." Lil took a breath and plunged on. "It's behind St. Paul's, we can take the carriage and leave it in Paternoster Row. Wear no jewelry but our clothes must show we have money. If he's on the common felons' side, it's not fit for a baboon. They have their wrists and ankles shackled and drag about in chains. Still, he won't have it as hard as a female would. Do you know it's barbaric the way they treat poor women in these places. The poor unfortunate girls who get with child without benefit of wedlock are whipped through the streets at the cart's tail. They are naked from the waist up. Lords and ladies of the court sometimes make up parties and go and watch the poor girls for sport. Oh, darling, there I go again running off at the mouth so tactlessly when you are breeding."

Summer sighed. There was hardly any point in continuing to deny she was pregnant, for Lil believed what she wanted to believe.

"Now, let's see, we'll need vizard masks so we won't be recognized. We'll need snood nets on our hair so we don't pick up lice, and spiced pomander balls to ward off the stench, and—oh yes, I'll find you a pair of the lastest fashion: pattens. Little wooden platforms that fit onto your shoes to keep your skirts from trailing in the mire. They make you feel taller than high-heeled shoes!"

* * *

Summer looked at Lil Richwood in amazement as they stepped up into the carriage. Though she had advised Summer to dress conservatively, she wore pale blue brocade with an elaborate underskirt embroidered with golden thread. Her snood covering her blond curls was gold mesh and her vizard matched exactly.

Summer wore a gray walking dress with a black snood and velvet mask. Lil had given her the pattens, which she would definitely have to get used to, and she'd also handed her an orange studded with cloves and threaded onto a black satin ribbon. Summer carried a small clutch purse with her money inside, since a reticule on a string would have been too tempting to prison inmates.

The carriage let them off on the doorstep of Newgate so they didn't have far to walk, but Summer saw with horror that the gutters running from the prison were dankly clogged and black with flies. The moment they knocked, they were admitted by a turnkey and taken to the common room. This was a very large, open place like a yard where prisoners who were not dangerous could gather and socialize. A high catwalk ran around the perimeter, where guards idly watched the gathering below. Summer scanned the faces in the crowd, hoping to encounter her brother. She felt anything but hopeful.

"Ho there—you down below!" Summer looked up at an exquisitely dressed man on the catwalk who had been standing talking with a guard. Apparently they had been trying to get her attention for quite a few minutes. He held up two ten-pound notes and raised his eyebrows. In shock, she looked at Lil for confirmation of what she thought he meant. "How dare you, sir, go away!" she called.

The man held up two more ten-pound notes, and the guard with him called down, "This is Lord Peregrine Howard."

"Tell him no—go away!" shouted Summer.

Lil explained, "Prostitutes ply their trade here day and night."

The guard called down, "He says you don't even need to take off your clothes."

"No!" cried Summer.

"He'll settle for a French," shouted the guard.

Summer put her hands on her hips angrily and looked up at Lord Howard. "You don't seem to understand English very well. Let me put it more succinctly—piss off!"

Lord Howard waved and shrugged his disappointment.

"What on earth is a French?" whispered Summer.

Lil pantomimed licking ice cream and Summer shuddered with horror. It propelled her, however, to get someone in authority and demand to know where they were keeping her brother. After an interminable wait while records were checked she finally learned that he was imprisoned in the old section. The guard also explained that to go over there she would have to pay a guard to protect her, as it was very rough. It was rapidly turning into the nightmare she had feared as they were lighted down a dark stone tunnel which she feared would lead to the bowels of hell. When she saw where they were keeping him, however, it was not the large cell, which stank of urine and excrement, that upset her, but the cell's inhabitants. An iron grille separated the men from the women and she saw her brother immediately. His face was a mass of bruises. He also sported a black eye and split, swollen lip. He came toward her with anger blazing in his eyes. "Cat, what in the name of hellfire are you doing in this hole? I forbid you ever to come here again. Lil, for Christ's sake, surely you have enough brains if she doesn't. You should have used a go-between."

"Did the guards do that to your face Spider?"

"No. I had to beat the shit out of a couple of the prisoners." She looked about and saw battered and bleeding men. Some lay naked in the corners on stinking heaps of straw.

"Why? Did they think you had money?" she asked innocently.

He did not disabuse her of her ideas. Not for the world would he tell her that he must guard against rape every hour of the day and night. "I suppose so, Cat. Did you bring money?" he asked hopefully. She nodded and immediately he bargained with the turnkey to be taken to the affluent side of the prison.

Summer could not keep her eyes from straying into the women's cell. They were filthy drabs. The pregnant ones with swollen bellies were the most pathetic. Some wore rags; other were less fortunate and lay naked covered by dirt and suppurating sores. Their faces were hopeless, their eyes empty.

The cell door was unlocked and Spencer was permitted to accompany them. Halfway down the passage Summer felt the nausea grip her and she vomited her heart up. Spider held her until the spasm passed. " 'Fore God, you must promise me you'll not come again, love. Did you tell Ruark what Oswald did?"

"Don't ever speak that man's name to me again. He did nothing to prevent Oswald from shipping you here."

"Nay, he knew nothing of it. Oswald learned Ruark was coming to Falmouth jail and had to get rid of me before Ruark arrived. Cat, he'd never do a bastardly thing like that. He's your husband, for Christ's sake."

"Not for long, I hope. I'm going to the King. I'll have you out of here as soon as I possibly can. I swear it!"

"Come along of me, missus, while I tally up what's owin'," said the turnkey. Reluctantly Summer left her brother in the common cell, which was patrolled from the catwalk. When she protested at the ridiculous rates she was being charged for the week Spider had been incarcerated in such a hellhole, the guard growled, "We ain't runnin' a bleedin' charity, ye know." They even charged for him to use the piss stone twice a day and as an afterthought added on another ten shillings for her "puking."

She paid twenty pounds for him to have a private cell with water to bathe and shave and all his meals brought in. She said that she would be back again next week if he had not been released.

The moment she arrived back at the fashionable house in Cockspur Street Summer ordered a bath. She bade the servant take away every stitch of her clothing to be washed then proceeded to scour her body and hair to rid herself of the odor of the place which seemed to cling to her.

A message was brought to the house from Edward Progers that if Lady Helford would come to the privy garden at Whitehall tomorrow night between the hours of eleven and midnight, there was every chance that His Majesty would see her.

Summer conjured a mental picture of Whitehall. It was a sprawling red-brick mass in the old Tudor style. Its hallways and apartments opened one into another like a vast honeycomb. She knew where the kitchens were because at high tide they sometimes flooded and could be seen from the river. Ah yes, now she remembered. To get into the privy garden you had to go through a gateway into the Stone Gallery. She wished he had agreed to see her tonight, but she supposed she was extremely fortunate to be seen at all.

Actually Charles had granted a private meeting to his friend Ruark Helford tonight and he'd set aside an hour for their business. "The Dutch have outfitted two war fleets. They intend to make war on our ships in America off the coast of New Amsterdam and our East India Company ships will be attacked off the Guinea coast of Africa. Michael de Ruyter is in charge of the

Guinea Fleet. He's a genius at sea, Sire, make no mistake about it," warned Helford.

"Well, forewarned is forearmed. We are at war, even though it's still being fought in distant ports. I'll try my best to double the fleet and I think we'd better be about building ships on a greater scale. We are bound to suffer losses." Charles had few illusions. "Bloody Parliament controls the purse strings. Christ, Ru, it's like walking a tightrope dealing with the tightfisted bastards. In open confrontation they win every time, so I have to outwit them or deceive them. Ah well, that's not your problem." Charles took off his periwig and scratched his head. He glanced at Ruark's clubbed-back hair. "Are you wearing one of these?" he asked.

Ruark laughed and shook his head. "I hate the damned things. I wear my own hair, Sire."

"They're all the rage at the French court, so my sister says, and my hair is getting as gray as a badger's arse these days, but it feels wonderful to take the damned thing off and scratch my head."

"Sire, through a comedy of errors at my headquarters in Falmouth, my wife's young brother, Lord St. Catherine, was arrested and shipped to Newgate. I'd like your permission to get him released."

"Arrested for smuggling?" Charles laughed. "No doubt working for that reprobate brother of yours. Speak to Shaftsbury, he'll write you out a release for the young devil."

"Thank you, Sire, Lady Helford will be relieved."

"You are a lucky dog, Helford. My wife thinks a bedchamber is for displaying pious pictures of saints and books of devotion. She sleeps with holy water at the head of the bed."

Ruark grinned. "For what you are about to receive, may the lord make you truly thankful. Amen!"

"Exactly!" said Charles, appreciating the witticism. "Are you staying at Whitehall tonight?"

Ruark nodded then bethought himself to tell Charles something others might keep from him. "I'm afraid plague has been brought to London and it's spreading. There've been many reports of sickness among ships' crews."

"Damnation! I'd heard rumors, but nothing confirmed. Let's hope it confines itself to the dock area. I'll speak to Sandwich; the Navy Office should put a quarantine on any ships suspected of carrying plague."

"Good night, Sire." Ruark bowed.

"Hold on. I'll walk with you. Your room's down by the bowling green, isn't it?"

Ruark nodded, aware that Charles was on his way to Barbara's even though it was past midnight.

Summer awoke at dawn with nausea once again. Finally she faced the indisputable fact that she was probably going to have a baby. She had been intimate with Ruark and also with her husband's brother Rory and she had no way whatsoever of knowing who had fathered the child. This truth was so shocking she simply hadn't been able to accept it. Now that she was trying to face up to it, she was deeply ashamed of herself. It was too appalling to share with Auntie Lil. She would let her assume it was Lord Helford's child, as of course would everyone else. Summer, however, was less sure about what she should disclose to Ruark, or for that matter to Rory. For the present she would keep her mouth shut.

If she was to be a mother, it was time to take practical steps for her own welfare and the well-being of the child. The first practical thing she must do is put her money where it was safe and where it would earn interest. Solomon Storm was the only person who came to mind. She dressed in her richest walking suit with matching hat and gloves and asked if she could use the carriage.

Since she was carrying a fortune of twenty thousand pounds, she took along two of Lil Richwood's six-foot servants. She was ushered in with deference and served refreshments before they began their business. Solomon Storm called her Lady Helford so many times she began to realize just how impressive the name was in London.

"Lord Helford wished to surprise you by discharging the mortgage on Roseland." He nodded, pleased he'd had a hand in it.

"Oh, he surprised me all right," replied Summer, wondering why everyone assumed Ruark intended it as a gift for her. But to be fair, she was the one who had sprung the bigger surprise regarding Roseland and its heavy mortgage. When she left, she had deposited her money with him at six-percent interest. He had offered five, but Summer wasn't quite the green girl she had been on her first trip to London.

33

Lord Helford visited the house in Cockspur Street with very mixed feelings. He hoped his wife would not shut the door in his face, yet he knew he would risk more than the sharp edge of Summer's tongue to keep her from the King's lusty advances.

"Oh, my lord, you have just missed her," said Lil Richwood, bursting to ask him a dozen questions. "Do come and have a drink, darling, and satisfy my insatiable curiosity."

"What has she told you?" he asked bluntly.

"Ah, I can't begin to catalog all your faults, Ruark my dear, but I've been playing devil's advocate. I told her it was all a silly misunderstanding . . . that you would never in a million years kick her out without a penny . . . especially not in her condition—" Lil's drawling voice halted as if she had revealed something she shouldn't have.

"Condition?" he questioned quickly. "Is she . . . ?"

Lil held up her hands. "She swears she is not."

His mouth hardened. "Where has she gone?"

"She took the carriage up into the city. I really don't think she'll be back for hours and hours, my lord."

"I'll write her a note," he said with decisiveness. "Perhaps it's best we don't meet face-to-face today. We have this unfortunate knack of exacerbating each other's tempers the moment we are in the same room together." He emptied his glass and refused to let her refill it. "I've seen the King and Shaftsbury about young Spencer. I've arranged to have him released, so there's no need for her to petition His Majesty about this."

Lil brought him paper and quill and he wrote that under no circumstances was it necessary to meet with the King to beg his favors. "When she learns what you have done for her brother, I'm sure she'll be ready to forgive everything, darling," assured Lil.

"I do have to beg her pardon for a few things I said to her," he explained, "then perhaps we can begin again." He handed Lady Richwood the letter and after he left she took it up to Summer's chamber and laid it on the pretty French desk.

After Summer left Solomon Storm she went on a shopping spree in the Exchange. All she bought for herself were some pretty hair ornaments and a pair of delicious, dangling earrings which caught her fancy, but for Spider she bought soap, towels, a razor, underclothing, shirts, breeches, doublets, waistcoats, and vests, the very latest fashion from Paris. She knew the hours would stretch interminably until she must be at the gateway of the privy garden, so she lingered in the vast arcade, enjoying the display of articles from around the world.

There were wig shops, tobacconists with their strange masculine aromas, French glove shops, lace vendors, goldsmiths, rainbow displays of Venetian glass and Moroccan leather. By the time she returned to Cockspur Street, Lil's escort for the evening had already called to take her to Lady Somerset's ball.

Summer took a bath while she mulled over what would be the right outfit to wear tonight. She chose her gown for her meeting with the King very carefully. Red was out, it was far too provocative and bold. Black was very regal, but with her dark coloring it was not her best color. In white or pastel she would stick out like a sore thumb, and when one had a secret, midnight meeting through the privy garden and up the backstairs, one did not wish to advertise the fact. She finally settled on an apricot silk with a taffeta cape of amber.

She had a light supper of cold meat and fruit and decided against taking any wine. She would need all her wits about her for tonight's encounter. Finally at the hour of ten o'clock she bade a footman call her a linkboy to light her way to Whitehall. It lay just across Pall Mall and along through the Holbein Gateway. She hadn't even noticed the letter from her husband lying on the desk.

Lord Helford at this fashionable hour was about to take a short-cut through St. James Park over to the palace, where he had business with Chancellor Hyde. He couldn't believe his eyes as he saw Edward Progers speaking with a fashionably dressed young woman who looked suspiciously like his wife. He was furious. Obviously she had completely ignored his letter telling her not to ask the King for favors, but what was most damning was the method she had chosen for the meeting.

It was nothing but a rendezvous arranged through Charles's pimp, Progers! By the time he reached the privy garden, Summer had disappeared inside. He went all the way up to the King's apartments, encountering none but red-coated yeomen of the guard who stood at the main archways. He decided to wait for her, even if it took all night.

He slipped into a shadowed alcove near Charles's apartments and propped himself against the wall.

Progers took Summer through no less than three salons before he knocked discreetly upon a door, bowed, and withdrew, leaving her to her fate. Almost immediately the door was opened wide by Charles, who was dressed quite informally in shirt sleeves topped by a brocaded vest. His eyes kindled warmly as he drew her inside and kissed her hand in the most breathtaking manner. Without doubt, Charles was the most charming cavalier in the whole nation.

As he put his hands to her shoulders to remove her cape, she noticed how extraordinarily long were his beringed fingers. His hands were very large and strong, almost like a peasant's, and looked capable of heavy physical labor. His manners, however, were impeccable. His hands did not linger about her person in a lascivious way. Charles relied upon charm alone to seduce a lady.

Summer curtsied low and Charles raised her immediately. "That's quite unnecessary, my dear, when we are private."

"Your Majesty, thank you for agreeing to see me so quickly," she breathed.

"Lady Helford . . . Summer, it is a pleasure. Please don't be a stranger to the court now that you are in London."

"Thank you, Sire," she murmured, wondering how soon she could petition him for help without seeming rude.

"Allow me to wait upon you for a change. Would you join me in a glass of port?" He led her to a chair and stood against the mantelpiece, where he could observe her beauty. The room, filled with priceless furniture, paintings, and art objects, could only be described as opulent. Summer was grateful that he had not received her in his bedchamber.

Her eyes glanced over the masterpieces on the walls as she composed what she should say to him, but suddenly her eyes came to stop on a magnificent portrait and she blurted, "Oh, is that a Raphael?"

"Yes. My father had the greatest art collection in England. That damned usurper sold off priceless works of art as if they were coconuts at the fair. I'm trying my best to restore his collections of Raphael, Titian, Guido, and the like."

"We used to own a Raphael at Roseland but my father gambled away everything," she said with candor.

"Well, I've been both prince and pauper and know what it's like to have to sell heirlooms for practical purposes, but to sacrifice them for gambling is an obscenity."

"Sire, I cannot ask you for a favor without offering something in return; my pride won't allow it."

He smiled down at her with jaded eyes. "Pride is a luxury we sometimes cannot afford. Summer, you neither flatter me nor flirt with me, as all other women do, so I must assume you are not offering the usual fare."

She blushed, then plunged on. "My husband spies for you. I, too, could do that. Think how much a woman could learn and pass on for the good of her country. I know information is leaking to the Dutch, and perhaps I could find the source of that leak. Baron Arlington, your secretary of state, is married to a Dutchwoman."

Charles laughed. "Egad, Arlington is after Hyde's job, he'd better not be married to a traitor."

"I didn't mean to imply the baroness was a traitor, Sire; I'm simply using her as an example."

"Yes, yes, I do understand and what you suggest has a great deal of merit I am in need of someone here at Court who will gather information for me and it would be best if we were just friends rather than intimate."

She blushed again.

"Summer, you are that rare phenomenon—a woman who is in love with her husband."

Summer's flush deepened. If only he knew the truth about her, she was certain he would be very shocked.

"I feel I can be very open and frank with you and you will keep my confidence," he said low.

"You may trust me implicitly, Sire," she assured him.

"There is a young lady my sister brought home from France. Her name is Frances Stewart. I have a special interest in the lady, but she rebuffs every advance. She professes to be an innocent maid, a virgin, and I would know if this is true or if she spurns me for another."

Summer was dismayed. "Oh, Sire, I don't mean that sort of spying!"

"Well, my dearest Summer, while you get this information for me, perhaps you will learn other things regarding the security of the realm."

"I think you are just playing with me."

"Sweetheart, I'd like to play with you but you hold me at arm's length like la belle Stewart." He chuckled. "Tell me what it is I may do for you."

"My brother was wrongly imprisoned in Falmouth and sent to Newgate. I was there yesterday, Sire, and it broke my heart to see his condition."

"My dear, Ruark has already spoken to me about this. I gave my permission for him to get your brother released."

She was so surprised her mouth fell open a little.

"Haven't you spoken with your husband?"

"N-no, Sire, I thought he was in Falmouth."

"Well, no doubt he wants to surprise you."

"P-perhaps," she whispered.

"I believe he's here at Whitehall tonight."

She was frightened to think Lord Helford might have seen her with Progers. "Thank you for your kindness toward my brother, Your Majesty, I shall never forget it. Good night, Sire."

He wrapped her cloak about her and bestowed a chaste kiss upon her brow. "*Au revoir,* Summer."

She found her way back through the three salons, but Edward Progers didn't seem to be anywhere in evidence. Annoyed, she supposed the wretched man had assumed she would be staying the night. She stepped out into the dim hallway and a man emerged from the shadows to block her path. Fear sketched its ugly finger across her brow. "Ruark, this isn't what it seems, my lord," she protested.

His face was dark and brooding in the dim light. He contemplated her in silence for a moment, managed to gain control over his temper, and answered, "I believe you. If I'd been making love to you, an hour wouldn't satisfy me . . . it would be the same for Charles."

She bit back a cutting remark. "Thank you for seeing the King about Spencer. I've been mad with worry for him."

"Didn't you get my letter?" he asked.

"What letter?"

"I came to Cockspur Street to see you today. I gave Lady Richwood a letter for you."

"She had already gone out for the evening by the time I returned," she said.

"We can't talk here. Summer, I have rooms here at Whitehall. Will you come with me there so that we may talk?"

She was amazed that he was not shouting at her, calling her names. He seemed to be in a quiet enough mood. Perhaps there was more she should know about her brother's imprisonment and release. "I'll come for half an hour, my lord, but it's very late. It's not really safe for me to be on the streets at this time of night."

"I shall see you safely home, Summer," he assured her.

He led her through the labyrinth of Whitehall, then outside and past the bowling green. They entered his apartment from the grounds, but she knew the two small rooms must open onto an inner corridor of the maze that was called Whitehall.

When Ruark lit the candles, she smiled to herself. The chambers reflected his taste exactly. It was so warm and welcoming, she had the peculiar feeling of coming home. He removed her cloak and offered her a comfortable chair. He poured them both a glass of sack and took the chair opposite her.

"I came to see you today to tell you that I had the King's permission to get Spencer released from Newgate. The last thing in the world I wanted was for you to go begging favors from Charles."

"Why can you ask him, but not me?" she asked reasonably.

"Because you are a very beautiful woman. Because I have first-hand knowledge that he is attracted to you. I'm being very honest with you, Summer . . . I didn't want you giving yourself to him out of gratitude." His eyes searched hers.

"Why should you care? It's over between us, you said as much yourself."

"It isn't over between us, Summer . . . not yet . . . perhaps not ever. I know I have the devil's own temper but I'd give anything in the world if we could go back to being the way we were." His voice was so sincere, so regretful, it made a lump come into her throat.

"What we had together was so fine . . . so special . . . so rare. I want us to begin again if you'll give me another chance, my darling."

She looked down into her wineglass and saw the candlelight reflected in the deep amber. She felt her heartbeat quicken in her throat.

"I'm my own worst enemy, you know. I flew into a rage when you told me about your brother being imprisoned and about the mortgage on Roseland, but I regretted it almost immediately and that same afternoon I made it possible for Spencer—Spider as you affectionately call him—to escape through the open window of the interrogation room. Then I went to London and redeemed the mortgage on Roseland for you."

A tear slipped down Summer's cheek. They had been so deeply in love, they had been totally immersed in one another, why hadn't she realized Ru had done these things for her?

He reached over and took hold of her hand. He gazed at it as if it were made of precious porcelain. "When the King and court came to Helford Hall, I was so proud of the way you handled everything. I saw immediately that it didn't matter how you'd been brought up . . . you do everything with such a natural, inborn grace that to know you is to love you. And I also realized that you did it for me. I nearly went mad for the taste of you, the feel of you. That last night I approached you so clumsily, we quarreled again. I was a brute to force you. All I really wanted was to tell you, show you how much I loved you."

"Oh, Ru," she cried softly.

"Hush, darling, I should be horsewhipped for making you cry." He stood up and came behind her chair, rubbing a strand of her silken hair between thumb and forefingers. "I apologize for the things I said and did to you, and beg your forgiveness."

She stood up to face him. "It wasn't all your fault. I lied to you and lured you into marriage under false pretenses, but Ru, I swear to you I always loved you." She swayed involuntarily toward him, her eyes closed.

His powerful hands grasped her about the waist and he drew her toward him, then crushed her softness against his hard length. Her head fell back and her mouth parted to receive his kiss. Passion rose like a flame between them. "Oh, my darling, stay with me tonight?" he begged. "Let's never, ever have secrets between us again . . . promise me."

Reality intruded itself upon her consciousness and she realized how wickedly promiscuous she had been with Rory. More than anything in the world, she wanted her husband's love, and she knew how he had reacted when she confessed all to him before. She had learned her lesson. Never again would she confess anything to him. "I should go now, Ruark, Auntie Lil will be worried for me."

In response, his mouth came down upon hers to ravish it. They were like two people starving with the need for each other. Her gown was drawn over her head and she heard its whisper as it was banished to the floor. He picked her up, held her against his heart, and carried her to his bed. She was stunned that his touch had set all her senses quivering with expectant eagerness.

Once he held her naked body, his mouth was relentless in its demands. Breathlessly between kisses she begged, "Ru, please undress, you have no idea how much pleasure I get from touching you." The moment he unbuttoned his shirt her hands slid inside to trace the hard sinewy muscles which covered his rib cage. Then his hands were at the waistband of his breeches to slide them down and her eager mouth followed his hands, raining tiny kisses on his flat belly. He was groaning hoarsely from her play, and the moment he managed to rid himself of the tight breeches his shaft rose up to brush her cheek. Then she let herself go and unleashed all the pent-up longings she had in a sensual excess that carried them both to the brink of madness.

All her kisses were now reserved for the marblelike phallus with the velvet head which had unfailingly brought her rapture. Then her lips parted and slid over him to let him explore her soft mouth. The tip of her tongue encircled him beneath the ridge, then licked at the tiny opening at its very tip.

Ruark didn't want his seed to start, though he knew she was too aroused to mind, so he quickly lifted her high to stand on the bed before him. Then his mouth received the sweet pleasure as her arms went about him and she pressed his head into her body to feast wherever he desired.

Finally neither could wait a second longer for their bodies to fuse. His hands were on her silken thighs, spreading them wide so that he could impale her savagely. She screamed with the sensitive pleasure his fullness created inside of her. Both of them prolonged the loving, endlessly building and receding until neither could bear it a moment longer. She writhed beneath him and begged, "Ru, now! Now! Now!"

They came together as they always did, but he refused to release her and withdraw and she thanked God for it. The amazing thing about her and Ruark making love with each other was that it was always better than the time before. Each successive mating reached a higher degree of passion with a more explosive and prolonged climax.

During the next few hours Ruark whispered such words of love, she felt her very bones would melt. The entire universe narrowed down to their bed. The world disappeared and nothing else mattered to them but their newfound intimacy. Ruark's mouth became unbearably tender as he kissed her cheekbones, eyelids, throat, and lips. For once his mouth was so gentle she felt tears start in her eyes. Before dawn Summer experienced the total devastation of his possession and they fell asleep, curled together, limbs entwined, bound by love.

When they awoke, Ruark's hot cheek was pressed to her breast. She stirred, luxuriating in his warmth, and immediately she was assailed by nausea. She groaned, and when he sat up to look down at her with concern, she said, "The fish I had for dinner didn't agree with me, I'm afraid."

His dark eyebrows drew together immediately. "Why are you lying to me?" he demanded.

"What do you mean?" she asked, desperately trying to control the nausea.

"You are having my child," he stated.

"Whatever makes you think that?" she asked lightly.

"Because I made love to you day and night for two whole weeks when we were married." His eyes narrowed dangerously. "You weren't going to tell me, were you?"

"There's nothing to tell," she insisted. She could contain it no longer. She reached under the bed and was indelicately sick in the chamber pot.

"Lil told me," he said quietly, bringing her a towel to wipe her mouth.

"Is that what this reconciliation is all about?" she demanded angrily. "If I bear you a son, you'll reconsider annulling our marriage?" she flared.

He gripped her shoulders and shook her angrily. "You came to London knowing you were with child. I should take my belt to your bottom. I'm sending you home to Helford Hall today. There's plague in London, it isn't safe for the baby."

She shook off his hands and stood defying him, stark naked. "You are *sending* me home today? *Sending* me home? I don't believe I heard you correctly, Lord Bloody Helford!" The nausea vanished in the face of her anger. "Well, let me make something perfectly clear to you—I won't be sent anywhere. You can take Helford Hall and you can take your precious marriage and you can shove them where the monkey shoved his nuts. This child is mine . . . this life is mine . . . I'll decide where we'll live and where we won't live. And since you insist there be no more secrets between us, let me confess what you forced me to do. When you swore I'd get none of your money and you told me to get my own, I did exactly that. I took to the road, I dressed as a highwayman. I robbed your guests of their money and jewels until I had enough to pay off the mortgage on Roseland."

"Oh, my God," he ground out.

"I am the Black Cat. Your bloody Sergeant Oswald arrested the wrong St. Catherine." She sneered.

Ruark's face was dark with fury. He began to threaten her. "I'll take the child away from you."

She bared her teeth like a female wolf protecting its young. "Then I'll have to prove that it isn't your child!"

The palm of his hand made contact with her cheek in a stinging slap. She sank to the bed and spat, "Whoreson, I'll never forgive you for that."

In a murderous mood he dressed and quit Whitehall.

34

Summer looked around the chamber until her eyes picked out exactly the right objects. She picked them up and hurled them against the wall. As the pair of priceless Ming porcelain figurines shattered into a thousand shards she felt even worse. She was thoroughly sick and then she fell to the bed and sobbed her heart out. Damn, damn, damn—they'd patched things up so beautifully last night, why did all the seams have to come unglued in the bleak light of day?

In the privacy of the night he'd told her how deeply he loved her, missed her, needed her, and then at dawn he'd lost his temper and actually struck her. Well, she was really finished with him this time. Now she was the one who wanted an annulment.

By the time she bathed and dressed and walked back to Cock-spur Street, Spider had arrived. She did not fall upon his neck and sob her relief but put up her chin and said, "I see you found the new clothes I bought for you. I hope you deloused before you put them on."

He grinned at her cheekily and said, "Give me a few pounds for a stake, I'm about to embark on my new career. I've heard of a fashionable gaming house in Bell Yard."

She gave him the money but not without a warning. "If you intend to follow in your father's footsteps, don't be stupid enough to get caught. I don't want you coming back feetfirst with a lead ball in your gut."

"How elegantly you put it, Cat."

"If you want elegance, you've got the wrong woman. At least try to act civilized while we're under Auntie Lil's roof. Perhaps I should get us a place of our own."

"Then I can act uncivilized?" he questioned innocently.

"Since you're a bloody man, I have no doubt of it," she retorted.

"Ah, you've obviously had an encounter with Lord Helford recently. Only he can manage to put you in such a bitch of a mood."

"I'm sorry, Spider, you're right, of course. Oh, God, I was just sick when that swine Oswald sent you to Newgate. Rory brought me to London on the *Phantom* in the dead of night. I saw the King about getting you released and he told me Ruark had already arranged it. I was so very grateful to him and we almost got to the point where we were acting civilized toward each other again. Until he found out about the baby. We ended up threatening each other, as usual."

"You're having a baby, Cat?" asked Spencer with concern.

"I wish to God I wasn't!" she whispered.

He was shocked. "You don't want your baby, Cat?"

"Oh, Spider, of course I want my baby, it's just that—well, I don't know exactly . . . which Helford is the father."

She stole a glance at his face and saw that he was more than shocked, he was appalled at her promiscuity.

"Oh, what does a fifteen-year-old know about these things anyway?" she said crossly.

He stiffened. "I know what's more or less right is more or less right. What the hell will you do if the child's Black Jack's?"

"There'll be no trouble if it's Rory's," she said defiantly.

"Oh, really? He has to sail into London in the dead of night. When do you suppose you'll see him again?"

She picked up his plumed hat and handed it to him. "I think we're both adult enough not to interfere in each other's lives, don't you?" she asked pointedly.

Lil would not hear of Summer getting a place of her own. "Darling, what could possibly be more convenient for you? This house is in the most fashionable part of town and it's within spitting distance of Whitehall. Whenever you're at Court late at night, you can stay there in Helford's rooms."

"But Lil, are you sure you won't mind having Spencer live here? He's used to coming and going at any hour he chooses and he's likely to have disreputable friends," warned Summer.

"Darling, I'm particularly partial to attractive men, especially young ones."

"And what about when the baby comes?" Summer asked bluntly.

Lil Richwood clapped her hands. "At last we are making progress. At least you admit there's going to be a baby. We shall pick you a good midwife, and when the time comes, you'll have your lying-in there at her house, and when the child is old enough to go abroad, it shall come to live with us. We'll be a family, with a nursemaid and everything."

Summer hugged her warmly. She was the most generous woman Summer had ever encountered. Some way she intended to get Roseland back. She wasn't quite sure yet how she would accomplish such a feat, but she vowed that by fair means or foul, she would get it back. After all it was Spencer's birthright, and though the young wretch seemed years away from marriage, when he did take a wife, Roseland should belong to Lord St. Catherine and his heirs.

Since Lil had been so accommodating and Summer knew she was dying to go to a court reception, she invited her aunt to accompany her there tonight. A reception and ball were planned for each night that Charles's mother and sister were in England.

Lil consulted with both Summer and Dora, the mistress of her extensive wardrobe. Finally a royal blue taffeta with yards of silver ribbon was chosen. "A woman nearing fifty shouldn't wear ribbons, but I don't give a damn," declared Lil. "You don't think I'll look like mutton dressed as lamb, even though I am exactly that, do you, darling?"

At the ball Charles introduced Summer to his little queen Catherine. Her heart went out to the sallow-faced young woman who skillfully plied her fan so that when she smiled, it covered her prominent little teeth.

Catherine said, "We have much in common, Summair . . . your husband and mine are far too attractive to other ladies, no? Is your husband faithful to you?"

Summer was slightly taken aback at the Queen's frank question, but obviously fidelity occupied most of her thoughts and brought her much misery. She chose her words carefully. "Yes, Lord Helford is a tall, dark cavalier like His Majesty but I have never asked myself if he is faithful. Probably he is not, but I am wise enough to know that brief encounters or even longer liaisons are no threat to a wife if her husband treats her well."

The Queen put her head on one side and said, "There is someone I want very much for you to meet with. She is called Frances Stewart. My husband thinks he is in love with her. After you meet her I want you to tell me honestly if you think she is his latest mistress."

Summer was amazed to see how young Frances Stewart was. She was a tall, painfully slim girl with pale blond coloring. Catherine invited Summer and Frances to accompany her to a play the next day and left them to become acquainted. Summer found her puzzling. On the surface she seemed nothing more than a simple girl; for one who had spent years at the dissolute French court she seemed naive in the extreme.

"You are so lucky to be married, it is the one dream I cherish in my heart," said Frances.

Just then Summer noticed Barbara Castlemaine with three gentlemen in tow enter the card room. She stopped to greet Summer, swept her dark eyes over Frances in an insolent examination, and invited, "Come and play dice, Lady Helford, I'm determined to have those rubies off you before I'm done, y'know."

Frances whispered behind her fan, "Oh, Lord, I wish she hadn't stopped to speak with us. My reputation will be smirched forever."

"Lady Castlemaine is the King's mistress, there's no dishonor in that at this court," explained Summer.

"Lady Helford, I am a maiden. If my name is not totally unblemished, I will never receive an offer of marriage."

"I see," said Summer, trying to keep from laughing. "Who is the lucky gentleman?"

"Why, any gentleman of the court who is in possession of a title and unencumbered by a wife," confided Frances.

Later Summer told the Queen, "Your Grace, I can assure you Frances Stewart will never become any man's mistress. She is obsessed by the notion she must keep her reputation spotless so she will receive an honorable proposal of marriage."

The Queen said, "How clever you are. You shall be my spy."

Summer groaned inwardly. She longed for adventure and intrigue and the delicious danger connected with spying, but the only spying she had been asked to do was to find out who was sleeping with whom. From personal experience Summer felt such intimate information was nobody's goddamn business but the lovers' themselves!

Thus began a social whirl for Summer whereby she rode in the park each morning, saw a different play each afternoon, and spent her evenings at Court getting up to nonsensical escapades with the Queen and her ladies. They went about on what they called "frolics." They thought it the height of daring to dress up as orange girls and go abroad pretending to sell their wares to the cheeky Londoners. Along with the rest of London they flocked to see a baboon brought from Guinea and thought it could be taught the King's good English.

Summer was growing weary of the whole pointless rigmarole. Here was Frances Stewart being a silly professional virgin, making the King jump through hoops, and there was Barbara Castlemaine opening her legs and holding out her greedy hand at the time so he'd pay her gambling debts of thirty or forty thousand, while children picked rags for threepence a bushel and the plague was devastating the poorer districts, which were a breeding ground for rats and vermin.

The war was spoken of quite openly now. Ships were being built and fitted out for war as fast as the money could be found. Prince Rupert fit himself out with a ship named *Henrietta* after the King's mother and Lord Sandwich escorted Charles's sister and mother back to France while it was still safe to cross the Channel.

Charles received the Dutch ambassador to warn him that England had been pushed too far and intended to retaliate. Reports came in that England had beat the Dutch at Guinea and also in America at New Netherlands and in fact were doing the Dutch fleet damage all over the world.

Uniforms were seen everywhere. Companys of soldiers in white doublets roamed the streets of London, navy garb was seen everywhere, and one company of the militia actually dressed like Turks. Naturally fashion was influenced by all the talk of war and navy blue and brass buttons and jaunty red jackets were worn to court functions. On slim ladies the male attire was provocative, but on the majority, whose figures tended to be on the plump side, the fashions were disastrous.

It was fashionable to speak of war, but not to speak of plague, so people spoke in whispers. A tally had begun to be taken, because the dreaded scourge had begun to seep into some of the fashionable districts and it seemed like the church bells which tolled for the dead were ringing night and day. Now when the courtiers went to the theater in Drury Lane, they could no longer close their eyes to the red crosses on the doors and their breaths caught in their throats as they read the pitiful signs scrawled across houses that begged, "Lord Have Mercy Upon Us."

Whispers were turned into full-voiced concern, then became loud cries. Plague! Plague! Suddenly it became apparent that death played no favorites. London could not stop the Reaper whose skull grinned and gave the gravediggers employment.

The theaters began to close. Ships' crews were kept aboard and not allowed to roam London's taverns, and the King decided to remove his court from Whitehall to Hampton Court away up the Thames past Richmond.

Fanatics preached that it was a divine judgment being handed down from above because the whole court was profligate and infected the whole of society. Others blamed the populace at large for its loose morals. It was said that all Londoners had murderous tempers, would cheat even a blind man, and steal the copper pennies from the eyes of a corpse. It was all true, of course, but Londoners, be they prince or pauper, did not mend their ways. Rather they became almost frenzied in their pursuit of pleasure and dangerous diversion.

Summer had deserted the bland company of Queen Catherine and Frances Stewart for the faster crowd of Barbara Castlemaine and Anne Carnegie. Accompanied by Buckingham and big-headed Henry Jermyn, they took a boat over to Southwark one evening to attend something reported to be very exciting. It was a knife fight, much more bloodthirsty than cockfights or bear baitings. The preliminary bouts were sword fights where first blood drawn won, but the main bout was whispered to be a fight to the death!

Their party arrived accompanied by a dozen swaggering gallants, all laughing too loudly. Linkboys with their flares led them from their boat to the secret place of the knife fight. Summer wore a hat with a sweeping feather which concealed her left cheek, and she had stolen a page from the book of Black Jack Flash and wore dramatic black and white. The very air was charged with excitement and Summer could feel her pulses racing. This was a welcome change from the company she usually kept. They had become dull as a damned sermon.

She had just accepted a silver flask from one of her admirers and was about to tip its fiery contents down her throat when a powerful hand took her wrist and made it immobile. "Hell and furies," she swore, "let go or I'll have you beaten and kicked!"

"Indeed, madame?" said Lord Helford in a voice so menacing, a shiver ran up her spine. "I don't believe a knife fight is a fit place for the mother of my child . . . or have you conveniently rid yourself of it?" He sneered as he raked her slim figure from head to toe.

His words cut her to the heart. "What makes you such a cruel bastard?" she asked low, her throat swollen with unshed tears.

Desire flared in him. She was more temptingly beautiful than she had ever been. She was still extremely slim-waisted, but her breasts could only be described as voluptuous. He pictured her naked and ached to experience her new ripeness. His green eyes glittered with suppressed fury. "I didn't mind your frolics with the Queen, she is always well guarded and chaperoned, even when she isn't aware of it, but the company you keep tonight is unacceptable. If you are allowed to associate with such, you will become as notorious as the whores you are with. I'm taking you home."

"Plague take you, Helford!" It was a most obscene epithet to throw at him in such times of horror.

"It may take you, madame. I hear pregnant women are particularly vulnerable."

She gasped. Real fear had been with her for some time now. He took her elbow in a firm grip.

"Take your hands from me, sir," she ordered angrily.

"If you don't come willingly, I shall simply carry you off. The choice is yours," he said in a tone that brooked no denial. She glanced about to see who was watching her encounter with her husband and thought better of refusing him. Helford was capable of any atrocity that crossed his mind. He had his carriage waiting. He helped her inside and she sank back against the velvet squabs. Being confined together in such a small space was almost unbearable. The very air between them was charged with sexual tension until finally, when she could bear the silence no longer, she spat, "I hate you!"

His deep voice filled the coach, filled her very head. "The opposite of love isn't hate, Summer—it's indifference—and indifference is one thing we'll never feel toward each other."

"How could you say such a thing to me about the child?" she asked in anguish.

"Because I wanted to hurt you, of course. I don't think for one moment you would ever do such a thing," he admitted. His voice hardened again. "You heeded me not about leaving London."

Her mind working like quicksilver, she said, "If Roseland were still mine, I would consider going there to get away from this terrible plague . . ." Her words hung in the air. As he turned toward her in the dark coach, his hand brushed her breast and she cried out as if she had been scalded. Suddenly she found herself enfolded in his embrace; his arms were like steel bands crushing her to his heart, his mouth fused to hers as if he had been starving for her. "Ru," she cried breathlessly, uncertain if it was lust or love that drove him.

"My darling, my honey love," he said hoarsely, "why do we torture each other so? When I see you out with other men, laughing up into their faces, I want to kill them—aye, and kill you, too," he said fiercely.

Her guilt over Rory overwhelmed her. "I would much rather be home in Cornwall where there is no danger."

His arms tightened. "No danger? Wherever you are there is danger. If I sent you home the minute you got bored, you'd be dressing up as the Black Cat," he accused.

"Soon I'll have too big a belly to play highwayman."

"I hope so," he said, his hands roaming her belly and thighs possessively.

"If I'm being truthful, Spencer would be better off at home. London has been a very bad influence on him."

"What's the young devil up to now?" he demanded.

"Oh, nothing," she said faintly.

"Whoring, gambling, drinking, I have no doubt. Worrying you half to death, I suppose."

"No, really, it's his friends who are such rakes," she protested.

"Like your own friends?" he pointed out.

"Damn you, Ruark, you must be the only man on earth arrogant enough to insult me while trying to make love to me!"

Her words fueled his need for her. "Stay with me tonight at Whitehall," he demanded.

She pretended indifference. "Why on earth would I want to do that?"

"We have an unquenchable thirst for each other," he said, rubbing his thumb across a taut nipple.

"You might," she said lightly.

"We need to lie naked in each other's arms all night."

"You might," she repeated. But he had a power over her that set her shivering.

"We've always been more like lovers than husband and wife," he murmured against her neck. He ached to be deep inside her and vowed to have her this night. He knew he'd give much if she'd yield to him. "All I ask is one night."

She pulled away from him, truly offended now. "How dare you treat me like a strumpet?"

"God's flesh, Summer, what do you want? You won't behave like a decent wife and go home where you belong, so I'm reduced to begging your favors one night at a time. You lure me then rebuff me, daring my manhood. I don't know whether to strangle you or ravish you, or both." He tipped her face up to his and kissed her gently. "Come to Whitehall with me . . . on your own terms."

"Absolutely not," she said without hesitation. "You will take me to Cockspur Street or you can set me down in the street here."

"Dammit, Summer, why are you so willful?"

"If I were a passive woman, you'd crush me in a minute."

"Little chance of that, you're headstrong as ten men."

The coachdriver slowed at Whitehall, but Ruark instructed him to drive over to Cockspur Street. He helped Summer out of the carriage and instructed his driver to leave him.

"I didn't invite you in," she said pointedly.

"I don't need an invitation, you are my wife."

"I've been meaning to ask you to expedite that annulment," she said in a brittle voice.

He clamped his hand around her arm and half dragged her up the front steps of the house. "You are the most maddening creature a man was ever cursed with," he swore.

"Then why do you bother with me? I thought it was over."

They stood in the entrance hall at the foot of the stairs. "It will never be over between us." He entangled his fingers in her hair. "You're still the most beautiful woman I've ever seen. I bought you a waterfall diamond necklace for our first week's anniversary, but we couldn't even make the honeymoon last one week without savaging each other," he said with deep regret in his voice. "If you let me stay with you tonight, it's yours."

"I don't bribe so easily. Now, if you were thinking of offering me Roseland, I might reconsider."

He swept her up into his arms and carried her up the stairs. Her protests availed her nothing. He was finished asking. He was a man, she was his wife. He had decided to exercise his rights. He set her on her feet when he entered her bedchamber and began to remove his clothes.

"No, Ruark! I won't! I'll fight you."

"The choice is yours. I intend to have you, willing or no," he said quietly.

She backed away from him across the room, watching him undress in a leisurely fashion. She told herself not to be a fool. She could get Roseland deeded to her if she played her cards right.

When he was naked, he began to stalk her as if she were his prey. Summer knew he was dangerous, but danger always excited her. She ran from him, but watched over her shoulder in a most inviting way his pursuit of her. When his arms closed about her and he tried to remove her gown, she struggled so fiercely they fell to the carpet and rolled about. In less than a minute he had her pinned down and began to remove her clothing in as leisurely a way as he'd removed his own.

Her breasts were full and sensitive and she moaned helplessly as he dipped his head to tongue the rose-pink crests. She struggled again and managed to get to her feet, but he clasped his hands tightly behind her thighs and forced her forward until his mouth touched her most secret part. She arched forward so he could taste her and cried over and over "Ru, Ru." Then they were lost in each other, exploring and reexploring all the different ways they'd discovered to love each other.

Suddenly there was a crash, followed by a lot of giggling. They both sat up in bed and Summer searched frantically in the dark to find her bedrobe. They stared in disbelief as their door opened and three figures staggered in. "She's not here, I tell you, she's at Court." The man's words were so slurred they were almost indecipherable.

Ruark lit the bedside lamp and its light illuminated Summer's brother, dressed like a town gallant with his arms about two young street prostitutes. Ruark confronted him instantly. "What the hell is the meaning of this drunk and disorderly display, Spencer? How

dare you worry your sister like this! I can't believe you'd bring
these drabs to defile your sister's bed."

"Well, well," said Spider, swaying on his feet, "if it isn't the
Helford brothers' whore." He bowed to her mockingly.

Ruark's fist smashed into his face and he went down into unconsciousness. His companions had run from the house the moment
they'd seen Lord Helford's fury.

"Ruark, don't! My God, you've killed him, you brute," cried
Summer, going on her knees to cradle Spider's bleeding face.

"Get up, dammit, he needs a good thrashing. It's obvious you
can't handle him. He's out of control, sowing a crop of bastards
across London, bringing the pox home to you."

"It is you and your temper that's out of control. He's only a boy,
did you have to be so brutal?" she cried.

His fury was only exacerbated as he saw her pity for the young
lout. "He needs discipline. By God, I'll have him impressed into
the navy. I'd soon whip him into shape if he served on one of my
vessels."

"Get out—get out now! I hate you."

He turned on her angrily. "You, my lady, can get your things
packed. You're going home!" His voice was so implacable, it was
an order, and she was too distraught to argue. "I'll give you
twenty-four hours."

35

Later, as she bathed Spider's black eye and tried to sober him up with a foul-smelling concoction of Auntie Lil's, she wished she had taken her pistol to Ruark Helford. He had given her an ultimatum and there was no way she was going to be meekly packed off home, wherever that might be!

Spider was sullen. They exchanged unpleasant words until finally he informed her he was taking rooms in the city where he'd be free from damned meddling women who clocked him in and out like a felon on parole. She argued with him, threatened him, and saw he would do exactly as he pleased, no matter what she said. "Spider, I won't try to stop you if you promise to let me know where you are living when you get settled," she bargained desperately. He left without committing himself. "Typical male behavior," she raged aloud to the empty room. "Ruark Helford is the author of all my problems. I hope he rots in hell!"

Lil Richwood, dressed to the nines, swept in with a dramatic announcement. "Forgive me, darling, I didn't want to interrupt your delicious rendezvous with your husband last night; I thought the reunion was heaven-sent. How was I to know it would degenerate into a brawl before daylight?"

Summer sighed, realizing the whole debacle must look like a farce acted out on a stage. "I'm sorry, Auntie Lil. Spencer's moving into the city, so perhaps things will be a little more peaceful around here."

Lil waved a negligent hand weighted down by all her fine rings. "I'm moving the household to Southampton and I want you to come with us. I've had a letter from my very good friend Lady Worthing who insists I visit until this dreaded plague is gone from London."

"Oh, Lil, I couldn't impose on your friend," Summer protested.

"Nonsense, darling, she's as rich as a potentate and rattles about in a country mansion with fifty bedchambers. I'm the one who introduced her to Lord Worthing and they are both particularly partial to me. Pamela is the pampered darling of an older man and Lord Worthing appears virile as a stallion to all his peers. A match made in heaven," Lil drawled.

"Like mine," said Summer, her voice dripping acid.

"Well, no, that's more a volatile mix of love, hate, and explosive passion . . . a devastating combination!"

"Thank you for asking me, Lil, but I'll stay in London, I think, or perhaps I'll move to Court."

"I've inside information that Court is moving to Salisbury for the duration. If they do, I'd advise you to move with them, darling. Salisbury and Southampton are within spitting distance."

"I'm sure as soon as cold weather arrives it will stop the spread of this filthy disease," said Summer, repeating what was said at every gathering lately.

Lady Richwood took all her servants and naturally they traveled in her carriage, so Summer would have to hire chairs if she planned on going any distance. The house seemed deserted and she couldn't help feeling she was rattling around in it aimlessly, even after they'd been gone only an hour. Her practical nature soon took over, however, when she realized she would need food. The day seemed overcast, so she slipped on her pattens in case of a downpour and walked toward Piccadilly, where she knew there were shops to fill all her needs. She chose a cookshop where the food was already prepared.

Inside the cookshop all was in an uproar. There was something tangible in the frantic air which she soon learned was fear. The man and woman behind the counter spoke in shrill agitated voices to their customers.

"Last day, lydies . . . the shutters are goin' up the minute we've sold the last tripe 'n trotters. Droppin' like bleedin' flies around 'ere. Did ye see the comet in the sky last night? An omen of doom if there ever was one!"

The minute the man stopped talking, his wife began. "The butcher put up 'is shutters yesterday . . . dead today! They had nine children . . . all lived over the shop . . . bowled down like ninepins." Some of the women waiting their turn quickly left the shop. When it was Summer's turn, all they had left were meat pies and pickles. The woman behind the counter wiped the sweat from her face with her apron and took Summer's money. As she glanced out the window a look of horror crossed her face. The woman crossed herself quickly. "Christ Almighty, look at that . . . the death cart's come in broad daylight!"

Summer wished she'd never come; in fact, she wished now that she'd left London with Auntie Lil and the servants. The cart stood at the butcher's door; its driver rang a big hand bell and shouted, "Bring out yer dead, bring out yer dead."

The cookshop proprietors and the last few customers crowded about the window in horrified fascination as the little bodies were brought down and chucked into the wagon. Summer knew she was going to faint if she didn't get away. She pushed through the small avid crowd and bolted through the door to gulp fresh air. London's air today, however, was anything but fresh.

A pall of smoke hung about from the chimneys and from street fires which had been lit to destroy plague-contaminated furniture. She tried to hurry, but the pattens hampered her badly. She stopped, leaned against a wall, and unfastened them from her shoes, then she began to run and didn't stop until she was behind the door of the house in Cockspur Street.

It was like a nightmare. Why hadn't she left with Lil? Her throat felt dry and sore and fear rose up in her to rob her of coherent thought. Ruark Helford was to blame for her plight. He should have told her he loved her and taken her home to Cornwall after he'd made love to her last night. Instead he'd beaten and alienated poor Spider and given her another ultimatum. Now she was going to die of the plague and her precious burden would die with her.

She shook her head to rid it of such appalling thoughts and took the food into the kitchen. She looked at it with distaste, thinking she would never be hungry again. As she climbed the stairs her legs felt weak and shaky and she knew she must lie down or fall down. Well, it would serve Lord Bloody Helford right . . . when he arrived tomorrow, she would be dead!

She had caught the plague. She staggered off the bed to look at herself in the mirror. Her face was scarlet as if it had been boiled and she was hot as fire. She fell back upon the bed, her fingers frantically searching her groin for the black plague boil which would swell up like a balloon and burst. She sank into oblivion. Later she swam up out of the blackness, feeling herself being lifted, but she could not open her mouth to protest. She could not even open her eyes and she knew with horrified certainty they thought she was dead. They carried her out to the death cart and she could not lift a limb in protest. Her mind screamed in dread at her horrific plight. Stop, please, I beg you, her mind screamed, but no words came. Children's bodies were being thrown on top of her, and suddenly, shocked by the hideousness of the act, she found her voice and cried, "Stop, please, I beg you!"

"Cat, sweetheart, wake up," a very worried voice urged.

Her eyes flew open and stared into those of Black Jack Flash. She clutched him about the neck. "Rory . . . oh, my God . . . Rory."

He held her against his heart and stroked her tumbled hair. Her body trembled uncontrollably. "Cat, sweetheart, you were having a nightmare."

Her face was wet with tears. "I . . . I don't have the plague?"

"Of course not, the devil himself looks after sinners like you and me," he said, laughing down at her.

She clung to him thankfully. He was her savior. Gradually she relaxed against his powerful chest and murmured, "Rory, thank you. I'm so glad you came."

"What happened to my brave little hellcat? Where have all these fearful, fanciful thoughts sprung from?" he gently chided.

She sighed in his arms. How gentle he could be; how sweetly understanding. In that moment she felt so secure in his strength and his good nature, she felt she could tell him anything. Her voice was very low with a slight hint of apprehension as she said, "I'm going to have a baby, Rory."

"That's wonderful, darling," he said, clasping her close and pressing his lips to the curling tendrils that framed her brow.

"Perhaps you won't think so when I confess that I don't know if you are the father, or if it's Ruark's," she said low.

For a long moment he didn't speak and she eased her cheek away from his shoulder and looked up at him. He smiled down at her. "That makes no difference to me, love, and I'm damned sure it will make no difference to you."

"Oh, Rory, you can't mean it, surely every time you looked at the child, you would have doubts."

He put his fingers beneath her chin and brought his face closer to hers. "Do you think me incapable of loving my brother's child?" he asked seriously.

She knew in that moment he was a very special man. She lifted her mouth to his and was amazed at the tenderness he showed her.

"Come sail away with me," he tempted. "London is too foul a place for you at the moment. I'll take you to France and Holland," he coaxed.

Her eyes opened wide. "I thought we were at war with the Dutch."

He laughed. "We are, but I fly any flag I please, remember?"

What a difference a day made. If he'd asked such an outrageous thing yesterday, she would have refused, for hadn't she vowed that nothing more must happen between them? But now she was eager to get away from London, eager to be with a man who accepted her totally with all her faults, eager to make love with such a magnificent male as Rory Helford.

She glanced to the window, saw it was dark, and knew he must be away before light. "Do I have time to pack some things and change my clothes?" she asked, feeling excitement rise within her.

"Let me undress you, darling, we have all the time in the world." He rubbed his thumbs across the worry lines in her brow and said huskily, "You need to play, my love, have some fun." He pulled the gown from her shoulders and brushed his lips across the bared skin in reverent appreciation. This close, his eyes were deepest green and the skin seemed to be stretched taut across his deeply bronzed cheekbones. She held her breath, waiting for his reaction when he uncovered her breasts, for she knew their size and fullness had increased this last week. His mouth curved into a deep smile and he rolled his eyes and groaned in exaggerated bliss.

Summer laughed with pleasure and he bent his head to taste them as if they were luscious fruits. "I'm glad I can make you laugh," he murmured. "When's the last time you had any fun?"

"I can't remember," she said, smiling up at him. He made a game of undressing her. Each silken body part he uncovered received a dozen tiny kisses and then she joined in the fun and returned the bed play.

"Cat, life is a game. Love is a game. Lovemaking can be a thousand different games. Shall we play one?" he challenged, lifting an amused eyebrow. She was lying nude upon the bed. He, too, was now nude and he leaned his weight upon his hands on either side of her, filling his eyes with a lover's vision of a lifetime. "You are almost too beautiful," he whispered.

Her eyes traveled the length of his magnificent body, marveling at the perfection of muscle and sinew. "Are you ready?" he asked.

She caught her breath in anticipation, then nodded.

"I'm going to make love to you without moving in and out. If I bring you to climax, I win."

She laughed shyly. "Rory, that's impossible."

He grasped her ankles and pulled her gently from the bed onto the floor. Then he reached up and pulled down a pillow for her. She thought he would put it beneath her head, but instead he lifted her hips and positioned it beneath her buttocks. Her mons stood out invitingly. He went on his knees before her and she couldn't resist reaching out her fingers to touch his proud, crimson-headed shaft. It jumped wildly when her fingers came into contact with the hard center of him; he spread her rose-colored center and slowly inserted himself deep inside her until she was filled with him. He stayed absolutely motionless to let her get used to his fullness, then his mouth closed over hers and his tongue penetrated the sweetness of her mouth, and he held it motionless also.

It felt strange at first not to feel him moving in and out, but after about five minutes of stillness she became more aware of her body than she had ever been before. She became so sensitive she could feel her blood running through her veins. Then she became aware of her heartbeat, then his, and realized they pulsed against each other. Suddenly she felt him growing inside her and was both amazed and pleased that she could affect him so profoundly.

When he had lengthened and thickened to his full potential, he began to flex the great muscle of his manroot inside of her. Her honeyed walls clung to him, setting up a deep pulsing within her as they fused together. He fit so tightly that when the head of his phallus pulsed, it forced her to pulse also. The rhythm he set up inside her body was fast and strong. Incredibly she began to build to an intense degree, then his tongue began to pulse against hers and she knew a desire to suck him which she could not deny. Then a feeling she had never experienced before began deep within her and she knew her other lips were sucking him as wildly as her mouth clung to his tongue. Finally she let go to cry out her rapture and Rory's cry also filled the chamber. "Oh oh . . . Rory . . . you win and I win . . . mmm . . . yes, yes, yes!"

"I love playing games with you," he murmured against her ear. They slept curled together for a half hour, then he stirred and awakened her with love words. "Cat, sweetheart, you'd better pack a few things."

She groaned. "Brute, I can't lift a finger, I'd rather stay here in bed with you."

"I know another game," he tempted.

The corners of her mouth curved up irresistibly. "What?" she asked curiously.

"Don't dress. Pack the things you think you'll need but stay naked so I can watch you move about the room. Then we'll play half-and-half."

She laughed. "What's half-and-half?"

"I'll make love to you half in your bed here and the other half in my bed aboard the *Phantom*."

"Will you be able to stop halfway?" she teased.

"Indeed, my darling. I have perfected the technique. Only you must just slip a cloak over your nakedness so I can caress you in the coach and keep you in readiness for the finale."

"Rory Helford, you are a very wicked man." She laughed.

"Tell the truth and shame the devil—you love to play my wicked games."

Black Jack Flash was at the helm of the *Phantom* as it silently glided out on the flood tide. He seemed to have no difficulty finding his way in the dark, but he did not move from the forecastle until his sure hands and keen eyes had maneuvered the long, low ship past Margate into the open sea. He then turned the ship's wheel over to his second mate and slipped belowdecks.

Summer was always bemused at the contrast between Rory's two cabins. The outer room was exactly what one would expect of a sea captain, with comfortable leather chairs, map tables, and a desk filled with charts and papers. The inner cabin had his own unique, strong personality stamped all over it. The black silken carpet had a pile so thick, her feet sank into it. The black-and-red-lacquered cabinets were probably priceless, and when the heavy, mirrored door of the wardrobe was opened, it displayed the clothes of a vain, flamboyant male, selected to match his striking black hair with its startling streak of white.

Some of the items were strange and had obviously come from foreign lands, others were magnificently embroidered with jewels, yet always in the same colors of jet, pearl, diamonds, and crystal. Even the plain shirts and breeches were hand-sewn from the finest, most expensive materials.

Summer hung her clothes beside his, glad that she had not brought many with her since the space was so limited. Finally she turned toward the bed which dominated the room. The red silk panels floated about like smoke and she wondered with a stab of jealousy how many women had been inside that silken cocoon. She knew full well that if she was experiencing pangs of the green monster, she must be falling in love.

Suddenly she heard him step into his outer cabin and felt shy as a new bride, but the moment his tall figure stood in the doorway and they looked at each other, everything was all right. He carried a huge platter of food, which smelled delicious, and she smiled as she remembered that Rory always fed her. He set the tray on the bed and came to her. "You haven't eaten all day, have you?" he asked as he gently took her into his arms and held her against him. She shivered. "You're cold, love," he said, untying her cloak and casting it across the room. "Come to bed."

He reached for an enormous white djellaba with a hood and wrapped it about her, then held open the red silk panels as she climbed upon the huge bed. He undressed quickly, slipped in the other side, and closed the silken drapes to seal them off from the rest of the world.

He grinned down at her wickedly. "All that love play in the coach has gone to waste now that you are cold. I'll have to begin all over again." His brown hand reached for the platter and pulled it between them. They sat cross-legged on the bed so they could share the food and wine. Summer devoured half a chicken then sighed and licked her fingers. She knew from experience that Rory did everything in a leisurely manner. One by one all their hungers would be satisfied and all their thirsts quenched. Soon he was feeding her various spicy delicacies, and laughed with knowing eyes as she grew warmer.

His hand slipped inside the white djellaba to fondle her breasts and belly and thighs and he knew she no longer needed the robe. He pulled off the hood and ran his fingers through her silken black tresses, then he peeled it from her breasts and shoulders and tossed it negligently after her cloak. He poured them a goblet of hot, mulled cider spiced with cinnamon, cloves, and myrrh, and set the empty platter down on the floor. With one strong arm about her he drew her across to his side of the wide bed and held the goblet to her lips. She sipped obediently, then he, too, drank, carefully placing his lips on the same spot where hers had been.

She reclined against him, one breast pressed into the curling mat of hair on his broad chest, her cheek resting against his shoulder so she could gaze up at him. One hand cupped her breast and his strong fingers played tantalizing games with her rose-pink nipple. His other hand moved the spiced wine from his lips to hers, allowing them to share the loving cup.

Summer hadn't felt this warm and secure for a long time. She hadn't felt this loved since the first rapturous days with Ruark when he had married her. She closed her eyes as Rory's mouth took hers in a deep kiss. She wondered briefly if she was substituting Rory for her husband. After all Ruark had been her first love and she had loved him totally. She did not want to cheat this man. The thought melted away as his tongue began its game of arousal. He inflamed her desire and her senses so quickly, so deeply, that she knew without a doubt that she loved him.

They lay on their sides with every part of their bodies touching as he kissed her over and over. When her legs wrapped about his marble-hard thigh to rub her mons against him, he placed strong hands on her waist and lifted her over him. He held her high and allowed the tip of his erection to enter her. She plunged down and he playfully withdrew. They did it over and over, each time he went up inside her just a fraction of an inch further, slowly, blissfully going all the way up until he was seated where he longed to be. Then she drew up her legs on either side of him until she was on her knees. In this fantastic position his hands were free to cup her breasts, trace delicious fingers about her navel, or dip lower to touch the tiny erect bud of her womanhood just slightly above the place where his thick manroot entered her. She was free to arch backward, bringing an almost unbearable fullness to the sensitive area at the front of her sheath, or bend over him to tongue and lick his erect bronze nipples while his shaft moved up into the deepest

part of her and his hands cupped her buttocks to hold her imprisoned while he thrust in and out. Their cries of love were mingled
with the cries of the seabirds which had spotted the *Phantom* in the
early pink dawn.

36

Their days together were happy; their nights paradise. Rory knew they belonged together. This woman gave all of herself to their passion and he felt overwhelmed by her giving. Also, she was honest with him to a marked degree. There was no subject she could not discuss with him.

Summer spent time at his side up on deck. She never strayed to more distant parts of the ship and the crew simply grinned and gave the captain as much privacy as was possible. He had found her some white canvas pants belonging to a cabin boy and she had cut the sleeves from one of Rory's shirts and tied its tails at her waist. She leaned far out over the rail to watch some dolphins at play when she felt his arm steal about her. She seemed slimmer than ever to him and he bent to her ear and asked, "Are you sure about the baby?" She looked up at him quickly to see if she could catch a glimpse of regret, but all she saw was joy mixed with concern.

"I'm sure. Thank God I'm over the morning sickness or this voyage would be more like hell than heaven."

His arm tightened. "I love you, Cat."

"I believe you," she said, lifting her hand to smooth back the white flash of hair at his temple. "Rory, your brother Ruark is aware that we've met. I was at a knife fight across the river in

Southwark. My husband was angry to find me there and insisted on taking me home. My young brother came in drunk and said something offensive. He called me . . . he called me the Helford brothers' whore. Ru didn't question me about you, but he was so angry he savagely knocked down Spider. Then we did what we always do, had a terrible fight. I told him I hated him."

He looked down at her with amusement in his eyes. "Do you hate him?" he asked, wanting her to tell him the truth.

"Rory, you deserve the truth, the whole truth, not just part of it. I loved Ruark Helford with all my heart and soul. I fell so deeply in love, I walked about in a perpetual garden where he was the sun and the moon and the stars. When he made me Lady Helford, I thought he loved me, too. After he initiated me into the mysteries of love, I thought he was a god! But the truth is, now that I've met you, I've fallen out of love with him as suddenly as waking from a dream. I see all his faults in the clear light of day, and there are actually moments when, yes, I truly hate him. I know you are brothers and you have similarities, but the differences between you are amazing. He is arrogant, demanding, and he has a cruel streak which frightens me."

He looked down at her and she saw that the amusement had left him. He said carefully, "I am quite capable of arrogance and cruelty, Cat; don't deceive yourself, I beg you, love."

"But he also has a brooding moodiness sometimes which you are incapable of. Your eyes show only amusement . . . you laugh all the time. That's probably the reason I love you, Rory."

His green eyes were smiling again. "Ru knows all about us. I don't want you to worry about it . . . it's between Ru and me and we'll settle it once and for all, but I don't want you to be mistaken about him either. He must have loved you with all his heart or he wouldn't have made you Lady Helford in a million years."

"But when I confessed that I wasn't a wealthy, strictly brought up lady, I've never seen such fury. The things he said to me were unbelievable. They were enough to shatter my love forever."

"Ru had a couple of bad experiences with women who tried to take him for everything he had. It made him cynical toward all women."

A spark of anger flared in Summer. "You play devil's advocate very well. Are you trying to make me go back to him?"

He laughed, kissed her quickly, and said, "I just want you to understand, and if you refuse to understand, then it's my gain and his loss and I'm a big enough bastard to take full advantage."

"He was the one who spoke of an annulment, but it's what I want more than anything." She added quickly, "Not so that you'll have to marry me."

"Don't you want me for your husband?" he asked seriously. "You can't have a child and remain unmarried, I won't allow it."

"Of course I want you for my husband."

"Cat darling, I want you to think about it carefully. An annulment will mean giving up the title of Lady Helford, giving up Helford Hall and all Ruark's wealth and position with the King's court."

"Hell and furies, why won't you Helfords believe money and titles mean nothing to me? I only wanted money to save Roseland, and even then it wasn't really for myself but for my brother, who is Lord St. Catherine and deserves some sort of inheritance."

"I believe you, darling. Why else would you take up with a pirate who steals and smuggles for a living?"

"Anyway, I have friends of my own at Court and I'm a particular favorite of Charles. He doesn't give a damn if I'm Lady Helford or Cat St. Catherine!"

Rory's eyes had narrowed at mention of the King. A hardness had come about his mouth that she had never seen before. She felt a slight flutter of fear and came to the conclusion that she had misjudged his carefree manner. He was obviously jealous of her. Simply because he had not seemed jealous of his brother, she assumed he was not possessive by nature; she was wrong.

One of the sailors in the rigging had spotted a sail and all eyes were on Black Jack Flash to await his reaction and his orders. Rory adjusted his spyglass and shouted "She's Dutch," which only confirmed what his crew had suspected. Summer felt a great excitement well up within her. "Let me see!" she cried. He handed her the instrument and pointed out the small sail on the horizon, then shouted some strange foreign words to his men.

"Oooh"—Summer let out a long breath—"are you going to take her?"

Rory shook his head and laughed as the total look of disappointment covered her face. "Why not?" she demanded. "We're at war with the bastards."

"England is at war; I am not England. How could I take the ship and tomorrow go sailing into The Hague with a Dutchman in tow?"

She felt a keen disappointment but grudgingly admitted that what he said made sense. She felt his amused eyes upon her as she glanced up to see that the *Phantom* was flying the Dutch flag.

When they arrived in port, Rory took her below to his cabin while a crewman named Hans took care of the customs official. He kissed her nose. "If you'll change out of those cabin boy's trousers, I'll take you to the warehouses. I'm sure when you see the fabulous goods stored there, you'll make a poor man out of me."

"I'll make you a pauper," she promised. "But I can only speak English," she reminded him.

He grinned down at her. "In the warehouses the only language they understand is money. On the streets it's different. You can pretend to be French. Whatever I say to you, just answer *'oui.'*"

"You devil, I know better. I assure you that whatever you say, I will answer *non, non, non!*"

The warehouses were filled with varied and exotic goods from all parts of the world. The aromas were pungent enough to fill the senses and send the imagination off on flights of fantasy about strange lands and customs. One warehouse held nothing but wine, its floors stained purple from spillage. Every conceivable shape of bottle and cask held the best that Spain, Portugal, and France produced in their vineyards. Rory explained that Holland made gin to export or trade for the wine. The air was so heady Summer felt intoxicated simply breathing the fumes.

They passed into another warehouse whose contents could be identified by aroma. Large wooden boxes, lined with lead, held layers of tea from India, Ceylon, and even as far away as China. At the back of the warehouse the aroma changed to chocolate from sacks filled with cacao beans. Rory simply pointed to the things he wanted and two clerks followed him to jot down and tally his purchases. The haggling would come later when he must pay for the cargo he selected.

The smells in the next warehouse were so strange and pungent, they made Summer's nostrils quiver. Rory explained, "What you smell are drugs—benjamin, frankincense, galingale, mirabolans, aloes zocotrina, camphire. Other drugs are illegal—hashish, opium, even worse things which men will pay a king's ransom for, simply to make them mindless." He spoke rapidly to the clerks, giving them his drug order, and they nodded quickly, understanding immediately.

Summer wondered what he was buying and thought perhaps it was best if she did not know. The spice warehouse was unbelievable. Mountainous piles of peppercorns, nutmeg, and cloves stood beside heaps of licorice root and green ginger and sticks of cinnamon.

There was one vast warehouse filled to the rafters with weapons and ammunition. Knives, daggers, swords, and rapiers were displayed beside scimitars, sabers, and strange Oriental weapons and instruments of torture. Across from the knives were the pistols, guns, even cannons in every shape and size with their corresponding cannonballs.

Rory told her he had things to order which would bore her, so he left her to browse about among the material. He summoned a small Chinese woman in black trousers to take Summer's order for whatever struck her fancy. The array of colors and textures was beyond anything she had ever imagined. Silks, damasks, taffetas, cloth of gold, and curled cypresse hung beside ribbons and feathers and ornaments for hats and shoes. Chintz and calico vied with Egyptian cotton as fine as spiderwebs. Cloth embroidered with silken silver and gold thread was hung beside more elaborate beaded cloth decorated with flowers and butterflies and birds. Suddenly she was back aboard the *Golden Goddess* in the halcyon days of her honeymoon when her husband would have given her the whole world, had she asked for it. Her heartstrings tightened painfully as she thought of Ruark, then quickly she banished all thought of him before the teardrops gathered to cloud her vision. Finally Summer saw something which fired her imagination for a gown and she knew she must have some. Vases filled with ostrich feathers, dyed every hue of the rainbow, took her breath away. Ribbon dresses were so popular that now they had become commonplace. Summer wanted a gown trimmed with pale turquoise ostrich feathers. She ordered enough to encircle the neckline and float about the hem. The Chinese woman brought her a fan made from the same shade of feathers and she nodded her acceptance.

Through another door was a room filled with curio cabinets, some from India, others from the Orient. Summer remembered that Queen Catherine had many such cabinets at Hampton Court. The center of the warehouse was filled with the curious objects which made the curio cabinets interesting. There were agates, onyxes, intaglios, a lump of amber with a toad enclosed, shells, rare bird's eggs, and porcelain miniatures.

She wandered into a cavelike room where guards trained their guns upon her person and she realized with awe that she walked among trays of diamonds, emeralds, rubies, pearls, turquoise, sapphires, onyxes, and opals. Hundreds of other trays held gems so exotic she had never heard tell of them. Rory found her here and told her to choose a pair of jewels to be made into earrings. She chose tear-shaped rubies as large as pigeon eggs. "There are many more costly jewels than rubies, sweetheart, are you sure?"

She nodded and said emphatically, "I'm particularly partial to rubies."

He tallied up his purchases and grinned to himself as he noticed she had chosen ostrich feathers. She had no idea how wildly expensive they were or she would never have bought five dozen, but he wasn't about to enlighten her. "Your earrings will be ready in half an hour. Why don't you wait in the carriage while I haggle over prices for what I've bought today?"

A clerk escorted her back to the waiting vehicle and she was startled to come face-to-face with the man she had seen at Stowe who was so obviously a Grenvile.

"Oh, hello," she said, "we bumped into each other at Stowe."

The man uttered the identical words to her as he had the last time they met. "Madame, you are mistaken."

Her mind flashed about quick as mercury. Each time she had seen him she had angered him. Why did he not wish to be recognized either here or in Cornwall? The Grenviles were high in the King's favor and Jack had recently been created Earl of Bath. What was a Grenvile doing in The Hague when England was at war with the country?

When Rory returned to the coach with her earrings, the encounter was momentarily forgotten. "Oh, Rory, I've never had anything so lovely in my whole life."

"Here, let me put them on for you," he offered, brushing her hair back from her ears.

"They don't go very well with this peach-colored gown, I'm afraid."

"We can remedy that easily enough," he said, and in a flash his arms went about her to undo the gown's fastenings.

"Rory, stop," she gasped, pulling the gown back up to cover her breasts.

"I can't stop," he said huskily, lifting her into his lap. A thrill ran through her because he was bold enough to undress her in a coach. When she finally allowed his hands to roam freely beneath the gown, he was momentarily satisfied to simply hold and kiss her. She sighed and clung to him, thankful that his desire for her raged hotter each day they spent together.

He opened the carriage window and instructed the driver to stop at an inn. Cat was surprised because the ship lay at anchor only a few miles away. She concluded he must be hungry and was taking her to the inn to dine. When the coach rolled to a stop in the busy inn yard, he pulled up her gown to cover her shoulders and, without bothering to fasten it, lifted her up into strong arms and swept into the inn. If the proprietor was startled to see the black-clad pirate with the startling streak of white hair carry in a female like a piece of prize booty, he hid it the moment he caught the gold piece tossed to him. He showed them up to the best room and discreetly closed the door on them. Rory was on fire. His tongue darted out to part her soft lips and the top of her gown fell away to expose her lovely breasts. A groan escaped his throat as he gently laid her across the bed and pulled the gown all the way down her hips and off her legs. He was enflamed as he saw she wore nothing beneath the gown but lacy stockings held up by peach-colored garters.

She watched his eyes turn to green flame as they licked over her bare skin. As he bent over to remove her shoes, his black hair brushed her soft belly and she sucked in her breath at the exquisite sensation. Then his mouth was taking tiny nips across her bare stomach and she fastened her fingers in his magnificent hair and pressed him closer.

She was panting with her need for him, crying his name over and over as his mouth went lower and lower until he opened the pink petals of her secret flower and tongued the tiny hidden bud until it stood erect. She let go of his head and fell back to allow him full rein. She knew he loved to do this to her and abandoned herself to his pleasure totally. Her body arched up to his mouth of its own volition and he began to suck on the hard little fruit until wave after wave of pure, shattering sensation spread up from her mons, inside her belly, and up to her breasts like threads of fire. His hands went beneath her bottom to lift her closer to his mouth and he plunged his tongue deep within to gather all her honeyed sweetness. She screamed as her endurance reached its limit and she plunged over the edge to pulsating climax after climax. She came up off the bed, clinging to him tightly, her hot mouth pressed against his throat.

Their hands came together to divest him of his clothes, then he lay full length on top of her so that their bodies touched from head to toe. His phallus throbbed against her soft thigh and she whispered, "Darling, you've made me so sensitive, I don't think I can take you inside of me now." She was dreamy-eyed and languorous with fulfillment.

"Hush, precious love, open your mouth to me." They curled together and she obeyed him implicitly. First the tip of his tongue entered her mouth, then it slid in all the way and she tasted herself on it. Immediately she wanted him again and the knowledge that she was oversensitized and slightly swollen nearly drove her mad with desire. Suddenly she wanted him more than she'd ever wanted anything before and she begged him not to be gentle.

He thanked the gods that he had found a mate who was woman enough to explore the limits of her sexuality and allow him to indulge every raging need. Before he finished loving her, her beautiful blushes tinged her ivory skin all the way to her rose-tipped nipples. He had never known a woman so perfectly attuned to his body's demands. She opened to him and her wild movements urged him on to total domination. His lovemaking had been fiercely demanding, yet her body had complied to every ultimatum. She slitted him a look of adoration and he ran the back of his fingers down her throat. "You have satisfied all my cravings, little hellcat. I love you with all of my heart."

Her fingertips traced the heavy muscles of his shoulders and he dipped his head to touch her lips with infinite tenderness. "You were magnificent, like a great raging storm."

The mocking amusement was back in his eyes. "And you, my darling, were insatiable."

She laughed and blushed. "You take me beyond control so that my needs scream aloud for fulfillment."

"They no doubt heard your screams below," he teased unmercifully.

"Oh, Rory, how will I ever be able to face them?" she asked contritely.

"Any man who saw me sweep you up those stairs must have been green with envy. Any who heard your cries of love would die for one night in your bed. Come, sweet, we must return to the ship."

"Beast! I can't move a finger. You'll have to dress me," she teased.

Dutifully he propped her up and put her gown on over her head. His lips tickled her ear and he whispered wickedly, "I'm not finished with you yet tonight."

37

❦

"**R**ory," she said the next morning as he came back down to the cabin from the quarterdeck, "yesterday I saw a man who was quite obviously a Grenvile." She let the statement hang in the air to see what he would say.

A quick frown came between his brows. "At the warehouses? You don't think he saw me, do you?"

"I don't think so . . . I don't know. Who is he?"

"It must have been Richard . . . Sir Richard Grenvile. He was a general in the late King's army, but he and Chancellor Hyde hated each other with a vengeance. When he offered his services to Charles, they were not accepted because of the ill feeling with his chief minister. It embittered Richard so much he chose to live in exile and swore never to set foot in England again."

"That's strange—I saw him at Stowe a few weeks ago." As soon as she said it, she knew that Richard Grenvile was a spy. This was important information which she could pass on to the King. Actually she was unsure where Rory's loyalties lay and it made her uneasy now that she had begun to think about it. He certainly was no stranger to Dutch soil. Though she sometimes lusted for adventure and was usually ready for any madcap risk, she was deeply loyal to king and country. One of the things she most admired about her husband was his commitment to duty. She probed lightly: "Rory, is your first loyalty to Charles?"

He grinned at her. "My first loyalty is to myself, Cat." He changed the subject immediately. "I've arranged for you to go shopping today. I can't leave myself, I have to wait for the goods I ordered yesterday, but I've asked Hans to accompany you to interpret the language. I think you'll be astounded when you see the fashionable shops. I've given him enough gilder to pay for anything you desire."

"You are very lavish with your money, sir. Do you come by it so easily?"

His eyes showed their amusement. "Sometimes yes, sometimes no, but I hope I'm man enough to afford whatever my woman desires." He looked into her eyes. "You are my woman, Cat, aren't you?"

She lowered her lashes. "You know I am, Rory."

"You'd better hurry and put your gown on before I prove it to you." He winked. He closed the bedroom door as he went into the cabin he used as his office. She wondered if Hans spoke any English and ran after him to ask, but he had already left the outer office. Suddenly she heard his deep voice just outside the door. "Keep her away from the ship until three. I don't want her to be here when de Ruyter comes."

Summer was stunned. Everyone in England knew that the famed de Ruyter was the mastermind of the Dutch fleet and England's premier enemy. She couldn't believe that Rory would have dealings with the famed sea captain—no wonder he didn't want her to know anything about it! Her first thought was that she should inform the King. She shuddered . . . she knew she could never betray Rory. When they had first met, he had warned her that he was a scoundrel, that he had always been the black sheep of the family, and for the first time she was ready to believe it.

She went ashore with Hans, a blond giant who had been ordered to protect her with his life. He looked incongruous in the ladies' shops, doling out gilder for Summer's purchases, but she would have been unable to manage without his ability to interpret Dutch and French to English. As Rory had predicted, she was amazed at the high style and vast number of establishments which were mostly run by French couturiers.

She bought a flame-colored gown which opened down the front to reveal a petticoat of gold lace tissue. It was a spectacular gown,

one which needed the confidence of a queen to wear, but Summer
had always possessed that quality. At another establishment she
chose a beaded gown of clinging material which changed colors
with the light. One moment it was pale green, the next it was a
shimmering silver. She couldn't resist a wrap made of fox fur,
outrageously dyed a pale green shade to match the gown. She knew
no one in London had a pastel fur and reasoned that someone like
Barbara would be willing to kill for such a garment.

It began to rain, and when it rained in Holland, it did a thorough job of it. The heavy pewter sky made Summer's spirits sink
and no matter how she tried to push away the disturbing thoughts
about Rory, they crept back insidiously, fueling her active imagination with one unsavory plot after another. She almost insisted that
Hans return her to the ship so she would walk in on Rory and de
Ruyter, but she thought better of it and allowed the blond giant to
escort her to a fine restaurant for a good hot meal to ward off the
chill of the wet weather.

She decided she needed a drink to banish the darklings, and
when a light golden wine was suggested, she shook her head emphatically and ordered gin. Hans looked alarmed. If he had dared
to refuse her, he would have done so. He was all too aware of the
potent and immediate effects of the clear, strong liquor. By the
time he guided her back to the *Phantom,* Summer was in the state
of intoxication which made the timid bold. In Summer's case it
made her downright aggressive. She boarded the *Phantom* and
watched with knowing eyes as the faithful Hans went up on the
quarterdeck and reported to Black Jack Flash that she had almost
disgraced herself by guzzling gin.

She divested herself of her gown and high heels and donned the
white duck pants and knotted his white lace shirt at her waist. She
tied a red kerchief about her hair and, barefoot, went up on deck to
beard the lion in his den.

Rory's eyes followed her progress with amusement as she took
extra-careful steps to match the ship's roll as it rode at anchor.
Today his amusement annoyed her. She'd wipe that damned smile
off his face if it was the last thing she did.

She swaggered up to him insolently, fists dug into her hips, and
said, "I've decided I don't like this stinking country, when are we
leaving?"

Rory's eyebrows went up slightly. "When I give the order to
leave."

She uttered a stable oath and he looked down at her from at least six feet and said in a mocking voice, "I should teach you how to curse in another language, it sounds so coarse in English." He was filled with arrogance, dash, and swagger. He could be rude or charming, but she knew he would never be anything other than self-assured, and today it simply grated on her nerves.

"English is quite good enough for me," she said with narrowed eyes. "*I* hate fraternizing with my enemies even if you do not!"

"I believe you are slightly drunk, Cat. Seek your cabin," he said quietly.

"You give orders so well, sir, let's see if you can take them. I order you to weigh anchor now!" she shouted recklessly.

"Cat, I warn you I will not tolerate your impudence before my men. Go below," he ordered.

She took an aggressive step toward him, daring his manhood. "And if I don't?"

He took two strides toward her and lifted her in his arms. Her mouth curved with satisfaction. Now he would carry her below and try to make love to her, but she would refuse him! He carried her to the rail, lifted her over, and let her drop straight down into the water.

She came to the surface gasping for air. She couldn't believe what he'd just done to her. God damn all Helford men to hellfire! The dunking had sobered her up in one hell of a hurry, but there was no way on God's earth she was going to haul herself up on the seawall and board the *Phantom* looking like a defeated drowned rat.

He wasn't even looking over the rail to see if she was all right. She trod water for what she estimated would be ten minutes, then she filled her lungs with air and pushed herself out from the side of the ship in a deadman's float. Her arms spread wide, her hair drifted out from the red kerchief, and she hung facedown, half-submerged in the water. She heard the cry go up—"Captain! Captain!"—and forced herself to remain still and use up as a little oxygen as possible. She heard Rory's frantic "Christ Almighty!" Then she heard him plunge down from the deck thirty feet above her. She felt his strong hands lift and turn her so that she was faceup in the water. "Sweetheart, speak to me," he ordered. She lay with eyes closed in a seeming state of unconsciousness. "My God, I'm sorry, I didn't mean to hurt you," he gasped. She fluttered open her eyes, whispered his name pitifully, and closing them again, let out all her breath and stopped breathing. He was frantic now to get her out of the water. He floated her over to the seawall and allowed a half dozen of his crew to help him lift her, cursing them to be careful not to scratch her delicate skin on the sharp barnacles and crustaceans massed everywhere.

He carried her dripping body down to his cabin, flung back the red silk curtains, and lay her gently upon the bed. He knelt down beside her, pinched her nostrils together, and gently pried open her mouth. He covered her mouth with his and gave her his own breath to try to revive her. "Please, please," he murmured between breaths. Her chest rose and fell as he breathed life into her and Summer found it almost impossible to keep from giggling. The next time he fused his mouth to hers, she wrapped her arms around his neck and kissed him in a most suggestive fashion.

"You little hellcat, I should beat you to a jelly playing such damned tricks."

She began to laugh and found she could not stop. Finally she drew up her knees and, hugging them, rolled about the bed in mirthful glee. Rory regained his sense of humor and began to laugh with her. "You little bitch, you hate to be bested, don't you?"

"I haven't found the man yet who could do it."

In a flash he dragged her across his knee and pulled down her soaking pants. Then he gave her bare bottom one resounding smack which he knew would smart like hell.

"Rory, don't be fierce with me, you forget I'm with child."

He turned her over quickly and dropped a quick kiss upon her stomach. "Your little belly is too big for me to forget such a thing," he teased.

"You brute, how could you?" she protested.

He grinned down at her. "Serves you right. The bed is drenched, we'll have to sleep on the floor tonight."

"Mmmm . . . delicious," she said wickedly.

Rory however was nowhere to be found that night. She fell asleep on the window seat waiting for him and didn't awaken until the small hours of the night. When at last she heard him, his movements were so furtive she became suspicious. She pretended sleep until he changed into a robe and stretched himself out full length on the floor.

In less than an hour, light from the dawn crept into the cabin and she arose quietly. Her throat closed as she noticed his blood-stained knife lying with the black garments he had removed. She slipped out to go up on deck to get some air. As she leaned against the taffrail in the half-light she saw something floating in the water. It was too dark to make out what is was at first, then slowly she was filled with horror. She knew it was a body because of its auburn hair floating like seaweed. The shade of auburn matched that of the Grenviles exactly.

Within the hour the *Phantom* was on its way and soon they had left the sodden skies of Holland behind for the sun-drenched coast of France. Summer's peace of mine had fled. Her suspicions about him grew when they sighted Dutch merchantmen and Rory refused to attack them. Now that suspicion had raised its ugly head she could not content herself with his explanation that he did not want to jeopardize her safety.

When he took midnight watch at the ship's wheel, she decided to go through his desk. She was convinced that he had unlawful dealings with the Dutch and hoped and prayed that he was not selling England's secrets for money.

What she found was a diplomatic pouch with sealed documents addressed to King Louis of France from King Charles of England. She dared not disturb the seal further, for to her keen eyes it already looked as if it had been tampered with. Here was a puzzle indeed. Had Rory Helford been entrusted to deliver a message from England to France or had he come by the documents by piracy? If the documents were genuine, had he stopped off in Holland to reveal their contents to de Ruyter? Or were they fake documents to France's king, only ostensibly from the King of England?

The next time they made love she would pry in a subtle way to see if he would let anything slip.

The *Phantom* lay at anchor in a secluded cove. The crew had gone ashore in the longboats. They were familiar with many wineries in the vicinity which had provided vintages to slake their thirst in the past and the vineyards stretched back for miles.

Summer and Rory had swum naked together in the warm azure sea the moment they had their privacy and now lay on deck sunning themselves and drowsing in the heat of the day. Summer had modestly wrapped a towel about her, but Rory hadn't bothered with such an encumbrance. She reclined against soft red cushions he had brought from their cabin and Rory lay stretched out full length with his head resting in her lap. The wooden planks of the deck were deliciously warm beneath her buttocks and the sun had kissed her face until her skin had turned golden.

His cheek stirred against her thighs and she peeped from beneath half-closed lashes. Her eyes ran over the splendid length of him. He had such a superb body, it gave her deep pleasure to see the great slabs of bronzed muscle flex and relax as he breathed. Then she became aware that he was watching her admire his body, for his manhood stirred and the great shaft began to thicken and lengthen. Her body heat almost scorched his cheek as it pressed against her soft thigh. Slowly his hand reached up and removed the towel which separated her bare flesh from his. He turned his face into her body and pressed a kiss just above her triangle of curls. "You are so lovely," he said huskily, letting the tip of his tongue trace her secret places. "Your skin tastes salty from the sea." Suddenly she knew a strong need—his body was so beautiful, she wanted to worship it.

"Rory, I want to taste you," she said intensely. Their eyes met and held and in that moment the whole universe melted away until there was just the two of them and their great hungry need to devour each other. She knew all barriers between them must come down before he would reveal the truth to her. She knew they must merge and become one. He lifted her up until they stood pressed together in a close embrace. Her face when she stood on tiptoe reached to the base of his throat. She kissed the place where his pulse throbbed then her tongue began to lick his bronzed skin. He held his body motionless for her as she traced her lips lower across his pectoral muscles, his flat nipples, then her tongue traced down his ribs until she bent low enough to dip it in and out of the deep cleft of his navel.

Slowly she slid down his body until she was on her knees before him. His sex stood up rigidly, slightly higher than her mouth. She looked up to see him gazing down at her with adoration. This was the most intimate thing she'd ever done for a man and it would shatter the last barrier between them. She reached up gentle fingers to lever his shaft downward and kiss its velvet crown. He moaned with unbelievable pleasure and she took the head into her mouth and ran the tip of her tongue under its prominent ledge. She marveled that the head of his phallus was heart-shaped, and if she held her soft tongue pressed to him, she could feel every wild heartbeat and pulse of his magnificent body.

His head was thrown back now, the columns of his strong neck arched until they stood out, straining his control to the limit. She nibbled and sucked on him for a few minutes then her tongue traced the full length of his shaft and he cried out, "Don't!"

She had had a foretaste of lavish sensuality and now she needed him to fill her so she would never feel empty again. One last time she ran her tongue over the swollen crest of his manhood. She felt him swell and go solid. She removed her lips and saw how unbelievably large he had grown. She trembled with need. If she didn't have him, she would die.

He pulled her face up to his before it was too late, then lifted her by the buttocks onto his marble-hard weapon and thrust it to the hilt. If she hadn't been so completely aroused, she would never have been able to accommodate his great size. Their passion scorned convention and leaped the barriers of normal morality. They fell writhing to the hot deck and she wrapped her legs high about his back as he savagely thrust harder and deeper, impaling her to the limit of her endurance. It was torture, but a blissful torture of shivering, mounting, sumptuous response as he brutally carved out his own place inside of her.

She began to sob for the culmination, then she heard his command, "Now!" and he took her mouth in a bruising kiss which made her whole body throb from the tip of her tongue to her toes. She felt his explosion deep within and she felt herself implode upon him as he emptied himself inside her. It was as if he had opened the floodgates to paradise.

They clung together, dreading the inevitable separation that must come when they returned to being two again. He diminished in size and hardness until his erection was half what it had been at the height of their passion, yet he was still large enough in this semiaroused state to almost fill her. He rolled his weight from her but took her with him so that he could remain inside her. He could not bear to withdraw just yet. She lay in a wanton sprawl atop his great body and felt the delicious black crisp hairs beneath her cheek. The sun beat down upon her bared back and his beloved hands came up to massage her bottom, then he relaxed his hands so that he cupped her lightly. As she lay there, a captive to their lust, she began to feel guilty. What if this man was a traitor to his country? If she faced the truth, she knew he had killed a man. What if he was a danger to her husband, Ruark? She knew Ruark was involved in spying for the King. If Rory worked for the other side, was he ruthlessly using his brother to learn England's secrets?

She looked at his face and for the first time it looked dangerous, hard, brutal.

When she could speak again, she said low, "Rory, I saw the sealed documents you carry."

"Leave it!" His voice, like a whiplash, stunned her. How could he keep secrets from her while their bodies were still joined?

"Did you kill Richard Grenvile?" She felt enormous guilt over the death, since she'd been the one to tell him of sighting Grenvile. "Tell me!" she cried.

Very deliberately his hands tightened on her bottom and he rotated her erotically upon his hardening shaft. She gasped at the thrill which shot up inside her and knew he was trying to make her mindless, using his sex as his weapon. She had mistakenly thought all barriers between them had been swept away. He had given her all of his body and part of his soul, but his mind was locked away from her.

She reached her hand down between them, felt the crisp hairs of his groin, and withdrew him from her sheath. She cried out at the sharp, quick loss of exquisite fullness, and as their eyes met she saw his were filled with furious anger.

"You deliberately spoiled the most beautiful fucking either one of us ever experienced in our lives!" he ground out between clenched teeth.

She was covered with guilt, for indeed it had come close to being the most beautiful loving she'd ever experienced and she couldn't bear it to be so. Ruark's lovemaking had been the best and that's the way she wanted it to stay. She was momentarily overwhelmed by her faithlessness to her husband. As if she'd done it deliberately to hurt him. My God, even if she'd lain with the King, it wouldn't have been as bad as giving herself to his brother! She snatched up the towel to cover herself and ran belowdecks, feeling the fury in his accusing green eyes burning into her back as she ran. She slumped down upon the bed with both her mind and her emotions in chaos. A tear slipped down her cheek. She didn't like herself very much at the moment and knew she needed to take a good hard look at herself.

Why had she let herself fall into another man's arms so quickly? When Ruark rejected her, her loss had been so devastating that she had immediately replaced him with a replica of himself. She felt ashamed that she had needed a man so badly. Hell and furies, she'd always managed on her own before she'd met Lord Ruark

Helford. Admittedly she'd cheated, stolen, and lied, but in a man's world you did these things to even the odds a little. She'd found the courage to smuggle, she'd had guts enough even to play highwayman, therefore she should have had enough spirit to go on alone without a man in her life. She didn't need either of them. To hellfire with all men!

38

That night the ship docked at Le Havre and she saw Rory leave the ship in black cloak and mask. She had no idea what time he returned, she only knew that he did not join her in the exotic silk-hung bed. When she emerged into the bright morning light, Rory stood at the wheel garbed in white from head to foot, with the Union Jack flapping in the stiff breeze from the top of the mast.

Yesterday seemed like a specter seen through a glass darkly. Today there was nothing sinister about the ship or the man at its helm. He looked boyish, carefree. He waved and called to her, "Come up and navigate." She was about to shake her head when out of nowhere came a deafening boom and a splash. A great cry went up as the deck suddenly filled with the crew and two went up the masts quick as monkeys.

Summer's heart drummed in her ears as a quick stab of fear shot through her, but it was immediately replaced by an excitement she could hardly contain. She saw Rory gesture for her to go below but she blithely ignored the order and ran up to the quarterdeck. She did not run to him for protection, but went there to get a better view. Rory was looking through his telescope and his voice boomed to every corner of the *Phantom:* "It's a Dutchman." She imagined she heard relief in his voice, and relief on the faces of the crewmen.

"We'll fight!" He shouted his decision, and the crew let out a cheer that was deafening. "Get below," he told Summer.

"No!" she defied him.

"This deck will run with blood," he told her graphically.

Her eyes narrowed with the excitement of danger. He was so bold, so brave, she wanted to watch him take the prize. "I want to see you fight!"

"You may see me die," he pointed out.

"Heaven doesn't want you and the devil is afraid you'll take over," she threw his own words at him.

He looked at her and grinned widely—she was every bit as courageous as he and he admired and loved her for it. Then he had no more time to think of her and knew she would understand. He thundered his orders and every last man anticipated them. Skillfully he maneuvered the ship quickly enough to allow one of his gunners to put a broadsider into the oncoming vessel, and Summer could taste the pitch he had used to light the gunpowder in the cannon. A victory shout went up as the cannonball found its target in their enemy's belly. There was no way such a small hole would sink them, but it would keep some of the Dutch crew busy stopping the seawater from gushing in.

Summer's hand went to her waist and she felt relief as she felt the hilt of her knife safely tucked there. Rory's crew comprised every nationality, but whether they were black, yellow, or brown, they were armed in identical fashion. Each man held a cutlass in one hand, a pistol in the other, and a belaying pin or cudgel tucked into his belt alongside his knife.

They climbed the lines of the rigging like circus performers, some even holding their weapons in their teeth while they got a better grip on the lines with their hands and knees. Summer's head fell back to watch them and she shaded her eyes with her hand. She assumed they were climbing the rigging so that when the two ships came alongside, they would swing over to the Dutchman and board her, but as the tall sailing ship loomed over them she realized in a moment of panic that the smaller *Phantom* was much lower than the tall merchantman and it would be the Dutch who would board the *Phantom* and the battle would be waged on her decks.

Rory and his crew had known this all along and were high in the rigging so they could jump the sailors once they came aboard the *Phantom*. There was a sickening thud and shudder as the two vessels came together and Summer realized she stood alone on the deck of the *Phantom* as the Dutchmen swarmed aboard. Should she flee or stand and fight? Her feet were rooted to the spot as she watched two men advance upon her. From nowhere a line swung down past her and the sailor on the end of it kicked one of the enemy in the throat while disemboweling the other with a low cutlass slash across his stomach. The man's innards spewed out and splattered Summer's canvas pants while she looked on in helpless horror.

Screams and shouts intermingled with curses, cries, and wild laughter. Shots whistled through the air and steel clashed against steel and flesh. Men everywhere were engaged in desperate battle but she had no way of telling which were the enemy. A sailor advanced upon her with glinting sword, but her feet slipped on the blood of the deck and she ducked her head under his arm. Her knife was in her palm and she whirled about and brought it up in a vicious slash to rip open his arm from wrist to elbow.

This was no exciting adventure; the reality was a living nightmare. It was blood and guts and brains. It was death and maiming and gaping wounds. It was screaming and groaning and weeping. It was madness!

Three men were almost upon her when Rory swung down and knocked her from their path. She sprawled onto the blood-slippery deck, the wind knocked from her lungs. Rory stood over her and fought off the enemy. One took a ball through the temple, another lost an arm as Rory slashed his heavy cutlass with all his powerful strength. The third man he disarmed and ran him at swordpoint up onto the quarterdeck, where he lashed him to the mast with a rope. Then in a flash he was back to scan her anxiously then thrust her behind him while he dispatched another to hellfire.

With their captain taken and half their number slaughtered, the Dutch surrendered. The crew of the *Phantom* prodded them overboard and a magnanimous Black Jack Flash cut the ropes which sent a longboat splashing down among them. Only two of Rory's crew were dead. Eight were wounded and a dozen had minor injuries which they ignored from sheer bravado.

Summer was shaking all over as she helped to bind up the wounded. Rory's white clothes were stained red from head to foot. "You were very brave," he said solemnly.

"I didn't know . . . I had no idea what it would be like," she said shakily.

"I know, love . . . you wouldn't listen . . . you had to learn the hard way."

"Rory . . . forgive me . . . I thought you had gone over to the enemy."

He shook his head. "You still don't understand. I didn't take the ship because she was a Dutchman, I took her because she fired across my bow. If she'd been English, I would have taken her just the same. I am a pirate."

Her eyes lifted to the captain still lashed to the mast. "What will you do with him?"

"Probably turn him over to Ruark along with the ship." He grinned at her. "But not before I strip her of every last piece of booty."

She staggered a little. "Go below and bathe and rest if you can. We have our work cut out for us up here," he said.

She looked down at herself in dismay. "Does the smell of blood ever wash off?" she asked him quietly.

"Not really," he said, shaking his head sadly.

That night they didn't make love, but he clung to her in the great bed in a towering need. Their closeness brought him some small measure of sanity in an uncivilized universe. It was hours before peaceful calm descended to slow his thudding heart and racing pulse. By dawn she had given him back his powerful strength.

"I think you'll be glad to get back on land again, won't you?" he questioned.

She hesitated, not wanting to hurt him. "I love the sea . . . but perhaps we are too close to Holland in these particular waters."

"I've been thinking about sailing to New Guinea for gold. Would you go with me, Cat?"

She thought of her baby and wondered how he could ask such reckless behavior of her. "I don't know," she said truthfully. "I would need time to consider such a thing."

He stretched and laughed and kissed her deeply before he went abovedecks to again take over the helm of the *Phantom.* By late afternoon they had sighted England and Summer came up on deck. She was vastly relieved to see everything had been swabbed and scrubbed to remove all evidence of the recent carnage. The gulls and terns circled and screamed overhead as she climbed to stand beside Rory. A stiff breeze was blowing his black-and-white-streaked hair about his shoulders and he seemed lost in thought.

"Where are we?" she asked, and her words brought him back from the distant place his mind explored.

"That's the Isle of Wight," he answered.

"When will we arrive in London?" she asked.

His eyes sought hers. "I'm not taking you to London. When it's dark, we'll sail into Southampton, which is only twenty miles from Salisbury where the court has moved."

"To hell with the court, I want to go to London," she argued.

"London is still a pest hole. Believe me, the moment the plague starts to disappear Charles and the court will return to the city."

"But I must see if my brother is all right. I've been away too long now."

"Cat, your duty is to yourself and my son that you are carrying. My business is in Southampton and yours is in Salisbury, and you will obey me for once." His face was stormy and she thought better of arguing with him. She also realized that his self-assurance was so great he didn't believe the child she carried could be anyone's but his.

It took most of the night to make port, for first, of course, he moored the Dutch merchantman in a safe haven where he could empty her of the spices, ivory, and gold she had brought from the Guinea coast of Africa.

Summer went below to write a letter. She could not bring herself to tell him to his face the decision she had made. Her thoughts had slowly sorted themselves out day by day until she had come to a final conclusion. There were more foul days at sea than fair, and though they had enjoyed a fantastic liaison, it was over.

Black Jack Flash was a superb adventurer and lover, but he was not the right stuff for husband or father. Summer and her baby would become anchors about his neck until resentment would destroy them. She faced the truth for once. She wanted Lord Ruark Helford for husband or she would do without.

In the note she bade him goodbye and told him she loved him too much to chain him. She bade him sail the seven seas and urged him to go to Guinea for the gold he so much wanted. Then she hid the note where he would not find it until they had parted.

At dawn he put Summer on the coach for Salisbury and told her he would make contact with her in a week's time. He lingered over his goodbyes, kissing her deeply, then grinned and dropped a pouch of gold coins into her lap. "You'll need this," he whispered. "Gambling will be the only diversion in Salisbury."

She waved until he was out of sight. Then she sighed deeply and resolutely opened the heavy coach door and climbed down.

"Hey, missus, get back inside, we're ready to leave!" ordered the coachman.

She gave him a cold glance. "Are you speaking with me or chewing a brick? You'd be better occupied unloading my trunks and putting them on the coach for London."

Summer was set down in deserted streets upon arrival in London. Its citizens had barricaded themselves against the horrible death, so that it looked like a ghost town. A disgusting smell hovered over the city like a charnel house. Vendors no longer hawked their goods in the streets. Horse-drawn drays and wagons no longer plowed a path between crowds of citizens bustling about London in pursuit of her wealth. Most of the shops were shut up tight as a drum, for who would purchase a wig when the hair likely came from a corpse? Who would buy clothes or even jewelry which had adorned a plague victim? Who wanted furniture from an infected house? Summer was unable to hire a chair to carry her to Cockspur Street, since the chair stands had all closed, so she offered an old man with a handcart a gold piece to cart her trunks through the empty streets while she walked beside him.

"The courtyard at Whitehall has grass growin' up between the cobbles," he said.

"Aren't there any businesses left open?" she asked, worried about where she would get food.

"The wheel of fortune turns," he told her philosophically. "Londoners have lived high for so long, thumbing their noses at the rest of humanity, but now that luck has deserted them they are overwhelmed with grief. Once the King and Queen deserted her, the rest followed suit like a pack of cards. The court fled, then every other citizen with the means to do so fled. The theaters closed, its actresses thrown out of work turned to whoring, but for once even that trade didn't thrive, for who would couple with a diseased body? The gravediggers are thriving, thieves are doing a bang-up business looting deserted houses. Anybody willing to nurse the sick can make a fortune. Any cookshops left open are charging ten times normal for food and folk are fightin' to pay it. Even poor old

sods like me are collectin' gold pieces." He winked at her as they
turned into Cockspur Street.

"I suppose there are many like me," she said absently, listening
with only half an ear

"Nay, lass—I earn gold every night cartin' off the corpses."

"Oh, my God." She shrank back from him in horror as she
realized her trunks were being carried on a death cart. She paid
him his money, glad to be rid of him. She unlocked the front door
and dragged her trunks into the beautifully appointed entrance
hall. It was a cool haven for her and she leaned her back against
the door, thankful that she could withdraw safely and shut out the
whole of the plague-riddled city.

A note had been shoved through the letter box in the front door
and she bent to retrieve it. Her heart gave a jolt as she saw the
handwriting was Spider's. She took it through to the small salon,
where she drew back the curtains to let in the daylight. She slipped
her shoes off her aching feet and anxiously scanned the lines from
her brother. A great knot of anxiety formed inside her chest as she
read his note.

Dear Cat:
I'm sorry I went off half-cocked last week and dropped by to tell
you that Edwin Bruckner and I have taken rooms together in
the city. (He is Lord Bruckner's younger brother whom you met
at Court.) I found the house locked up and assume you have
gone with the court to Salisbury. When you return, you will find
us at number 13 Warwick Lane, close by St. Paul's. We were
going to Bruckner Hall in Oxford for a fortnight until the plague
settles down, but Edwin was under the weather this morning, so
we'll go tomorrow. Please don't be angry with me.
                                    Spider

His friend had been under the weather . . . what if he'd been
sickening with the plague? The premonition of danger to her
brother was so strong that she knew she must go to him. The only
thing she found in the cupboards was some dry biscuit, and as she
choked it down she wondered where she would find the courage to
go out into the streets of London and look boldly into the face of
the Grim Reaper.

39

Lord Helford was early for his appointment with King Charles, but the King was seldom tardy and had been up since the crack of dawn. Actually Salisbury was beginning to wear on his nerves. The town had opened its heart to him and his court, but the confines hemmed him in considerably and the respectability and even the sheer cleanliness of the place set him longing for brawling, sprawling London.

The King's brother, the Duke of York, arrived with his father-in-law, Chancellor Hyde, and Charles gave Ruark a speaking glance to be careful of what he said. "I take it you've been in contact with your brother Rory?" said Charles, cutting to the heart of the matter.

"I have, Sire. The *Phantom* slipped in and out of Southampton last night. He delivered the secret messages to The Hague suggesting negotiations to a peaceful settlement of this war and I regret that they were rejected."

Charles flushed angrily at the affront to his pride. "We should never have lowered ourselves to make the offer!"

Chancellor Hyde held up his hand to soothe Charles. "There is no shame in offering a means to an honorable peace."

"God damn Parliament for tying my hands. I'd like to blow the Dutch out of the water, and would do so if they didn't control every damned penny in the Exchequer." His big fist cracked down onto the table to emphasize his frustration.

Hyde placated as best he could. "I will go back to Parliament and demand money for this war. If they know I am committed to it, perhaps they will loosen the purse strings."

Ruark Helford chose his words carefully. "My brother arranged a secret meeting with de Ruyter himself." The three men riveted their attention upon him. "De Ruyter concludes, as my brother and I conclude, that our sea power is too evenly matched for a clear and decisive victory in this war."

Charles gave a short bark of laughter. "Well, Helford, at least you tell me the unvarnished truth and not just what I want to hear. Well, Chancellor, you must feel most gratified that you were right and hotheads like Buckingham, Lauderdale, and myself were wrong."

The old man's hand went up again. "No, no, if they are not yet ready to negotiate a peace, then I must get money from Parliament and we must pursue and harry them with a vengeance until they are damned glad to open negotiations."

Charles gave his brother a signal to leave and take his father-in-law with him. When he was at last private with his friend Helford, he asked, "And the other delicate matter I entrusted to that damned pirate?"

Ruark Helford grinned. He reached inside a leather case and withdrew a sealed document from the King of France. "He jumped at the chance to buy back the city of Dunkirk."

Charles ripped open the letter. "He offers double what I asked . . . two hundred thousand pounds!" he said with pleased disbelief.

"Er . . . that was Rory's idea. He's a most devious fellow, I'm afraid; he told him you asked two hundred thousand."

Charles was elated. "I'm glad you had sense enough not to mention it in front of the others. They'll know only when it's a fait accompli. After all, bloody Dunkirk belongs to France . . . just because Cromwell's army captured it doesn't make it part and parcel of England. You've no idea how sick and tired I am of being penniless and going hat in hand to Parliament like a sodding beggar with a tin cup. I'm so poor, I haven't a pot to piss in or a window to throw it through. When do you think I'll get the money?"

Lord Helford grinned again. "The gold was transferred from the *Phantom* to the *Pagan Goddess* last night."

"God's flesh, the Helford brothers are mighty good to know," he said, winking.

"If you'll excuse me, Sire, I shall seek out Lady Helford and remind her of her wifely duties."

"Summer isn't here in Salisbury," corrected Charles.

"You must be mistaken, Sire. I don't think she's been here long. Stubborn wench had to be pried away from London, but my brother assures me he gave her safe passage here."

Charles shook his head and winked at Ruark. "I know Summer isn't here or I wouldn't be so damned bored."

"She must be staying with Lady Richwood," said Lord Helford, unable to keep the annoyance from his voice.

Charles grinned. "Get her with child, it will effectively clip her wings."

"I've already done that, Sire, but it doesn't stop her from running off on her adventures."

Before Summer left the security of Cockspur Street, she wanted to be sure she had everything she might need. First and foremost was money; it was ever so. Then she decided if she was carrying a tidy sum of money through half-empty streets, she would need her pistol. She found a valise and put in a package of the dry biscuits and a bottle of full-bodied port wine. She put in a fresh change of clothes and a pair of soft slippers along with her toilet articles. Knowing she would likely have to walk for two or three miles into the city proper, she knew she could not carry more.

She set off along Northumberland to the Thames. Perhaps she would be lucky enough to find traffic on the river which would take her to Paul's Wharfe. There was an occasional wherry passed in midstream, but no matter how loudly she hailed it, she was totally ignored. Finally she gave up and resigned herself to walking. As she made her way along the Embankment she noticed all kinds of disgusting rubbish had collected and where the filth had fallen into the water, it had turned into a loathsome broth. Emaciated dogs rummaged in reeking piles of rotting filth and Summer had to avert her eyes. Gulls and even crows were picking at bloated objects floating farther out in the Thames and Summer's graphic imagination made her gorge rise.

Between White Friars Stairs and Black Friars a navy patrol boat pulled close enough to call out to her. "If you enter the city, you will not be allowed to leave, and there is a curfew."

"I must find my brother," she called back.

"Over seven thousand died last week. Guards are posted in the streets to keep people inside." He did not await her reply. He had warned her and if she was pig ignorant enough not to heed him, then plague take the wench.

She turned north from the river at Bridewell Prison and wished to God she hadn't. What furniture and mattresses had been supplied the prisoners were now heaped into the street on bonfires and guards were in the process of carrying out the corpses of women who were dying like flies. The bodies were half-naked. All had bare legs and feet; the rest of their emaciated bodies were garbed in tattered rags. The stench was unbearable and every last one was smeared with the grime and filth of years.

She began to shake uncontrollably and turned back to the river to cut through by Baynard's Castle. That also was a mistake. Seamen lay in the street. At first she thought they were plague victims, but before she could avoid them, they crawled after her and clawed at her skirts, begging for food. A few were drunk, but most were genuinely starving, for no ship would take back its crew members once they had been in the City of London and sailors by the score had nowhere to go, no money, and no food. Their eyes were filled with apathy and misery and malice.

Summer gave them all the dry biscuits she had and literally pulled her skirts from their beseeching hands. She ran from the river all the way to St. Paul's then turned into Warwick Lane and looked for number 13. There was a yard with a water pump, but it seemed deserted. All the ground-floor houses which had the even numbers were empty. Her eyes lifted to the odd-numbered dwellings upstairs and she spotted the ominously numbered 13. With her heart in her mouth she hammered on the door and was swept with a wave of relief when no one answered her knock. He must be safely in Oxford. She sat down on the landing of the outside staircase to catch her breath. Now that she was past the halfway mark of her pregnancy she found she wasn't as quick and agile as she had been and exertion left her quite breathless.

As she sat resting the sound of someone softly crying came to her. She lifted her head warily like an animal scenting danger. Suddenly she knew it was her brother, even though she hadn't heard him cry since he was three. She looked through the window which was slightly ajar and saw him sitting with his head in his hands, rocking back and forth.

"Spider, it's me, Cat," she called to him. When he didn't seem to hear her, she pushed hard against the door and found that it was not locked after all. The stench which met her nostrils was so offensive it staggered her. She went on her knees before him. "Spider, it's Cat . . . what's the matter?" she demanded. He lifted his head slowly and looked at her with glazed eyes. Then he seemed to become aware of her for the first time. "Is your friend sick?" she demanded.

He nodded his head. "Edwin . . . he's got the plague," he whispered in a terrified voice.

"Where is he? Through here?" she asked, standing up and going toward an inner door.

"No, Cat, for Christ's sake don't go in there. He's finally gone to sleep."

"The stench in here is unbearable; come on, you'll have to help me clean it up," she said, looking with distaste at a pile of soiled towels and sheets. "These should be burned. Do you have more?" she asked. He shook his head wearily. "Well then, I'll just throw them down into the courtyard and wash them later. I'm going down for water from the pump. We'll have to scrub this place to eliminate some of the stink." She had to busy herself or her thoughts would have driven her mad. If Spider had nursed Edwin, he was sure to have been infected. She struggled up the steps with the heavy bucket of water and called, "Damn, Spider, get off your arse and help me." It was then she noticed he was not just filled with apathy, he was flushed.

The silence in the fashionably appointed bachelor apartment gave her a creepy feeling. On impulse she opened the hall doorway and went into the first bedroom. This was definitely the source of the stench. The floor was slippery with excrement and vomit. In fascinated horror she drew closer to the bed. The young man's face was bloated and going black. She had no way of knowing how long he had been dead.

She ran back into the salon. "Spider, Edwin is dead!" she cried.

"No . . . no . . . he's just gone to sleep," Spider mumbled.

"Come on," she said decisively, "we're getting out of here." As Spencer stood up his knees buckled beneath him and he vomited.

"Oh, dear God, no, please no," Summer begged under her breath. He staggered down the hallway and into a second small bedchamber, which mercifully held a clean bed. He fell down upon it and Summer quickly stripped him down to his shirt and placed a chamber pot beside the bed ready for a second round of vomiting.

She remembered the wine she had brought and poured out a small glass and fed it to him. It seemed to settle his stomach for the moment, but he was still very flushed and his eyelids closed heavily. She had no idea how long he'd been fighting off Edwin's death, but realized he was exhausted. She heard a cry from the street and dimly realized it was a death cart. She ran out to the balcony and cried, "Up here, please, I need help."

The cockney shouted back, "We only pick up from the street . . . we ain't obliged to come into yer bleedin' house, missus."

"Wait . . . wait right there!" she ordered in her most commanding voice. She held her breath and plunged into the first bedroom. She forced her mind to dwell on other things as she lifted and hauled the bloated, black thing that had been Edwin Bruckner from the bed to the floor. She then pulled him by the bedclothes he'd fallen onto. Some reserve of strength she never knew she had enabled her to drag him outside onto the landing. "You'll have to come up and get him," she panted, holding a painful stitch in her side.

"Do ye fink yer the bloody Queen an' I'm yer lady-in-waitin'?" he asked in outrage. "Rules is rules . . . I pick 'em up from the street."

Summer was so angry she wanted to get her pistol and shoot the bastard, but then she would have a cartload of bodies instead of one to dispose of. With her last ounce of strength she dragged Edwin to the top of the stairs, placed her foot in the middle of his back, and kicked with all her strength. The body toppled down the stairs and landed in the courtyard with a sickening splosh.

"Christ Almighty, yer stupid cow, now I'll 'ave ter use a shovel."

She closed her eyes and uttered a prayer. It was for poor Edwin Bruckner, a great lord's brother being carted off in such an ignoble manner, it was for her own beloved brother so deathly ill inside the dreaded number 13, and it was for herself and her precious unborn child.

She had descended to the pump eight times before she had scrubbed the rooms enough to remove some of their putrid offensiveness. Between buckets she continually checked on Spider's condition, but he was sleeping heavily and she shoved from her mind the suspicion that he might be unconscious. She had pushed herself far beyond the limits of her strength and knew she needed some sort of sustenance, but she did not dare to rest until she had lit the fire and set the kettle to boil. She would make some tea and force herself to sit and rest before the fire while she drank it.

Absently she moved a chessman on a board which had been set up before the fire. A tear slid down her face. The boys must have been playing an innocent game of chess before the angel of death paid them a visit.

A sudden hammering on the door nearly made her jump out of her skin. She grabbed the pistol, not knowing what to expect, and cautiously approached the door. It was going dark and the lord mayor of London had ordered a curfew, so she knew whoever was at the door spelled trouble.

She opened it slowly. Ruark Helford stood on the threshold, dressed in black with a powder blue ostrich feather in his wide-brimmed cavalier's hat, exactly as she had seen him the first time they'd met. Her heart turned over in her breast at sight of him. His eyes were blazing with anger. He shoved the door open all the way and demanded, "What the hell do you think you're doing in a place like this?" He grabbed her roughly. "I'm taking you out of here *now,* this minute, madame."

"No, Ruark, I can't leave," she said wearily.

He raised his voice. "I've nearly gone mad looking for you. Finally I broke into Cockspur Street and found this address on a piece of paper. If you don't give a damn about yourself, at least think of my child! To be in London this week is your death warrant."

Her heart cried out to him to take her into his arms because she was so afraid, but her lips uttered very different words. "So all you care about is this baby—you don't give a tinker's damn about me!"

"Like a bloody fool I ran all over Salisbury looking for you and now, to add insult to injury, I've spent two days running all over London for you."

"Why were you looking for me—to tell me the annulment has gone through?" she demanded sarcastically.

He was so angry he lied. "Yes, as a matter of fact, it has."

"Oh," she whispered, all the wind taken from her sails.

As he looked at her he saw her face was tinged with gray like a dirty gown. Her beautiful hair was a disheveled mess and she looked weary beyond belief. "Are you coming or do I have to carry you?" His voice brooked no disobedience.

She raised her pistol and said between her teeth, "Get the hell out of here, Helford, or I'll blow your bloody head off!"

The anger set like stone in his face. He brought his hand up and struck her in the face. She fell down and at the same time pulled the trigger. As the acrid smell of gunpowder filled her nostrils she thought wildly, I've killed him . . . I love him! The ball had ripped open the shoulder of his coat. It was the only damage apart from his pride. He snatched the gun from her. "I'm going to beat you for that," he said very deliberately, and reached down for a handful of her hair.

Remembering his violent temper, she cried out, "Ru, please help me . . . my brother is dying with plague." She buried her face in her hands and began to sob brokenly.

"My God," he said hoarsely, and stepped over the threshold to pick her up. He carried her to the fire and gently sat her in a chair. His nose had already told him what she had been battling all day.

"When I got here, I found Edwin already dead," she choked.

"Young Edwin Bruckner?" he asked in disbelief.

"I had to get rid of the body . . . the death cart came . . . I had to do it, Ruark." She clutched at him.

"Of course you did. The plague doesn't respect wealth or title, sweetheart, that's why I have to get you out of here. I have my coach and driver below." He brushed back her hair and stroked the cheek he had slapped so hard. "Darling, listen to me. I'll get Spencer a nurse. I wouldn't let you stay here even if you weren't in a delicate condition."

She shook her head. "I won't leave him."

"You will *die* if you stay," he said emphatically.

"Then I will die," she said simply.

He knew she meant it. Every instinct told him to pick her up and forcefully remove her from such a pest hole, yet he knew if he did so, she would hate him forever. He took off his coat and rolled up his shirt sleeves. "If you are staying, I'm staying with you. Where is he?"

"No," she cried. "You will die if you stay."

"Then I will die," he said flatly.

She laughed through her tears. "Come, he's been sleeping for hours."

Ruark strode up to the bed and was alarmed at the dark red

flush on the boy's face. "He's not asleep, Summer . . . I think he's unconscious. He cannot last much longer. The choice is yours —will we allow him to slip away peacefully or will we try to revive him and put up a hell of a battle with the Grim Reaper? A battle, I might add, which we'll probably lose in the end."

"Fight and survive or fight and die . . . we'll fight, I know no other way."

"Good girl," he encouraged. "What do you have to drink here?"

"Water . . . tea . . . port wine . . ."

"We'll give him all three. We'll start with water."

Summer ran to fetch the water and Ruark flung open the window and pulled the covers off the bed. Spencer was burning hot, and when Ruark lifted him into a sitting position, he began to mumble and then to rave. Ruark took the water from Summer and held it to Spencer's mouth. He almost knocked it from Ruark's hand in his raving, but Ruark persisted until the boy took some of the water. The minute he tasted it, he drank greedily until it was finished, then began thrashing about again.

"More," ordered Ruark, and Summer ran to do his bidding. With infinite patience Ruark fed him the water, and bade Summer make some tea. After he got some of the hot tea into him, Spencer began to sweat so heavily he drenched the sheet upon which he lay.

"We'll bathe him, fetch some water."

Summer picked up the empty bucket.

"What the hell are you doing?"

"The water pump's in the yard," she explained.

He strode toward her. "Never, ever let me see you haul water again." His voice was like the crack of a whip and she gladly relinquished her hold on the handle and let him take over. They bathed him, fed him more tea, then bathed him again. They had no clean sheets and made do with the bare ticking of the mattress.

Ruark felt the swollen glands in his neck and examined his groin for the telltale plague boil. Spencer's groin was only slightly swollen and Ruark took it as a bad sign. Anyone who had ever survived the plague had done so because the carbuncle came to a head quickly and burst, releasing the body's poison. He said nothing to Summer save, "Let's try him with some wine and water."

He held the boy in one strong arm and fed him the watered port wine with his free hand. After three glasses, Spencer stopped thrashing about and his breathing became slightly more regular.

"He'll sleep for a while. I must go out and get you food, Summer. I know damned well you've had nothing all day."

"I'm not hungry, Ruark, I'm too tired and worried to eat."

"That is beside the point. I will get food and you will eat it," he said as if speaking to a child of five.

She nodded. His strength and determination were too much for her. "There's a curfew, the guard will stop you."

"You mean he'll try," said Ruark.

It seemed that she just dozed off for a moment and Ruark was back. He brought a roasted capon and a bottle of cider, which brought memories of Cornwall flooding back to her. She smiled sadly as she nibbled on the crisp brown skin of the bird. "Once, when my brother and I were starving, we survived by stealing one of your prize cockerels."

"At last! You can be yourself with me. I like you best when you are honest with me, Summer."

She knew better. She knew being honest and having no secrets was just one of those things men paid lip service to. She knew that if he found out she had been intimate with his scoundrel brother, he was capable of killing them both.

As if he knew she was thinking of Rory, he said, "I asked Rory to take you to Salisbury, why did you deceive him?"

She wondered wildly if he knew Rory had lured her to Holland and France before delivering her to Southampton. She doubted it very much. She shrugged. "He's easier to deceive than you."

"I should have taken you myself, but I knew you'd listen to my suggestion and do exactly the opposite just on principle. We've been like gunpowder and match lately."

"A dangerous combination," she murmured, looking at the firm set of his mouth.

"You seemed to get along with Rory so comfortably, like old friends, I thought you'd be more amenable to his suggestions."

Her heart screamed, We're not friends, we're lovers! Are you blind? She wanted to tell him not to trust Rory because his first loyalty was to himself and he made no bones about it. Brothers, kings, and countries were the last things he cared about.

"How did he get the wound which put the white streak in his hair?" she asked.

He was silent for a while, then almost reluctantly he recounted events from the past. "My father and I had quarreled as usual. He was such a fierce loyalist, he would have climbed the scaffold with

King Charles I . . . except by the time that regicide took place he'd already sacrificed himself to the cause." He was quiet for a minute or two, but she knew he wasn't finished.

"We had agreed to mortgage all the Cornwall holdings to raise money for the Stuart cause. I had the gall to tell him that was enough, that he was too old to fight and he should leave that to us younger men. We almost came to blows that day and he never forgave me." He stood and kicked a burning log to the back of the fireplace with his elegantly booted foot. "Cromwell's army finally penetrated Cornwall. They set fire to our town of Helston then swarmed over Helford Hall. They drove my father and a few defenders into the raging waters of the Helford River. They fought valiantly, but of course they were outnumbered. Rory rode into the raging torrent to help Father and instantly received a sword slash which cleaved his scalp in two. They thought him dead, but he was washed out to sea and deposited unconscious on the beach below the house."

"Our beach," she said softly.

"Yes, our beach," he said, his eyes licking over her like candle flame.

Summer saw Rory's amused face in her mind and knew she could never betray him to the King, but her husband Ruark was another thing entirely. She knew a great need to warn him, caution him about the black sheep of the family. "Ru, I think Rory uses the cellars at Roseland to smuggle people in and out of the country."

His eyebrows went up and the muscle in his jaw stood out like a lump of iron.

"I . . . I think he sells secrets to the Dutch . . . to the French . . . to anybody."

He looked outraged at her words. "I thought you were his friend! You're betraying him!" he accused angrily.

"Not to the King . . . I wouldn't . . . I couldn't . . . only to you, so you can protect yourself," she said, faltering.

"So, you have chosen between us, and I'm the lucky man to receive your favors, am I?" he mocked.

"No, damn you. I choose neither of you. You can both go to hell!"

She drained her cup of strong cider and then threw it at him. He pulled her from the chair into his lap. His lips seared her throat and he whispered, "What will we do to pass the long hours of the night?" She could feel his sex, hard as marble against the softness of her buttocks. The heat from his body seeped into hers and she almost succumbed to his powerful strength. "We could play"—she felt his shaft jump—"*chess,*" she finished repressively.

"Winner's choice," he insisted.

She was too weary to argue with him. The fire and the cider were making her drowsy, and as she leaned against his shoulder she longed for his love and his protection. She wanted him to make the world safe for her brother, herself, and her unborn child nestled beneath her heart. Her moves were clumsy, uncalculated, and in no time at all he had the advantage and would easily win the match. After her last move her hand came to rest upon his thigh and he had no more interest in chess than flying to the moon. He covered her hand with his and slowly moved it up his thigh until it came to rest along the hard length of his shaft. When she didn't pull away, he was encouraged. His lips brushed the top of her head. "You have a magic touch," he murmured huskily. "Lord God, how you make me quiver." His other hand stole to the hem of her gown and began to slip up her leg beneath the gown. When she did not thrust his hand away, he felt triumphant. His triumph was short-lived, however, for as he looked down at her he saw she was asleep against his shoulder. He schooled his lust, promising himself they would finish this chess game through to its natural conclusion at a more propitious time.

40

He held her until the first gray light of dawn, then gently arose to check on Spencer, who must have survived the night because he could hear him coughing. He looked down at the youth with disbelief. Spencer was awake, his eyes glassy, and he was covered from head to toe with bright red dots.

"Summer, sweetheart, come quickly," he shouted.

She came awake with a jolt. It took only a moment to adjust to her surroundings and her heart plummeted as she recalled her brother's peril. "What's wrong?" she called fearfully.

"Come and see for yourself," Ruark bade.

With dragging feet she went to the bedroom door.

"He hasn't got the plague at all," he said. "It's spotted fever!"

She blinked. "What do you mean?"

"He's got the bloody measles," Ruark shouted, unable to contain his elation any longer. He swept her up into the air, swung her about, and planted a hearty kiss on her lips. Suddenly he stopped, turned an accusing finger on poor Spencer, and said, "When you recover, I'm going to beat the shit out of you." Then he swung her into the air again and said, "I'm taking you both out of here."

Despite the guards and the unloaded pistol, they decided to risk it. He bundled up Spencer and handed Summer a small bag of gold. They were only halfway down the steps when two guards carrying muskets came into the yard. "Halt!" they ordered in unison, running to the foot of the stairs to block their leaving.

Ruark's empty pistol stuck out from beneath the cloak and he said in a deadly quiet tone, "Gentlemen, the lady has bribes, I have balls, the choice is yours." It was a double entendre which they understood immediately. They glanced at Ruark's driver, who was clutching an iron bar, and capitulated instantly.

Summer handed over the money and climbed into the coach. "It's terrible, I can feel frost in the air," she said worriedly.

"No, that's wonderful. Freezing cold is the only thing that will put an end to this pestilence." He laid Spencer on the carriage seat, and as he sat down beside her he slipped his arm about her and cuddled her to his side. "Just look at you, you're worn out."

She wanted to melt against him, to lean on his great strength, but she knew the physical effect they had on each other. Just being enclosed in a carriage together was a sensual experience. She sat stiffly, not daring to look up into his darkly handsome face. "Thank you for staying with me, Ruark. I'll be all right now."

"I'm going to get you a woman to look after you. She can nurse Spencer for a few days until he's on his feet again, but then I want you to keep her on to look after you. In your condition it won't be long before you're unable to do for yourself."

"Nurses are asking a fortune and then they'll steal you blind the moment your back's turned. Londoners can't be trusted, especially now."

"I know a good woman. She lives in the country. She used to be my housekeeper before I went back to Cornwall. She's a capable, no-nonsense woman who'll keep an eye on you. God's flesh, someone has to. Don't worry, I'll pay her wages, I know what a mercenary little bitch you are."

Stung, she gave him an immediate comeback. "Just consider it part of my settlement for agreeing to the annulment."

Why did he allow the things she said to nettle him so much? He wanted to shake her like a rag doll, but he knew if he put his hands on her, desire would flare up in him and threaten to consume him. When they arrived in Cockspur Street, he carried Spencer upstairs to one of the elegant bedchambers, undressed him, and slipped him between cool, fresh sheets. Then he dispatched his driver for food, wine, and a supply of medicinal herbs. He sent him to the storehouse which had just victualed his ship. The house felt cold and damp, so Ruark lit fires in every room. "Summer, I would feel much better if you would promise to keep arm's length from your brother. I know measles isn't nearly as terrifying as the plague, but how do we know how it will affect our child? If you get sick or overdo, you could miscarry. I want you to bathe and rest while I go and fetch Mrs. Bishop."

She had a defiant look on her face and for once in his life he controlled his temper and tried gentle persuasion. "Summer love, I know you don't take very kindly to orders and that's why I'm asking you, nay begging you, to have a care for your delicate condition."

She placed both hands upon her abdomen and said hotly, "This baby means more to me than all the rest of you lumped together—the whole bloody world can go to hell in a handbasket for all I care!"

"Here comes the carriage with the supplies. Tell him where you want everything. I'll go and see to Spencer and then I'm off. I promise to be back this afternoon."

When she caught a glimpse of herself in the mirror, she was horrified that Ruark had seen her looking her very worst. A rush of love and gratitude swept over her. Whatever would she have done if Ru hadn't found her? She knew she didn't want her marriage to him annulled. She wanted to be his very precious love, exactly as she had been until they came back from their honeymoon at Stowe and she'd ruined her whole life by confessing the truth to him. She leaned her head against the doorjamb. Perhaps she could persuade him to stay with her again tonight. If she bathed and changed into an alluring gown and acted sweet and feminine, perhaps she could dissuade him from going through with the annulment. She had seduced him into marriage once, why not again? The trick was to make him think she wanted the annulment desperately.

By the time Lord Helford returned with Mrs. Bishop it was three o'clock in the afternoon. Summer liked her immediately. She had a comfortable figure with a large expanse of bosom and seemed to take charge immediately. Summer could see she was kind and generous but not above using bullying tactics if that's what it took to make people obey her. In a glance Mrs. Bishop took in Summer's expanded waistline and said firmly, "No more climbing stairs for you, young lady."

Ruark laughed. "Bish will get obedience from you, even if I can't."

"But I must show you to your bedchamber, Mrs. Bishop."

Bish pointed to her trunk and gave Ruark a speaking glance. "He's got two strong legs, he can show me my room and the patient. Then I'll be in the kitchen getting us all some supper."

Summer hid a smile. "Lord Helford will help you, he's very good at hauling wood for the fires."

"I can haul my own wood. Lord Helford can look after his wife. A woman needs pampering when she's carrying her first child."

Ruark carried up Mrs. Bishop's trunk and returned immediately. Summer felt so shy with him that she actually blushed. He had obviously stopped somewhere to shave and change his clothes, and as always he was immaculate. She had set up a chessboard in front of the fire and the elegantly appointed room was intimately inviting. She had brushed her hair until its silken black mass cloaked her shoulders and she had chosen a silk gown the color of crushed raspberries, which outlined her breasts and fell in soft folds to her feet.

Ruark's eyes smoldered as they lingered on her luscious breasts. He glanced at the chessboard and she said breathlessly, "We didn't finish our play." She saw him harden at her words and averted her eyes as if she were still a maiden. Summer sat down on the love seat before the fire, and reaching behind a cushion, pulled out the leather-bound volume her father had given to her. "Ruark, you know I want this annulment every bit as much as you do, but I see no reason why we can't remain friends." Her voice had a whispery, seductive quality which sent shivers up Ruark's back. "As a parting gift . . . as a token between friends . . . I want you to have this journal. It will probably make your job in Cornwall much easier and perhaps less dangerous."

He sat down beside her and opened the book curiously. "What is it?" he asked as he saw the dates and places and names.

"It's a record of wrongdoing . . . of smuggling . . . of wrecking . . . of selling information to the highest bidder. There's everything in there from murder to treason and I'm ashamed to say that nearly every prominent family in Cornwall had one or more members involved. When my father died, he gave it to me so I could blackmail these rich families for money."

"Summer, didn't you trust me enough when we married to give it to me?" he asked.

"Ruark, when you married me, I fancied myself so much in love, I would have trusted you to the ends of the earth. I always meant you to have it, only I was so ashamed that my father was involved in such vile things."

He put a finger beneath her chin and lifted her face so that he looked deeply into her eyes. "I know you well enough to know you have the guts to blackmail someone."

"Damn you, blackmail isn't my style!" she cried, forgetting her resolve not to swear in front of him. "Don't you think it would have been easier for me to get money from the journal than dressing up as a highwayman and robbing coaches?" she demanded. "All because you left me penniless," she added, outraged.

"Have you any idea how magnificently beautiful you are when you lose your temper? I get you angry on purpose sometimes just to watch you." He took hold of her hand and lifted it to his lips, lingering over each fingertip, each perfect nail oval. "Thank you for trusting me with the journal. I have discovered some of the treachery, of course, but it might have taken me years to ferret out all the bastards."

His arm slid along the back of the love seat and his fingers began to play with her hair. "Ruark, I think Richard Grenvile is dead. I told you I saw him at Stowe when we were on our honeymoon. Do you remember?"

His arm came around her and he drew her to him. "Do I remember our honeymoon?" he asked huskily, a thousand erotic images stealing into his mind.

"I believe now that Grenvile was involved in treachery against the King. I think Rory killed him. I think you should be extremely careful around Rory."

"Darling, I don't intend to waste our lovely evening talking about that young devil, but I'll put your mind at ease by telling you that Charles and I trust him completely. Don't go sticking your pretty little nose in and messing things up," he warned.

She brought her hands up against his chest; she could feel the crisp hairs beneath the snowy linen. She had warned him and it would be up to him to guard himself. She had no fear for him, for in a fight with any man, king or brother, he would emerge the victor. His closeness was having an unbelievable effect on her. Her senses were dizzy with the feel of him, the scent of him. "Now that the danger to Spencer is past, I suppose you'll have to leave. . . ." she said wistfully.

"I'm staying," he asserted.

"Staying to eat?" she asked innocently.

"Longer," he said firmly.

Summer didn't allow her expression to change but she was willing to bet he was "longer," and if she teased him just a little more, she would feel his full length. "Oh, of course, I forgot our game," she said, removing herself from the love seat.

He, too, stood up to remove his coat and pour them a little Chablis. "Winner's choice," he reminded her.

She took the proffered glass, accidentally brushing his hand with her fingertips, and said, "Let's see, what do I want if I win?"

The tip of her tongue played about the edge of the glass and he said in a low, intense voice. "You know what I want."

She teased him by giving him a hot, slanting glance and saying breathlessly, "I think you know what I want, Ru!"

He drained his glass and, slipping his hands around her back, pressed her buttocks forward so that her sensitive mons rubbed against his swollen sex. "What do you want, darling, tell me."

She lifted her lips to within an inch of his and whispered, "The annulment, of course."

"Damn," he cursed, "you play the game well."

"I had a superb teacher," she said, tracing the outline of his top lip with her tongue. He swept her up into his arms, one hand going swiftly up her skirts to caress between her legs.

Mrs. Bishop pushed through the door, holding an enormous tray. "That's right, carry her to the fire and I'll set this tray right here in front of the love seat." She gave Ruark a warning glance. "Don't eat everything in sight; remember, she's eating for two now."

Ruark scowled blackly and jerked his head in a signal for her to leave.

"You needn't mee-maw at me, Lord Helford. I'm not so obtuse I don't know when lovers want to be alone. I'll just take myself upstairs now," she said, winking broadly.

"Bloody woman—why the hell did I fetch her?" he muttered, and Summer buried her head against his throat to stifle her laughter. He sat her down and fed her. Tonight even eating was a sensual experience for them. Each time he put a morsel of food into her mouth she either licked his fingers, bit his fingers, or sucked his fingers. After each sip of wine he gave her, he touched his mouth to hers. Each of them savored the tantalizing arousal.

When they finished the food, they began a slow game of chess. Each knew they played two games at one time and the game of seduction was infinitely more absorbing. When he took a pawn, he also took the liberty of taking off a stocking. When she took his rook, she slowly removed his shirt.

He pulled the cushions from the love seat to make a nest for them on the floor. She agreed to join him, but only if they kept the board between them. He distracted her by playing with her bare toes, then running a fingertip across her bare sole. "Tickling is against the rules," she purred.

"I always break the rules," he warned as his strong fingers encircled her bare ankle and inched up her leg. The wine and the fire and the teasing heightened the sensual tension between them and one by one the barriers began to fall. Imperceptibly they drew closer to each other until his fingers were trailing the neckline of her gown and dipping into the deep cleft between her breasts.

Her own hands had begun to roam pleasurably over the rippling muscles of his shoulders and back. Then her hand slid down below the waistband of his breeches and her finger traced the cleft between his hard buttocks. She thought she had totally distracted him into moving his king into a vulnerable position and quickly moved her queen to take advantage of him. "Check," he said triumphantly, "and mate," he added, pushing her down onto the cushions and opening her gown to the waist. Her ripe breasts thrust upward into his waiting hands and he lifted them one at a time to receive a reverent kiss. The game was forgotten in the heat of the moment. In the game they now played, there would be no losers, they would each win their heart's desire. When she made a pretense of clinging to her garments, he lured her into allowing him to remove them completely by whispering, "We only have till dawn!" He was entranced by the way the flickering firelight played over her satin skin, turning it to golden flame on her swelling breasts and belly, and darkest vermilion in the valley between luscious globes, and the much deeper, more intimate valley between her thighs. His fingers traced every curve, his eyes devoured her as she writhed seductively for him, opening and closing her legs like a tempting pagan goddess who would lure him to the very limit of his virility.

Ruark knew that foreplay for a woman was every bit as pleasurable as the consummation. When his shaft could swell and lengthen no further because of the confines of his tight breeches, he slipped them off and closed his eyes at the pleasurable sensation he experienced as his shaft filled until he was rigid. He gently rolled her onto her stomach and straddled her back, then he lowered himself until his face was buried in the silken, scented mass of her hair. His throbbing member pulsed against her back and his hands slipped beneath her to capture her sensitive breasts and brush his thumbs across her taut nipples.

Summer was determined not to moan and reveal her great need to be filled, but when Ruark whispered, "Tell me what it feels like when I'm deep inside you," a small moan escaped her throat and he smiled triumphantly into the semidarkness. He climbed off her and gathered her into his lap so he could enjoy her mouth. His lips touched hers tentatively as if pleading, begging, then they became firm and gave her the hard kisses her senses craved at this moment. They they changed again, stopped giving and started taking until his mouth was scalding her in its fierce demands. As he became totally aggressive, she became totally submissive—all soft and womanly and willing—ready and eager to obey his body's demands.

He watched her face through half-closed eyes and knew she was the loveliest woman who would ever come into his life. She attracted him like a lodestone and he was intimately aware of how deeply she was aroused by him. Together they were physically perfect. Their mating was like an erotic ballet, a dance of love they could draw out for hours of titillating bliss. How could she keep reminding him of the annulment when all he wanted to do was bind her to him forever?

He shifted her in his lap, lifting one bottom cheek to allow his erection to slide along the cleft between her legs. She moved back and forth upon him, teasing and tantalizing him to the point where he was now moaning deep in his throat. "Summer," he whispered urgently, "I can't live without you. When it's official that we're no longer married, will you be my mistress?"

She became still as death. She stopped moving, stopped breathing; she could have sworn that her heart stopped beating. With the pride of a Siamese cat she arched her body away from his and stood to face him. This wasn't the first time he had done this to her, and it was like another slap in the face. "I'm not good enough to be Lady Helford, but you don't want to lose me because I make such a damned good whore!"

"You're the one who wants the annulment," he ground out.

"You have never been more right," she hissed. "Get out and don't bother to come back!"

"I'll leave after I get what I came for," he growled.

"If you think I would allow you to make love to me now, you are mad!" she cried.

"Yes, mad . . . madder than I've been in my entire life. You're nothing but a cockteaser to lead me on this far and then stop cold. What the hell do you think I am, some sort of machine? I'm flesh and blood, Summer. I'm a man!" Slowly, determinedly, he began to stalk her across the room. She moved quickly, managing to elude him each time he cornered her. At first she ran and repeatedly turned to look over her shoulder, but he always managed to gain on her. Now she dared not take her eyes from him. He was like a stealthy animal, circling his prey, sure of his victory. She backed away, hating him in that moment, yet incredibly she was still aware that he had the most superb male torso in all England.

Ruark moved slowly, blocking her escape, and suddenly she knew without a doubt that like the game of chess they'd played, he would check and mate. They tumbled to the carpet, but he was careful to cushion her fall with his body. He carried her back to the cushions and stood towering above her. His voice was rough with desire. "Darling, I'm not going to force you, but I am going to make love to you." He went on his knees before her and she flew at him, biting, scratching, clawing, then taking fistfuls of hair and finally pounding at his chest with tight fists. He waited passively until she had exhausted herself. Then he spread her thighs apart and delicately traced the folds there with one fingertip. "You are slippery for me," he said softly, then he deliberately licked his finger and slid it up inside her.

She was breathless from her exertions and hoped angrily he would not think he was arousing her. Her luscious breasts rose and fell with each deep breath she drew and she resented the pleasure he was receiving from simply looking at her nudity. His strong thumb unerringly found the little bud of her womanhood and stroked it relentlessly. She would not give him the satisfaction of a reaction, although it sent shock waves pulsing deep within. She lay limp and totally passive, sending him a message that he could do anything to her and she would receive no pleasure from it.

Very gently he took her legs and placed one on each of his shoulders then he dipped his head until his mouth took possession of her secret place. He began to suck gently, and though she willed it otherwise, she climaxed more strongly than she had since their honeymoon. Swiftly he lowered her from his insatiable mouth and impaled her deeply with his marble-hard weapon. He didn't kiss her but held his mouth barely an inch from hers to feel every sigh, every delicious intake of breath, and his eyes caressed hers with love.

She was stubbornly determined not to let on that she was building to climax and Ruark scythed in and out, in and out, determinedly holding back until he brought her fulfillment. It seemed to go on forever, but Ruark knew he was fast reaching the peak of his endurance and would plunge over the abyss at any moment. His muscles strained tautly, his brain was on fire, his breathing became harsh and ragged, yet still he held himself under control. If he couldn't master this woman, he didn't deserve her. Then he felt it. Her sheath began to spasm, squeezing the sensitive head of his shaft, contracting tightly upon him, over and over until he lost control. Not by word, sound, or gesture did she let him know that she had come completely. With a smug little look of triumph she said, "I felt nothing."

He allowed her her small deception. "I'm sorry, sweetheart, that I couldn't satisfy you."

"I'm not your sweetheart! I never want to see you again!"

"As you wish . . . but you will always be my sweetheart." His lips brushed hers in a heartbreakingly tender kiss. Then he arose and quietly dressed himself.

41

After a week of frosty mornings the number of plague victims dropped dramatically to under five hundred. Spencer recovered quickly and knew the first thing he must do was go to Bruckner Hall in Oxford to tell the dreadful news about Edwin.

Mrs. Bishop now turned all her motherly attention upon Summer, feeding her until she felt like a goose being fattened for Christmas. Then one morning Lil Richwood returned from Southampton and the house was turned into a beehive of activity by all the servants. There was trouble in the kitchens with the pecking order because Mrs. Bishop was determined that she owned Summer body and soul and no one was allowed to trespass on her private domain. Summer's peace was shattered and she wondered why Auntie Lil needed a dozen people to run her household when she had been perfectly content with just Mrs. Bishop.

She did, however, enjoy Lil's company and listened eagerly to all her outrageous stories. Apparently her dearest friend's husband, Lord Worthing, had chased her until she slowed down long enough to let him catch her. With sparkling eyes she told Summer, "I don't think it will be long before he invents business in London and shows up at Cockspur Street."

Lil prophesied, "Mark my words, we are in for the most outra-

geous season London has enjoyed since Charles's restoration. The
court has absolutely stagnated in Salisbury and like a pack of wild
beasts is ready to be let loose from its cage." Within a month all
the theaters reopened and shopkeepers didn't know what to do
with the profits they were making since London had gone on a
buying spree. New businesses flourished. Moneylenders, gambling
houses, and brothels were in competition to take over empty buildings.

The small house on Cockspur Street was bulging at the seams
and Summer decided it was high time she took a small house of her
own. Rents were climbing every week and she decided to pay Solomon Storm a visit to see if her finances were healthy enough to
allow her to acquire a place of her own.

Summer had ignored the many invitations she'd received for
balls, masquerades, and parties, feeling most virtuous in leading a
secluded life until after the birth of her child. She thought she
looked ungainly, and even though Lady Richwood swore she
looked no such thing, she certainly felt ungainly now that she was
in the late months of her pregnancy.

Solomon Storm provided her with a comfortable chair and insisted she put her feet up on a footstool when he saw her condition.
She explained what she wanted and Solomon pursed his lips and
made steeples out of his fingers as he explained to her that the
fashionable districts were now beyond the means of most citizens.
"Westminster, St. James, and Mayfair are bringing astronomical
sums. I'm afraid you'll have to ask your husband to make you a
present of a house again."

"Mr. Storm . . . Solomon . . . Lord Helford never made me
a present of a house. As a matter of fact he's no longer my husband. I've reverted to using my own name of St. Catherine since
our marriage is annulled."

Solomon Storm looked most concerned. "How can he possibly
get the marriage annulled when you are so obviously enceinte—if
you will forgive my indelicacy—my lady?"

"It's a mutual agreement," she insisted. "It was my own decision."

"Then let me say it is a terrible decision. In my business I need
to know the law and my son is an attorney. I don't know what
went wrong in your marriage, my lady, and I have no desire to
know, but Lord Helford is legally responsible for any issue of the
marriage whether it is his or not, as so often is the case in these

times." He cleared his throat delicately. "If the marriage is to be put aside, at least you should wait until after the child is born. Then it will be Lord Helford's legal heir and, if it proves to be a male issue, will inherit his title as well as his property."

"Oh, I couldn't do a mercenary thing like that. He already thinks I married him for his money. I'm quite sure Ruark Helford will do the right thing by his son—or daughter—without my blackmailing him into it."

"I beg to differ, my lady. In my experience gentlemen seldom do the right thing from generosity of the heart. Rather they do the right thing only when pressed to do so."

"Perhaps I could afford a house here in the city in a less fashionable locale?" she suggested.

"I have no doubt of it, my lady, and I shall find a couple of suitable properties immediately, but I would feel much better about things if you allowed me to approach Lord Helford. You should have a house as part of your settlement. It is scandalous that it has not already been provided."

"Well, I'll give it some thought, but I really don't think I want to be obligated to any man, Mr. Storm."

Within the week Solomon Storm showed her some suitable houses and she chose the one on Friday Street beside St. Matthew's Church opposite the Old Exchange. It was a tall, narrow house like Lil Richwood's and it had been newly decorated in lovely shades of peach and pale green and all the fireplaces had been freshly painted cream. The kitchen, pantry, and laundry were in the basement. On the main floor was a reception room, a dining room, and a comfortable salon, while upstairs held only two large bedchambers and a bathing room. Its attics had dormer windows perched above the bedchambers and she thought Spencer might like these for his own. Mrs. Bishop would sleep in the nursery and talked of nothing these days but the baby.

Summer told Lil about the new house and she immediately insisted upon helping her choose furniture and transforming one of the large bedrooms into a nursery. She couldn't wait until Spencer arrived home to tell him of the house on Friday Street, but when she gave him the news, he looked a little sheepish and she knew he had no intention of coming to live with her. She could tell he was reluctant to tell her something, so she sat down, propped her feet on a footstool, and said, "Spider, you know you can tell me anything . . . what is it, love?"

He took a deep breath and plunged in. "Ruark has offered me a place on one of his ships."

She jumped to her feet. "The swine! You're not taking it!"

"Well, actually, I am, Cat."

"You have no idea what sort of authoritarian he is. I've seen him flog a sailor bloody for taking a drink. Don't you remember he knocked you down for a remark you made to me?" She was incensed.

"Well, actually, I sort of deserved it," he temporized.

"Spencer, there's a war on. Lightning blast the man—he once threatened to have you impressed into the navy. This is his way of hitting back at me!"

"For what. for Christ's sake?" he demanded.

"For not letting him have his way with me."

Spencer's bark of laughter shocked her. "All he has to do is look at you and you roll on your back."

She slapped him then. It was the first time she had ever struck him.

"You are about to bear the fruit of his labor," he said, pointing to her stomach. "Stop pretending."

"The child isn't his," she denied hotly.

Spencer said slowly, "You'd better not let him ever hear you say that. Not if you value your life."

"It's your life we are discussing. I refuse to let you go on one of his ships to become cannon fodder in this escalating war with Holland," she shouted, then burst into frustrated tears.

He knew he should not have upset her in her condition. "Cat, it's on one of his merchantmen for the East India Company."

"What! You'd be sailing halfway around the world! I'll kill him!"

"Cat, please don't upset yourself like this."

She felt a painful stitch in her side and her hand pressed her abdomen until it passed. "Where is he?" she demanded.

"I'm not telling you. Forget all about it," he said dismissively.

"He's at the bloody Pool of London readying the ship, isn't he?" she guessed.

"Mrs. Bishop," called Spider, going through into the kitchen. "My sister will be off to the London docks if you don't forcibly prevent her."

"That she won't, your lordship, not now you've tipped me the wink. Be off, you young scoundrel, it seems you've done enough damage for one night."

Summer put up an argument with Mrs. Bishop, but she lost and found herself packed off to bed early. Even Lil sided with the servant and refused to entertain any scheme which involved Summer's going out of the house that night. Up in her chamber Summer knelt before her old trunk and pulled out the black velvet disguise she had worn as a highwayman. She was determined to leave by the window and forbid Ruark Helford to lure her brother to sea. She looked at the tight black breeches in dismay and sat back on her heels, defeated. She knew she could not climb through a window out onto a roof and dash off on a mad scheme simply to rail at Ruark Helford, but come hell or high water, she would go first thing in the morning.

The weather was blustery and cold, so she wore her favorite gray cloak with the soft fox fur around the hood and a large matching muff to keep her hands from freezing. She made her face up carefully and chose the ruby earrings, then at the last moment donned ruby shoes and stockings which were sure to catch the eye and draw attention away from her rounded midsection. Lil ordered the carriage for her and wanted to accompany her, but Summer said she would have quite enough interference from Mrs. Bishop, thank you very much. When Summer told the driver to take her to the London docks, Bish opened her mouth to protest and Summer said crisply, "Not one word or I shall give you back to Lord Helford."

Mrs. Bishop pressed her lips together in undisguised disapproval and sniffed loudly every few minutes. Summer put up with it all the way down the Strand, then finally she said, "Stop it! You can bully me all you want to tomorrow, but today I'm going to have my say!" Mrs. Bishop decided to let her have her own way. Besides, Summer would need all her energy for the shouting match with Ruark, whom Bish had never yet seen lose a battle.

All the ships looked alike to Mrs. Bishop, but Summer's keen eye spotted the *Pagan Goddess* immediately and she rapped sharply for the driver to stop. He jumped down and assisted her to alight and hid a smile as she turned to Mrs. Bishop and said, "Keep your bum on that cushion, even if I'm gone an hour. I don't need you to interfere for me." When she walked up the gangplank as if she owned the ship, he turned to Mrs. Bishop and said, "She's one beautiful, headstrong woman. I feel sorry for the poor bastard."

Poor Mrs. Bishop was pulled between two loyalties. She had grown obsessive about the baby Summer was carrying and felt maternal to both mother and child, but she felt undying loyalty to Lord Helford and considered him the master.

Ruark was belowdecks, but when he heard the distinctive tapping of high heels on his polished deck, he raised his head to see who had dared. The foul word died on his lips as he saw his lovely Summer sweep down the stairs. She raised her skirts prettily and he was allowed a generous glimpse of alluring red stockings and slippers. She froze him with a glance and suddenly he knew exactly why she was here.

"I want you to tell Spencer you have changed your mind about letting him sail."

"Summer, be sensible. It will make a man of him."

"I didn't save him from the plague only to have you send him halfway across the world to die," she said, her eyes blazing with anger.

"It wasn't the plague, it was the measles."

"That is irrelevant, you monster. Taking your revenge on me in this manner is wicked. He's a defenseless boy who will suffer nothing aboard one of your vessels but hardship."

"Come into the cabin and sit down, love."

"I will stand," she said, drawing herself up to her full height. "My God, someone must stand up to you."

As she clutched the soft fur muff to her breasts he thought he'd never seen her looking lovelier. He felt so protective toward her he wanted to cradle her in his arms and lift her against his heart. He crushed down the soft feelings and said, "If he's left to whore and gamble his way around London every night, he'll turn into his father. He needs discipline, responsibility, a purpose in life."

"We managed well enough before you came into our lives!" she hissed.

"Did you?" he said bluntly. "He saw the inside of a prison twice before he was fifteen. The only thing he'll accomplish in London is sowing a crop of bastards and getting a dose of the clap."

"There's no need to use filthy language to me, sir," she said primly, forgetting she had the vocabulary of a sailor. "You will tell him he cannot go!" She turned to go.

"It's too late for that," he said quietly. "The *Golden Goddess* left on the morning tide for Madagascar. He'll get a share of the priceless cargo she'll bring. He could return with wealth. But rich or poor, he'll return a man."

She staggered slightly and he moved toward her protectively.

"Don't touch me! Don't you dare to touch me!" she cried. "I'll make you pay for this," she swore.

Her driver assisted her into the coach and Mrs. Bishop opened her mouth to ask how she had fared. "Not one word or I am undone," she said, choking back her tears. "Cheapside," she told the driver.

By the time she sat across the desk from Solomon Storm her tears had dried and her resolve hardened. "You gave me excellent advice the other day, Solomon. I would be a fool to ignore it. I should like you to inform Lord Helford that he can pay for the house in Friday Street and I'll also be submitting the bills for the furnishings. Let's see, what else will I need? Of course I'll need a carriage and horses and their stabling. Perhaps I'll have need of your son's services, too, Solomon, for after my child is born I don't wish Lord Helford to have any visiting privileges whatsoever."

42

Once again Barbara Castlemaine redecorated her bedchamber in her magnificent house just a stone's throw from Whitehall. The bed was massive, its great feather mattresses covered by purple satin sheets, embroidered with crowns. The headboard had two naked cherubs holding a golden crown between them in the Restoration design that had come to be known as boys and crown.

When Charles had arrived, she saw that swift demanding impatience on his face which gave her such a feeling of power. Now, two hours later, he lay sprawled naked against her, his slack mouth touching one opulent breast.

Barbara took careful aim and tossed a candied violet onto his groin. Like a great beast his flaccid member awoke and stretched itself. "Surely you don't think me capable of another joust?" he murmured huskily, a sweet smile curving his mouth.

"You are the King, darling," she purred. "You are omnipotent." She picked up her garters from the floor, where they had been so hastily discarded, giving him a tempting view of her derriere. She tossed a garter so that it encircled his semiaroused cock like a ring toss at a fair. By the time she looped the second garter over his enormous shaft, it was standing at attention like a six-foot yeoman of the guard. "Turnabout is fair play," she said throatily. "Since you did all the work the first three times, it's my turn." She lifted herself above him, straddled his thighs, then bent forward to remove her lacy garters from his maypole with her sharp little teeth, then she positioned herself so that she slowly swallowed him until all nine inches were thrust up inside her.

Charles had missed these afternoons of endurance while they had been holed up at the inn in Salisbury where the walls had been paper thin. Barbara was unmatched in bed. When it came to lovemaking, she was aggressive, with a lusty passion that struck a chord in his own deep sensuality, and she was very, very vocal. Her cries of pleasure filled the house as she plunged down upon him, as if she wanted all the world to know her body was joined to that of the King of England.

Charles cupped her magnificent buttocks to help balance her in her wild ride to satiety. Her melon-shaped breasts swung forward with each gyration and Charles's mouth gave them small love bites, enjoying her little screams interspersed with deep moans. In actuality they were perfectly matched sexually, for Charles usually had delayed climax, which allowed Barbara a full thirty minutes of creamy friction to indulge and satisfy her carnality.

Ironically this was the reason lovemaking was so unsatisfactory between Charles and his little queen Catherine. Because of her strict religious upbringing, she was crippled by her inhibitions and she was never aroused enough to take all nine inches of her husband. She was too dry and he often became lodged halfway inside her. All his endearments and whispered encouragement that she relax had little effect because she usually experienced very real pain. Charles was ever patient and kind, but he more or less had to masturbate after their unsatisfactory attempts to get her with child, and he despaired that in the royal bed his rampant virility would always go to waste.

He sighed as he thought of Catherine's delayed return to London so that she could visit the wells at Tonbridge, said to be a tonic to aid conception. He also knew she planned a pilgrimage to Our Lady's Shrine at Southwark Priory to pray for a child. Charles knew the only way to make a woman conceive was by planting his seed in her. Hadn't he proved it often enough with Barbara?

At that moment he felt his seed start and Barbara milked him until he was drained of every last drop. Now, if she'd just allow him an hour's slumber to regain his vigor in time for tonight's bachelor party for Charles Berkeley . . .

At Barbara's instigation her cousin Buckingham had been urging Charles to set Catherine aside and marry again so there would be a legitimate heir to the throne. But while the court had been at Salisbury, Charles had kept Barbara at arm's length and seemed to prefer the company of silly Frances Stewart, who trumpeted her virginity at every opportunity until Barbara feared that if Charles did choose another wife, she would have to be virgin. She must get her head together with Buckingham again to see what they could do to destroy Frances Stewart's reputation.

George Villiers, Duke of Buckingham, didn't realize it but he was skating on very thin ice with the King at the moment. Live and let live was Charles's attitude toward most of his courtiers, but George had been involved lately in what amounted to plots against the Queen, which was tantamount to hatching plots against the King. He was also creating a public scandal with Anna Maria Shrewsbury and a private one with his invitations for his favorites to dine at his "high" table.

Tonight, however, Charles chose to be in a magnanimous mood toward Buckingham as they sat around the large oval gambling table with a dozen other courtiers. The entire chorus from the King's Theatre Royal had been invited to entertain at Berkeley's bachelor party and almost every man at the table had a scantily clad actress perched on his knee. The byplay and bawdy remarks were most diverting, but Edward Montagu, the Earl of Sandwich, one of the few men without a companion, had been winning and was growing impatient with their antics. "God's flesh, Lauderdale, keep your fingers out of her, you're getting the cards all sticky," he drawled wittily.

The Scot, Lauderdale, was one of the coarsest men in the kingdom, but he amused the King and of course that was his saving grace in everyone's eyes. He asked Sandwich, "Can't ye get yer prick up these days, laddie? D'ye have a dent in yer balls?"

Sandwich threw him an amused glance. "Actually I'm off sex for the moment. Did you never notice that as the bills of a mistress mount, the pleasure diminishes?"

Buckingham drawled, "I should tempt you by inviting you to dine at my 'high' table."

"I've heard whispers about that. What's it all about?" asked Sandwich.

Buckingham said mockingly, "We dine and place high-stakes bets at the table. We are served by Oriental girls. How about tomorrow evening? Sandwich? Lauderdale? Your Majesty? Shall we make a foursome?"

The King looked at him quizzically. "I remember a Chinese girl once; did an unbelievably erotic trick with a string of pearls. Well, why not, George, you've dined at my high table for years."

The Duchess of Buckingham was now living in the country because Villiers had made it plain that conjugal bliss was not and never would be to his jaded taste. He had taken the first steps down deviation road and found it to his liking.

When all three of his guests had assembled the following evening, he asked each of them to change into a black silk robe embroidered with golden dragons then led them to an intimate dining room whose centerpiece was indeed a "high" table inlaid with lapis lazuli. The room was paneled in silver and gold and needed little illumination.

The table was set with delicate porcelain and at each setting was a jade dice box which held carved ivory dice. The gentlemen had to sit on tall stools because of the dining table's height. An air of expectation filled the air as a houseboy entered the room to light incense and theatrically strike a brass gong. Then four Oriental girls, naked even of body hair, entered the room in a procession. Each balanced three golden chafing dishes upon each arm and each girl served only one man. They were served a potent rice wine, and as the anticipation for what would follow piqued their curiosities, Lauderdale opened his mouth to ask a lewd question. Buckingham placed a finger to his lips and said, "Silence is golden. When we do not speak, all our other senses are heightened. We'll play a simple game of hazard—the dice will speak for us. The wrinkle is, gentlemen, the first to utter a sound pays a fine of five hundred crowns."

Lauderdale and Sandwich opened their mouths to protest, then thought better of it. Charles's eyes were like black obsidian as he watched Buckingham with moody cynicism. When the Oriental girls had satisfied one appetite, they prepared themselves to satisfy another. Their slim, naked beauty in the silver and gold light turned their skins to iridescent pearl. They went to the far end of the "high" table, opened a low door, and disappeared inside. Suddenly three pairs of eyes opened wide in shocked surprise as the men felt their robes opened and their sex organs manipulated by the exquisite touch of fingers and lips.

Lauderdale moaned his pleasure in a thick, unintelligible brogue and Buckingham said smoothly, "That will be five hundred crowns, John. I hope this game doesn't prove too rich for your blood!"

Charles stood up and said with distaste, "George, I like women. I have a reputation for being a womanizer, as you all know. But I have never knowingly degraded a woman in my life and I'm not about to start doing so now." He reached a hand below the table and helped the beautiful girl to climb out from underneath. "Come, my dear, I'm sure we can find a bedchamber where we can be private." He swept George with a look of contempt and led the girl from the room.

Just before Christmas, Buckingham was the central figure in a quarrel with Shrewsbury. Both King and Court were shocked that he fought a forbidden duel with the old earl and killed him, and at last Charles lost his temper and banished his old friend Villiers from Court.

That winter turned out to be the coldest that England had experienced in a century. Rather than hampering the frivolities of the court, however, it aided them in their voracious quest for new and unique diversions. The canal which Charles had designed in St. James Park froze solid and the place was turned into a winter wonderland. A carnival atmosphere prevailed, where skating, sliding, and snowball fights became the fashionable thing to do. The pathways were crowded with sleighs pulled by colorfully decorated miniature horses and a great ice house was constructed where the revelers could warm up with buttered ale, hot rum toddies, and partridge pies.

In January even the River Thames froze over and Londoners imitated the antics of the King's court and frolicked on the ice like children. Booths sprang up offering food and potent drink to ward off the chill, and of course entrepreneurs offered everything from skates to roast chestnuts. Punch and Judy shows vied for space next to fortune-tellers' booths. Betting on trotter races became all the rage; surely a pig on ice was the funniest thing Londoners had seen since dancing dogs performed on heated metal platforms.

Summer was far too involved with her own small world to attend the festivities of the winter season. With the help of Auntie Lil she furnished the new house in Friday Street and hibernated there with Mrs. Bishop to await the birth of her child. She noted with grim satisfaction that all the bills presented to Lord Helford through Solomon Storm were paid without question.

The first week of February the midwife moved in, bringing her

birthing stool and all the tools of her trade, and Mrs. Bishop fussed
about until Summer thought she would go mad. She longed to
escape her confines some days and her imagination flew her off to
the isolated beach in Cornwall where she rode Ebony through the
azure sea, warmed by the gulf stream. Her beloved Cornwall,
where the ever-blooming flowers turned the soft air to scented seduction and every fantasy ended in memories of the first time she
had offered her naked breasts to Ru in that perfect pink dawn so
long ago.

She was brought back to the present by a sudden agonizing pain
which seared through her midsection like a slash from a cutlass.
Mrs. Bishop and the midwife urged her to lie back on the slanted
birthing stool with its cutout seat, but after an hour's ordeal she
pushed herself to her feet, using the armrests, and paced about like
a caged lionness. Day turned into night and labor almost cut her in
half, hour after relentless hour. The only relief she felt was when
she threw her head back and screamed curses upon Ruark
Helford's head, then as an afterthought she did the same to Rory
just in case he was the author of her misery.

Like millions of women before her she swore off men for the rest
of her life. Before she had finished she experienced every emotion
known to woman, from helpless tears to hysterical laughter at the
cruel joke nature played on females to make a child come out the
same way it had gone in!

Finally, when she was at the end of her endurance and stopped
fighting it, the baby was born. Mrs. Bishop held the male child
with reverence. It was as dark and lusty as its father and she feared
that its fierce hunger would be too much for the fragile-looking girl
the midwife had just tucked into bed. Also, after the curses Summer had rained on the Helfords all day, poor Bish wondered how
she would react to a child who was a miniature Helford from its
startling green eyes to its prominent male appendage. She needn't
have worried. Summer held up amazingly strong arms. "My son,
please, Mrs. Bishop!" She clasped him to her heart fiercely, kissing
the fuzzy dark hair which covered his beautifully shaped head, and
the baby's instinct sought her nipple immediately. A selfish little
smile curved her lips. The ultimate revenge would be to refuse to
share him.

During the next couple of weeks she was swamped by visitors.
Maids of honor from Court came calling bringing their cavaliers,
then when her address became known, gentlemen dropped by con-

tinually to invite her to supper and a play since she was only a hop, skip, and a jump away from London's playhouses. Whispers had spread about her that she was no longer married and of course Whitehall thrived on rumor and gossip. She had been steeped in domesticity so long she had forgotten what it was like to dance, to flirt, to fend off a flattering advance from an ardent male admirer.

Lord Helford sent her a note asking when it would be convenient for him to see his son. She picked up a feather quill and answered with one word. "Never!" Then she realized he would immediately rise to the challenge, so she tore up the note and answered evasively, saying she was taking little Ryan to the countryside for the fresh air and would let him know when they came back to town.

When the Queen sent her an invitation to attend her drawing room for an evening of cards, Summer felt the old excitement rise within her. It had been so long since she'd worn anything more elaborate than a day dress and it seemed like years since she had painted her face.

Mrs. Bishop had been urging her to get out and about more. It wasn't natural for a beautiful young woman to devote every waking moment to a child, she insisted. Summer hid a smile. She knew Bish was dying to get the child to herself more often and in truth she knew she could never leave him in better hands. She wondered if she would be able to fit into her gowns and was amazed to find that her waist was smaller than it had been, although her breasts certainly were not. In the end she chose something they'd never seen her in before. She took a womanlike pleasure in choosing something spectacular, which would make the other ladies mad with envy. She had decided to wear the pale green creation which shimmered to silvery green when candlelight struck it. However, she found that she had to nurse Ryan a second time to reduce her breasts before she could fit into it. She swept high her dark, silken mass of curls and fastened it by carved jade combs and hairpins, then she made up her face, using kohl on her long dark lashes and bright poppy-colored lip rouge. She had some powder which contained gold dust and she patted it across her cheekbones and on the swell of her exposed breasts. Then she carefully selected her patches. She ignored the usual black ones and instead chose tiny gold ones in the shape of crowns. One went high on a cheekbone, the other she stuck on her breast just above and to side of a nipple which the gown barely covered. Then she wrapped herself in the pièce de résistance, the pale green fur wrap.

The carriage was brought from its stables behind St. Matthew's Church and she threw the baby a kiss and told Mrs. Bishop not to wait up for her. Summer took a deep breath, held her head high, and walked into the gallery. She heard gasps and whispers, and when she told the uniformed herald to announce her as Lady Summer St. Catherine, the buzz of the crowd became louder and every head swiveled in her direction.

The King gallantly stood beside Catherine to welcome the guests she had invited, and when Summer made her curtsy, she felt his amused eyes upon her. Only after she had exchanged kisses with Catherine did she look into his eyes. She saw appreciation writ plainly for her great beauty and she also saw speculation prompted by her advertisement that she was no longer Lady Helford.

The crowd swallowed her. They were all there, and she had no trouble keeping them apart tonight as she had when she first arrived in London. Lord Sandwich, head of the King's Fleet; Cornwallis, who flung silver coins at Royal Ceremonies; Albermarle, who tasted the King's food. The Duke of Ormond, who had once ridden his horse right into Westminster. Ned Hyde, the aging chancellor, and his plain daughter, Ann, Duchess of York. Summer's eyes swept the room as she nodded to Rochester, Clifford, Ashley, and Arlington.

Then she went suddenly cold, for watching her through narrowed eyes was none other than Ruark Helford. "Death and damnation," she swore, "if I'd known he'd be here, I wouldn't have come." She heard the King's deep chuckle from his great height and knew that he'd heard her. She looked up at him and said, "I swear to give me confidence, Sire."

"I know," he said, tucking her hand in his. "Don't worry, I'll stand by you in the face of the enemy."

She thanked him with a brilliant smile and whispered, "Damn 'em and ram 'em and sink 'em to hell."

He threw back his head and his great laughter rolled out. She clung desperately to his big hand as Ruark walked a direct path to them and said in deadly quiet tones, "I see the country air wasn't to your liking, madame."

"A barefaced lie, I'm afraid, Lord Helford," she said smugly, bolstered by the King's protection.

His voice was silky with menace. "I hope you don't think you can keep me from my own son."

"It's a wise father who knows his own child!" she dared to utter.

"God's flesh, Summer, is that remark intended for me or your husband?" the King asked, pretending injury, for rumor was rife that not all Barbara's offspring belonged to Charles.

Ruark gave the King a mock look of pity. "Can't be directed at me, Sire, my son is reported to be my living, breathing image."

Charles disengaged his hand from Summer's and murmured, "I wish you joy of each other," as he left the antagonists at daggers drawn.

Ruark's eyes swept over her with smoldering anger, then he said with contempt, "Pale green fur is decadent."

"Isn't it?" she said, looking immensely pleased with herself, and let the fur fall to her hips, affording him an unimpeded view of her breasts. She knew he was fighting a losing battle with his temper, but felt secure in a roomful of people, many of whom were watching the pair with avid interest.

He took a step closer and in spite of the crowd she felt a thrill of danger. The muscle in his jaw clenched like a lump of iron. "That gown was designed with one purpose in mind. It invites a man to play with your breasts."

"Yes," she agreed, goading him purposely, "unfortunately you are not the man I had in mind."

He reached out a deliberate thumb and forefinger. She gasped as she thought he intended to expose her nipple, but when she glanced down in alarm, she saw he had picked off the golden crown. "No, madame, it's patently obvious which man you had in mind." He took hold of her wrist in a viselike grip and led her back to the King. He said low, "I don't take leftovers from the royal table." He placed her hand in that of Charles and gave the King back his words: "I wish you joy of each other." Then he stalked off to soothe his injured pride with the first attractive woman to cross his path.

"It's the Helford temper, Your Majesty," Summer explained, humiliation staining her cheeks.

"Damned fellow almost challenged me. I warrant you're a match for him any day . . . or night," teased Charles.

Ruark Helford soon found that the company of the ladies present palled quickly. During each dance, before he could broach the subject of dalliance, his partner had touched him suggestively with her fan to let him know she was eager to lie with him. The hunter became the hunted and it was distasteful to his dominant nature.

He hated to admit it but Summer's face, exquisite as a cameo, made the beauty of other women seem overblown. Too, she had an elusive quality which made a man want more from her than she was willing to give. He soon gravitated to the men, whose conversations of sea battles and politics were infinitely more interesting.

Ned Hyde, the old chancellor, looked most pleased when Ruark thanked him for getting Parliament to vote in favor of spending two and a half million on the war. Ruark told him, "We get all the glory when we bring in enemy ships, but in truth the credit is yours, Chancellor."

Charles approached them and it was only his impeccable manners which prevented Ruark from turning away. "Ned, the Queen is looking for you. She wants to personally thank you for helping me find favor with Parliament for once." When they were alone, Charles said to a stone-faced Helford, "If looks could kill, I'd be a dead man. I'm probably a fool to tell you this, but I haven't cuckolded you . . . at least not yet. What's all this nonsense about Summer using her maiden name? You haven't really dissolved the marriage, have you?"

"No. She'll remain Lady Helford whether she chafes at the bonds of matrimony or not," he said flatly.

"Then I suggest you put your brand of ownership on her," drawled Charles, "before some other man plucks the fruit for which you lust."

Ruark Helford watched her covertly for the next hour. The men were attracted like flies to a honeypot. He watched her fend off Jack Grenvile, the King's brother James, Wild Harry Killigrew, and Sir Antony Deane, the great shipbuilder who had just finished two new vessels, the *Hampshire* and the *Nonesuch,* and was one of the guests of honor this evening. Ruark's brows drew together as Summer greeted Sir George Digby, Earl of Bristol, with a kiss. He estimated him to be close to fifty years old, but he had a youthful air and was good looking in the extreme. Summer did not dismiss his attentions and in fact allowed Digby to tuck her arm beneath his as he led her into a card room. The earl had been a widower for well over a year now and no woman had been lucky enough to snare him. If Summer was fancying herself a countess, he'd soon disabuse her of such delusions of grandeur, he thought grimly as he entered the card room.

He heard her say, "I'd love to try some clary—I hear it's become all the rage since I was last at Court."

Clary was a very potent concoction of brandy, sugar, clary flowers, and the aphrodisiac ambergris. No wonder Digby lost no time running to fetch it for her, thought Ruark angrily. He stepped up behind her. "I will escort you home, madame."

She whirled to face him. "Oh, I'm so sorry, I've just told the Earl of Bristol that he could have that honor." She had emphasized the title to annoy him.

"I will escort you home now. I've decided to take a look at my son."

She stiffened. She was in a panic, for she knew that once he set his mind to do something, he did it! "I couldn't possibly disappoint George," she protested.

"I'll do it for you," he said with firm resolve. As the handsome earl returned carrying two glasses of clary, Helford relieved him of one and drained it. "Thanks, George, Summer can't have brandy at the moment, it would get into her milk."

Summer gasped, George Digby flushed, and Ruark Helford flashed his wolf's grin. "Excuse us, George, we're leaving."

The whoreson had deliberately spoiled her evening. She planted her feet firmly and glared at him. "We can't leave before the Queen," protested Summer.

His hand had a firm grip on her elbow and he almost dragged her from the card room into the gallery. "No one will see us leave in this crush." But they did, of course. The men envied him and the women envied her. It looked as if they couldn't wait a moment longer to lie with each other as they rushed from the gallery.

She knew what would happen if he got her alone. The same thing that happened last time, the thing that always happened between them. She wanted to fly at him and rend his dark face to ribbons. Instead she tried an evasive tactic. With honeyed voice she said, "Ru, come tomorrow and spend some time with us. It would be so selfish to wake a sleeping babe."

"I am known to be selfish," he said implacably.

"Not just selfish," she railed, losing her carefully held temper, "you are an arrogant, ill-tempered, rampant swine."

"Rampant?" he echoed. "I haven't laid a hand on you for almost three months." Almost implicit in his words was the promise "until tonight." Her mind raced about for an avenue of escape. If she could get home before he arrived, she could keep Mrs. Bishop with her. "I'll ride in my own carriage," Summer insisted.

"That will be difficult. I dismissed your driver hours ago."

Her eyes blazed her outrage. "How dare you do such a high-handed thing?" she demanded, stamping her high-heeled foot on the marble steps.

He raised a dark eyebrow. "Since I pay the man's wages, I believe I am merely exercising my rights." His words set off warning bells as they echoed in her brain: "Exercising my rights . . . exercising my rights." The last thing she wanted was to be alone with him in his carriage. He was far too bold and sensual a man to be trusted on even a short ride. He hailed his driver and opened the carriage door for her. She stood resolute and actually opened her mouth to blurt "I'm afraid to be alone with you" when he looked down at her mockingly and said, "You're not afraid to be alone with me, are you?"

"Afraid? You must be mad! I'm afraid of neither man nor beast."

His mouth curved wickedly. "And you haven't quite decided which I am yet."

She shook off his hands as she climbed into the carriage and sat stiffly against the velvet squabs. When he sat down next to her she felt his thigh against hers and tried to move away, but he was sitting firmly on the material of her gown and she found herself effectively pinned like a butterfly. She was furious with herself for letting him have such a physical impact on her, alone together in the intimate darkness of the carriage. Her mouth was dry, her breasts, now heavy with milk, ached unbearably, and her mind vividly recalled his scalding mouth when it made love to her.

His maleness silently overwhelmed her. It had been almost three months since he'd made love to her and her traitorous body had begun to tingle the moment his muscled thigh brushed hers. The tingle grew to hunger as the carriage swayed and she fell against him. She recoiled as if she'd been shot.

"I just want you to leave me alone," she cried.

His voice was deep, smooth, knowing, as he said, "I haven't seen you or touched you for three months. I think that's long enough—overlong for a woman as sensual as you are, Summer darling." Her name on his lips sent shivers running up inside her. She dug her clenched nails into the palms of her hands and the sharp pain stopped her resolve from weakening. She bit down on her lip to revive her hatred of him.

"Why are you angry with me?" he asked, his lips only an inch above her ear.

"Damn you, I'm more than angry—I hate you!"

"Why?" he whispered.

"Spencer, of course, and for ravishing me. I'll never forgive you!"

He didn't touch her, but she expected to feel his roving hands any moment. Quietly he said, "You know how the war has escalated. I sent him off to Madagascar on a merchant ship to keep him safe. How long do you think you could have kept him out of the fighting? And it's going to get worse, much worse."

He was actually trying to make her believe that he had done the noble thing by Spencer. "And the ravishment?" she demanded. "Talk your way out of that one!"

"Mea culpa," he crooned, knowing he was close to committing the offense again.

The carriage stopped and she knew she must get out instantly. She tried to bolt through the door and heard a sickening rip as the delicate fabric of her gown was torn open from ankle to hip. She looked at him in dismay and he smiled into her eyes with unconcealed lust. With one smooth movement he swung her legs up onto the seat and his strong brown hands went up inside the gaping gown to slither up her thighs and beyond. His mouth sought hers and she withdrew from it until she was lying full length upon the carriage seat. Her breasts swelled from the overtight bodice until one popped out and his avid mouth had captured its rosy crown before her hand could cover it. Too late! He tasted the drop of fluid and it was such an unbelievably erotic experience he almost ejaculated.

She shuddered. "No, no, no," she cried.

"Darling, I know your body so well, it's crying out to mine right now."

"Not anymore, Ruark. I've fallen in love with someone else."

The words had the same effect as a slap in the face. He withdrew from her immediately. She sat up shakily and covered her naked breast. The silence stretched between them unbearably. She had gained a few minutes' respite, perhaps she could gain longer. "If I let you see Ryan, will you promise to leave us in peace for another three months?"

THE PIRATE AND THE PAGAN

His voice was cool, distant. "I think I can safely say I'll be occupied elsewhere. The Dutch are going to hit back and hit back hard."

The baby was crying when they entered the house. The moment she heard his cry, drops of milk ran from her swollen breasts and wet the bodice of her gown. Mrs. Bishop carried him down the stairs, secretly delighted to see Ruark was with her.

Ruark held out his arms for his son and naturally Mrs. Bishop proudly handed him over to his father. Self-interest made Summer keep a close watch on his face. A finger of fear touched her heart as she saw the possessive look on Ruark's face. His dark eyes sent a quick message to Bish to leave them private and she retreated up the stairs unobtrusively.

"My sweetheart," whispered Summer, her heart turning over with love at the sight of her child. The moment he heard his mother's voice, baby Ryan had eyes for no one else. He began to cry lustily, demandingly, and Summer knew she must somehow get rid of Ruark so she could feed him. "It's late," she said apologetically. "You do understand, Ruark?"

Still holding his son, he lowered his eyes to her breasts, which swelled lusciously from the tight bodice. The two wet spots grew larger as he watched.

"I understand perfectly," he said hoarsely.

Her cheeks grew warm. She took the child from him firmly and said pointedly, "I have to feed him, as you can see. If you have looked your fill, sir, would you leave?"

"No," he said quietly, "I'm going to watch you . . . I'll never have my fill."

Her breasts ached so much she knew she had no choice. She carried Ryan into the salon and sat down in a rocking chair. She turned her shoulder away from Ruark to partially conceal herself, gently withdrew a full breast, and offered it to her baby. For the first few seconds he made little noises of distress as if he feared he would be deprived of the source of his happiness. Then he quieted as he gripped it firmly with his tiny hands.

Ruark moved around in front of them with a look of awe on his face. Never in his life had he felt so protective before. He wanted them both, and of course he knew a sure way to get what he wanted. If he took his son, he knew the mother would follow.

"Ru, I beg you, leave us in peace," she begged.

"A baby belongs with his mother, but later on, you know I will want him, Summer. I won't allow my son to be brought up in London. You know as well as I that he belongs at Helford Hall."

Tears glistened in her eyes as they fiercely challenged each other over the precious burden. Rather than hurt her child, she was willing to hand him over now. Then she saw Ruark's eyes soften. "I'm sorry, Summer, I can be such a swine at times. I'll leave you in peace," he promised sadly.

43

Summer entered that period of her life where she sought to know herself. Since that fateful day long ago when she arrived in London and glimpsed Lord Ruark Helford, her life had been tumultuous. The passion which had almost consumed them had been too scorching not to cool and by his rejection he had sent her headlong into the arms and bed of his brother. She had committed the mortal sin of letting both men make love to her until it had culminated in a child.

She was now completely celibate and at last her conscience was at rest. It was such a relief to have everything sorted out, to get off the seesaw of loving two men. The only one she loved now was Ryan. He was the only male in her life who meant anything and everything to her. Peace and quiet had brought her contentment, especially now that she had been able to put the ghost of her excessive love for Lord Ruark Helford to rest.

Her contentment was short-lived. The Earl of Bristol was taking her to the King's Playhouse on Drury Lane to see Ben Jonson's *Volpone*. It was the talk of the town and she dressed with great care because she knew the house would be packed with fashionable women. She chose a sophisticated black gown to set off her rubies and swept her hair up in a rather severe, yet most elegant fashion.

Summer was amused by the envious glances she received from

the other women at the play and knew it was because of the earl's
devastating good looks. She liked George immensely; they were
good friends because she wasn't the least bit infatuated by his
handsome face. It took a more rugged countenance to set Summer's pulses beating. The earl held her seat in the private box and
she gave him a dazzling smile as she shrugged the black fox fur
from her shoulders and looked across the theater to see a small
group arrive. It was the King, and Summer was amused to see that
he had escorted both Barbara Castlemaine and Frances Stewart to
see the fashionable play. Barbara was resplendent in purple; she
laid claim to the color because of its association with royalty. She
flaunted her diamonds and Summer grudgingly admired her. Sitting there, filled with another royal bastard, she had more than
earned her diamonds. Summer's eye fell on Frances Stewart and
again she wondered what possible attraction the girl could hold for
a voluptuary like Charles. She was so young, so slim, so pale. Only
a prim little strand of pearls adorned her small bosom. She felt a
fleeting stab of pity for poor Charles caught between two loves,
then the pity was swept away as she saw clearly that Charles was
an aging roué who lusted for the girl's extreme youth and virginity.
Her lip curled and she was about to make a cynical remark to her
escort when her eyes traveled to the next box. "Good God!" she
exclaimed.

"What's amiss, my dear?" asked George, who saw clearly her
look of distress.

"It's Helford. He's with a chit young enough to be his daughter!" An unreasoning hot jealousy swept her with such ferocity it
deprived her of breath.

George chuckled and she turned to bestow a look of outrage
upon him. "Actually it's *my* daughter."

Her brain had ceased to function. "Your daughter?" she repeated stupidly.

"Georgie. She's up from the country for the first time and Ruark
has taken her under his protective wing . . . to keep off the fortune hunters," he added confidentially.

"Georgie?" she echoed with unconcealed loathing. She felt
acutely unwell. A sudden pain almost cut her in half and she realized with dismay that it was her heart which was hurting. Her
throat constricted so much she began to pant. Her eyes narrowed
and swung between Helford and the King. Both dark faces smiled
down at little girls and she saw Charles reach out to fondle

Frances's knee. They were like two peas from the same disgusting pod! Whoremongers! Lechers! It was unbearable; she was outraged.

Good God, in the eyes of the court it would look as if two men had conspired obscenely to swap a daughter for a wife, yet the Earl of Bristol sat there with a fatuous look on his face as if the world were unfolding as it should, when in reality it was hurtling toward destruction!

Ben Jonson's masterpiece made little sense to Summer as she tapped her foot, impatiently waiting for intermission. The actors droned on until she wanted to scream, then mercifully the velvet curtains swung closed and the applause burst forth like thunder. Summer clapped her hands enthusiastically, glad that the damned thing was at least half over. As the occupants of the boxes mingled in the circular promenade where wine was served, George and Summer came face-to-face with Ruark and Georgie. Why in the name of heaven had she worn black? It turned her skin sallow and aged her unbelievably. Her coiffure, which had seemed elegant at the outset of the evening, now seemed hideous.

Digby's daughter wore baby blue. Summer thought the clusters of blond ringlets bouncing upon her shoulders looked like disgusting sausages. "Oh, Daddy," she said, bubbling, "I'm having a simply divine evening." She glanced adoringly up at Ruark and said, "Lord Helford's eyes match the emeralds you gave me for my birthday."

"Really?" drawled Summer. "They always remind me of gooseberries floating in syrup."

Ruark's face was impassive, his manners impeccable, as he said, "Lady Georgina Digby, may I present Lady Summer St. Catherine."

"Oh," said Georgina, suddenly looking very sulky, then remembering her manners, she curtsied to the older woman.

Summer's eyes narrowed. "I'm not quite a dowager yet, darling."

"Daddy, Lord Helford has asked me to the Countess of Lauderdale's party after the play. May I go, Daddy, please?" she begged prettily.

"It's unlike you to play gadfly," George remarked to Ruark.

Summer said sweetly, "It's hard to be yourself when you're trying to make a good impression." The currents between Summer and Ruark flowed furiously, yet amazingly father and daughter seemed unaware.

The earl could deny his child nothing. "You may go to your party if you're home at a respectable hour."

Ruark's eyes caught Summer's as he said smoothly, "I'll have her in bed before eleven." Summer gasped in disbelief at the double entendre, but Helford had swept the girl off on his arm to enjoy the rest of the play. The girl hadn't the vaguest notion that Lord Helford had ever been married. As he took her empty glass from her Georgie whispered to Ruark, "So that's Summer St. Catherine. My father's in love with her, you know, and I'm dreadfully afraid she's got her hooks well into him."

Ruark's hands balled into fists. The empty wineglass was crushed into minute shards.

Georgie was aghast. "Oh, my lord, did you cut yourself?"

He shook his head and replied through his teeth, "Didn't draw blood . . . though I might before I'm finished."

Summer said to George, "I cannot approve your choice of escort, milord."

"Helford? Why, he's the most honorable fellow I know."

"That damns your friends with faint praise indeed," she said coolly, struggling in vain with the green-eyed monster who had her by the throat. "I wouldn't trust him in a convent."

George hugged her to him, his eyes laughing down into hers. "Your wicked wit is devastating. 'Tis one of the things about you which utterly fascinates me."

The next day she lost no time paying a visit to Lil Richwood. Her aunt had an uncanny ability at picking up whispers before they became common gossip, and Summer bombarded her with questions about the Earl of Bristol's daughter. "She's obviously a sly little bitch who has her father wrapped about her little finger. He actually bought her emeralds, the other day . . . emeralds begod!"

"She's his only heiress, darling, and she got a fortune when her mother died."

"Well, you'd never know it by her clothes," said Summer with a shudder. "She was as commonplace as mud. 'Fore God, she was in predictable baby blue."

"She was in pastels because she's not yet sixteen," soothed Auntie Lil.

"For Christ's sake, is that supposed to make me feel better?"

"Stop it, Summer! Next you'll be fancying he annulled the marriage so he could take another wife."

"Is that what you've heard? Is that what you're trying to keep from me?" demanded Summer.

Lil rolled her eyes heavenward, desperately seeking divine help. " 'Tis as plain as a pikestaff that you're still mad in love with him. If I can see it, it only stands to reason that he's well aware of it. It's beyond me why he doesn't drag you by the scruff of the neck to Cornwall to make more babies."

Summer burst into tears.

"What's the matter now?" asked Lil, softening.

"Tomcats drag females by the scruff of the neck. That's exactly what he is, a tomcat!"

Lil was exasperated. "I've only so much patience and you've had the lot. What you need is a damn good roll in the hay. Take a lover. Let him fill you with cream until you purr."

"Who?" asked Summer blankly.

Lil laughed. "You're like someone at a banquet who starves! The court is chocablock with randy males; you have your choice from the King down . . . or up, whichever your perspective. Or better yet, marry George Digby and become a countess."

Summer suddenly became very still. After a few moments she gathered her fan and her muff and departed, her mind far off in deepest thought.

"Good God, what maggot have I unleashed in her brain?" muttered Lil to no one in particular.

To a casual observer it appeared that Summer was taking Lil Richwood's advice as she readied some of her more elaborate gowns to take to Court. She needed a man and the place to find a man, of course, was Court. In a few days there was to be a gala reception honoring ambassadors from France, Spain, and Russia, and Summer decided the occasion definitely called for ostrich feathers. Ryan was six months old and just about weaned, but the day before she left for Court she spent the whole day cuddling him. Mrs. Bishop shook her head over Summer's behavior. " 'Tis most unfashionable for a lady to be constantly seen with a babe in her arms. Soon he won't just be spoiled, he'll be ruinated! He has too many women fussing about him night and day."

"You're quite right, of course, Bish. He needs a father as well as a mother. I think it's time I did something about it. I'm going to be spending more time at Court. I wouldn't be able to do that if I didn't have you, Mrs. Bishop."

The older woman was worried. She didn't see what was wrong with the father he already had. There would be hell to pay if Ruark knew she was husband hunting. Bish knew he would take his son in a minute rather than let another man have him, and she felt in her heart that he would be justified.

Summer stood inside the wardrobe in the Helford rooms down by Whitehall's bowling green. For a moment she was lost in another world, her hand on one of Ruark's old doublets, its scent of sandalwood filling her nostrils, stirring half-forgotten dreams from the past, then briskly she pushed it aside to make room for the clothes from her trunk. She planned to arrive after the banquet but before the dancing. There was no way she was going to sit through an interminable dinner where the speeches would be fatuous and the food cold.

Two hours later she arrived in the great banqueting hall. Her ostrich-feathered fan wafted frangipani about her beautiful shoulders and every eye was riveted upon her. Everything about her gown was outrageous, from its cost to its vivid color of peacock. Every breath of air wafted the delicate downy tendrils of her hair into a fluttering, floating mass which caressed her breasts and shoulders with shivering, shuddering undulation and alternately revealed and concealed as she was greeted by one man after another. Her wicked juices bubbled tonight. She was there for one purpose only, to torment Ruark Helford and make him as miserable as she had been since he'd begun his liaison with Lady Georgina Digby. The corners of her mouth turned up in a secret, delicious smile as she spotted him at the far end of the hall laughing with the King, while the little grubworm made a polite effort to make sense of the Queen's fractured English.

Jack Grenvile came to her side as soon as he saw her. He kissed her hand and tickled her palm suggestively with the tip of his tongue. She tucked her arm in his and invited, "Come, you handsome brute, let's do some husband baiting."

When he saw where she was heading, he whispered, "I don't think Bristol's little gel is any competition for you, sweetheart."

"No, poor little mouse," purred Summer. She had eyes only for the King as he looked at her with undisguised admiration mixed with lust. She curtsied to the Queen and enjoyed the stone face of

Ruark as Charles looked down the front of her gown. The King said, "You are a vision of loveliness tonight, Summer."

Grenvile agreed heartily. "The plumes look a lot better adorning Summer than the ostrich."

Lady Georgina pressed her lips together in disapproval and said, "How cruel."

Summer bestowed a dazzling smile upon the girl and traced her finger along the expensive ermine trim of her gown. "That rabbit died for you. My ostrich is merely running around in the nude."

The King and Grenvile laughed, but Ruark Helford did not. "I believe this is our dance," he said to Summer in a tone which brooked no refusal.

"You are mistaken," she said softly, flirting outrageously with Charles. "I believe I'm yours, Sire." The King swept her into a courante and Jack Grenvile partnered Georgina. Ruark bowed to the Queen and begged her to dance with him. When the dance ended, they were all in approximately the same place they had started. Summer looked at Georgina Digby's emerald pendant and said, "Your emerald is lovely. If I were you, I'd get Daddy to give you matching earrings. When he takes a countess, I'm afraid she'll claim all future jewels."

Georgina looked alarmed.

Summer saw the Earl of Bristol emerge from the crush. "Darling," she said, lifting her face for his kiss. *"Je suis désolée sans toi."*

A tall footman offered a silver tray to His Majesty and Charles reached for a glass of champagne. Summer took two, draining them both while the men adored her with their eyes. The music started up and she said gaily to Helford, "An ugly fellow like you deserves to stand against the wall, but if I don't take pity on you, who will?"

The King and Jack Grenvile laughed again and Ruark knew he would look a churlish swine if he refused her. "What in hell were you thinking of to kiss Digby in a public place?" he demanded harshly.

"Because if I'd kissed him in a private place, his little girl would have fainted." His hand tightened on hers dangerously, threatening to crack her delicate bones. "Or perhaps not . . . perhaps she's your latest whore."

"God's flesh, the girl is only sixteen years old," he protested, shocked.

"George thinks she needs a mother . . . perhaps I'll apply," she said lightly.

Lids low over glittering green eyes, he sneered. "You used your body to become Lady Helford, so you'd probably stop at nothing to become the Countess of Bristol."

His cruel words hurt her, but she would have died rather than show it. She gave him a glorious smile and said low, "You know, it would be worth it if I could talk George into naming Ryan his heir."

Ruark stiffened and warned between clenched teeth, "I'll give you the benefit of the doubt and believe you are playing teasing games, because if I thought for one moment you were serious, the consequences would be deadly." The music changed to a kissing dance. Both Ruark and Summer glanced back toward the Digbys as they stood together, eagerly awaiting the return of their partners. Both Ruark and Summer heartily wished the Digbys in hell. But Summer was in far too dangerous a mood to allow Helford a kiss tonight even though it was just a playful dance. She swept off the dance floor, not even glancing back to see if he followed, and took George's hand eagerly as if she couldn't wait for him to take her in his arms.

She glanced down the hall to see Georgina Digby lift her oh-so-innocent face up to receive Ruark's kiss and she felt totally defenseless. "Whoremonger!" she whispered furiously, and the Earl of Bristol, who was about to delicately brush her tempting breast as he kissed her, drew back his hand as if he had been caught.

By midnight most of the guests in the banqueting hall who were still on their feet were inebriated—or "disguised," as they called it. Assignations were being made, and couples were emerging from alcoves to slip away down the honeycombed passageways of Whitehall or outdoors into the warm September night. Summer had partnered the King more often than she had any other man and was perfectly amenable when he manuevered her out onto the stone balcony for a little air. A hot breeze wafted the fragile feathers about her shoulders and Charles responded to her beauty in his usual physical way. His big arm swept about her and he pressed her to the hard length of him to gauge her reaction. "You little minx, it is nothing novel to you to have a man rise to the occasion."

She laughed up at him. " 'Tis a great compliment to have a king stand at attention for me."

"Summer, you disappoint me. I thought we knew each other well enough to dispense with this King and subject nonsense . . . I thought we were just a man and a woman."

"We know each other too well to be anything but good friends," she said quietly.

He sighed. "Ah, I thought you came out here with me just to get Ruark's goat; now, there's no need for me to ask if you're serious about George, it's just a brutal stratagem to make Helford suffer and come to heel."

She ran her fingers through her plumes. "He shouldn't have ruffled my feathers with the little goosegirl."

"He's going out with the fleet in a couple of days, in an all-out offensive. Why don't you forgive the poor devil before he goes into battle?"

She shook her head. "He hasn't suffered nearly enough," she said decisively. She went up on tiptoe to kiss him. "Thank you for sharing state secrets with me, Sire."

"You should be thrown in the Tower for leaving me in this condition," Charles whispered as they quit the stone balcony.

Ruark Helford had seen her leave the hall with Charles and had felt an impotent fury seething in his veins. Normally he would have taken Georgina home hours ago but he had not dared to leave Summer when she was acting in such a dangerous manner. He was on the point of going out onto the balcony and dragging her back inside by the hair. At the moment his temper was out of control and he was actually contemplating knocking his monarch over the stone balcony. Barbara Castlemaine, wise in the way of women, knew Summer had gone out there to plague Helford. She reached out a firm hand to stay him and said low, "He sleeps in my bed tonight . . . not hers."

They came back into the blazing lights of the hall separately. As soon as Charles entered, Barbara slipped her arm through his and moved away from Helford. Ruark was ready for her the moment she came through the balcony doors. He took hold of her arm and forcefully dragged her at least thirty feet down the hall to an alcove. He shoved her ungently against the wall and put up his arm as a barrier.

"You've bruised me," she accused with blazing eyes.

"I certainly hope so," he ground out.

She could see and even feel the fury just barely held in check. She had incited him to it and secretly gloried in her power over him. His fingers actually tingled as he envisioned putting them about her slender neck and throttling her. Never had she needed such a strong lesson in learning which of them was master. He knew an urge to put a destructive hand into the neck of her provocative gown and tear it to its hem. His fury almost choked him. He growled, "All night you have acted like a common trollop, a little whore!"

The very devil danced in her eyes as she ran the tip of her pink tongue over her lips. "Wine makes me insatiable," she said huskily.

He snarled like a wolf. "You're drunk . . . I wouldn't bother to lay you."

She smiled and her knowing eyes glanced down his body. She had never been more aware of his powerful anger combined with lust. "Your prick makes a liar out of you. You'd give your soul to fuck me right now," she breathed.

Ruark hovered on the brink of violence, yet under it all he knew she spoke the truth. This thing between them was a volatile mixture of love and hate. Their feelings for each other were too intense, too violent, too darkly passionate. He knew he must keep his hands to himself or he would do her an injury. He turned away with a foul oath and saw a wide-eyed Georgina had witnessed the exchange with his wife. "Come," he said stiffly, "I must return you to your father. I am no fit company tonight."

Summer knew this thing which had blazed up between them was not finished. She knew without a doubt that once he had rid himself of Digby's daughter, he would stalk her to finish what he had started. Then a bubble of laughter escaped her lips as she realized he had no idea she was spending the night in his rooms. How delicious! She would sleep in his bed while he drove into the city to wait all night for her outside her house on Friday Street.

Quickly, while she had the opportunity, she scooped up the hem of her gown with its magnificent ostrich plumes and ran outside into the stone gallery. Ruark was right, she had had far too much to drink, she realized as a dizziness threatened to steal away her balance. On her way to the rooms by the bowling green she saw two people making their stealthy way in the same direction. Immediately she recognized the black and white stripes of Frances Stewart's gown. The pious little bitch, thought Summer. Pretending to be so pure and virginal while opening her legs for the King in secret! Then Summer heard the man speak with a Scottish burr and she realized it was not the King, but his cousin the Duke of

Richmond who had apartments by the bowling green. She realized Frances Stewart was risking everything to become a wife. Then she became angry. Life was so damned unfair to women. They were forced to do anything and everything to trap a man into marriage, then spend the rest of their lives paying the price!

She let herself into the apartment and secured the door. She undressed and hung up the costly peacock gown then she threw herself on the bed and swore she was finished playing games. What was the point of the frivolous life she was leading? She may be able to convince others that she wanted to be Countess of Bristol, but she couldn't convince herself. She knew she loved Ruark Helford beyond reason. Next week he was going to war. Tomorrow she would go to him. She would swallow her pride and beg him to take her back as his wife. It was time she grew up. She would do it before one more day of her life was ruined. When she put her head on her pillow and closed her eyes, the room spun about and she cursed herself for drinking so much champagne.

44

Summer slept like a log until well past noon. She awoke with a groan and gingerly lifted her head from the pillow. When she did so, it felt like someone had taken a meat cleaver to split her head in half. She sat up slowly, holding both halves of her head together. Never had she experienced anything like this champagne hangover. Even her eyebrows hurt when she winced. Her mouth felt like the bottom of a monkey's cage and her tongue tasted as if she'd been sucking on a shepherd's stocking.

When she recalled last night's behavior, she moaned with despair. How could she face Lord Ruark Helford after drunkenly goading him to madness? Her language had been appalling. He must have a fine disgust of her. She pledged never to drink again. She pledged never to swear again. She pledged never to breathe again. She sat huddled in a miserable heap for over an hour before she could manage to wash and to cleanse her mouth. Another hour passed before she could muster enough ambition to dress herself. She looked at the clothes she had brought and shuddered at the outrageous styles and impractical glittery material.

She chose the least elaborate gown she had brought, a cream-colored watered silk with cherry underskirt and cherry ribbons threaded through the enormous sleeves, and concentrated upon making her face look less ravished. Her makeup did miracles and managed to make her look only half dead. She realized she would not feel better until she put something in her stomach. As she threaded her way back to Whitehall's center she found the passages were singularly deserted and she thought cynically that after last night's debauch everyone was likely still abed nursing their heads. She climbed the stairs slowly and wondered if she would have to go all the way up to the King's closet before she encountered a footman. At last she came upon a yeoman of the guard. "Lud, where is everyone today?"

"Her Majesty and her ladies are up on the top floor watching the fire, ma'am."

"Fire?" she muttered. "It never ceases to amaze me what these people do for entertainment."

Against her better judgment Summer climbed higher and saw about thirty women clustered about the east windows. Their chatter was so loud and excited she pressed her hands against her ears. Elizabeth Hamilton moved over to make room at the window for her. Far off in the City of London proper an ugly pall of gray smoke had blanketed the sky. The voices were beginning to penetrate now and Summer heard one say, "Imagine last night we were dancing and didn't know a thing about it." Another said, "I heard it was started by a baker in Pudding Lane, is that true?" Someone answered, "I don't believe it. I heard that it was started by the Dutch. The warehouses down Thames Street hold all our war supplies."

Queen Catherine was wringing her hands. As soon as she saw Barbara Castlemaine arrive on the scene she swallowed her pride and said, "Lady Castlemaine, I have been told that Charles and James have gone into the city to fight the fire. Have you heard aught of the King?"

"Your Majesty, I only hear the same rumors you do." Barbara glanced at Summer and saw that all the color had drained from her face and her hands were shaking like leaves. Barbara took hold of her arm and steered her away from the others. She used bracing words so the girl would not faint. "Zounds, you Helfords give me nothing but trouble. That damned husband of yours dragged the King from my bed at three o'clock this morning."

Summer stared at her wildly. "Barbara . . . my baby . . . my house is on Friday Street!"

"Oh, Lud," said Barbara with sinking heart. "Look, they've

probably got it under control by now. All the able-bodied men went over twelve hours ago."

"What did Ruark say?" Summer begged.

There was no way Barbara was going to repeat the graphic horror stories Helford had relayed to Charles, but she didn't lie when she told her, "The moment he alerted the King, Ruark was off to Woolwich and Deptford to the naval yards for workmen and seamen and all the militia. Summer, where are you going?" she demanded.

What a ridiculous question, thought Summer, lifting her petticoats and flying down the stairs of Whitehall Palace. Forgotten was the throbbing head and delicate stomach. They had been replaced by a hard knot of fear which threatened to choke her. She ran down to the water stairs thinking to take a boat into the city, but this far out the Thames was deserted. She had no choice but to set off on foot. The four miles did not daunt her, she would have walked had it been forty.

She could smell the smoke from the fire on the warm wind and prayed that the fire would be out before she reached the city. By the time she rounded the bend of the River Thames, she could hear something roaring, and the wind had picked up considerably. Now she was so hot and walking so quickly that she began to perspire. Her breathing became labored, but she thought it was from her exertion coupled with her apprehensiveness. She had no idea that fire used up all the available oxygen and the smoke was a potential killer.

As she approached the city, the Thames was clogged by small boats and lighters filled with household goods which people were bringing out of their homes as fast as they could. The streets were unpassable because of the number of horses and wagons and carts evacuating people and the possessions they had accumulated over their lifetimes. If one and all were fleeing the fire, who remained to put it out, to stop it from spreading across the entire city? It seemed to be every man for himself, thought Summer with despair. Almost there, almost there, Summer kept repeating to herself as the wind and the fire roared.

She could feel the heat of the pavement through her satin slippers and the air was filled with black soot. She glanced down at her skirt and feet and saw they were no longer cream-colored. She was begrimed with soot and sweat, but there was far more to contend with. She could see the flames of the fire now; surely every warehouse along Lower Thames Street was ablaze. Showers of fire drops rained down, burning her cheeks and singeing her hair. Two Duke of York's horse guards were forcing everyone back and would not allow them to enter Upper Thames Street.

Without hesitation she ran up to the guard and grabbed the horse's bridle to get his attention. "My baby is in danger, I have to get through," she begged.

He shouted, "Warehouses are full of pitch, tar, oil, brandy— can't you hear the explosions?"

She turned up Blackfriars toward Ludgate Hill, but the crush of people heading to the river so they could get across to Bankside made progress almost impossible. The people were black. They had stayed in their houses until the last possible minute, until the top stories had actually set on fire. She had to fight her way through the throng. Almost there, almost there, she thought, and knew it was the only thing which kept her from screaming. Tears ran down her face freely at the suffering she witnessed. She saw sick children being carried out in their beds, old people being knocked to their knees as younger, stronger ones fled the malicious, bloody flames.

She looked up and saw church steeples ablaze; she looked down to see a cat fly past with all its tail ablaze. Even the poor pigeons had circled and circled the ledges of the burning buildings until their wings caught fire and they dropped down to the pavement to be crushed underfoot. By the time she reached St. Paul's Cathedral her lungs felt as if they would burst. She stopped to press her aching side where she felt a cramp beneath her ribs. The massive church gave her a sense of calm. It was immense, it was the heart of London. Surely this building which covered over ten acres would stand its ground in the face of the terrifying conflagration. Summer crossed herself and ran along the south side of St. Paul's toward Friday Street, muttering, "I'm there, I'm there." Then she saw a sight that almost drove her mad. One side of Friday Street was ablaze; the opposite side, where her house had stood, no longer existed.

As she stood there unable to comprehend the enormity of her loss, she wondered why her feet were in such pain. She looked down to see her very shoes on fire. She kicked them off and the pavement scorched the bare soles of her feet. She saw a woman huddled in the middle of the road, but when she bent down to aid her, she saw the woman was dead, her face charred black, her hair still crackling. She screamed, "Mrs. Bishop, Mrs. Bishop." Debris was falling about her and she took to her heels as if she had just gotten her second wind. She ran into Canning Street blindly, sobbing, not knowing or caring where she was or what she did. A large crowd of men were working furiously, pulling down houses in an effort to thwart the raging inferno. She saw a familiar tall, dark figure stripped to the waist, lifting heavy timbers. She flew to his side through the crowd of men. "Ru, Ru," she cried, now oblivious to all danger.

Charles turned to see who grabbed him and couldn't believe his eyes when he looked through the sweat and grime and recognized Summer. "Sweetheart, what in the name of hellfire are you doing here? Get back to the palace immediately."

"Oh, my God, I thought you were Ruark. Where is he? My baby, my baby, my house is gone," she babbled. "I must find my husband and my baby!"

He sat down on a doorstep and took her onto his knee. "Listen to me now, Summer," he said as if speaking to a distraught child. "Ruark had your son and his nurse in his carriage when he came for me at three o'clock this morning. You are in the way here, we are trying to prevent the total destruction of St. Paul's and the rest of my city. Be a good girl and get the hell out of here. For Christ's sake, be careful. If anything happens to you, how am I to face Helford?" he demanded.

Her face beamed up at him as her heart overflowed with joy. His big hand covered her hair to crush out the burning flakes of fire. "Go in that direction, through Doctor's Common and straight down to Paul's Wharfe. The water is the only place that's safe." The water stairs had scores of people clinging to them. The crowd's temper was turning nasty as they realized over half the boats had been hired to remove expensive furnishings rather than help the poorer families burdened by too many children. Summer found herself actually helping to tip a pair of virginals out of a boat so that a dozen terrified children could be taken across to Bankside. Eventually someone made room for her in a boat and she gladly went across the Thames to safety.

It had begun to get dark and the fire seemed an evil, insatiable monster. The flames smoldered and crackled, seeming to enjoy their wicked orgy of destruction.

As Summer watched London all ablaze from the opposite shore she could feel the presence of death's angel. She saw the fire grow, fresh blazes breaking out every minute. It was easier to see in the darkness. One corner after another caught fire, jumping across streets, arching across roofs, dropping down from blazing church steeples. It ran for well over a mile up the hill of the city. It devoured everything in its path—houses, churches, factories, prisons, alehouses, brothels. London was surely a city damned. It was still staggering from the devastation of the plague when the devil reached down to torch Sin City.

She sat on the grass all night watching the holocaust annihilate, ravage, and destroy the greatest city in the world. By morning even St. Paul's had caught fire and the King, the Duke of York, and the lord mayor of London decided to blow up whole rows of houses so the insatiable fire would have nothing to feed upon. Summer hugged her knees, wondering why she had been blessed. It was a miracle that Ruark had gone to Friday Street in time to save Ryan and Mrs. Bishop. She felt very guilty over her good fortune in the face of so much misery. The fact that she had lost her home and all her possessions never entered her head.

Eventually she got back to the palace, but it took her most of the day. Some of the stories she heard were hard to believe. Stories of suffering and heroism and impossibilities the mind could hardly grasp, like the lead roof of St. Paul's melting in the inferno, sending molten lead spewing down Watling Street.

Every stitch she wore went into the midden, then she bathed and washed the black soot from her singed hair. She was so tired she found it a great effort to lift her hands high enough to shampoo her head. The bed looked very inviting, but she knew she must get to Cockspur Street because that was the most likely place Ruark had taken Ryan. She cut through Pall Mall, which was the shortest distance to Auntie Lil's, and when the familiar condescending footman opened the door, she could have kissed him.

The minute Lady Richwood glided into the reception room in oyster-colored silk Summer asked anxiously, "Did Ruark bring Ryan here in the middle of the night?"

"Yes, darling, but wherever have you been? We've been out of our minds with worry!"

"Oh, Lil, it will take me a week to tell you of my ordeal by fire." Suddenly she broke down and sobbed. Lil saw that she needed the release of tears and quietly let her get it all out. Finally Summer sniffed and gulped. "I'm sorry, I suppose it's the relief of knowing my baby is here."

"Darling," said Lil with understandable reluctance, "I said

Ruark brought the baby and Mrs. Bishop in the middle of the night. I didn't say they were still here."

"Where are they?" asked Summer blankly.

"Darling, you look absolutely done in. Why don't I put you to bed and I'll tell you all about it in the morning."

Summer shuddered as a goose walked over her grave. She looked Lil straight in the eye and said, "I walked into Dante's Inferno today looking for my son and it seems I still haven't found him."

"Lord Helford came back at midday with a traveling coach and took the baby and his nurse away with him. He left a note for you." Lil bit her lip as she handed her the sealed letter. She dreaded Summer's reaction. Her relationship with her husband had always been volatile, to say the least, and by the looks of her niece the last thing she needed was another emotional upheaval.

Summer tore open the note with impatient fingers and read the words in disbelief.

I am removing my son from your care for reasons which are obvious. London is unfit and his permanent home will be Helford Hall. I have made my wishes on this clear to you in the past, so it should come as no surprise. I also rescued the Helford rubies, which you carelessly left behind in your haste to return to Court.

R.

She crumpled the note in a clenched fist and jumped to her feet so quickly the white Persian cat ran straight up the curtains. "Whoreson! Swine! May lightning blast the man from the face of the earth!" She sloshed wine from a decanter and drained it. Then she wailed, "I gave an oath not to drink or swear and the bloody man has me doing both!" She paced up and down the small salon as if it caged her. "Well, here's another oath—if my son's permanent home is to be Helford Hall, then so is mine. I'll stick closer than fog on London Bridge, aye, and he'll fasten the Helford rubies about my throat before I've done with him!"

If only Ruark Helford could have been there to hear her reaction to his note, he would have smiled with deep satisfaction, for it was exactly the reaction he had hoped to provoke.

"Darling, can we go to bed now? I was particularly partial to those curtains."

"Lil Richwood, you should be ashamed. Half of London have no windows tonight and you're worried about bloody curtains."

It took until Thursday to put out the great fire of London and even then some places still burned. The Clothmakers Hall had a cellar filled with oil and would have to burn itself out. The entire fleet had been ordered from the Pool of London into the Channel as soon as the fire started and now reports were everywhere that the Dutch and English fleets were in sight of one another.

Summer and Auntie Lil took the coach into the city to see if they could learn the whereabouts of Solomon Storm. His place of business had been in Cheapside and, alas, Cheapside now lay in black ruins. "Summer, I have a ghastly feeling that the gold we had on deposit has gone up in smoke." They sat in the coach, stunned.

It took Summer a few moments before the full impact hit her, then she said slowly, "I've lost my son, my jewels, my house, my gold . . . I've even lost all my beautiful clothes, save that damned feathered creation. How the hell will I get to Cornwall?"

Lil shook her head, too stunned by her own losses to consider Summer's plight. The first person Summer thought of was Black Jack Flash. Oh, how she needed him now! She closed her eyes and saw his lazy, amused smile, his unshaven beard, his flash of silver hair. If only it were possible to locate the *Phantom*.

Back at Cockspur Street Summer knelt down before her old trunk and lifted its heavy leather lid. The black garb which lay folded there seemed symbolic.

She remembered once before when she had been stripped of everything and had been reduced to relying on her wits. She took out the black breeches and doublet and was relieved when she could squeeze herself into them. She put on the boots, then brushed her hair up into a tight knot and lifted up the wide-brimmed black hat. Beneath it lay her pistol and mask. She shoved them inside her doublet and strode in front of the mirror. The male attire gave her a surge of confidence she hadn't felt in an age. She strutted about admiring herself, a devilish smile curving the corners of her lips.

With a long-legged, male swagger, she strolled to the palace stables. She didn't have the luxury of picking and choosing, she simply stole a horse which wasn't being attended. She went down to the London docks, offering to exchange gold if anyone could get a message to Black Jack Flash, who sailed the *Phantom*. She had no gold, of course, but it didn't matter since she was soon convinced Rory was not in London. She knew she preferred a port like

Southampton or Portsmouth if he'd illegally taken any ships. That's where she'd last seen him, and she made her decision quickly, firmly. She had nothing to lose. If she didn't find Rory, at least she would be halfway to Cornwall.

Lil Richwood did her utmost to dissuade Summer from such reckless behavior. She laid out her arguments one by one. It was too far to ride, she was a woman alone, she had no money, bad weather and gales threatened, but she finally realized the more Summer was told she couldn't do a thing, the firmer her resolve became.

The first night she only made it as far as Dorking. She selected a field with haystacks next to a stream. She watered her horse and let him crop the grass beside the water, then she curled up beneath one of the stacks and ate the bread and cheese she'd brought. She awoke before dawn to the crowing of a cock and realized she was freezing. She rubbed her arms and legs furiously and stamped about until her blood warmed a little. To hell with this, she thought. Tonight I need a bed and Dobbin here will need some oats or he'll be in danger of floundering.

She rode doggedly through a bitter wind blowing in from the Channel. At dusk she chose a carriage heading out of Portsmouth to eliminate the chance of coming face-to-face with her victim later on. She tied on her mask, pulled her hat low, and halted the startled carriage driver. Portsmouth was a rough seaport where you had to look over your shoulder every minute, but the driver had relaxed once he'd left the crime-ridden streets behind him. The occupant of the carriage was outraged. "Why didn't you shoot the fellow?" he demanded of his driver.

"Because he's got more brains than you," growled Summer, "and he doesn't want them spilled all over the road."

"I'll have you whipped for this!" he told his driver. "And as for you, I'll see you hanged, drawn, and quartered."

"Shut your cake hole and empty your pockets," she said, waving the pistol in his face. She relieved him of his money, but to her great consternation the minute she let the carriage go on its way, the driver must have received orders to turn about and head back into Portsmouth. Summer had little stomach for this highway robbery; she would try to make the coins last.

When she rode into the inn yard at the Three Cranes and dismounted, she'd been so long in the saddle she thought she'd never be able to make her knees touch again. She paid for oats and stabling the horse, paid for a bed and a bowl of hot stew, then walked out along the quay to see what ships lay at anchor. Wobbly on her legs from fatigue, she almost decided to turn back to the inn when a large ungainly vessel caught her eye. As she drew closer she saw it was unloading women in chains. "What in the name of God is going on?" she asked a seaman who was taking a keen interest in the unloading.

"Prisoners from London," he told her. "Jails all burned . . . women from Bridewell and Fleet Debtors' Prison to be housed here and Southampton."

She stared up at the women in fascinated horror as their chains clanked together. Suddenly she got the weirdest feeling, as if someone were staring at her. She glanced about quickly, then froze. Looking straight down into her eyes was Sergeant Oswald.

45

***

"Grab him!" he shouted to the men on the dock. Summer bolted immediately, but her legs betrayed her, turning to rubber as she tried to escape. Before she knew it, four burly seamen closed in on her to block her escape. She swept off her hat and shook her head. The black silken mass of hair tumbled to her shoulders and she begged them with her eyes. "Please, please, if any of you know Black Jack Flash of the *Phantom*, get a message to him. I'm his woman, I'm Cat."

The men were startled by her beauty and touched by her low urgent plea. They looked at each other, ready to let her go, but before she could get to her feet, Oswald had his beefy hands on her. "Well, well, well, if it isn't the notorious highwayman the Black Cat," he ridiculed.

"Let me go, Sergeant Oswald, or I shall report you to the King himself," she vowed.

He gave her arm a savage twist. "It's Sergeant-Major now, Lady Bitch." He quick-marched her to the end of the line of women who now stood on the dock and shackled her to the last one. A combination of hatred and pride kept her on her legs as Oswald and six militiamen under his command marched the women from the ship, through the port, and down to Portsmouth Prison. The forty women were made to stand in the prison yard until all the paperwork was sorted out. The fact that it had begun to rain and the cold wind slanted icy raindrops against their faces made little difference to the harassed jailer.

"I'm overcrowded now," argued Bludwart in the cluttered room he used for office cum living quarters. "The magistrate that looks after Hampshire and Dorset counties has been ailing for over a year. There's been no hangings here in all that time. The prisoners just sit and eat their bloody heads off!"

A well-dressed man stood beside a cluttered desk with a look of disgusted outrage on his face. "Bludwart, I'm trying to report a criminal act. How dare you make me wait? If you ordered militiamen out now, you'd apprehend the fellow! I don't know what the country's coming to!"

"You'll have to wait your turn, Mr. Blackthorn. I can't be expected to do everything. I'm short of militiamen, short of guards, short of victuals, and what do they do? Send me forty bleeding drabs to feed and house—I tell you I've not room for four, let let alone forty!"

Oswald's brain was working overtime to see how he could take advantage of this situation. His insides seethed with excitement at the prospect of having Helford's whore in his power. Of the forty women who stood outside in the downpour only one obsessed him, the rest didn't matter one iota. He rustled the official list of prisoners in his beefy hands and said low, "If I pull strings to get you out of this mess, Bludwart, I'll expect something in return."

The warden's eyes narrowed and he stepped closer to Oswald. The sergeant-major almost recoiled at the reek of the man. He smelled of filth and sweat and gin. His eyes were bulging and bloodshot, the veins continually breaking down from his love affair with the bottle. "Most of these female felons are pickpockets, thieves, prostitutes, and I can take them over to Southampton. Half a dozen are murderers and I've orders to jail them here in Portsmouth because its security is stronger. You give me a private room for interrogation any time I want it and I'll lumber you with only six of them. What do you say?"

"Done! Fetch 'em in," said Bludwart. "I'll get my records clerk."

Mr. Blackthorn stepped forward. "It's an outrage," he thundered. "Bringing in more murderers to live off the fat of the land. When will they be executed, I ask you?"

"Mr. Blackthorn, half my prisoners haven't even been tried and sentenced since the magistrate took to his bed. Everything has to go by the book. I can't hang 'em out of hand, you know. I'm here to uphold English justice, Mr. Blackthorn. Did ye never hear of the Magna Carta?"

Oswald walked out into the cold rain. The women set up a protest of catcalls. "You pisspot, get us inside. Whoreson . . . Bastard . . . Pricklouse."

Summer shuddered as he walked a direct path to her. She knew the names they threw at Oswald were inadequate. She knew he was evil. He just looked at her. He walked down the line a short distance and began to unshackle women. He had selected five before he came back to unlock her chains.

Summer looked at the other women and was surprised to see they had not been chosen for their attractions. One was a short fat woman, as broad as she was long, another looked no more than a little girl. One of the women was great with child and Summer's heart constricted for her. The fourth woman was old, she had scraggly gray hair and no teeth. The fifth woman was not ugly, she was rather comely in fact, but nothing could hide the fact that she was tough, like a hardened criminal. As Oswald returned for Summer he smiled. He couldn't help it, he was so damned pleased with himself.

As the six drenched women filed into Bludwart's office, Mr. Blackthorn's mouth fell open. "That's him . . . her! That's the highwayman that robbed me! Do something, damn you!"

"Mr. Blackthorn, we've arrested your dangerous criminal, what more do you want?"

"I'll tell you what I want, sirrah . . . I want him—her—it . . . I want it hanged!"

Oswald wanted no interference with his private brand of justice. He stepped up to the irate citizen and said, "These women are all murderers. Be assured every last one of the creatures will be hanged. This is maximum security. Everything must go by the letter of the law. All names strictly recorded in the journal. Not one will ever slip through the cracks. Please accept our deepest thanks for your positive identification."

Bludwart scratched his lice-ridden head. "The only empty cell I 'ave is in the cellar and on nights like this the floor is ankle-deep in water."

"Plenty good enough for these dregs of humanity, Bludwart. Lock 'em up. I'll need two wagons to take the rest over to Southampton, but I'll be back tomorrow for that nice private room you promised me."

Summer's eyes never left Oswald. He was out for revenge. He relished the very idea of it. He would take his pound of flesh, of that she had no doubt whatsoever.

The women were taken down stone steps inside the fortresslike building to what could only be described as a dungeon. All six were locked in a cell which measured roughly four by ten feet.

"Well, at least we have running water," quipped Sidney, the hard-faced one.

Summer had never seen anything like it. The stone walls dripped with water which formed a rivulet on the floor and emptied down a smelly drain. The cell was empty except for tallow candles in wall sconces, two heaps of moldy, damp straw, and a slop bucket in the corner. When the six women lay down, Summer knew their bodies would have to touch each other and she shuddered uncontrollably. She could smell their unwashed bodies, which surprised her, for the dungeon reeked heavily from rot, decay, moldering hay, and the open drain.

They were all drenched through to the skin and they took off their gray worsted smocks and tied them to the prison bars to dry. Underneath they wore black cotton stockings and knickers. Most of them pulled the knickers up to cover their breasts with the tops now sitting just underneath their armpits. The only one who couldn't do this was the fat woman called "Lardy," and her breasts hung down over her fat belly in an obscene overabundance of quivering flesh. Summer averted her eyes. She made no attempt to remove her shirt and breeches, though they were plastered to her body. If she got pneumonia, then so be it, she thought stubbornly.

"What's yer name?" demanded Sidney.

"Cat," Summer said shortly.

"You look like a bleedin' cat," Sidney said.

"I know," said Summer, turning the full impact of her green eyes upon her.

"We call the old hag Granny and the little one is Gert. The one 'avin the kid is Nellie."

Summer glanced at them one by one then murmured, "I'm pleased to meet you, ladies."

"La-de-dah, ye talk like we was in a bleedin' drawing room," said Sidney.

"That's 'cause she's a lady," said Lardy.

"Oh, really? And 'ow the bleedin' hell do ye know I'm not a lady?"

"Ye can't make a silk purse out of a sow's ear," said Lardy.

"You should know." Sidney laughed. "If you lay on that bleedin' straw, you'd just look like a sow ready to farrow."

"Well, if I had a face as hard as yours, I'd give kids pennies to throw shit at me!"

Sidney's eyes narrowed dangerously. She walked over to Cat and felt the silk material of her shirt. "I like that black shirt . . . how'd ye like to make me a present of it?" It was not a request, it was an order.

"In a pig's arse," said Cat, giving Sidney an aggressive shove against the wall. "The only present I'll give you is a black eye; maybe two."

Sidney grinned. "He was right when he called you Lady Bitch, wasn't he?"

Cat smiled back, ready to call a truce. "I'm afraid he's not finished with me yet. Look, we're all in this together, so let's not make it unbearable for each other. I think Nellie should sit down."

Lardy helped Nellie to the straw and sat beside her. Both women began to crack things between their thumbnails and Summer realized with horror they were fleas which had immediately jumped on them from the straw. Nellie's face was ashen, her eyes were circled by black rings. She was skeleton thin except for her great belly and her swollen ankles. "It's an outrage for a pregnant woman to be imprisoned. What will happen when she goes into labor?" asked Cat.

They shrugged. The old woman said, "She'll 'ave another unwanted kid, won't she? An' why am I in 'ere? I botched an abortion as kilt the slut, but she's better off dead, don't ye think?"

Cat was almost ready to agree with her. "I don't think Charles has the vaguest notion how abominably women are treated in these places."

"Charles who?" asked Sidney.

"The King," explained Cat. "When I get out of here, I'll go to him immediately. I won't rest until something is done about it."

"When you get out of here you'll be on the end of a hempen rope," said Sidney.

"Do you know the King?" asked Gert, wide-eyed.

"Yes, I was at Whitehall two days ago." Granny and Lardy began to laugh.

"La-de-dah," mocked Sidney. "What did you do for your bleedin' hobby, m'lady, stitch embroidery?"

Cat looked off into the distance, remembering some of the unbelievable things that had happened to her. Then she smiled sadly at the women and said, "Actually I collected rubies."

Gert's mouth gaped open and Granny made a gesture to indicate that Cat had lost her wits.

"Do you think they'll feed us?" asked Lardy wistfully.

"Not tonight," said Sidney. "In London at least we were entitled to a penny loaf and pump water. Here, God only knows."

Cat had bought stew at the inn so she wasn't hungry, but how would she be able to face this misery when hunger was added to the other deprivations? One by one the women sat, crouched on the dank floor, their backs against the slimed walls. Cat was glad she was bone tired, for sleep would be a blessed relief from this living nightmare. She crossed her arms above her knees and laid her head down. The women quieted, the tallow candles guttered out, and she was about to drift off to a gentler place when she realized the cell had visitors. Rats! They climbed up the drain hole by the dozen. She screamed and they stood up on their hind legs in cheeky curiosity.

"Put the piss bucket over the hole and go to sleep," grumbled Sidney.

Cat did the first thing Sidney advised, but she found it impossible to do the last. In the morning, when Cat tried to stand, every bone in her body ached. They were served wooden spoons and bowls containing thin gruel. When Granny found a cockroach in hers and ate it with relish, Cat could not bring herself to eat in spite of the fact that her common sense told her she would need food if she was to survive this ordeal. Cat gave her bowl to Nellie and Lardy looked deeply offended. "She's eating for two," Cat said lamely.

Sidney looked at her with contempt. "You'll never survive if you put others before yourself. They didn't teach you much at Whitehall."

Cat gave her a sad half smile. "Believe me, the rules there are precisely the same as here." Cat could bear the hunger, what she could not bear was being unclean. "Won't they let us wash?" she asked.

"A few layers of dirt'll keep you warm." Lardy laughed.

"A few layers of fat, ye mean," said Sidney.

Cat realized sadly that the women's gibes, oaths, and shameless talk offered them the only means of defense against a savage, pitiless world that cared nothing whether they lived or died. Cat gathered up the empty bowls and spoons and shoved them through the small hole in the wall through which they'd been served. She kept one of the wooden spoons, and when the other women were busy putting on their damp gray smocks, she showed Sidney. "If we could wedge this against the stones in that small opening they push the food through, it might split in half."

Sidney eyed her with approval. "It might make us a couple of pig stickers at that, but don't expect help from me if you have any half-assed ideas of escaping."

Cat alternated sitting and standing all day long. Her mind escaped to her beautiful Cornwall where her baby was. Her thoughts were pleasant as she pictured how he must be growing. Her mind's eye saw Mrs. Bishop bathing him and feeding him and she laughed out loud when she thought of Mrs. Bishop's will coming up against Mr. Burke's. She rode Ebony along the sands and pictured Ruark riding down to meet her, because he could not bear to have her out of his sight too long. She sighed and dozed a little. It was easier for her to sleep in the daylight.

Supper was watered-down cabbage soup and this time Cat forced herself to swallow the vile stuff. She knew as soon as it began to grow dark that Oswald would come for her.

He threw open the cell door and looked at the women one by one. Cat stepped toward him and said, "Nellie is near her labor time . . . she shouldn't be here like this."

"She shouldn't have got knocked up, should she? Don't waste your pity on her, Lady Bitch, save it for yourself. Come with me."

Sidney threw him a threatening glance, and he challenged, "Do you have something to say, maggot face?"

She curled her lip and said, "Suck my duck till it quacks!"

He smashed her across the bridge of her nose and they all heard the bone crack. Though she fell to her knees, she didn't let out so much as a whimper. He took Cat's arm viciously and shoved her out the cell door. He took her up two flights of steps and through a part of the prison which housed men. She never even heard the whistles and bawdy compliments thrown her way, for Oswald filled her head. He opened a door to a room with a fire where Bludwart had just brought a trayful of hot food. "Will ye need any help with 'er?" Bludwart leered.

"None at all, thank you. Women only need be treated like horses."

"Ye mean ye ride em?" he said, licking his lips.

"No, Bludwart, I mean no such thing. You break them. You let them know who's master, then they will obey any command at the slightest touch of the whip."

Fear ate at her belly as she heard his words and the threat in the tone of voice. Cat probably had as much spirit as any woman alive. Oh, how she had enjoyed defying Ruark. Even with that flaring, uncontrolled temper of his, she had goaded him to madness and she had dared do that she realized suddenly because he loved her. It was a game; the game of love. Without love a woman had no rights. She tried to keep her lips from trembling as Bludwart closed the door and left her alone with her enemy.

"There's no need to fear me, if you obey me. I follow the letter of the law. I can do nothing to you except what is laid down in prison regulations." Her eyes were liquid with apprehension.

"Take off your clothes," he ordered. She closed her eyes, wondering how she would get through such an ordeal. She opened them quickly as he took hold of her breast.

"I have found nothing gets obedience so quickly as a good tit twist," he said, viciously twisting her soft, pliant breast.

She gasped and moaned softly as he let go of her.

"From now on when I give you an order you say 'Yes, Sergeant-Major,' do you understand?" he repeated.

"Yes, Sergeant-Major." She seethed inwardly, awaiting an opportunity to defy him.

"Very good. It's in the prison regulations that I may conduct a strip search. Take off your clothes."

"Go to hell!"

Both hands reached for her breasts this time and she whispered, "Yes, Sergeant-Major." She removed her boots, then slowly took off her black shirt and pants. Her left breast was marred by blue finger bruises. Her lids lowered over hate-filled eyes as she watched his face. He was power mad.

He smiled. "I'm going to enjoy our visits. I'm stationed at Southampton, so I'll be able to come every week. Next week you'll know the routine. If you forget, I'll have to touch you up with the whip. Now you may serve me my dinner while you are still naked and then you may get dressed."

She wanted to spit on him and spit on his food. She had grown used to standing up to men and fighting back. But real fear of this man made her cautious. She must think before she acted . . . must swallow her insults before she uttered them, at least until she was no longer naked.

She felt such a sweeping sense of relief when she had her clothes back on it almost made her giddy. Her chin went up in defiance. "Are you finished with me, Sergeant-Major?" She made his rank sound pitiful.

"Not quite." Then his words sent a chill up her back and into her very brain. "This highway robbery isn't your first offense. A thief always gets burned on the thumb, branded, so that if you return a second time, it's automatically a hanging matter. Show me your thumb," he ordered. When she hesitated, he grabbed her hand.

"Just as I feared. We have neglected you shamefully, Lady Bitch." He got up, selected a long metal rod from a holder, and inserted it into the fire.

"No!" she cried.

He had no mercy for her whatsoever. He grabbed her by the hair on her head and forced her down before the fire. He straddled her and let her bear his full weight. Then he pressed the glowing iron brand into the soft flesh of her thumb. Cat screamed and fainted. He picked her up and carried her back down to the cellar. He opened the cell door and threw her in a heap among the other women.

They saw and smelled her burned flesh, then each woman dropped her eyes to her thumb to examine her own brand. Mercifully Cat stayed unconscious for almost two hours, but by morning she was crying and fevered.

46

≈≈⟶⟶ ≈⟶⟶

Lord Ruark Helford was a happy man. He had just watched Mrs. Bishop give Ryan his morning bath, then he had enjoyed a substantial breakfast served by Mr. Burke. He was filled with anticipation. It excited him, excited his blood. Soon, he told himself, soon. After breakfast he climbed up on Helford Hall's widow's walk among the chimneys and sailboat weathervanes. As he looked out to sea a crease formed between his brows. Why hadn't she arrived yet? What was the delay? He couldn't wait for his beauteous wife to come sweeping in like a tropical storm demanding their son. This time he would keep her. What an idiotic fool he'd been to ever let her get further away than kissing distance. A smile curved his mouth. He should lock her in their bedchamber and keep her abed for a month. His manhood stirred and began to fill and he called into the sea wind like a lovesick youth, "Summer . . . hurry!"

As the day wore on the warm expectant feeling grew into one of anxiety. What the hell would he do if she didn't arrive by tomorrow? He was neglecting his duty shamefully, a thing that rankled a man as hidebound as Helford. He'd promised to fight the Dutch in this last all-out offensive, and though his ships were privately owned and not part of the navy, he was committed to Charles, his monarch and his friend.

Two days back when he arrived home, he had found the *Golden
Goddess* sitting at anchor, newly arrived back from Madagascar.
When its valuable cargo had been unloaded, he'd sent it straight off
into the Channel to look for Dutchmen, promising to sail the *Pagan
Goddess* in its wake. Summer wouldn't recognize Spencer. He
had filled out and was bronzed by the fierce sun. Ruark had shown
him his nephew Ryan and told him Summer was on her way from
London. He omitted to tell him that he had stolen his son. A pang
of guilt touched his conscience. Perhaps he shouldn't have sent
him off to war. Perhaps he should have insisted Spencer stay in
Cornwall until Summer had had a chance to see that he had grown
into a man, but upon reflection he knew he would have had to lock
him up to keep him from sailing with the *Golden Goddess*.

That night Ruark Helford's bed was cold and lonely. Doubt
assailed him on all sides. It was a thing with which he'd rarely
grappled. Why was she dallying in London? If she was playing
house with George Digby, he'd throttle her. He knew Digby meant
nothing to her, but he wasn't sure about the title of countess. Most
women would sell their souls to become an earl's wife. No, he
knew her better than that. She was Ruark Helford's woman and
she knew it. They only had to be in the same room for the sparks to
fly and ignite into a firestorm. He wouldn't put it past her, however, to let him cool his heels here in Cornwall while he ate his
heart out wondering how many kisses she'd allowed the King to
steal. No, dammit, she may be heartless enough to keep herself
from her husband, but not from her baby; he was her whole life.

Sleep eluded him until just before dawn. He fell into the arms of
Morpheus, wishing fervently he'd reacted differently to her cry for
help that morning when they were fresh back from their honeymoon at Stowe. The bed curtains still cloaked them in intimate
darkness. Summer sat up to push them back and let in the early-
morning sun. Ruark reached up to pull her back to their warm
cocoon and she lay in the curve of his arm, knowing he could never
love her more than he did at this moment. The waterfall diamond
necklace was in a cabinet beside the bed and he wanted to give it to
her now. He dipped his head to steal a kiss, but she stopped him.
"First, I have something to tell you, darling." She hesitated, her
heart beating rapidly now that the moment was here. "I have some
secrets that I have to confess to you," she said softly.

His look bathed her with love and tolerant amusement for her
great confession.

She knelt before him with bent head and lowered lashes. "My brother Spencer was arrested on suspicion of smuggling with some other men . . ."

His voice like a whiplash cut off her words. "When?" he demanded.

"He . . . I . . . the night before we were married," she answered truthfully. "He's in Falmouth prison and I told him . . . I hoped . . . you would be able to release him." No one could have guessed at the panic that was rising within her. Ruark flung from the bed and reached for his breeches. The silence in the room was terrible. She felt under so much stress that the only thing she wanted to do was confess all and receive her absolution. "Ruark, we had to dabble in smuggling, we were starving! My father gambled away everything we had. He sold the horses, the paintings, the furnishings. Roseland hasn't had servants in years, the stables are falling down, the grounds are overgrown, and the house is in total disrepair. When I met you in London, I'd just learned that it was mortgaged for eighteen thousand pounds. That debt has now grown to twenty thousand and it's due next week or the London moneylender Solomon Storm will sell it." She took a great trembling breath.

He came back to the bed and enfolded her in his arms. "My little love, why didn't you tell me all this before? Didn't you think I'd help you when you were in trouble? Darling, how long have you carried this burden? Hush, it doesn't matter, love," he said, kissing her eyelids. "If Roseland is precious to you, we'll restore it to its original condition. Will that make you happy? God's flesh, sweetheart, I can't bear to think of you going hungry." His arms tightened about her protectively.

"What about Spencer?" she whispered.

He cupped her face with his strong hands and looked down at her delicate beauty with reverence. "I'll have him out before lunchtime," he promised.

Tears of gratitude welled in her eyes and he quickly kissed them away. "Precious love, don't weep. I never want you to weep again. See here, see what I have for you." He reached into the little cabinet and drew out the waterfall of diamonds. They only made her cry harder.

"Oh, Ru, you are so good to me." She smiled through her tears. "I don't want you to give me diamonds."

"What do you want, beloved?" he murmured.

Her arms slipped up about his neck. "I want you to fill me with your babe."

Ruark jerked awake, saw the empty place in the bed, then reality washed over him. What a cruel bastard he'd been to take her baby away from her. He threw back the covers. To hell with the Dutch, he was returning to London for his wife.

It took a whole week before the unbearable pain of the burn began to dull. Summer suffered alternate chills and fever, gave most of her gruel to Nellie, and managed to steal one more wooden spoon. Ironically, the first day she began to feel better physically, she was almost distraught, for she knew Oswald's promised return visit was upon her. When he entered the cell, the other five women shrank back from him, each fearing he might choose her, but when he took Summer again, even the hardened Sidney wished she could have done something to help the girl.

"You know the routine. Take off your clothes."

Summer had done everything he'd demanded of her last time, answering each command with a submissive "Yes, Sergeant-Major," and still he had tortured her with the hot iron. Perhaps the outcome would be no worse if she defied him. When she didn't obey him immediately, however, he took hold of her breast and twisted it viciously. She cried out with pain and cursed herself for being weak. Slowly she removed her soiled clothes, almost glad to be out of them. When he ordered her to serve his dinner, the delicious smell of the food made her mouth water, then her empty stomach cramped painfully. She gathered her courage. "May I bathe, Sergeant-Major?"

"No, you may not," he said pleasantly.

"How can you bear to have me serve your food when I'm so soiled?" she cried angrily.

"I am amazed that the first thing you beg of me is a bath. That tells me that cleanliness is more important to you than food." He smiled. "The filthier you become, the happier I'll be. When you are so begrimed with dirt that no soap will ever get you clean again, I shall be content, Lady Bitch. You may put your grimy rags back on now."

This time she did not relax once she was dressed. She remembered too vividly what happened last week and expected him to have some cruelty planned again.

He finished his ale and surveyed her through narrowed eyes. "I bet you thought you'd be able to bribe me with sexual favors. You don't know me very well yet . . . but you'll learn. I'll bet your hair drives Helford mad with lust. Does he spread it across the pillows before he makes love to you? Too bad," he said with mock regret, "regulations say I may cut your hair to stop lice." He reached for a bone-handled razor and licked his lips with excitement as he chopped it so short it barely covered her ears. She knew if she struggled or defied him, he might shave her bald.

When Summer was shoved back into the cell, she saw sadly that the other women had suffered the same fate. Sidney said, "Bloody pervert!"

"Never mind," Lardy said, "it'll grow again. We were crawling with lice anyway."

Summer took heart at their comments. It showed they were beginning to care what happened to one another. She had no time to mourn her lost beauty because around midnight Nellie went into labor.

The moment the *Pagan Goddess* dropped anchor in the London Pool, Ruark Helford went directly to Lil Richwood's house in Cockspur Street. He held up his hand in hopes she wouldn't launch into a long list of his shortcomings. "Lil, before you say anything, I know it was wrong to take Ryan like I did. I want you to know I'm finished with all these damned silly games. I want to ask her . . . beg her . . . to come back to me."

"That's wonderful, darling," drawled Auntie Lil. "Summer lost absolutely everything, you know—her house, her gold, all her clothes."

Ruark was beginning to understand why she hadn't rushed to Cornwall. "Then you think she'll agree to come to Helford Hall?" he asked hopefully.

"Darling, she went. She was absolutely incensed with you for taking her son."

"How could she travel without money?" he asked, a feeling of alarm growing steadily inside his chest.

Lil Richwood shrugged her elegant shoulders. "You know Summer, darling. I tried to tell her she couldn't go off alone, but that was like waving a red flag at a bull!"

"I know how headstrong she is, Lil," he supplied, both hope and dread warring inside him. "Tell me her plans."

"She 'borrowed' a horse from the palace stables and was riding to Portsmouth to take ship for Cornwall," said Lil.

"I knew she would come after Ryan, that's why I took him, but where under heaven and hell is she?" he demanded. He felt Lil was keeping something back from him. Suddenly all the churchbells began to ring. The servants ran into the street to see what was amiss. Everyone knew it was an alarm signal of some sort. Since the disaster of the London fire everyone was alert to unexpected calamity befalling.

A footman came back into the house, ashen-faced. "What is it, man?" demanded Ruark.

"They say we are attacked! The Dutch have landed!" he cried.

Ruark clapped on his wide-brimmed hat. "I'll go across to Whitehall and find out what this is all about," he said grimly. He went directly up to the King's closet and found Charles in his shirt sleeves with his brother James, Chancellor Hyde, and some men from the Navy Office.

"Helford! What news?" asked Charles.

It was one of the few times in his life he was at a loss for words and he felt his neck. "None, Sire. I had no indication aught was amiss last night when I anchored in the Thames. Rumors are everywhere that we are attacked," he said with a question in his voice.

"The reports I received said that all last week we ravaged the coast of Holland with over a hundred ships. The Dutch lost six thousand men. Can you verify these reports?"

"I can verify them, Sire," said Sandwich, who had joint command of the English fleet. "Unfortunately they sank the *Hector* and the *Mary* suffered damage and only managed to limp home, but I swear we only lost two hundred men to their six thousand."

The Duke of York, who held joint command with Sandwich, but never bothered going to sea, was covered with shame at the moment. His face was very flushed as he cut into the conversation. "What of the rumors we are attacked?"

"Du Ruyter and a handful of his most reckless captains have followed us home and are trying to blockade us in the Thames and the River Medway, where our larger vessels are anchored."

"A handful?" shouted James. "Why haven't you sailed out of the estuary and blasted them out of the water?"

"Because rumor has it the French are standing off the coast of Dover," said Sandwich simply.

James's face went ashen. Charles saw his brother's agitation and knew he would be useless to Sandwich in spite of his high command. The King exchanged glances with Helford. "You're thinking what I'm thinking. We need Rupert."

"I saw his ship *Henrietta* at Portsmouth yesterday. I want my old command back under Prince Rupert," said Ruark without hesitation, caring little if he offended Sandwich.

Charles looked at his elderly chancellor. "Get them to stop ringing those infernal bells, man. We should be listening for gunfire."

Edward Progers, His Majesty's page of the backstairs, came into the King's closet. "Sire, there are so many courtiers gathering I thought it best not to let any more up here, but now that Buckingham and Lauderdale are below, I can't control them. It seems everyone wishes to volunteer his services."

"I'll be down directly. Ask the two of them to control everyone until I get there. They will relish the authority," Charles said shrewdly.

Sandwich said, "We'll stretch a boom across the River Medway to stop their ships."

"If I know de Ruyter, a boom won't stop him," said Helford. "We'll have to sink some ships to block them coming upriver."

"We need our ships," said Sandwich, glaring at Helford.

James said, "Upnor Castle has a fortress. It will defend the Medway."

Charles said ruefully, "Upnor has been totally reglected since the Civil War. We should have built flanking batteries to raise its firepower. I don't have much faith in a small fort rendering the tidal Medway impassable to a seaborne enemy."

"Albermarle's fleet at Chatham will be the most vulnerable," said Sandwich, shaking his head, "if it's not already destroyed."

"Send all volunteers to Chatham under Albermarle, until Rupert can get here," suggested Helford.

"I'll go," offered the Duke of York helpfully.

"James, you'd be more use here as liaison," Charles said smoothly so as not to ruffle his feathers. "Draw up a list of ships and who commands them. I think Albermarle has *Sovereign of the Seas* and William Penn commands the *Royal Charles*." The King headed for his bedchamber. "Excuse me, gentlemen. Helford, attend me while I shave and make myself more presentable."

Ruark followed him through the inner door of the privy closet which led to the King's bedchamber. He grinned widely at the disarray of the King's enormous curtained bed. Sheets and pillows were strewn everywhere and two of his spaniels were having a tug-of-war with Barbara's satin slipper, which she'd lost in her hurry to depart when the churchbells had sounded the alarm.

"I need the services of the *Phantom,*" said Charles quietly. "You don't think it's trapped in the Medway, do you?"

"My brother has many shortcomings, but stupidity isn't one of them," said Ruark.

"Rory still uses the Isle of Sheppey?" asked Charles.

"Your spies keep you well informed, Sire," said Ruark noncommittally.

"Oh, obviously." Charles laughed, jerking his head toward the rumpled bed. "The Dutch attack and catch me with my pants down." Charles sat down at a writing desk and dipped a quill in the inkwell. "I don't believe the French are standing off Dover. I think they are enemies of Holland, not allies. I want Rory to confirm for me this is a last-ditch effort by de Ruyter. I believe their entire fleet is decimated and this farce is being staged to wring better terms from us in the inevitable peace negotiations."

Ruark Helford knew the King was more shrewd than all his ministers rolled over.

"Ru, I'm entrusting Rory with two secret letters. One for Holland, the other for France. I must caution you this mission is different from the others." Charles sighed. "Old Hyde will have to step down. He's outlived his usefulness. I'm going to replace him with a cabal of four or five so that full power never rests with one man again."

"Secretary of State Arlington?" asked Ruark. "Buckingham and Lauderdale?"

Charles nodded. "I don't want any of them, not even my brother James, to know about these secret treaties with Holland and France. Not until they're faits accomplis. They will give England the balance of power in Europe."

"Accomplished by the grossest political chicanery," said Ruark Helford grimly.

"God's flesh, why can't you be more like your brother Rory?" groaned Charles.

The two dark-visaged men glared at one another for a full minute, before their challenge to each other dissolved into laughter. Each knew they'd gone through too much together to walk separate paths at this late stage of the game.

47

Nellie's screams were enough to awaken the dead. When Bludwart came to investigate the hullabaloo, Cat said, "She's giving birth. We can deliver her, but not without hot water and some clean sheets and blankets." Bludwart knew the cell wasn't even a fit place for the rats that came up the drain at night. He should never have put the women there, but Oswald had insisted. Someday someone with higher authority might come and inspect and he wanted no trouble. Everyone must be accounted for; he didn't want the woman dying when she'd been there less than a month.

Cat knew young Gert would be useless and she didn't fancy Granny the abortionist having a hand in the matter. She looked at Sidney's face set in its hard lines and knew she wasn't about to help anyone. It would have to be Lardy. When they got the bucket of hot water, they used it to wash Nellie from head to foot. Bludwart had supplied one sheet and one blanket, and they knew it was a miracle they'd gotten anything at all.

They wrapped Nellie in the sheet and tried to make her as comfortable as was possible under the circumstances. Her cries grew fainter with the long labor, and by the time the small, bluish baby was delivered she seemed to have sunk into an exhausted stupor. Nellie had bled a lot and as a result the sheet was now saturated.

Cat washed the blood from the tiny baby girl, then dropped the fouled sheet into what now looked like a bucket of blood. They wrapped Nellie and the baby in the sole blanket and Cat stayed awake to keep the rats away.

When the gruel arrived in the morning, Lardy said, "I can live off my fat."

Cat smiled at her. "She's got to get her strength back or her milk might not come in." They spooned the gruel into Nellie's mouth, but she seemed completely apathetic and somehow detached. She didn't speak, or look at her child, but at least she clasped the baby to her thin breast and they could hear it making tiny sucking sounds.

Cat kept another wooden spoon. Now she had three. Bludwart said nothing, but they got no more spoons. Cat knew she was much thinner than she had been a month past. She also felt so damned weak and weary she often wished she could sit against the wall and go to sleep forever. The smell of the place became a part of her. She soon adapted so that she could tolerate the abrasive company of the other women, and eventually when her stomach didn't get enough food, it shrank and diminished her appetite. She experienced a dull gnawing in her gut which never went away but she trained herself to ignore it. She even began to get used to the dirt. If you resisted and railed against a thing night and day, you used up every last ounce of strength. The way to get through this ordeal, she told herself, if indeed there was a way to get through it, was acceptance. Quiet acceptance.

She used the power of her mind to free her from her cage. Each day and every night she spent long, pleasant hours in flights of fancy, far removed from the slimed wall of the dungeon she was propped against. She spent hours remembering her baby—the soft feel of the black down upon his head, the tiny black eyelashes forming crescents on his cheeks when he slept, the rosebud mouth which could smile or pucker or open in a rage to make a racket loud enough to raise the rent. And she remembered the sweet, clean smell of him and the way his dark green eyes followed her about the room, never leaving her.

Sometimes she would sail the *Phantom* to warm climes while the swarthy, grinning crew played merry tunes on their tin whistles and concertinas. Rory must have gathered his men from all over the world, for they looked Spanish, Turkish, Moorish, Sicilian. Corsairs signed on at the waterfronts of Marseilles or Genoa. Black

Jack Flash—she could feel his hands covering hers while she stood at the ship's wheel, feel his warm breath on her cheek and his rough beard brush against her throat. Whenever he had stood behind her, she had felt him quicken against her buttocks, then, oh how she'd enjoyed being carried down to the red, silk-draped bed. She could still feel his beard brush against her breast, her belly, her thighs. There had been no resisting Rory Helford and now she was glad she hadn't resisted him. She realized that a woman never regrets the things she's done in life; only the things she's never done.

She would never be wholly imprisoned so long as she could picture him standing at the wheel on his slanting deck, his face wet with spray, his flash of hair wildly blowing in a gale as he trimmed his sails. A storm at sea exhilharated him as much as it did her, so she pictured him in that reckless way he had with his amused eyes laughing at something, everything.

One of her favorite escapes was on Ebony's back. Their beach ever beckoned. The warm scented breeze, the azure sea, the coves where playful otters balanced crustaceans on their tummies. She could feel the soft velvet of Ebony's nose, see his black, shiny flanks quiver to discourage an inquisitive wasp or dragonfly. If she ever had the chance again to greet the dawn astride her beloved animal, she would do so naked, in true pagan fashion. To be free—to be unfettered again would perhaps only come with death. She no longer feared death. Death was easy. It was life she feared. Living was hell. Except for the dreams, the daydreams.

The single most pleasurable thing she remembered in her entire life was Lord Ruark Helford. How he had loved to gather her into his lap so they could share a single chair. She could still feel the hardness of his mouth on hers, hear his words against her hair: "I love you, Summer, I love you with all my heart. I have never loved another woman." When their mating was finished and his dark head rested against her breast and when he lifted his head to worship her with his eyes, she knew he was neither hard nor cruel. No one knows a man like a woman who shares his bed. The rare moments when she had caught the unfamiliar look of tenderness on his face, just for her, was enough to take her breath away. She remembered again and again how, in the dead of night, he lay deep within her, then spent the violence of his passion, unleashed and savage and never-to-be-forgotten. The single most precious memory was that rapt moment of silence when they looked into each other's eyes, their smiles faded away, and the aching fire sprang to life between them.

She didn't really give a tinker's damn what happened to her, for she had had it all. She'd felt his love words whispered against her throat, felt his dark head between her hands as she'd held it close to her breast. She'd known the exhilaration of bantering words and arguing with him—aye, and sometimes besting him. So long as he walked proud and free, his dark head held high with unhumbled arrogance and she knew that he lived and laughed, it didn't matter about herself, for she was part of him and would be throughout eternity.

Something woke Cat before morning had quite arrived. She was filled with an inexplicable dread, then she remembered this was the day of Oswald's weekly visit. Her numbed mind became fully alert and she heard the squeaking and obscene rustling of the rats in Nellie's corner. She sprang up and reached for the guttering stub of tallow candle from its iron bracket. She rushed to the corner, thrusting the meager flame at the long, sleek creatures, and fell back in horror. The baby's body was covered by rat bites. She lifted the tiny blue body from its sleeping mother and saw that it had been dead for hours. Summer stood stunned and silent, biting her lips until the scream choking her throat subsided and did not escape. If she began to cry now, she would break, and she knew she must not break until after she'd seen Oswald.

When Nellie awoke, she seemed in a stupor. She simply set the little blue body aside as if it didn't exist. Lardy was concerned about Nellie. She could see clearly the Grim Reaper hadn't finished his business with them quite yet. Sidney's face was set hard. "Death's kingdom is the night. When the owl hunts, death reigns. The smell of death hovers like a charnel house." Summer's stomach heaved, but she had nothing in it to evacuate. After a few painful spasms the dry heaves ceased and she turned her face to the wall, trying not to think of Sergeant-Major Oswald.

By evening, when Bludwart came to remove the dead baby, Nellie had followed the child into the next world. Summer averted her eyes from the unpalatable sight of Bludwart dragging out her body. He showed great alarm and concern, but only for his own neck, of course. Sidney was in sole possession of Nellie's blanket before her heels were dragged clear of the threshold.

Something inside Summer snapped. She went to the corner

where she had hidden the three wooden spoons beneath the straw. She wedged each one between the iron candle bracket and the stone wall until it splintered in half lengthwise. Only one did not splinter the way she wanted it to, but before she was done she had five jagged wooden stakes which, wielded in the proper hands, could become five ugly lethal weapons. The other women pretended indifference, yet she knew each was aware of exactly what she did, and why. Cat had only enough time to cover the stakes with moldy straw before Oswald unlocked their cell door.

She did not look at him, instead she looked Gert in the eye, then Lardy. She turned her eyes upon Granny and then finally she looked long and deep at Sidney. She communicated without words. The message was crystal clear in its simplicity. They would all die, one by one, unless they helped each other.

When they were safely behind the locked door, Oswald surveyed with satisfaction the wraith she had become. Where she had been attractively slim, she was now a thin specter. Her short, dirty hair stuck out at odd angles and her beautiful face, once exquisite, was now haggard. Her cheekbones stood out and beneath them were sallow hollows. She almost had the look of a village idiot.

"Remove your clothes," he ordered smoothly.

Cat didn't move. She'd never take orders from him again. He'd have to kill her.

He came toward her and pulled open her shirt to survey her breasts. They had shrunk in size and were marred by dying bruises, yellow and green and purple. "You look and smell like a street whore from the slums. Did you know it is within regulations for me to brand you with the letter *H* for harlot?"

When he uttered the word "brand" a raw burning pain streaked from her thumb straight to her heart. He rummaged through the cast-iron rods for the iron, growing angry because he could not find the one he wanted. "Tomorrow night I will fetch the brand which imprints the scarlet letter. I think I will put it upon your breasts. Yes, an *H* upon each. Two *H*'s. They will brand you forever as Helford's Harlot!"

He shoved her through the door and she hurriedly buttoned her shirt before they passed by the male prisoners, though in truth they no longer cast her a glance. She knew her time was running out. If only the others would help her. He unlocked the cell door and pushed her through, then he noticed that the woman who had been swollen with child was missing. He took an aggressive step through the doorway and demanded, "Where's the pregnant bitch?"

Young Gert showed courage for the first time. "She's dead . . . you killed her!"

His fist smashed her mouth so viciously he knocked her front teeth out and marred her young face forever. Then he heard the cell door crash behind him and at the same moment the old hag launched herself at him like a screaming banshee. Summer knew the old woman was no match for the burly Oswald. His big arm flung her off against the wall with a sickening thud, but when he looked down at his chest he was surprised to see a stream of blood coming from a small hole made by what looked like a pig sticker. He was off balance and fell to one knee. Lardy knocked him over and sat on him, jabbing him viciously in the throat with her stake.

Sidney handed Cat a weapon and she looked in horror at what he had done to Granny. Then she realized she had no choice whatsoever. If they didn't kill him, they would all die. In unison, Sidney and Cat fell upon him and stabbed his face, his eyes, his throat. His screams of agony were terrible, then, when Gert stabbed him over and over between the legs, his screams rose in a crescendo of agony. Cat was beginning to despair. She knew he could not have sustained a mortal wound if he was making such an outcry. In desperation she felt for the vital artery in his neck. Then with her last ounce of strength and courage she plunged in the splintered stake to rip and sever everything it touched. Sergeant-Major Oswald made an unearthly, gurgling bubbling sound and began to twitch uncontrollably. The four women did not get off him until he lay absolutely still. Beside his body lay that of Granny in a grotesque heap. They had killed him, but not before he had taken another of their pack.

King Charles was furious and humiliated. Dutch war ships had actually broken through the boom strung across the Medway and bold landing parties had silenced the guns of Upnor Castle. Upnor, which was thought to be formidable enough to guard the dog leg on the Medway leading from the lower estuary to where the English fleet lay at anchor in Chatham.

Charles loved ships and the sea and had a good technical knowledge. His navy had always been his pride. In just a few short years, years in which Parliament's purse strings had been mostly closed, he had built a stronger and bigger navy. It was his plan and the hope of his reign that England should sail supreme, unchallenged mistress of all the waters on earth.

The King's cousin, Prince Rupert, had the best military mind of the age, and England's finest soldiers and sailors had always clamored to serve under him. He preferred privateers to regular navy, so Ruark Helford's *Pagan Goddess* joined Rupert's *Henrietta* to fight off an attack on Sheerness.

The Dutch seized the *Royal Charles,* captained by William Penn, then sailed up the Medway and set fire to half a dozen man-of-wars. Rupert and Helford concocted a brilliant plan. Under cover of dark they boarded the burning ships, maneuvered them behind the Dutch vessels, and scuttled them so they sank. They made an effective barrier, neatly trapping the Dutch in the tidal waterway. It was rapidly becoming an impasse. The two navies were deadlocked and peace negotiations began in earnest.

The King signed a peace treaty with Holland which gave England all of the Guinea coast of Africa. The Dutch forts along that coast were surrendered to the English, who would now be able to bring out gold without being harassed. The Dutch also agreed to turn over the greatest port in the Americas to England; thus New Amsterdam was renamed New York after the King's brother.

England yielded the Spice Islands to the Dutch and agreed to confine her eastern trade to India. Rory Helford negotiated two highly secret and private agreements between Charles and Holland, and Charles and France.

On the surface England and Holland drew closer together to form a common resistance to France. Charles, however, had always been friendly to France and accepted money from King Louis in return for a promise to desert Holland and allow English soldiers to join with the French army if war between France and Holland broke out.

He also made a secret treaty with Holland promising that in the event of war he would keep England neutral. An air of victory pervaded the whole of London in general and the court in particular. All things nautical became the rage and ladies wore navy blue sailor dresses with crown and anchor emblems upon them.

Barbara Castlemaine threw a private victory party for the King and her closest friends and caused quite a stir with her specially decorated cakes and confections. She had cakes in the shape of battleships and red, white, and blue victory flags, but Barbara, being Barbara, was not satisfied with merely a nautical theme. She knew what would amuse her prurient-minded guests and ordered small round cakes with white icing and red cherries in the middle designed to resemble female breasts which she promptly dubbed "maids of honor," and for the gentlemen she caused great merriment with cakes resembling a man's cock and balls. Then she had the gall to pretend they were supposed to be cannons and cannonballs.

Later, as she lay abed with Charles, he chuckled. "Nautical doesn't mean naughty, Barbara. I'll give you some English lessons."

"Well, I certainly caught on to the French lessons you gave me," she teased bawdily.

He reached for a delicious red apple from a bowl beside the bed. She snatched it from him playfully. "Oh, no you don't, I'm not finished with you yet. I have other uses for that sensual mouth of yours."

"Insatiable wench to make me satisfy your appetite before I satisfy my own."

"Mayhap we can do both at the same time," she teased, gripping the apple between her plump knees and lying back against the pillows. "Let's see if you can finish the apple before a more delectable fruit distracts you."

As Charles bit into the apple its sweet juice ran down from her knees to the insides of her thighs and his tongue tickled her as he licked it off. He finished off the apple, then lowered himself to lie full length upon her with a laugh and a sigh. "Barbara, you are a delicious baggage." He kissed her then brushed the dark red curls from her brow. "Pretty too," he murmured, observing her voluptuous beauty from beneath lowered lids.

"Pretty enough to pose for Brittania on the new Guinea gold pieces?" she asked.

Damn! he thought. Why do women always want something and without fail ask for it in bed? "The model hasn't been selected yet," he demurred.

"In that case, you can select me," she pressed, using both hands to roll his large shaft between her palms.

He groaned. "The final selection rests with the artist, Babs; let's not talk of it now."

"Now," she insisted, brushing his velvety tip with her thumb. "Charles, who has a better right than I?" she demanded.

He realized that she must have gotten wind of his choice of

Frances Stewart for Brittania. "Who has a better right?" he repeated. "Why, the Queen, of course," he said, trying to distract her with a red herring.

"Piffle!" shouted Barbara, pushing at his hard chest to dislodge his body from between her legs. "I know the rabbit-toothed little Queen is the last person you have in mind!"

"Barbara!" he warned.

She ignored his tone of voice completely, working herself into a fine breathless passion. "You've chosen that prim little Stewart bitch over me," she said, her breasts heaving.

He tried to defend his choice. "The artists all agree she has a most noble profile."

"Oh!" Barbara cried, jumping from the bed and flinging her slippers across the room. "You make a laughingstock of yourself. She teases you with her virginity so you'll run panting after her."

"You're doing a damn good job of cockteasing yourself at this moment," he complained.

"You beast! How can you call me that when I make myself available to you day and night? If you think for one minute she'd be able to satisfy your lusty appetite, you're completely mistaken in her. You are as randy and as big as your damned stallion, Old Rowley. Why, that narrow-hipped little bitch wouldn't even be able to take you. She'd wear white gloves to bed in case she had to handle the beastly thing, and she certainly wouldn't 'French' you whenever you fancied it, like I do."

"Barbara . . . darling . . . come and do it now. Let's not fight, you know how I hate these scenes," he pleaded.

"Then you'll arrange it so that I can be Brittania?" she pressed.

"Barbara, no, you can't have everything you want under the sun, and bargaining with your body when you know I'm hot for you is acting like a strumpet."

"Oh, you brute!" She picked up a crystal bottle of heliotrope and flung it across the bed. "Take back your gifts, I don't want them!" she cried.

He noticed with a jaundiced eye that she never flung back any of the jewels he had given her.

"I hate you, Charles! Get out of my house and never come back," she shouted as if he were the meanest lackey.

His temper snapped and he slapped her face, hard. She began to sob, and when he held out his arms she went into them and buried her face against his neck. His lips nuzzled her ear and he whispered, "Go on and cry, you'll piss less."

Her tears turned to laughter and she turned her face up to his and said provocatively, "A man who doesn't give his woman a hard slap when she's begging for it doesn't have that woman's respect."

"You know I'm not a violent man, but you drive me to it on purpose," he said, stroking her generous curves until she almost purred. She reached up to rub her body full length against him then lowered her hands to knead his hard buttocks. His hands and mouth moved across her flesh so temptingly that her knees buckled and they fell entwined onto the bed. He rolled her under him and she immediately separated and lifted her knees in blatant invitation, then he dove into her and the heavy seas of passion rolled through them and over them.

48

After Lord Lord Ruark Helford had served his king and country, he immediately set sail for Cornwall. His mouth curved whenever he thought of Summer and how she had taken her own sweet time in returning to Helford Hall from London. It was her way of showing him that even when he held all the cards, she wouldn't come begging. Well, he'd been away almost three months—long enough for her to have had some private time at Helford Hall with Ryan. Now, however, she was going to have to learn to share their son. She was also going to have to learn to be a wife again as well as a mother.

He swore that from now on he would tell her and show her exactly how deep his love for her ran and in return he wanted all of her love, given without reserve. He anticipated with lusty relish a second honeymoon.

However, when Mr. Burke and Mrs. Bishop claimed that Summer was not there, that she had never been there, he was stunned. He immediately sailed back to London and by now he was frantic with worry. Straightaway he went to Court and made inquiries. No one had seen her for months, since before the fire, and he went to Lil Richwood's house on Cockspur Street with dread in his heart. He wasted no time bantering with Lil. "She never turned up at

Helford Hall. She must have been in touch with you," he insisted
grimly.

"Ruark, darling, I do believe you are accusing me of lying," she
drawled.

"Not lying, precisely, but there's something you're not telling
me," he insisted.

"Whatever makes you say such a thing to me, Ruark?"

"Because you're not frantic with worry over her. If you had no
idea where she might be, you would be mad with anxiety—filled
with mental anguish, as I am, until you went out of your mind."

Lil cast him an apprehensive little glance. "Ru, darling, sit
down." She patted the satin-covered love seat coaxingly as if she
were about to divulge a confidence. She looked at his dark brows
and thought he looked like Lucifer after his fall from grace. His
black hair was in wild disarray from running his distraught fingers
through it.

"I hoped I wouldn't have to be the one to tell you this. I don't
want to hurt you, Ruark. I believe that Summer went off with your
brother, Rory. I believe she is in love with him."

A wail of anguish came from Helford's throat which sounded
like a wounded wolf. Lil wished with all her heart she had never
told him, for he was plainly devastated by the news.

Summer had stopped living. She had stopped daydreaming,
stopped wishing, even stopped thinking. She existed—barely. In
her heart she knew she would never again know a moonlit night on
the balcony overlooking the garden at Helford Hall. Ebony and her
dawn ritual were lost to her forever. When she had first been imprisoned, she felt outrage at the injustice of it all, but since then she
had killed; she had become unclean, evil. Her son would be better
off without her, so it was only right that she had lost him.

She had lost her husband. She had lost her lover. She had lost
her looks, her youth, her health. She no longer cared. She was
numbed to passivity; frozen, encased in ice, impervious to any further pain or torment.

She was so thin, her wrists and ankles looked delicate enough to
snap. Her clothes and skin were layered with so much dirt she was
unrecognizable. Her hair had grown but the lank, greasy shags
were now plastered down the back of her neck.

* * *

Under cover of darkness the *Phantom* slipped silently up the Solent, past the Isle of Wight, into Portsmouth Harbor. Prince Rupert, disguised as an ordinary seaman, disembarked and was soon swallowed up by a waiting carriage. Black Jack Flash had safely delivered him to France and returned him twice in the last month without one soul being the wiser. He was acting as proxy for his cousin King Charles in a secret matter, namely handling the transfer of money from Louis to Charles for favors rendered.

Rory Helford never lingered in a port. Before dawn his *Phantom* would be safely out of Portsmouth, tucked snugly in a hidden cove off the Isle of Wight. Though he never appeared to be in a hurry, he wasted no time returning to his ship. He knew immediately he was being followed and his hand slipped over the carved handle of his long knife to caress it intimately. Damn and blast the man, thought Rory. I hate to take life unnecessarily.

He was in black from head to foot and easily concealed himself by slipping behind an iron capstan. As the seaman stood glancing about in the dark, Rory stepped silently forward and wrapped his forearm about the man's throat. His knife, palmed in his other hand, pricked into the man's kidney. "Talk fast and make it good," he threatened.

"Black Jack, it's me, Gitan. I sailed with you once. I lost an arm, remember?"

Rory's hand slipped down the man's shoulder to feel the empty sleeve. "Turn about slowly," he ordered, "so I can see your face."

The swarthy Breton was indeed Gitan. Rory grinned. He could let him live. The only people he allowed to know his identity were those few who had sailed with him. "You need money, Gitan." It wasn't a question.

"That's not why I've been watching for you," he denied. Rory arched a black brow.

"It's a woman. Four or five months back they brought in women prisoners on a ship from London. The soldiers arrested a woman right here on Portsmouth dock and shackled her to the others. She gave me a message for you. She said she was your woman."

"Cat?" demanded Black Jack Flash.

"Aye, that's the one." Gitan nodded.

"Christ Almighty," swore Rory, "so that's why she seemed to drop from the face of the earth." He slipped his knife back into its sheath. "Can the warden be bribed?" he asked.

Gitan shook his head emphatically.

"Is there a way I can get in?" Rory asked.

Gitan shook his head again. "There's no way in and no way out except through death's door."

"You've earned yourself a bag of gold this night. Come aboard and tell me the whole tale again in minutest detail," invited Rory.

He took the risk of staying in port, but after three visits to the prison, Rory Helford was convinced he would get absolutely nowhere. Bludwart would answer no questions, give no hints, take no bribes. Short of storming the stronghold with the entire crew of the *Phantom,* Rory had no way of helping Cat. Lord Ruark Helford, however, should be able to come up with some sort of plan which would allow him to walk in and at least try to assert his authority. A vile curse dropped from Rory's lips. He was loath to leave Cat incarcerated for one more hour while he sailed to London, but he knew in his heart it was a job for Lord Helford and not Black Jack Flash.

Ruark was in danger of letting his anger and his impatience get the better of him. It was a platitude to say that knowing the fate of a loved one was better than being left wondering. In this case it simply wasn't so. To think of his sweet, precious Summer in a prison cell, and worse, to think that she had been moldering there five months, was unendurable to him.

A knife was twisting inside his heart, the pain made more unbearable because of the great burden of guilt which threatened to crush him. If only Lil Richwood's suspicions had been correct. If only Summer had sailed off with Rory five months ago. Well, he wouldn't enlighten her—wouldn't inflict even a small part of the pain he was suffering on her. Somehow, someway, he would free her, and no one would ever know she had spent one shameful, degrading hour in an English prison.

He paced about the anteroom to the King's closet like a caged animal. His body cried out for action, yet here he was trapped with all his excessive energy coiled tight within him. At last he saw the door open and Charles emerge and he schooled himself to patience.

Charles smiled at his friend. "All was accomplished with the precision of a well-oiled machine."

Ruark looked at him blankly for a moment. Then he recalled he must be speaking of the covert operation involving Rory and Rupert. "I'm here about a totally unrelated matter," he said with what he hoped was an affable grin. "The high magistrate in Hampshire has been indisposed for over a year and as a result there have been no trials in Southampton and Portsmouth. The prisons are bulging at the seams and I think I could do something to ease the backlog before I return to my own district."

"Find a suitable replacement for the magistrate if you will. That is a ridiculous situation which should never have been allowed to go on this long. All the seaports are overcrowded, unspeakably evil and filled to the rafters with scoundrels who daily break the law, but they should not be incarcerated without trials."

"Sire, all I need is a letter of authority."

"See Cornwallis for that. I've appointed him head of the justice system. Apparently it stands in need of a damn good overhaul. He has some scheme under way which transports petty criminals to the Americas. Apparently there is a grievous shortage of laborers and a crying need for women in the colonies."

"It sounds like the scheme has merit," said Helford, his brain already at work on a scheme of his own.

"Makes more sense than letting them sit on their backsides, eating their heads off at my expense," said Charles.

Ruark Helford lost no time visiting Cornwallis. He put it in such a way that he would assume the King had ordered him to Portsmouth. "Some women were shipped to prisons in other counties after the London fire. That was five months since and they haven't even been tried for their offenses."

Cornwallis warned him. "The selection must be a careful one. We don't want cutthroats and murderers overrunning our colonies, but I see no reason why women who were arrested for small debts or stealing bread to feed their children cannot be given a chance to help populate the New World. I'm still undecided about prostitutes. What do you think, Helford?" he asked, raising bushy eyebrows.

It was the closest Ruark had come to smiling since he'd learned the whereabouts of his wife. To think the fate of perhaps hundreds of ladies of the night rested with him. He considered the matter gravely, then said without the least hint of mockery, "Since men in the colonies are in need of women to warm their beds and make a harsh life more bearable, I think women who have loose morals would be welcomed with open arms."

"Mmm. Man does not live by bread alone," agreed Cornwallis, remembering many of his own irregular pleasures.

"Give me the necessary letter of authority and I'll be off to Portsmouth. Which vessel will transport the women I select?" he pressed.

"Goddammit, Helford, you're in a tearing hurry. Don't you realize the wheels of justice grind slowly?"

"Well, now that the war's over, I see no reason for the navy to sit about on their backsides eating their heads off," he said, borrowing a phrase from the King.

"You're right of course," said Cornwallis, still smarting at navy men like Sandwich and Albermarle who had kept him in the background during the late nasty business with Holland. "I suppose I have full authority to pick and choose any vessels from the fleet I might need."

"I don't think there's any question of it," replied Helford smoothly. "How about the *Neptune*? I believe it's riding at anchor in Portsmouth this very day, doing nothing more than gathering barnacles." He picked the slow, cumbersome *Neptune* for its dearth of cannon.

"The *Neptune* you say?" asked Cornwallis, beginning to see the humorous side to Helford's choice. "God's flesh, that's the ship they gave William Penn to command after he lost the *Royal Charles*. I don't think our rigidly religious Penn will appreciate transporting a shipload of drabs."

"On the contrary," said Helford, "I don't think we could put our women in safer hands."

Lord Helford arrived at Portsmouth Prison with half a dozen young militiamen under his command. When he dismounted in the prison yard, he realized that for the first time in his life he knew real fear. His guts threatened to turn to jelly and he almost contemplated bolting. When he entered the building, he had to clench his jaw to keep his gorge from rising at the stench of humanity which oozed from the very stones. One glance at Bludwart made him assert total authority immediately. He flashed his legal letters signed by Cornwallis and sealed by the Crown and decided then and there he would give no further explanation of his actions.

Earlier in the day he had ordered the *Neptune* readied for its voyage to America and had curtly dismissed William Penn's objections to transporting prisoners. He took over Bludwart's office, throwing the man and his furnishings out until the room stood bare. He ordered his militiamen to scrub it down as if it had been the deck of his ship and bade them burn brimstone and saltpeter to disinfect the air.

One table was placed in the room to hold the great ledger of records. One immaculately uniformed militiaman presided over those records. When all was ready, he had all the women who were incarcerated brought before him. They numbered between fifty and sixty. As they filed in they were told to stand against the wall.

Lord Helford's keen eyes searched each and every face as it entered the room. He had hardened himself to the fact that she would be changed. Try as he might, however, he could not accept that any one of these poor wretches was his wife. His man read out each name, and as the woman stepped forward the catalog of her crimes was read aloud.

Ruark Helford was well known for his hardness, his discipline, his strong belief in right and wrong, crime and punishment, but this day he felt nothing so much as pity for these women who had spent months in shame and degradation, suffering slow starvation in filth because of their sinful misbehavior. He felt shame, too, that the reason he experienced compassion now was because his beloved was one of them.

He felt panic rise within him. She was not here. Please God she had not died before he could save her. His distraught fingers went through his hair over and over in frustrated alarm. He took the ledger and scanned it distractedly. "Are there any names unaccounted for?" he demanded grimly.

The efficient militiaman had put a neat tick beside each woman's name who had come forward. He had also ticked off the names of the deceased, who had a black line through their names. His finger went down the columns rapidly and he pointed out four names which were unaccounted for. The name St. Catherine jumped off the page. "Bludwart!" Ruark thundered, striding from the room. "There are four women I have not yet seen."

The warden wrung his hands, opened his mouth, and closed it again.

"Well? Is this a dumbshow?" he demanded.

"Your lordship, they are vicious killers," he babbled. "I've kept them confined, but they have even murdered one another. Originally there were six and a child, now there are but four."

Ruark closed his eyes and prayed. "Please God, not this close only to find you have taken her." When he opened his eyes, they bored into Bludwart's. "Fetch them," he croaked hoarsely.

He was again standing in the roomful of women when the four wraiths slipped through the door. His heart stopped beating and he momentarily died when he saw that Summer was not one of the women. Then suddenly his hard mask almost crumbled with the force of his rage as he recognized the exquisitely delicate cheekbones. Then the knife twisted in his heart as he saw that she would rather die than have him recognize her.

He cleared his throat to gain some measure of control over his voice and his emotions, then in a matter-of-face tone explained to the women the reason for his being there. When he mentioned America, when he spoke of freedom, he saw hope rekindle in their eyes where there had been no hope. His eyes slid over Summer and on to the next face with no slightest hint of recognition. "I hereby reduce every sentence in this room to transportation to America. The phantom of death has stalked you long enough. I charge all of you to henceforth abide strictly by the letter of the law. I charge you to become useful members of society. I charge you to watch out for the *Phantom*." He turned his back upon the women, no longer able to look at her without breaking. He instructed his men to see that the women were fed a decent meal and bedded down with sufficient blankets. With his back still turned, he raised his voice over the whispered murmurs of the women. "Tomorrow you will all be bathed and disinfected and issued clean clothing before you board the *Neptune*."

When she saw his ramrod back quit the room, Summer felt only relief. Thank God his eyes had not even flickered as they passed over her. She would never have been able to bear being humbled and humiliated by his revulsion. It was then that she realized her damnable pride was still intact. Prison hadn't been able to destroy it, even though she had felt numb for the last months, thinking her pride had been destroyed forever. In her great relief at the prospect of escaping this horrific prison, her spirit and pride were restored.

The thought of going to America, however, filled her with such anguish, she didn't know how she would bear it. It would prevent her from seeing Ryan again, but she must endure it because he was probably better off without her.

Something drove Ruark to see for himself the dungeon where she had endured half a year. He took a lantern and went below to the cellars. The stench down here was worse by a thousandfold. In one corner was a heap of something unspeakable which at one time must have been straw before it became fouled with blood and excrement. He recoiled instinctively from the open drain and the slop bucket, but more horrific to him than the putrescence was the mean size of the room in which she'd been caged. Lord Ruark Helford slid down in a corner against the slimed stones, and the rats gathered curiously at the sound of his sobbing.

49

Captain William Penn had almost a hundred women aboard the *Neptune*. They took up over half of the hold space, which had been fitted with narrow, tiered bunks. Food and water supplies for the monthlong voyage took up the rest of the space. The women were not shackled, but they were only allowed up on deck during daylight hours, then locked below-decks at dusk.

Most of them had never been to sea and it frightened them enough to keep them huddled below, fighting off the misery of mal de mer. But if they had been given a choice between staying in England and sailing to America, there wasn't one who would have chosen to remain behind.

Summer spent every moment that she could up on deck. She sat quietly in a corner, speaking to no one. It was like paradise simply to breathe in the clean fresh air of the wind and the sea. The iodine smell of tidewrack, the taste of salt on her lips, the sound of creaking timbers and the chain rattling through the hawse hole were music to her ears. She had not yet begun to speak or even think, but she had begun to feel.

When the *Neptune* sailed past the Isles of Scilly, she caught the fragrance of its flowers upon the sea breeze and realized with amazement that it was spring. Two days past the Scillies a murmur rippled through the ship that another vessel had been sighted. It flew a Union Jack, so Sir William Penn was not disturbed when it veered toward the *Neptune*, drawing close enough to exchange greetings. He was more than disturbed, however, when the sleek, well-armed vessel put a ball across his bow and ordered him to heave to.

"Clear the decks for action! Gun crew to stations!" bellowed Penn, but he knew it was too late. The colors she'd been flying had completely lured him into complacency, and as the *Phantom* came alongside and he saw the swarthy, grinning faces and noted with alarm the carronade guns capable of smashing through a three-foot-thick hull, he realized they were pirates.

"Prepare to repel boarders!" he shouted at the top of his lungs, then he was stunned to hear himself hailed from the deck of the *Phantom*.

"Captain Penn," came the booming voice of the pirate, "I wish the *Neptune* no harm and will allow you to sail on in peace."

"What do you want?" demanded Penn in a skeptical voice.

"I want a woman," called the pirate.

"These women are being transported to America. They are under my protection."

"One woman only, Captain Penn. I'll even buy her from you . . . name your price."

Penn eyed the guns trained on his decks and was almost tempted. "You godless swine, women cannot be sold!"

Black Jack Flash swung across the ship's rail and landed, sword in hand, lithe as a panther on the deck of the *Neptune*. Black, calf-skin boots reached to his thighs. A ruffled shirt opened to the navel was tucked into black, skintight breeches. His unshaven face contrasted sharply with the silver streak of hair which zigzagged above his temple. He bowed low to William Penn. "Never trust a religious man, he hides behind his God; an atheist, however, stands before you naked." When he received no rejoinder to his sally, he explained himself further. "My woman is aboard your ship. I am here to collect her."

"What is this woman's name?" asked Penn.

Rory glanced about the decks for Cat. "She knows who she is, Captain."

When no woman came forward, Penn became almost defiant. "Apparently she does not wish to go with you."

Rory flashed his wolf's grin. "Unfortunately, Captain, she has no choice in the matter." He strode unerringly toward a dark, thin female and held out his hand. "Cat," he said simply.

She felt as if she were awakening from a nightmare. Lord Helford had recognized her after all. His last words came back to her clearly. "Watch out for the *Phantom*." Ruark and Rory, together, had planned her escape. The dark vivid face and green eyes had the look of a wild hawk. He was so shamelessly arrogant that all other men suffered by comparison. Her fingers reached tentatively toward his outstretched hand and his warm fingers closed over hers and drew her to her feet. Then everything blurred together. They ran lightly across the deck, his strong arms holding her securely as they swung across to the deck of the *Phantom* and the space between the two vessels widened quickly as the *Phantom*'s top gallants filled with wind to carry the graceful marauder out of sight within minutes.

His arm still steadied her as she gazed up at him in disbelief, then she whispered the first words that had passed her lips in months. "You should have let me go."

Sea green eyes looked deeply into hers and then they smiled at her. "I will never let you go," he said simply. "As captain of this ship I order you below to bed. You will do nothing but eat and sleep for a week." Then he added a phrase to give her peace of mind. "None will disturb you."

Without a backward glance she gratefully went below to the well-remembered cabin. Gone were the silken red panels which used to float about like smoke. In their place were pristine white bed curtains, and the linen spread upon the wide bed was clean and white as driven snow.

She slept heavily for three days and nights. On the fourth day she began to eat between long naps and on the fifth day she added another delicious pleasure to her regimen. She bathed.

The sixth day she ventured up on deck and realized they lay at anchor in a sun-bathed cove of the Scilly Isles. Rory wisely kept his distance and allowed her to approach him. "The sunshine and sea air will help to heal you. Already your cheeks have roses in them."

She wandered ashore, basking for hours on the hot sand, then she would go for solitary walks, picking up exquisite shells, letting tiny crabs run across her bare toes while the seabirds wheeled and screamed above her head.

She allowed herself to think again. It was painful at first until she got back into the habit of it. And the thought that came again and again to her lifted the corners of her mouth in a sad smile. Fate had chosen for her, and it had chosen Rory. Soon she would go to him, and she would go willingly. He had saved her life and she owed him everything.

Late one warm afternoon she felt strong enough to swim again. Rory watched over her anxiously, but when she climbed back aboard and toweled her dark curls into a soft halo about her head, he grinned at her and said, "I think it's time I took you home to Helford Hall."

She recoiled from him. "No!" she said sharply. "I don't want to see him."

"You must. We struck a bargain, you see. I was to rescue you, then I was to take you home to him."

"No!" she cried in great panic. "Why would you force me to this?" she demanded.

"Hellcat, when are you going to face the truth? It is he you love, and only he."

She stared at him aghast.

He was the first to lower his eyes. "You know which cabin I'm using. When you are ready to face the truth, you know where to find me."

She sat with her knees drawn up, resting her chin upon them as she watched the crimson sunset. When the night sky turned from crimson to black, she stood up and fetched a sigh to her very toes. What was the use of pretending? It seemed everyone knew anyway.

She gathered Rory's white djellaba robe about her and padded down the companionway to his cabin. She opened the door and gasped in shock. "Ruark!"

He had just finished shaving and he was brushing a black substance into his hair. "Where's Rory?" she demanded.

"There is no Rory," he said quietly. "There is only me, Ruark Rory Helford."

She stared at him in disbelief. That could not be. He was surely taller and broader than Rory, and he held his dark head with a greater pride. Ruark had a dark heritage in his blood, that heritage of violence and disquiet which seethed through the men of Cornwall but had not touched the youthful, carefree Rory. Lord Ruark Helford seethed with a dark vein of passion. Yet she suddenly knew he spoke the truth. Her eyes had been opened at last and she wondered unbelievably how she had not seen it before. Her hand went to her throat. "Does any but your crew know?" she whispered.

"The King," he said quietly. "It was Charles's suggestion in the first place to assume two identities. Whenever he wants to resurrect Black Jack Flash, I always tell him Rory is dead, but he flashes that charming smile and says, 'A convenient rumor the scoundrel circulates for some dark reason of his own, I have no doubt.'"

She almost smiled.

He held out his hand. "Lady Helford . . . Summer . . . will you let me take you home?"

She moved forward slowly and at last placed her hand in his. "If you will give me time to adjust." She withdrew her hand shyly. "I just can't comprehend it all at once."

He wanted to pledge to her that he would spend the rest of his life loving her, that he would make it up to her somehow, or die in the attempt, but he knew she was not ready for impassioned speeches and vows.

When the *Phantom* dropped anchor in a sheltered cove of the Helford River in the late afternoon, Summer's heart began to thud uncontrollably at the thought of seeing Ryan again. She was certain he wouldn't even remember her, but that wouldn't matter at all so long as he was healthy and happy. She donned a lavender silk gown she had left aboard the *Phantom* when she had bought all the fancy clothes in The Hague, but she scrupulously avoided the mirror. She did not need to be reminded that her clothes hung on her and her hair was still too unfashionably short.

Ruark came down to the cabin to escort her home. A slight frown formed between his brows as he watched her wash her hands for the third time. There was still such a gulf between them. They hadn't even talked yet. Oh, they exchanged polite pleasantries whenever they encountered one another but they hadn't *talked*, they hadn't *touched*. His brow cleared. He would have to be the one to breach the gap. Perhaps when she got the baby back, it would go a long way to healing her.

She felt his strong arm supporting her back as they went through the front doors of Helford Hall and she was most grateful for it. Her knees had been threatening to turn into butter ever since she'd stepped off the ship. The hall was filled with masses of cream-colored roses and there stood Mrs. Bishop holding a small, sturdy replica of Ruark Helford. He was not really a baby, he was a one-year-old scrap of Satan with black silk curls and a laughing, red mouth.

Summer's throat closed painfully and she found it almost impossible to speak. Mrs. Bishop tried not to stare too rudely at Lady Helford. She realized that she must have been ill and was still so fragile a strong wind would blow her away. Nevertheless, she held out her son to her. Summer shook her head and quickly put her hands behind her back to conceal her burned thumb. Then in a low voice she said, "Mrs. Bishop, you have done such a wonderful job with him. I thank you from the bottom of my heart."

Mr. Burke came forward then. He and Summer looked at each for long silent moments then his right eyelid lowered in a conspiratorial wink and she knew that everything was going to be all right. He took her arm possessively and said, "Come up to your chamber, my lady, and tell me if there is anything I've forgotten."

She was grateful that he had not assembled all the servants to gawk at her and she realized in that moment that the goodwill of this man meant more to her than that of the King and all the court.

Ruark took his son from the arms of Mrs. Bishop and lifted him onto his shoulders, then they galloped around the house and out into the gardens like wildmen. It was impossible to tell which Helford was enjoying himself more. When they got to the fountain, Ruark set him on his feet and watched his son fondly as he reached into the water to try to catch the flashing fish. "Ryan, old man, we have a big job ahead of us. Somehow we have to pierce the protective carapace she's built about herself." His hand rested momentarily on the black silk curls, so like Summer's. "Well, you've stolen my heart and I believe you will steal your mother's."

Ryan sloshed water all over his father and laughed recklessly.

"You little sod!"

"Sod! Sod!" cried Ryan in imitation.

"How come you learn swear words quicker than other words?" Ruark demanded, laughing, but Ryan was busy climbing over the edge of the fountain and his father had to fish him out.

Mrs. Bishop was outraged when they returned to the house and scolded Ruark loudly for wetting the child.

"You're going to bathe him before you put him to bed, aren't you?" inquired Ruark.

"Of course," said Mrs. Bishop.

"So what's the difference?" he asked with annoying male logic.

Then he said, "Bish, after you've had your dinner I want you to take yourself off to Roseland for the night. You can take a letter for me to Spencer. He'll bring you back tomorrow."

"But Ryan might need me," she pointed out.

"He needs his mother more, Bish. And she needs him," he added.

Mr. Burke had a supper tray sent up to Lady Helford's chamber and Summer had just finished eating when Ruark came in, in shirt sleeves. She betrayed her thoughts by the blush upon her cheek, which told Ruark she was wondering if he intended to sleep in this chamber. He had no intentions of forcing himself upon her, but he knew that intimacy had to be reestablished between them. He glanced at the food she had left on the tray and said, "Can't you eat more than that, love?" He took the cover from a silver dish and saw the first strawberries of the season. He helped himself to one and took the dish across to her. She was sitting beside the open French door which led to the balcony. That balcony she had thought never to enjoy again.

"You were always particularly partial to strawberries," he reminded her as he held one out for her. She smiled and let him put it into her mouth.

"Mmm," she sighed. "I'll be spoiled rotten within twenty-four hours."

"It will give me the greatest pleasure in the world to spoil you," he said, putting the silver dish in her hands and going to the bedside cabinet to take out her rubies. He opened the velvet cases for her and she touched the glowing jewels with a tentative finger.

"How lovely they are," she murmured.

"They are lovelier when you are wearing them. May I put them on for you?" he asked softly.

She remembered how she'd vowed that he would clasp them about her neck again before she was done with him. How willful and worldly she'd been in those days. How selfish and greedy she had allowed herself to become. Now it was like getting a second chance in life. Never again would she take a beautiful gown or a sumptuous meal for granted. She would be deeply appreciative of the life she would have with this man.

His hands fastened the necklace at the nape of her neck and his fingers could not resist touching the springy little curls which lay there. "You are beautiful," he breathed.

"I know I'm not," she said wistfully. "You're just being kind."

"Me? Kind?" he asked in mock amazement.

She giggled, but sobered quickly. "I must let Auntie Lil know I'm rescued."

Ruark drew up a chair close to hers. His eyes were filled with teasing amusement.

"Lil told me you'd gone off with Rory, that you were in love with him."

"And so I was," she teased back.

He grew serious. "She really believes you've been with Rory. She has no idea you were imprisoned. There's no need to enlighten her, nor anyone, for that matter."

A great weight was removed from her and relief showed in her eyes.

Then he added gently, "Anyone, that is, except me. How did you come to be there, love?"

Her eyes flew to his. "It was Oswald," she said at last.

"God's flesh, I might have guessed," he said furiously. "The man hated me with a vengeance. I'm so very, very sorry, my little love, that he took his hatred for me out on you." He went on his knees before her. "I swear to you, Summer, I will track him down and kill the bastard."

"He's dead," she said low. "I killed him."

He stared at her in horror. "Christ! What did he do to you?" Then his voice took on a tender, sad note. "Did he rape you?" His hands covered hers gently, trying to lend her courage to tell him the worst.

She shook her head. "He made no sexual demands on me." She smiled a sad half smile. "Perhaps that would have been easier, but Oswald wasn't a normal man."

Ruark's throat closed in frustrated fury as a teardrop rolled down her cheek. He brushed it away with gentle fingers and braced himself while she got it all out.

Summer loved him far too much to cause him much more distress, so she said softly, "He simply enjoyed being cruel. He branded my thumb and degraded us by cutting our hair and starving us. Let's never speak of it again."

His arms enfolded her and clasped her to his heart. "I'll try to make it up to you, beloved."

"Ru, you already have," she assured him with all her heart.

50

Ruark took her small hand to his lips and kissed her scarred thumb, then he gathered her into his arms and held her until long after her sobs had subsided. She lay in his lap, sharing the big chair like they had done in the early days of their marriage.

Finally she lifted her head and braved looking into his eyes. She saw only compassion and love. "I'm so very tired," she said simply.

He lifted her against his heart and took her to their great bed. With gentle hands he helped to undress her and pulled the soft covers up about her neck as he tucked her in securely. "Sleep, darling," he murmured. "I love you very much."

Totally safe for the first time since they had had their first quarrel, she fell into an undisturbed sleep. In the middle of the night something woke her and she sat up quickly, sensing that something was wrong. Ruark stood naked, distractedly running one hand through his hair, while his other arm clutched a wailing Ryan.

Ruark called to her helplessly, "Summer, Summer, the young bugger won't stop howling."

"Where's Mrs. Bishop?"

"I banished her to Roseland for the night. I thought we could handle him ourselves," he said sheepishly. "I went down to get him some milk; I even warmed it, but the young bugger threw it on the floor."

For a moment she panicked, then she laughed and held out her arms to them. In three great strides he was beside the bed. He handed her their agitated son and climbed in beside her. Summer's arms gathered the baby to her breast and she rocked him back and forth, making soothing, motherly noises which Ryan found much to his liking. He clung to her desperately, no longer the willful one-year-old, but a baby again for the darkest hours of the night, needing to be cuddled and loved until he drifted off into a trustful sleep.

Their baby lay enfolded between their two bodies. Ruark's fingers entwined with Summer's and they spent the lovely warm, dark hours of the night whispering love words and exchanging thousands of gentle kisses, while their three heartbeats mingled and bonded forever. Ruark prayed silently, Dear God, I don't ask for anything more, just don't take anything away.

In the morning when her brother Spider arrived, she couldn't believe the change in him. He was so tall and broad; the boy had disappeared forever and in his place stood a man.

"I sold Roseland to him." Ruark laughed. "You'll have enough to do looking after Helford Hall."

Spider grinned. "He sold it to me for five gold crowns so I could afford my own ship with my profits from Madagascar."

"You have no regrets about the voyage then?" asked Summer.

"Of course I have regrets; I missed out on the war!"

Summer smiled, understanding at last. "Ruark planned it that way to keep you safe for me."

Spider looked at her keenly. "I'm going to say this, Cat, whether you like it or not. I hope to God you're ready to stop leading a dissolute life, racketing about London. You're as thin as a damned rail. I don't think you've tried very damned hard to be a good wife and mother either." He looked pointedly at Ruark. "If she were my wife, I'd be tempted to take my hand to her backside. If you give her an inch, you know, she'll take whole bloody mile."

Ruark tried unsuccessfully to conceal a grin. "You've no idea how much I've been tempted to take my hand to her backside."

She slanted him a glance and a fierce wildness pulsed in her blood.

Spider stayed for lunch and Summer allowed Ryan to sit at the big table with the adults. She could see that her brother and her

son were already fast friends and her heart swelled with thankful-
ness for all her blessings until she thought it might burst.

In the afternoon Ruark slung a hammock for her in the secluded
part of the garden that was the most headily fragrant. She lay back
in it obediently and Ruark sat on its edge gazing down at her. She
lifted her hand to touch his clean-shaven cheek. "I can't understand why I never guessed Rory was you," she said, remembering
the unshaven beard and the zigzag of white hair. "Why did you
play such a damnable trick on me?"

"I couldn't breach the antagonism between us. After I lost my
damnable temper and said all those cruel things to you, I regretted
it almost immediately. But it was too late. Every time we spoke, we
fought like cat and dog. You were much more amenable to Rory.
You were completely yourself—no lies, no subterfuge. You certainly weren't about to let Ruark make love to you, so I seduced
you as Rory."

"Have you any idea how guilty I felt about having an affair?"
She searched his face, then her lashes dropped to her cheeks. "I
almost died when I discovered I was going to have a baby and
didn't know which of you was the father."

He studied her face, so exquisitely lovely in the dappled shade of
the flowering almond. "You confessed to Rory you didn't know
which of us was the father, but I noted with amusement you didn't
breathe a word to your husband," he said with a teasing light in his
green eyes.

"Oh, Lord," she breathed, "I didn't dare."

He looked at her quizzically. "Darling, were you afraid of me?"

Her lashes went up. "Yes, a little . . . perhaps more than a
little."

He dipped his head to steal a very gentle kiss. "But surely you're
not afraid of me anymore, are you?"

"Of course not," she breathed. "Well, perhaps just a little," she
admitted.

He lifted her hand to his mouth and placed an intimate kiss in
her palm. She raised her hand to his temple and ran her fingers
through his hair, where his scar was hidden. She wondered how
she'd missed feeling it when they'd been first married. Perhaps
subconsciously she had known Ruark and Rory were one. She'd
never really know the answer. "So it was you who rode into the
raging Helford River to save your father."

"Our damnable tempers were so much alike. He went to his death before we had healed the rift between us," he said ruefully. "God's flesh, the same thing almost happened to us," he said, fiercely gripping her shoulders. "I'm so sorry I made you afraid, threatened you, said cruel things to you."

"Did you have our marriage annulled?" she asked him quietly.

He groaned. "Of course not, sweetheart. You are my heart's desire. Surely by now you know my bark is worse than my bite?"

"Mmmm," she said with a little moue of longing, "you haven't bitten me lately."

In spite of his good intentions, desire was running rampant through his blood. With a great deal of willpower he tried to bank the fires within, for he did not think she was ready yet for lovemaking. In a light teasing voice he said, "Someday I will show you how to make love in a hammock. There is a knack to it, you know."

She slanted him a provocative glance. "What's wrong with today?" she tempted.

His laugh was slightly ragged as his hands closed about her tiny waist. "Little pagan!" His fingers easily spanned her and it reminded him just how gentle he must be with her, lest he hurt her. Slowly, slowly, he undid the fastenings on her gown and slipped it off. It fell to the lush green grass with a whisper and was soon followed by her shift and stockings. Her mass of silken curls came just to her shoulders and they both remembered in that moment how her hair had been long enough to cloak her breasts whenever she was naked.

"Don't move," he begged, "I'll be right back." He selected the largest cream-colored roses he could find and plucked an exotic scarlet hibiscus flower. With tender hands he placed a rose upon each breast and tucked the vivid blossom in the lovely dark curls between her legs. Summer has been so anxious about Ruark's reaction to her thin body, but suddenly he had made her feel utterly beautiful and she loved him for it. She sighed as he worshiped her with his eyes.

"This garden is lovelier than Eden, I warrant."

"And you are lovelier than Eve . . . who was that legendary enchantress who was thought to be Eve's mother? Lilith, that's the one . . . a true pagan, I'll warrant."

He quickly removed his clothes and lowered himself carefully into the slowly swaying hammock. He cautioned himself again to go slowly, to take his time with her. He clenched his fist on nothing, wondering if he was insane to think he could remember caution once he'd touched her. He lifted her into his lap as they lay back in the hammock, nuzzling her neck and letting his hands gently explore her slight curves.

All the most vulnerable parts of her body were open to his seeking hands when they lay this way. He caressed her skin, murmuring, "Sunshine . . . silk . . . sweetness . . . scent." He breathed deeply to inhale the delicious fragrance of her. As they lay beneath the heady pink almond, lazily swaying in the hammock, he knew an exquisite torture. Each time the hammock swung, her buttocks moved slightly against the tip of his swollen phallus, until finally he cried out with the sheer pleasure it gave him.

He took her hand to his lips, kissed the palm, and traced his tongue along the curves of her fingers. "I love to touch you and taste you and I know you love it . . . want it." He guided her hand down to the place where the scarlet blossom lay. He took her fingers and dipped their tips deeply inside her. Then he took those honey-drenched fingers to his hot mouth and sucked her sweetness from them.

"Oh, Ru, the things you do to me make me feel wicked as sin."

"I hope so," he murmured, repeating the erotic act.

Her other hand slipped beneath her buttocks to close over his imperious hardness, and as her fingers teased him the world went dim around him. Her fingers caressed him with the delicacy of butterfly wings, feeling his shape and long thick dimensions. "Oh, God . . ." he gasped. "How I've missed waking up naked in bed with you."

She slid over so that her breasts pressed into his hard-muscled chest, their bellies touched and the length of his marble shaft lay between her legs, against her hot moist cleft. She had been without him so long, she felt her whole body was fiery with a combination of shyness and pulsing need.

He moved gently up and down along her cleft, slipping deliciously on the moistness that was spreading into her tight curls. His tip, like carmine velvet, penetrated her and she cried his name over and over for the sheer pleasure of tasting it on her lips. "Ru, Ru!"

His rigid head slid and pleasured her in a more gentle way than she'd ever been loved in her life. She arched up to him, stretching and straining her mouth to reach his so he could cover it with his demanding kisses, but his mouth, too, was so tender with the deep love he felt for her that her mouth wasn't even bruised.

She spread her legs as wide as she could and pressed down onto him, but his hands were so gently firm he would not allow her to impale herself upon him and risk hurting her. A few times he felt as if he was losing control, but his iron willpower enabled him to regain it even in the face of his great need. He had always encouraged her to cry out her needs and be vocal in their lovemaking, as indeed he himself was. He could tell by her moans and little cries that she needed to be brought to fulfillment, so with strong tender hands he lifted and lowered her hips onto him gently, not allowing deep, full penetration.

Summer was almost mad with a frenzy of need. Finally she realized he was watching her face intently, then as he lifted her body each time, he watched his shaft go up inside her and withdraw again. He didn't wish to miss one single expression of pleasure on her face as he made love to her, while the bees droned in the blossoms above and the erotic rhythm of the swaying hammock brought them to their final bliss in a delicately sensual fashion. She clung to him shuddering for a long, long time and the nectar of their love felt warm and slippery between their fused bodies.

As their blissful days together blended into a week he knew he had never known such happiness. If they were in a room with other people, they began by making love with their eyes. Then he could not resist touching her, kissing her, caressing her, but always with such infinite gentleness it had a poignancy about it. Before Ryan's bedtime they always retired to their bedchamber with him so the three of them could spend a private, intimate hour together.

Sometimes they played on the floor with him or sometimes all three romped on the great bed, with Ruark only pretending to be fierce. He was as gentle with Summer as he was with their baby, his heart almost bursting in his chest with the love he felt for them.

Tonight Summer lay stretched upon their bed in her nightgown, watching Ryan raptly as he sat on the floor playing with her jewels. Ruark knelt on the bed behind her and, wrapping one possessive arm about her, drew her back to lean against him. With gentle hands he lifted her hair so that his lips could feather kisses from her nape down her back. He glanced at Ryan. "Apparently he is particularly partial to rubies, like his mother."

Summer laughed softly. "Jewels aren't as important to me as they used to be."

"Mmm, that's too bad," he said, his mouth against her back, "for I have a waterfall of diamonds I've been waiting an eternity to give you."

She slanted him a glance over her shoulder. "Well, perhaps you can persuade me to take them, if you bribe me."

His hands began to caress her gently and his voice became low and husky in anticipation of their bed play. "Let's put Ryan to bed and then I'll do my utmost to make you model the diamonds for me."

Ryan made the usual protest, so they allowed him to keep the rubies to play with until he was tucked into the sturdy cradle in his own chamber. Mrs. Bishop shook her head in wonder as Lord Helford swept his scantily clad wife in his arms and carried her to bed. Oh, they might be all lovely-dovey for a while since they'd been parted so long, but she knew them well enough to know that one of these days the sparks would fly and they'd have another fight to end all fights, and she'd lead him a merry chase all over England or God-knows-which country. There would be the threats and the jealousies and the screaming matches at the top of their lungs, then he'd take her to bed and bend her to his will and tame her again. A calm, peaceful life wasn't the Helfords style at all.

Alone in their bedroom, Ruark dangled the waterfall of diamonds in his fingers, playfully tempting and seducing her to let him make love to her in return for them.

"That would be wicked of me," she protested innocently.

"Didn't they teach you in church that the devil makes wickedness attractive for the sole purpose of corrupting the virtuous?"

She looked at him from beneath half-closed lids. He was a reckless breed of man who had taught her to commit her sins in the grand manner, disdaining pettiness.

"I've decided to have them after all," she said, reaching out a hand.

"Uh-uh—you have to be completely naked before I'll let you wear them."

"Unfair! If I'm to be naked, so are you," she decreed.

He grinned his wolf's grin and wasted no time in throwing off his garments. Freed from the confines of his tight breeches, his great manroot sprang up, filling, expanding, hardening, and quivering with anticipation. He drew her so close against his body she could see the tiny image of her face reflected in the black pupils of his eyes. With reverent hands he drew off her nightgown and gently clasped the diamond waterfall about her slender throat. Then his lips touched hers in a gentle kiss.

She slid against him provocatively and whispered, "Ru, I'm tired of you touching me with gentleness."

He drew back and looked down into her face. Suddenly his emerald eyes were stained black with passion as he took her meaning.

Her lips half parted beneath his. "Lord God, I think I'll die if you don't take me, take me!"

Her language acted like an aphrodisiac on him. She'd seemed too fragile both in body and spirit for him to be savagely demanding in his lovemaking, but now she was making demands of her own and he couldn't wait to satisfy those demands. He swept her up and carried her in front of the great mirrored wardrobe so she could watch his body make love to hers. He set her down in front of him and turned her to the glass. "See how lovely your breasts look adorned with a waterfall of diamonds?"

"Mmmm," she said, deliberately moving her bum against his erection. She smiled as she heard his great intake of breath above her ear. Then her eyes widened as she saw his hand come between her legs from behind to cup her whole sensitive mound of Venus. Her breath caught in her throat as she watched his hands, capable of such brutal strength, toy and play upon her body so intimately. In that moment she learned what women had learned down through the ages . . . that a man wasn't devastatingly attractive and irresistible unless he was dangerous.

Ruark applied a strong, delicious pressure as he cupped her, and ground his palm in a slow rotating motion until she thought she might climax into his hand, but he was a superbly skilled lover and withdrew his hand, trailing the pads of his fingertips across her hot center. The peaks of sensation receded and he immediately set to work rebuilding them. He knew that one of the most pleasurable parts of making love was penetration and so he showed her all the different ways to go about the sensual business.

At first her cheeks and throat were suffused with blushes at his boldness, but she soon lost her ability to think clearly. She could only feel and she let herself go and gave herself up totally, absorbing his masculinity to the full, high up inside her. Each time he withdrew totally and each time her body mourned the loss. He penetrated her over and over again, burying himself to the hilt,

then his tongue filled her mouth with the same dominant insistence
before withdrawing completely.

Finally she could bear the torture of separation no longer and
her body closed over him, tightening, squeezing, not permitting
him to withdraw. She did the same with his delicious tongue, sucking hard so that he couldn't bear to withdraw it from her honey-
drenched mouth. He pressed her up against the mirrored wardrobe, thrusting up into her so savagely that her feet no longer
touched the floor.

Their gyrations became so frenzied that suddenly her waterfall
of diamonds broke and showered down over their fused nakedness.
"I'll buy you more diamonds . . . emeralds . . . rubies," he
vowed.

"Ru, I don't want jewels," she whispered huskily.

"What do you want?" He knew he would give her anything.

"Fill me with another babe," she said simply.

His hands slipped beneath her buttocks and she wrapped her
legs about his back, then he walked to the bed and spread her
beneath him. They wanted it to last all night, but they were both
out of control and in a few minutes they were both shuddering as
he began flooding into her.

Later, as they lay talking in the privacy of the great curtained
bed, her hand absently cupping and fondling him so that he remained aroused, he murmured, "Will you miss London?"

"Of course I shall miss it. But every year you will take me back
so that I can shop, see all the plays, and have a flirtation with the
King."

"There was a great scandal at Court recently," he told her.
"Charles caught the virtuous little Frances Stewart in bed with
Richmond, so Richmond had to marry her."

"I knew they were having an affair. I saw him take her to his
rooms one night, down by the bowling green."

"You never breathed a word," he said, marveling.

"I couldn't betray another woman. After all I was having an
affair myself with that damned pirate. Well, if Frances is married,
that should make Barbara Castlemaine happy."

"Not a bit of it." He laughed. "Married to the Duke of Richmond makes Frances a duchess and Barbara is only a countess.
She's nagging Charles to death to make her Duchess of Portsmouth. He's given her Berkshire House to keep her quiet."

Summer stretched like a cat in the warm bed and ran her bare foot up Ruark's leg. She wouldn't change places with anyone in the whole wide world and she had the powerful knowledge that neither would her husband. She leaned over him so that her breasts lay on his hard-muscled chest and ran her fingers along his jaw. "Don't shave today, and remove that black stuff from your silver flash of hair."

"Ah, you fancy being made love to by Rory, do you?"

"Well, it's not every woman who is lucky enough to be married to two men . . . after all, variety is the spice of life," she purred.

He was insanely happy that she was over her ordeal and that they were more in love than they had ever been. He looked down into her eyes and said softly, "Darling, do you forgive me for all the grief I caused you?"

"Forgive you? Forgive you? Hell no, I haven't even forgiven you for the bloody oysters and champagne you fed me!" she cried as she reached up to pull handfuls of his dark hair.

He captured her hands and pulled her down to him. His deep kisses had the ability to make her forget everything. He was her rock, her strength. She would cleave to him forever and there would be no more nightmares in his safe arms.

Experience the Passion and the Ecstasy

Meagan McKinney

☐ 16412-5 No Choice But
        Surrender $4.99

☐ 20301-5 My Wicked
        Enchantress $4.99

☐ 20521-2 When Angels Fall $5.99

☐ 20870-X Till Dawn Tames
        the Night $4.99

☐ 21230-8 Lions and Lace $4.99

☐ 20913-7 Fair Is The Rose $5.99

At your local bookstore or use this handy page for ordering:

DELL READERS SERVICE, DEPT. DFH
2451 S. Wolf Rd., Des Plaines, IL . 60018

Please send me the above title(s). I am enclosing $_____
(Please add $2.50 per order to cover shipping and handling.) Send
check or money order—no cash or C.O.D.s please.

Ms./Mrs./Mr._____

Address _____

City/State _____ Zip _____
                                         DFH - 11/93

Prices and availability subject to change without notice. Please allow four to six
weeks for delivery.

ST. MARTIN'S

MINOTAUR
MYSTERIES

"Agatha Raisin, a cranky, crude, and raunchy woman, somehow (and this reviewer doesn't have a clue) manages to worm her way into the reader's heart and elicit sympathy. The latest installment in this long-running series is funny, breezy, and very enjoyable."

—*Midwest Book Review*

AGATHA RAISIN AND THE LOVE FROM HELL

"Among the many joys of all Agatha Raisin adventures are Beaton's sweetly formal prose and her vivid descriptions of colorful villagers. This one, however, adds a crackerjack plot and a delightfully comic ending to the mix, making it clearly the best of the lot."

—*Booklist* (starred review)

"M. C. Beaton's eleventh Agatha Raisin book is a reason to celebrate ... [It has all] the vitality and robustness of a new series."

—*Tulsa World*

AGATHA RAISIN AND THE FAIRIES OF FRYFAM

"Witty ... [a] highly amusing cozy."

—*Publishers Weekly*

"Agatha is as fractious and funny as ever. Don't miss this one."
—*Tulsa World*

"Outwardly bossy and vain, inwardly insecure and vulnerable, Agatha grows more endearing with each installment."

—*Cleveland Plain Dealer*

"More great fun from an endearing heroine."

—*Library Journal*

AGATHA RAISIN AND THE WIZARD OF EVESHAM

"Another delightful cozy featuring Cotswolds surroundings, a bit of history, and buoyant characters."

—*Library Journal*

"[A] smartly updated Miss Marple . . . Beaton's books about this tough little Raisin cookie are well-made and smoothly oiled entertainment machines . . . trust Agatha to solve it all in style."

—Amazon.com

"The return of Agatha Raisin, amateur sleuth extraordinaire, is always a treat and M. C. Beaton does not miss a beat . . . another fabulous English cozy by the great M. C. Beaton."

—Harriet Klausner, *Painted Rock Reviews*

AGATHA RAISIN AND THE WELLSPRING OF DEATH

"Tourists are advised to watch their back in the bucolic villages where M. C. Beaton sets her sly British mysteries . . . outsiders always spell trouble for the inbred societies Beaton observes with such cynical humor."

—*The New York Times Book Review*

"Outspoken, chain-smoking, aggravating Agatha roars back for a[n] . . . outing that will keep fans cheering. Must be something in the water."

—*The Poisoned Pen*

Writing as M. C. Beaton

Agatha Raisin and the Haunted House

Agatha Raisin and the Case of the Curious Curate

Agatha Raisin and the Day the Floods Came

Agatha Raisin and the Love from Hell

Agatha Raisin and the Fairies of Fryfam

Agatha Raisin and the Witch of Wyckhadden

Agatha Raisin and the Wizard of Evesham

Agatha Raisin and the Wellspring of Death

Agatha Raisin and the Terrible Tourist

Agatha Raisin and the Murderous Marriage

Agatha Raisin and the Walkers of Dembley

Agatha Raisin and the Potted Gardener

Agatha Raisin and the Vicious Vet

Agatha Raisin and the Quiche of Death

The Skeleton in the Closet

Writing as Marion Chesney

Snobbery with Violence

Hasty Death

AGATHA RAISIN
AND THE
CASE OF THE
CURIOUS CURATE

†

M. C. BEATON

St. Martin's Paperbacks

AGATHA RAISIN AND THE CASE OF THE CURIOUS CURATE

Copyright © 2003 by M. C. Beaton.
Excerpt from *Agatha Raisin and the Haunted House* copyright © 2003 by M. C. Beaton.

Library of Congress Catalog Card Number: 2002031885

ISBN: 0-312-99061-8
EAN: 80312-99061-9

Printed in the United States of America

St. Martin's Press hardcover edition / October 2003
St. Martin's Paperbacks edition / October 2004

St. Martin's Paperbacks are published by St. Martin's Press, 175 Fifth Avenue, New York, NY 10010.

10 9 8 7 6 5 4 3 2 1

This book is dedicated to Mrs. Nancy Stubbs of Woore, near Crewe, with many thanks for her description of the village duck races, which were much more decorous than the one described in this book.

ONE

✝

AGATHA Raisin was beginning to feel that nothing would ever interest her again. She had written to a monastery in France, to her ex-husband, James Lacey, who, she believed, was taking holy orders, only to receive a letter a month later saying that they had not heard from Mr. Lacey. Yes, he had left and promised to return, but they had heard or seen nothing of him.

So, she thought miserably, James had simply been sick of her and had wanted a divorce and had used the monastery as a way to get out of the marriage. She swore she would never be interested in a man again, and that included her neighbour, John Armitage. He had propositioned her and had been turned down. Agatha had been hurt because he had professed no admiration or love for her. They talked from time to time when they met in the village, but Agatha refused all invitations to dinner and so he had finally given up asking her.

So the news that the vicar, Alf Bloxby, was to get a curate buzzed around the village, but left Agatha unmoved. She went regularly to church because of her friendship with the vicar's wife, regarding it more as a duty that anything to do with spiritual uplift. Also because of her friendship with Mrs. Bloxby, she felt compelled to attend the Carsely Ladies' Society where the village women discussed their latest fund-raising projects.

It was a warm August evening when Agatha trotted wearily along to the vicarage. She looked a changed Agatha. No make-up, sensible flat sandals and a loose cotton dress.

Miss Simms, the secretary, read the minutes of the last meeting. They were all out in the vicarage garden. Agatha barely listened, watching instead how Miss Simms's stiletto heels sank lower and lower into the grass.

Mrs. Bloxby had recently been elected chairwoman. Definitely the title of chairwoman. No chairpersons in Carsely. After tea and cakes had been passed round, she addressed the group. "As you know, ladies, our new curate will be arriving next week. His name is Tristan Delon and I am sure we all want to give him a warm welcome. We shall have a reception here on the following Wednesday. Everyone in the village of Carsely has been invited."

"Won't that be rather a crush?" asked Miss Jellop, a thin, middle-aged lady with a lisping voice and large protruding eyes. Agatha thought unkindly that she looked like a rabbit with myxomatosis.

"I don't think there will be all that much interest," said Mrs. Bloxby ruefully. "I am afraid church attendances are not very high these days."

Agatha thought cynically that the lure of free food and

drinks would bring them in hordes. She wondered whether to say anything, and then a great weariness assailed her. It didn't matter. She herself would not be going. She had recently returned from London, where she had taken on a free-lance public relations job for the launch of a new soap called Mystic Health, supposed to be made from Chinese herbs. Agatha had balked at the name, saying that people didn't want healthy soap, they wanted pampering soap, but the makers were adamant. She was about to go back to London for the launch party and intended to stay for a week and do some shopping.

At the end of the following week, Agatha made her way to Paddington Station, wondering, as she had wondered before, why London did not hold any magic for her anymore. It seemed dusty and dingy, noisy and threatening. She had not particularly enjoyed the launch of the new soap, feeling she was moving in a world to which she no longer belonged. But what was waiting for her in her home village of Carsely? Nothing. Nothing but domestic chores, the ladies' society, and pottering about the village.

But when she collected her car at Moreton-in-Marsh Station and began the short drive home, she felt a lightening of her spirits. She would call on Mrs. Bloxby and sit in the cool green of the vicarage garden and feel soothed.

Mrs. Bloxby was pleased to see her. "Come in, Mrs. Raisin," she said. Although she and Agatha had been friends for some time, they still used the formal "Mrs." when addressing each other, a tradition of the ladies' society, which fought a rearguard action against modern times and modern manners. "Isn't it hot?" exclaimed the vicar's wife, pushing a damp tendril of grey hair away from her face. "We'll sit in the garden. What is your news?"

Over the teacups Agatha regaled her with a highly embroidered account of her experiences in London. "And how's the new curate?" she finally asked.

"Getting along splendidly. Poor Alf is laid low with a summer cold and Mr. Delon has been taking the services." She giggled. "I haven't told Alf, but last Sunday there was standing room only in the church. Women had come from far and wide."

"Why? Is he such a good preacher?"

"It's not that. More tea? Help yourself to milk and sugar. No, I think it is because he is so very beautiful."

"Beautiful? A beautiful curate? Is he gay?"

"Now why should you assume that a beautiful young man must be gay?"

"Because they usually are," said Agatha gloomily.

"No, I don't think he's gay. He is very charming. You should come to church this Sunday and see for yourself."

"I might do that. Nothing else to do here."

"I hate it when you get bored," said the vicar's wife anxiously. "It seems to me that every time you get bored, a murder happens somewhere."

"Murder happens every day all over the place."

"I meant close by."

"I'm not interested in murders. That last case I nearly got myself killed. I had a letter from that Detective Inspector Brudge in Worcester just before I left. He suggested I should go legit and set up my own detective agency."

"Now that's a good idea."

"I would spend my days investigating nasty divorces or working undercover in firms to find out which typist has been nicking the office stationery. No, it's not for me. Is this curate living with you?"

"We found him a room in the village with old Mrs. Feathers. As you know, she lives opposite the church, so we were

4

lucky. Of course, we were prepared to house him here, we have plenty of room, but he would not hear of it. He says he is quite comfortably off. He has a small income from a family trust."

"I'd better get back to my cats," said Agatha, rising. "I think they prefer Doris Simpson to me." Mrs. Simpson was Agatha's cleaner, who looked after the cats when Agatha was away.

"So you will come to church on Sunday?" asked Mrs. Bloxby. "I am curious to learn what you make of our curate."

"Why, I wonder," said Agatha, her bearlike eyes sharpening with interest. "You have reservations about him?"

"I feel he's too good to be true. I shouldn't carp. We are very lucky to have him. Truth to tell, I think my poor Alf is a little jealous. Though I said nothing about it, he heard from the parishioners about the crowds in the church."

"Must be awful to be a vicar and to be expected to act like a saint," said Agatha. "All right. I'll be there on Sunday."

When she got back to her cottage, Agatha opened all the windows and the kitchen door as well and let her cats, Hodge and Boswell, out into the garden. I don't think they even missed me, thought Agatha, watching them roll on the warm grass. Doris comes in and feeds them and lets them in and out and they are perfectly happy with her. There was a ring at the doorbell and she went to answer it. John Armitage, her neighbour, stood there.

"I just came to welcome you back," he said.

"Thanks," retorted Agatha. "Oh, well, you may as well come in and have a drink."

She was always surprised, every time she saw him, at how good-looking he was with his lightly tanned face, fair hair and green eyes. Although he was about the same age as she was herself, his face was smooth and he looked younger, a fact that annoyed her almost as much as the fact that he had propositioned her because he had thought she would be an easy lay. He was a successful detective story writer.

They carried their drinks out into the garden. "The chairs are a bit dusty," said Agatha. "Everything in the garden's dusty. So what's been going on?"

"Writing and walking. Oh, and tired to death of all the women in the village babbling about how wonderful the new curate is."

"And is he wonderful?"

"Smarmy bastard."

"You're just cross because you're no longer flavour of the month."

"Could be. Haven't you seen him?"

"I haven't had time. I'm going to church on Sunday to have a look."

"Let me know what you think. There's something wrong there."

"Like what?"

"Can't put my finger on it. He doesn't seem quite real."

"Neither do you," commented Agatha rudely.

"In what way?"

"You're . . . what? Fifty-three? And yet your skin is smooth and tanned and there's something robotic about you."

"I did apologize for having made a pass at you. You haven't forgiven me, obviously."

"Yes, I have," said Agatha quickly, although she had not. "It's just . . . you never betray any emotions. You don't have much small talk."

"I can't think of anything smaller than speculation about a new village vicar. Have you ever tried just accepting people as they are instead of as something you want them to be?"

"You mean what I see is what I get?"

"Exactly."

What Agatha really wanted was a substitute for her ex-husband and was often irritated that there was nothing romantic about John, but as she hardly ever thought things through, she crossly dismissed him as a bore.

"So is it possible we could be friends?" asked John. "I mean, I only made that one gaffe."

"Yes, all right," said Agatha. She was about to add ungraciously that she had plenty of friends, but remembered in time that before she had moved to the Cotswolds from London, she hadn't had any friends at all.

"In that case, have lunch with me after church on Sunday."

"Right," said Agatha. "Thanks."

She and John arrived at the church on Sunday exactly five minutes before the service was due to begin and found there were no seats left in the pews and they had to stand at the back.

The tenor bell in the steeple above their heads fell silent. There was a rustle of anticipation in the church. Then Tristan Delon walked up to the altar and turned around. Agatha peered round the large hat of the woman in front of her and let out a gasp of amazement.

The curate *was* beautiful. He stood there, at the altar, with a shaft of sunlight lighting up the gold curls of his hair, his pale white skin, his large blue eyes, and his perfect mouth. Agatha stood there in a daze. Mechanically, she sang the opening hymn and listened to the readings from the Bible. Then the curate mounted the pulpit and began a sermon about loving thy neighbour. He had a well-modulated voice. Agatha listened to every word of a sermon she would normally have damned as mawkish and boring.

At the end of the service, it took ages to get out of the church. So many wanted to chat to the curate, now stationed on the porch. At last, it was Agatha's turn. Tristan gazed into her eyes and held her hand firmly.

"Beautiful sermon," gushed Agatha.

He smiled warmly at her. "I am glad you could come to church," he said. "Do you live far away or are you from the village?"

"I live here. In Lilac Lane," gabbled Agatha. "Last cottage."

John coughed impatiently behind her and Agatha reluctantly moved on.

"Isn't he incredible?" exclaimed Agatha as they walked to the local pub, the Red Lion, where they had agreed earlier to have lunch.

"Humph," was John's only reply.

So when they were seated in the pub over lunch, Agatha went on, "I don't think I have ever seen such a beautiful man. And he's tall, too! About six feet, would you say?"

"There's something not quite right about him," said John. "It wasn't a sparkling sermon, either."

"Oh, you're just jealous."

"Believe it or not, Agatha, I am not in the slightest jealous. I would have thought that you, of all people, would not fall for a young man simply because of his looks like all those other silly women."

"Oh, let's talk about something else," said Agatha sulkily. "How's the new book going?"

John began to talk and Agatha let his words drift in and out of her brain while she plotted about ways and means to see the curate alone. Could she ask for spiritual guidance? No, he might tell Mrs. Bloxby and Mrs. Bloxby would see through that ruse. Maybe dinner? But she was sure he would be entertained and fêted by every woman in not only Carsely, but in the villages around.

8

"Don't you think so?" she realized John was asking.

"Think what?"

"Agatha, you haven't been listening to a word I've said. I think I'll write a book and call it *Death of a Curate*."

"I've got a headache," lied Agatha. "That's why I wasn't concentrating on what you were saying."

After lunch, Agatha was glad to get rid of John so that she could wrap herself in brightly coloured dreams of the curate. She longed to call on Mrs. Bloxby, but Sundays were busy days for the vicar's wife and so she had to bide her time with impatience until Monday morning. She hurried along to the vicarage, but only Alf, the vicar, was there and he told her curtly that his wife was out on her rounds.

"I went to church on Sunday," said Agatha. "I've never seen such a large congregation."

"Oh, really," he said coldly. "Let's hope it is still large when I resume my duties next Sunday. Now if you will excuse me . . ."

He gently closed the door.

Agatha stood there seething with frustration. Across the road from the church stood the house where Tristan had a room. But she could not possibly call on him. She had no excuse.

She was just walking away when she saw Mrs. Bloxby coming towards her. Agatha hailed her with delight. "Want to see me?" asked Mrs. Bloxby. "Come inside and I'll put the kettle on."

Mrs. Bloxby opened the vicarage door. The vicar's voice sounded from his study with dreadful clarity. "Is that you, dear? That awful woman's just called."

"Excuse me," said Mrs. Bloxby and darted into the study and shut the door behind her.

She emerged a few moments later, rather pink in the face.

"Poor Alf, some gypsy woman's been round pestering him to buy white heather. He's rather tetchy with the heat. I'll make tea."

"Coffee, please." Agatha followed her into the kitchen.

"We'll go into the garden and you can have a cigarette."

"You forget. I've given up smoking. That trip to the hypnotist worked. Cigarettes still taste like burning rubber, the way he said they would."

Mrs. Bloxby made coffee, put two mugs of it on a tray and carried the tray out into the garden. "This dreadful heat," she said, putting the tray down on the garden table. "It does make everyone so crotchety."

"I was at church on Sunday," began Agatha.

"So many people. Did you enjoy it?"

"Very much. Very impressed with the curate."

"Ah, our Mr. Delon. Did you see anything past his extraordinary good looks?"

"I spoke to him on the porch. He seems charming."

"He's all of that."

"You don't like him, and I know why," said Agatha.

"Why?"

"Because he is filling up the church the way Mr. Bloxby never could."

"Mrs. Raisin, when have I ever been *petty*?"

"Sorry, but he does seem such a wonderful preacher."

"Indeed! I forget what the sermon was about. Refresh my memory."

But try as she could, Agatha could not remember what it had all been about and she reddened under Mrs. Bloxby's mild gaze.

"You know, Mrs. Raisin, beauty is such a dangerous thing. It can slow character formation because people are always willing to credit the beautiful with character attributes they do not have."

"You really don't like him!"

"I do not know him or understand him. Let's leave it at that."

Agatha felt restless and discontented when she returned home. She had started to make up her face again and wear her most elegant clothes. Surely her meetings with the curate were not going to be confined to one-minute talks on a Sunday on the church porch.

The doorbell rang. Ever hopeful, Agatha checked her hair and make-up in the hall mirror before opening the door. Miss Simms, the secretary of the ladies' society, stood there.

"Come in," urged Agatha, glad of any diversion.

Miss Simms teetered after Agatha on her high heels. Because of the heat of the day, she was wearing the minimum: tube top, tiny skirt and no tights. Agatha envied women who were able to go around in hot weather without stockings or tights. When she went barelegged, her shoes rubbed her heels and the top of her feet and raised blisters.

"Isn't he gorgeous," gasped Miss Simms, flopping down on a kitchen chair. "I saw you in church."

"The curate? Yes, he's quite something to look at."

"He's more than that," breathed Miss Simms. "He's got the gift."

"What gift? Speaking in tongues?"

"Nah! Healing. I had this terrible pain in me back and I met him in the village and told him about it. He took me back to his place and he laid his hands on my back and I could feel a surge of heat."

I'll bet you could, thought Agatha, sour with jealousy.

"And the pain had gone, just like that!"

There was a clatter as Agatha's cleaner, Doris Simpson, came down the stairs carrying the vacuum cleaner. "Just going to do the sitting room and then I'll be off," she said, putting her head round the kitchen door.

"We was just talking about the new curate," said Miss Simms.

"Oh, him," snorted Doris. "Slimy bastard."

"Come back here," shouted Agatha as Doris retreated.

"What?" Doris stood in the doorway, her arms folded over her apron, Agatha's cats purring and winding their way around her legs.

"Why did you call Tristan a slimy bastard?" asked Agatha.

"I dunno." Doris scratched her grey hair. "There's something about him that gives me the creeps."

"But you don't know him, surely," complained Agatha.

"No, just an impression. Now I must get on."

"What does *she* know about anything?" grumbled Miss Simms. "She's only a cleaner," she added, forgetting that she herself was sometimes reduced to cleaning houses when she was between what she euphemistically called "gentlemen friends."

"Exactly," agreed Agatha. "What's his place like?"

"Well, Mrs. Feathers's cottage is ever so dark, but he's brightened up the room with pictures and throw rugs and that. He doesn't have his own kitchen, but old Mrs. Feathers, she cooks for him."

"Lucky Mrs. Feathers," said Agatha.

"I was wondering if there was any chance of a date."

Agatha stiffened. "He's a man of the cloth," she said severely.

"But he ain't Catholic. He can go out with girls same as anybody."

"What about your gentleman friend in bathroom fittings?"

Miss Simms giggled. "He wouldn't have to know. Anyway, he's married."

The normally pushy Agatha was beginning to feel out classed. Besides, Tristan was young—well, maybe thirty-something, and Miss Simms was in her late twenties.

When Miss Simms had left, Agatha nervously paced up and down. She jerked open a kitchen drawer and found herself looking down at a packet of cigarettes. She took it out, opened it and lit one. Glory be! It tasted marvellous. The hypnotist's curse had gone. She hung on to the kitchen table until the first wave of dizziness had passed. Think what you're doing to your health, your lungs, screamed the governess in her head. "Shove off," muttered Agatha to the inner voice.

There was another ring at the doorbell. Probably some other woman come to gloat about a laying-on of hands by the curate, thought Agatha sourly.

She jerked open the door.

Tristan stood there, smiling at her.

Agatha blinked at the vision in blue shirt and blue chinos. "Oh, Mr. Delon," she said weakly. "How nice."

"Call me Tristan," he said. "I noticed you at church on Sunday. And I heard that you used to live in London. I'm still a city boy and still out of my depth in the country. This is very last minute, but I wondered whether you would be free to have dinner with me tonight?"

"Yes, that would be lovely," said Agatha, wishing she had put on a thicker layer of make-up. "Where?"

"Oh, just at my place, if that's all right."

"Lovely. What time?"

"Eight o'clock."

"Fine. Won't you come in?"

"Not now. On my rounds. See you this evening."

He gave her a sunny smile and waved and walked off down the lane.

Agatha retreated to the kitchen. Her knees were trembling. Remember your age, snarled the voice in her head. Agatha ignored it and lit another cigarette while she planned what to wear. No more sensible clothes. She did not stop to consider what gossip the curate had heard that had prompted him to ask her to dinner. Agatha considered herself a very important person, which was her way of lacquering-over her feelings of inferiority.

By the time she stepped out into the balmy summer evening some hours later in a gold silk dress, the bedroom behind her in the cottage was a wreck of discarded clothes. The dress was a plain shirt-waister, Agatha having decided that full evening rig would not be suitable for dinner in a village cottage.

She kept her face averted as she passed the vicarage and knocked at Mrs. Feathers's door. She had not told Mrs. Bloxby about the invitation, feeling that lady would not approve.

Old Mrs. Feathers answered the door. She was grey-haired and stooped and had a mild, innocent face. "Just go on upstairs," she said.

Agatha mounted the narrow cottage stairs. Tristan opened a door at the top. "Welcome," he said. "How nice and cool you look."

He ushered Agatha into a small room where a table had been laid with a white cloth for dinner.

"We'll start right away," he said. He opened the door and shouted down the stairs, "You can start serving now, Mrs. Feathers."

"Doesn't she need some help?" asked Agatha anxiously.

"Oh, no. Don't spoil her fun. She likes looking after me."

But Agatha felt awkward as Mrs. Feathers subsequently

appeared carrying a heavy tray. She laid out two plates of pâté de foie gras, toast melba, a chilled bottle of wine and two glasses. "Just call when you're ready for your next course," she said.

Agatha sat down. Mrs. Feathers spread a large white napkin on Agatha's lap before creaking off.

Tristan poured wine and sat down opposite her. "Now," he said, "tell me what brings a sophisticated lady like yourself to a Cotswold village?"

Agatha told him that she had always had a dream of living in a Cotswold village. She left out the bit about taking early retirement because she did not want to refer to her age. And all the time she talked and ate, she admired the beauty of the curate opposite. He had the face of an angel come to earth with his cherubic, almost androgynous face framed by his gold curls, but his athletic, well-formed body was all masculine.

Tristan rose and called for the second course. Mrs. Feathers appeared bearing tournedos Rossini, new potatoes and salad.

"Isn't Mrs. Feathers an excellent cook?" said Tristan when they were alone again.

"Very," said Agatha. "This steak is excellent. Where did you buy it?"

"I leave all the shopping to Mrs. Feathers. I told her to make a special effort."

"She didn't pay for all this, I hope?"

"Mrs. Feathers insists on paying for my food."

Agatha looked at him uneasily. Surely an old widow like Mrs. Feathers could not afford all this expensive food and wine. But Tristan seemed to take it as his due and he continued to question her about her life until the steak was finished and Mrs. Feathers brought in baked Alaska.

"I've talked about nothing but myself," said Agatha ruefully. "I don't know a thing about you."

"Nothing much to know," said Tristan.

"Where were you before you came down here?"

"At a church in New Cross in London. I ran a boys' club there, you know, get them off the streets. It was going well until I was attacked."

"What on earth happened?"

"One of the gang leaders felt I was taking his members away. Five of them jumped me one night when I was walking home. I was badly beaten up, cracked ribs, all that. To tell the truth, I had a minor nervous breakdown and I felt a spell in the country would be just what I needed."

"How awful for you," said Agatha.

"I'm over it now. These things happen."

"What made you want to join the church?"

"I felt I could help people."

"And are you happy here?"

"I don't think Mr. Bloxby likes me. I think he's a bit jealous."

"He's a difficult man. I'm afraid he doesn't like me either." Both of them laughed, drawn together by the vicar's dislike of both of them.

"You were saying you had been involved in some detection. Tell me about that?"

So Agatha bragged away happily over dessert, over coffee, until, noticing it was nearly midnight, she reluctantly said she should leave.

"Before you go," he said, "I have a talent for playing the stock exchange. I make fortunes for others. Want me to help you?"

"I've got a very good stockbroker," said Agatha. "But I'll let you know."

Somehow, she expected him to offer to walk her home,

but he led the way downstairs and then stood facing her at the bottom. "My turn next time," said Agatha.

"I'll keep you to that." He bent and kissed her gently on the mouth. She stared up at him, dazed. He opened the door. "Good night, Agatha."

"Good night, Tristan," she said faintly.

The door shut behind her. Over at the vicarage, Mrs. Bloxby's face appeared briefly at an upstairs window and then disappeared.

Agatha walked home sedately although she felt like running and jumping and cheering.

It was only when she reached her cottage that she realized she had not set a date for another dinner. She did not even know his phone number. She searched the phone book until she found a listing for Mrs. Feathers. He would not be asleep already. She dialled. Mrs. Feathers answered the phone. Agatha asked to speak to Tristan and waited anxiously.

Then she heard his voice. "Yes?"

"This is Agatha. We forgot to set a date for dinner."

There was a silence. Then he gave a mocking little laugh and said, "Keen, aren't you? I'll let you know."

"Good night," said Agatha quickly and dropped the receiver like a hot potato.

She walked slowly into her kitchen and sat down at the table, her face flaming with mortification.

"You silly old fool," said the voice in her head, and for once Agatha sadly agreed.

Her first feeling when she awoke the next day was that she never wanted to see the curate again. She felt he had led her on to make a fool of herself. A wind had got up and rattled through the dry thatch on the roof overhead and sent small dust devils dancing down Lilac Lane outside. She forced herself to get out of bed and face the day ahead. What if Tristan was joking with Mrs. Bloxby about her? She made herself her customary breakfast of black coffee and decided to fill up the watering cans and water the garden as the radio had announced a hose-pipe ban. She was half-way down the garden when she heard sirens rending the quiet of the village. She slowly put down the watering can and stood, listening. The sirens swept past the end of Lilac Lane and up in the direction of the church and stopped.

Agatha dropped the watering can and fled through the house and out into the lane. Her flat sandals sending up spirals of dust; she ran on in the direction of the vicarage. Please God, she prayed, let it not be Mrs. Bloxby.

There were three police cars and an ambulance. A crowd was gathering. Agatha saw John Fletcher, the landlord from the Red Lion and asked him, "Is someone hurt? What's happened?"

"I don't know," he said.

They waited a long time. Hazy clouds covered the hot sun overhead. The wind had died and all was still. Rumour buzzed through the crowd. It was the vicar, it was Mrs. Bloxby, it was the curate.

A stone-faced policeman was on duty outside the vicarage. He refused to answer questions, simply saying, "Move along there. Nothing to see."

A white-coated forensic unit arrived. People began to drift off. "I'd better open up," said the publican. "We'll find out sooner or later."

Agatha was joined by John Armitage. "What's going on?" he asked.

"I don't know," said Agatha. "I'm terrified something's happened to Mrs. Bloxby."

Then Agatha's friend, Detective Sergeant Bill Wong, came out of the vicarage accompanied by a policewoman.

"Bill!" called Agatha.

"Later," he said. He and the policewoman went to Mrs. Feathers's small cottage and knocked at the door. The old lady opened the door to them. They said something. She put a trembling hand up to her mouth and they disappeared inside and shut the door.

"There's your answer," said John Armitage.

"It's the curate and he's dead because that ambulance hasn't moved!"

TWO

✝

JOHN and Agatha decided to go back to Agatha's cottage and then return to the vicarage later.

"Who would want to kill the curate—if it was the curate," asked John.

Me, thought Agatha. I could have killed him last night.

Aloud, she said, "I hate this waiting." Then she thought, they'll have questioned Mrs. Feathers and she'll tell them about that dinner last night. I don't want John to know about it. I've got to get rid of him.

"I'm restless," she said, getting to her feet. "I think I'll go for a walk."

"Good idea."

"Alone."

"Oh, all right."

They walked together to the door. Agatha opened it. Detective Inspector Wilkes of the Mircester CID stood there, accompanied by Bill Wong and a policewoman.

"May we come in?" asked Wilkes.

"Yes," said Agatha, flustered. "See you later, John."

He was urged on his way by a push in the back from Agatha.

Agatha led the police into her living-room and sat down feeling, irrationally, like a guilty schoolgirl.

"What's happened?" she asked.

"Mr. Delon, the curate, was found this morning in the vicar's study. He had been stabbed."

Agatha felt hysterical. "Was he stabbed with a rare oriental dagger?" She stifled a giggle.

Wilkes glared at her. "He was stabbed with a paper-knife on the vicar's desk."

Agatha fought down the hysteria. "You can't kill someone with a paper-knife."

"You can with this one. It's very sharp. Mr. Bloxby said he kept it sharp. The church box, the one people put donations in for the upkeep of the church, was lying open. The money had gone."

"I know the vicar took it from the church from time to time to record what had been donated," said Agatha. "But Mr. Delon couldn't have surprised a burglar. I don't think there were ever any donations in there worth bothering about."

"Evidently, according to the vicar, there were this time. The curate had delivered a sermon the Sunday before last about the importance of donating to the upkeep of the church. There were several hundred pounds in there. The vicar hadn't got around to counting it. He says he just checked inside and planned to get down to counting the takings today."

"But what was Mr. Delon doing in the vicar's study?" asked Agatha.

"If we can stop the speculation and get to your movements, Mrs. Raisin. You had dinner with Mr. Delon in his flat last night. You left around midnight."

"Yes."

"Were you intimate with him?"

Agatha's face flamed. "Of course not! I barely knew the man."

"And yet he asked you for dinner."

"Oh, I thought it was a parish thing. I assume it was his way of getting to know everybody."

"So what did you talk about?"

"He was a good listener," said Agatha. "I'm afraid I talked mostly about myself. I asked him about himself and he said he had been at a church in New Cross in London and that he had formed a boys' club and that one of the gang leaders had become angry, thinking he was taking the youth of the area away and had had him beaten up. He said he'd had a nervous breakdown."

"And you left at midnight and that was that?"

"Of course."

"Do you know of any other women in the village he was particularly friendly with?"

"No. I mean, I'd been away and then I was up in London, working. The first time I met him was on Sunday, outside the church. Then he turned up on my doorstep yesterday and invited me to dinner."

"Let's go over it again," said Wilkes.

Agatha went through the whole business again and then felt her face going red. They would check phone calls to Mrs.

Feathers's phone and would know she had phoned him when she got home.

"What is it?" demanded Wilkes, studying her red face.

"When I got home, I realized I had asked him for dinner but hadn't fixed a date, so I phoned him and he said he would let me know."

"Those were his only words?"

"Exactly," said Agatha with all the firmness of one used to lying.

"That will be all for the moment. We would like you to come down to headquarters and sign a statement, say, tomorrow morning, and to hold yourself in readiness for further questioning."

As they rose to leave, Agatha's friend, Detective Sergeant Bill Wong, gave her the ghost of a wink.

"Call me later," mouthed Agatha silently.

As Wilkes was leaving, Agatha called, "When was Mr. Delon killed?"

He turned. "We don't know. Mrs. Bloxby rose at six-thirty this morning. She went out into the garden and noticed the French windows to the study were wide open. She could see papers were blowing about. She went in to close the window and found the curate dead."

Agatha felt a great wave of relief. She realized she had been afraid the vicar might have lost his temper and struck out at Tristan.

"So someone came in from outside?"

"Or someone made it look that way."

Agatha sat down shakily when they had left. Then she rose and phoned the vicarage. A policeman answered and said curtly that neither the vicar nor his wife were free to come to the phone.

The doorbell rang and she rushed to answer it. For once John Armitage got a warm welcome. "Oh, John," cried Agatha, grabbing his arm and dragging him indoors. "Isn't this too awful? Do you think Alf did it and made it look like a burglary?"

"I cannot believe our vicar would harm a fly," said John, shutting the door behind them. "Let's sit down calmly and think about it. Why did the police want to see you?"

"As far as they know, I was the last one to see Tristan alive. I went to his place for dinner and left around midnight."

"Oho. He's a fast worker. How did that come about?"

"He just turned up on the doorstep and asked me, just like that."

"Tell me about it."

"I've already gone over and over it with the police." She started to describe her evening again.

"Wait a minute," he interrupted. "Mrs. Feathers supplied a dinner of pâté de foie gras, tournedos Rossini, and baked Alaska. She can't be rich and she's a widow. Didn't you think it was a bit much of him?"

"I did a bit," said Agatha ruefully.

"Sounds a bit of a taker to me. Did he try to get money out of you?"

"You do underrate my charms, don't you? Oh, Lord. I've just remembered something. He said something about being a whiz at playing the stock exchange and that he could invest money for me. I said I'd a very good stockbroker but that I'd let him know."

"So *that* was why he asked you for dinner."

"What do you mean?" demanded Agatha huffily.

"Look at it this way. He'd conned old Mrs. Feathers into supplying an expensive meal. Who knows? He may have got his hands on her savings. You know what the gossip in this village is like. He'd have heard you're rich. You've got a bit of a reputation when it comes to men."

"Undeserved," snapped Agatha.

"And you're a divorcée. You should tell the police."

"Must I?" asked Agatha bleakly.

"Yes, of course. And just think. They're probably still up at the vicarage and it'll be an excuse for us to get in there."

The policeman on guard at the door of the vicarage listened to Agatha's request to see Wilkes because she had something to tell him relevant to the murder. He disappeared indoors and reappeared a few minutes later. "Follow me," he said. "They're in the garden." The vicar's study door was standing open. Men in white overalls were swarming all over the place.

They followed the policeman out through the French windows and into the garden where Wilkes, a policewoman, the vicar and Mrs. Bloxby sat round a garden table. There was no sign of Bill Wong.

Mrs. Bloxby was holding her husband's hand. Both looked strained.

"What is it?" asked Wilkes.

Agatha drew up a chair and sat down. She told him about the expensive dinner and about the offer to invest money for her.

"This might give us an angle," said Wilkes slowly. "He may have been successful with some of the other women. We'll be checking his bank account. Now Mrs. Feathers says you were the only one he invited home for dinner and he told her to make a special effort and you were very rich and probably used to the best."

Agatha felt herself grow red yet again with mortification.

Wilkes turned to Mrs. Bloxby. "Was he particularly friendly with any other women in the village?"

"It's hard to say," she said wearily. "I think they mostly invited him for meals. Miss Jellop was one. Then there was Peggy Slither over in Ancombe. Oh dear, let me think. Old Colonel Tremp's widow, Mrs. Tremp, she lives up the hill out of the village in that converted barn. So many were smitten with him. He was very handsome."

"And what about the both of you? Did he offer to invest any money?"

"No, he said he had a little money from a family trust. He didn't ask us for any."

"How come you got him as a curate?" asked Agatha.

"I was told he'd had a nervous breakdown," said the vicar. "I was glad of help in the parish work."

"And did you find him helpful?" asked Wilkes.

"The first week was fine. But then he became—selective."

"What do you mean—selective?"

"I found he had not been calling on any of the elderly or sick, unless—I now realize—they were wealthy. I took him to task for neglect of duty and he simply smiled and said of course he would attend to it. Then I fell ill and he took over the services in the church. I felt it churlish of me to dislike him—for I was beginning to dislike him—and I feared I was envious of the way he could pack the church."

"It looks as if he might have surprised a burglar," said Wilkes.

"Or," interrupted Agatha suddenly, "been robbing the cash box himself."

"If he had a private income and if, as we fear, he had been taking money from gullible women, why would he want a few hundred pounds?"

"He was very vain," said Mrs. Bloxby. "It was because of his sermon that there was such a large donation. I think he probably saw that money as rightly his."

"And he had a key to the vicarage," said Wilkes, who had already established that fact. "Those long windows into the study, do you keep them locked?"

Mrs. Bloxby looked guilty. "We do try to remember to lock them, but sometimes we forget. Up until recently, we never bothered to lock up at night, but with the police station having been closed down along with all the other local stations, there have been a lot of burglaries recently."

"So far, we can't find any sign of a break-in and no fingerprints at all, not even the vicar's," said Wilkes. "Excuse me, I'll see how they're getting on. Come with me, Reverend, and check again to see if there is anything else missing."

The vicar, the policewoman, and Wilkes went indoors. "Is there anything I can do for you?" asked Agatha, taking Mrs. Bloxby's hand in hers. "You've helped me so much in the past when horrible things have happened to me."

"You can find out who did it," said Mrs. Bloxby. "Because they suspect Alf. You see, a lot of the women were smitten by Mr. Delon, and before he died, there was a lot of talk about how Alf should step down and leave the sermons to Mr. Delon. My husband," she sighed, "can be, well, not very tactful and when Miss Jellop suggested such an arrangement to him, he told her not to be such a silly woman. The police are already beginning to think that Alf was jealous of Mr. Delon. He was in bed with me when the murder took place and so I told them, but they look at me in that way which seems to say, 'You would say that.'"

"We'll do our best," said John. Agatha looked at him in surprise. She had forgotten he was there. A man as good-looking as John had no right to be so forgettable.

"I think," pursued John, "that we should start off with whichever church he was at in New Cross in London before he came down here."

"But the police will dig all that up," protested Agatha.

"I still think we might be able to find out things the police don't know. They'll be sticking to facts. We can find out if he conned any of the women in New Cross out of money. One of them could have been watching Mrs. Feathers's cottage and seen him slip out. She may have entered the study by the French windows. There's no flower-bed in front of the windows to leave footprints, only grass."

"It all sounds far-fetched to me," said Agatha crossly, cross because she expected everyone at all times to play Dr. Watson to her Sherlock Holmes. "I mean, what sort of person would watch the cottage all night?"

"A jealous, furious woman," said John. "Come on, Agatha, don't knock it down just because it wasn't your idea. We'll hang around another day to be available for the police and then we'll go off."

"I think that's a very good idea," said Mrs. Bloxby quietly.

"All right," said Agatha sulkily. Mrs. Bloxby, despite her fear for her husband and her shock at the murder, could not help but feel amused. There was something childlike about Agatha Raisin with her bearlike eyes under a heavy fringe of glossy brown hair registering a pouting disappointment that someone else was getting in on the act.

"Now, have you eaten?" asked Agatha. "I've got some microwave meals at home I could bring along."

"No, thank you," said the vicar's wife. "Neither of us feels like eating." She privately thought that even if she and her husband had been starving, they could not have faced one of Agatha's shop-bought frozen meals.

Agatha lit a cigarette. "Agatha!" exclaimed Mrs. Bloxby, startled into the use of Agatha's first name. "You're smoking again!"

"Tastes all right now," mumbled Agatha.

John produced a small notebook. "I'll just make a note of these women who were close to Tristan. Let me see—there was a Miss Jellop, and then there were two others."

"Peggy Slither and Mrs. Tremp," said Mrs. Bloxby.

"You call her Peggy?" asked Agatha. "First name?"

"She is not a member of the ladies' society."

"What's she like and where does she live?" asked John.

"In Ancombe. A cottage called Shangri-la."

"That's a bit twee."

"I think she means it to be a sort of joke. She finds it fashionable to adopt the unfashionable. She has gnomes in her garden. That sort of thing. Rather loud and busty. About fifty. Her money comes from fish and chips. She never married. Her father had a profitable chain of fish and chip shops and she sold them when her father died."

"I know Miss Jellop," snapped Agatha, who did not like John's taking over the investigation.

Mrs. Bloxby leaned back and closed her eyes.

"We'd better go," said John.

"Phone me if there is anything I can do," said Agatha.

Mrs. Bloxby opened her eyes. "Just find out who did it."

When John and Agatha arrived back at Agatha's cottage it was to find Bill Wong waiting outside for them. "Thought I'd drop in for a chat. Trust you to land in trouble again, Agatha."

Agatha unlocked the door. "Come in and we'll have coffee in the garden."

Bill Wong was Agatha's first friend, a young police detective, half Chinese and half English. When they were seated in the garden, he surveyed Agatha with his brown slanting eyes. "I know you've already made a statement, but I'd like to know a bit more about your evening with Tristan. Did he come on to you?"

"Well, he kissed me."

"And didn't that let you know there was something funny about him?" demanded John sharply. "I mean, the difference in ages and all that."

"I have attracted younger men before," said Agatha waspishly.

"So he kissed you. When?" asked Bill.

"When I was leaving."

"What sort of kiss? Social peck?"

"No, a warm one, on the lips. What's all this about?"

"It's this money business. He was after money, we think. I wondered how far he was prepared to go. If he'd had a full-blown affair with any of them, that might have been a reason for murder."

"He didn't have an affair with me," said Agatha. "I'd have sussed him out sooner or later. I'm not *stupid*, you know."

"Women can become very stupid faced with such beauty. I saw him preach. My girl-friend heard all about him and dragged me along to church."

"Girl-friend?" Agatha was momentarily distracted.

"Alice. Alice Bryan. She works as a teller in Lloyds bank in Mircester."

"Serious?"

"It always is," said Bill sadly.

And it'll be over like a shot when she meets your parents, thought Agatha. Bill's parents could repel any girl-friend.

"Anyway," said Bill briskly, "what did you talk about?"

"Me, mostly," said Agatha ruefully. "When I realized it was all about me and nothing about him, I asked him about himself. He told me about working in New Cross and forming a boys' club and how the gang leaders thought they were losing members because of him. Five of them had attacked him one night and injured him and then he had a nervous breakdown."

"Which church in New Cross was it?" asked John.

"Saint Edmund's. Here! I don't want you pair poking your nose in and interfering with police work."

"As if we would," said Agatha, flashing John a warning look.

"What did you think of Tristan when you heard him preach?" John asked Bill.

"I thought him stupid and vain and the sermon was a load of nothing. On the other hand, I could have been jealous. Alice was gazing at him as if an angel had come to earth. So, Agatha, he didn't try to persuade you in any determined way to let him have money?"

"No, apart from suggesting he could invest some for me, he let the subject drop."

"Strikes me as odd from the little I know of him. Any suggestion of a future dinner date?"

"No!" Agatha flushed angrily. Bill eyed her shrewdly.

"He got Mrs. Feathers to go to a lot of trouble producing an expensive dinner and nothing came of it. I'll bet he thought you were a waste of space."

"If he thought so, he didn't tell me."

"We'll find out more when we study his bank account and find out who's been giving him money, and if he invested any of it, I'll eat my hat."

"It still seems odd, this idea of someone watching the cottage during the night and then following Tristan to the vicarage," said John. "If he'd cheated old Mrs. Feathers and she'd just found out about it, she could have heard him going out and followed him. The old sleep lightly."

"I can't see old Mrs. Feathers at her age going to tackle a young man like that."

"She could simply have meant to berate him if she found him taking the church money," pursued John, "and seized that letter opener and stabbed him. I mean, how many people would know that letter opener was so sharp? Did you, Agatha?"

"I was there one day talking to Mrs. Bloxby when he came in carrying the post. He was slicing open the letters and I remember thinking then that the letter opener must have been sharp. It was a silver one in the shape of a dagger. Not a real dagger."

"And what about the vicar himself?" asked John quietly. "I mean, he could have caught him at it. Was there any sign of a struggle?"

"No, Tristan was stabbed with one blow to the back of the neck."

"Yes, that would take a lot of force," said Agatha.

"Not necessarily," said Bill. "As the knife was sharp, once the skin was penetrated then the blade would sink in easily and it was sunk in up to the haft. Rather like stabbing a melon. But we'll know more after the post-mortem."

"I read somewhere," said John, "that victims of stab wounds don't often die immediately. Say the vicar did it, not in his study but at Tristan's. Wonder if he has a key to that cottage? Anyway, some people stabbed with a sharp thin blade can walk around for a couple of hours afterwards. Say the vicar stabbed Tristan and Tristan doesn't know how bad he's hurt. So he decides to clear off, but first of all, he's going to get that money out of the cash box and take it with him and he collapses in the vicar's study."

Agatha gave him an impatient look. "With the knife still in his neck?"

"Maybe he knew it was safer to leave it in until he got to a hospital."

"Oh, really? And some doctor looks at the knife in the back of his neck and promptly calls the police."

"Oh, shut up, you two," said Bill. "That's where amateurs

are such a menace. Stick to the facts, to what you know."

But John, undeterred, volunteered, "Maybe Alf Bloxby summoned him and made it look as if Tristan was robbing the church box."

"You're forgetting Mrs. Bloxby," said Agatha. "She would never cover up for her husband if he'd committed a murder."

"But she might not have known. They both probably claim to have slept through the whole business, but maybe she was heavily asleep."

"I've had enough," said Bill. "I'm off. Agatha, report to police headquarters tomorrow morning and sign a statement."

Agatha was driving the next morning. "Look out for that child on a bicycle!" shouted John at one point and at another, "You're going too fast."

Agatha sighed. "This is like a marriage without the nookie."

"May I point out that no sex was your choice?"

Agatha stared at him.

"Look at the road, Agatha, for God's sake!"

"What is up with you, John? You're usually so . . . so *placid*. Now you're bitching and whining like an old grump."

"I made some reasonable suggestions to Bill Wong yesterday and all you did was sneer."

"I thought they were a bit far-fetched. I'm entitled to my opinion."

"You could have told me afterwards. Look, Agatha. We are both amateurs at this game. There is no need to go on as if I am some sort of office boy."

"I never . . . Oh, let's drop the whole thing. I don't want to quarrel."

They continued in an uneasy silence.

After Agatha had made her statement, John said, "We should start off by going straight to New Cross."

"What? Right away?"

"Why not?"

"Oh, all right. But I don't like driving up to London."

"Then I'll drive, if your insurance covers me. Unless, of course, you have to be in the driver's seat all the time, both literally and metaphorically."

"Drive if you like," said Agatha huffily. "My insurance does cover you driving."

What had come over him? wondered Agatha, as they drove towards London. She was used to a rather colourless John. He had been going on as if he thought she was bossy. Like most high-powered people with a soft, shivering interior, Agatha considered herself a gentle lady, sensitive and sympathetic.

But by the time they reached New Cross, the driving seemed to have soothed John and he appeared to have reverted to his usual equable self. Probably his bad mood was nothing to do with me, thought Agatha. I don't upset people. Must have been someone or something else and he took it out on me.

John stopped the car and asked directions to St. Edmund's until he found a man who actually knew where the church was.

St. Edmund's was in a leafy backstreet. It was a Victorian building, still black from the soot of former coal-burning decades. White streaks of pigeon droppings cut through the soot up at the roof. It had four crenellated spires with weather vanes of gold pennants. Beside the church was a Victorian villa, also black with soot, which, they guessed, must be the vicarage.

John pressed the old-fashioned brass bell-push sunk into the stone wall beside the door.

The door was opened after a few moments by a heavy-set woman with her hair wound up in pink plastic rollers. She had a massive bosom under an overall and a large, truculent red face.

"Whatissit?"

"We would like to see the vicar," said John.

" 'Sinerstudy."

"Would you mind telling him we're here?"

Without asking them who they were, the woman shuffled off. "Poor man," murmured John. "What a housekeeper!"

The vicar arrived and peered at them curiously. He had what Agatha always thought of as a Church of England face: weak eyes behind thick glasses, sparse grey hair, grey skin, a bulbous nose and a fleshy mouth with thick pale lips.

"What do you want to see me about?" he asked. His voice was beautiful, the old Oxford accent, so pleasant to listen to that it sounds like no accent at all.

"I am Agatha Raisin and this is John Armitage. We both live in Carsely and are friends of the vicar there, Mr. Alfred Bloxby."

"Oh, dear." His face creased up in distress. "I heard about that dreadful murder on the news this morning. Terrible, terrible. How do you do. I am Fred Lancing. Do come in."

He led them into the study, a shabby book-lined room. "I should really take you through to the sitting-room," he said apologetically, "but I only really use this room and the others are rather damp and dusty. Would you like tea?"

"Yes, please," said Agatha.

He opened the door of the study and shouted, "Mrs. Buggy!"

"What yer want?" came the answering shout.

"Tea for three."

"Think I've got nothing better ter do?"

"Just do it!" shouted the vicar, turning pink.

He came back and sat down behind his desk. Agatha and

John sat side by side on an old black horsehair sofa. "It was those evening classes on feminism," he sighed. "Mrs. Buggy was much taken with them. She has regarded me as a tyrant ever since. How can I help you? Poor Tristan."

Agatha outlined what had happened and said they were afraid that the police suspected Mr. Bloxby and she and John wanted to help to clear his name.

The police called on me yesterday evening," said the vicar mildly. "But I really couldn't tell them anything much."

"Did Tristan really get beaten up by a gang and have a nervous breakdown?" asked Agatha.

"I gather that is what he said."

At that moment, the door crashed open and Mrs. Buggy entered with three cups of milky tea on a tray, which she crashed down on the vicar's desk.

"No biscuits," she snarled on her road out.

"I do hate bossy women," murmured the vicar.

"I do so agree with you," said John, flashing a look at Agatha.

"I did not know the vicar of Carsely—Mr. Bloxby, did you say?—was under suspicion."

"I'm afraid so," said Agatha. "Please tell us the truth about Tristan Delon. It could help. Someone murdered him and it could be someone from his past."

The vicar stood up and handed each of them a cup of tea before retreating behind his desk.

"I am wondering what to tell you," he said. "You see, if I tell you more than I have told the police, they will be very angry."

"I am a private detective," said Agatha. "I will not tell the police anything you say. I promise."

"I, I, I," murmured John, and Agatha threw him a fulminating look.

"De mortuis . . ." said the vicar. "I always think it is cruel to speak ill of the dead."

"But surely it is necessary if it can help bring justice to the living. I gather Tristan was gay," said John. Agatha stared at him in amazement.

"I believe so," said Mr. Lancing. "There are so many temptations in town for a young man."

"What temptations?" demanded Agatha sharply.

"He bragged about having a rich businessman as a friend and showed off a gold Rolex. But his homosexuality was not the problem. He should really have gone on the stage. He was very flamboyant in the pulpit. He charmed the parishioners—at first."

"And then what happened?" asked John.

"He seemed to become bored after he had been with me for a few weeks. It was then he developed a, well, nasty streak. He would find out some parishioner's vulnerable point and lean on it, if you know what I mean."

"Blackmail?" demanded Agatha eagerly.

"No, no. Just . . . well, to put it in one word . . . spite."

"Do you know the name of this businessman?" asked John.

There was a long silence, and then the vicar said, "No, although he bragged, he was very secretive about the details."

He does know who it is, thought John.

Agatha sat forward on the sofa, her bearlike eyes glistening. "So he didn't have a nervous breakdown. He didn't get beaten up."

"He did get beaten up."

"Because of his boys' club?"

"He didn't have a boys' club. He appeared very frightened, however. He said he had to get away. He seemed to become quite demented. He was also very penitent and said he wanted

37

to make a new start. I made inquiries and hit on the idea of removing him to a quiet country village. He had done nothing criminal, you see. And he did seem determined to become a better person."

"Did he have any particular friend in the parish?"

"He did have one, Sol MacGuire, a builder. He lives over the shops on Briory Road. Number sixteen. It's just around the corner if you turn left when you leave the vicarage."

Agatha rounded on John as soon as they had left the vicarage. "How did you know he was gay?"

"I didn't. It was just a wild guess."

"Humph!"

"And I'll bet he knows the name of that businessman."

"He wouldn't lie."

"Because he's a vicar? Come *on*, Agatha. You can be surprisingly naïve at times."

"I don't believe you," said Agatha furiously.

They walked in silence round the corner to Briory Road. It was a shabbier street with smaller houses. Number 16 had an excuse for a front garden: a sagging privet hedge, a broken bicycle, rank grass and weeds.

No one answered their knock. They tried the neighbours and were told he was probably out working but that he usually came home around six in the evening.

"Four hours to kill," said John, looking at his watch. "But we haven't eaten anything. Let's find a pub."

They found one out in the main road where traffic shimmered in the heat. John pushed open the door and they walked into the gloom. It was fairly empty. It was an old-fashioned London pub which had not yet been "bistro-fied" like many others. Sunlight shone dimly through the dusty windows. Fruit machines winked and blinked. But at least there was no pipe-in Muzak. The landlord, a thin, sour man, said lunches were over but that he could make them some sandwiches. They ordered ham sandwiches and beer and when their order arrived, retreated to a corner table.

"At least we're a bit ahead of the police," said Agatha.

"Only a bit ahead. They'll be back again sometime to ask the vicar more questions, and having told us, he'll probably now tell them."

"Do you really think so? He might not want to tell them now and let them know he was withholding informations in the first place."

"Maybe. These sandwiches are awful. I haven't had pub sandwiches like these in years. The ham is slimy and the bread's dry."

"Keeping up the good old English pub traditions," said Agatha gloomily.

"This news about the rich man is interesting, though," said John. "I mean, if he's really someone important, he might have wanted to get rid of Tristan. Maybe Tristan was blackmailing him."

"We forgot to ask how long it was between Tristan leaving New Cross and Tristan arriving in Carsely."

"How would that help?"

"If it was a long period, he might not have that much left in his bank account. You see, he wasn't in Carsely long enough to fleece anyone to any significant degree. I think he liked to spend money on himself. Whatever he had got, he might have dissipated so his bank account won't give much of a clue."

"It will," said John, "if it shows cheques from any of the villagers, or from this businessman, whoever he is."

They debated the mystery and then left the pub and wandered around the streets of New Cross, past Indian shops and Turkish restaurants until John looked at his watch and said, "Time to go back to see if Sol MacGuire is at home."

THREE

✝

SOL MacGuire was another Adonis, but a black-haired, blue-eyed one. He looked shocked when they told him they were investigating the murder of Tristan Delon.

"Sure, now, isn't that the big shock you've given me," he said. "Come on in."

They followed him into a small living-room which seemed to be full of old beer cans and old copies of newspapers and magazines.

"Find a space and sit yourselves down," said Sol. "How was he murdered? I haven't kept up with the news."

John told him and then asked what he knew about Tristan. "Not that much," said Sol. "He saw me working on a local building site and kept coming round to chat. I told him flat-out I wasn't gay and he just laughed and said he wasn't gay either."

"I couldn't be bothered much with him at first, but he kept coming round. He was funny in a malicious way, know what I mean?"

"Give us an example?" asked Agatha.

"He was adored by the women in the parish, but he seemed to despise them."

"Anyone in particular?"

"He'd talk about a Mrs. Hill. Said she used to look at him like a dog. He said he felt like snapping his fingers and tossing her a biscuit. Things like that."

Agatha leaned forward. "Did Tristan ever talk about some businessman, someone who gave him presents?"

"Oh, that. Mind if I get myself a beer?"

"Go ahead."

"Want one?"

"Not for me," said John. "I've already had some beer and I'm driving. What about you, Agatha?"

"Not for me either."

Sol disappeared and returned after a few moments with a can of beer which he popped open. After a hearty swig, he wiped his mouth with the back of his hand and said, "He showed me a gold Rolex. Said it was a present from Richard Binser."

Agatha's eyes opened wide in amazement. "Richard Binser, the tycoon?"

"That's what he said. But then, he was a terrible liar."

"Do you know who beat him up?"

"He said it was one of the gangs, but he didn't know any gangs. Trust me. Maybe one of them women got wise to him and took a club to him. I dunno."

"Do you know where this Mrs. Hill lives?"

"He told me. It's a big house round in Jeves Place. You cross the main road, take Gladstone Street, turn right on Palmerston, then first left is Jeves. Don't know the number, but it's a big place on its own. I'm curious, like," went on Sol, his accent an odd mixture of Irish and south London. "Why ask questions around here, and why you? You his relatives?"

"No," said Agatha. "We are private detectives."

"Got a licence?"

"Pending," lied Agatha.

"Well, good luck to you. But if he was murdered in that village, stands to reason someone down there killed him."

"Do you know how long it was," asked Agatha, "between the attack and him leaving here?"

"He came round once after the attack. Said he was going abroad. Would be about six months ago."

"That long!"

"See what I mean?" said Sol. "He was old history far as New Cross was concerned."

When they left Sol, Agatha said, "Let's go after Binser."

"It's late. We can find his offices—I think they're in Cheapside in the City. As we're here, shouldn't we try Mrs. Hill?"

"All right, though mark my words, she'll just turn out to be a sad middle-aged woman, duped by Tristan."

"Like you," murmured John.

Agatha glared at him and stalked on in an angry silence.

When they found the villa in Jeves Place, it appeared there was no one at home. Far in the distance came the menacing rumble of thunder.

"I think we should leave things for tonight," said John, "drive back to Carsely and try Binser tomorrow and then Mrs. Hill."

Agatha agreed because she was tired.

The storm burst halfway to Carsely and John had to drive very slowly through the torrents of rain. As he turned at last into the road leading down into Carsely, the storm clouds rolled away. He opened the car window and a chilly little breeze blew in.

"End of summer," said Agatha. "What time do we set off in the morning?"

"Early. About six-thirty. Beat the rush. Don't groan. We'll take my car and you can sleep on the road up to town if you're still tired."

Agatha said good night to him when they reached Lilac Lane. Her cats came to meet her, yawning and purring. She fed them and then put a lasagne—Mama Livia's Special—in the microwave.

After she had eaten, she bathed and went to bed. Before she went to sleep, she fought down nagging jabs of conscience that were telling her that she should have phoned Bill Wong and brought him up-to-date on what they had found.

"If Binser is in his office, we'll be lucky," said John as he joined the traffic heading for London on the M25 the next morning. "He travels a lot."

"Maybe we should have waited at home and phoned him," said Agatha sleepily.

"Best to surprise him."

"How are we going to get past all the minions he'll surely have to protect him?"

"We'll send in a note saying we want to see him about Tristan Delon."

"And if he doesn't see us?"

"Oh, do shut up, Agatha. We have to try."

"It will be difficult," pursued Agatha. "I remember seeing pictures of him in *Celeb* magazine. Wife and two children."

"Like I said, we must try."

Richard Binser's offices were in an impressive modern

building of steel and glass with a great tree growing up to the glass roof from the entrance hall.

"Here goes," said Agatha, marching up to the long reception desk where four beautiful and fashionably thin young ladies were answering phones.

"Mr. Binser," said Agatha to the one she considered the least intimidating.

"What time is your appointment?"

"We don't have one," said Agatha. She produced a sealed envelope which contained a note she had written in the car. It was marked "Urgent, Private & Confidential." "See that he gets this right away. I am sure he will want to see us."

"Take a seat," said the receptionist, indicating a bank of sofas and chairs over by the entrance doors.

They sat down and waited, and waited.

At last the receptionist they had spoken to approached them and said, "I will take you up. Follow me."

A glass elevator bore them up and up to the top of the building. It opened into another reception area. A middle-aged secretary greeted them and asked them to wait.

Again, they sat down. The receptionist had gone back downstairs and the secretary had retreated through a door leading off the reception. It was very quiet.

Agatha was just beginning to wonder if everyone had forgotten about them, when the secretary came back and said, "Mr. Binser will see you now."

She led them through an inner office and then opened a heavy door leading off it and ushered them into a room where a small, balding man sat behind a large Georgian desk.

He did not rise to meet them, simply surveyed them coldly, then said, "That will be all, Miss Partle. I will call you if I need you."

The secretary left and closed the door behind her.

"Sit!" commanded Richard Binser, indicating two low chairs in front of his desk.

Agatha and John sat down.

"You are not quite what I expected. I am taping this and I warn you both if you try to blackmail me, I will call the police."

"We are not here to blackmail you," said John. "We are investigating the death of Tristan Delon."

"And you are?"

"John Armitage and Agatha Raisin."

"John Armitage. The writer?"

"Yes."

"I've read all your books." The tycoon visibly thawed.

John explained that they both lived in Carsely and were friends of the vicar and anxious to clear his name; that they had learned that Binser had given Tristan presents.

Binser switched off the tape recorder and passed a hand over his forehead. "I thought you were his relatives."

"Was Tristan trying to blackmail you?"

"Oh, yes, but he didn't get anywhere. I may as well tell you what happened. I suppose the police will find out about me eventually. Where shall I begin? I give a lot of money to charities, but my employees sift through the applications, type up a report and I decide how much each should get. Therefore I was a bit taken aback when my senior secretary, Miss Partle, insisted that I should see Tristan in person. It seemed he wanted to raise funds to start a boys' club in New Cross. I was amused that my usually stern secretary appeared to have been bowled over by this Tristan and so I agreed to see him. He was so beautiful and so charming that I began at times to doubt my own sexuality. He flattered me very cleverly. I do not have a son and it amused me to see the way Tristan's eyes lit up when I gave him a present. Then I cut off the friendship."

"Why?" asked Agatha.

"I went down to the church in New Cross one day to find out how the boys' club was getting along. I had given Tristan a cheque for ten thousand pounds to rent a hall and buy equipment. He had asked for more money, but being first and last a businessman, I wanted to see how he had used the money he already had. He was out when I called, but the vicar was there. He said he'd never heard of a boys' club. Tristan came in at that point and waffled and protested that he had meant it to be a surprise but it became clear to me that he had done nothing. I did not want anyone to know how I had been suckered and so I left the vicar to deal with him. Then Tristan wrote to me, threatening to tell my wife that we'd had an affair—which we most certainly had not—and saying he would show her the presents I had given him. I told him if he approached me again I would go straight to the police and that I'd taped his call. All my calls are taped. I never heard from him again. But I was puzzled at being so easily taken in. I consulted a psychiatrist friend and outlined what I knew of Tristan's character. He asked me if Tristan was fascinated by mirrors. It seemed an odd question, but I remembered that on the few occasions I had taken Tristan out for dinner to a restaurant with a lot of mirrors that he would sit gazing fascinated at his own reflection.

"The psychiatrist said he was probably a somatic narcissist and that this type of narcissist could charm people by exuding that warm, fuzzy emotional feeling of well-being you get on a good day. He said this type could be prone to violence.

"Anyway, that was Tristan's charm. He made me feel good about myself. I was sure, however, that I would hear from him again, but not a word. When I received your note, I thought he had left some journal about our friendship and that you had come to blackmail me. But that's all there was to it. I pride myself on being a good judge of character and yet Tristan had me completely fooled."

"I don't think the police need to know about this," said John, "unless the vicar tells them. We certainly won't. Will we, Agatha?"

Again those jabs of conscience. But Agatha said reluctantly, "No."

"I liked him," said John, as they joined the stream of traffic heading for south London.

"Binser? I suppose."

"You don't seem too sure."

"I had it in my mind that whoever beat him up or had him beaten up had something to do with his murder. A powerful man like Binser could have had him beaten up."

"You've been watching too many left-wing dramas on the box about sinister company executives, Agatha."

"It could have happened that way," said Agatha stubbornly.

A glaring, watery sunlight was bathing London. Agatha glanced sideways at John and noticed for the first time the loosening of the skin under his chin and the network of wrinkles at the side of his eyes. This for some reason made her feel cheerful and she began to whistle tunelessly until John told her to stop.

Back at New Cross, they drove round to Jeves Place and parked in front of the villa. The front door was standing a few inches open. "Someone's at home," said Agatha.

"Good," said John. "Let's go."

A thin voice was singing a hymn somewhere in the interior of the house. John rang the bell. A very small woman with greying hair and a sallow skin came to the door carrying a feather duster.

"Mrs. Hill?" asked Agatha, pushing in front of John who,

she obscurely felt, was taking over too much of this investigation.

"Yes. I am Mrs. Hill."

Agatha introduced both of them and launched into their reasons for wanting to speak to her.

Mrs. Hill stepped out on the doorstep and looked nervously up and down the street. "You'd better come in," she whispered, although the street was empty.

She led them into a large dark room full of heavy old furniture. "I was shocked about poor Tristan's death," she said. "Such a good young man."

"May we sit down?" asked Agatha.

"Oh, please do."

John and Agatha sat in hard high-backed chairs and Mrs. Hill sank down on the edge of an armchair and looked at them with all the fascination of a bird confronted with a snake.

"He wasn't very good at all, as it turns out," said Agatha bluntly. "He conned a respectable businessman out of money to set up a boys' club, and of course he kept the money. No boys' club."

John glared at Agatha and mouthed, "Shut up!" The business about Binser should surely be kept private.

But tears welled up in little Mrs. Hill's eyes and rolled down her cheeks. "I'm so glad I wasn't the only one," she choked out. "I've felt such a fool."

John passed her a large clean handkerchief and she dried her eyes and blew her nose. "Tell us about him," said Agatha gently.

"I felt so silly, so betrayed. You see, I adored him. I saw later what must have happened. All the houses in this street are split up into flats except mine. I have the reputation of being wealthy. I am referred to as the rich Mrs. Hill. But to go back

49

to the beginning. Tristan flattered me. He made me feel good, made me feel worthwhile. I was quite dazed by the impact he had on me. We occasionally went out together, but somewhere where no one would recognize us. He said he didn't want me making the other women of the parish jealous. He said he cared for me. He said that he thought age difference was no barrier when two people respected each other." She wiped away a tear. "I lived and breathed for him. Then he asked me for a donation for this boys' club he said he was setting up. I confided in him that I had no money to spare. I lived on very little. I said I hoped my savings would last until I died. He asked me a lot of questions about how much I was worth, seemingly sympathetically. And then he stopped calling. I thought he loved me," she wailed. "He said he loved me. And I . . . I would have died for him."

She gave a great gulp and then went on. "I waited outside the vicarage one day until I saw him coming out and I asked him why he had been avoiding me. I reminded him he'd said he loved me. He laughed in my face. He said he was gay. He said a lot of things I don't want to repeat. I could have killed him. But I didn't."

"Do you think he did get money out of anyone else?" asked John quietly.

"I don't know. It was, before he came, a tiny congregation. When he preached instead of the vicar, a lot of people came but mostly silly young girls. Please, you won't tell anyone what I've told you. I couldn't bear it."

"We won't unless we have to," said Agatha. "You've got a lot of rooms here, haven't you?"

"Too many," she said in a hollow voice.

"You should let a few rooms out," said Agatha bracingly. "Give you an income."

"But I might get, well, bad people."

"Use an estate agent to handle the renting for you. You couldn't charge all that much because they wouldn't have private kitchens or bathrooms, not unless you spent a lot of money on renovation. I saw an estate agent's out in the main road that handles rentals. They could vet the people for you. Means you wouldn't be alone in this house either. I mean, no children, no pets; just collect the money."

"I couldn't . . ."

"Oh, yes, you could. Look, get your coat and we'll go with you to that estate agent and see what they say."

John Armitage wanted to question the vicar again. The vicar had deliberately lied to them about Richard Binser. He knew Binser because Binser had said he called on him. The vicar had also said that Tristan had done nothing criminal and yet he had. He had pocketed ten thousand pounds. But John had to fret with impatience while Agatha plunged happily into room rentals with Mrs. Hill, who was looking happier by the minute. A representative from the estate agent's then had to come back to the house with them and inspect the rooms. He said for a modest sum she could have wash-basins installed in the bedrooms and allow tenants the use of the kitchen. He seemed as bossy and managing as Agatha Raisin, and Mrs. Hill was delighted to be ordered what to do. When Agatha finally decided she had done enough, a grateful and tearful Mrs. Hill hugged her and said she had given her a new start in life. Agatha said gruffly it was her pleasure, but looked every bit as bored as she was beginning to feel.

"Well, now that waste of space is over," said John crossly, "I want to see that vicar again."

"I had to do something for the poor soul," snapped Agatha.

"That poor soul, as you call her, could have stabbed Tristan. We never asked her what she was doing on the night he was murdered. If you are going to be so trusting about every suspect, we may as well pack it in."

"I'm beginning to think I don't really know you," said Agatha. "You're quite nasty."

"You don't even know yourself, Agatha Raisin."

"Are we going to stand here all day bickering?"

"I want to talk to that vicar again."

"So let's get on with it, for God's sake!"

"I'm tired and we haven't eaten."

"We'll get something after we grill the vicar. But not that pub again."

The vicar of St. Edmund's looked distinctly unhappy to see them again. There was no sign of his ferocious housekeeper.

"I am rather busy writing my sermon," he began.

"We will only take a few minutes of your time, Mr. Lancing," said Agatha. "We want to know why you lied to us."

"Dear me. You'd better come in."

When they were once more seated in his study, Agatha began. "You told us that Tristan had done nothing criminal. Yet he had conned Mr. Binser out of ten thousand pounds. You also told us that you did not know Mr. Binser and yet he said he called on you."

"He did call on me but he urged me not to tell anyone how he had been fooled by Tristan. He said it would be bad for his business image. And Tristan was so truly penitent. He assured me he would pay back every penny."

"Well, we gather he didn't."

"I am sorry I lied to you, but I did give Mr. Binser my solemn word that I would not say anything."

"Is there anything else you have not told us?"

"Not that I can think of." Mr. Lancing gave them a strained look. "Surely what I have told you is enough." His voice became angry. "You are not the police. I should never have spoken to you in the first place. You have no authority."

"We are merely trying to help our local vicar, Mr. Bloxby," said John gently. "Surely you can see that. The police will not hear of anything you have told us unless it is really necessary."

"Then would you mind leaving? You have upset me very much."

"And that's that," said Agatha wearily. "Let's get something to eat."

They stopped at a service station on the A40 for a greasy all-day breakfast of egg, sausage and chips.

"I keep having a feeling we're wasting our time up in London," said John. "The murder was committed in Carsely and I'm sure our murderer lives in the village or round about."

"No, I think the clues lie in London," said Agatha, more out of a desire to contradict John than because she really believed it.

They took to the road again and Agatha fell asleep and did not wake until they were going through Woodstock. "Goodness, have I been asleep all that time?" she said, sitting upright.

"Yes," said John, "and you snored terribly."

"I've had enough of you for one day," snarled Agatha. "You're always nit-picking about something."

"I was merely stating a fact," he said stiffly.

Agatha stifled a yawn and thought longingly of the comfort and peace of her cottage.

When John finally drove into the village, it was to see the narrow main street almost blocked by two television vans.

"I thought the press would have given up by now," said John.

He turned into Lilac Lane. A police car was standing outside Agatha's cottage. "Listen," said John fiercely, "I don't know what's going on, but tell them we simply went up to London for the day to look at the shops and have a meal. No, wait, they'll check restaurants. We can tell them about the service station and then just say we had taken a picnic lunch and ate it in Green Park."

When they parked, Bill Wong and a detective constable and a policewoman got out of the waiting car.

Bill looked grim. "Where were you, Mrs. Raisin?" he demanded. Agatha's heart sank at the formal use of her second name.

"In London, going around the shops," she said. "Why?"

"We'd better go inside," said Bill. "You come along as well, Mr. Armitage."

Agatha unlocked her cottage door. "Come into the kitchen," she said, nearly tripping over her cats, which were winding themselves around her ankles.

When they were all seated around the kitchen table, Agatha said, "What's this about? I've made a statement."

"There has been a further development," said Bill, his eyes hard. Then he winced as Hodge dug his nails into his trouser leg.

"Miss Jellop has been murdered."

FOUR

✝

"HOW? When?" asked Agatha.

"We cannot ascertain the exact time of death at the moment, but sometime early this evening. She was strangled. She lives alone and might not have been found for some time except Mrs. Bloxby went to call on her and found the door open and then found Miss Jellop."

"Poor Mrs. Bloxby!" Agatha half-rose. "I'd better go to her."

"Sit down! Detective Inspector Wilkes is with her. Let's go through your movements."

"But we're not suspects, surely?"

"You stir things up and I would like to know just what you've been stirring."

John took over. "We decided to get out of the village. We

took a picnic and had that in the Green Park. We went round the shops, window-gazing. Then we stopped at that service station on the A40 and had an all-day breakfast."

"When?"

"About an hour and a half ago."

"You weren't up in New Cross trying to play detective?"

"No," said John, praying that the vicar would keep silent.

"So you went off together for the day. Why?"

"We wanted to look at the shops. That's all." John desperately improvised. "As a matter of fact, we took a walk around Kensington as well to see if there was a location that might suit us."

"What location? Why?"

John took a deep breath. He was tired and the news of this second murder had rattled him. "Because we're thinking of getting married."

Cursing him inside, Agatha forced a cheesy smile onto her face and said, "I didn't tell you before. I wanted it to be a surprise."

"And when is this wedding to take place?"

"We haven't fixed the date yet," said Agatha. "But when the time comes, Bill, I hope you'll give me away."

Bill's almond-shaped eyes fixed on both their faces. "I don't believe this," he said flatly. "But we will check out your alibi."

The questions continued. Had anyone talked to them in the shops, in Green Park, at Kensington? They were both tired and began to find it easy to lie, both sticking to their stories until Agatha almost began to believe they really were going to get married.

When the questions had finished, Agatha asked, "So does that mean Mr. Bloxby is in the clear?"

"No one is in the clear," said Bill. "Don't take any more trips in the next few days."

When they had gone, John could see that Agatha was about to round on him about their supposed forthcoming marriage.

"Save it," he snapped. "We've got to get on the phone to that vicar and to Mrs. Hill and tell them to keep quiet."

"You do it, O future husband of mine," said Agatha. "I'm going to get a drink."

"Get a large whisky for me at the same time. Before you do that, give me Mrs. Hill's number. I saw you taking a note of it."

Agatha gave him the number. She went into the sitting-room and poured a large gin and tonic for herself and a whisky for John and then sat down, hearing his voice talking on the phone, but unable to make out the words because she had closed the sitting-room door. They should have told Bill the truth, she thought wearily. It looked as if John had been right and that the murderer was down here in the Cotswolds.

The doorbell rang. She peered through the curtains and saw several members of the press outside.

She let the doorbell ring and sat sipping her drink until John joined her.

"That the press outside?" he asked.

"Yes, lots of them. Why on earth did you say we were getting married?"

"On impulse. This second murder rattled me. We can go along with it for the moment and then say we broke up."

"Bill didn't believe us."

"He will. All we have to do is look a bit lover-like when he calls again—which he will. Feel up to it?"

"I don't feel up to anything at the moment," said Agatha. "Why was Miss Jellop murdered?"

"She obviously knew something. I think the best thing for us to do is lie low and let things quieten down. We can go and see Mrs. Bloxby when the coast is clear. She'll know all about Miss Jellop. Who were the two others Mrs. Bloxby talked about?"

"Peggy Slither over at Ancombe and Colonel Tremp's widow."

"We can't very well talk to them with police and press swarming all over the place. Do you want me to stay the night?"

"No," said Agatha. "I thought we had sorted all that out."

"I only meant for protection. Someone might want to shut you up as well."

Agatha gave a shudder but said, "I'll be all right."

The phone rang. "You get it," said Agatha.

John went out to the phone in the hall and then returned a few moments later. "Press," he said. "I thought your number was ex-directory."

"It is, but the press have ways of finding out ex-directory numbers. Unplug it from the wall as you go."

"Meaning you want to be alone?"

"Exactly."

John took a gulp of the whisky in his glass, placed the glass carefully on the table and made for the door.

"Scream if you want me," he called.

Agatha sat nursing her drink after he had left. From time to time the doorbell shrilled. The press were persistent. They must have seen the police car outside her cottage earlier.

Then she rose stiffly and went up to bed. She carefully removed her make-up and peered at her face in the magnifying mirror in the bathroom. The lines around her mouth seemed to have got deeper. She undressed, took a quick shower, pulled on a night-dress and crawled into bed and lay staring up at the beams in the ceiling. At last the shrilling of the doorbell fell silent and she sank into an uneasy sleep.

It was early afternoon the next day when she remembered the phone was still unplugged and reconnected it. She dialled John's number. "What are you doing?" she asked.

"Writing. But I've got something for you. I'll be right over."

"Knock the door, then, don't ring and I'll know it's you."

Agatha was wearing an old blue linen dress and flat sandals. She wondered whether to change into something more fashionable, but then reminded herself—it was only John.

When the knock came at the door, she answered it. John followed her through to the kitchen and put a small jeweller's box on the table. "I think you'd better start wearing that to keep up the fiction."

Agatha opened the box and found herself looking down at an engagement ring, a large sapphire surrounded by diamond chips.

"When did you get this?" she asked.

"Years ago. It's my ex-wife's. She flung it in my face just before we broke up. Try it on."

Agatha slid it on over the wedding band she still wore. It was a perfect fit.

A tear rolled down her face and plopped on the kitchen table.

"What's up?" said John.

Agatha gave a shaky laugh. "I still have the engagement ring James gave me. I couldn't bear to wear it although I still wear his wedding ring."

John gave her a brief hug. "Best you wear a different one. Unless I'm mistaken, Bill Wong will be back soon. I'll make us

59

some coffee. Those cats of yours are prancing all over the kitchen table. Do you allow that?"

"I'm afraid I let them do what they like. The table's scrubbed regularly. Still, you're right." She lifted both cats off the table, opened the door to the garden and shooed them out.

John was spooning coffee into the percolator when the doorbell rang.

"I wonder if that's the press again." Agatha went to the front door and peered through the spy-hole. "It's Mrs. Bloxby," she called.

She swung open the door. "Come in. Poor you. What a nightmare. Where is your husband?"

"Helping the police with their inquiries."

Mrs. Bloxby sat down at the kitchen table. "Coffee?" asked John. "It'll be ready in a moment."

"Yes, please," said Mrs. Bloxby. "Milk and no sugar."

"Why Miss Jellop?"

"I just don't know," said Mrs. Bloxby. She accepted a cup of coffee from John. "Such a silly, harmless woman."

"Where did she come from? Everyone in Cotswold villages these days seems to come from outside. No wonder the locals complain about the villages losing their character."

"Miss Jellop moved here from somewhere in Staffordshire. I believe she was comfortably off. Her family were in jam. Jellop's Jams and Jellies. Not much known around here but very popular in the north."

"Does Alf have an alibi?"

"They don't know the exact time of death, sometime in the evening. Alf was working in his study and I remembered that Miss Jellop had phoned in the morning. She wanted me to call round because she said she wanted to talk to me about something. She was always complaining about happenings in the parish and she wanted the church livened up, as she put it.

Wanted to hire a steel band from Birmingham to perform at the services, that sort of thing. I phoned back late afternoon and said I would be around about nine in the evening. The door of her house was slightly open. There was no answer when I rang the doorbell and I went in, worried that she might have met with an accident." Mrs. Bloxby raised a trembling hand to her mouth. "And there she was."

"Did she have anything around her neck?"

"I couldn't see. I mean, I forced myself to check her pulse and then I phoned for the police and ambulance. But I couldn't bear to look at her closely."

"Villages are getting like the city," said John. "Nobody notices things the way they would have done in the old days, when everyone minded everyone else's business. There's a high hedge on either side of her garden, as I remember, that effectively screens the door from the neighbours on either side."

"Let's see," said Agatha. "She lived in a terraced cottage on Dover Rise up behind the general stores. It's a cul-de-sac. Surely someone must have seen someone walking along."

"If you remember, there are only four cottages in that row. Mr. and Mrs. Witherspoon were away in Evesham visiting their daughter. That's the first cottage you come to. Then there's Mr. and Mrs. Partington. They were in their back parlour away from the road for a good part of the evening watching a couple of rented videos and eating TV dinners. Then comes Miss Jellop, and at the end of the row, Miss Debenham, who was with her sister in Cheltenham and stayed there the night."

"How come you're so well-informed?" asked Agatha.

"I've had police in the vicarage half the night and they often talk as if I'm not there."

"So we come back to Miss Jellop," said John. "Did you overhear the police say anything about Tristan's bank account?"

"Yes, I did, as a matter of fact. He paid several sums into

his account over the past few weeks, but all in cash. Before this murder, they interviewed several of the women they think he might have preyed on, but they all swear they gave him nothing. They say they had been thinking about it. They even checked old Mrs. Feathers's bank account, but the only large sum—large sum to her—she had drawn out recently was to supply you with dinner, Mrs. Raisin. She evidently said he had promised to invest money for her, but women like Mrs. Feathers are frightened of old age and harvest every penny. The fact that Tristan even got her to pay for his meals says a lot for his charm."

"So did you hear how much he had in his account?" asked Agatha.

Mrs. Bloxby shook her head. Her usually mild grey eyes were full of worry and pain. "I am so worried about poor Alf. Did you find out anything?"

"We don't want the police to know," cautioned Agatha, "because they would give us a rocket for interfering." She told Mrs. Bloxby about the visit to New Cross and to Binser.

"If only it would turn out to be someone from London," sighed the vicar's wife. "The atmosphere in the village is poisonous, all these silly women telling the police that Alf was jealous of Mr. Delon."

Pale sunlight shining in through the kitchen window sparkled on the ring on Agatha's finger.

"That's a new ring," exclaimed Mrs. Bloxby.

"John got rattled and told Bill Wong we were engaged to cover up what we were doing in London," said Agatha.

"Perhaps you should have told him the truth," said Mrs. Bloxby. "Anything to get the investigation away from poor Alf."

"I really don't think Mr. Bloxby has anything to worry about," said John soothingly. "In order to suspect him of the first murder, they would need to think you were lying to protect him and no one could believe that."

Agatha was about to point out waspishly that John *had* suggested to her Mrs. Bloxby might be lying, but with rare tact refrained from saying anything.

"I'd better get back," said Mrs. Bloxby, rising to her feet. "Alf might be back any time and I wouldn't want him to find the vicarage empty."

"Do you want us to come with you? Aren't the press pestering you?"

"They've gone, apart from a few local reporters."

Agatha saw Mrs. Bloxby out and returned to John. "Let's switch on television and look at the news," he said. "Something big must have happened to send them running off."

"Wait until the top of the hour," said Agatha. "It's twenty to three. It'll be sport on every channel."

She lit a cigarette. "That's a filthy habit," remarked John.

"I know," she sighed, "but one I love a lot."

"We'll just need to wait. Things'll be easier if the press have gone. We could leave it until tomorrow and then try to see what we can get out of this Peggy Slither. She's in Ancombe and the police won't be hanging around there. Did Mrs. Bloxby say where she lived?"

"I can't remember. Wait and I'll get the phone-book." Agatha went out and came back with the telephone directory.

As Agatha turned the pages, John said, "I remember. Shangri-la. That was the name of her place."

"That's right. Gnomes in the garden. I remember. Here it is. Doesn't give a street, just the name of the bloody house, as if the snobby cow lived in a manor. Well, Ancombe's a small place. Should be easy to find."

They turned over various bits and pieces of what they knew until Agatha noticed it was almost three o'clock. "Let's look at the television news now."

They went into Agatha's sitting-room and she switched on

the television set and selected the BBC *24-Hour News* pro-
gramme.

The announcer said, "The Liberal Democrats, the Scottish
Nationalists, and the Unionists have combined to table a motion
of no confidence in the government following the revelations
that the defence minister, Joseph Demerall, had been accepting
large sums of money from Colonel Gadaffi."

"So that's it," said Agatha. "The press won't be interested
in a village murder, or murders. At least we should get some
peace."

"I think I'll go and get on with my writing," said John,
getting to his feet. "I'll call for you in the morning, say around
ten."

"All right," said Agatha, although she suddenly did not
want to be left alone.

"See you."

Agatha wondered what to do. A pile of shiny new paperbacks she had bought in Evesham lay on the coffee-table. She
picked up the first one. *Jerry's Mistake,* it was called. Agatha
sighed as she skimmed the pages. She shouldn't have wasted
her money. It was a chic-fic book, which meant it would be
about thirty-something women in London. There would be one
Cinderella character who would have a gay best friend and the
best friend would die from AIDS in the penultimate chapter.
The hero would have muscled legs and be bad-tempered. She
tossed it aside. The next was the first Harry Potter book. Agatha
had bought it out of curiosity. She settled down to read and
became dimly aware an hour later that the doorbell was ringing.
She looked through the spy-hole and saw Bill Wong. With feelings of guilt and reluctance she opened the door. He was alone.

"I think it's time you and I had a chat, Agatha."

"Come in and bring the thumbscrews with you. We'll sit
in the garden. It doesn't look too cold."

"No, it's nice and fresh after that storm."

Agatha collected two mugs of coffee and carried them out into the garden. Hodge and Boswell climbed up on Bill. Hodge settled on his lap and Boswell draped himself around Bill's neck.

"Amazing how those cats like you," said Agatha.

"I'd like to concentrate on the matter in hand, however." Bill gently removed both cats and put them down on the grass. "Now, Agatha, I see you already have the ring. But why do I get the impression that the pair of you were lying to me?"

"Because you've got a nasty, suspicious policeman's mind. We are very much in love. No, I'll be honest with you. We get along together very well and neither of us wants to go into old age alone. So we decided to get hitched."

"If you say so. No word of James?"

"I may as well tell you. That lying bastard never returned to that monastery."

"He'll turn up again. With your luck, probably on your wedding day."

"Forget about him. Any ideas why Miss Jellop was murdered?"

"I think she might have found out something. I think that was why she phoned Mrs. Bloxby. And yet Mrs. Bloxby said Miss Jellop was always summoning her to make some complaint or another."

"Was she rich?"

"Very comfortably off."

"Anyone inherit?"

"She hadn't left a will. Her nearest relative was a sister who lives in Stoke-on-Trent."

"Tell me, Bill—anything funny in Tristan's bank account?"

"Large sums of money, not great—five hundred here, six hundred there, all deposited in cash. Total around fifteen thousand. Seems he invented that family trust. He was born Terence

65

Biles. Father was a post-office worker, mother a housewife. Both dead. Tristan changed his name by deed poll when he was seventeen. His parents were dead then. Nothing in his past. Good exam results at school. Studied divinity. Had the curacy of a church in Kensington for a few years. Nothing sinister there. Vicar said Tristan had declared he wanted to work in a rougher area. He seemed genuinely sorry to let him go.

"So, Agatha, you haven't been poking your nose in where you shouldn't?"

"No. I really have gone off the idea of detecting. I want to live a long and quiet life."

Bill stood up. "If you hadn't said that, I might actually have begun to believe you really were getting married. But you wanting a quiet life? Never! Just make sure if you do find anything that you tell me."

After he had gone, Agatha sat on in the garden, deep in thought. What had happened to that ten thousand? The police would not have asked the bank about it because they didn't know about it. Perhaps Tristan had asked for it in bits and pieces so as not to alert the income tax.

Agatha phoned Binser's office and asked to speak to him. She finally got through to his personal secretary, Miss Partle. "I really do wish you would leave him alone," said the secretary sharply. "He is very busy."

Agatha drew a deep breath. "Look, lady, just get off your bum and tell him that Agatha Raisin wishes to speak to him."

"Well, *really*."

Agatha waited and then Binser's voice came on the line. "What now?" he said. "I've told you all I know."

"It's just about that ten thousand pounds. How did you pay it?"

"Cash."

"Cash!" echoed Agatha. "That's odd."

"I know it's odd, but I think Tristan twisted my mind. He said he was setting up a special account with a bank in New Cross. He could get started right away if he didn't have to wait to get the cheque to clear."

"I know you didn't want anyone to know you had been conned. Still, I would have thought a man like you would have sued him to get the money back."

"He sent it back."

"What! You didn't say anything about that. When?"

"About a month after I had confronted him. The money was delivered downstairs in a large envelope, addressed to me."

"Was there any letter with the money? Perhaps he was hoping to resume the friendship."

"No, there was no letter. I heard from him a week after that when he threatened to blackmail me. And as I told you, I said I would report him to the police if he did, and heard no more from him. Now, if you don't mind, Mrs. Raisin, as far as I am concerned the matter is closed. I have heard on the news about the other murder in your village. Obviously the murderer is in your neck of the woods. Goodbye."

Agatha replaced the receiver and stood thinking hard. What would have made Tristan return that money? Mr. Lancing, his vicar? No, it would have been more like Tristan to fake penitence and claim to have returned the money while keeping it.

She reached out to the phone again, meaning to call John and discuss this with him, but changed her mind. Tomorrow morning would be time enough. She didn't want to fall into the trap of needing John's company.

But when she lay awake in bed that night, she felt frightened at the thought that there was some unknown murderer out there. And a thatched cottage was the last place you wanted to try to get to sleep in when you were scared. Things rustled in the thatch overhead and the beams creaked. She decided, just before she fell asleep, that she would forget about the whole thing, see the police in the morning and ask permission to go abroad. She would stay in some foreign country, far away from danger.

In the morning, however, after two cups of black coffee and three cigarettes for breakfast, Agatha felt strong again. The fears of the night had gone. At ten o'clock, she heard the beep of John's car horn outside, locked up the cottage and went to join him.

As they drove to Ancombe, she told him about the visit from Bill and her phone call to Binser and the surprising news of the return of the money.

"There's something that man isn't telling us," said John. "Tristan wouldn't return the money like that. He must have threatened him."

"I dunno. There's something very straightforward about him."

"If he's all that straightforward, then why did he give us the impression that Tristan kept the money?"

"He didn't lie about it."

"Only by omission. Here's Ancombe. Look for a twee cottage."

"Nothing in the main street that I can see. Stop at the post office there and I'll ask."

John waited until Agatha returned with the news that Peggy Slither lived at the far end of the village in Sheep Street.

"There must be hundreds of Sheep Streets in the Cotswolds," said John, letting in the clutch and moving off.

At the end of the village, he turned right into Sheep Street.

"Only a few houses here. Oh, that must be it up ahead on the right."

Shangri-la was a modern bungalow. The front garden was bright with flowers and plaster gnomes. They parked outside and then made their way up a crazy-paving path to the front door. The doormat bore the legend GO AWAY. No doubt Peggy found it humorous. John pressed the bell and they waited while it rang out the chimes of Big Ben. "Is she Mrs. or Miss?" asked John.

"Don't know."

The door was opened by a dark-haired middle-aged woman. She had a sallow skin and the sort of twinkling humorous eyes of people who do not have much of a sense of humour at all.

Agatha introduced herself and John.

"Oh, the snoops of Carsely," she said in a husky voice. "I was just about to make a cup of tea. Come in."

The living-room was full of knick-knacks and plants. Beside the window, a palm tree grew out of an old toilet. One wall was covered in those tin advertising signs that antique dealers love to fake. On the other side of the window from the palm tree was a copy of the boy of Bruges, peeing into a stone basin. The three-piece suite was upholstered in slippery green silk and decorated with gold fringe.

"I'll get the tea," said Peggy.

John looked at the stone boy of Bruges. "I wonder how the water circulates?" he said.

"Awful thing to have in your living room," said Agatha. "Makes me want to pee myself."

"Do you think she is really trying to be funny with all this kitsch?" whispered John.

"No, I have a feeling she really likes it. Shhh! Here she comes."

Peggy entered carrying a tray. The teapot was in the shape of a squat fat man. The spout was his penis. Agatha suddenly decided she did not want tea. When Peggy handed her a cup, she placed it on a side-table.

"All this murder is quite exciting," said Peggy.

"Exciting?" Agatha looked at her in surprise. "I thought you were very fond of Tristan."

"Oh, we all were, dear. Such a gorgeous young man."

"When's the funeral?" asked John. "I forgot to ask."

"Some cousin's having the body taken to London for cremation."

"I would like to attend that funeral," said Agatha. "Do you know when it's going to be?"

"I don't think anyone will know until the body is released by the police. Of course, you had a thing with him, didn't you?"

"If you mean an affair," said Agatha stiffly, "I most certainly did not."

"But Mrs. Feathers is telling everyone she peered round the kitchen door and saw him kissing you good night."

"It was a social peck, that's all," said Agatha, becoming angry. "I thought you were close to him."

"Not close. He amused me. And women of our decaying ages, Agatha, do like to be seen around with beautiful young men."

"I do not need beautiful young men. I am engaged to John, here."

"Really?" Peggy surveyed John from top to bottom before turning back to Agatha. "How did you manage that?"

John said quickly, "Did you give Tristan any money?"

"Not a penny. Not that the poor lamb didn't try. Cost him a good few dinners before he gave up on me."

I hate you, thought Agatha.

"Where were you on the night he died?" asked John.

"Silly man. You're not the police, so I'm not even bothering to answer you. I thought it would be funny to see how you two snoops went about your business, but I'm beginning to find the whole thing rather boring."

Agatha stood up. Rage was making her intuitive faculties work overtime. "It's a good act you're putting on, Peggy, *dear*. But you were in love with him and somehow he suckered you and I'm going to find out how. Oh, by the way, did you know he was gay? Come along, John."

Peggy sat staring after them as they made their exit.

"That last remark of yours hit the old bag hard," said John when they were back in the car. "How did you guess all that casual jeering was a front?"

"Tristan, it turns out, was a complete rat and a blackmailer," said Agatha. "But he was glorious and charming. He made me feel fascinating and desirable. That was why he was so dangerous. People who have been conned by him—and to be honest, I could have been—will pretend he had no effect on them. But I can't imagine any woman being unaffected by Tristan."

"Except Mrs. Bloxby," said John. "Let's go and see Mrs. Tremp."

FIVE

✝

MRS. Tremp lived in a converted barn outside the village. Agatha remembered seeing her at various village events. She was a small, mousy woman, and when the colonel was alive, the locals reported that he bullied her.

They bumped down the pot-holed drive leading to her home. As they got out of the car, Agatha slammed the door, and rooks, roosting in a nearby lightning-blasted tree, swirled up to the heavens, cawing in alarm. The harvest was in, and the large field beside the house was full of pheasant pecking among the golden stubble.

The converted barn looked large and solid. Agatha rang the bell and they waited. The rooks came swirling back to their tree and stared down at Agatha and John with beady eyes. Agatha shivered. "I don't like rooks. Birds of ill omen."

"You mean ravens," said John.

The door opened and Mrs. Tremp stood there, blinking myopically up at them in the sunlight.

"It's Mrs. Raisin and Mr. Armitage, is it not?"

"Yes," said Agatha. "May we come in? We want to talk about Tristan Delon."

"Oh dear. I was just making jam ... and ... I suppose you'd better." She turned and walked indoors and they followed her into a huge sitting-room with long French windows. The furnishings were a comfortable mixture of old and new. The air was redolent with the smell of plum jam.

"Do sit down," said Mrs. Tremp. "I hope you don't mind, I keep the windows closed when I am making jam or I get plagued by wasps. What do you want to know about Mr. Delon?"

"We heard you were friendly with him," said Agatha.

"Yes, I was, and I was most distressed to hear of his death. And now this other terrible murder. There was never anything like this before you arrived in our village, Mrs. Raisin."

"Nothing to do with me. I don't go around murdering people. But I'd like to know who is for Mr. Bloxby's sake."

"He has only himself to blame for being a suspect," said Mrs. Tremp. "He was so jealous of Mr. Delon."

"I suppose Tristan told you that."

"He did let slip that he was having a difficult time with the vicar, yes."

"Did you know that he was gay?" asked John. "And that he tried to get women to give him money?"

She raised a gnarled and veined hand up to her suddenly trembling mouth. "I don't believe it. That's a wicked thing to say."

"I'm afraid it's true," said Agatha. "Did he try to get you to give him money?"

"He did tell me he had this project to start a club for the youth of the village. He said he would need help. I did offer to support him. In fact, I had a cheque ready for him. But he was killed, so he could not collect it. But I am sure he really did want to start this club. You must be mistaken. He was a real Christian."

"Mrs. Tremp," said Agatha firmly, "you are very lucky that he never collected that cheque. He would have pocketed the money. How much was the cheque for?"

"Five thousand pounds."

"That's a lot of money."

"I can afford it. My dear George left me very comfortably off. He did not like me spending money. I made all our jam and cakes and bread. He insisted on it. And he would go over my housekeeping books every week, and goodness me, he would get so angry if he thought I had spent a penny too much. We lived in that poky little cottage on the Ancombe road for years. So full of junk I could hardly move! He never threw anything away. I craved space and light. The cottage was so dark. When he died, I rented a skip and threw everything out and then I bought this place."

She gave a little smile. "Nice, isn't it?"

"How did your husband die?" asked John.

"In a fit of temper. I was always saying, do watch your blood pressure. I'm afraid it was the cigarettes that did it."

"He smoked too much?" Agatha thought guiltily of the packet of cigarettes in her handbag.

"No. What happened was I suddenly craved cigarettes. He wouldn't let me smoke. There was a new cut-price grocery shop in Evesham. I realized if I shopped there instead of the village shop, I could enter the village-shop prices in the housekeeping book, but save enough for a packet of cigarettes. He had said he was going for a round of golf. I had just lit one up when he

74

came crashing in. He had forgotten something. He started to rant and rave about my smoking and then he made some strange gargling sounds and dropped dead."

She gave another little smile. "I sat down and watched him for quite a while before I phoned the ambulance. He was quiet for the first time."

"To get back to Tristan," said Agatha, "how did he first get in touch with you?"

"He called on me. He said he was doing the rounds for the vicar. He was so charming. He loved this house. He said he could live here forever. He said Alf Bloxby was a bully. I said I knew all about bullying and told him about my life with George."

"Alf Bloxby is not a bully," said Agatha firmly. "You have known him a long time. Can you see Mrs. Bloxby putting up with a bully?"

"Mr. Delon said she was very long-suffering. I think you have been listening to malicious gossip, Mrs. Raisin. Even if he were gay, where's the shame in that?"

"None whatsoever, except it was a fact he kept from the women he was tricking out of their money."

A mulish looked firmed Mrs. Tremp's normally weak features. "I think you had both better go. I am not going to listen to any more slander and lies."

She rose and went and held open the front door. "And don't come round here again."

"I think she deliberately smoked that cigarette to make her husband have an apoplexy," said Agatha waspishly. "Terrifying woman."

"There's one thing that came out of it," said John.

"What?"

"She said she had a cheque ready for him. If he was prepared to take cheques rather than cash, then our Tristan planned to get as much as he could and then disappear."

"Maybe. But if he'd taken village people's money and disappeared, he would need to leave the church, and it was his position as a churchman that made it easier for him to get money out of people."

"But if he had received some sort of threat on his life, he might have planned to leave the country."

"Humph," said Agatha, annoyed that she had not thought of any of that. "We've not got much. What do we do now?"

"It's early yet. We could go back up to London to try whatever church it was in Kensington that Tristan used to work at."

"Bill didn't say what church it was."

"We could ask around."

"It might be in west Kensington. Might take us all day."

"I'm willing to bet it's somewhere around south Ken," said John. "Our Tristan would want somewhere fashionable."

"What if the police call round again?"

"Well, maybe we'll leave it until tomorrow. Let's find out how Mrs. Bloxby is getting along."

Mrs. Bloxby led them through to the vicarage garden. "Alf is lying down," she said. "This has all been a nightmare."

They sat down in the garden. "And no word of anyone seeing a stranger in the village?" asked Agatha.

"Nothing at all. It's television, you see. So many people appear to have been indoors, glued to their sets. I often wonder what it was Miss Jellop wanted to talk to me about. Was it something important, or just one of her usual complaints?" Mrs. Bloxby sighed. "Well, I'll never know now."

"What about the press?" asked Agatha. "Some of them must have still been around. People might remember someone with a camera and think, oh it's just another one of them and not bother saying anything to the police. By the way, Tristan started off at a church in Kensington. Any idea which one?"

"It might be in the letter that Mr. Lancing wrote to Alf to introduce Tristan. Wait here and I'll look."

When Mrs. Bloxby went inside, John said, "We've been neglecting our local pub. That must be a hotbed of gossip at the moment. We'd better try there after we've finished with Mrs. Bloxby and get some lunch at the same time."

Mrs. Bloxby came back holding a letter. She held it out to John, much to Agatha's irritation. Agatha pushed her chair up next to John and they both read it at the same time. It described Tristan's need to move to the country for his mental health. It then said in the last paragraph that he had previously worked at St. David's in south Kensington before moving to New Cross.

"We'll go there tomorrow," said John. "It's probably someone from Tristan's past."

"I think poor Miss Jellop was very much from Tristan's present," pointed out Mrs. Bloxby.

"But she might have found out something," John persisted.

"Has that sister arrived?" asked Agatha. "Miss Jellop's sister? The one from Stoke-on-Trent?"

"I haven't heard anything," said Mrs. Bloxby. "If I do, I'll let you know."

"We're going to the pub for lunch," said Agatha. "Care to join us?"

"No, Alf will be up and about soon."

John and Agatha left her and drove the short distance to the pub. "We're getting lazy," commented Agatha. "I used to walk everywhere." This was not true, but Agatha only remembered her rare bursts of exercise. She even had a bicycle rusting in the shed at the bottom of her garden that she had not taken out for over a year. She remembered cycling with Roy Silver, her one-time assistant in the days when she had her own company. Strange, she thought, that he hasn't phoned. He must have read about the murders in the newspapers. And what of Sir Charles Fraith, her one-time friend and "Watson"? She gave a little shiver. Her friends were deserting her. Even Bill Wong looked at her with a policeman's eyes these days rather than with the eyes of a friend.

The pub was noisy and full of smoke, not from cigarettes but from the open fire. The landlord, John Fletcher, was bending over it, coughing and spluttering. "It's that last load of wood," he said when he saw them. "Green." He lit a fire-lighter and threw it in among the logs. Reluctant flames started to lick up round the wood. "That should do it." He straightened up, wiping his hands on his trousers. "Now, what can I get you?"

They both ordered beer and sandwiches and retreated to a table in the corner by a window, propped open to let out the smoke. The fire crackled, a comforting sound. Outside the open window and beyond the small car-park, golden fields of stubble stretched out under a pale sun. The air coming in through the window held the chill of autumn. If only these murders hadn't happened, thought Agatha, forgetting how bored she had been recently, it would be nice to sit here and eat sandwiches and drink beer and then go home and play with the cats.

John brought over their beer and sandwiches. "So what's the gossip?" asked Agatha.

"Nothing much," said the landlord. "At first they all thought the vicar did it, but there's been talk that our curate wasn't really a very nice person, and so people think it was someone outside the village."

A customer at the bar shouted that he wanted a drink and John left.

Agatha took a sip of her beer and made a face. She preferred gin and tonic but often ordered beer, knowing she wouldn't finish her half pint or want another. Alcohol was just about the most ageing thing a middle-aged woman could take.

There was the brisk tap of high heels on the stone-flagged floor to herald the arrival of Miss Simms, secretary of the ladies' society.

She was clutching a glass of rum and vodka. "Mind if I join you?"

"Please do," said John Armitage.

Miss Simms sat down on a chair next to Agatha. "Terrible about Miss Jellop, innit? But she had it coming to her."

"How's that?" asked Agatha.

"Always complaining and poking her nose into things. Terrible gossip, she was. You should have heard the things she said about you, Mrs. Raisin."

"I don't want to know," snapped Agatha. "Do you still think Tristan was a saint?"

"No, he did a nasty thing."

"What?"

"I met him in the village on the day before he was murdered. He asked me out. Said he was tired of all those old women in the village. Now, that wasn't a nice thing to say, but at the time, like, I was so flattered that he wanted my company because he asked me out for dinner."

"But that was for the evening I had dinner with him!" exclaimed Agatha.

"I know. I'm coming to that. I was to meet him in that new restaurant, Stavros, in Chipping Norton, at eight o'clock. By ten past eight, I'd ordered a drink. He still didn't show. By eight-thirty, I decided to leave. Well, I'd had a look at the menu and I knew I couldn't afford their prices, so I just paid for the drink, picked myself up some fish and chips in Sheep Street and went home. I phoned and Mrs. Feathers said he was entertaining you and couldn't be disturbed. When did he invite you?"

"The day before he was murdered."

"But he asked me out for dinner in the afternoon of that day," wailed Miss Simms. "I just don't understand it."

"Maybe he did it deliberately," said John. "He'd already made a dinner date with Agatha here. Maybe he enjoyed the thought of you sitting, waiting."

"But he seemed so nice, ever so nice, but now there's some murmurs that he could be a bit, well, cruel, like."

"Got any examples?" asked Agatha.

"Well, Mrs. Brown, her what comes with the mobile library, she said he was charming to her one week and then, the next, he announced in front of the other customers that the selection of books was for morons and some moron must have chosen them. Mrs. Brown chooses most of the books herself, everyone knows that. There was a bit of a shocked silence, but he stood there, looking so gorgeous and smiling so sweetly, that everyone sort of decided they must have misheard. Then old Mr. Crinsted near me at the council houses, Tristan used to call round and play chess with him. Mr. Crinsted said he was so glad of the company that he let Tristan win the first couple of times, but on the third, he beat him and he said Tristan got very angry and accused him of cheating."

"There's one good thing about stories like that going round the village," said Agatha: "people can't be thinking Alf Bloxby murdered Tristan in a fit of jealousy."

"No, not anymore. But then, people do say things like—but who else could have done it?"

"What about Miss Jellop?" asked John. "What's being said about her?"

"She wasn't very popular. Always complaining. I mean, she irritated people. But I can't see anyone wanting to murder her. Of course, people are saying she was being spiteful about the vicar, saying he murdered Tristan, things like that."

And what that amounts to, thought Agatha wearily, is that people will still be thinking of Alf Bloxby as a murderer. I must do something. But what? Just keep on ferreting around and hope I find something out.

Miss Simms finished her drink and left. "What should we do now?" asked Agatha.

"I don't know. We'll try that church in London tomorrow. In the meantime, let's go down to the library and look up the name 'Jellop' in the Stoke-on-Trent directory. We might get the sister's number and we could call her. Tristan obviously told Miss Jellop something that made her dangerous."

"Nothing here," said Agatha, half an hour later. "Not in the residential addresses."

"Jellop's Jams and Jellies. Try under the business addresses," said John.

Agatha searched the book. "Got it," she said.

"Write it down and we'll go back and phone in comfort."

Back at Agatha's cottage, she said, "Who's going to phone? You or me?"

"I'll do it."

Agatha went into the kitchen and petted her cats and let them out in the garden. She stood for a moment surveying the scene in front of her, and thinking the garden looked rather dull. Not having green fingers herself, she had hired a gardener, but he turned out to be expensive and lazy, so she had fired him and replaced the flowers with shrubs. Next year, she thought, she would start all over again and have a colourful display of flowers.

John came out to join her. "Miss Jellop's sister is a Mrs. Essex. A nice woman in personnel even gave me her home address. You want to try it?"

"No, you do it."

John gave her a surprised look, but went back indoors.

Agatha was suddenly tired of the whole business. She should leave it to the police. She wanted something else to occupy her mind. Anything else. She could not, somehow, relax in John's company. Agatha could not understand that it was John's regular good looks which fazed her. Such men were usually interested in prettier and younger women. Such men were not for the likes of Agatha Raisin. And Agatha was old-fashioned in that she could only relate to men when there was a sexual undercurrent.

When John returned again, he said, "I spoke to the husband. Mrs. Essex is down here, at Mircester police headquarters. Let's go. We might catch her as she comes out."

"We might not recognize her," said Agatha, reluctant to move.

"With luck, there'll be some sort of family resemblance."

"She might have left Mircester and be up at the cottage."

"I doubt it. I took a walk up there early this morning. It's still taped off and the forensic people are still working on it. Come on, Agatha!"

They waited in the car-park outside Mircester police headquarters, studying all the people coming out. After an hour, Agatha yawned and then shifted restlessly. "No one who even looks like her. I say we should go home. She probably left ages ago."

"That might be her," said John. A middle-aged woman had just emerged accompanied by a policewoman. She had protruding eyes and a ferrety appearance. A police car drove up and both women got in the back.

"Now what?" said Agatha.

"We follow them. She might be staying somewhere locally."

John, who was driving, followed the police car at a safe

distance. "They're going in the Carsely direction," said John after a few miles. "Maybe the police have finished with the cottage and she's going to stay there."

"Must be tough if she is," retorted Agatha. "I don't know that I'd want to stay in a house where my sister had been murdered."

"Maybe keeping an eye on her assets. She'll probably inherit."

Sure enough, the police car drove on down into Carsely.

"We'd best go home," said John, "and wait, and then walk up later when we're sure the police have gone. We'll go to my place."

Agatha always experienced a pang of loss when she entered John's cottage. There was no feel, no trace of her missing ex-husband's personality. James Lacey's books had spilled from the shelves. John's books were all in neat order, according to subject. He worked at a metal computer desk placed in front of the window. There were two armchairs covered in bright chintz and an oak coffee-table, shining and bare.

"Like a drink?" asked John.

"Gin and tonic."

"I don't have lemon or ice."

"How British! I'll drink it warm."

While John went into the kitchen, Agatha sat down and closed her eyes, trying to conjure up an image of James and of the room as it used to be. She had nearly succeeded when John came back in. She opened her eyes and accepted a glass of gin and tonic. He carefully put two coasters down on the coffee-table.

"You live like a bachelor," commented Agatha. "Neatness everywhere."

"It's the only way I can live. If I let it go for one day, then sloppiness sets in. There's a police car just gone past." He went to the door and opened it and looked out. "Bill!" he shouted. "In here."

"I feel guilty every time I look at him," grumbled Agatha.

Bill came in. He was on his own. "Was that you following us from Mircester?" he asked.

"We just happened to be in Mircester doing some shopping," said Agatha defensively. "We saw the police car in front of us. I didn't know you were in it."

"I wasn't. I was in the car behind you."

"Anyway, now you're here, what can we do for you?"

Bill studied Agatha's face and noticed the way she dropped her eyes and reached for her drink.

"I think you pair have been up to something. I've never known you to let things alone before, Agatha."

"It's this engagement," said John. "We've got so much to deal with. We don't know whether to keep one of our cottages or buy somewhere bigger."

"So you say. Have you heard anything?"

"Only that the villagers have been sharing views about Tristan and seem to be coming to the conclusion that he was rather nasty."

"Give me an example."

Agatha told him about Miss Simms. "Now, that *is* odd," said Bill. "I mean, what would a gay man want with a woman without money?"

"Probably did it out of spite."

"It still seems out of character. If he was out to fleece rich women, then he would be anxious to keep up his front of being sweet and charming. He must have known that Miss Simms would talk about it."

"Unless," said Agatha slowly, "someone or something frightened him and he'd decided to leave. That was why he wanted the church money. He probably hoped to get a cheque from me."

"Or he decided to dump Miss Simms because you provided a possibility of good pickings."

"But he asked Miss Simms out for dinner after he'd invited me. Did Miss Feathers say if he had received any calls during the night?"

"Not that she knows of, apart from the one from you."

"Miss Simms must have been very flustered and excited about that invitation," said Bill. "I wonder if she got the evening wrong. You had dinner with him on the Tuesday. I wonder if he said tomorrow evening and in her excitement, Miss Simms misunderstood him."

"I'll phone up the restaurant and see when he made the booking for," said John.

"You'll need an Oxfordshire phone-book," said Agatha.

"I've got one. You two go on talking; I'll phone from the bedroom."

"So you're really going to get married again," said Bill, scrutinizing Agatha's face.

"Seems like a good idea."

"Women of your age often marry because they want companionship, or someone to go into pubs and restaurants with, or to mend fuses; but not you, Agatha."

"I've decided I'll never fall in love again," said Agatha. "So I may as well settle for companionship. Can we talk about something else? Like is Miss Jellop's sister going to stay in her cottage?"

"How did you know it was Miss Jellop's sister?"

"The police car turned off in the direction of Dover Rise. Simple."

"Now, why do I get the feeling that the pair of you found

out that she was at police headquarters and waited outside and tailed her back here?"

"Because you've got a nasty, suspicious copper's mind. Oh, here's John."

"Mystery solved," said John, coming down the stairs. "Tristan booked a table for the Friday evening, not Thursday. The restaurant was quiet, so when Miss Simms turned up, saying she was waiting for a gentleman friend, but not giving any name, they put her at a table for two."

"Another dead end," said Bill. "I'd best be off. Don't go bothering Mrs. Essex."

"Who's she?" asked Agatha innocently.

"As if you didn't know!"

When Bill had left, John asked, "Are we going to bother Mrs. Essex?"

"Of course," said Agatha.

"Better leave it a bit until we're sure the police have gone. That's Mrs. Bloxby just gone past the window. She's probably on her way to your place."

He opened the window and called, "Mrs. Bloxby!" She turned and smiled and then walked up to the door. John opened it and ushered her in. Mrs. Bloxby was looking so relaxed and cheerful that Agatha cried, "You look great. You must have heard some good news."

"I haven't heard any good news. But I've been in church and I have renewed my faith."

Agatha felt embarrassed. She said, "Bill Wong has just been here." She told the vicar's wife about Miss Simms's date, ending up with, "But I don't see why he even asked her in the first place."

"I think," said Mrs. Bloxby slowly, "that perhaps he was not gay."

"But by all accounts he said so himself," exclaimed Agatha.

"He may have said that as one of his ways of rejecting and hurting people. Men who are very beautiful are naturally assumed to be gay. I must confess I made that mistake myself. Think, Mrs. Raisin, when you had dinner with him, did you ever think he might be gay?"

"No, I didn't," said Agatha. "He was exuding sexual vibes."

"If he was as cruel as he seems to have been, it might have delighted him to lead both men and women on. To the men, he could imply he was gay and then reject them if they made any advances. To the women, he could say he was gay, and reject them that way. He liked manipulating people. He did at first imply that I was wasted on Alf, but, you see, that didn't work with me, for I have never fallen out of love with my husband."

Agatha felt a sour pang of jealousy which she quickly dismissed. Mrs. Bloxby deserved the rewards of a good woman. Maybe I should pray myself, thought Agatha.

They all went over what they knew about Tristan without getting any further.

When Mrs. Bloxby had left, John glanced at his wristwatch. "Perhaps we should try Mrs. Essex now."

They walked up through the village to Dover Rise. "If she was well off," said John, "it's a wonder she didn't choose somewhere a bit more expensive to live. I think these used to be workers' cottages at one time."

"She was on her own and probably didn't feel she needed anywhere larger. One of these terraced cottages costs nearly two hundred thousand pounds. Living in the Cotswolds is expensive. Everyone wants to live here. A lot of people who had second homes in the Cotswolds during the last recession opted to sell their London homes and commute from here. It's only an hour and a half on the train from Moreton. If you live in Hampstead, say, it can take you all that just to get into the City."

They stood at the end of the cul-de-sac and looked along it. "No police cars," said John. "I can't see a copper on duty either."

"Why are they called coppers?" asked Agatha.

"It comes from an old acronym, COP, constable on patrol. Why are you playing Trivial Pursuits, Agatha?"

"Because I'm nervous. I expect Bill Wong to leap out of the bushes at me."

"Looks all-clear."

"I hate this business of being unauthorized," Agatha burst out. "We look like a couple of Nosy Parkers."

"The curse of the amateur detective," remarked John cheerfully. "Buck up, Agatha. Where's your stiff upper lip?"

"To quote the Goons, it's over my loose wobbly lower one."

They arrived at the cottage. The door was standing open. "Here goes!" said Agatha.

She rang the bell beside the door, suddenly aware that she was wearing trousers, a shirt blouse and flat sandals. I'm letting my appearance slip, thought Agatha. I haven't been to the beautician in ages. I hope to God I'm not growing a moustache. She nervously felt her upper lip. Was that a hair? She fumbled in her handbag and took out a powder compact and peered in the little mirror.

"Yes? Can I help you?"

Agatha lowered the compact and found Mrs. Essex staring curiously at her.

Agatha tucked the compact hurriedly in her handbag. She introduced both of them as friends of Miss Jellop and said they had come to offer their condolences.

"Too kind," said Mrs. Essex. Her protruding eyes stared at Agatha's face with such intensity that Agatha wondered if she was, after all, sprouting a moustache.

"We would like to talk to you about your sister," said Agatha.

"Why?"

Agatha took a deep breath. Where had all her old confidence gone? "I have helped the police on murder cases before," she said. "I thought we might be able to help find out who murdered your sister if we could ask you a few questions."

"But I have already told the police all I know!"

John edged in front of Agatha. He gave Mrs. Essex a charming smile. "As you may know, I write detective stories."

"What's your name again?"

"John Armitage."

Her pale lips parted in a smile. "Why, I saw you on the *South Bank Show* last year. Please come in. This is exciting."

Hardly the grieving sister, thought Agatha sourly as she followed John into the cottage.

"I'm just making an inventory of everything," said Mrs. Essex. "Poor Ruby never spent much on herself."

Ruby, thought Agatha. So that was her first name. Momentarily distracted, she began to wonder about the first names of other women in the ladies' society where the tradition was to use second names.

Then she realized John was speaking. "Your sister phoned Mrs. Bloxby, the vicar's wife, asking her to call round as she had something to tell her, but by the time Mrs. Bloxby got here, your sister was dead. Did Miss Jellop say anything at all to you that might indicate she knew something dangerous about someone?"

"No, because we didn't speak. We had a falling-out. I was amazed when the police told me they had found Ruby's will

89

and that she had left everything to me. In fact, she had changed her will the day before she died."

Agatha's bearlike eyes gleamed. "Who had she left her money to in the previous will?"

"To that curate. The one who was murdered. Poor Ruby. She was always getting these schoolgirl crushes on some man or another."

"And you didn't know anything about it?" asked Agatha.

Those protruding eyes fastened on Agatha's face with a flash of malicious intelligence. "Meaning did I murder my sister the minute I knew she'd changed her will? You should leave detecting to your friend here."

"Might there be something among her papers?" put in John quickly. "Letters or diary or something?"

"You'll need to ask the police. They took all her papers away. Now, if you'll excuse me, I have a lot to do."

"Will you sell the cottage?" asked Agatha.

"I don't know. Maybe keep it for holidays and weekends. My husband's due to retire soon."

"When did you last speak to your sister?" asked Agatha.

"Must have been about three years ago."

"Not much there," said John gloomily as they walked back down through the village. "You know, the car has caused a decline in gossip in English villages. I suppose not so long ago one would see people standing gossiping and walking about. Now a lot of them even use their cars to drive a few yards to the village stores."

"But that means empty roads and lanes," said Agatha impatiently. "Surely a stranger would have been noticed. Unless it was someone masquerading as a local reporter. The village is fed up with the press. They see someone that looks like a journalist and they shy away. I can tell a genuine journalist a mile off."

"How?"

"Even if they're well-dressed, they carry a shabby sort of people-pleasing alcoholism about with them."

"You're sour because you were a public relations officer."

"You're right," said Agatha reluctantly. "I hated crawling to the bastards."

"I can't imagine you crawling," said John. "I can imagine you frightening them into writing what you wanted them to write."

This was in fact true but Agatha didn't want to hear it or believe it. She still saw herself as a waiflike creature—shy, vulnerable and much put-upon. Sometimes when she looked in a full-length mirror, she could not believe that the stocky, well-groomed woman looking back at her was really herself.

They walked on in silence and then Agatha said, "What next?"

"Just keep on trying. London tomorrow."

SIX

†

"YOU look very nice," commented John when Agatha got into his car the next morning. Agatha was wearing a silky gold jersey suit. It had a short skirt. Her best feature, her legs, were encased in sheer tights and her feet in high-heeled sandals.

"Thanks," said Agatha gruffly. She had decided it was time she started dressing up again, not, she told herself, that this sudden desire to smarten her appearance had anything to do with John Armitage. She wished she had elected to drive them herself. There was something about John doing all the driving that was making her feel diminished. Agatha liked to feel in charge at all times. Subconsciously she had felt that putting on her best clothes might prompt some sexual interest in her from John, and in that way, she would have the upper hand. But what Agatha's subconscious decided hardly ever reached the conscious part of her brain.

"Look at that dreadful advertisement," exclaimed John, driving along the M40.

"What? Where?"

"We passed it. It said, 'Only ninety-one shopping days to Christmas.' "

"The shops are full of Christmas crackers and wrapping already," said Agatha. "The adults have ruined Christmas for the children with all this commercialism."

"Wrong. The children have ruined Christmas for the adults."

Agatha looked at him, puzzled. "How do you explain that?"

"They've come to expect to get exactly what they want. I know all this from friends of mine with children. Something new comes out in July, say. They clamour for it. No use saying, 'Wait till Christmas.' They have to have it right away because it'll be old hat by Christmas. They don't want surprises. They want what they demand. So there are no shining faces under the Christmas tree, radiant with surprise and gratitude. Only complaints like, 'Why did you buy me this computer game? It's *months* old.' Greedy children and disappointed parents, that's Christmas."

"But surely it's the parents' fault. Can't they put their foot down and say, 'You'll get what we give you and nothing costing more than five pounds'?"

"And never, ever be forgiven? It's the kids these days who have to keep up with the Joneses. They don't want to go back to school after the holidays and be unable to compete with the others. I'm going away for Christmas."

"Where?"

"Don't know. Stick a pin in the map."

93

"I'll probably go away somewhere myself, but only for a short time. I don't like leaving my cats."

"Your cats seem to adore Doris Simpson."

"They're my cats!"

"Possessive, aren't you? We may as well think of going somewhere together."

"Why?"

"Well, why not? Unless you prefer to go places on your own."

"Actually, I like my own company when I'm travelling."

"Suit yourself. I'll find someone else. Look at that idiot in front, veering from lane to lane like a maniac."

I should grow up, mourned Agatha. It would have been nice to have company. Why did I get miffed because he didn't say anything affectionate? Why should he? Why should I want him to?

She ruthlessly shifted her mind onto the problems of the Carsely murders. Why had John decided that Tristan was gay? Jealousy? Agatha thought back to that dinner. She had largely blotted it out of her mind because of that final rejection. No, he had not struck her as gay. She was sure he masqueraded as one to lead women on and then rebuff them. Perhaps he had lured men on and then told them he was heterosexual. It could be that he had behaved himself while at the church in South Ken. Could he have been twisted and spoilt by his exceptional looks? Hardly. There must have been something twisted in him from the beginning.

How did those journalists that she had been so bitchy about cope with day-to-day rejections and dead ends? Perhaps she should have been nicer to them during her career as a public relations officer. Perhaps, had she done so, she might have been even more successful.

Agatha hardly ever questioned her own behaviour, but this rare introspection was caused by a longing to forget about the whole case. She felt obscurely that it was because John kept taking over. He didn't have to suffer from the same setbacks as she did. People mostly recognized his name and were prepared to speak to him. And because he was a man, she thought sourly. Men investigated. Women were regarded as interfering. Had women's lib all been a myth? All that seemed to have been achieved was that women were expected to work as well as raise families. Respect for women had gone.

She roused herself from her meditations to realize they were approaching south Kensington and John was saying, "Look out for a free parking meter." They cruised around until they struck it lucky. A man was just moving his car out from a parking meter two streets away from the church.

"I hope it turns out to be someone from Tristan's past in London," said Agatha. "I want Carsely to go back to being its old time-warp-dull sort of place."

"I might agree with you," said John, "had it not been for the murder of Miss Jellop. I hope we can find someone at the church. With all the thefts these days, a lot of these churches stay locked up."

Agatha looked at her watch. "It's getting on for lunch-time. Some of them have a lunch-time service."

St. David's was a small Victorian church tucked in between two blocks of flats. To Agatha's relief, the door was standing open.

She followed John in, noticing with irritation that John as usual was leading the way. The church was dark and smelt of incense. Agatha looked at the burning candles and at the Stations of the Cross. "Isn't this a Catholic church?" she asked.

"No, Church of England. Very High. All bells and smells."

A man in shirt-sleeves came out of a side door and approached the altar. "Excuse me," called John.

He approached them down the aisle. He was wearing a grey shirt and black trousers. He had a thin intelligent face.

John introduced them and explained why they were anxious to find out all they could about Tristan.

"I am Hugh Beresford," he said. "I am the vicar here."

"And were you here when Tristan was curate?" asked Agatha.

"Yes. I was distressed to read about his murder. So sad."

"What was his behaviour like when he was here?"

"Exemplary, until . . ."

"Until what?" demanded Agatha sharply.

"I should not speak ill of the dead, although it was not entirely his fault."

"You'd better tell us," said John. "We're desperate for any morsel which might help us find out what happened to him." At that moment a woman entered the church, sat in a back pew and then knelt down in prayer. "Is there anywhere private we can talk?"

"Yes, follow me."

He led them up the aisle and through a heavy oak door at the left of the altar, down a stone passage where surplices hung on hooks, and through another door into a small wood-panelled room furnished with a plain desk and chairs. "Please sit down," said the vicar. "I will tell you what I know, but I really don't think it has much bearing on the case. I feel I should really not be telling you anything I have not said to the police, but as you explained, your local vicar is in danger of being falsely accused and so I suppose I should do everything to help. Now where shall I begin?"

The room was dark and stuffy. Agatha could hear the muted roar of the traffic on the Old Brompton Road. The chair she was sitting on was hard and pinched her thighs. She was getting pins and needles in one foot and eased her bottom from side to side.

"Tristan was a very charming young man. At first, he seemed a great asset to the parish. But I suppose having such good looks could only lead to trouble. Before I go on, you must assure me that everything I tell you is in confidence."

"Absolutely," said Agatha and John nodded.

"Right. A very attractive lady started attending the services. She started to get friendly with Tristan. Of course, other ladies in the congregation became jealous and one told me that Tristan was having an affair with this lady. I challenged him. He said they were going to be married. Now this lady was a divorcée in her late forties. I pointed out the age difference and the difference in circumstances."

"Such as?" asked Agatha.

"She was very wealthy and high-class. I told Tristan he would be damned as a toy-boy. But he would not listen. I thought of reporting the matter to the bishop, but I kept putting it off. He was so very much in love, you see."

Agatha raised her eyebrows. "Tristan? In love?"

"Possibly I should not have done what I did, but I called on this lady. The minute I explained the difficulties there would be for her in marrying someone so young she burst out laughing and said Tristan was a dear boy and very amusing but she had no intention of marrying him. I said if that was the case, she should leave him alone. She was raising hopes in him that could not be fulfilled."

He fell silent. Did Tristan really love this woman? wondered Agatha. Or was he dazzled with the thought of wealth and a sophisticated life?

The vicar took up the story again.

"In telling him that all was off and that she had no intention of marrying him, she let fall that I had been to see her. Tristan came back in a rage and accused me of ruining his life. He said he was sick of being poor."

"So he wasn't really in love with her," exclaimed Agatha. "It *was* her money he was after."

"Dear me," said the vicar. "I never thought of it like that. Before it all came to an end, he was . . . glowing."

"And who was this woman?" asked John.

"I really do not think I should tell you. She has moved from this parish anyway."

"We really will be discreet," said John. "We are neither journalists nor the police."

Again the vicar fell silent.

At last he said, "It was Lady Charlotte Bellinge."

"And do you know where she is now?" asked Agatha.

"I am afraid I do not."

They thanked him and made their way out of the church. "So how do we find this Charlotte Bellinge?" asked John.

"I've got friends in newspapers who could look up the files, but they would want to interview us about the murders. I know—*Gossip* magazine. I know the social editor. We'll try her."

Tanya Cartwright, the social editor of *Gossip,* quailed when she learned that a Miss Agatha Raisin wanted to see her. Agatha had once done public relations for a businessman who wanted to break into London's social scene. Tanya had caved in and had written him up in her column just to get rid of the terrifying Agatha Raisin. "Tell her I'm out," she was saying to her secretary just as the door of her office opened and Agatha and John walked in.

"Some woman's bothering me," she said brightly. "How

nice to see you, Agatha." She dismissed her secretary with a wave of her hand. "Take a seat."

John was amused. Tanya was a brittle, thin woman with a hard face, which her latest face-lift had done nothing to soften. Her eyes were disconcertingly huge. Gold bracelets dangled from one bony wrist. But she looked terrified of Agatha.

Agatha introduced John and Tanya relaxed a fraction. "So pleased to meet you," she said. "We must do a profile on you sometime."

"Delighted," said John. "May I explain why we're here?"

"I'll explain," said Agatha harshly. She outlined the tale of the murders and then asked if Tanya knew where Charlotte Bellinge could be found. Relief that Agatha was not going to badger her to put some social-climbing nobody into her column flooded Tanya's face. She switched on her computer. "Wait a bit. I should have an address here. She gets mentioned in the social columns quite a lot." She moved the mouse and clicked. "Let me see. Yes, here she is. Number Twenty-five Parrot Street. It's off the King's Road in Chelsea."

"I know where it is," said Agatha. "Thanks a lot, Tanya. We'd best be off."

They had just left Tanya's office when the social editor opened her door and cooed, "A word with you, Mr. Armitage."

John went back in and Tanya closed the door firmly, leaving Agatha on the outside.

John emerged after only a few moments. "What was that about?" demanded Agatha.

"She just wanted to meet me for lunch sometime."

"Oh," grunted Agatha. "She might have asked me."

"She's not attracted to you," said John with a certain air of smugness.

They had left the car in an underground car-park. "Better

leave it where it is," said John. "I don't want to have to drive around Chelsea looking for a parking place. We'll take the tube to Sloane Square and walk along."

The King's Road in Chelsea always reminded Agatha of her youth, when she was struggling to claw her way up the business ladder. That had been during the days when a good address mattered and she had paid an expensive rent for a flat in Draycott Gardens and had very little money left over for anything else. In the evenings, the restaurants had been crammed with trendy young people, laughing and drinking, and Agatha, on the outside looking in, would feel intensely lonely, with only her ambition to keep her warm.

She shrugged off her memories as they turned the corner of Parrot Street. Charlotte Bellinge lived in a thin white-stuccoed house. "At least someone's at home," she remarked. "One of the downstairs windows is open."

John rang the bell and they waited. The door swung open and a young girl stood there. She had a pale spotty face, a stud in her nose and five little silver earrings in each ear. She was wearing a short tube-top exposing a pierced belly-button.

"What?" she asked.

"Is Lady Bellinge at home?" asked Agatha.

"Who wants her?"

"Here's my card," said John, stepping in front of Agatha. The girl disappeared, only to reappear a few moments later to say, "Come in."

She opened the door to a sitting-room on the ground floor and Charlotte Bellinge came forward to meet them. She was exquisite: small, dainty, perfectly groomed. Her face was unlined and her large eyes were of an intense blue. Her hair was tinted a pale shade of gold. She was wearing a loose white silk shirt and tight black trousers.

"Now, why is a famous detective writer calling on me?" she asked.

Agatha and John sat down and John explained the reason for their visit while Agatha felt sulkily that she was been pushed to the sidelines, again.

"But how fascinating!" drawled Charlotte when John had finished. "Quite like one of your detective stories. I don't see how I can help you. Tristan was a gorgeous boy and yes, he did have a crush on me."

"Did you have an affair?" demanded Agatha, not liking the way John was staring at Charlotte with a dazed smile on his face.

"No, I did not. But he amused me and he was so very beautiful. He did, however, become demanding. I am not made of money."

"He asked you for money?" Agatha leaned forward.

"Not in so many words. But when I took him out to some smart restaurant, he would complain his clothes were too shabby, so I paid to have him tailored and all that." She waved one perfectly manicured little hand. "But then he began to ask for things as if he had some sort of right. So I got bored and said he ought to be going around with people of his own age and to leave me alone. He made some feeble attempt to black-mail me, threatening to tell the social columns that I had been having an affair with a curate. I told him if he did, I would sue him. I wanted to move to Chelsea anyway, so I moved and was glad to get away from him. He had become . . . quite frighten-ing. I think he lived in fantasies. I think he believed I would actually marry him and he would live in the lap of luxury. He did crave the good life. I remember once when we were in a shop, he was looking at a cashmere sweater and he kept stroking it like a lover. He begged me to buy it for him and became so shrill that I did, to avoid a scene."

"Were you surprised when you learned he was murdered?" asked Agatha.

"Yes, very surprised. If I had learned that Tristan had murdered someone, I would not have been nearly so surprised. So boring, all this raking over the past." She turned a dazzling smile on John. "Do tell me about your books."

And so John did and at great length, while Agatha shifted restlessly. When he had finally finished, Charlotte looked curiously at Agatha. "Are you two an item?"

Agatha opened her mouth to say they were engaged, but John said quickly, "We're only pretending to be. You see, we didn't want the police to know we had been up in London finding out things, so I invented the lie we were engaged to divert their suspicions."

Charlotte gave a tinkling laugh. "How funny! You are very amusing, John." She picked up her handbag, opened it and extracted a card. "My mobile-phone number and e-mail address are there. We should meet up for dinner one evening."

"That would be wonderful," said John.

"Excuse *me*," snapped Agatha. "*If* we could get back to the matter in hand: Did Tristan court any other women in the parish that you knew of?"

"No." The beautiful eyes drifted back to John. "He seemed totally wrapped up in me."

"Hardly surprising," commented John. They gazed at each other and Agatha could have slapped them both.

She stood up, stocky and militant. "We'd best be going, *dear*."

"What? Oh, yes, of course."

"Sophie will show you out."

"Your daughter?" asked Agatha.

Charlotte let out a trill of laughter. "No, my maid. They

don't wear caps and aprons like they did in your day, Mrs. Raisin."

Agatha led the way. John hung back. She heard him saying, "I'll phone you soon," and then the amused murmur of Charlotte's voice, "Next time leave your dragon behind."

"She could have done it, mark my words," said a truculent Agatha as she stomped her way along the King's Road.

"Nonsense, Agatha. She wouldn't hurt a fly. But we know one thing. Tristan was just the same sort of person in London as he was in New Cross."

"I suppose so," conceded Agatha, suddenly not wanting to appear jealous. "Where do we go from here?"

"Back to Carsely. I feel we let Peggy Slither's nastiness put us off. Perhaps if I saw her on her own . . . ?"

"By all means, try," said Agatha, thinking that John in Carsely was at least not John entertaining Charlotte Bellinge in London. "But there's one thing we've been forgetting. Who attacked Tristan in New Cross? Were the police called in? I wish we could ask them."

"We could try that vicar, Lancing, again. I mean, he didn't tell us at first about Binser, so he may be holding back other information."

"Okay," said Agatha, "back to New Cross."

"I really don't think you should keep coming round here," said Mr. Lancing an hour later, when they were once more seated in his study. "I have told you all I know."

"The thing that puzzles us," said Agatha, "is this business about the attack on Tristan. Was it reported to the police?"

"No, it was not. Tristan became almost hysterical. He had to go to hospital and he told them there that he had suffered a bad fall. He kept saying over and over again that he wanted to get away. He seemed truly repentant about that business with Binser."

"Did you know he had returned the money?" pursued Agatha.

"Yes, because he assured me he had."

Agatha gave a click of annoyance. "You didn't tell us that. You let us assume he had not."

"I am afraid that after he had left, and on calmer reflection, I came to the conclusion that he had not. Now you tell me he did return the money, which relieves my conscience. He must indeed have been truly repentant."

"I doubt it," said John. "I don't think repentance was in his nature. I'm beginning to think the return of the money and the beating were connected. I think we should have another word with Mr. Binser."

But this time there was no audience with the businessman. His formidable secretary, Miss Partle, received them instead. She said that Mr. Binser was abroad on business but that he would no longer be available to answer their questions. "He has done enough, considering you have no official status," said Miss Partle. "But as a matter of interest, what brought you back here?"

John tried delicately to put the case of the beatings and the return of the money while Agatha studied Miss Partle. She was typical of an executive secretary. Plain, middle-aged, sensibly dressed with intelligent eyes behind thick glasses. Those eyes were surveying John with increasing contempt. When he had finished, she said, "I think you should keep fiction for your books, Mr. Armitage. We are not the Mafia. We do not hire people to beat anyone who annoys us. We believe in dealing with the law. And talking about the law, do the police know that you are investigating?"

"I have helped the police in the past," said Agatha defensively.

"Meaning that in this case, they do not know, and I think they should be told. Please do not trouble us again."

On the road home, Agatha and John anxiously debated whether Miss Partle would actually tell the police. By the time John turned the car into Lilac Lane, they had come to the comfortable conclusion that she would not. Neither she nor Binser would want his friendship with Tristan exposed.

And then they saw the police car outside Agatha's cottage.

They drew up and Wilkes and Bill Wong got out of the car. "Probably something else," John reassured Agatha. But Agatha reflected uneasily that it had taken them nearly three hours to get back because of an accident on the M40—time enough for Miss Partle to have consulted her boss and then phoned the police.

Wilkes looked grim. "I think we should talk about this inside," he said.

Agatha opened her cottage door and led the way into the kitchen with her cats at her heels. She opened the kitchen door and let them out into the garden.

"Now," she said with false brightness, "what can I do for you? Would you like a coffee, or maybe something stronger?"

"Sit down," commanded Wilkes. "We have just had a certain Mr. Binser's lawyers on the phone. Mr. Binser is making a statement which they are faxing over. As you evidently already know, he was conned out of ten thousand pounds by Delon, money which was returned. He told you this and hoped that would be the end of it because he said being tricked in such a way might bring his business judgement into disrepute. He says that as the murder took place here and had nothing to do with him, he did not feel obliged to contact us before this. He says the reason he is doing so now is that you both had the temerity to suggest to his secretary that he had hired people to beat Delon up. What all this amounts to is that you have been withholding valuable information and interfering in a police investigation. I should charge you both and arrest you.

"But I will admit you have been a little help to us in the past, Mrs. Raisin, so I will tell you this. You are not to conduct any more investigations into this case."

"If we had not found out about Binser," said Agatha crossly, "then you wouldn't either."

"Perhaps. But as far as I can judge, Binser has nothing to do with the case. He is a very powerful man with powerful friends in high places and I would like to keep my job until it is time for me to retire. Do not approach him again, do you understand me?"

"Yes," said Agatha meekly.

"So what else have you found out? What else have you been keeping to yourselves?"

Agatha was about to say, "Nothing," but John told them all about Charlotte Bellinge. "I know she's got nothing to do with this," he said, "but we thought if we could get a better picture of what Tristan was really like, we could maybe discover the type of person who would kill him."

"Miss Jellop's connections were all in Stoke," said Bill, speaking for the first time. "I cannot see that she could have anything to do with such as Mr. Binser or Charlotte Bellinge. All you have done is to tread on the toes of the rich and powerful, Agatha, and, incidentally, lie to me about it."

Agatha turned red.

"You will both come with us now to police headquarters," said Wilkes, "and make full statements, and I mean full statements, and then I hope you will both get on with your respective lives and leave policing to the police."

"And that's that," said Agatha, three hours later when they emerged from Mircester police headquarters. "It's one in the morning and I'm starving."

"There's an all-night place on the Mircester bypass," said John. "Let's go there and go over what we've got."

"Don't see much point in going on," said Agatha. "And you'd better have your ring back."

"Not right away. I think it would be the last straw for Bill if he knew we had been lying to him about that as well."

The all-night restaurant was a depressing place, redolent with the smell of old grease. They collected plates of sausage, egg and chips and sat down at a window, their tired faces lit by the harsh fluorescent lighting.

"It lets Binser out," said John.

"I suppose it does," agreed Agatha. "All we did was goad him into going to the police, and if he had anything to hide and had previously used criminal means to hide it, he wouldn't have opened up to the law. Damn! I should have trusted my first judgement. I thought he was a nice man and honest and one that was only furious that he'd been so taken in by Tristan."

"Which brings us straight back to the Cotswolds," said John. "You know, that rudeness of Peggy Slither could have been to keep us away. I'll try her tomorrow and you can see if you can get anything more out of Mrs. Tremp."

"And what if they phone the police?" said Agatha miserably.

"Well, maybe not tomorrow. Tell you what, I'll get on with my writing and you get on with whatever it is you usually get on with and we'll let the police settle down."

Agatha slept late the next day and awoke feeling still tired and still guilty about having lied to Bill. She phoned John to see if he would like to join her for dinner that evening but he said he had just checked his contract and he was going to be late delivering his latest book if he didn't get down to it. "So I'll need to leave real-life murder for a bit. See you around. In fact, I've got to go up to London to see my agent and publishers tomorrow and I may stay there for a few days. All right if I leave my keys with you? Just in case there's a gas leak or something like that."

"Sure," said Agatha.

"I'll pop them through the letter-box tomorrow."

"I've got to go," said Agatha. "Someone at the door."

It was Mrs. Bloxby. "I heard you had the police round last night, Agatha. Anything up?"

"Come in. It's amazing. Someone bumps off Miss Jellop and nobody sees a thing, and yet you know I had the police here last night." Agatha told her about Binser's complaint.

Mrs. Bloxby sighed and sat down and placed her battered handbag on the kitchen table. Look at her, thought Agatha, mangy old handbag, droopy cardigan, baggy tweed skirt, and yet she always appears the picture of a lady. "If only you could find out who did these dreadful murders," said the vicar's wife. "Nothing in the village will ever be the same if you don't."

"I'm shackled at the moment," said Agatha. "The police will be furious if I carry on, and I think they'll charge me next time."

"Did you find out anything else?"

Agatha told her about Charlotte Bellinge. "Tristan must have been furious," said Mrs. Bloxby. "Beauty, titled lady, wealth, and all snatched from him."

"He thought he was using her and all the while she was just using him," said Agatha.

"So he was probably not gay although it is so hard to tell, with all of us being such a mixture of masculine and feminine."

"Anyway, it appears the London end is closed."

"I don't think that matters. Surely it is something to do with someone here."

"Tell me about Peggy Slither," said Agatha. "Is there a Mr. Slither?"

"She's divorced. Her husband, Harry, was a wealthy businessman. He was having an affair. She hired a private detective and when she'd gathered enough evidence, she sued him for divorce. She already had money of her own, but she took a lot from him, including the house. He had evidently once jeered at her over what he called her vulgar taste and the minute the house was hers, she redecorated—I think—in a way that would infuriate him."

"I think John is going to try her again on his own. Do you know her very well?"

"Only through charity work or when the Ancombe Ladies' Society and our own get together. She is not popular."

"She evidently was with Tristan."

"I don't think he really cared what women were like as long as they had money."

Ouch, thought Agatha, so much for my charms.

"But," continued the vicar's wife, "the parish work must go on. We need some event which will raise a good sum for Save the Children. We seem to have done everything in the past—jumble sales, whist drives, fêtes, country and western dances—there must be something else."

"People like to gamble," said Agatha.

"I thought of a fishing competition." Mrs. Bloxby opened her handbag and drew out a small yellow plastic duck with a hook in its head. "The scouts use these for fishing contests—you know, fishing lines and tanks of water and a prize for the person who hooks the most ducks."

"No money in it," said Agatha. She took the duck from

Mrs. Bloxby and examined it. "I've got an idea," she said. "If you took the hook off and weighted the duck underneath for balance and put a cocktail stick with a flag on the head instead of the hook, you could have duck races."

"Duck races?"

"Yes, you see, that would bring in the gambling element. We could ask Farmer Brent if we could use the stream on his land. We run, say, six races and get people to sponsor each race and get their name on it. John Fletcher at the Red Lion could sponsor a John Fletcher race, and so on. Have a refreshment tent. Have a gate with entrance fees. Planks laid across the stream for starting and finishing points. I'll be bookie and get them to place bets on the ducks. Small prizes for the winners. Take the ducks back at the end of each race, dry them out and sell them again for the next one."

"It could work," said Mrs. Bloxby. "We'd be awfully dependent on the weather."

"The long-range forecast says October is going to be a good month. Put posters up in all the villages."

"I'll get to work on it," said Mrs. Bloxby. "It will take my mind off things. You are a great loss to public relations, Mrs. Raisin."

"I'll talk to Farmer Brent and get his permission, I'll arrange the posters and publicity."

"Do you know what you mean to do next?" asked Mrs. Bloxby. "I mean, in finding out who committed these murders?"

"I'll keep digging around," said Agatha.

The next morning, Agatha found John's keys lying inside her front door. She picked them up and put them in the pocket of her slacks. Perhaps, she thought, Mrs. Essex might have discovered or remembered something. I might get more out of her on my own. After a breakfast of two cigarettes and two cups of black coffee, she fed her cats and then set out for Dover Rise.

As she was passing John's door, she noticed a package sticking out of his letter-box. Better pop it inside, thought Agatha. Like that, it's an invitation to thieves.

She fished out his keys, extracted the package, picked up letters from the floor and placed them all on his desk. The phone began to ring. She stood listening to it, wondering whether to answer it when it clicked over onto the answering machine. A voice said, "John, dear, this is Charlotte Bellinge. Looking forward to seeing you for dinner tonight. Would you be a dear and bring me a signed copy of one of your books? 'Bye."

Agatha sat down by the desk and twisted the bright engagement ring round and round on her finger. Of course John must be investigating further, she tried to tell herself. But then she thought of the beautiful and exquisite Charlotte and shook her head dismally. It was obvious John couldn't wait to see Charlotte again. And he hadn't told her.

Feeling very much on her own, she locked up and left and went to her own cottage. What of her former Watsons—Charles Fraith and Roy Silver? She would get one of them on the case with her and show John Armitage that she did not need him.

But when she phoned Roy's office, it was to be told he was working out of the New York office, and Charles Fraith's aunt informed her that Charles was in Paris.

Agatha stood up and squared her shoulders and set her mouth in a grim line. She would solve this case herself.

SEVEN

✝

AGATHA had decided that Mrs. Essex would have probably returned to the north before she arrived at the cottage, but Mrs. Essex herself answered the door.

"Oh, it's you," she said. "Come in. Maybe you can tell me what I should do with this lot. They're down in the cellar," she said, leading the way to a door under the stairs.

As Agatha bent her head to follow her through the low door and down shallow stone steps, she wondered if Mrs. Essex had found something gruesome.

"There they are," said Mrs. Essex.

The small cellar was full of metal wine racks stacked with dusty bottles.

"I wouldn't have thought your sister would be a wine collector," said Agatha.

"If you mean fine wines, forget it. This lot is all home-made. See!" She took a bottle out of the nearest rack. A faded white label with the inscription "Jellop's Brew" had been stuck on the greenish glass.

"Is it any good?" asked Agatha.

"I never touch alcohol, so I wouldn't know."

Agatha thought of the duck races. Nothing like a bit of alcohol to get the punters going. And home-made wine would not be considered sinful.

"If it tastes all right, I could maybe take the lot off you for a church fête."

"What! All of it?"

"Yes, how much would you want?"

"If it's for the church, you can have it. I could turn this cellar into a big kitchen. The one upstairs is like a cupboard. But you'd better try some first. We'll take this bottle upstairs and I'll find you a glass."

Agatha reflected it was a bit early in the day for alcohol. On the other hand, it was probably pretty mild.

She led the way upstairs and Mrs. Essex followed her carrying the bottle. The living-room smelt damp and musty. "Ruby was too mean to get central heating in," said Mrs. Essex, as if reading her thoughts. "Have a seat and I'll get a glass."

At least she's being friendly, thought Agatha. I might just find out something.

Mrs. Essex returned with a corkscrew and a glass. She drew the cork and poured Agatha a glass of golden liquid. Agatha sniffed it cautiously. Then she took a sip. It was sweet and she normally didn't like sweet wine, but it slid pleasantly down her throat and sent a warm glow coursing through her veins.

"So have you found out anything relevant to my sister's murder?" asked Mrs. Essex.

"No, nothing. All I can think of is that Tristan told her

something about somebody and that somebody found out she knew and decided to silence her. Would she keep such information to herself without telling the police?"

Agatha took another large gulp of the wine.

"If she did know something, she might not realize how important it was. She liked secrets and she liked power. Ruby wasn't a nice person. I know she's dead. But the fact is that she tormented the life out of me when we were growing up. I remember once . . ."

Her voice went on, describing the iniquities of Ruby while Agatha refilled her glass, enjoying the effect of the wine. It was as if all the golden warmth of summer were surging through her body.

She realized Mrs. Essex was asking her a question. "I beg your pardon," said Agatha dreamily.

"I was asking how you pass your time in this village. It seems so cut off."

"Oh, there's the ladies' society. We're always arranging events to raise money for charity."

"Forgive me, but you don't look the type to enjoy that sort of thing. Are you married?"

"I was."

"Where is he now?"

"I don't know," said Agatha. A dark tide of misery flooded her. She told Mrs. Essex all about James, all about how he had pretended to be taking holy orders while fat tears coursed down her cheeks. She went on to tell the bemused lady about her past, about her struggles, about her life, until she realized that somewhere in this sad tale, Mrs. Essex had gone into the kitchen, taking the remains of the bottle of wine and had replaced it with a steaming mug of coffee.

"Drink that," said Mrs. Essex. "You must forgive me for saying so, but you are drunk."

Shock sobered Agatha somewhat. "I'm sorry," she said. "I don't know what came over me."

"Alcohol's what came over you. It looks as if that stuff's pretty lethal. Do you still want it?"

"Oh, yes. I'll get John at the pub to collect it and we can stack it somewhere in the church hall. I'll ask Mrs. Bloxby where it should be stored." Agatha rose unsteadily to her feet. "I'll jusht be on my way."

Mrs. Essex scribbled something on a piece of paper and held it out. "That's my phone number. Give me a ring when they're coming to collect the wine."

Agatha looked at her helplessly. "Shorry."

"It's all right. I think you should go home and sleep it off."

Agatha was sure the fresh air would restore her, but she had to walk home very slowly and carefully as her legs were showing an alarming tendency to give way.

With a sigh of relief she opened her front door and went into the sitting-room. She would just lie down on the sofa until her head cleared.

When she awoke, the room was in darkness. Her cats were sitting on her stomach looking down at her, their eyes gleaming.

Agatha straightened up and they jumped down on the floor and headed for the kitchen, mewing crossly.

What time is it? wondered Agatha. She stumbled to the door and switched on the light and stared in amazement at her watch. Eight o'clock in the evening. She hurried into the kitchen and opened cans of cat food. Once the cats were fed, she made herself a cup of coffee and sat down at the kitchen table and lit a cigarette. With the first puff, memory came flooding back. With dreadful clarity she remembered telling Mrs. Essex everything about her life. Her face flooded with colour and she let out a groan. She wondered what proof that wine was. It had seemed such a good idea for the duck races. She picked up the phone in the kitchen and dialled the vicarage number. When Mrs. Bloxby answered, Agatha told her all about the wine. "It's heady stuff. Do you know I gave Mrs. Essex my life story after only a couple of glasses? Do you think it would be safe to serve it?"

"It's in a good cause," said the vicar's wife. "And she is giving it away. We'll sell it by the small glass and warn everyone it's very strong."

"I feel such a fool," wailed Agatha.

There was a long silence.

"Are you still there?" asked Agatha anxiously.

"Yes. I'm thinking. Something just struck me. If it loosened your tongue so effectively, it might have done the same to Tristan Delon's."

"So it might," said Agatha slowly. "I've never behaved like that before. He might have been blackmailing someone we don't know about. John was going to see Peggy Slither again, but he's gone off to London. I might try her myself. I'm going to phone John Fletcher and ask him if he can pick up the wine tomorrow. Where do you want it stored?"

"In the church hall. I'll leave it open tomorrow morning. We could really do with a proper church hall. That one is too small for events and we always have to use the school hall."

"Maybe the duck races could be used to raise money for a new one."

"Tempting. But Save the Children comes first."

"Okay. Can you think of any excuse I could use to talk to Peggy Slither again?"

Mrs. Bloxby sat in thought. Then she said, "We could involve the Ancombe lot in the duck races. Old Mrs. Green is the chairwoman of the Ancombe Ladies' Society, but she is poorly at the moment. Peggy is the secretary. You could call on her as my emissary and propose to her that we join forces."

"Excellent. I'll do that."

"I'll phone John Fletcher at the pub and ask him if he'll send the truck round to pick up the wine," said Mrs. Bloxby. "If the wine is as powerful as you say, perhaps we should mix it with fruit juice and serve a punch."

"Might be safer," conceded Agatha. "Tell John to call Mrs. Essex and tell her what time the truck will be there. I'll try Peggy Slither tomorrow. I'm still feeling shaky."

After Mrs. Bloxby rang off, Agatha put a frozen shepherd's pie in the microwave. It never struck her as odd that she should be prepared to spend time cooking for her cats and yet be content with microwave meals for herself.

Agatha had tried to get interested in cooking. The Sunday supplements for the newspapers were full of recipes and coloured photos of delicious meals. Everyone who was anyone knew how to cook exotic dishes these days.

But it was very hard to plan exotic meals for one. She poked at the microwaved mess on her plate, forcing herself to eat some of it so that she would not wake up hungry during the night.

It's just as well I'm not in love with John, she thought, as she finally settled down for the night. I wish him well with that tart, Charlotte Bellinge. But as if to give the lie to this thought, her cats sidled into the bedroom and leaped onto the bed, something they only did when they sensed she was upset.

Agatha drove reluctantly to Ancombe the next morning to face Peggy Slither. She now wished she had waited for John's return and sent him instead. After all, he was the one who had promised to go. She found herself hoping that Peggy was not at home. But as she parked, got out, and approached the garden gate of the bungalow, she saw Peggy stooped over a flower-bed.

"Hi!" said Agatha.

Peggy straightened up from her task of planting winter pansies and surveyed Agatha with disfavour. "Why do British people keep saying hi, as if they were Americans? I blame television."

"Oh, really. Well, a good day to you and how *do* you do," said Agatha acidly, forgetting that she had meant to be nice to Peggy and so encourage her to talk.

"So what do you want?" demanded Peggy.

Agatha outlined the idea for the duck races and Peggy visibly thawed. "I'll make the decision to join forces with Carsely," she said. "Mrs. Green should never have been made chairwoman. Come inside and let's discuss dates and arrangements."

Back into that horrible living-room. Agatha said that the twenty-third of October, a Saturday, would be a good day.

"What if it rains?" asked Peggy.

"I'll get a marquee set up in the field for refreshments. If it rains, the races will just need to take place all the same."

"Will Farmer Brent agree to let us hold it on his land?"

"I'll go and see him," said Agatha. "I only know him slightly. I was introduced to him in the pub. He seems a friendly sort. Mrs. Essex, Miss Jellop's sister, is contributing home-made wine."

"Is she living in her sister's house already?"

"She's just clearing up. I think she and her husband plan to use it for weekends."

"Must say it's pretty insensitive of her, her sister being recently murdered and all. I think the Jellop woman was slightly off her head."

"Did you know her?"

"Not very well. Sort of in the way I know the rest of you women from Carsely."

"Tristan knew her well. Did he talk about her?"

118

"Had a giggle with me about several of the old biddies in the parish. I can't remember him saying anything about her in particular. You detecting again?"

Agatha was suddenly sure that she was lying. She was sure that Tristan had said something about Miss Jellop.

"I'm curious," she said. "There's a murderer on the loose."

"You've done this sort of thing before, if I remember."

"Yes."

"Is this how you go about it? Ask questions? Any questions?"

"Something like that," said Agatha. "People sometimes remember things they haven't told the police."

"I could do that."

"Why should you?" demanded Agatha crossly.

"Because I'd probably be better at it than you." Peggy's eyes gleamed with a competitive light.

God, I really do *hate* this woman, thought Agatha.

"I have a lot of experience in these cases," said Agatha stiffly.

"Yes, but I knew Tristan very well."

"Not well enough to find out anything that might relate to his murder," said Agatha, hoping to goad her into some revelation.

"That's what you think. If you can find out things, so can I. I remember, you even got your picture in the newspapers a couple of times."

"I didn't do it for fame or glory. As a matter of fact, the police took the credit in nearly every case."

"So you say," jeered Peggy.

Agatha had had enough. She stood up. "The police don't like amateurs interfering in their investigation."

"Oh, really? So what about you? You have no professional status."

"I am discreet."

"Agatha Raisin discreet!" Peggy gave a great horse laugh and that braying laugh followed Agatha as she marched out of the door. She gave a fishing gnome a savage kick as she passed and it tumbled into a small pool.

"I'll show her," muttered Agatha as she got into her car. "But how? I'm at a dead end."

Once home again, she sat down at her computer and began to type out everything she had learned. As she typed, the engagement ring on her finger winked and flashed. She took it off and put it in the desk drawer.

The doorbell rang. She saved what she had typed and went to answer it.

Bill Wong said, "I think it's time we had a chat, Agatha."

"Come in," said Agatha reluctantly. "I'll make coffee."

"Instant will do."

Agatha switched on the kettle. Her cats jumped up on Bill, purring loudly. He patted them and then removed Hodge from his shoulder and Boswell from his knee and placed them gently on the floor.

Agatha made two cups of coffee and placed them on the table along with milk and sugar. "I think I've some cake left," she said.

"Never mind the cake. Sit down. I want to talk to you. I see you're not wearing your ring."

"I was typing on the computer and it kept flashing in the light and distracting me. What do you want to talk to me about?"

"I've never known you before to let things lie in a murder case," said Bill. "I feel damn sure you've been ferreting around. Is there anything you haven't been telling me?"

"You know about Binser. Yes, I've been asking a few questions but not getting anywhere. Someone Tristan knew, like Miss Jellop, learned something about the murderer."

"I should think that's pretty obvious."

"Unless it wasn't related. Unless maybe her sister bumped her off."

"Mrs. Essex has a cast-iron alibi. Now out with it. Who have you been talking to?"

"You may as well know. I went to see a Mrs. Peggy Slither this morning."

"Why her?"

"That repulsive woman was friendly with Tristan. But she won't tell me anything. The silly cow has decided to turn detective herself."

"I'd better see her. If she's holding anything back, she might tell me. Where does she live?"

Agatha gave him directions. Then she said, "There was Mrs. Tremp."

"We spoke to her. Apart from the fact she was about to give Tristan money and was saved by his murder is all we know. Think, Agatha. Has anyone else in this village got enough money to have attracted Tristan's attentions?"

"There are a good few around. I can't bring anyone to mind. I mean, sometimes in the Cotswolds, people with a good amount put by for their retirement live in quite modest homes. People are living so long these days and they all dread the inevitable high fees of a nursing home."

"I'll ask Mrs. Bloxby," said Bill. "She might be able to think of someone. Where's John Armitage?"

"He's up in London." Agatha coloured faintly. Had she told Bill about Charlotte Bellinge? Better keep some bits of the investigation to herself. Pride would not let her confess to Bill that John had gone up to London to see an attractive woman.

"There's a favour I want to ask you," said Bill. "You know I told you about my girl-friend, Alice."

"Oh, yes. That still on?"

"Very much so," said Bill, beaming.

"Been to meet your parents yet?"

"No."

Obviously not, thought Agatha, or it wouldn't still be on. "You see," continued Bill, "I feel I've made mistakes in the past by introducing my girl-friends to my parents too early on. Makes them think I'm getting too heavy. But I would like Alice to meet my friends. I've got the evening off. May I bring her over?"

"I'd be honoured," said Agatha. "Bring her for dinner."

"Maybe not. She's a vegan."

"Oh dear. But I think I can cope."

"No need to do that. What if I bring her for drinks, say, for an hour about seven o'clock and then I can take her for dinner somewhere."

"Right you are."

When Bill had left, Agatha returned to her computer and ran over what she had already written.

If Miss Jellop had learned something from Tristan, something dangerous, then it must be about someone in Carsely or one of the other nearby villages.

And what of Mrs. Tremp? Perhaps it would be a good idea to try that lady again. She decided to walk. Too much driving everywhere meant she wasn't getting enough exercise. But as she trudged up out of the village, she was assailed again by the old longing to just let herself go, stop chasing after men, give up the battle against age. John Armitage, whom she had almost come to think of as asexual, had fled off to London, apparently smitten by Charlotte Bellinge. There was a faint hope that he might be trying to find out something relevant to the case, but Agatha doubted it. And how could a stocky, middle-aged woman compete with a porcelain blonde? Not that I want to, thought Agatha. I mean, I'm not at all interested in John. I wonder if I should go blonde. Do blondes really have more fun? Why not try? She tugged her mobile phone out of her handbag and called her hairdresser. Yes, they had a cancellation and could fit her in at three that afternoon.

Mrs. Tremp was at home and not at all pleased to see Agatha. "If you've called to ask me about the murders, I don't know anything," she said.

"I actually called to see if you could help with the duck races," lied Angela.

Mrs. Tremp looked diverted. "Duck races? What on earth are they?"

Agatha explained.

"That does sound a good idea and I do like to help in charity work. Come in. What is it you would like me to do?"

"Last time I was here you said you were making jam," said Agatha. "I wondered if you would consider setting up a table at the races and selling some of your home-made jam? You need not contribute what you make for any sales to the charity if you do not want to. It's just that stands with home-made jams and cakes lend a country air to the proceedings."

"Oh, no, I'll be glad to contribute. Who is making the cakes?"

"I thought I might ask the members of the ladies' society."

"No need for that. Do sit down, Mrs. Raisin. I will bake cakes as well. To be honest, time does lie heavily on my hands. The colonel when he was alive kept me so busy. As a matter of fact, I've just made some carrot cake. Would you like some?"

"That would be very nice."

"Tea?"

"Yes, please."

When Mrs. Tremp retreated to the kitchen, Agatha wondered how to broach the subject of Tristan. Perhaps just talk about the races and village matters and see if Mrs. Tremp herself volunteered anything.

The carrot cake proved to be delicious. Agatha ate two large slices, comforting herself with the thought that the walk home might counteract the calories. She talked further about the plans for the races and then volunteered the information that Mrs. Essex was contributing a cellar-full of home-made wine.

"Who is this Mrs. Essex?" asked Mrs. Tremp.

"Miss Jellop's sister."

"How odd! She is staying at her sister's home?"

"Only, I think, to clear up. I believe she and her husband plan to use it for weekends and holidays."

"Sad, that. I mean, the life is draining out of the villages. I mean, the community life. Soon the whole of the Cotswolds will be some sort of theme park full of tourists, incomers and weekenders. There are few like you, Mrs. Raisin, who are prepared to do their bit. I am sorry I was so cross with you, but the murder of poor Tristan upset me. He had a way of making me feel good about myself. I suppose the secret is to feel good about oneself without relying on other people, but that is a very hard thing to do. Of course, I have wondered and wondered what could have brought about his death. He was extremely attractive. Perhaps it was a crime of passion."

"Could be. Somehow I think it was to do with money and somehow I get a feeling that after I left him on his last night something happened to make him want to run for it. Has anyone said anything about anyone strange being seen in the village?"

"I only usually speak to people in church or people in the general stores. They are all mystified."

"If you can think of anything, let me know." Agatha tactfully turned the conversation back to village matters and then took her leave.

When she returned home, she checked her supply of drinks to see if she had a good-enough selection, ate a hurried lunch of microwaved lasagne and got into her car and drove to the hairdresser's in Evesham, all the while telling herself that she did not really need to go blonde, she could always change her mind at the last minute.

Early that evening, she rushed up to the fright magnifying mirror in the bathroom for yet another look. Her thick hair was a warm honey-blonde . . . and yet . . . and yet . . . she did not feel like Agatha Raisin. Agatha went into the bedroom for a look in the wardrobe mirror. A stranger looked back at her. She was wearing a plain black georgette dress, cleverly cut to make her look slimmer than she was. Perhaps some eye-shadow? She went back to the bathroom. She carefully applied beige eye-shadow, then liner and mascara, and had just finished when the doorbell rang.

"You've gone blonde!" said Bill, goggling at her. "This is Alice."

"Come along in," said Agatha.

As she led the way to the sitting-room, she heard Alice mutter, "You said she was *old*."

And then Bill's quiet rejoinder, "I said older than me."

Agatha crossed to the drinks trolley. "What will you have, Alice?"

"Rum and Coke."

"Oh dear," said Agatha. "I don't know if I've got any Coke."

"Sherry will do, if you've got that," said Alice.

"I'll have a soft drink," said Bill.

"Tonic water?"

"That'll be fine."

Agatha busied herself with the drinks, handed them round, and sat down opposite Alice and Bill, who were seated side by side on the sofa. It was the first occasion since their arrival that Agatha was able to get a good look at Alice. She had curly brown hair, wide eyes and a pugnacious jaw. She had a generous bosom, a thick waist and chubby legs.

"Have you known Bill long?" asked Alice. She took Bill's hand in hers and held it firmly.

"Ever since I came down here. Bill was my first friend."

"Seems odd." Alice took a sip of her drink and wrinkled her nose. "I like sweet sherry," she said.

"I don't have any of that. May I offer you something else?"

"Don't bother. Just put this in a bigger glass and add some tonic water."

Oh dear, thought Agatha, but did as requested. "What's odd?" she asked.

"Well, I mean, Bill being young and you old."

"We were not having an affair," said Agatha acidly.

"Found out anything more about the case?" asked Bill hurriedly. Why, oh why, he wondered, did Agatha Raisin have to go blonde and put on a slinky dress?

Agatha shook her head. She told them about the duck races. Alice laughed, a harsh and brittle sound. "Kids' stuff."

I will not be nasty to this girl for Bill's sake, no matter what she says, vowed Agatha. "Oh, it will be amusing, I assure you," she said lightly. "How do you enjoy working in the bank, Alice?"

" 'Sawright."

"Interesting customers?"

"Some of them. Some of them think the bank's a bottomless pit of money. They come in saying the machine outside won't give them anything. I just tell them, 'You're wasting my time and your own. If that machine says you can't have any money, then you can't.' " She laughed. "You should see their faces."

How can Bill like such a creature? marvelled Agatha. But Bill was smiling at Alice fondly.

Alice stood up. "Can I use the little girls' room?"

"It's at the top of the stairs."

When Alice had left, Bill grinned. "I'm rather enjoying this."

"Why?" demanded Agatha.

"I've never seen Alice jealous before. You would choose this night to turn yourself into a blonde bombshell."

"I should find it flattering, but I'm finding this visit awkward, Bill. Are you really keen on her?"

"I think this is the one, Agatha. You're seeing her at her worst. You should be flattered."

Agatha opened her mouth to say she wasn't feeling flattered at all when Alice returned. Deciding to keep the conversation away from Alice, Agatha discussed the case with Bill while all the time she thought, he really mustn't get tied up with such a creature. But she promised herself she would not interfere in his life.

But as they were leaving, Agatha said politely, "Give my regards to your parents, Bill."

Alice, who had reached the front door ahead of Bill, swung round. "*I* haven't met your parents. *I* would like to meet your parents."

"And so you shall," said Bill. "Thanks for the drinks, Agatha. I'll call you soon."

Agatha slammed the door behind them. Bill's formidable mother would soon send Alice packing, but what a horror she was. Agatha surveyed herself in the hall mirror. She sighed. It just wouldn't do. Then she was struck by the thought that John, seeing her as a blonde, might get the idea that she was trying to compete with Charlotte and she would look pathetic. Agatha resolved to get it all dyed back the way it was as soon a possible.

She had arranged so that the phone would not ring during Bill's visit. She picked up the receiver to put it back on the ringing tone and found she had a message. She dialled 1-5-7-1 and waited. "You have one message," said the carefully elocuted voice of British Telecom. "To listen to your messages, please press one." Agatha did that and Peggy Slither's voice sounded, "I'm streets ahead of you. You'll never guess what I found out. I'm just going to check a few more facts and then I'm going to the police."

Agatha saved the message. I don't think she knows anything at all, she thought. She bit her lip. She picked up the receiver again and arranged the ringing tone and replaced it again. She was just turning away when it rang. It was Mrs. Bloxby. "How are things with you, Mrs. Raisin?"

"I'm not getting any further. Oh, Bill was just round with his latest love and she's horrible. Nasty bullying sort of girl."

"Well, as you've pointed out before, they never last after a visit to his parents."

"He hasn't taken her to see them yet but he's going to, so that should be the end of that."

"I gather from what you've told me that he usually favours nice quiet girls. Maybe this one will be a match for his mother."

"No one," said Agatha with feeling, "is a match for Bill's mother. Oh, there's something else." She told the vicar's wife about her visit to Peggy and the message she had just received.

There was a silence and then Mrs. Bloxby said, "I don't like this. I can't help remembering the time when Miss Jellop phoned me up. Do you think she could be in danger?"

"I don't know. She did know Tristan pretty well. I tell you

what, I'll phone her and see what she's up to. Probably just bragging. I'll let you know."

Agatha rang off and looked up Peggy's number in the phone-book and dialled. She got the engaged signal. She went into the kitchen and looked in the freezer for something to microwave. The cats wove their wave around her ankles. "You've been fed—twice," complained Agatha. She picked out a packet of frozen steak-and-kidney pudding and put it in the microwave to defrost. She tried Peggy's number again, but it was still engaged. She returned to the kitchen and heated the steak-and-kidney pudding and shovelled the mess onto a plate. The cats sniffed the air and then slunk off, uninterested. Agatha picked at her food with a fork. After she had managed to eat most of it, she dialled Peggy's number. Still engaged.

I'll drive along and see her, thought Agatha. She went upstairs and changed into a sweater, slacks and flat shoes. She tied a scarf over her hair because the more she looked at it, the more it began to seem too vulgar-bright.

The night was blustery with wind. The lilac tree at the gate dipped and swayed, sending leaves scurrying off down the lane. A tiny moon sailed in and out of the clouds above.

Agatha looked ruefully at John's dark cottage. She felt that she would have liked him to go along with her. The road to Ancombe was quiet. She passed only two cars on the way and one late-night rambler, trudging along, scarf over the lower part of the face as protection against the wind.

When Agatha parked outside Peggy's cottage and saw that all the lights were on and music was blaring out, she experienced a feeling of relief. Peggy was obviously entertaining. Still, thought Agatha, having come this far, I may as well see if she'll give me a hint of what she has found out. If I handle it properly, she may be tempted to brag.

She walked up the garden path where plaster gnomes

leered at her from the shrubbery. The Village People were belting out "Y.M.C.A." The door was standing slightly ajar. Agatha walked into the little hall. The music crashed about her ears but she could not hear any voices.

Suddenly frightened, she pushed open the door of the living-room and reeled before the increased blast of noise. She walked over to the stereo and switched it off. Now the silence, broken only by the sound of the peeing statue and the wind outside, was more frightening than the noise of the music.

"Peggy!" croaked Agatha. She cleared her throat and shouted loudly, "Peggy!"

Agatha looked longingly at the phone, which was in the shape of a shoe. Call the police before you look any further, she told herself. But something impelled her to go out and across the hall and push open the kitchen door at the back . . . She fumbled inside the door for a light switch and, finding it, pressed it down. Fluorescent light blazed down on the kitchen . . . on the blood on the white walls, on the blood on the floor and on the savagely cut body of Peggy Slither lying by the back door.

Agatha let out a whimper and stood with her hand to her mouth. She forced herself to kneel down by that terrible body and feel for a pulse. No life. No life at all.

She rose and scrambled back to the living-room and seized the phone and dialled the police. Then she went outside and leaned her head against the cold wall of the cottage.

EIGHT

✝

FOR the next two weeks, Carsely was a village under siege. It was flooded by press and by sightseers. Finally rough weather drove the sightseers away, leaving behind them soda cans and sandwich wrappers, and another Balkan uprising sent the press rushing back to London. It was a relief to walk down the village streets without being accosted by reporters. The members of the ladies' society picked up all the rubbish left behind and bagged it. Even John Fletcher, landlord of the Red Lion, who had done a roaring trade, was glad to see the last of the press and the gawking public.

John Armitage had returned from London as soon as he had heard the news of the latest murder. Agatha was once more restored to a brunette, having gone straight to the hairdresser's the day after the murder and right after signing her statement at police headquarters in Mircester. Only the dogged police were left, still going from house to house in Carsely and in the neighbouring villages, questioning everyone over and over again. The weapon with which Peggy had been so brutally murdered had never been found.

Agatha had expected John to be a frequent caller to discuss the case, but he seemed quiet and withdrawn, saying he was behind with his writing and had to catch up. She herself had been frightened into inactivity, although she would not admit it to herself. Such as Agatha Raisin hardly ever admitted to being frightened. She persuaded herself that three murders were just too much. Out there was a madman who should be left to the police. But she lost weight through nerves, waking up during the night at the slightest sound and picking at her food during the day.

Mrs. Bloxby had given up urging Agatha to find the killer. "It really is not safe for you, Mrs. Raisin," she said. "What if this dreadful murderer should decide you knew something as well?"

The day after the press had gone, John Armitage called round. "Are you eating?" he asked anxiously, as if noticing Agatha properly for the first time since his return from London. "You look haggard."

Agatha glared at him. Despite her fright, she had been pleased with her new slimline figure. "I did find the body," she snapped.

John sat down at her kitchen table. "And what about you?" asked Agatha. "What have you been doing?"

"I told you. Writing and more writing."

"But you've never said anything about how you got on in London."

"There's nothing much to tell. I saw my publisher, I saw my agent, I saw my friends . . ."

"And you had at least one dinner with Charlotte Bellinge."

"How did you know that?"

"There was a parcel sticking out of your letter-box. I opened your door to put it on the table and heard her dulcet tones on your answering machine."

He coloured faintly. "I thought there might be a lead there, but there was nothing further to add. I did go back to see that vicar at New Cross, but he said he was busy and slammed the door in my face."

"Don't you find that suspicious?"

"Not really. I think he's guilty about having lied to us in the first place. Anyway, to get back to Peggy Slither. She thought she had found out something. And you saw nothing around her home before you found the body? No sinister men?"

"Nothing."

"Any cars on the road?"

Agatha frowned in thought. "Two passed me going away from Ancombe but don't ask me the colour or make. It was dark and I didn't notice them in particular."

Suddenly, in her mind's eye, she was driving towards Ancombe that evening. "The rambler," she exclaimed. "I forgot about the rambler."

"What rambler? Did you tell the police?"

"No, I forgot about him. The shock of finding Peggy lying in all that blood drove him right out of my head."

"What was he like?" asked John eagerly.

"I just got a glimpse. One of those dark woolly hats and a scarf over the lower part of his face. An anorak, a backpack, dark trousers."

"A scarf over his face and you didn't think that suspicious?"

"There was a freezing wind that night. Oh, God, I'd better tell the police. They'll think me such a fool for forgetting."

The doorbell rang. "You get it, John," said Agatha. "Probably some lingering local reporter. To think of the days when I cultivated the press!"

John went to the door and came back a few moments later followed by Bill Wong.

"There you are Agatha, you want the police and here's Bill."

"Why do you want the police?" asked Bill, shrugging off his raincoat and placing it on a chair.

"I've just remembered something." Agatha told him about the rambler.

"Agatha!" Bill sounded exasperated. "Why didn't you remember this before? I'm off duty, but get me a piece of paper. I'll need to take this down."

Agatha went through to her desk and came back with a sheet of paper and then sat down and described the rambler.

"Do you know what I think?" Bill put down his pen with a sigh. "I think our murderer was very lucky. Wilkes is going to be furious when I tell him this. If you had told us right away on the night of the murder, we could have put up road-blocks, we could have scoured the countryside for him. I'd best get off. We'll put out a police bulletin asking him to come forward." He got to his feet and put on his coat.

"Where was Alf Bloxby on the evening of the murder?" asked John.

"According to his wife, he was out on his rounds all evening. We've interviewed all the people he said he'd been to see, but it still leaves an hour unaccounted for."

"Mrs. Bloxby never told me that." Agatha experienced a pang of unease. "What does the vicar say he was doing during that hour?"

"He says he was just walking about. He says the whole business of Tristan's murder had upset him dreadfully and he felt like taking a good walk before bedtime to clear his head."

"Sounds reasonable," said Agatha. She followed him to the door. "Why did you call?"

"Social visit."

"How's Alice?"

"She's fine."

"Take her to see your parents?"

"Yes. They loved her."

Oh dear, thought Agatha.

She saw him out and returned to the kitchen. "Why did you ask about Alf Bloxby?" she demanded.

"I've been thinking. Just because we love Mrs. Bloxby doesn't mean we know anything about Alf. Do you?"

"No, I don't know much, but I do know this. Such as Mrs. Bloxby would never, ever stay married to any man capable of murder."

"She might not know he was capable of murder."

"Rubbish."

"I mean, did she say anything to you about Alf being unable to account for an hour of his movements?"

"He did account for them!"

"But only his word. No witnesses. Let's go and see her."

"All right. If it'll make you feel any better."

"You're not wearing your ring."

"Oh, that. I'd forgotten about it. Do you want me to put it on?"

"May as well maintain the fiction."

"We don't need to maintain it in front of Mrs. Bloxby."

"But we do in front of other people," said John.

Agatha went through to her desk and fished out the ring and put it on her finger. It felt loose. Good heavens, she thought, I'm even losing weight on my fingers.

Leaves wheeled and whirled about them as they walked to

the vicarage. To Agatha, the village no longer felt like a safe haven. She felt there was menace lurking around every corner. She longed for a cigarette and remembered the days when one never, ever smoked in the street. Now the street was about the only place outside one's own home where one could smoke.

Mrs. Bloxby opened the door to them. "Come in quietly," she said. "Alf is resting."

They followed her into the vicarage sitting-room. Agatha and Mrs. Bloxby surveyed each other. Mrs. Bloxby noticed that Agatha was considerably thinner and Agatha noticed that Mrs. Bloxby's usually mild eyes held a haunted look. They had talked since the murder, but only briefly.

Agatha told her about the rambler and Mrs. Bloxby clasped her hands as if in prayer. "If only you had remembered this earlier, Mrs. Raisin."

"They're putting out a bulletin, asking him to come forward," said John. "If he's innocent, he will."

"I've been thinking about ramblers," said Agatha. "I mean, one never really notices them."

"Not groups of ramblers," commented Mrs. Bloxby with a certain edge in her voice. "But one, on his own, at night!"

"I know, I know," mourned Agatha. "But the horror of Peggy's murder drove it right out of my mind until today."

"Bill was round this morning," said John. "He says there is a whole hour your husband can't account for."

"Most of us have whole hours in our lives we can't account for," said Mrs. Bloxby. "It's just unlucky for Alf his hour should have happened on the evening Peggy was murdered. All this is wearing my husband down. I could do without your suspicions being added to our worries, Mr. Armitage."

"I didn't—"

"Yes, you did," interrupted Mrs. Bloxby. She rounded on Agatha. "I thought you had given up investigating."

"I had," said Agatha, silently cursing John.

"Whoever is committing these murders is highly dangerous. I suggest you both leave it to the police. Now, if you don't mind, I have things to do."

They both left the vicarage, Agatha furious with John. "I never should have gone along with you," she said. "Mrs. Bloxby is my best friend."

"Never mind. It's lunch-time and you look a ghost of your former self. We'll go to the pub and have something."

Agatha was about to say pettishly that she didn't want to go with him, but realized she was reluctant to be on her own. "All right," she said ungraciously. "But I don't want much."

In the pub, they both ordered shepherd's pie. Although there were quite a few regulars at the bar, there wasn't much conversation. The murders had poisoned the atmosphere.

Agatha surprised herself by eating all the food on her plate. She decided it was time she went in for some decent home cooking instead of microwave meals.

When they had finished, she looked curiously at John. "You are strangely reticent about Charlotte Bellinge."

"If I had anything relating to the case to tell you, Agatha, I would."

"I don't think you went to see her because you thought she had anything to add. I think you're smitten with her."

"She is a very attractive woman, but no, I am not smitten with her."

"So she rejected your advances?"

"Don't be cheeky, Agatha. We're only pretending to be engaged. You have no right to question me on my personal life."

This was indeed true but for some reason Agatha did not want to be reminded of it.

"So you told me briefly before that you'd been to see Mrs. Essex and Mrs. Tremp. Nothing there, I gathered."

"No, except the wine."

"What wine?"

Agatha told him about the home-made wine and the odd effect it had had on her.

"That's interesting," said John. "You mean, Miss Jellop may have given Tristan some and he might have told her things he wouldn't otherwise have said?"

"Could be."

John sighed. "And now she's dead, we'll never know. What about Mrs. Tremp? There was something cold-blooded about the way she talked about her husband's death. If a woman can sit looking at her husband who's just had a stroke without immediately calling an ambulance, then she must be really pretty tough."

"I don't know. I kept the discussion to the duck races. She seemed pretty friendly and normal."

"Did she know Peggy Slither?"

"I don't know."

"Let's go and ask her."

"I somehow don't want anyone to know we're still investigating," said Agatha.

"You told me she was going to bake cakes for the big event. We'll ask her how she's getting on."

"I suppose we could do that."

After they had returned to Lilac Lane and had driven off in John's car, Agatha felt the black edges of depression hovering around her. For years she had been driven by her obsession for James Lacey, getting James Lacey, and marrying James Lacey. Then she had been divorced by him. After that, she lived in dreams that one day he would return to her. Cold reality was telling her he would never return. Carsely had become a sinister place. She was going to interview a woman who probably did not know anything at all relevant to the case with a man she was pretending to be engaged to. Bill Wong, who had been a sort of soul mate in that he was always being rejected by the loves of his life, had at last found one who evidently could stand up to his parents.

"What's up?" asked John.

"Nothing. Why?"

"This car's filling up with gloom and it's coming from you."

"I've got a bit of a headache, that's all."

"Want to go back home and take some aspirin?"

"No, I'll be all right. Here we are. She's probably at home. I don't think she goes out much."

They parked and got out of the car. The door was standing open. Agatha rang the bell beside the door. The bell shrilled somewhere inside the house.

"That's odd," said John. "She must be in. Try again."

Agatha rang the bell and waited.

"I think we'd better take a look inside," said John uneasily.

Agatha walked in first. "Mrs. Tremp!" she called. No reply. Outside, the rooks cawed from their tree and the wind rushed around the converted barn.

Followed by John, she walked into the kitchen and let out a scream. Mrs. Tremp was lying stretched out on the floor, her eyes closed and her hands folded on her breast.

"See if she's alive," said John, tugging a mobile phone out of his pocket. "I'll call the police."

Mrs. Tremp opened her eyes at that moment and struggled to her feet. "It is my meditation hour," she said crossly. "I do not like to be disturbed. I hoped you would go away." She smoothed down her tweed skirt with her hands. "What do you want?"

Agatha sank down onto a kitchen chair. "I just wanted to

ask if you could cope with all the cake baking for the duck race."

"Of course," said Mrs. Tremp. "I would have told you if I could not. How are the arrangements going?"

"I'm on my way to see Farmer Brent," said Agatha.

"You mean you haven't got permission from him yet? You'd better hurry up. It's only three weeks to the races."

"Isn't it terrible about Peggy Slither?" said John.

"Oh, her." Mrs. Tremp gave a disdainful sniff. "Probably her ex-husband. He was furious at having to pay out so much after the divorce proceedings."

"Did you know her?" asked Agatha.

"Tristan took me over to meet her once. Disgusting, vulgar woman."

"I gather Tristan was friendly with her."

"She was so rude to me that Tristan assured me he would have nothing more to do with her."

"And you haven't heard from her since?"

"Why should I? Such as Mrs. Slither and such as myself have absolutely nothing in common. Now I do have things to do. I suggest you get Mr. Brent's permission as soon as possible."

"We couldn't really stay to get more out of her," said John as they drove on to Brent's farm at the top of the hill.

"She's got a study off the hall," said Agatha. "The door was open and I looked in as we went out. There's a desk there with letters and correspondence. I'd love to have a look at them. I think she's hiding something. I wonder if Tristan ever wrote to her."

"Why should he?" asked John. "I mean, he was in the same village."

"Still, I wouldn't mind having a look. Maybe she wrote to someone about him."

"Then the someone will have the letter. Not Mrs. Tremp."

"There was a computer on the desk. Maybe she's got letters logged in it. The days when it was considered bad manners to type a letter to a friend have long gone."

"I don't know how you're ever going to have a chance to look at them."

"Maybe. I wonder if she locks her door at night."

"Meaning," said John, "you plan to creep in one night and have a look? Don't be silly. There'd be all hell to pay if you were caught. Is that the entrance to Brent's farm on the left?"

"Yes, let's hope he's at home. I don't feel like trekking over muddy fields looking for him."

To her relief, Mark Brent opened the door to them himself.

"I was just about to have a cup of tea," he said. He was a tall, thin man with long arms and stooped shoulders. His thick hair was grey and his long face burnt red by working outdoors. "The wife's off visiting her sister," he said. He prepared a pot of tea and put mugs and milk and sugar on the table. "Sit down," he said. "Isn't it awful about these murders? Is that why you're here, Mrs. Raisin?"

"No," said Agatha. "It's about these duck races. I remember you had an event for the boy scouts in one of your fields with a pretty stream running through it." She told him all about the duck races.

"It's all yours," said Brent. "There's cattle in that field but I'll move them for the day. When is it to be held?"

"October twenty-third."

"Fine. I like to do my bit. Help yourselves. I'm glad I'm outside the village. It's as if that there damned curate and his poncy ways brought something evil in with him."

"You knew Tristan?" asked Agatha.

"My wife, Gladys, was friendly with him. I'd come in from the fields and there they'd be, laughing and joking, and Gladys looking like a dog's dinner, all tarted up in her Sunday best although it was a weekday. Then she tells me she wants a cheque for this Tristan. She says he could invest money for us and make a killing. I said the only killing was going to be Tristan himself. There was something slimy about him. So I got him one day in the village and told him if he came near my wife again I'd set the dogs on him. Poor Gladys cried and cried when I told her and called me a monster.

" 'I put up with it,' I says, 'until he tried to get money out of you.' Fact is, she thought he fancied her. Now don't get me wrong. My Gladys is a fine-looking woman but she's in her fifties." He looked at Agatha. "Didn't have you fooled as well, did he, Mrs. Raisin? I heard how you had dinner with him the night he was murdered."

"No," said Agatha. "He did suggest investing money for me but I refused."

"And I hear you pair are engaged?"

"That's right," said Agatha. "How did you hear that?"

"All over the village, it is. Good on you. I wish you both well. You'll be getting married in the church. Nothing like a good old-fashioned village wedding."

"You didn't threaten to kill Tristan?" asked John.

"Meaning, did I stick a knife in him? No, that's not my way. A telling-off was enough."

"I didn't mean . . ."

"I know what you meant," said the farmer with unimpaired good humour. "Our Mrs. Raisin here has made a name for herself as a detective. Seems as if you're well-suited."

"I found Peggy Slither," said Agatha. "On the road to Ancombe, I noticed this rambler. I've only just remembered and told the police. You didn't at any time see anyone strange about the village?"

"Not on the days of the murders. We're not a tourist place like Broadway. We get these chaps selling kitchen stuff round the doors. Then there are women from the Red Cross and the Lifeboat people come round collecting. Ramblers, of course. Few outsiders at the bed-and-breakfast places, but I gather the police have checked them all out. I think all of us have had the police round asking questions three or four times. But I tell you this, Mrs. Raisin." His voice became hard. "Whoever is doing these here murders is a dangerous man. I think you should sit this one out and leave it to the police. Don't want you getting hurt."

"Sounds like a threat," said John.

"Just a bit of sensible advice. Now I'd best get out there. There's fencing to be repaired."

"I think that *was* a threat," said Agatha as they drove off.

"I don't know. Seems a straightforward-enough man to me."

Agatha sighed. "Well, I'd better throw myself into the publicity for these duck races. I'll be round at Mrs. Bloxby's if you want me."

"Right. I'll get on with some more writing."

Agatha spent the afternoon discussing arrangements such as the hiring of a marquee with Mrs. Bloxby and phoning up local papers, arranging advertisements for the duck races to go in and also for free publicity. But once a public relations officer, always a public relations officer. She also sent press handouts to all the nationals and TV stations to the effect that the murder village was returning to normal. Might get a few of them down from London.

It was only that evening that her thoughts turned to Mrs. Tremp's desk. No one in the village would leave their doors open at night after three murders. But country people often left a spare key in the gutter or under the doormat or in a flowerpot. Had Agatha not felt the black edges of depression returning, she would never have decided to try to break into Mrs. Tremp's home. But action and thoughts of action kept the depression at bay. She set her alarm for two in the morning but she was so restless that she only fell asleep at twelve-thirty and woke at the alarm's shrill sound feeling groggy.

She dressed in dark clothes and decided to walk. Thank goodness Mrs. Tremp doesn't keep a dog, she thought, as she finally reached the converted barn. The guttering was too high up for anyone to reach and there was no doormat or flowerpot. Frustrated and not wanting to turn back now she had come so far, she walked round the side of the house. That must be the study window, she thought. Easy to break a pane of glass and release the catch, but that would mean Mrs. Tremp might hear the noise. Shining the light of a pencil torch at the ground to make sure she did not trip over anything, she made her way round to the back of the house. At the back there was a trapdoor in the ground with coal dust around it. She eased back the bolt and lifted the trapdoor and looked down. Coal had been delivered recently and glittered with reptilian blackness in the faint beam of her torch. She eased herself down onto the top of the pile. The coal began to slide under her feet. She reached upwards trying to catch the top of the trapdoor but she was descending too fast, crashing down among rumbling lumps of coal to finally land at the bottom of the cellar. She lay there, her heart thumping. She had lost her torch but there was faint light from the open trapdoor. She crawled to her feet, feeling bruised. She could dimly make out a stone staircase.

Agatha was just creeping towards it when she heard from

above someone running down the stairs and then a key being turned in the cellar door. Then she heard the front door of the house opening and footsteps hurrying round the side of the house. Agatha scrambled away from the coal and into a corner piled with old suitcases and boxes. Mrs. Tremp's voice said triumphantly, "Got you. You can wait in there until the police come." She slammed down the trapdoor and Agatha could hear her shooting the bolt across.

Agatha felt her way across the floor on her hands and knees with the mad idea of trying to climb up the coal stack and force the trapdoor. Her hand touched her lost torch and she grabbed it eagerly. No, she could not force the trapdoor. She must hide somewhere, somewhere the police would not find her. The beam of the torch lit on a rusty suit of armour covered in coal dust. In a mad panic, Agatha hauled the suit upright. It was unusually light. Probably a replica. She lifted off the helmet and headpiece. Standing on one of the old suitcases, and putting the legs of the suit at an angle, she eased herself into them. She put on the breastplate and fastened it with the leather straps at the back. Then she put on the gauntlets and lifted the headpiece over her head and with a trembling hand forced the rusty visor down, shuffled off into the corner and stood there.

It was then she realized that because of the murders it wouldn't be one local policeman from Moreton-in-Marsh who would arrive but probably the whole squad from Mircester.

She stood there, trembling with cold and fright until she heard the wail of police sirens drawing closer and closer. Then Mrs. Tremp's voice shrill with excitement. "I've got him locked in the cellar. He can't get out."

The cellar door opened, the light was switched on. There was a light switch at the top of the stairs, thought Agatha. But Mrs. Tremp had sounded the alarm before I could have reached it. Bill Wong was there with Wilkes. Four policemen were systematically going through the cellar, turning over boxes, raking over the coal. Coal dust rose in the air. Agatha prayed she would not sneeze.

And then Bill Wong walked over to the suit of armour which encased the trembling Agatha. He raised the visor. A pair of terrified bearlike eyes stared back at him. Bill slammed down the visor.

"Nothing here," he said.

After the search was over, Agatha could hear Wilkes complaining that everyone around was getting hysterical and that Mrs. Tremp had probably left the trapdoor open herself or the coalman had. She had said a load of coal had been delivered only that day. The coal must have shifted and tumbled down in the night. At last Agatha was left alone. She lifted off the visor, took off the gauntlets and headpiece, and lay against a pile of boxes and eased out of the armoured legs. The house was silent again. She crept up the cellar stairs and tried the door. It was unlocked. Agatha walked through a laundry room and then into the hall. All she wanted to do now was escape. She tiptoed to the front door and gently unlocked it and slid back the bolt. Mrs. Tremp would just have to think that in all the excitement she had forgotten to lock the door.

She hurried down the hill, keeping to the shadow of the trees. She let out a sob of relief when she turned into Lilac Lane. She reached her cottage door and put her key in the lock. A voice in her ear said, "What the hell were you playing at?"

Agatha gave a stifled scream and turned round. Bill Wong's eyes gleamed at her in the darkness.

"Oh, Bill," babbled Agatha. "I'm so sorry. So very sorry."

"Let's go inside. You've some explaining to do."

In the fluorescent light of the kitchen, Agatha was a sorry

sight. She was black with coal dust. "I'd let you clean yourself up first," said Bill. "But I'm in a hurry."

Agatha seized a handful of kitchen paper and ran it under the cold tap and then wiped her face and hands.

She sat down at the kitchen table. "Bill, thank you for not betraying me."

"I should have done," he said grimly. "This could cost me my job if anything came out. Lucky for you that Mrs. Tremp came to the conclusion that the coalman had left that trapdoor open and rats or something had shifted the coal during the night. She was most apologetic. So, what have you been up to?"

In a halting voice, Agatha told him all about her plan to look at the papers on Mrs. Tremp's desk and also to see what was in her computer.

"Now, listen to me very carefully," said Bill. "If I ever catch you doing anything like that again, I will not only have you arrested, our friendship will be at an end. I risked my job for you, Agatha. Of all the stupid things to do! This is one case you are going to leave strictly alone from now on. If you do hear of anything relevant to the case, then you are to tell me immediately. I am going to get some sleep with what is left of the night."

"Any news of the rambler?"

"Lucky for you, there is. He walked into police headquarters around seven o'clock this evening—I mean, yesterday evening. Respectable computer nerd, member of a rambling society, said he liked night walking on his own occasionally. No record."

"Why lucky for me?"

"If no one had turned up, it would have looked as if that faulty memory of yours had lost us the chance of getting the killer. Before I go. Why Mrs. Tremp? Did she say something you aren't telling me about?"

"John and I saw her earlier in the day. Tristan had taken her once to meet Peggy Slither. There's something not quite right about Mrs. Tremp. When her husband had his fatal stroke, she sat watching him for a bit before calling the ambulance. She seemed to be . . . well . . . gleeful that he was dead."

"And that's all you had to go on?"

"I know it sounds silly, but I've had good hunches before."

"Agatha, for the last time, leave it alone."

"Okay," said Agatha wearily. She saw him to the door. "Give my regards to Alice."

His tired face lit up. "Thanks. I will."

Agatha shut and locked the door behind him and set the burglar alarm. Then she crawled wearily up the stairs and stripped off her dirty clothes and threw them in the laundry basket before taking a shower and scrubbing off all the coal dust.

Her last thought before she fell asleep was that she was actually relieved she could leave this messy and dreadful case alone.

Next day Agatha went to a printer's where she got a flyer she had run off on her computer enlarged. She collected two hundred copies and spent an afternoon posting them up in shop windows and on trees in Carsely and in the villages round about.

When she returned home, John rang and said he'd be round in a few minutes.

"I've been thinking," he said as he walked in, "that perhaps we've been neglecting the London end. We never found out who beat Tristan up in New Cross."

"Forget it," said Agatha. "I have been told in no uncertain terms to keep away from everything and anything to do with the case. And by the way, that rambler I saw was kosher. A respectable citizen."

"Why are you warned off? What's been happening?"

"I may as well tell you." Agatha described the events of the night. John was hardly able to hear the rest of her story, he was laughing so hard. "You are an idiot," he said finally. "Thank goodness you didn't drag me into it. Not that I would have gone with you. But I haven't been warned off."

"I should think the warning applies to you as well."

"So you're just giving up? Have you ever given up before?"

"No, but I've never been at such a dead end before. I tell you, John, I'm going to concentrate on these duck races and make it all a success for Mrs. Bloxby and then find something safe and pleasant to do with my time."

"Like what?"

"I'll think of something."

"I think I'll go back up to London," said John, "and see what I can find out. Want to come with me?"

Agatha shook her head. "I've given up."

NINE

✝

THE day of the duck races was fine. Hazy sunshine gilded the countryside. Agatha was there early to supervise the arrangements. John had said he would join her later.

Miss Simms was to sell programmes at the field gate. Six races were to be run. The entrance fee was one pound, but as Agatha had put a sign up on the main road saying FREE DRINKS, she was sure that the entrance charge would not deter the crowd. The free drinks were to be fruit punch laced with Miss Jellop's wine. The bottles of wine could be bought for three pounds each. The ducks, for anyone wanting to take part in the race, were to be sold for two pounds each. One of Miss Simms's ex-lovers, a bookie, had volunteered to take the racing bets. Agatha had donated small engraved silver cups to be given to the winner of each race. Agatha was glad the day was warm because the three men who had volunteered to start the duck races would have to stand in the stream in their bare feet to lift the restraining plank across the stream which held the ducks at the starting line.

Agatha was glad she had trusted the weather report and had cancelled the marquee. The day set fair without a breath of wind. The sun sparkled on the rushing stream and shone on the red and yellow leaves of the trees bordering the field.

Some of the local farmers, along with Farmer Brent, had set up tables to sell meat and local vegetables. Mrs. Tremp had two tables, one with home-made jam and the other with cakes.

Agatha mixed fruit juice and two bottles of Miss Jellop's wine into a giant punch-bowl, ready to be ladled into small plastic cups. The event was to start at ten. A small trickle of people began to enter the field. Agatha noticed old Mrs. Feathers. Why didn't I think to question her about Tristan? she wondered. But deep down she knew it was because Mrs. Feathers was old and frail and Agatha was ashamed when she remembered the trouble the old woman had gone to producing that expensive dinner. More people arrived and Agatha was suddenly very busy ladling out punch and selling wine. John appeared and she appealed to him for help because a large crowd of people were demanding punch.

Although Agatha had vowed to have nothing more to do with the case, she could not help turning over what she knew in her mind. There were noisy cheers from the stream where the races were taking place. The bookie was doing well, taking bets. After the first hour, Mrs. Tremp had sold practically everything. More and more people were arriving, drawn by the offer of free drink. Agatha began to feel marginalized. After all, she had paid for the cups. She should be the one to present them. But it was Mrs. Bloxby who was making the presentations.

Agatha tried to console herself with the thought that the day had turned out to be a roaring success. But the press were there in force and she was getting none of the glory.

John tugged out his mobile phone. "Won't be moment," he said. "Just phoning home to see if there are any messages."

"All right. But hurry up," said Agatha sulkily. Then she thought about mobile phones. What had people ever done without them? A thin woman a little away from her was shouting into one. Doesn't need a phone, thought Agatha. Her voice is loud enough to carry miles.

And then she stood with her mouth a little open, the ladle in her hand while a customer looked at her impatiently.

Had Tristan had a mobile phone? If he had, could someone have phoned him the night he died and threatened him? But the police would have found it and checked the numbers.

"Are you going to give me any of that punch or not?" demanded a man in front of her.

"Sure." Agatha ladled some into a cup. She realized she had served the same man about five times before. The crowd was getting noisy and boisterous. Agatha, seeing the punch-bowl was nearly empty, added a bottle of wine and fruit juice to fill it up again. Perhaps two bottles of the stuff had been too strong. A team of Morris dancers had just arrived in their flow-ered hats and jingling bells and started buying bottles of wine. "I don't have a spare corkscrew," said Agatha uneasily. She had not imagined that anyone would drink that lethal stuff until they got home. "Got one here," said a red-faced Morris dancer and his friends all cheered.

Over the Tannoy came an announcement that there would be a break for lunch. Agatha picked a placard off the ground at her feet which said CLOSED FOR LUNCH and placed it on the table. "Do you think anyone will pinch anything?" asked John.

"We'll put the bottles back in the boxes for now and tape them over."

The members of the ladies' societies had set up a buffet at the far corner of the field and had laid out tables and chairs.

Mrs. Bloxby came up to Agatha, her eyes shining. "Such a success," she said. "We were going to confine it to six races, but we've decided to hold more in the afternoon and finish with the Morris dancers.

"What about prizes?" asked Agatha. "Surely all the cups have gone."

"I thought we might present each winner with two bottles of wine."

"Good idea," said Agatha in a flat voice because she still thought that she should have been the one to present the prizes.

"And seeing as the organization has been largely done by you, Mrs. Raisin, I thought it would be nice if you could address the crowd at the end."

Agatha brightened visibly.

When Mrs. Bloxby had left, John said, "What now? Do we go over there and fight for something to eat?"

"I wonder if you could get me a plate of something, John. I want to speak to Mrs. Feathers."

"What about?" he demanded sharply. "I thought you had given up."

"Just one question. I'll tell you later."

Agatha began to search. Mrs. Feathers was not with the lunch crowd nor among the people still crowding in front of the farmers' stalls, Agatha being the only one who had packed up for lunch. And then she saw her grey head bobbing along in the direction of the gate. She ran after her, shouting, "Mrs. Feathers!"

The old lady turned around slowly, blinking in the sunlight. "Oh, it's you, Mrs. Raisin. Lovely day."

"Yes, it is. We're very lucky. Mrs. Feathers, did Tristan have a mobile phone?"

"I was sure he had. But I must have been mistaken. He always used mine."

"What makes you think he had one?"

"I went into his flat one day when I thought he was out, to change the bed linen. But he was in and he was using a mobile phone. He put it away quickly when he saw me. Later when he came down to use the phone, I asked him why he didn't use his own phone and he said it had been a friend's and he had returned it. It was a terrible business, that murder. It really shook me up."

"And Tristan never at any time said anything that you might think would give the police a clue to his murder?"

"Oh, no, they've asked me and asked me. Dear Tristan. He said I was like a mother to him."

"I'm sure you were," said Agatha. "When's the funeral?"

"That took place some time ago. A cousin arranged it."

Drat, thought Agatha, I'd forgotten all about the funeral. But what good would that have done me?

"Do you have a name and address for this cousin?"

"Reckon as how you'll need to ask the police, m'dear. They took away all his stuff and then I think they sent it on to the cousin."

Agatha thanked her and was about to turn away when she saw Bill and Alice just paying their entrance fees.

"Bill," said Agatha, approaching him. "Could I have a word?"

"What about?" demanded Alice.

Agatha looked at Bill pleadingly. "It's a police matter."

"All right. Alice, go and see if there's anything at the stall that Mother would like."

Alice shot Agatha a venomous look and trudged off.

Agatha told Bill about the mobile phone. "Good work," he said. "I'll get them on to it. They can check all the mobile phone companies and see which one he was registered with. But I thought I told you to stop investigating."

"It just came up in conversation with Mrs. Feathers," said Agatha. "Oh, here's your beloved back again."

"I want a drink," said Alice, "but that stall is closed."

God forgive me for what I am about to do, thought Agatha. "I'll get you a drink, Alice." She went to her stall and drew the cork on a bottle of home-made wine while Bill had pulled out his mobile and was phoning headquarters. She picked up one of the large tumblers she had kept for people who only wanted fruit juice and filled it up. "I'd tell Bill that's just punch," said Agatha. "It's pretty strong stuff."

"I can drink any man under the table," sneered Alice. She went back to join Bill.

John came back with a plate of ham and salad, which he handed to Agatha. "Thanks," she said.

"What's going on?" asked John. "When I was queuing up, I saw you talking to Bill and he looked very serious."

Agatha told him about the mobile phone. "That might be something," said John. "Say he had his phone beside the bed. Someone phones him after you left and frightens him. He decides to make a run for it, but first of all, he thinks he'll take that money out of the church box. Whoever threatened him is watching the house, follows him to the vicar's study and stabs him."

"Could be. Oh, they're starting up again and I haven't had time to eat."

"You go ahead. I'll cope with the first lot and then you take over so that I can eat something."

Agatha walked over towards the duck races carrying her plate. People were cheering on the ducks, bets were being laid. The little yellow plastic ducks were bobbing down the stream, occasionally swirling round in the eddies. Agatha found it too difficult to eat with just one plastic fork, so she headed for the lunch tables and found a chair. A little way away from her the Morris men were downing glasses of Miss Jellop's wine, their faces flushed and their voices loud.

"Mrs. Raisin? It is Agatha Raisin, isn't it?"

Agatha looked up. A pretty young woman was standing over her holding a child by the hand. With a wrench of memory, Agatha said, "Bunty! How are you?"

The woman seated next to Agatha moved away and Bunty sat down and put the child on her knee.

Bunty had been Agatha's last secretary before she retired. "Is that yours?" asked Agatha, pointing with her fork to the little girl Bunty was holding.

"Yes, this is Philippa."

"Who did you marry?"

"Philip Jervsey."

"Of Jervsey Advertising?"

"That's the one. After you packed up and retired, I took a job as his secretary."

Agatha frowned. "I thought he was married."

"Yes, he was . . . then."

"Did he get a divorce to marry you?" asked Agatha, ever curious.

"Yes. I feel guilty about it. But I was mad about him. Still am. I took my time about saying yes. You know how it is, Agatha, secretaries and bosses. It gets like a marriage. You get to know them better than their wives."

"Was it a bitter divorce?"

"Not too bad. Cost him a lot, though. But there were no children. We've got a place over in Cirencester we use for weekends. Give Philippa here some country air. And what about you? I see your name from time to time in the newspapers. Death does seem to follow you around." She looked at the ring sparkling on Agatha's finger. "Are you married?"

"I was. I'm divorced. I still wear my rings." Agatha did not want to talk about John.

Bunty looked around. "It all looks so peaceful here. You wouldn't think there had been any murders in such a quiet rural spot. Have the police any idea who did it?"

Agatha shook her head. Philippa squirmed on her mother's knee. "I want to see the ducks," she wailed.

"I'd better take her or I'll get no peace." Bunty rose to her feet. "Nice to see you again."

Agatha saw Alice sitting a little way away on her own, drinking wine. She must have bought a whole bottle from John. There was no sign of Bill. He was probably off somewhere phoning to see if there was any news about that mobile phone. She finished her food and went back to where John was ladling out punch. "We'd better stop selling that wine," he said when he saw her. "The Morris men won't be able to dance if they have any more."

"Are we selling much?"

"Yes, quite a lot. But people are mostly taking it home."

"We'll put the bottles on the table in the boxes and if the Morris men come back, tell them we're sold out and we'll keep on selling it when they go away."

The afternoon wore on and a chill crept into the air. Mrs. Bloxby came up. "The Morris men are getting ready to perform and then it's your speech, Agatha. You may as well close up here. You've done splendidly."

Agatha thankfully put a CLOSED sign on the table and she and John put the remaining plastic cups in a box.

They walked to where the crowd was gathering to watch the Morris men. Bill and Alice were standing just behind the crowd and Alice was red-faced and shouting at him. "You're nothing but a mother's boy."

"Let's go round the other side. I don't want to listen to this," said Agatha. She felt guilty. She should have warned Alice about the effects of the wine.

They found a space where they could watch the Morris men. Alf Bloxby's voice sounded over the crowd. "We will now see a performance of the stick dance by the Mircester Morris Men. Morris dancing is one of the characteristic folk dances of England. We do not know its origins, although we know it was derived from agrarian traditions of fertility rites and celebrations at sowing and at harvest time."

A Morris man fell over and lay on the grass.

"Though well-known during Shakespeare's time," continued the vicar, "it almost died away during the Industrial Revolution, but has now thankfully been revived. You will enjoy the colourful sight of the dancers with their bells and waving hankies dancing to tunes played on the fiddle, pipe and tabor and melodeon. Over to you, boys."

The Morris man who had fallen over was dragged to his feet and he stood there, blinking in the fading sunlight. A tape was put into a player and the jingly, jaunty tune of Morris music sounded out. The dancers with flowers in their hats and silver bells at their knees clutched their sticks and faced each other. They were supposed to bang their crossed sticks as they met in the dance but two of them missed and hit their opposite number a thwack. "You did that o' purpose, Fred," yelled one, and seizing his stick brought it down on the unfortunate Fred's head. Soon the dance had degenerated into a rumble.

Alf Bloxby tried to separate the warring dancers but was thrust aside with cries of "Get away, you murderer."

The vicar, his face flaming, looked around for help, shouting to the crowd to stop laughing and do something.

"Police!" shouted Bill Wong. Alf switched off the music. The dancers stopped hitting each other and stood there sheepishly.

Bill shouted to the crowd. "All of you, go home. Show's over."

The crowd began to stream off towards the gate. "My speech," wailed Agatha.

"Too late," said John. "We'd better get back and start loading up the rest of the wine and stuff." John had borrowed a trailer which was hitched to his car, parked at the edge of the field.

John stared at the ground behind the table. "Agatha, the wine's gone. Someone's nicked the rest of it."

"I don't care," said Agatha. "I hope it poisons them."

"But we'd better tell Bill!"

"Bill's got his hands full. You didn't leave the money behind?"

"No, I've got it here in a bag. We'll count it out at home and then take it along to the vicarage. Are you sure you don't want to report the missing wine?"

"I'm sure. Just let's hope it wasn't a married couple who took it. A few slugs of that wine and they'll be in the divorce courts in no time at all. I don't like Alice, but I should have never let her drink that wine."

"Better Bill finds out what she's really like now instead of later," said John. "Hurry up and help me, Agatha. It's getting cold."

The sun had turned red and was low on the horizon. They

loaded up the trailer with the remainder of the plastic cups, the glasses, the punch-bowl, and then the table itself. As they drove out of the field, Agatha said, "I should have told Bill as well about Brent and his wife."

"I really don't think they had anything to do with it, Agatha."

"Someone had. Someone somewhere. Someone who could have been at this very fête."

They drove to the church hall first and carried the table in. There was still plenty of wine, stacked in boxes. "Just as well we didn't take the whole lot along," said John. "Where did you get the punch-bowl from?"

"I bought it."

"No one could call you mean, Agatha Raisin. It must have cost you a lot, what with the silver cups and all."

"Just doing my bit," said Agatha wearily.

"Will Bill book the Morris dancers?"

"No, I think he'll give them a warning and tell them not to dare drive until they've sobered up."

"That's all right. They'd hired a minibus. As long as the bus driver didn't have any of the wine, they'll be all right."

"We'll leave the cups and glasses here," said Agatha. "They can be used another time. I was too upset to notice. I hope the press had all gone by the time the dancers started fighting."

"Sorry. There was at least one television camera in action and I saw two press photographers."

"Damn."

"Let's go to my place and have a drink."

"No, mine," said Agatha. "I want to let my cats out."

After they had finished their drinks, they counted out the money on the kitchen table. "Nearly one hundred and fifty pounds, and that for the wine alone," said John. "Not bad. There must have been about only two boxes of wine left for them to steal."

"Miss Jellop must have brought most of the wine down here with her when she moved. It must have taken years to make a cellar-full of the stuff," said Agatha. "Let's take this money along to Mrs. Bloxby. She could raise a lot of money for the church with the wine that's left. But I think someone in the village who knows about home-made wine should figure out how to weaken it before any more is sold. At least that should be the end of Alice. I never could figure out what Bill saw in her."

"Maybe she's good in bed."

Agatha shuddered. For some reason she did not want to imagine Bill Wong in bed with anyone, least of all Alice.

Mrs. Bloxby welcomed them at the vicarage and took the bag of money from John. "I'll give this to Alf. He's in his study counting out the takings. From the initial look of things, we've done very well. It is all thanks to you, Agatha, and Alf is going to say so in his sermon next Sunday. I saw you talking to old Mrs. Feathers. Did she have anything interesting to say?"

"I should have spoken to her before," said Agatha. "She said she was sure Tristan had a mobile phone."

"And how does that help?"

"Because Mrs. Feathers said he had no calls the night after I left. But if, say, he had a mobile in his bedroom, someone could have rung him up and threatened him. He could have decided to flee and decided at the same time to take the church takings with him. He was too mean, I think, to let Mrs. Feathers know he had a phone of his own. He preferred to run up bills on hers."

"Did you tell Bill?"

"Yes, for once, I did. He's getting the police to check it."

"If only, oh, if only these murders could be solved."

"If they ever are," said Agatha, "I'll never complain of being bored again. But Bill has definitely warned me off for the last time, so I'll need to leave it to the police."

"He didn't warn me off," John pointed out.

But Agatha didn't like the idea of John playing detective when she herself was not allowed to.

"Mind you," she said, "there would be no harm in continuing to ask around the village. Look at the news I got from Mrs. Feathers. Might do no harm to go and talk to Mr. Crinsted, the man Tristan used to play chess with."

"I'll come with you," said John. "We'll try him in the morning."

"What do you know of Mark Brent?" Agatha asked Mrs. Bloxby.

"Nothing bad. Nice man. Always willing to help out. Why?"

"He was upset with Tristan. Seems his wife, Gladys, got a crush on Tristan and Brent warned him off."

"I cannot imagine for a moment that such as Mr. Brent or his wife would resort to violence of any kind," said Mrs. Bloxby.

"Well, we'll try Mr. Crinsted. Oh, and the mobile library is due round during the week. I'll have a word with Mrs. Brown."

"Do you think it will do any good?" asked the vicar's wife wearily.

Agatha could feel a resurgence of her old energy for investigation which had so recently deserted her. "I've blundered around asking questions before. Something's got to break."

Agatha and John drove to the council estate on Monday morning. "Do you think he'll be at home?" asked John.

"He's very old," replied Agatha. "Bound to be."

Mr. Crinsted answered the door to them. He was stooped and frail with a thin, lined face and mild eyes behind thick glasses. "Do come in," he said. "Dear me, how nice to have some company. The only company I usually have is the television set."

His living-room was neat and clean. Agatha looked at photographs on the mantelpiece of couples with children.

"How many children do you have?" she asked.

"A son and daughter and six grandchildren."

"Must be nice for you when they come on a visit."

"I'm afraid I only see them at Christmas. I think they find visits to me rather boring. The children are dreadfully spoilt."

How awful, thought Agatha, to be trapped here, never seeing anyone. Her mind worked busily. She would suggest to Mrs. Bloxby that they start an old folks' club.. Her stocks and shares had been doing very well. Maybe she could see about getting the church hall renovated, turn it into an old folks' club.

"The reason we called," said John, "is to ask you for your opinion of Tristan Delon."

"Oh dear. Do sit down. I'll make some tea."

Agatha glanced at her watch. "Don't worry. It's nearly lunch-time. Tell you what, we'll chat for a bit and then we'll go down to Moreton for some lunch. My treat."

John stared at Agatha in surprise, but Mr. Crinsted was obviously delighted. "Goodness me, it does seem an age since I've been out of the village. So what can I tell you about our late curate? Well, he called round one day when I was working out some chess moves and offered to play. I was so delighted to have a partner that I let him win on a couple of occasions. He was such good company. I thought he really liked me and that was very flattering to an old man like me. Then the last time, I became absorbed in the game and forgot to let him win. I have never in my life before seen anyone change personality so completely. He accused me of cheating. I patiently began to explain to him the moves I had made and he said, 'You're lying, you silly old fool,' and he upset the chessboard and sent the pieces flying and stalked out of the house. I was very disappointed. You see, I did think we might be friends."

"Before he became upset with you," said John, "did he let fall anything about his private life?"

"Not really. Chess is such a *silent* game. He did say once that people were like chess pieces, easily moved around. I pointed out that people could be very unpredictable."

"Let's continue this over lunch," said Agatha.

They went to a pub in Moreton and ate great helpings of steak-and-kidney pie. Agatha ordered wine. To John's amazement, she sparkled for Mr. Crinsted's benefit, telling him stories about her public relations jobs. Warmed by the wine and food, Mr. Crinsted talked in turn about his own life. He had been a nuclear physicist, working at Los Alamos, and then in Vienna. He had married an Austrian wife, Gerda, but she had died of breast cancer after their second child was born. "I spent a lot of money sending my son and daughter to the best schools and then university. Freda, my daughter, became a nurse and then married a doctor, and my son, Gerald, he became an accountant and married his secretary." Mr. Crinsted sighed. "I never saved any money and I was lucky to get that council house. I have a comfortable pension and my needs are small. I am glad both my children are very comfortably off."

"Don't they help you out?" asked John.

"I never ask them. I don't have any expensive needs. Perhaps I did too much for them and taught them to be selfish."

"You know the church hall?" asked Agatha.

"I know where it is, but that's all."

"I thought I might see about getting it repaired. The roof needs doing. I could start an old folks' club—films, bingo, stuff like that. You could give chess lessons. We'd need a minibus, too, to take people to the shops in Stratford, maybe the theatre."

"That would be wonderful. I would love to give chess lessons."

Again John looked at Agatha in surprise. He had recently come to think of her as a bossy, occasionally grumpy woman. But her eyes were sparkling with enthusiasm and old Mr. Crinsted looked positively rejuvenated.

He had to remind her after two hours of conversation that if they didn't hurry up, they would miss the mobile library.

After they had left Mr. Crinsted, John said, "Are you really going ahead with this old folks' club?"

"Yes, it'll be fun to have something to do."

"You surprise me."

"I can believe that. You have me down as a pushy, selfish woman."

"I have not," said John, reddening.

"There's the mobile library. Let's see what Mrs. Brown has to say."

They had to wait patiently while various villagers returned books, took out more books, and discussed books. At last they were left alone with Mrs. Brown.

"Mr. Delon?" Mrs. Brown looked at them thoughtfully over her half-moon glasses. "Now there was a young man just waiting to be murdered."

"Why do you say that?" asked John.

The plump little librarian picked a book off her desk and put it back on the shelves. "I've often thought about the way he humiliated me, jeering at my choice of books. There was no reason for it. It was an exercise in spite. I thought after I'd heard he had been murdered that if he could be bothered to go out of his way to be nasty to a country librarian, then he had probably been extremely nasty to someone who was prepared to retaliate."

"And you can think of no reason why he should suddenly have sounded off at you?" asked Agatha.

"There was one silly little thing. Mrs. Feathers likes romances, so I always choose one of the more innocent ones and keep it for her. She doesn't like the ones with explicit sex. We got talking one day and she said that Mr. Delon wanted to invest her savings for her. I told her that she should hang on to them, Mr. Delon was not a stockbroker. Perhaps that was what made him angry. But when Mrs. Feathers thanked me for my advice, I asked her not to tell Mr. Delon it came from me and she promised me she wouldn't tell him. That is why I thought his malice was unprompted."

"I think she probably did tell him," said Agatha. "What's the gossip about these murders?"

"I'm afraid a lot of people still suspect the vicar. They say Mr. Delon was murdered in the vicarage and that Miss Jellop and Mrs. Slither may have known something incriminating and Mr. Bloxby might have silenced them. It's ridiculous, I know, but frightened people do talk such rubbish and people *are* frightened. I see the duck races made the front page of the *Daily Bugle*."

"I haven't seen the papers today," said Agatha. "Have you got a copy?"

"Yes, I've one in my desk." Mrs. Brown pulled open a drawer. "Here it is."

There was a coloured photograph of the Morris men fighting. The headline read: THE PEACE OF THE ENGLISH COUNTRYSIDE. "Oh dear," said Agatha. "Never mind. We raised quite a bit of money."

There was nothing more about Tristan to be got from Mrs. Brown. "Two more dead ends," said John when he dropped Agatha off at her cottage. "Now what?"

"I'm going back to see Mrs. Bloxby," said Agatha. "I'm going to put forward my idea for the old folks' club."

"You're on your own, then. Maybe see you tomorrow."

"Yes, maybe," said Agatha vaguely, her mind full of plans.

"It really is too generous of you, Mrs. Raisin," said Mrs. Bloxby. "But what about all that wine? We'll need to find a new home for it."

"I've had an idea about that," said Agatha. "The wine is very heavy and sweet. We could relabel it and call it Cotswold Liqueur. I could ask John Fletcher if he would buy the wine. He could sell it by the glass as a liqueur. I could get a write-up on it in the local paper, do a bit of promotion in return. Tell him the proceeds will go to the old folks' home."

"That's a brilliant idea. I don't think all your money should go into the repairs. Now we have done so well for Save the Children, I think we should organize the next fund-raising venture to go to repairing the hall."

"I'll think of something good," said Agatha confidently.

"I am so glad to see you looking like your old self," said Mrs. Bloxby.

"I think I've finally got fed up with suffering over James. I'm going to have fun."

Agatha was hungry when she got home. Once more she scrabbled in the deep-freeze, scraping frost off labels in her search for something to eat. She was so tired, she did not notice that the tray of faggots she placed in the microwave was on a foil dish. She had not read the instructions properly and so did not know that foil was deemed unsuitable for microwaves. She had only read the time by dint of screwing up her eyes. Agatha should have realized that forty-five minutes in a microwave is a long time. While the dish spun round, she went into the garden and took a deep breath of the cold night air.

Was the murderer somewhere in the village? Was it possible to sleep easy at night after having committed three murders? As she stood there, lost in thought, she finally became aware of the frantic mewing of her cats and turned round. Black smoke was billowing out through the open kitchen door.

She rushed in. Flames were beginning to lick around the inside of the microwave. She switched it off and unplugged it and opened the door, coughing and waving her arms to try to clear the smoke. The foil tray had melted under a congealed black heap of food. Agatha lifted up the microwave and put it outside the kitchen door.

She found some slightly hard bread and cut two slices and toasted them with cheese under the grill. A film of black was lying over all the surfaces in the kitchen. When she had finished eating, she began to clean the kitchen. It was nearly midnight by the time she had finished.

Agatha went upstairs and had a hot bath and then changed into a long cotton night-dress. She climbed into bed and settled down with a weary sigh. What a day! At least the duck races had raised a lot of money. Pity about the bad publicity. So Bunty was married. She had achieved the dream of many secretaries by marrying the boss. Agatha's thoughts drifted back to the days when she herself had been a secretary. Her boss, an advertising manager, had been tall and blond and charming. Agatha had slavishly spent some of her small pay packet on buying special brands of coffee to please him. But he had never seemed to pay any more attention to her than if she were some sort of piece of office machinery. Mr. Crinsted's son had married his secretary.

She sat up, her mind racing. Miss Partle, Binser's secretary. What if she was so in love with her boss that she would defend him every way she could?

TEN

✝

WITHOUT even bothering to put on a dressing-gown, Agatha fled down the stairs, out into the night, straight to John's cottage and rang the bell and then hammered on the door.

"I'm coming," she heard John's cross voice shouting. He opened the door and stared at Agatha in her night-gown.

"Why, Agatha, this is so sudden."

"Don't be silly," said Agatha. "I've just got to talk to you."

He stood back and she walked into his living-room. John was bare-chested, wearing only a pair of blue silk pyjama trousers. His smooth chest was strong and muscled. Agatha wondered briefly what he did to keep so fit before plunging in. "Secretaries," she gasped.

"Sit down. Calm down. Begin at the beginning."

"I met my former secretary, Bunty, at the duck races. She'd married her boss. Mad about him."

"That's nice," said John soothingly. "But why come dashing in here in the middle of the night?"

"I just remembered how secretaries can obsess about their bosses. What about Miss Partle?"

"Binser's secretary?"

"Yes, her. Do you remember it was because of her that Binser met Tristan in the first place?"

"I think I do."

"Well, think of this. She could have been charmed by Tristan, enough to effect the introduction, but her real passion was for her boss. When Tristan conned Binser out of ten thousand, she must have been determined to get it back. She may have arranged to get him beaten up. So the ten thousand is returned. Still, Tristan tried a bit of blackmail. He loved money. He was desperate for money and more money. Miss Partle thought it was all over. But somehow Tristan gets his hands on a real piece of blackmail material concerning Binser. He phones Miss Partle. Say he speaks to her because Binser is away. She decides to silence him. She phones him in the middle of the night after you leave. Maybe she reminds Tristan of the beating in New Cross. He decides to make a break for it. He leaves the house and goes to the vicarage. She follows him quietly, not wanting to attack him in the street. Let's say he doesn't use his key to the vicarage but goes through the French windows. She sees him open the church box and take the money. She suddenly sees it would be to her advantage to get rid of him in such circumstances. She seizes the paper-knife, and bingo!"

"And what about Peggy Slither and Miss Jellop?"

"Tristan must have told them about what he had, or hinted at it. Miss Jellop, upset at his death, decides to phone Miss

Partle. Maybe she thinks Miss Jellop knew more than she did; same with Peggy. She panics. Two more murders."

"Agatha, Agatha, think calmly. It's all too improbable. You're clutching at straws."

"Nevertheless, I am going up there tomorrow and I'm going to have a word with her and see her reaction. She can't do anything to me in a busy office."

John was about to point out that Binser's offices were in a quiet executive suite but restrained himself.

"Go back to bed," he said soothingly. "We'll talk about it tomorrow."

"Maybe I won't confront her right away," said Agatha. "I'll follow her after work, see where she lives, try to find out what sort of person she is."

"Yes, dear. Just go home," said John as if humouring a child.

"So you aren't coming with me?"

Unknown to Agatha, John had a dinner date for the following evening with Charlotte Bellinge, but he wasn't going to tell Agatha that. "I have a book to finish."

"Very well," said Agatha huffily. "I'll investigate on my own."

Agatha decided to be in London when Binser's offices closed for the night. That way she could follow Miss Partle, see where she lived, perhaps get some idea of her real character. She put on a disguise she had worn before of a blonde wig and spectacles with non-magnifying lenses.

Before she went, she was tempted to phone Bill, but then she remembered John's sheer disbelief at her deductions and realized Bill would probably feel the same.

Once at Binser's offices, she took one of the many seats in the large reception area, confident that no one would ask her what she was doing there. People came and went and the seats around her began to empty. Staff began to pour out of the building. The receptionists began to pack up for the night, their places being taken by two security guards. Agatha knew she was beginning to look conspicuous and so she left and lurked outside.

Time dragged on. A cold wind blew along Cheapside. Then suddenly Miss Partle appeared. Agatha sighed with relief. She had been worried that Miss Partle might be wearing a hat or something that might make her difficult to recognize. Keeping well behind her, Agatha followed Miss Partle along to St. Paul's tube and then down the long escalators to the Central Line platform. Now what to do? she wondered. Get into the same carriage? Why not, she decided. Miss Partle would not recognize her, disguised as she was.

They were travelling west. The carriage was crowded. Agatha straphung, peering occasionally through the press of bodies to where Miss Partle was standing, farther down the carriage.

The secretary got out at Notting Hill Gate and Agatha doggedly followed her. Miss Partle went quickly along Pembridge Road and to Agatha's disappointment went into a Turkish restaurant. Still, I'm disguised and I may as well eat something, thought Agatha. The restaurant was quiet. Agatha was placed three tables away from Miss Partle.

The secretary took the *Evening Standard* out of her briefcase and began to read. Agatha ordered kebab and rice and a glass of house wine. The restaurant began to fill up. Finally Miss Partle finished eating and reading and called for her bill. Agatha did the same. As Miss Partle was paying her bill, Agatha was overcome by a desire to pee. Cursing, she dived down the stairs to the toilet. When she emerged upstairs again, it was to find Miss Partle gone. Agatha paid her bill and rushed out into the night, looking to right and left. She saw the figure of Miss Partle turning left into Chepstow Villas and set off in pursuit. She paused at the end of the street and looked along. The sturdy figure of Miss Partle moved from pool of lamplight to pool of lamplight. Apart from a woman walking her dog, the street was empty. Then Agatha saw Miss Partle turn in at the gate of one of the early-Victorian houses. It had a holly tree at the gate. Agatha waited and then walked slowly along and once outside looked up at the house, wondering what to do next. She had learned nothing. Miss Partle had met no one, talked to no one. Agatha knew as little about her as she had always done.

She missed John. She missed someone to talk to. She took a notebook out of her handbag and made a note of the address. Perhaps she should check into a hotel for the night and try again the next day. Try what? jeered a voice in her head.

The more Agatha stood there and thought about Miss Partle being the killer, the more ridiculous it began to seem.

She decided to go home. After all, she hadn't told Doris Simpson to look after her cats. She had left dried food out for them, which her spoilt cats hated. No, it was time to go home and leave it all to the police.

John Armitage had endured a humiliating evening. He had arranged to meet Charlotte in a smart restaurant in the Kings Road. Charlotte had turned up half an hour late accompanied by a handsome young man. "This is Giles," she said. "Giles, John Armitage. You don't mind if Giles joins us, do you, darling?"

So John, who had hoped for a romantic evening, was forced to entertain Giles as well as Charlotte, and Giles was a man of few words. Apart from saying he thought reading books was a waste of time, he drank a lot and said little else. John began to hope that when the meal was over, maybe Charlotte would get rid of this boring young man and invite him home.

The price of the meal made him blink, but ever hopeful, he paid up. To his chagrin, once outside the restaurant, Charlotte thanked him firmly but sweetly for dinner, tucked her arm in Giles's and walked off with him down the Kings Road in the direction of her home.

John cursed himself for a fool. He found himself missing Agatha. He would have been better off to have gone with her on whatever mad-goose chase she was on. Agatha could be infuriating and bossy, but she was never boring. He had tried to discuss the case with Charlotte until he realized her beautiful eyes were glazing over with boredom. Charlotte, when not talking about herself, only liked to hear things she was interested in, like which restaurant or fashion designer was in and which was out.

The lights were out in Agatha's cottage when he arrived home. He decided that on the following day he would drive to Mircester where there was an excellent butcher and buy some steak and invite Agatha for dinner.

Agatha awoke the next day with the beginning of a sniffle. She was afraid she must have caught a cold with all that hanging around Cheapside in the cold wind. But somehow her belief that the murderer might be Miss Partle was renewed. She paced up and down her kitchen. Perhaps the thing she should have done was simply to confront the woman and see if she betrayed herself in any way.

Determination rose in her. She swept the morning's mail off the mat, including a note from John inviting her for dinner, and placed it on the hall table without looking at any of it. She served her cats chopped lambs' liver and then put a warm coat on and made her way out to her car.

In London, she parked her car in the underground car-park at Hyde Park and took the tube to Notting Hill Gate. The area was crowded as people made their way to the antiques market in the Portobello Road.

Agatha went straight to the house in Chepstow Villas and rang the bell and waited. There was no reply. She stood for a moment, irresolute, and then decided to take a look at the stalls in the Portobello Market. It felt odd to be surrounded once more by the smells and crowds of London. Agatha walked from stall to stall, examining jewellery, military badges and old clothes. She saw a handsome silver paper-knife and decided to buy it for Alf Bloxby. He would need a new one. The stall owner wrapped it up in tissue paper and Agatha slid it into her coat pocket.

She was just making her way through the crowds, past a man with a hurdy-gurdy and with a parrot on his shoulder when a voice in her ear said, "Mrs. Raisin?"

Agatha swung round. There was Miss Partle, surveying her.

"What a surprise!" said Agatha. "Isn't this market fascinating?"

"It is, if you can tell fake from genuine. But I like looking," said Miss Partle. "Like a coffee?"

"Thanks," said Agatha. "Where shall we go? It's so long since I've been here."

"I live close by. I was just going home."

They walked together chatting amiably about how London had changed and all the while Agatha was thinking, I must have been mad to suspect this nice woman.

In Chepstow Villas, Miss Partle unlocked the door. Agatha followed her into a sitting-room which led off a narrow entrance corridor. It was furnished with good antiques and some fine paintings. The room, which had originally consisted of front and back parlours, was now one long room with long windows front and back.

Miss Partle went to a thermostat on the wall and turned it up. "Keep your coat on. It's chilly in here but it will soon warm up. Come downstairs to the kitchen and I'll make coffee."

"This is a fine house," said Agatha when they were downstairs, looking around the gleaming modern kitchen. "You've put a lot of work into it."

"I bought it with an inheritance from an aunt back when Notting Hill was still pretty unfashionable and got work done on it every time I could afford it. Take a seat and tell me why you were following me yesterday in that strange disguise. The coffee will be ready in a minute."

Agatha laughed. "You are never going to believe this. I must have had a rush of blood to the head. I didn't know you had spotted me last night."

"That's a very distinctive ring you are wearing. You should have left it off. And the wind must have disarranged your wig. I noticed in the restaurant that a strand of brown hair had escaped. I studied you when you thought I wasn't looking and finally I was able to place you and then I saw you standing outside my house. So what were you doing?"

"I may as well tell you. I hope you are not going to be too furious with me. It all started at the duck races."

"This sounds weird. Duck races? What has that got to do with me? Oh, the coffee is ready. How do you take it?"

"Just black. Do you mind if I smoke?"

"Yes, I do."

"I'll live without one."

"Here's your coffee. Now tell me why you were following me."

"Well, at these duck races in the village, I met my former secretary, Bunty, who had married her boss. I got to thinking about secretaries who were in love with their bosses and I thought that if Mr. Binser had been under some sort of threat from Tristan, you might have stepped in to protect him. It all seems fantastic now I'm here talking to you."

"I should be angry but I suppose three murders in and around your village must have made you want to grasp at straws. So the police have no leads?"

"Not unless the one I've just given them comes to anything."

"And what was that?"

"Mrs. Feathers, the elderly lady Tristan was living with, she told me she had once seen him using a mobile phone. I told the police. You see, he might have got a phone call on the night he died that frightened him. I think he broke into the church box to take the money because he planned to make a run for it and wanted some petty cash. So if there was a call, they'll be able to trace who it was."

A cloud crossed the sun, darkening the garden outside, where two starlings pecked for worms in the small lawn.

"You don't see many of them nowadays," said Agatha.

"What? Mobile phones?"

"No, starlings. London used to be full of them. I was looking at the starlings on your lawn."

"Tell me about these duck races," said Miss Partle. "It sounds very primitive. It's a wonder you didn't have the animal-rights people after you or the Royal Society for the Protection of Birds."

"These were plastic ducks, the little yellow ones." Agatha told her all about the races and the drunken Morris men.

"I didn't realize there was so much fun to be had in a village," said Miss Partle. "What on earth made you decide to poke around in murder?"

"Insatiable curiosity, I guess. But I have no intention of giving up until I find out who did it."

"Well, you know what they say: curiosity killed the cat. Would you like to see the rest of the house?"

"Not really," said Agatha. "I think I'd better be getting back down to the country."

"You were talking about all that wine the dead woman's sister gave to the races. I've built up quite a cellar. Not homemade, mind. Good stuff."

"You have a cellar?"

"Yes, here." Miss Partle opened a door in the kitchen. "Come on. You can choose a bottle."

Agatha walked to the cellar door and peered down some stone steps. "You go on down," said Miss Partle behind her. "I'll just switch off the percolator."

"Is there a light switch?" said Agatha, uneasily reminded of being trapped in Mrs. Tremp's coal cellar.

"On the inside of the door on your right." Agatha was searching inside the door for the switch when a massive blow struck her on the back of the head and she fell headlong down the steps and lay in a heap at the bottom.

Agatha could feel pain all over though she was still conscious, but as she heard Miss Partle coming down the stairs, with what was left of her wits she realized she had better look as if she were unconscious.

Then she felt her ankles being bound and then her wrists. A piece of strong adhesive tape was put over her mouth. "Interfering bitch," hissed Miss Partle. "I thought that phone had been got rid of. I phoned from a call-box round the corner. I hope they don't realize the phone-box is near where I live. What'll I do now? I'll be back. Oh, God, why couldn't you leave things alone!"

Agatha heard her footsteps mounting the stairs and then the cellar door banged shut. At first Agatha was in such a state of pain and fright that her brain did not seem to be able to work at all. Then she thought dismally that she should have told Bill her suspicions. When she went missing, John would tell him, and he would then question Miss Partle and maybe her body would be found.

John Armitage carried his groceries to his car parked in the public car-park in front of Mircester police headquarters. Bill Wong hailed him. "On your own? Where's your fiancée?"

For one split second, John wondered whom he was taking about and then rallied and said, "Oh, Agatha. She must still be up in London. Any luck with that mobile phone?"

"There was a call to him the night he was murdered. It came from a call-box in Notting Hill."

"Pity. Look, Bill, I hope she isn't getting herself into trouble."

"You'd better tell me."

"It's just that she had this mad idea that the murderer was Miss Partle—you know, Binser's secretary."

"Why on earth should she think that?"

"It's because she met her former secretary at the duck races. Former secretary married her boss. Agatha starts thinking about secretaries who are in love with their bosses and comes to the mad conclusion that the respectable Miss Partle must have gone around bumping off people to protect Binser. I just hope she doesn't get into trouble. She's gone to find out about her. Binser's got powerful friends."

Bill stood very still. "I've often thought," he said slowly, "that although Agatha might sometimes do silly things, she is possessed of an almost psychic ability to leap to the right conclusion."

John looked unconvinced. "Unless Miss Partle has any

connection with Notting Hill, the whole idea remains far-fetched."

"I have the addresses of everyone concerned with the murder cases in the station," said Bill. "Do no harm to have a look."

"I'll come with you."

"All right." Bill led the way into police headquarters and told John to take a seat and wait.

John waited and waited, feeling increasingly uneasy. Bill was taking an unusually long time.

At last Bill came out. "Miss Partle lives in Notting Hill," he said. "I've phoned Kensington to pull her in for questioning just in case, and hope Binser doesn't sue us."

"Give me the address," said John.

"No, one amateur is enough. Leave it to the police."

John raced to the post office and asked for the London phone directory. He located Miss Partle's address, got back into his car and set off at speed for London.

Agatha was in a state of sheer terror. For a long time she was unable to think. Then she remembered that paper-knife she had bought and put in the pocket of her coat. She twisted her bound hands, trying to get her fingers inside her coat pocket.

Then the cellar door opened again. This is it, thought Agatha. Miss Partle came down the stairs carrying a hammer. "I'll just put an end to you," she said, "and then worry about getting rid of the body later."

She hefted the hammer and Agatha closed her eyes. Then, above their heads, the doorbell shrilled.

Miss Partle lowered the hammer. Should she answer it or wait for them to go away? But sometimes Mr. Binser sent important documents to her home for her to study. She dropped the hammer on the floor beside Agatha and went back up the stairs.

She opened the street door. Two policemen stood there. "Miss Partle?"

"Yes?"

"I wonder if you would accompany us to the police station. Just a few more questions concerning the murder of Tristan Delon."

"But I have already answered all your questions. Mr. Binser will be most displeased."

"It won't take long."

The desire to get them away from the house prompted Miss Partle to say, "I'll fetch my handbag."

Agatha heard the voices but could not make out what they were saying. She heard Miss Partle go back into the kitchen, and then back to the front door. Agatha began to bang her feet on the floor. But the door slammed shut behind Miss Partle and the house was quiet.

Bill and Detective Chief Inspector Wilkes were speeding for London, siren blaring. "I told them to hold this Miss Partle until we got there," said Wilkes.

"I've been thinking," said Bill, "what if Agatha's gone to her house?"

"They say she seemed to be alone."

"Might be an idea to call at the house first and ask the neighbours if they saw anyone like Agatha call at the door. Only take a minute," he pleaded.

Wilkes sighed. "Well, all right. But I've got a feeling we'll have Binser's lawyers on top of us by the end of the day. Agatha Raisin. Pah! Why can't she mind her own business?"

"She's often blundered onto something in the past."

"If there's nothing in this, I'll charge that damn woman with interfering in police business and I really will do it this time!"

• • •

Down in the cellar, Agatha rolled onto her back again with a groan. Why wasn't real life like the movies? In a movie, the heroine would have been able to get her hands on that knife and free her bonds.

She lay still for a moment and tried again. Her pockets were deep. She got a finger on the edge of the tissue paper and gently tugged. Bit by bit the knife began to emerge from her pocket. She gave a final tug and the knife in its tissue-paper wrapping popped out and fell on the floor. She rolled on her side and felt for it. But the tissue-paper wrapping had been Sellotaped around the knife and she could not get enough movement in her fingers to tear it off. Tears began to roll down her cheeks.

John Armitage was caught up in a traffic jam. He heard the sound of a police siren and saw the cars in front twist to the side of the road. A police car roared past. He got a glimpse of Bill Wong's face. He suddenly felt that Agatha had made a terrible mistake and the police would never forgive her.

"This is the house," said Bill. "Let's try next door and find out if Agatha's been seen."

A young woman with two children hanging on her skirts opened the door. Bill described Agatha. She shook her head. "I've been busy with the children. Ask old Mrs. Wirtle across the street. She never misses anything."

Mrs. Wirtle took ages to answer the door. She was leaning on a zimmer frame, peering up at them from under a bird's nest of uncombed grey hair. Once more, Bill described Agatha.

"Yes, I saw a woman like that go in with Miss Partle," said Mrs. Wirtle. "Then Miss Partle was taken away by the police. What's going on?"

"And you did not see the other woman come out?" demanded Bill in a loud voice.

"No need to shout. I'm not deaf. No, I didn't see her."

They thanked her and went and stood in front of Miss Partle's house. "Might take too long to get a search warrant," said Wilkes.

"Try the door," suggested Bill.

Wilkes turned the handle. "It's open."

"Then we can go in," said Bill. "Responsible policemen checking unlocked premises."

Agatha heard men's voices. Had Miss Partle associates? But she was desperate. She made choking noises behind her gag and banged her feet on the floor.

"You hear something?" asked Bill, as they stood in the narrow entrance corridor.

They stood and listened. Again a faint banging sound followed by a moan.

They walked down to the kitchen. "Agatha!" called Bill sharply.

A stifled gurgling moan.

"That door over there is open," said Bill.

He fumbled inside the door and located the light switch and pressed down.

There down on the cellar floor lay Agatha Raisin, her face blotched with tears.

The two men hurried down. Bill ripped the gag from her mouth and then, producing a clasp knife, cut the ropes that bound her.

"She was going to kill me," gasped Agatha. "She's coming back to kill me."

Bill helped her to her feet. Agatha staggered and winced at the pain in her feet and hands, for the ropes had nearly cut off her circulation.

"Get her upstairs and give her some tea," said Wilkes. "I'll phone Kensington. They've got Miss Partle there."

The Kensington police were becoming increasingly worried. This Miss Partle was formidable and business-like. She seemed to have powerful friends and her boss was a tycoon.

Miss Partle sensed their unease and was becoming increasingly confident. All she had to do was sit tight and sooner or later they would release her. She was not under arrest. All she had to do was answer the questions put to her by the clowns from Mircester police, go home, and decide what to do with Agatha Raisin's body. If she and Agatha had been spotted together at the market, then she might have more questions to answer, but so long as there was no body to be found, there was not much they could do. It might be an idea to put the body in the boot of her car and dump it somewhere in Carsely.

A policewoman had been sitting with her. But the door of the interview room opened and two detectives came in. They looked at her grimly. One said, "We'll start the questioning when Detective Chief Inspector Wilkes of the Mircester CID arrives."

It was then that Miss Partle realized she could not remember locking her front door.

John Armitage arrived just as Bill and Wilkes were ushering Agatha into their police car.

"Come with us," said Bill, "and look after your fiancée. She was nearly killed."

As they drove to the police station, Agatha told her story.

"I wonder why she attacked you?" said John when Agatha had finished. "I mean, you didn't say anything that might lead her to think you had any proof at all, did you?"

Agatha shook her head. "Mind you, I did tell her about

the mobile phone and I did say I would never give up trying to find out who did it." She was beginning to recover. The old Agatha Raisin was coming back. And the old Agatha Raisin was thinking what a pill John was. No glad hugs or kisses. No cries of "Darling, are you all right?" Sod him.

At the police station, John was told to wait while Agatha was led off by a detective to give her statement.

Bill and Wilkes entered the interview room where Miss Partle was sitting.

Wilkes said, "I am charging you with the attempted murder of Mrs. Agatha Raisin . . ."

And Miss Partle began to scream.

ELEVEN

†

BILL began to think she had gone mad and that they were never going to get a coherent statement out of her, but at last she calmed and it all came out.

"I am devoted to my boss," she said in a flat, even voice. "I did everything for him, more than his wife. I made him the best coffee, I put his shirts in the laundry, I bought the Christmas and birthday presents for his children as well as dealing with his business affairs. Then I received a message one day to say there was a Mr. Tristan Delon in reception. He wished to see Mr. Binser with a view to getting a charitable donation towards a boys' club. I sent down a message that he should put his request in writing."

Wilkes occasionally interrupted to ask for times and dates.

"He must have somehow got a description of me from one

of the receptionists, for when I left that evening, he was waiting for me. He invited me for dinner. He was very charming and I knew that Mr. Binser would never love me the way I wanted him to, and it was like a perpetual ache at my heart. Tristan made me feel attractive. I found myself promising him an interview with my boss. And then suddenly Mr. Binser and Tristan seemed to be going everywhere, but Tristan was still careful to take me out as well from time to time.

"Then Mr. Binser came to me and told me how he had been cheated out of ten thousand pounds. I told Tristan to visit me at my home. I took a cricket bat to him and said that was only a taste of what he would get if he didn't return the money, and I thought that was the end of it. I checked with his vicar and found he had moved to the country.

"And then, when I had all but forgotten about him, he phoned me. He said he and Mr. Binser had gone to a gay bar and a friend who worked there had sent pictures of Tristan and Mr. Binser. Tristan said to tell Mr. Binser that if he did not pay up two hundred and fifty thousand, the photographs would go to his wife. Much as I thought Mr. Binser's wife was not worthy of him, I knew he would be devastated. I hated Tristan Delon. He had fooled me. He had let me think he cared for me. I went down to Carsely in disguise, dressed as a rambler. I saw a group of ramblers and tagged on to them until I got a plan of the village in my head. I was still thinking what to do. You see, I told him I had money saved and I would pay him the money myself. I watched and waited. I saw that Raisin woman leave his house around midnight. And then I wondered if I could frighten him into leaving. So I phoned him and told him I would call on him the following day and I would shoot him. You see, I was beginning to wonder if there really were any photographs. Because I'd asked my boss if he'd ever been to a gay bar and he said he hadn't, and Mr. Binser," she said, all mad pride, "*never* lies.

"Tristan did sound frightened. But I waited. I saw him slip out and walk to the vicarage. He entered by the French windows. I slipped in after him. I saw him open a box and take money out and at the same time I saw the paper-knife, gleaming in the moonlight. I seized it and stabbed him and left. I had parked my car among woods at the top of the hill and I made my way across the fields to it."

She fell silent.

"Miss Jellop?" prompted Wilkes. "Why her?"

"Tristan had told her. She said he had left the photos with a Mrs. Slither but that she, Miss Jellop, knew all about it. She said he had got drunk one day and told her. She said she was going to the police. She said she was up in London and calling from a phone-box. I couldn't have that. I said I would call on her and give her a full explanation. I was so lucky to get to her first. But would it never end? Then I had that Slither woman saying she was sure Tristan had told her that he had enough evidence to ruin Mr. Binser. I hoped it was over but then I began to worry about Peggy Slither. Getting rid of her would make sure there would be an end to it. I carefully looked through her house after I had killed her without disturbing anything, but could not see any photographs. I waited and prayed, but it became evident that the police had not found any either. You won't tell Mr. Binser about any of this? I would not want to lose his respect."

"I'm afraid we'll have to," said Wilkes and Miss Partle began to cry.

Agatha, for the next few weeks, was frightened into domesticity. Doris Simpson, her cleaner, had gone on holiday to Spain, leaving Agatha to look after her cat, Scrabble. Agatha had brought back Scrabble from one of her cases, had *rescued* Scrabble, but the ungrateful cat seemed to be pining for the missing Doris, and did not appear to remember Agatha at all. Agatha polished and cleaned and had a brave try at making apple jelly from a basket of windfall apples which Farmer Brent had given her but it would not set, so she gave the jars of runny liquid to Mrs. Bloxby, who miraculously did something to them to turn them into golden jelly.

The vicar, Alf Bloxby, had called in person to thank Agatha for her help. He made such a polite and formal speech that Agatha wryly thought that his wife had coached him in what to say.

John Armitage was often up in London and she saw little of him.

Then Bill Wong called round to tell Agatha that Miss Partle had gone completely mad and it was doubtful if she would ever stand trial.

"It was a visit from Binser that seems to have sent her over the edge," said Bill. "He'd got her the best lawyer, but she kept asking to see him. I don't know what was said, but after his visit, they had to put her in a strait-jacket. One always thinks of romantic people as suffering from undying passion, not plain, middle-aged secretaries."

"Those gay photographs that Wilkes told me about, had Binser known anything about them?"

"No, evidently all he remembers is her asking him if he'd ever gone to a gay bar, and he was surprised, said no, and asked her why. She had responded with something non-committal. As for Jellop and Slither, their end was partly your fault, Agatha."

"How come?"

"I think both of them were jealous of you and wanted to show they could be detectives as well. It's very dangerous to keep things from the police. You should have told me about your suspicions, not gone to see her yourself. I mean, what on earth were you thinking of, going back with her to her house?"

"It was when I met her in the Portobello Market," said Agatha. "She seemed so normal that I decided I must have been fantasizing."

"But it was a leap in the dark to suspect her."

"It was this secretary business," said Agatha. "I was a secretary once. People think because of women's lib that secretaries no longer make the coffee or things like that. But the top-flight go on more like wives. Some of them even choose schools for the boss's children. There's an intimacy springs up. Often boss and secretary work together late. Men like to talk about their work and secretaries make good listeners while wives at home get bored with it all. He probably saw Miss Partle as a cross between mother and helper. And she probably lived on romantic dreams of him. Tristan must have provided a brief holiday from her obsession until she found out that he had been using her. Then all her passion for Binser would return and engulf her."

Bill's eyes were shrewd. "You sound as if you're speaking from personal experience."

"No, just speculation. How's Alice?"

"She's fine."

"I thought after that scene at the duck races that it would all be over."

"She was drunk. She cried so hard and apologized so sincerely that I was quite touched."

"You're touched in the head," said Agatha acidly.

"What's that supposed to mean?"

"Bill, trust me, Alice is one cast-iron bitch. She wants to get married and with that mouth of hers, I doubt if anyone else would have her."

Bill stood up and jerked on his coat. "Just because you've

been crossed in love, Agatha, you see the worst in anyone else's romance. You should be ashamed of yourself. Who I see or what I do is none of your business."

"But, Bill . . ." wailed Agatha.

"I'm off."

After he had gone, Agatha sat feeling miserable. If she wanted to retain his friendship, she would need to apologize to him. But what on earth did he see in the awful Alice?

Restless, she looked around her gleaming cottage. Better to get started on the old folks' club and take her mind off things.

She walked along to the vicarage. Mrs. Bloxby was out in the garden planting winter pansies.

"You look upset, Mrs. Raisin," she said, straightening up from a flower-bed. "It's not too cold today. I'll bring some coffee out into the garden so you can have a cigarette and you can tell me what's been going on."

When they were seated at the garden table with mugs of coffee, Mrs. Bloxby asked, "What's up?"

"It's Bill," said Agatha. "You'll never believe this. He's still devoted to Alice."

"And what's that got to do with you?"

"He's my friend and he's making a terrible mistake. I told him she was a cast-iron bitch."

"Oh, Mrs. Raisin, you cannot interfere in a relationship."

"Really? It was you who told me my marriage to James would be a disaster."

The vicar's wife looked rueful. "So I did. But I was so worried about you."

"As I am about Bill."

"True. But you'd better apologize. He is too good a friend to lose."

Agatha sighed. "I'm tired of blundering around other people's lives. I thought I would sound out some builders about getting the church-hall roof repaired for a start."

"I am so glad you are still going to go on with that. John Fletcher, at the pub, is going to take the wine and label it as a liqueur. He says half of the price of each glass sold will go to the new club."

"That's handsome of him. I'll make a push and try to get it all ready by Christmas. Have some sort of party."

"When is the trial?" asked Mrs. Bloxby.

"It seems as if there isn't going to be one. Miss Partle has lost her marbles and will be considered unfit to stand trial. You know, I had one thought when I was lying in that cellar—I haven't made a will. Maybe I'll leave it all to the church and go straight to heaven."

"You'll want to leave it to your husband."

"What husband?"

"I cannot imagine you staying single for the rest of your life."

Agatha grinned. "Maybe I'll marry John Armitage after all."

"There's not enough of a spark there."

"Does one need a spark at my age?"

"At any age."

"I'll think about it. I'll go home and phone around some builders."

Agatha went to feed her cats because their bowls were empty and she couldn't remember feeding them. I'm turning into a compulsive cat feeder, she thought as she poached fish for them and then set it aside to cool. She saw John's keys lying on the kitchen counter and decided to go next door and pick up his mail from the doormat and put it on his desk.

In his cottage, she scooped up the pile of post. She looked thoughtfully at his answering machine. Why all these trips to

London? Feeling guilty, she laid down the post on his desk and crossed to the answering machine. There were several messages, and all from Charlotte Bellinge. He must have saved them, thought Agatha dismally. The first one was Charlotte apologizing for bringing some man called Giles to dinner. "Do forgive me, dear John," she cooed. "Do let me take you out for dinner and make it up to you." The second said, "What a wonderful time we had. Pippa is giving a party tomorrow night. Do say you'll come." And the third, "I'm running a bit late. Can you pick me up at nine instead of eight? Dying to see you."

So that's that, thought Agatha. No heading into the sunset of middle age with John Armitage.

She went home and arranged the cooled fish in bowls for the cats. The loneliness of the cottage seemed to press down on her.

Agatha picked up the phone and dialled old Mr. Crinsted's number. "Feel like coming out for dinner?" she asked.

"Delighted," said the old man.

"I'll pick you up in half an hour," said Agatha.

Agatha found she was enjoying herself in Mr. Crinsted's company. They discussed plans for the old folks' club and Mr. Crinsted promised to teach Agatha chess.

"I am so glad you called, Mrs. Raisin," he said. "I wanted to hear all about the murders."

"I would have called earlier," lied Agatha, who had practically until that evening forgotten Mr. Crinsted's existence, "but I've been settling down after the shock of it all."

"Tell me about it, Mrs. Raisin."

"Agatha."

"Right, my name is Ralph."

So Agatha did while Ralph Crinsted listened intently. When she had finished, he said, "It's odd, all the same."

"What's odd?"

"This Miss Partle must have been so used to discussing everything with him, I'm surprised she decided to take matters into her own hands."

"I've met Binser. He's a straightforward man. He probably never noticed much about her. Thought of her as a bit of office machinery."

"I think any man who had a secretary so much in love with him would have noticed something."

"Maybe he did and took it as his due. Men do, you know."

"Some men."

"I'm just glad it's all over and Alf Bloxby is in the clear. Not that there was ever any evidence against him, but there was gossip, and gossip in a small village can be very dangerous."

"True. Have you ever played chess before?"

"No, never."

"Like to learn?"

"I wouldn't mind."

"Then I'll give you lessons."

After she had dropped Mr. Crinsted off at his home, Agatha reflected that it was a long time since she had enjoyed such a carefree evening.

She had promised to call on Ralph Crinsted in a couple of days' time and start her chess lessons. Then tomorrow, she would see what estimate the builders came up with for the roof. The ring on her finger sparkled. "Masquerade over," said Agatha ruefully to her cats. She took off the ring and put it in the kitchen drawer. She wondered how John was getting on with Charlotte and realized with relief that his relationship didn't bother her in the slightest. Or that was what she believed. Almost impossible to imagine John getting passionate about anyone. Like Miss Partle. Poor Miss Partle. Now why think that?

This was a woman who was a stone-cold murderess and who was probably faking insanity.

John Armitage was at another hot and noisy party in Chelsea with Charlotte flirting with a group of men across the room. But he could bear it. Tonight was going to be the night. Hadn't she said they would just drop in for an hour and then go home together? He remembered fondly the seductive look in her eyes when she had said those words and the caress in her voice.

He had been disappointed that she had still shown no interest in the murders except to laugh and say that Agatha Raisin was a formidable woman.

John looked at his watch, only half listening to the woman next to him, who was telling him that she was sure she could sit down and write a book if she only had the time. They had been there two hours and Charlotte showed no signs of leaving. Time to take charge. He crossed the room and took her arm in a possessive grip. "Time we were leaving."

"Oh, darling." Charlotte pouted prettily. "We're all going on to Jilly's party."

John did not know who this Jilly was and he did not care. He said stiffly, "Either we leave now or I'm going home."

"Then you'd better go. But why not come with us? It'll be fun."

"Good night," snapped John.

As he strode to the door, he heard one of the men with Charlotte laugh and say, "There goes another of Charlotte's walkers."

His face flamed. That had been all she had really wanted from him, an escort to walk her to the endless social functions she loved.

His thoughts turned to Agatha on the road home. He had been neglecting her along with his work. He would get going on the book for a couple of days and then take her out for dinner. But, damn Charlotte Bellinge. She had really led him a fine dance.

Agatha was busy with the builders next day and with looking around the church hall. Old people like comfort and dignity. The floor would need a carpet and she would need to supply comfortable chairs and tables. Bookshelves along one wall for books, games and jigsaws. What else? The walls painted, of course, but not in those dreadful pink and pale-blue pastel colours do-gooders liked to inflict on the old as if catering for a second childhood. Plain white would do, with pictures. It should really be called the Agatha Raisin Club, considering all the work and money she was putting into it. But Mrs. Bloxby would think she was being grandiose. Of course, she had promised to think up some fund-raising venture so that she would not have to bear all the cost herself. Agatha's mind worked busily. An auction would be a good idea. She had raised a lot of money for one of those before by going around the country houses and getting them to contribute. Or what about getting some well-known pop group to put on a concert? No, scrub that. It would bring in too much mess and probably drugs as well. She must think of something.

She walked back to her cottage in the pouring rain, trying to avoid the puddles gathering amongst the fallen leaves.

In her cottage, there was a note lying on the kitchen table from Doris Simpson, one of the few women in Carsely to use Agatha's first name. "Dear Agatha," she read, "Have taken poor Scrabble home to feed. Cat looks half-starved. Be round to clean as usual next week. Doris."

"Bloody cat ate like a horse," muttered Agatha.

The doorbell rang. Agatha answered it. John stood there. He had suddenly decided he wanted to see Agatha.

"Yes?" asked Agatha coldly.

"Can I come in? It's bucketing with rain."

He followed her into the kitchen.

"So what were you doing in London?" asked Agatha.

"This and that. Bookshops, agent, publisher, the usual round. Are you free for dinner this evening?"

"I think I've got a date," lied Agatha. "I'll check."

She dialled Mr. Crinsted's number. "Is our date for tonight, Ralph, sweetie?" asked Agatha in a husky voice.

"I thought we'd arranged to play chess tomorrow," came the surprised voice at the other end. "But tonight, any time is fine."

"Look forward to it," said Agatha. "See you then." She put down the receiver and turned to John.

"Sorry, I've got a date."

"Well, what about tomorrow?"

"Sorry, going to be busy for some time." And I am not interested in Charlotte Bellinge's leavings, thought Agatha. She must have ditched him.

"I'll leave you to it." John marched out, feeling doubly rejected. The rain poured down. What am I doing stuck in this village? thought John angrily. It doesn't help a bit with the writing. I was better off in London.

After he had gone, Agatha took the ring he had given her out of the drawer and put it in an envelope. On her way out that evening, she popped it through his letter-box. Not that she was jealous of Charlotte Bellinge.

For Ralph Crinsted's sake, Agatha tried to concentrate on her chess lesson while privately wondering what could be the fun in playing such a boring game. There seemed to be so much to memorize. "I don't think you're going to make a chess player," said Ralph finally. "You're not enjoying this one bit."

"I will, I will," said Agatha. And with a rare burst of honesty, she added, "You see, I'm not used to concentrating on anything other than people—what motivates them, why they commit murder, that sort of thing. Let's try again another night. I'll buy some sort of book, *Chess Made Easy,* or something like that, so I'll be geared-up next time."

"If you say so. Do you play cards?"

"Don't know many games. Poker. I once played poker."

"Like a game?"

"Sure."

Agatha actually won the first game and began to enjoy herself. It had reached midnight when she finally put down the cards and said ruefully, "I'm keeping you up late."

"Doesn't matter. I don't sleep much. The old don't, you know."

As Agatha drove home, she thought with a shiver of impending old age and loneliness, would she endure white nights and long days? Would her joints seize up with arthritis?

Tomorrow, she thought gloomily, I'll draft out my will. I'm not immortal.

Had the weather cleared up, Agatha might have put off thoughts of making out a will, but another day of rain blurred the windows of her cottage and thudded down on the already rain-soaked garden.

She went into the sitting-room, carrying her cigarettes and a mug of coffee and sat down at her desk. She took a small tape recorder out of her drawer and had got as far as "This is the last will and testament of Mrs. Agatha Raisin" when there was a ring at the doorbell.

"Blast," muttered Agatha and went to answer it.

Mr. Binser stood there. "Good heavens," said Agatha. "Come in out of this dreadful rain. What brings you?"

"I just came to see you and thank you for clearing up those dreadful murders," said the tycoon. "I'm curious. How did you arrive at the truth?"

Agatha took his coat and ushered him into the sitting-room. "Coffee?"

"No," he said, sitting down on the sofa. "I haven't much time. So how did you guess it was my Miss Partle?"

Agatha, glad of an opportunity to brag, told him how she had managed to leap to the conclusion that the culprit was Miss Partle.

"Interesting," he said when she had finished. "You seem such a confident lady. Are you never wrong?"

"I pride myself I'm not."

"You were certainly right about Miss Partle's adoration of me."

Agatha felt a lurch in her stomach. "You mean I was wrong about something else?"

"If there is one thing I hate, it is busy-body interfering women."

The rain drummed against the windows and dripped from the thatch outside. The day was growing darker. Agatha switched on a lamp next to her. "That's better," she said with a lightness she did not feel. "At least you don't go around killing them."

There was a long silence while Binser studied her. Agatha broke it by saying sharply, "I have a feeling you came to tell me something."

"Yes. You are so unbearably smug. You see, Miss Partle didn't commit these murders. I did."

Agatha goggled at him. "Why? How?"

"In all my life," he said calmly, "no one has ever managed to put one over on me—except Tristan Delon. I suppose, in my way, I was as infatuated with that young man as Miss Partle was with me. I married for money, the daughter of a wealthy company director. I never had any real friends. I felt I could be honest with Tristan, I could relax with him. Then he cheated me. All he had ever wanted from me was money. I hated him. I have certain underworld contacts which come in useful from time to time. I arranged to have him beaten up. I got Miss Partle to tell him who had done it. He returned the money and I thought that was that. But the leech wouldn't let go. He phoned Miss Partle and said he was going to tell my wife unless I paid up. I found he had gone to the country. I went down to Carsely. I had already studied ordnance survey maps of the area. I dressed as a rambler and left my car hidden some distance outside the village and crossed the fields so that I would get down to where he was living without being seen. I decided to give him one more chance. I had his mobile phone number. I phoned Miss Partle and told her to go out to the nearest phone-box and call him and tell him I was coming to kill him. I thought I would give him a chance to run for it.

"I hid behind one of the gravestones in the churchyard where I could watch the entrance to his cottage. The door is clearly illuminated by that one streetlight. I saw him slip out and head for the vicarage. I saw him enter by those French windows and followed him. There he stood in the moonlight like a fallen angel, rifling the contents of the church box. I saw that paper-knife. I was in such a blinding rage. I did not know it was so sharp. I drove it down into his neck.

"And then I ran. I told Miss Partle what I had done and she said that no one would ever suspect me. And then you came to see me. I thought I had shut you up with my statement to the police, and then I found myself being threatened by a village spinster called Jellop who Tristan had told about me. She said she felt she should go to the police with what she knew. She said Tristan had photographs of the pair of us in a gay bar. Now

Tristan had taken me to one once. I said I would call and see her and she was not to go to the police until I explained things. So that was the end of her. When Peggy Slither told me she actually had the photographs, I thought the nightmare would never end. I said I would pay her two hundred thousand for the photos and she agreed. I didn't trust her. She kept crowing about what a great detective she was. I felt she might take my money and tell the police all the same. After she had handed me the photographs and I had given her the money, she suddenly snatched back the photographs. 'This isn't right,' she said. 'I told someone I would go to the police and so I will.' I found out that she had not mentioned my name. I said mildly, 'All right, but what about a cup of tea?' What a triumphant bully she was. I followed her quietly into her kitchen and slid a carving knife out of the drawer. She turned just as I was raising the knife and screamed." He shrugged. "But it was too late."

Agatha felt cold sweat trickling down the back of her neck.

"I made an arrangement with Miss Partle that should anything break, she was to take the blame."

"But why should she do that?" demanded Agatha hoarsely while her frightened eyes roamed around the room looking for a weapon.

"I told her if she took the rap, with good behaviour she would be out in ten years' time and I would marry her. I knew she would go through hell if only I married her."

"Are you going to kill me?" asked Agatha.

"No, you silly cow, I am not. You have no proof. And poor Miss Partle is now stone-mad. You won't get anything out of her. If it hadn't been for you, she wouldn't be in prison. I couldn't bear the idea of you sitting smugly in your cottage thinking what a great detective you are."

"I'll tell the police!" panted Agatha.

"And what proof will they find? Nothing. You will find

that the police, having got her confession, will not thank you for trying to re-open the case. I have powerful friends. Goodbye, Mrs. Raisin."

Agatha sat very still. She heard the door slam. She heard him driving off. She tried to stand up but her legs were trembling so much, she collapsed back into her chair.

And then she saw her tape recorder sitting on the desk.

She had forgotten to turn it off.

Now a burst of rage and energy flooded her body. She went to the desk and re-ran the tape and switched it on. It was all there.

Agatha picked up the phone and dialled Mircester police headquarters and explained she had the real murderer. She got put straight through to Wilkes, who listened in astonished silence and then began to rap out questions: When had he left; what car was he driving?

When Agatha replaced the phone, she wondered whether to call John and then decided against it. Although she would never admit it to herself, she viewed his pursuit of Charlotte Bellinge as a rejection of herself. She phoned the vicarage instead, only to learn that Mrs. Bloxby was out. The doorbell went. It couldn't be the police already. Agatha went into the kitchen and slid a knife out of the drawer and approached the door. She peered through the peep-hole in the door and saw, with a flood of relief, the elderly face of Ralph Crinsted under a dripping hat.

"You'll never guess what's happened!" she cried, brandishing the kitchen knife in her excitement.

"Be careful with that knife, Agatha," he said nervously.

"Oh, what? Gosh, I was frightened. The police are on their way."

"May I come in? It's awfully wet."

"Yes, come along."

"I hope I'm not disturbing you; I thought up a few ideas for the old folks' club. You seem to be in the middle of a drama."

Agatha led him into the sitting-room. "I don't know about you, but I would like a large brandy. Care to join me?"

"Why not."

Once the drinks were poured, Agatha got half-way through the story when Bill Wong arrived with another detective.

He asked to hear the tape. Agatha switched it on, wincing at the earlier bit, which included the start of her will, and then all her bragging. But then Binser's dry precise voice describing the murders sounded in the room.

"We'll get him," said Bill. "We have his registration number. He'll be stopped before he reaches London. I think we'd better start ferreting in his background. He was up for a knighthood, you know.

"You'd better come back with us to Mircester, Agatha, and make a full statement."

Agatha was taken over her statement again and again until she was gratefully able to sign it. She then had a long talk with Bill which depressed her. He was doubtful whether the tape alone would be enough to convict Binser.

Poor Miss Partle. Had Binser said something to her during his prison visit that had finally tipped her over the edge? Had he always been respectable?

John Armitage watched her climbing out of a police car that evening. He hurried round to her cottage and listened amazed to the story that Agatha was now heartily tired of telling.

"Did they get Binser?" John asked when she had finished.

"He was stopped on the road to London. He's denying everything. He's got a team of lawyers. Bill says they are digging into his past. He says Binser seems always to have been a pretty ruthless person."

"And you thought he was straightforward and decent."

"I got there in the end," said Agatha crossly. "Get your ring all right?"

"Thank you. As a matter of fact, I'm thinking of moving back to London."

"Not a good time to sell. The house market's in a slump at the moment."

"I'll take what I can get, and," John added with a tinge of malice, "I shall think of you down here busy at work on your old folks' club. So Miss Partle's off the hook?"

"If she ever recovers her sanity, she'll probably be charged with aiding and abetting a murderer and attempting to murder me. I'm glad it's all over. It's up to the police now to prove he did it."

"They've got that taped confession."

"Bill told me after I'd made my statement that he might get away with it. He's saying he only told me a load of rubbish because he thought I was so smug. He's insisting it was a joke at my expense. Also, I don't know if that tape would stand up in court. There was no one in authority here, he wasn't cautioned and he wasn't on oath."

"You should be worried. If he gets away with it, he'll come looking for you."

"No, he won't," said Agatha. "I'm no threat to him. He seemed pretty confident I couldn't find out anything. And if they don't get him this time, then they can't charge him with the same crime twice."

"Well, I can't share your confidence. I'd best be off. I've got enough in the bank to rent somewhere in London until this place is sold."

Agatha wanted to say, "Will you miss me? Did you care

anything for me at all?" But fear of rejection kept her silent.

Instead, she said, "I suppose you'll be seeing a lot of Charlotte Bellinge."

"That silly woman," he said viciously. "No. She turned out to be a terrible bore. I shall be glad to return to all the fun and lights of London. The thought of being buried down here in the winter is an awful prospect. I don't know how you cope with it."

"Some people would think three murders was enough excitement for anyone."

"Anyway. See you around, maybe."

John went back to his cottage and stood looking around. May as well think of packing some things up. He'd be glad to get away. And whoever it was that Agatha was romancing, he wished her the joy of him. *He* didn't care. She meant nothing to him. Infuriating woman. And as a proof of his lack of interest in Agatha Raisin, he kicked the wastebasket clear across the room.

EPILOGUE

✝

DESPITE Agatha's assurances to John that she was not worried that Binser would come looking for her, she felt edgy and nervous.

She tried to call Bill several times only to be told that he was not available, and her heart sank. She really should have apologized to him about her remarks about Alice.

So when she opened the door to him a week after Binser had been arrested, she flew at him, crying, "Oh, Bill, I'm so sorry about those dreadful things I said about Alice."

"That's all right," he said. "Let's go in. I've some good news for you. Never mind about coffee," he said, walking with her into the kitchen to a glad welcome from the cats, "I want to tell you right away."

"What?"

"We've got Binser all sewn up."

"How? What happened?"

"Well, I phoned the top psychiatrist at that psychiatric prison she's in and asked how Miss Partle was getting on. He said he was just drafting a report. He said he was rapidly coming to the conclusion that she was faking madness. Maybe she was tired of keeping up the act, but he said twice he had surprised her reading a book with all the appearance of intelligent enjoyment. I talked to my superiors and arranged an interview. She sat drooling in front of me, all blank-eyed. I told her that Binser had confessed. I didn't tell her he might get away with it.

"She looked at me, startled, and then she began to cry. She switched the mad act right off. She said when he had visited her in prison, she had asked him whether he had told his wife yet that they were going to get married. He said, not yet. He would wait until she was free and then they would run off together. It was that, she said, that suddenly made her realize he was lying, for she knew he would never leave his work. He relished his position and he relished power. But she did not know what to do. She still loved him, however, still hoped. She said she had sunk so low that all she wanted to do was live in the hope of seeing him again. He told her if she faked madness, then she wouldn't stand trial.

"I was wondering how to get some actual proof of his culpability out of her, so I said there was no death penalty and she could wait for him, for the charge of conspiracy to murder plus attempted murder would carry less of a sentence. She said she would not have killed you. She had phoned him and he had said to frighten you as much as possible while he worked out what to do. She said she wouldn't actually have hit you with that hammer."

"So how did you get the goods on Binser out of her?" asked Agatha.

"I told her that Binser had told you that he had never loved her and she was easy to use, that he had no intention of ever leaving his wife. She started to cry again, and after a bit she became very angry. Miss Partle said that he had written a confession to the murders so that after his death, she would be exonerated. Why she fell for that one, I do not know, as he could have outlived her. I asked where the confession was. She said they had various subsidiary companies, and in the safe of an office in Docklands, we would find a confession.

"Once started, it seemed she could not stop. She told me about insider trading deals, intimidation of companies he wished to take over, the lot. I couldn't believe my luck. I phoned Wilkes, who said he would be down hotfoot with two detectives and a tape recorder. I was terrified while I waited that she would regret the whole thing and slip back into her pretended madness. We raided the safe of a company called Hyten Electronics, and there was the confession along with a set of account books he certainly would not want the income-tax people to see. So he's been charged."

"What a relief," said Agatha. "I told John I was sure he wouldn't come looking for me, but I'd begun to jump at every sound."

"Where is John? There's a FOR SALE sign outside his cottage."

"He's going to rent a flat in London. He's already sent off most of his stuff."

"That's quick work."

"Oh, it's easy to rent a flat in London if you've got the money."

"So no engagement?"

"No, there wasn't enough there. I gave him back his ring."

"Did that upset you?" Bill looked at her shrewdly.

"Not very much. He was a bore," said Agatha, unconsciously echoing John's remark about Charlotte Bellinge. "And I hope everything is all right with you and Alice?"

"Well, no, it isn't."

"I'm sorry, Bill. It was that dreadful wine. I should never have let her have any."

"I'd got over that. People say things when they are drunk they don't really mean. She was rude to Mother."

Agatha felt a pang of sympathy for Alice.

"What did she say?"

"Well, Mother always does jump the gun a bit. She was saying how Alice and me could save money after we were married by moving in with them—Mum and Dad, that is. Alice said to her, 'Don't be ridiculous. I've already picked out a nice bungalow for us.' I pointed out it was the first I'd heard of it. Alice said, 'I couldn't live here. They'd drive me mad.'

"I got very angry but I still thought it was maybe the wrong time of the month or something. Alice insisted we drive out of Mircester on the other side of the ring road, where she said this bungalow was. It was quite large. An estate agent was showing a couple round. I asked how much it was selling for and he said one hundred and eighty thousand. I pointed out to Alice I could never afford that. My pay isn't great, you know. She asked why I hadn't saved anything, living at home. I said I paid Mum and Dad for my keep. She went absolutely ballistic and called me all kinds of fool. So I told her I never wanted to see her again."

"Don't you want to live on your own?" asked Agatha curiously. "There's police accommodation in Mircester, isn't there? Get your independence."

"I have my independence," said Bill, puzzled. "All my meals are prepared for me and I have my own room at home."

Agatha decided to drop the subject. "I feel a fool the way

I went on," she said. "I was completely taken in by Binser."

"He's the fool," said Bill. "He was very lucky no one ever saw him. Mrs. Bloxby saw you leaving Tristan's at midnight. Pity she didn't look out of the window later on in the night. Miss Jellop's neighbours happened to be away or busy. Peggy Slither often played loud music and her neighbours aren't all that close to her. Maybe it takes an amateur to find an amateur."

"Except I got the wrong amateur. Did Binser say what he planned to do with me? I mean, I had told John I was going to see Miss Partle."

"He's already accused of enough, so he sticks to the story that he had told Miss Partle to frighten you so that you would drop the whole thing."

"I can't see her believing that."

"She was so much in love with him and already in such a state of panic that she didn't think clearly."

"I never saw a less frightened woman."

"Maybe he planned to dump your body somewhere and then arrange things so that it would look as if you had left the country. I don't know. I think you should take things easy from now on, Agatha."

"I plan to."

In the weeks leading up to Christmas, Agatha threw herself into preparations for the old folks' club. She raised money by deciding after all to hold an auction and then held several bingo evenings in the school hall, much to the distress of the vicar, who felt it was encouraging gambling.

The opening party on Christmas Eve was a great success. The ladies' society organized a roster of drivers to take the infirm elderly to the club.

In the new year, Ralph Crinsted started his chess classes.

Agatha felt mildly guilty that she had done nothing about taking further lessons from him, although he seemed to have a good few willing pupils.

It was the end of January before she realized that the FOR SALE sign outside John's cottage had gone.

Agatha hurried along to the vicarage. "Who's my new neighbour?" she asked Mrs. Bloxby.

"I believe it is a certain Mr. Paul Chatterton, some sort of computer expert."

"Oh, some computer nerd. Anyway, I'm not interested in men anymore. I thought John might have called at least once."

"I wouldn't worry about him. I think he was a bit of a lightweight."

Agatha looked at her in surprise. It was highly unusual for the vicar's wife to say anything critical about anyone.

Mrs. Bloxby coloured. "I do not like the way he treated you. I do wish you would find someone suitable."

"I tell you, I've given up. There aren't any suitable men when you get to my age, anyway."

"God will provide," said Mrs. Bloxby sententiously.

Agatha grinned as a vision of a handsome bachelor, gift-wrapped, and descending from heaven, entered her mind.

When she walked back to her cottage, she saw there was a removal van outside. Overseeing the unloading of it was what was obviously the new tenant. He was middle-aged but tall and fit-looking. He had a shock of white hair and a thin, clever face and sparkling black eyes.

Agatha hurried indoors. She picked up the phone and made an appointment with the hairdresser and then the beautician.

Not that she was interested in men anymore.

Still, it didn't do to let oneself go.

Read on for an excerpt from Agatha Raisin's next adventure

AGATHA RAISIN
AND THE
HAUNTED HOUSE

†

Now available in hardcover from St. Martin's Minotaur

FOOT-AND-MOUTH disease had closed down the countryside. Country walks and farm gates were padlocked. The spring was chilly and wet, with the first daffodils hanging their yellow heads under torrents of rain.

The thatch on Agatha Raisin's cottage dripped mournfully. She sat on the kitchen floor with her cats and wondered what to do to ward off a familiar feeling of approaching boredom. With boredom came nervous depression, as she well knew.

An interesting-looking man had moved into the cottage next door, formerly owned by her ex-husband, James, but interest in any man at all had died in Agatha's bosom. She had not joined the other village ladies in taking around cakes or homemade jam. Nor had she heard any of the gossip because she had just returned from London where, in her capacity as free-lance public relations officer, she had been helping to launch a new fashion line for young people called Mr. Harry. All it had served to do was make middle-aged Agatha feel old. Some of the skinny models—heroin-chic was still the fashion—had made her feel fatter and older. Her conscience had disturbed her because she knew the clothes were made in Taiwan out of the cheapest material and guaranteed to fall apart at the seams if worn for very long.

She got to her feet and went upstairs to her bedroom and studied herself in a full-length mirror. A stocky middle-aged woman with good legs, shiny brown hair, and small bearlike eyes stared back at her.

Action, she said to herself. She would put on make-up and go and see her friend Mrs. Bloxby, the vicar's wife, and catch up on the village gossip. Agatha put on a foundation base of pale make-up, reflecting that it was not so long ago when bronzed skin had been all the rage. Now that the unfashionable could afford to go abroad in the middle of winter, it was no longer smart to sport a tan or even to wear brownish make-up. She plucked nervously at the skin under her chin. Was it getting loose? She slapped herself under the chin sixty times and then was cross to see a red flush on her neck.

She changed out of the old trousers and sweater she had put on that morning and changed into a biscuit-coloured linen suit over a gold silk blouse. Not that this sudden desire to dress up had anything to do with the new tenant in the cottage next door, she told herself. At least, as the cliché went, time was a great healer. She hardly ever thought of James now and had given up any hope of seeing him again.

Downstairs again, she shrugged into her Burberry and picked up a golf umbrella and went out into the pouring rain. Why on earth had she worn high heels? she wondered, as she picked her way round the puddles on Lilac Lane and headed for the vicarage.

Mrs. Bloxby, a gentle-faced woman with grey hair, opened the door of the vicarage to her. "Mrs. Raisin!" she cried. "When did you get back?"

"Last night," said Agatha, reflecting that after London, the formal use of her second name sounded odd. But then the village ladies' society of which Agatha was a member always addressed one another formally.

"Come in. Such dreadful weather. And this foot-and-mouth plague is frightening. Ramblers have been told not to walk the countryside, but they won't listen. I really don't think some of those ramblers even like the countryside."

"Any foot-and-mouth around here yet?" asked Agatha, taking off her coat and hanging it on a peg in the hall.

"No, nothing round Carsely . . . yet."

She led the way into the sitting-room and Agatha followed. Agatha sank down into the feather cushions on the old sofa, took off her shoes and stretched her wet stockinged feet out to the fire.

"I'll lend you a pair of wellingtons when you leave," said Mrs. Bloxby. "I'll get some coffee."

Agatha leaned back and closed her eyes as Mrs. Bloxby went off to the kitchen. It suddenly felt good to be back.

Mrs. Bloxby came back with a tray with mugs of coffee.

"What's the gossip?" asked Agatha.

"Er . . . James was here when you were away."

Agatha sat bolt upright. "Where is he now?"

"I'm afraid I don't know. He only stayed for an afternoon. He said he was travelling abroad."

"Rats!" said Agatha gloomily, all the old pain flooding back. "Did you tell him where I was?"

"Yes, I did," said the vicar's wife awkwardly. "I told him where you were living in London and gave him your phone number."

"He didn't call," said Agatha miserably.

"He did seem in a bit of a rush. He sent his love."

"That's a joke," said Agatha bitterly.

"Now drink your coffee. I know it's early, but would you like something stronger?"

"I don't want to start down that road, especially for a creep like James," said Agatha.

"Have you met your new neighbour?"

"No. I saw him when he moved in, I mean from a distance, but then I got the chance of this PR job and took off for London. What's he like?"

"Seems pleasant and clever."

"What does he do?"

"He works in computers. Free-lance. He's just finished a big contract. He says he's glad it's over. He was commuting to Milton Keynes and back every day."

"That's a long haul. No murders?"

"No, Mrs. Raisin. I should think you've had enough of those. There is a small mystery, however."

"What's that?"

"Alf was recently asked to perform an exorcism, but he refused." Alf was the vicar. "Alf says he only believes in the divine spirit and no other kind."

"Where's the ghost?"

"It's a haunted house in Hebberdon—you know, that tiny village the other side of Ancombe. It belongs to an old lady, a Mrs. Witherspoon, a widow. She has heard strange voices and seen lights in the night. Alf has put it down to the village children playing tricks on the old lady and has suggested she call in the police. She did that, but they couldn't find anything. But Mrs. Witherspoon sticks to her story that she is being haunted. So, do you want to investigate?"

Agatha sat for a moment and then said, "No. I think Alf's

probably right. You know, sitting here I've decided to stop rushing around, finding things to ward off boredom. Time I broke the pattern. I'm going to become domesticated."

Mrs. Bloxby looked at her uneasily.

"You? Do you think that's a good idea?"

"The garden's full of weeds and this rain can't go on forever. I'm going to potter about and do a bit of gardening."

"You'll get fed up soon."

"You don't know me," said Agatha sharply.

"Possibly not. When did you make this decision?"

Agatha gave a reluctant grin. "Five minutes ago."

Her stubborn pride kept her from revealing that James's visit and the fact that he had not tried to contact her had hurt her deeply.

As the wet spring finally dried up, it did indeed look as if Agatha Raisin had settled into domesticity at last. Tired of lazy gardeners, she had decided to do the work herself and found it alleviated the pain she still felt over James. The ladies of the village of Carsely informed Agatha that her neighbour, Paul Chatterton, was a charming man but not at all sociable. For a moment, Agatha's competitive instincts were aroused, but then she thought dismally that men meant pain and complications. They were best left alone.

She was sprawled in a deck-chair in her garden one sunny day, covered in a careful application of sunblock and with her two cats, Hodge and Boswell, at her feet, when a tentative voice said, "Hullo."

Agatha opened her eyes. Her neighbour was leaning over the garden fence. He had a thick shock of pure white hair and sparkling black eyes in a thin, clever face.

"Yes?" demanded Agatha rudely.

"I'm your new neighbour, Paul Chatterton."

"So? What do you want?" asked Agatha, closing her eyes again.

"I wanted to say hullo."

"You've already said that." Agatha opened her eyes and stared at him. "What about trying goodbye?"

She closed her eyes again until she felt he would have fully appreciated the snub. She cautiously opened them again. He was still standing there, grinning at her.

"I must say you make a refreshing change," he said. "I've been besieged by village ladies since I arrived, and now I decide to be sociable, I happen to pick on the one person who doesn't want to know me."

"Bother someone else," said Agatha. "Why me?"

"You're the nearest. Besides, I hear you're the village sleuth."

"What's that got to do with it?"

"I read in the local papers that there's some old woman over at Hebberdon who is being frightened out of her wits by ghosts. I'm going over there to offer my services as a ghost buster."

Agatha's recently dormant competitive instincts rose. She sat up. "Come round the front and I'll let you in and we'll talk about it."

"See you in a few minutes." He waved and loped off.

Agatha struggled to her feet, thinking that old-fashioned canvas deck-chairs like the ones in the Green Park in London had been expressly designed to make one feel old. She found she could not struggle out of it and had to tip it sideways and roll over on the grass to get to her feet. She gave it a furious kick. "You're for the bonfire," she said. "I'll replace you with a sun lounger tomorrow."

She hurried into the house, stopping only in the kitchen for a moment to wipe the sunblock from her face.

Agatha hesitated before opening the door to him. She was wearing a faded house dress and loafers. Then she shrugged. Men! Who needed to bother about them?

She opened the door. "Come in," she said. "We'll have coffee in the kitchen."

"I'd rather have tea," he said, trotting in after her.

"What kind?" asked Agatha. "I've got Darjeeling, Assam, Earl Grey, and something called Afternoon Tea."

"Darjeeling will do."

Agatha put the kettle on. "Aren't you working at the moment?"

"No, I'm between contracts. Going to take a brief holiday."

Agatha leaned against the kitchen counter. Paul's intelligent black eyes surveyed her and Agatha suddenly wished she were wearing something more attractive, or, at least, had some make-up on. He was not strictly handsome, and yet there was something about that white hair combined with black eyes in a white face and a long athletic figure which, she thought, would disturb quite a lot of women—except, of course, she reminded herself, Agatha Raisin.

"I believe my cottage once belonged to your ex-husband, James Lacey," he said. The kettle began to boil. Agatha lifted down two mugs and put a tea-bag in one and a spoonful of instant coffee in the other.

"Yes," she said. She stirred the tea-bag, lifted it out and put the mug down in front of him. "There's sugar and milk in front of you."

"Thanks. Why Raisin? Did you get married again?"

"No, that was my first husband's name. I kept on using it even when I was married to James. Are you married?"

There was a short silence while Paul carefully added milk and sugar. He stirred his tea. "Yes, I am," he said.

"And so where is Mrs. Chatterton?"

Another silence. Then he said, "Visiting relatives in Spain."

"So she's Spanish?"

"Yes."

"What's her name?"

"Um . . . Juanita."

Agatha's bearlike eyes narrowed. "You know what I think? I think you're not married at all. I think there isn't any Juanita. Look, I invited you in here, not to get into your trousers, but because I'm interested in this ghost thing."

His black eyes sparkled with amusement. "Are you usually this blunt?"

"When I'm being lied to, yes."

"But there is a Juanita. She has long black hair—"

"And plays the castanets and has a rose between her teeth. Forget it," snapped Agatha. "So what do you plan to do about the haunting?"

"I thought I'd run over there and offer my services. Care to join me?"

"Don't see why not," said Agatha. "When shall we go?"

"What about now?"

"Okay. Finish your tea and I'll get changed."

"No need for that. Your housewifely appearance might reassure Mrs. Witherspoon."

"Tcha!" said Agatha. She left the kitchen and ran upstairs. She put on a cool pink-and-white-striped shirtwaister dress and then carefully applied make-up. She longed to wear high heels, but the day was hot and swollen ankles would not look chic. She sighed and pushed her feet into a pair of low-heeled sandals.

She was half-way down the stairs when she realized she had forgotten to put on tights. A hot day minus tights would mean the straps on her sandals would scrape across her feet and the skin of her thighs under the short dress might stick to the car seat. She went back to her bedroom and struggled into a pair of tights labelled "One Size Fits All," reflecting that whoever put that slogan on the packet had been thinking of a skinny fourteen-year-old. She looked in the mirror. The effort of putting on the tights in a hot bedroom had made her nose shine. She powdered it too vigorously and got a sneezing fit. By the time she had finished sneezing, her make-up was a wreck, so she had to redo it. Right! A last look in the full-length mirror. God! The buttons at the bosom of her shirtwaister were straining. She took it off and put on a white cotton blouse and a cotton skirt with an elasticated waist.

Fine. Ready to go. One more look in the mirror. Damn. She was wearing a black bra and it showed through the white cotton. Off with the blouse, on with a white bra, blouse back on again.

Resolutely not looking in the mirror this time, Agatha darted down the stairs.

"You shouldn't have gone to so much trouble," said Paul.

"I haven't gone to any trouble," growled Agatha.

"You were away ages and I thought . . . Never mind. Let's get going. You'd better take a pair of wellingtons."

"Why?"

"Because there's still foot-and-mouth around and she may live near a farm and we might have to wade through disinfectant."

"Right," said Agatha. "I've got a pair by the door. Whose car? Yours or mine?"

"I'll drive."

His car was a vintage MG. Agatha groaned inwardly as she lowered herself down into the low seat. She felt as if she were sitting on the road. He set off with a roar and Agatha's hair blew forward about her face.

"Why is it in films," she said, "that the heroine in an open car always has her hair streaming behind her?"

"Because she's filmed in a stationary car in a studio with a film of landscape rolling behind her and a studio fan directed on her hair. If it's bothering you, I can stop and put the top up."

"No," said Agatha sourly. "The damage is done. Whereabouts in Hebberdon does this Mrs. Witherspoon live?"

"Ivy Cottage, Bag End."

Agatha fell silent as the countryside streamed past, the ruined countryside, the countryside destroyed by foot-and-mouth. If she had still been in London, she wouldn't have given a damn. But somehow she now felt she belonged in the countryside and what happened there affected her deeply.

Hebberdon was a tiny picturesque village nestling at the foot of a valley. There were no shops, one pub, and a huddle of cottages. Paul stopped the car and looked around. "I'll knock at one of the doors and ask where Bag End is."

Agatha fished out a cigarette and lit up. There was a hole where she guessed the ashtray used to be. Still, it was an open car. He could hardly object.

He came back. "We can leave the car here. Bag End is just around the corner."

Getting out of the car to Agatha was reminiscent of getting out of the deck-chair, but she managed it without having to roll out on the road.

They walked round into Bag End, a narrow lane with only one cottage at the end. Agatha took a final puff at her cigarette and tossed it at the side of the road. Paul retrieved it and stubbed it out. "You'll set the countryside alight in this weather," he complained.

"Sorry," mumbled Agatha, reflecting that she was not really the countrywoman she had thought herself to be. "How old is this Mrs. Witherspoon?"

"Ninety-two, according to the newspapers."

"She might be gaga."

"Don't think so. Let's see anyway."

Ivy Cottage was indeed covered in ivy which rippled in the summer breeze. The roof was thatched. Paul seized the brass knocker and gave it a good few bangs. After a few moments, the letter-box opened and a woman's voice shouted, "Go away."

"We're here to help you," said Paul, crouched down by the letter-box. "We'll lay the ghost for you."

"I'm sick of cranks. Sod off!"

Paul grinned sideways at Agatha. "Sounds like a soul mate of yours." He turned back to the letter-box.

"We're not cranks, Mrs. Witherspoon. We really do want to help."

"How can you do that?"

"I am Paul Chatterton with Agatha Raisin. We live in Carsely. We're going to spend a night in your house and catch your ghost."

There was a long silence and then the rattle of bolts and chains. The door opened. Agatha found herself looking upwards. She had imagined that Mrs. Witherspoon would turn out to be a small, frail, stooped old lady. But it was a giantess that faced her.

Mrs. Witherspoon was a powerful woman, at least six feet tall, with dyed red hair and big strong hands.

She jerked her head by way of welcome and they followed her into a small dark parlour. The ivy clustered round the leaded windows cut out most of the light.

"So what makes you pair think you can find who is haunting me?" she asked. Her head almost touched the beamed ceiling. Agatha, who had sat down, stood up again, not liking the feeling of being loomed over.

"It's worth a try," said Paul easily. "I mean, what have you got to lose?"

Mrs. Witherspoon turned bright eyes on Agatha. "You said your name was Raisin?"

"He did. And yes, it is."

"Ah, you're the one from Carsely who fancies herself to be a detective. Your husband ran off and left you. Hardly surprising."

Agatha clenched her hands into fists. "And what happened to yours?"

"He died twenty years ago."

Agatha turned to Paul and began to say, "Maybe this is a silly idea after all . . ." but he hissed, "Let me handle it."

He turned to Mrs. Witherspoon. "We would be no trouble," he coaxed. "We could sit down here during the night and wait."

"Don't expect me to feed you," she said.

"Wouldn't dream of it. We'll come about ten."

"Oh, all right. I've lived in this cottage all my life and I am not going to be driven out of it."

"What form do these hauntings take?"

"Whispers, footsteps, a sort of grey mist seeping under the bedroom door. The police have been over the place, but there's no sign of forced entry."

"Have you any enemies?" asked Agatha.

"Not that I know of. I'm a friendly sort. Never anything about me to upset people." She fastened her eyes on Agatha's face with a contemptuous look as if to imply that there was a lot about Agatha Raisin to get people's backs up.

Paul edged Agatha to the door, seeing she was about to burst out with something. "We'll be back at ten," he said.

• • •

"I don't think I want to help that old bitch," she railed, when they got into the car. "Believe me, Count Dracula wouldn't even frighten that one."

"But it is interesting," protested Paul. "As a child, didn't you want to spend the night in a haunted house?"

Agatha thought briefly of the Birmingham slum she had been brought up in. There had been so much earthly terror and violence that as a child she had little need to scare herself with things supernatural.

She sighed and capitulated. "May as well give it a try."

"I'll bring a late supper and a Scrabble board to pass the time."

"A Ouija board might be better."

"Haven't got one of those. What would you like to eat?"

"I'll eat before we go. Lots of black coffee would be a good idea. I'll bring a large Thermos."

"Good, then. We're all set."

They drove back into Carsely under the watchful eyes of various villagers.

"I saw Mrs. Raisin out with that Paul Chatterton," complained Miss Simms, secretary of the ladies' society, to Mrs. Bloxby when she met her outside the village stores later that day. "I don't know how she does it! Here's all of us women trying to get a look in and she snaps him up. I mean ter say, she's no spring chicken."

"I believe men finds Mrs. Raisin sexy," said the vicar's wife and tripped off with her shopping basket over her arm, leaving Miss Simms staring after her.

"Would you believe it?" Miss Simms complained ten minutes later to Mrs. Davenport, a recent incomer and now a regular member of the ladies' society. "Mrs. Bloxby, the wife of a vicar, mark you, says that Mrs. Raisin is sexy."

"And what prompted that?" demanded Mrs. Davenport, looking every inch the British expatriate she had recently been—print dress, large Minnie Mouse white shoes, small white gloves and terrifying hat.

"Only that our Mrs. Raisin has been driving around with Paul Chatterton and the pair of them looking like an item." Under the shadow of the brim of her hat, Mrs. Davenport's face tightened in disapproval. Had she not presented Mr. Chatterton with one of her best chocolate cakes and followed it up with two jars of homemade jam? And hadn't he just politely accepted the gifts without even asking her in for a coffee?

Mrs. Davenport continued on her way. The news rankled. In the manner of British ex-patriates who lived on a diet of rumours, she stopped various people, embellishing the news as she went. By evening, it was all round the village that Agatha was having an affair with Paul Chatterton.

At six o'clock that evening, Agatha's doorbell rang. She hoped that perhaps it was Paul inviting her out for dinner. Detective Sergeant Bill Wong stood on the doorstep. Agatha felt immediately guilty. Bill had been her first friend when she had moved down to the country. She didn't want to tell him about the search for the ghost in case he would try to stop her.

"Come in," she said. "I haven't seen you for while. How are things going?"

"Apart from chasing and fining ramblers who will try to walk their dogs across farmland, nothing much. What have you been getting up to?"

They walked into the kitchen. "I've just made some coffee. Like some?"

"Thanks. That's the biggest Thermos I've ever seen."

"Just making some coffee for the ladies' society," lied Agatha.

"I hear James was back in Carsely—briefly."

"Yes," said Agatha. "I don't want to talk about it."

"Still hurts?"

"I said, I don't want to talk about it."

"Okay. How's the new neighbour?"

"Paul Chatterton? Seems pleasant enough."

Bill's round face, a mixture of Asian and Western features, looked at her curiously. Agatha's face was slightly flushed.

"So you haven't been getting up to anything exciting?"

"Not me," said Agatha. "I did some PR work in London, but down here I've been concentrating on the garden. I made some scones. Would you like one with your coffee?"

Bill knew Agatha's baking was bad, to say the least. He looked doubtful. "Go on," urged Agatha. "They're awfully good."

"All right."

Agatha put a scone on a plate and then put butter and jam in front of him.

Bill bit into it cautiously. It was delicious, as light as a feather. "You've really excelled yourself, Agatha," he said.

And Agatha, who had received the scones as a gift from Mrs. Bloxby, smiled sweetly at him. "You'll never believe how domesticated I've become. Oh, there's the doorbell."

She hurried to open the door, hoping it would not be Paul Chatterton who might start talking about their planned vigil at the haunted house. But it was Mrs. Bloxby.

"Come in," said Agatha. "Bill's here." She hoped Bill had finished that scone.

But to her horror, as she entered the kitchen with Mrs. Bloxby, Bill said, "I wouldn't mind another of those scones, Agatha."

"Oh, do you like them?" asked Mrs. Bloxby. "I gave Mrs. Raisin some this morning because I'd made too many."

"Coffee?" Agatha asked the vicar's wife.

"Not for me. The attendance at the ladies' society is not very good, so I called round to make sure you would be at it this evening."

"I can't," said Agatha, aware of Bill's amused eyes on her face.

"Why not?"

"I've got to see a man about some PR work."

"Working again so soon? I thought you wanted a quiet summer."

"Oh, well, it's just a little job."

"What is it this time? Fashion?"

"It's a new anti-wrinkle face cream."

"Really? Do you think those creams work?"

"I don't know," said Agatha loudly. "It's all too boring. Can we talk about something else?"

There was a silence. Agatha felt her face turning red.

"You're getting quite a name for yourself in the village," teased Mrs. Bloxby. "It's all over the place that you and Paul Chatterton are an item."

"Nonsense."

"You were seen out in his car."

"He was giving me a lift."

"Oh, is your car off the road?"

"Look," said Agatha, "I was leaving to go to Moreton and he came out of his house at the same time and said he was going to Moreton as well and offered me a lift. That's all. Honestly, the way people in this village gossip."

"Well," said the vicar's wife, "a lot of noses have been put out of joint by your apparent friendship with him. Why should you succeed when so many others have failed? I'd better go."

Agatha saw her out and then returned reluctantly to the

kitchen. "You haven't let me have another of those scones yet," said Bill.

"I must have made a mistake and given you one of Mrs. Bloxby's scones instead of one my own," said Agatha, who, once she was in a hole, never knew when to stop digging.

"Then I'll have one of yours."

Agatha went through the pantomime of opening an empty tin. "Sorry," she said. "Mine are all finished. What a pity."

She put another of Mrs. Bloxby's scones in front of him,

"Have you heard of a Mrs. Witherspoon who claims she is being haunted?" asked Bill.

"Yes, it was in the local papers."

"And you didn't feel impelled to do anything about it?"

"No, I want a quiet life. She's probably gaga."

"She's not. I went a couple of times to investigate. The police couldn't find anything. I've got this odd feeling you're hiding something from me, Agatha."

"Don't be silly."

"I mean, I ask you about this new neighbour of yours and you don't tell me he took you down to Moreton."

"What is this?" demanded Agatha. "The third degree?"

Bill laughed. "I still think you're holding out on me. Well, I'm sure a bit of ghost-hunting won't hurt you."

"I never said—"

"No, you didn't, did you? I would ask you about this face cream and where you are meeting this man, but I don't want to stretch your imagination any further."

"Bill!"

He grinned. "I'll see you around."

Agatha sighed with relief when he had left and went upstairs to take a shower. She felt hot and clammy after all her lies.

Now what did one wear for ghost-hunting?